PARALLEL TURNS

What was this Stefan going to be like? Her stomach knotted with apprehension as she thought of the hours of torture ahead of her.

An instructor with an Ecole de Ski jacket stood about twenty feet away from her. He was four feet tall, completely bald and the wrong side of sixty. Flora could tell he was a humourless crosspatch. Stefan. Her heart sank

'*Excusez-moi*' She jumped, The voice was husky, heavily accented. She shielded her eyes from the sun, unable to see properly. 'Are you Flora?'

She nodded, puzzled. The stranger towered over her. Her eyes were watering, his hidden behind dark glasses. He smiled a slow, lazy smile. She took in a mass of shoulder-length black hair pulled back in a ponytail, Slavic cheekbones and the long, lean body of an athlctc.

'You're Stefan? You can't be.'

'Even the snow-laden atmosphere does nothing to cool the passions in this steamy story of sex, snowploughing and chalet girls' *Marie Claire*

'Jauntily entertaining . . . A very well-written romp with more twists and turns than an off-piste run' *Ms London*

About the author

A former journalist, Sarah Ingham now writes full-time. *Parallel Turns* is her first novel.

Parallel Turns

Sarah Ingham

CORONET BOOKS
Hodder & Stoughton

First published in Great Britain in 1999
by Hodder and Stoughton
A division of Hodder Headline
First published in paperback in 1999
by Hodder and Stoughton

A Coronet Paperback
10 9 8 7 6 5 4 3

A CIP catalogue record for this title is available
from the British Library

ISBN 0 340 79400 3

Printed and bound in Great Britain by
Omnia Books Ltd, Glasgow

Hodder and Stoughton
A division of Hodder Headline
338 Euston Road
London NW1 3BH

CHAPTER ONE

Boxing Day

———◦◦◦———

'Smile, Flora. You're going skiing, not being sent to Death Row.'

Flora Rose ducked, to avoid being decapitated by the back end of her fiancé's skis.

'Got everything?' asked Jamie.

'Wedding file.' She rushed back inside, dashed up the narrow staircase and ran into the bedroom. Where was it? Out in the street, a horn honked.

'Come on,' called up Jamie, from the front door. 'We'll miss the plane.'

The heavy box file was under the bed. Grabbing it, she hurtled back down the stairs and out to the car. Jasper, Flora's brother had offered them a lift to the airport.

Jasper stared at his sister. 'That's my old jacket, isn't it? Haven't seen it for years.'

'Davos.' Flora shuddered.

'Must have been the last time you skied.' Jasper grinned. 'Or tried to. Not that you tried that hard. Not that any performance of yours on skis could ever be called skiing.' Flora pulled a face at him. He looked her up and down. 'Well, well. Jamie's working miracles. You look quite respectable. No bloody awful biker boots.'

'There's nothing wrong with them.'

'Nothing wrong if you're planning to invade Poland. Hair brushed . . .'

'You won't have any hair to brush soon,' retorted Flora.

'I'm not even thinning.'

'We'll miss the plane,' cut in Jamie. 'Get in, sweetheart.'

Chelsea's streets were deserted. As he and Jamie talked golf, the stock market and the Ashes tour, Jasper offered up a silent prayer of thanks that his future brother-in-law was such a good solid Englishman and all-round nice guy, rather than one of Flora's awful exes.

'What time should you arrive?'

'Oneish,' said Jamie. 'Hopefully ski this afternoon.'

In the back, Flora shivered. Jammed up against the door because of the skis, she tried to shift to a more comfortable position.

'You should have a great time,' said Jasper. 'Rain's forecast here until New Year.' For the past week, the sky had been overcast and gloomy. A battleship grey Christmas. 'Ma and pa were amazed when they heard Flora was going skiing.'

'So was I,' muttered Flora.

Jamie shot her a 'don't start' look.

They reached the M4. It was starting to get light. 'Planning to repeat Davos, Flora?' Jasper grinned into the mirror. 'Brave man, Jamie. Realise what you've let yourself in for?'

'I broke my leg,' protested Flora.

'Leg? A tiny bone in your foot. And we all know how that happened.'

'Shut up,' hissed his sister, blushing. 'I got vertigo. I hate heights.'

'Rubbish. All in the mind,' scoffed Jasper. 'Was it really ten years ago?'

'Ten years on, I still get vertigo,' said Flora. 'I still hate heights.'

'And I bet you still make a fuss about nothing.' He turned to Jamie. 'Day three in Davos, Flora refuses to ski. Why? She didn't like her instructor.'

'He was a sadistic, bullying monster.' That horrible morning in her ski school class came back. There were a dozen others, all German. The wizened instructor had taken them up in a cable car high above the town. At the top, Flora had the fear and was unable to move. Couldn't budge a centimetre. The instructor had tried cajoling, then persuasion, then a temper loss. The rest of the class thought her a joke, then became colder and more fed up. They had stood around staring at her, muttering in German. Whatever they said was way beyond her pre-GCSE level, but she knew they were unsympathetic. Eventually, the instructor had bundled her back into the cable car.

Flora had refused to go back to class. Her parents were furious that she was being so wet and wasting money on skis, a pass and lessons that she wasn't using. She was ordered to stay in her hotel room and get on with her studies. There she had stayed, bored rigid and smoking forbidden cigarettes next to an open window. She had written to her best friend Jem, pleading with her to contact Amnesty International or the SAS to release her. After a day speeding down black runs, Jasper would visit to cadge fags. And to gloat.

'Vertigo? Huh.' Jasper put his foot down. 'You were just a pain-in-the-arse teenager, Flora. She and Jem really fancied themselves, going round clutching books of metaphysical poetry and thinking they suffered existential angst. They didn't even know what metaphysical meant. Probably still don't.'

'I still get vertigo,' snapped Flora. 'I still hate skiing.'

'You don't have to ski. Pete and I will do it for you,' said Jamie, in his most soothing voice. 'You can sit on a balcony in the sunshine and read and drink hot chocolate.'

Flora thought how she'd prefer to sit on the beach in the sunshine and drink margaritas.

'You do know how she broke her foot, sorry leg, don't you?' asked Jasper.

Jamie was puzzled. 'Skiing wasn't it?'

'Shut up Jasper,' hissed Flora.

A lorry pulled out in front of them. Jasper swerved, causing the skis to slide and pin Flora more tightly against the door.

Outside the terminal, Flora wandered off to find a trolley, leaving the two men to unload the car. Coming back, they seemed amused. She had an uneasy feeling a joke was being told at her expense.

'Have a good time,' said Jasper.

'Thanks. We will.' Jamie suddenly felt far less guilty about the holiday.

Security announcements interrupted the piped Christmas carols. In the queue for check-in, those with skis had a definite air of oneupmanship about them.

'Come on,' muttered Jamie, hating to be held up. The man in front in a paisley cravat was demanding if there were such a thing as first class cargo for his skis. 'Don't know why he's so worried. Cheap, rubbishy things. Really short.'

Flora studied Jamie. She'd thought she knew everything there was to know about him. It had never really sunk in that he cared so much about skiing. 'Are you as good as Pete says you are?'

He smiled smugly. 'Probably better.'

She caught sight of the departure board. There was a last call for a flight to Pisa. After a rain-sodden week in Scotland, while Jamie caught salmon and she caught a raging cold, he had promised her the next time they went away, it would be her choice. 'Siena it is then. Scout's honour. Swear,' he had vowed.

How come she was getting a flight to Geneva?

The steward fussed over Jamie, offering to hang up his jacket and mixing his Bloody Mary with lingering care. With his thick blond hair curling round his head like laurel leaves, ice blue eyes

4

and aquiline nose, Jamie brought to mind one of the more noble Roman emperors.

'Nuts?' The steward's heart fluttered.

According to the captain, the plane was cruising high over the Channel, but it was impossible to know because of the thick cloud. The weather in St Marie promised to be bright and sunny. Cheered by the prospect, Flora smiled and squeezed Jamie's hand.

'Never thought you'd change your mind,' he said. 'Glad you did. We'll have a wonderful time. A week-long party.'

Her green eyes flickered momentary doubt. 'Still prefer to have you to myself.'

'Come on, you adore Pete.' Pete was Jamie's best friend. 'And the others are really nice people. Fun.'

Flora mentally counted off Miranda, Giles, Sam and Munchkin. One Clone Ranger and the three what? Graces? Wise men? Little pigs? She hardly knew them. What about the rest, whom she'd never met? What would they be like?

'There's nothing like spending a week together to really get to know people,' said Jamie, draining his glass. 'Another?' He leant over and kissed Flora's cheek. 'My beautiful wife.'

In Geneva, the train taking them to Annecy was waiting at the spotless airport station. It chuntered off towards the city centre the moment the clock hit 10.58. They peered out of the window, suddenly excited about being somewhere new. Later, as the train sped alongside the lake and towards the mountains, a buffet trolley was wheeled along the corridor. Jamie ordered a ham roll and a beer, then winced at the price. He was relieved to cross the border into France.

Like a dowager, Annecy seemed serene, well-established and well-heeled. A bone-chilling wind whipped down from the mountains and across the broad expanse of lake, freezing the water in the canals and the park fountains.

Waiting for the bus to take them to St Marie, Flora shivered inside Jasper's old jacket and stamped her feet. Across the deserted street, a digital display said the temperature was minus six degrees. Few cars were about and fewer people. The cold was making her nose run, and as usual, she didn't have any tissues. She sniffed. 'Has a neutron bomb fallen? Where's the bus?'

'It'll be here in a minute,' said Jamie with as much conviction as he could muster. He was wondering if they were in the right place, but there was no one to ask. 'If not, we'll get a taxi.'

'No taxis. Could hire a car.'

'No car hire.' Was Flora having a dig? As Jamie checked the timetable for the sixth time, she stamped her feet again and delved into her bag, pulled out Jasper's ski gloves and a pair of pink furry earmuffs Jamie had given her for a joke Christmas present. She put them on him. They laughed and began to cheer up. 'There's one thing missing. Apart from the bus.'

'Umm? What's that?' Jamie nuzzled her neck.

'Snow.'

'Not high enough. St Marie is a few thousand metres higher over there.' He pointed northeast. 'There'll be tons there.'

'Oh.'

A throaty rattle announced the arrival of a blue coach, which drew up next to them in a cloud of diesel fumes. The engine died. The driver climbed out.

'St Marie, monsieur?' asked Jamie anxiously.

'Oui. Cinq minutes.' The driver laughed.

Jamie slung their stuff into the hold. Flora smiled vaguely when the driver said something about the cold in rapid French. Teeth chattering, she got in and sat down, curling and uncurling her toes to get the circulation going. Just as the engine rumbled into life again, four panting teenagers piled on board, snowboards under their arms. Realising why they were sniggering, Jamie snatched off the earmuffs.

'Well organised Giles,' he sat back. When Giles had been told that Flora and Jamie would be going by plane, he had got his long-suffering secretary to find out the train and bus times. By the end of her research, she hoped his trip would be one way.

The bus climbed away from Annecy and into the country-side. As they had their first sighting of mountains and snow, their ears popped. Flora gazed up at the white capped peaks with a shiver of apprehension. The bus lurched around a hairpin bend.

'We're above cloud.' Jamie peered down. 'Look.'

'I can't.' There was a 100 metre drop, down, down to a boulder-strewn river bed. 'We'll go over the edge.' Flora closed her eyes and turned her head towards the aisle. 'It's like *The Italian Job.*'

'Stunning.' Jamie wiped the window with his sleeve to clear the condensation. 'I love mountains. I'll take you climbing.'

Flora went green.

The engine noise grew louder as the bus laboured climbing higher. They passed through villages and went alongside fields hidden under patchy layers of white. Sheer walls of rock dwarfed the farmhouses. The road cut through a thick pine forest. Green branches were weighed down by snow.

Ten minutes later Jamie nudged Flora and smiled. A road sign proclaimed St Marie.

'One of the oldest and prettiest of all the French resorts,' said the brochure, 'St Marie rightly remains a favourite holiday destination, offering an extensive network of runs to suit every skier from the novice to the expert. The village nestles at the foot of the mighty Diables, whose three peaks challenge the most experienced climbers.'

The bus trundled through the narrow streets, passing a fire station, apartment blocks and a small hospital, which had a helicopter pad beside it. Remembering the clinic in Davos, Flora grew pale.

Banks of snow separated the road from the pavements. Everywhere was thronged with people making their way to the lifts, walking clumsily in heavy boots, skis over their shoulders or carrying boards. Hidden behind hotels and more apartment blocks was a beautiful onion-domed church. Signs pointed to *Ecole de Ski*, *Patiner* and *Telecabine*.

They passed an open stretch of ground, covered by a patchy layer of grey snow. It was separated from the road by a metal crash barrier. To one side was a large concrete hanger. A long queue snaked around it. 'Must be the main chair lift,' said Jamie.

Flora's eyes followed the route of the chair lift's metal girders, strung across the white expanse of piste, stretching up towards the sky. Halfway up, the buildings flanking the slope gave way to trees. Skiers emerged from the green and darted across the snow like rabbits. She craned her neck as she gazed up and up. Smaller than pinheads, figures were silhouetted momentarily against the blue. She felt her stomach churning; it was so steep.

Jamie studied the piste map that Giles had faxed. 'That must be Les Pins. Nice easy blue run for you, angel.'

'Easy?' It looked like the north face of the Eiger to Flora. She remembered hitting a patch of ice on a blue run in Arosa, falling and hurtling down for what seemed like forever. When she had stopped her ski pants were shredded down one side. How old had she been? Ten?

The bus halted in the market square. Once a tranquil spot, it was now a traffic island, where the town's five main streets converged. Jumping out, Flora got a lungful of traffic fumes. Gaudy neon signs flashed *tabac*, *boulangerie*, pizza. The bustle around her was disorientating; she'd pictured a village out of *Heidi*, she'd arrived in a snowy Las Vegas.

She stood guard over their luggage as Jamie got on his mobile and called the chalet. Jamming his finger in his ear, shouting to make himself heard, he backed away and was almost mown down by the departing bus. 'Stay here.'

Suntanned skiers and boarders wrapped up against the cold went by en route to the lifts. Their ease, their confidence only underlined her misgivings. Flora wanted to run after the bus and bolt back to Annecy.

Jamie returned ten minutes later. 'Finally got through. On a land line.' He scowled at his mobile. 'Anyway the chalet girls are Hetty and Alice. Twins. Both sound really sweet. Hetty's meeting us over there.' He pointed at a shop across the square. 'Apparently it's the best.'

Flora's gaze followed his finger. 'Ski hire. What for? You've got skis.'

'For you, angel.' He interrupted her spluttering buts. 'Flora, if you change your mind, you'll be ready. No pressure. And it's a chance to warm up. Come on. Please. For me.'

Struggling with her bag heavy with books and the wedding file, she began walking.

Inside the hire shop, the Beach Boys blared from the speakers. Racks of skis lined the pine-clad wall. Flora eyed the rows of multi-coloured boots with suspicion; Frankenstein's monster should be wearing them. If only she were Surfing USA, at least California was warm.

The assistant sprouted short ginger dreadlocks and wore baggy green; a carrot in reverse. He stifled a yawn as Jamie explained the lady hadn't skied for years, was definitely no expert and probably needed quite short skis.

Flora grew uncomfortable as the Carrot looked her over, assessing her height and build, before demanding how much she weighed. She felt like a tailor's dummy as he and Jamie stood pair after pair of skis up against her and discussed their merits.

'Hold the pole properly,' said Jamie. 'No, too long. Hang on. Stand up straight.'

'Jamie,' pleaded Flora. 'I'm not going to ski.'

'You might change your mind. It's important to get it right. They seem OK. Now the boots. Put on the socks you'll be wearing.'

Tutting, Flora rummaged through her overflowing bag to find a pair of thermal socks. She stood up and wondered why the Carrot was grinning. At his feet were a pair of her knickers and a slightly grubby bra. She snatched them up as he asked her size.

'34B.'

'Shoe size.'

Flora blushed scarlet. 'Five. 38.' He climbed a ladder and pulled down a pair of shiny red boots. 'They're for a yeti,' she protested.

'Just try them on,' sighed Jamie. 'They have to be big to protect you. No, they clip up at the back these days.' He knelt down.

'Prince Charming,' said Flora.

'Then do try and be Cinderella, angel. Not an Ugly Sister.'

'Jamie. I don't want to . . . Ow.' She winced as he fastened the clips. The top of the boots bit into her shins.

'Walk round,' chivvied Jamie. They were so heavy she could hardly lift her leg. 'Comfortable?'

'No. Tight. Jamie, listen . . .'

'They're meant to be. What about the toes? Move them a bit? Good. We'll take them.'

As she watched the Carrot set them onto the skis and adjust the bindings, all her awful memories of fright, tears and being stranded on a mountainside rushed back. Why had she changed her mind?

'Hello?' The voice was tentative. A plump girl hovered by the door. She wore a lilac jacket and a beaming smile. 'Jamie Naze? I'm Hetty from the chalet. Welcome to St Marie.'

He bounded across to her, hand outstretched. 'Thanks. Hello. This is Flora. We're almost through here.'

He arranged terms with the Carrot. They followed Hetty out to an old Camper van. Flora got in a tangle carrying her skis and poles under her arm, rather than over her shoulder. She whacked herself on the shins, before trapping her fingers. Hetty suggested they'd want to arrange their passes while she went off to buy some potatoes. Knowing she had angst written all over her face, Flora tried to smile an eager, enthusiastic smile as if she could think of nothing nicer in the world.

The pass office was across the square. It shared premises with the ski school and was chaotically crowded. Jamie had brought passport photos of himself from London. Believing she would never, ever set foot in St Marie, Flora hadn't. She joined the queue for the booth behind a family from Birmingham. Each of the four images that dropped out of the machine showed up her apprehension.

'The incredible sulk,' said Jamie, looking at them. The ski school queue snaked around the building. He was desperate to be out on the slopes. 'You don't want to ski today, do you? We can arrange lessons for you later.'

'I thought you were teaching me,' said Flora. 'That's what you said.'

'I did?' He looked vague. 'A pro would be better.'

'You are a pro, aren't you? You taught in the Army.'

'That's different.' He handed over a huge wad of notes for two weekly passes, as Flora pleaded with him not to waste his money, she wasn't going to ski. 'Now put this round your neck and don't lose it.'

She examined the pass in its laminated coating. 'Abominable.'

'*Abonnement,*' corrected Jamie.

In the side mirror, Hetty watched them walk towards the van. A couple from a fairytale. Fragile, her long black hair snaking down her back, green-eyed, Flora had an air of vulnerability. Shy, slightly built, she was a head shorter than Jamie. An ethereal maiden in need of rescuing by a knight on a charger.

She was slowing down now, peering at the church which clearly intrigued her. Hetty felt a pang when she saw him put his arm around her and hurry her forward. He might be ancient — mid thirties — but was definitely — what was the word? —

distinguished. His straight back suggested Sandhurst, his jacket a tailor. An English pedigree chum. Looks, lineage and, she guessed, loot as well.

Climbing in beside her, he gave her another warm smile. Hetty melted.

They drove through St Marie. 'Nursery slope for the kinder-garten,' said Hetty. 'Skating rink. Chalet's up over there, quite close to the top of Les Pins. Loads of lifts there to take you up to the best runs.'

She changed down a gear as they left the town centre. The road became steeper and the buildings started to thin out. Snow lay to the side, surviving the gritters and tyres. Les Diables seemed closer, dwarfing everything.

'Didn't expect we'd be so far out. We can ski back to the chalet?' asked Jamie.

Hetty winced and sounded apologetic. 'Yes. Usually. If there's enough snow. But as you can see there isn't at the moment. It's forecast for later in the week. Don't worry it's only a short walk to Les Pins lift.'

'Walk?' said Flora cautiously.

'About ten minutes.'

Real time or brochure time? Flora remembered staying in a villa in Greece, described as minutes from the beach; minutes abseil down a cliff face more like.

St Marie was shrinking by the second as they climbed higher. The chalets on either side of the road had glorious views across the sun-filled valley. Up on the balconies, people were having lunch.

'What about the snow?' asked Jamie.

Hetty tried to sound reassuring. 'If you go high enough, absolutely no worries. Some of the lower slopes are getting a bit patchy. But the weather's been beautiful. Bright sunshine and blue skies every day for the past week.' She pointed. 'Top of Les Pins. See, the lift station.'

Through a clearing was a huge expanse of white piste, dazzling in the sunshine. Two skiers glided across the snow, heading for the lifts. The path connecting the road to the piste was rutted with ice. Imagining falling over on it, and ending up in plaster again, Flora winced.

'Les Landais.' Jamie read the gothic script on a sign outside a large wood-clad building. 'Restaurant?'

'Clients usually go there on our night off,' said Hetty, turning the van sharply to avoid a group of skiers ambling in the middle of road. 'Careful when you're walking. Some of these bends are completely blind.'

The road twisted and turned, going still higher. Jamie looked at his watch. It had just gone two. Where was the chalet? He'd miss his chance to ski. Hetty made an abrupt left and skidded up an icy driveway. 'Here we are.'

Chalet Juliette was three storeyed and whitewashed. A wooden balcony ran round the first floor. Behind the rails were huge picture windows looking down the valley towards Les Diables. To the back was a dense tangle of trees.

Flora jumped out, the ice-crust cracking under her feet. Apart from drip, drip, drip as tiny stalactites melted from the roof, there was silence. The cold, clean air hit her lungs like a punch.

'Need snow,' said Jamie, seeing clumps of yellowing grass peeking through the white.

Above them, a glass door slid back and Hetty's double came out onto the balcony. She was sturdily plump with the same kindly face and thick springy hair. She squinted against the glare and smiled. 'Hi. Alice. Welcome to Chalet Juliette.'

'Can I be Romeo?' called back Jamie.

The twins giggled. 'Everyone says that,' groaned Hetty, hauling a sack of potatoes out of the van. Flora, who had trouble lifting her bag, felt effete and useless in comparison.

'Let me,' said Jamie, grabbing the sack.

'Thanks.' Hetty led them through a pine door into a dark hallway. Next to a flight of stairs two single beds had been squeezed into a tiny bedroom. Clothes, toiletries, photos jumbled every surface. On the wall was a poster of Woodstock and Snoopy, next to another of Mel Gibson.

'Ours,' said an embarrassed Hetty, quickly closing the door. 'Bit of a mess. The last lot of clients left at eleven and we've been cleaning since then. Here's the storeroom, put your skis and boots in.' Jamie dumped the potatoes beside a huge freezer. A hot pipe led from a noisy boiler.

Bounding up the stairs into the sunny sitting room, Hetty introduced them to Alice, who was wearing a Garfield apron. Her hands were covered in flour from making a crumble.

The twins were in their gap year. They'd done a crash cooking course in the summer after A Levels. The tour firm director had hired them on the spot, impressed by their common sense, reliability and lack of obvious sex appeal. Experience had taught him to avoid pretty girls, who thought their main job was to bed clients and find husbands rather than make beds, and whose idea of washing up was to leave the dirty dishes out in a blizzard and hope for the best. For their part, the twins were quite happy to work hard and punishing hours in exchange for board, lodging and a season's ski pass.

'Festive in here,' said Jamie. A balding Christmas tree stood at the foot of the staircase to the second floor, its fairy lights out of action; tinsel and paper chains were draped around the pine walls and fireplace.

'It's so cosy when the fire's lit,' said Hetty. 'Now, bedrooms. As you've arrived first, you've got first pick.'

They followed her up the stairs. Two bathrooms, two twin rooms, two minute singles and a small double overlooking the trees at the back. Seeing it, Jamie raised an eyebrow. 'Bit pokey.' He counted up on his fingers. 'Where's the other room?'

'Clever of you,' said Hetty. 'Back downstairs.'

It was next to the sitting room. Large and bright, it had huge windows with views of Les Diables and a door leading to the balcony. The blue duvet matched the armchair upholstery.

'Great,' said Jamie, taking off his jacket and slinging it down as if staking his claim.

'Nicest room in the chalet,' said Hetty. 'Though it caused a rumpus the other week. One couple thought it wasn't fair that the other should have it all the time. They had to swap over. It was like musical chairs.'

'Don't worry. Won't happen this week,' said Jamie. 'First come, first served as Giles explained.' He began tearing through his bag. 'You'll unpack?'

'Later.' Flora was imagining the two of them enjoying a long, late, cosy, boozy lunch in Les Landais. 'Where are you going?'

'Skiing.' He pulled out a pair of long johns, gloves and socks. 'I've been waiting eight months for this.'

'Oh.'

'Tea before you go?' asked Hetty.

'Love a beer.'

Flora opened the door and went out onto the balcony, marvelling at the view. As the sun warmed her face, all her anxieties evaporated. Jamie could ski, she could sit and read in the warm sunshine. It was far better than being stuck indoors in grey, dreary England, feeling bloated from an excess of food and at a loose end because of the post-Christmas shut down.

Jamie managed to undress, dress and swallow his beer in less than three minutes. His jacket seemed tighter. Maybe it had shrunk in the wardrobe since April?

'See you later, angel.' He kissed Flora's cheek and pulled a face when she begged him to be careful.

She leant over the railings and watched him clomp down the drive in his heavy blue boots, skis over his shoulder, poles in his left hand. He put on his sunglasses and turned back to wave at her, his blond hair standing out against his navy jacket. Flora was bewildered by the transformation. Even when he was out of his pinstripes, she teased him that he always looked so stuffily, tweedily correct. Now he looked like a skier, as if he were born to it. As if he'd never been anything else.

Further along the balcony, Hetty waved too. 'He's wearing jeans. Pretty cool. And they're an even cooler set of skis. Racers aren't they?'

'Are they? Is there a difference?'

'Huge.' Hetty was shocked by Flora's ignorance. 'Don't you ski?'

'No. Not for years.'

'You're going to aren't you?'

'No.'

Hetty was dismayed. It was unthinkable that anyone wouldn't want to ski. 'What are you going to do all week?'

Flora smiled. 'Sit on a balcony in the sunshine and read and drink hot chocolate.'

'Oh.' There was a pause. 'Mr Thomas, Giles, mentioned a couple who are engaged. Is that you? Really? Congratulations. When's the wedding?'

'April.'

'Big wedding? Wow. Lots of work.'

'My ma's frantic.' Flora sighed. 'House is like Desert Storm headquarters, she's Stormin Norman. Plans, charts, lists.'

'Known Jamie long?'

'Since March. Not that long I guess. But it just seemed so right.'

Hetty glanced at Flora's tummy, but it was hidden under a bulky, surprisingly scruffy black sweater which had holes in the elbows. Her eye was caught by a sparkle. 'Your ring. Oh. Let's see.' Smiling shyly, Flora walked across the balcony and held out her long, thin fingers. 'That's so beautiful,' breathed Hetty, awestruck. 'Diamonds? They're huge.'

'Pretty, isn't it.' Flora couldn't quite believe it was hers. As soon as she had been given it, Jem had immediately done some research – 'guestimate, three times your annual salary according to my man in Hatton Garden' – and Flora had almost fainted.

'So, he's loaded as well as handsome and charming.' Hetty grinned wickedly. 'Go on, fess. He is, isn't he?' Flora laughed. 'Got a brother? No? Pity.' She sighed. 'Must get on. We're wondering what time your friends will arrive, so we can plan dinner.'

Flora had a vague stab of disquiet. 'Jamie said about eight.'

'Right. Tons to do. Ten staying.'

Flora collected some books, a blanket and sunglasses, opened up a faded deckchair and settled down for an afternoon's sun and fresh air. She wished she and Jamie had the place to themselves. Apart from Pete, none of the others were her friends, not real friends. Giles, Sam, Miranda and Munchkin she'd met perhaps once or twice; Martin, Nicky and Anna never. What would they all be like?

She thought back to that awful weekend in November when Jamie had told her he had arranged the holiday. On the Friday night she and Jem had been out with the girls. Dinner was followed by a packed, noisy club.

'A hen night? So, you'll be after some cock then,' a money broker had leered. It had been one of the better chat-up lines of the evening. How she had longed to see Jamie. When she had finally arrived at his tiny house in Chelsea, she had found him and Pete crashed out in the drawing room. Alcohol fumes filled the air.

Chinese takeaway was spilt on the carpet, a mirror and credit cards were on the table. And Rizla papers were scattered around. Jamie was sprawled on the sofa, snoring. He was like a Roman emperor — Caligula after a debauched night. Deciding it was easier to wake the dead than wake up the two men, Flora had gone to bed.

The next day, so hungover they wished they were dead, Jamie and Pete tried to piece together what had happened the night before. They gave up and switched on the racing. Just as they were about to go to the bookies to collect their winnings on the Hennessy at Newbury, Giles Thomas had called. To remind them that the night before they had agreed to join him for a week's holiday.

Flora was aghast when they told her she was going too.

A huge row had followed. Caught in the crossfire, Pete had made his escape. The row was bigger than the row after Jamie had trodden on one of her cherished paintings after a night on the sauce; more monstrous than when she collected him from the police station after the Test at Lords.

Flora tried to make Jamie understand that she was furious that he had arranged a holiday without consulting her, and that he'd arranged one with a group of people, most of them complete strangers. With him living in London and her based fifty miles away in Jaxley, they only really saw one another at the weekends. She wanted him to herself.

And why, why, if he had to book a holiday, why, why, why must it be a skiing holiday?

'What's the problem?' countered Jamie. 'Skiing's one of the best inventions in the world.'

'Better than the wheel? Better than penicillin? Better than chocolate?'

'Definitely better than chocolate. What's wrong with skiing?'

'It's loathsome. The cold, the boots, the queues, carrying the fucking skis, falling over on the fucking snow, falling over on the ice getting to the fucking snow. All of it.'

Skiing was the stuff of her worst childhood memories. If there wasn't a blizzard, there was an icy ledge of a path with a drop down hundreds of feet. When she didn't accidently let go of her poles on the chair lift, a ski would come off during a fall and shoot down the mountainside. Ski school classes hadn't taught her much about skiing, but she'd learnt a lot about humiliation. Her humiliation.

The weeks had passed. She refused to change her mind. Her colleagues in the newsroom of the *Jaxley Standard* all thought she was mad to turn down a holiday. Her friends said it would do her good to get away.

'You might be trying to be pale and interesting, but quite honestly you look washed out. Go,' said Jem.

Only Fred Quince had been on her side. 'Skiing? You?' He'd roared. 'Darling, no. No. No. No. All that horrible exercise, all that ghastly fresh air, those hideous dayglo clothes and the people, my dear, the people. Hearties of darkness. The horror. The horror.'

She had reported this back to Jamie as they walked round the Serpentine on the Sunday before Christmas.

'It's the French Alps, not the Congo,' he'd snapped, displeased. He didn't care for Fred, an artist, whom he dubbed Quince the Mince. Fred was a side of Flora that made Jamie nervous.

'You go. I can stay here and get on with the wedding,' she'd offered. 'Fred and Billy are giving a huge dinner on New Year's Eve.'

'Faggots on the menu?'

'They're recreating *Babette's Feast*.'

Jamie had rolled his eyes, then stopped and hugged her, wrapping her in his overcoat. 'Listen, angel. Supposing I hadn't got so wrecked that Friday night. Supposing I'd said I really need a break, will you come with me, because it would make me so happy? Supposing we'd talked about it properly. As we should have done. Surely I'd have persuaded you?'

Flora had felt herself thaw.

'It'd make me so happy. We'll have a wonderful week. Promise. You don't have to ski . . .'

Smiling, Flora stretched like a cat, took in another lungful of clean mountain air and marvelled at the view across the valley, glad that she'd relented.

'Jamie and Flora must have arrived by now.' W. Giles Thomas glanced at the dashboard of his company BMW. The miles per gallon ratio was poor; probably because of the roof box. They might have to make an unscheduled stop for petrol, which would mean losing valuable time and being further ripped off by the appalling exchange rate.

'Pete's probably there too,' piped up Sam Shaughnessy from the back seat.

'We're not racing,' said Giles crossly, pressing his foot down on the accelerator. An hour before he had been peeved when Pete's silver Porsche sped past with a flash of lights.

A farmyard smell filled the car. 'Farted again, Giles?' asked Sam with his Irish lilt.

'No I haven't.' He was indignant.

'Makes a change,' said Sam.

'Now, now. Mint?' offered Miranda Lake-ffrench. They raced past a juggernaut. 'Sure you wouldn't like me to take over, Giles?'

'Positive.' He wasn't going to entrust his precious car to anyone, not even Mirandy. Realising he sounded abrupt, he added a thank you and a smile.

As she smiled back, he once again thought that she'd make a perfect wife for him. The selection committees of the Constituency Associations would nod rapturously as she proclaimed that of course my husband will be a dedicated Member of Parliament working tirelessly for this constituency and I am 110 per cent behind him. Miranda was the sort that the biddies and buffers were charmed by; a pearl-wearing, charge-taking organiser who looked good in a head scarf.

Alas, it was never to be. Miranda was practically engaged to Charles Lyall, a bloodstock agent as well-bred as the horses he sold. 'How's Charles?'

'Charlie?' Miranda was studying the map, neatly folded on her lap. It was ripped and crumpled after Sam had got in a tangle with it near Rouen. 'Still in the Gulf. Boring. Won't be back for weeks.'

'Pity. Missing hunting then.'

'Um.' Miranda fiddled with a gilt button on her navy blazer.

'Like a word with him about it sometime,' said Giles.

'Planning to go out?'

'Giles? Hunt?' scoffed Sam, not taking his eyes from his Gameboy. 'The nearest he'll get is the Dog and Fox in Clapham. Not forgetting those Stag at Bay mats you picked up in Arding's sale. The sad ones you told Munchkin were family heirlooms.' Giles glanced testily in the rearview mirror. 'Giles wants the arguments for and against in case he ever goes for a rural seat. Poor seat.'

'How is Munchkin?' cut in Miranda. 'Did she make it to the get-together? Sorry I missed it, had to work late.'

'Didn't miss much,' said Sam. 'Only Munchkin turned up.'

'It's a very busy time of year,' snapped Giles. 'Few windows in anyone's diaries.'

'Shame really,' added Sam, 'after all the time you spent arranging the Christmas cards, making sure we could all see that one from the shadow minister.'

'If you must play with that thing, turn off the volume.' Giles was tempted to stop the car and make Sam walk.

Sam's big Irish mouth more than made up for his lack of height. Giles was recently finding him irksome. He was forever taking the piss, letting out Giles' secrets and showing him up. It was a mistake having him as a lodger. Of course, the money came in useful paying for all those extras like his bridge lessons and wine courses, which weren't part of everyday life where he was from. Not that anyone could tell where Giles was from, with the punnet of plums in his mouth. They had grown at university and flourished during his accountancy training.

'I forwarded your mail to Imogen's,' said Giles. 'Any sign of an offer?'

'None.' Sam was terse. 'Fuck.' Mario was crushed by a boulder.

'Move over.' Giles flashed his lights at a Citroen up ahead. 'Well, let's hope something turns up soon. I can't believe you'll claim housing benefit.'

Sam snapped off the Gameboy. 'Why not? I've paid in enough over the years.' He didn't need another pompous lecture about living off the State. 'Worried about declaring my rent?'

'That's got nothing to do with anything.'

'Hasn't it? Party won't like it. Future MP caught fiddling tax.'

'What future? Doubt if I'll ever get a seat.' Giles sighed. 'It's about as likely as you getting another job. How long's it now? Three months?'

'Who's counting?' demanded Sam. 'Best three months I've had in years. Nice to get off the treadmill. Take stock. Catch up with old mates . . .'

'Take stock?' Giles sniggered. 'You mean reading the *Racing Post* and hanging around the bookies all afternoon.'

'So?'

'So in your situation you shouldn't be gambling.'

'You mean I shouldn't have backed the winner of the Hennessy at twenty-to-one. Paid for this holiday, didn't it? Know something, Giles? I should've got you a tambourine for Christmas.'

Miranda turned round and winked. Sam's big brown eyes glinted merriment. 'Well, I do admire your optimism. The level of redundancies recently is quite frightening. Some chums think they'll never get another job.'

'At least I don't have a mortgage to worry about. Interest rates set to rise again, aren't they Rachman? I mean Giles.'

Miranda suppressed a giggle.

Giles scowled. 'You might've lost your job, but your singular sense of humour's still intact we see.'

'Something will turn up,' Sam yawned, 'always does.'

'That's hardly the attitude. The interest rate is a disgrace. There's no excuse. And did you see the latest factory gate prices . . .'

'More music?' interrupted Miranda. 'Simply Red?'

Giles hrrumped. 'Unfortunate name.'

'Stupid git,' muttered Sam.

Miranda stifled another giggle. Giles always took this politics business so seriously, his whole life one long march towards the green leather benches of the House of Commons. He had ambition, focus and prospects. If only he were more attractive, but those jowls, the almost white blond hair and matching lashes weren't for her. Pity. Pity she only went for bastards like Charlie.

She picked up the holiday brochure. On the cover were a sickening couple, bursting with good looks and health, their teeth as white as the snow on the mountains behind them. A week's skiing was just what she needed. Hard exercise through the day, cosy evenings unwinding in front of a fire followed by deep, deep sleep. It had been weeks since she'd enjoyed an uninterrupted night.

Up on the balcony of Chalet Juliette, Flora stretched like a cat. Her afternoon was passing to a background noise of scrubbing, vacuuming and clatters from the kitchen. She felt guilty that the twins were working so hard while she was idling in the sunshine with Dorothy Parker.

The sliding door opened. 'Hot chocolate?' asked Hetty. 'And there's some Sachertorte left.'

The chairlift swayed forty feet above the snow. Jamie's skis almost itched with excitement as he caught sight of the sparkling mounds of a mogul field. He loved going over the bumps. The twins were right; the snow was good higher up, although wearing very thin on the lower slopes. Even he had nearly come to grief. Flora's warning to take care had flashed through his mind. Eight months since he last skied; eight months of working at the bank, boozing and good food had taken their toll on his fitness and his waistline. Still, the coming week should put him right.

Taking a deep breath, he closed his eyes, turned his head up to the blue sky and got a faceful of sun. He was happy.

*　　*　　*

Pete Logan was unusually stressed. He drummed his fingers on the dashboard, fiddled with the stereo and took another look at the map. Two hundred more miles to go. Where the hell was Anna? He got out to check the skis on the roof, his eyes searching round the windswept service station for her.

'Hey. Gorgeous.' A shrill wolf whistle was followed by shrieks of teenage hysteria.

Preoccupied, Pete hadn't noticed the coach halting alongside him. Neither had he seen the ogling stares directed his way from the passengers, schoolgirls on a hockey tour. Or the excited nudges, and the movement as the girls on the right had rushed to the left hand window to get a better gawp.

'Nice,' called out the whistler, who had opened the emergency door at the back. 'Great bodywork. Any chance of a ride?'

Pete grinned. 'Anytime. Any of you.'

A cheer went up. 'You've got the Adonis award. Beaten Ralph Fiennes, Keanu Reeves, Brad . . .' The girl was yanked back by an angry games mistress, who glared at Pete and slammed the door. As the coach moved off, her two colleagues were storming up the aisle trying to restore order. Pete waved as the coach disappeared, the girls at the back blowing kisses at him.

Now in his early thirties, when some of his contemporaries were losing their hair and gaining paunches, Pete had retained his angelic good looks. The sweetness of his face was marred only by a crooked nose, which everyone assumed had been broken by a jealous husband. In fact, it had been smashed water skiing during the time he was running a bar in Antigua. With his shoulder-length, sand-coloured curls that he was always pushing out of his eyes, and his carefree, laidback sunniness, Pete seemed permanently on holiday. His girlfriends reckoned he was Australia's greatest export.

'Come on.' He looked round for Anna again. First, there had been a fifteen minute queue for petrol, then just as he'd been about to set off, she had disappeared to the ladies.

Why wasn't he with Jamie or Sam? They wouldn't have kept giving him earache about the speed limit, or lectured him about the earth's resources or global warming when he admitted the Porsche gobbled petrol. And if they'd been searching for a CD, they wouldn't have got the hump when a pair of black lace knickers belonging to he-didn't-know-who, fell out of the glove compartment.

'Thanks Giles.' Giles had suggested he drive down to St Marie with Anna Blake. Just longing to speed down the autoroutes, so he could speed down the slopes with Jamie, Pete hadn't cared who was in the passenger seat.

He'd been intrigued when he'd heard about Anna, at teacher training college up north, who was working in a hostel for down-and-outs over Christmas. She sounded far more interesting than the scores of girls he'd taken out in the past six months.

'Come on.' What was she doing? Half an hour had already been added to the journey when he'd got lost in the one-way system trying to find her friend's flat. King's Cross should've been renamed Pete's cross. And then she wasn't even ready; telling him some barmy story about trying to telephone her cats.

Chit-chat to the tunnel was stilted, after he told her he owned a bar in the City. She'd reacted as if he peddled smack rather than flogged fizz, before launching into an earbash about City parasites moving money around rather than creating anything of value. He had tried to talk films, but it seemed she only saw arty stuff out of Iceland or Tunisia.

On the M20, she had got out a book, asking him what he was currently reading. 'An Asterix collection. Jamie gave it to me for Christmas. Magnificent. What's that?'

'*The Brothers Karamazov*. And no,' she replied frostily, 'it's not about the Mafia.'

Anna Blake gazed at her reflection in the mirror and told herself to lighten up. Her thin face was devoid of make-up, her shrewd grey eyes masked by horn-rimmed glasses. Her mousy hair was Eton cropped.

As soon as she'd seen Pete at the door that morning, she had shrivelled up inside. Good looking, good-time guys like him always intimidated her. They were only interested in leggy blondes they could wear on their arms like an expensive watch. She noticed Pete had a Breitling, along with a Porsche, six feet three inches and an amazing smile. Feeling at a disadvantage, she had over-compensated and in self-defence played up her serious-minded, blue-stockinged side.

His driving was shocking. Anna felt she was at Le Mans or on a hurdy-gurdy at a funfair. She had looked forward to seeing the French countryside, but instead had spent most of the time with her eyes tight shut, gripping the side of her seat, alternately terrified or seething. Bloody testosterone. Exactly what were men trying to prove when they got behind a steering wheel?

She longed for the journey to end. Pete's chain-smoking made her feel sick, the roaring engine and the louder music was giving her a headache. Stopping for petrol, she seized her chance. She had tarried for as long as possible in the loo, hoping Giles might catch up and she could change cars.

From outside, she heard the blast of a horn and realised she couldn't dally another moment. Unable to look Pete in the eye, she had muttered something about a terrible queue as she fastened her seatbelt.

Pete revved the engine and they shot off, tyres squealing.

As the sun edged behind Les Diables and lights came on across the valley, Flora went inside and unpacked. A bathroom was next to their bedroom. She ran the taps, hoping a hot bath would ease the cold dread inside her.

It was almost five o'clock. Where was Jamie? She had taken his word that he could ski, but at what level? Supposing he had got out of his depth, pushed himself too far, taken unnecessary risks. Had he fallen over a precipice or into a crevasse? She would be widowed before she was married. Shivering in the rose scented water, she told herself to clam down, then wondered what a crevasse was.

Suddenly there was a knock at the door and Jamie came in with a huge slab of Sachertorte. Flora leapt up and threw her arms around him, as if he had returned from the Front.

'What a welcome. Angel, you're making the cake soggy. And me.'

'How was it?'

'Brilliant.' He sat on the edge of the bath and munched happily. 'Managed to cover three long runs. Legs feel it a bit. Out of practice.'

'Out of shape?' She smiled and poked him in his middle, which was starting to show the slightest of Winnie the Pooh bulges.

'Flora. This will go. Anyway, I can still run six miles straight off, which is six miles more than you. You smoke too much.'

'I know.' She pulled a face.

'New Year's resolution, remember?'

'Yes. I know.' She also knew she should go to a gym, but had never got round to it. Her attitude to exercise was unchanged since school; mentally she was still sitting on a radiator with Jem skiving off games.

Jamie gave her a bite of the cake. 'Make the most of that bath. Showers from now on. Can't be a hot hog, according to Giles. Got to think of the others.'

Crumbs of cake fell into the water. 'Wish we were here on our own.'

'We are.' Jamie grinned wickedly, suddenly got up and locked the door.

'What about the twins?'

'What about them?'

Hearing giggles, loud splashing and Flora's scream when Jamie accidently turned on the cold tap, Hetty and Alice wondered what was going on.

*   *   *

In the back seat of the Range Rover, Kate Williams took a quick bite of icing and marzipan. She had brought a Christmas cake, two flasks of coffee and a stack of turkey sandwiches for the journey.

Her resolution to lose weight and get fit for skiing had lasted one trip to the gym, where an aerobics class had proved the worst hour of her year. Pulse racing and exhausted after the five-minute warm-up, she'd been convinced she was only going to leave the studio on a stretcher, and then not necessarily alive. Her puce face had clashed revoltingly with her pink T-shirt. Her nickname should've been Babar, not Munchkin.

She had met Giles a year before at a Neighbourhood Watch meeting, just after she had bought her Clapham flat. When he invited her to join him and some friends for a week's skiing, she had accepted immediately.

The chalet looked beautiful; Giles, typically, had got an excellent deal and best of all, there would be five single men staying there. Well, four and a half, because unfortunately the dashing Jamie Naze was engaged to scruffy, arty Flora, a very unlikely choice. But that still left Giles and Sam, good mates and fun to spend the week with.

And Pete and Martin.

Munchkin had delicious daydreams about how she would be forced to choose between them. Sweet Pete, 100 per cent pure Aussie beefcake, with his blond ringlets and dreamy eyes, duck egg blue according to the colour chart for her bathroom paint. She had met him a few times and he was as easy to talk to as he was on the eye. But could she cope with the hours he put in at the bar and the hundreds of women chasing him?

Just as she was having doubts about Pete, Giles told her she would be driving down to St Marie with Martin June. The Martin June. Ex soccer star, now en route to tycoondom. Her luck was in. She described him to her envious colleagues as a cross between Richard Branson and Alan Shearer with a bit of Sean Connery thrown in. She immediately went on her cauliflower and water diet.

As December passed in a kaleidoscope of present buying and dos at the marketing company where she was a director, Munchkin became more and more excited at the thought of the holiday. Each day she had to restart the diet, which she would usually break by 11am, when she told herself it was personality that counted anyway. Her motto was bubbly not blubbery.

In idle moments she would speculate about the other women in the chalet. Flora was getting married in April. Miranda had been seeing some man for ages and was practically engaged, according to Giles. Munchkin, who didn't know Miranda well, conceded she was attractive but also quite bossy, which was a real no no as far as men were concerned. That left Anna and Imogen, Sam's sister. Both nice but not much competition. It was obvious that Anna read Wittgenstein rather than *Vogue*, and Imogen was so scatty, she thought she was going to St Tropez, not St Marie.

Munchkin's daydreams came to an abrupt end the week before Christmas.

To Giles' fury, Imogen pulled out. She had forgotten to put any oil in her car, which needed a new engine and could no longer afford to go away. After he slammed the phone down on her, Giles began a round of calls. Did they know anyone who could replace Imogen at such short notice?

When Munchkin rang back later that morning to say that someone from work may be a possible, a relaxed Giles assured her that everything was once again under control. Nikki Solange was coming. Munchkin's heart sank when she heard that Nikki was not only Martin's girlfriend, but a model who ran around town in a Mercedes convertible. From that moment, the cauliflower and water diet was history.

Munchkin had thought that Giles' pre-holiday get together might give her a chance to grab a lift from Pete. The evening was a washout. Expecting a party, she had rushed home and spent twenty minutes worrying about what to wear. Should she stick with her suit and be the time-pressed career girl or put on something more dressy in case they went on to a nightclub?

Arriving late and thinking she would find crowds of people, she'd been taken aback to find Giles and Sam tossing a coin to decide who would go to the corner shop and buy a tin of tomatoes for spag bog. After one drink, Giles had decided to have an early night and she and Sam had gone for a pizza. She'd paid. In more ways than one.

As the French countryside flashed past, she resolved to put her fretting on hold. She had another bite of cake. Although she would've loved sitting beside Pete, the Range Rover was incredibly comfortable. Martin was charm itself and had put himself out not to make her feel like a gooseberry.

He'd arrived at her flat just after seven that morning. Opening the door, her heart had soared. She had a moment to take in his black and silver hair and steel eyes, before he gave her a hug and kissed her on both cheeks.

'So you're Munchkin. We finally meet. About time. Why didn't Giles tell me you're gorgeous. And you're ready. My favourite kind of woman. Can't be doing with hanging around. Hey. Stop that. I carry the bags around here.'

She'd been left breathless by the energy crackling from him and quite weak-kneed as she followed him to the car. So often she'd asked God for a man, but He'd sent her boys. This time the prayer had been heard. Martin was Man with a whopping Times Roman capital M. Not conventionally handsome like Pete, or particularly tall, but so broad. He carried her two lead-heavy bags with ease. With those hooded eyes and the large, no strong, nose he reminded her of an eagle. A faint scar showed under his right cheekbone. Perhaps the result of a duel? Walking beside him, she felt incredibly feminine.

Nikki was sitting in the passenger seat, pouting beautifully into a compact as she retouched her lipstick. Munchkin felt the colourful fireworks of hope and joy fade to nothing.

At the sight of Nikki's legs, Munchkin cursed herself for not sticking to the cauliflower and water regime. Lithe thighs. They were lithe in cream cashmere leggings. The matching cream polo neck suited Nikki's long neck, her long sleek chestnut curtain of hair and her suntan. Munchkin hated polo necks because they accentuated her slight double chin and cream accentuated her every blemish and made her skin look grey. As they moved off, Munchkin reminded herself, bubbly not blubbery.

By the time they reached the tunnel, Munchkin had grown more relaxed about Nikki's glamour. Who needs a Hermès bag anyway? While perfectly pleasant, Nikki didn't have much to say for herself, whereas she and Martin talked non-stop as if they were old friends. He wolfed down the sandwiches and the cake.

'You made it? Really? What a star. Now fill us in. Who's Flora? Pretty-boy Pete's girlfriend? No? What do you make of him? Is it true some girl topped herself because of him?'

'You don't know? Well . . .' Munchkin poured herself some more coffee, warming to her task. There was nothing she liked better than a long, cosy gossip.

As Munchkin started, Martin winked at Nikki.

Nikki took out her compact again, wondering how long she could avoid any awkward questions.

The hours passed. Concentrating on the road occupied the drivers' minds, but their passengers grew fed up, the tedium worsening after dusk fell.

Giles talked about a recent by-election, going on about turn-out percentages and swings. Miranda had trouble staying awake, but she felt honour-bound to keep him entertained. Unlike Sam, snoring heavily in the back seat.

In the Range Rover, Munchkin scoffed more surreptitious chunks of cake, hoping that Martin and Nikki wouldn't catch her out in the mirrors.

'Let's make lots of money.' Pete was singing along to the Pet Shop Boys. 'Jamie's favourite song. What's that?' He turned down the stereo.

'I'm not sure this is right.' Anna peered out into the darkness.

'Giles said the road out of Annecy went alongside the lake.' She switched on the sidelight and picked up the map. They had just passed through Hiverette, so they were definitely on the wrong road. 'We should have taken a left.'

Muttering, Pete jammed on the brakes. The Porsche stopped in a screech.

Anna's hearing was acute. 'What do you mean why can't women ever read a bloody map? If you hadn't been going so ridiculously fast, you wouldn't have missed the turning.'

Flora had hidden her biker boots under the bed. Her thick black sweater was folded away in the wardrobe. When she was with Jamie, she'd make an effort. She liked it. Being on parade. If anyone had told her a year earlier she'd be wearing a pink twinset with violet velvet edging, she'd have laughed. Or huge pearl earrings, his Christmas present. She'd lived in black.

Pushing her tatty fabric friendship bracelets under her sleeve, she went into the sitting room. A log fire was burning. The twins were laying the table, telling Jamie about the best off-piste areas as he fiddled with the fairy lights. He'd already earned huge Brownie points by making the fire.

The smell of garlic and herbs wafted from the kitchen. With the curtains drawn, it was as cosy as Hettie had promised.

'Done.' Jamie settled into an armchair by the fire, gin and tonic at his elbow and smiled in satisfaction at the lights, now all working properly. He surveyed the L-shaped room, one half dominated by the stone fireplace. Shelves either side housed the stereo, a television and stacks of well thumbed blockbusters. The furniture, admittedly rather tatty, was upholstered in cheerful tartan. In the second half, a matching cloth covered the dining table laid for ten. Not a bad place to spend the week, he decided. Giles had chosen well,

Flora curled up into the armchair opposite him and picked up the wedding file. It was crammed with lists, shops catalogues, fabric swatches, colour charts and builders' estimates. She made a note to ask the twins for the Sachertorte recipe, then studied a thick cream swatch. 'Bedroom curtains, perhaps.'

'Anything.' Jamie lifted his eyes momentarily then returned to the *Spectator*. 'You decide. Just don't bankrupt me.'

Jamie had inherited his house off the Kings Road on his twenty-fifth birthday. Having suffered ten years of trashing, it needed a complete overhaul, a task he'd entrusted to her. Flora was anxious. 'It's like having a giant doll's house to play with. Wonderful. But I want you to like it.'

'I will. You've got the eye,' he murmured. 'My beautiful wife.'

She smiled contentedly. 'It's so peaceful. Marvellously peaceful.'

The BMW arrived in St Marie.

'Out of the way,' yelled Giles, hooting at a group of teenagers, ambling in the middle of the road. 'Bloody French. Think they own the place.' He drove into the square, which was as bright as if it were midday.

'Sweet church, all lit up like that,' said Miranda, catching sight of the onion dome.

'Think we'll find plenty of olde worlde charm here, unlike the purpose built resorts.' Giles missed a flashing pink neon Niteklub sign. 'And it shouldn't be chockful of plebs. Look out for the ice rink.'

Jamie stared into the fire, entranced by the flames that danced to the haunting violin concerto. Finishing his drink, he could feel himself unwinding. A glorious week lay ahead. No work, no crowded tube, no pressure. Just day after day of skiing.

He watched Flora, who had thankfully stopped fretting about colour schemes. She was sucking the top of her pen, trying to work out an anagram. *The Times* had its usual holiday jumbo crossword. She must be doing her usual two clues. She frowned. 'What are red caps? Birds? Mushrooms?'

'Military Police.'

'Really? M. P. So this must be rampage then. It is. Fits.'

'Perfectly.' Jamie grinned. He had spent three wonderful years in the Army on the rampage at the taxpayers' expense. Dull drills and tours of duty were long forgotten; sweeter memories remained. Mess nights, chopper rides to drinks parties and the Cresta Run.

'Another?' Getting up, he grabbed a handful of cheesy nibbles from a box on a side table. He was hungry, the delicious smells from the kitchen making him even hungrier. 'Found out about that cooking course?'

'Not yet.' Flora frowned.

Jamie's Guccied steps echoed off the wooden floor as he crossed the room to the sideboard, covered in half empty bottles of duty free left behind by earlier clients. Flora smiled as he ruffled her hair, putting another whisky at her elbow. She adored these times of cosy companionship with Jamie, whose hectic social life made them all too rare.

He stretched, yawning. 'Fire's making me drowsy. Wonderful week ahead. I think you should give it a go, angel.'

'Ski, you mean?' Flora shivered.

'I'll look after you.' His blue eyes were tender.

'Even thinking about it is scary.'

'Don't be silly.' Jamie was afraid of nothing except his grandmother. 'Flora, I'd never let . . .'

He was interrupted by the sound of a car braking and frantic hooting out in the drive. Going to the window, he pulled back the curtain and peered out into the darkness. 'Giles.' He waved him down, missing the minutest scowl from Flora. 'He's got Sam with him. And who's that? Miranda.' He tapped on the window and waved again. 'I'll go down and give them a hand with their stuff.'

Flora stood up, feeling she ought to help, but didn't really want to be bothered to go out into the cold.

Giles stormed in. 'Well, hello there you two. How the devil are you?' He seized Jamie's hand and gave Flora a slobbery kiss. His eyes caught the box of cheese nibbles. 'What's that? Tampax?' His whinnying laugh drowned out the music. He put his arm round Flora's waist and squeezed. 'Seven hours, not bad, eh? See we beat Pete Schumacher Logan. He'll go ballistic. Not bad, averaged 23 to the gallon and that's with Mirandy's arse weighing the car down. Axle practically dragging on the ground. Where's the beer?'

'I'll get you one,' offered Flora, wriggling free of him and rubbing her cheek, wet from his kiss. She had forgotten how loud and braying his voice was, as if he were always addressing a political rally packed with hostile hecklers.

'Miranda,' exclaimed Jamie. 'As gorgeous as ever.'

She beamed. 'I heard that, Giles. Beast. Jamie, darling hello. Mwah Mwah. And Flora. Lovely to see you. Isn't this fun?' Miranda's Sloane tones bounced off every surface. 'Super place. Well done Giles. What a journey we've had, still the man's a star. Now, simply must explore. Say hello to the girls. Hetty and Alice, isn't it? Something smells yummy. I'm bound to have put on tons over Christmas. Where's the kitchen. Ah here we are.'

Flora felt short and shaggy next to Miranda whose five feet ten inches were immaculately turned out, from her poker straight blonde hair held back by an Alice band to her polished navy loafers. Her jeans had pale vertical lines down them front and back. She irons them properly, thought Flora aghast.

'Hetty and Alice? Miranda Lake-ffrench. We spoke last week. I've got your stock cubes and some Marmite . . .' Miranda had stayed in chalets every year for simply yonks and knew the form. She had showers to save the hot water, and brought Trivial Pursuit. She always called the girls from her office to check on whether she could bring anything that might be hard to find 'Abroad'.

Giles's eyes under their white lashes followed Miranda across the room. With his string coloured hair and fat face ending in a pointed nose, he reminded Flora of a guinea pig.

'Nice fire. And a goggle box. Though Frog telly's supposed to be dreadful. Everything to your liking?' He was anxious. Organising the holiday had taken weeks of planning, getting together a mixed bag of friends and people he knew through work.

'Great.' Jamie raised his glass. 'Thanks for all your . . .'

A bellow came from downstairs. It sounded as if a cow in terminal distress had wandered into the chalet.

'Moo-ooo-ooo.' It got louder. 'Moo-ooo-ooo.'

'Where've you been?'

'Moo-ooo-ooo' replied Sam. 'Had to have a slash. Desperate. Thought I'd drown. Jamie, Flora. Wotcher. Good Christmas? Need a beer. Now.'

Flora suddenly felt taller. Sam was about five five, but always insisted he was perfectly formed where it mattered. With his curly brown hair, big brown eyes and button nose, combined with elfishness, many women thought him cute. Froth from his can arced high into the air before landing.

'Whoops. Christening the rug, someone has to.' He trod it in. 'Good flight? Ski at all?'

'Managed to go out this afternoon,' said Jamie. 'Found some nice runs.'

'You went with hubby?' asked Giles.

'No.' Flora shuddered. 'I . . .' She was silenced by a don't start look from Jamie.

'Village looks nice,' said Giles. 'Much better than all the purpose . . .'

The roar of an engine, screech of brakes and blast from a horn came from outside. Downstairs, the front door crashed against the hall wall and heavy footsteps bounded up the stairs. In strode Pete, broad shoulders matched by a broad smile.

'Pete,' cried Jamie joyfully.

'Jamie. My man.' They lurched round the room in a bearhug, crashing into Flora and knocking her sideways.

'Lizard of Oz. Beat you,' yelled Giles triumphantly. 'Beat you.'

'Only because of a wrong turning at Annecy. I was miles ahead, mate.'

'We wouldn't have missed it if you didn't drive like a lunatic.' The quiet voice was insistent. 'Hello.'

Pete turned to Flora and Jamie. 'Met Anna Blake, have you? Anna, Jamie and Flora. Anna couldn't navigate her way out of a paper bag. Recycled paper, right Anna?'

'Right.' She scowled at Pete, reached inside her turquoise ski jacket for a handkerchief and polished her glasses.

Flora saw Pete pull a face at Jamie. She was surprised. He was rarely ruffled by anything or anyone. Anna was clearly immune to the famous sweet Pete charm. What had happened on the journey?

'Hello Pete. Hello Anna. I'm up here. Unpacking,' called Miranda from the floor above. Flora wondered if she'd found a megaphone in her luggage.

'Brilliant.' Sam whooped. 'Giles said there was a stereo here. What's this?' He pressed the eject button. 'Mozart? Mozart? No thank you very much.' He rummaged through his bag. 'Now pump up the volume a bit.'

A techno beat blared out. Sam started to duckwalk across the room, bumped into a side table and overturned Flora's whisky onto her wedding file. Giles started to sing along. Seizing a gong from the sideboard, Sam whooped again.

Introducing themselves properly, Flora and Anna had to strain to hear what the other was saying. From upstairs, Miranda demanded to know what was going on. Sam held the gong up to Flora's ear and banged in time to the bass. Thinking she must look as if she'd seen something unpleasant in a lavatory, Flora gritted her teeth and forced a smile.

'My favourite song,' shouted a voice from the door. 'Hi guys.'

'Martin,' called Giles. 'Munchkin. And you must be the lovely Nikki.'

A dumpy blonde rushed into the room like a whirlwind. 'Party time.' Munchkin shrieked delightedly and blew the whistle hanging round her neck. An ear-shattering whistle. 'In case we get caught in an avalanche. Hi Sam.'

Giles introduced Flora to Nikki and Martin. Distracted by all the noise around her, she immediately forgot their names. The two men began comparing journeys, Martin wanting to know what time Giles had set off that morning. He took off his brown leather jacket and slung it on the sofa, as if marking his territory. His muscles bulged through his grey T-shirt.

Nikki stood mutely by his side. His bulk made her seem tiny, although they were shoulder to shoulder. Clutching her mink-lined parka, her lamplight eyes sometimes scanned the room, although mostly they were fused on Martin, as fixed as her wary half smile. Although stunning looking, and draped in expensive clothes and jewellery, she struck Flora as being ill at ease, like the wife of an errant MP standing by her man during a press conference after he'd been caught having an affair.

'More music someone,' called Martin.

Flora failed to be grateful to Munchkin and Sam for providing extra percussion with the avalanche whistle and dinner gong. The front door had been left open after all the luggage was hauled in, including Nikki's three massive Louis Vuitton bags. As case after case of beer was put out on the balcony, the temperature plummeted further.

While everyone rushed upstairs to unpack before dinner, Flora was tempted to pack up and flee into the night. All the peace she'd enjoyed with Jamie was shattered; so spacious earlier, the chalet now seemed hopelessly overcrowded.

'Another drink?' asked Jamie.

Flora's ears were still ringing from the assault from the whistle. She turned down the stereo, took a deep breath and picked up her drenched wedding file. She was about to sit down, but noticed an old white stain on the armchair. Ice cream? Or worse? Hastily, she moved to the sofa.

Jamie sat beside her and held her hand. 'We'll have a wonderful week.'

Trying to smile, she tracked the to-ing and fro-ing upstairs from the stomp of footsteps overhead. Was that Giles singing 'White Christmas'? 'Um.'

'You look gorgeous.' He fiddled with her engagement ring, the diamonds glittering in the firelight.

'Can't be a loveable scruff all your life,' quoted Flora. 'Jamie, I . . .'

'What?'

'Nothing.'

'White Christmas' grew louder.

Back in London, Giles had drawn lots out of a cleanish saucepan to decide who would have their own rooms and who would be sharing. 'Much fairer. Don't want any ructions on arrival,' he said to Sam, as he cut the paper with precision. 'You're the witness.'

Now Miranda laid out a row of face creams like a formation of model soldiers as Anna unpacked her books.

'Lovely place, isn't it? How was your journey? Being with Pete in the Porsche must've been fun. Sorry, seem to be hogging the wardrobe, carted far too much as usual. Bugger, forgotten my sunscreen.'

'Borrow some of mine.' Dodging round Miranda in the narrow room, Anna wished she didn't have to share. Her head was aching from the drive and she wasn't feeling up to chit-chat.

'Sweet of you. Now. Where did we meet? Imogen's party?'

Coming out of the bathroom which Miranda had decided was for the girls, Munchkin heard their muffled voices and felt a stab of social anxiety. Two's company, three's a crowd. If Anna and Miranda chummed up, what would become of her? Flora and

Nikki were with their men. Why did she have to be in a single? She'd miss out on all those girlie chats.

Wiping the steam from the boys' bathroom mirror, Giles ran a comb through his string-coloured hair and congratulated himself. The chalet was great, Hetty and Alice were sweet and here he was with a great bunch, all present and correct. It had been a long, hard slog getting the thing organised, but it would pay off.

A week like this was the best way of getting to know people and these were the sort of people he wanted to know. Jamie Naze, merchant banker, city whizz kid, family in *Burke's* — Giles had checked. Pete Logan, Aussie surfie and playboy about town. Martin June. Yes, *the* Martin June, now a property developer and one of his clients. It had been quite a coup getting them all along, the guys at work had been gratifyingly impressed.

What Giles hadn't let on was that it had been unexpectedly easy. After a Friday afternoon meeting back in November, Martin had come along for a drink at Pete's bar in Cheapside. Giles had arranged to meet Sam there. They'd bumped into Pete and Jamie. Although Giles couldn't claim closeness with either, he'd vaguely known both of them for a couple of years. They had people in common, such as Miranda. That night, the five men had got on well, one bottle leading to another. When Giles told them about the chalet and asked if they might be interested, Pete and Jamie had immediately got out their chequebooks. To his surprise, Martin had accepted too.

Giles examined his nostrils, which had got alarmingly hairier over the past year. As the resident property expert, Martin could give him some advice. The rung had broken almost as soon as Giles had moved up the property ladder and bought his new house. He had assumed it would be only weeks before the rest of the road was transformed into bijou residences for like-minded professionals, but had been sadly disappointed. Prices were plummeting by the day. The area that was up and coming, had been and gone.

Never mind that, he was on holiday. Martin was with the delicious Nikki, a *Vogue* model no less. She was much better to have around than the irritating Imogen, who was as much of a waste of space as her brother, Sam. He'd done nothing since he'd lost his job except moon about the house and run up huge heating and phone bills. His only outings were to Ladbrokes.

Nikki would introduce him to all her colleagues. He'd take one of them with him to Jamie's wedding. Would he be able to hack a week of being under the same roof as Mirandy? The Hon. Miranda Lake-ffrench, perfect in every way, apart from being practically engaged to Charles Lyall. The holiday would give him the chance to strengthen his friendship with her, if nothing else.

Anticipating the avalanche of invitations landing on his mat once he returned home, Giles burst into another chorus of 'White Christmas.'

Next door, in his tiny single room, Sam cursed the depreciation of sterling as he counted out his francs and hid them away in a sock drawer. He wished Giles would shut up and hurry up, he must have the three Ss before dinner.

Pete galloped down the stairs, went out onto the balcony and grabbed some beer for him and Jamie. A dose of Asterix had restored his usual sunny mood. 'Here's to hols. Never thought I'd see you here, Flora.'

'Neither did I,' said Jamie squeezing her hand.

'Neither did I,' she said dryly.

'Did I pitch up much after Giles?' Pete tried to sound casual.

'About ten minutes.' Jamie grinned. 'You made his day.'

'I bet. Just my luck to be with someone who's brought a library but can't read a roadmap.' He lowered his voice. 'Explain the difference between greenhouse effect, global warming and the hole in the ozone layer. No, don't bother.' He yawned,

shaking the hair out of his eyes like a sheepdog puppy.
'Knackered. Early bed, then out first thing. How long's it been
since we skied together?'

'Zermatt. January,' said Jamie.

'Right. Remember that night we got really stoned and ended
up playing strip poker with those four German nurses?'

Flora raised an eyebrow.

'Did we?' Jamie shot Pete a warning look. 'If we did, which I
doubt, I don't think Flora wants to hear about it, thank you.'

Upstairs, Nikki was brushing her long chestnut hair. Catching
herself frowning in the mirror, she tried to relax. Impulse had
made her agree to this holiday, just as impulse had made her go
out to the bar that Thursday night, where she had let herself be
picked up by Martin. And now here she was, only weeks later,
her life turned topsy turvy, in France with a man she hardly
knew.

Martin was lying on the bed, holding his strong wrist up to
the light to admire his new Rolex, Nikki's Christmas present to
him. He rolled onto his stomach and gazed at her reflection. 'I'll
get it sorted.'

'Good.' When she had seen their room, Nikki had been
unable to hide her disappointment. It was so small, with such
tiny windows. There wasn't enough hanging space for all her
stuff.

'Promise.' He had caught sight of Jamie and Flora's room.
'The other two will swap halfway through the week.'

'Couldn't you say something tonight?'

'Let's get settled in first, shall we?'

'My clothes'll be ruined crammed together like that.' Not
that she would be able to wear half of them, if her first
impressions of St Marie and the other women in the chalet
were correct.

Munchkin she knew. Only too well. She'd yakked away non-stop from the moment she'd got into the car, even when she'd been gobbling up Christmas cake on the sly. Nikki had caught her in the wing mirror. No wonder she was about two stone overweight. When Martin had asked if she'd mind driving down with someone else, Nikki had assumed the third would be an old friend of his. She'd been put out to learn that he'd never met Munchkin before today.

There was the quiet girl with the glasses. And the blonde, very lah-di-dah who'd gone on and on about the bathrooms. She must be the one engaged to Jamie. They seemed very well suited. Nikki made a note to check the engagement ring. Where did the arty looking one in pink fit in?

She wondered how she was going to cope with the coming week. 'I'm not sure about this modelling business, Martin. Why not say I temped or something?'

Martin propped himself up on his arm. 'Temping doesn't buy you a fur coat or your handbags or a Mercedes. Don't worry. You're beautiful enough to get away with it.'

'Why tell anyone about the car? It's gone now.'

'May your days be merry and bright.' Giles clomped downstairs. He'd changed into scarlet cords, a checked country shirt and wore a knitted yellow tie under his jersey. His hamster face was still red from the shower.

Settled on the sofa beside Flora, Miranda ssshed him. 'The twins said dinner would be at nine. Three hot courses, we're going to be incredibly spoilt. When I do a DP, everybody's lucky to get one. You and Jamie must come along to one of my young marrieds.'

Flora imagined the scene. Miranda's flat would be spotless, with framed photos of labradors. There would be lots of chat about weddings and skiing. She'd forget to post her thank you letter, which Jamie would have to remind her to write in the first place.

'Of course,' continued Miranda, 'people are so understanding if one's a career girl. Sir Graham, my boss, is such a sweetie, always lets me go early, but thank heavens the supermarkets are open late. But doesn't shopping take hours, one's always bumping into chums. Entre nous, have you noticed the standard of talent in Waitrose on the King's Road? Pretty a-mazing.'

Flora who avoided shopping as much as humanly possible, was at a loss.

'Talent. Where?' demanded Munchkin eagerly, plonking herself down in an armchair. She was wearing a pink and orange sweatshirt. 'Meribel – Powder and Glory' was emblazoned in day-glo yellow. Coming downstairs, she had planned to make a beeline for Pete, but he and Jamie were studying the piste map on the wall next to the dining table.

'Waitrose. Happy hour.'

'True. And the Cromwell Road Sainsbury's.' Munchkin's slight second chin quivered in excitement. 'Simon, one of my best friends met his girlfriend there. But you've got to check the trolleys. Nappies, family packs, don't bother.' Several times she had stalked her prey up and down the aisles, only to give up at baby foods.

'What are you girlies on about?' boomed Giles, swigging from a beer bottle.

'Shopping,' said Miranda.

'Men,' added Munchkin.

'Thermo-nuclear physics,' muttered Flora.

Giles groaned. 'Typical. All you lot ever think about.' He belched. 'Pardon. You, Miss Rosehagen, shouldn't smoke.' He snatched Flora's lighter, which she'd been about to pick up.

'Rose,' she muttered. Her heart sank. She didn't want to go into long, complicated explanations about her family history and, almost as bad, she realised that apart from Pete no-one else smoked. She put the unlit Marlboro back in the packet.

'Skiing tomorrow.' Giles began bending his knees and twisting his torso. 'Hope everyone's thighs are up to it. Have to arrange an inspection. Bet yours are, Mirandy. All that horizontal jogging with Charlie.'

Miranda blushed. 'Giles . . .'

Munchkin turned to her. 'Charlie's your man, isn't he? Involved in racing or something. Horse trader?'

'Bloodstock agent.' Miranda corrected her stiffly.

'From what Giles has said, he sounds very glam.' Munchkin had been dazzled by the description of Charlie, his title and his family estate, which Giles had given her in a Lavender Hill pizzeria. If she buttered up Miranda, maybe she'd be invited to one of the famous weekend house parties.

Miranda fiddled with her three string pearls as if they were worry beads. Why did Giles have to mention Charlie? He'd never met him. Or had he? Perhaps he could tell her what was going on. 'Didn't realise you know him.'

Puzzled, Munchkin stared at Giles. She remembered his talk of the King's bedroom and its Caneletto. 'You and he go back a long way, don't you?'

'Got hold of the wrong end of the stick, Munch.' Giles took a gulp of beer and smiled. The nearest he'd got to Charlie was when he paid £2 one afternoon to go round the grounds open to the public under the National Gardens Scheme. 'Never set eyes on the guy.'

'But . . .' Munchkin frowned.

'Are you having a marquee, Flora?' demanded Miranda, as Giles swiftly asked who would like another drink.

Upstairs, Anna lay on her bed, listening to the rumble of talk. She knew she ought to go down and join in, but it was such luxury to be with her own thoughts after the horrible drive, trying to be jolly when she arrived and as she unpacked with Miranda.

She wondered how Tom was, and whether the cats – Trotsky and Ortega – were enjoying their temporary new home.

She and Pete hadn't exactly hit it off, she realised. She knew he thought her po-faced. Perhaps she should've tried harder. Anyone else would've loved bombing across France in an expensive sports car with him. She guessed that Miranda and Munchkin would've swapped places with her immediately.

If only she had brought her flute and her music.

She knew she ought to be downstairs, being sociable. After all, she had decided to risk coming on holiday knowing no-one really, apart from Sam, Imogen's brother. Neither had ever warmed to the other, they were too different in outlook. When Imogen had called, wailing that she had to pull out, Anna had been in two minds as to whether she should too. But she had told herself not to be so wet. She had survived South America alone, she even went to the cinema by herself, which amazed her friends. Besides, she enjoyed skiing and needed a proper break before term started at college. And Imogen had called the day after she'd met Tom at a concert at the Trade Hall and she'd been in a complete daze.

Like a drinks party when the ice is broken, the voices downstairs were getting louder and jollier. Martin's was loudest of all, his arrival announced by increased volume from the stereo. Anna got up and found some painkillers.

'Was about to send a search party,' said Giles as Martin and Nikki came downstairs. 'What you drinking?'

'Tonic water.' Nikki had changed into skintight black leather trousers and a cropped black sweater which showed off her tanned midriff, tiny waist and pancake-flat stomach. 'Slimline tonic,' she insisted.

Munchkin's Gee and Tee suddenly tasted of a million calories, which she could feel going straight to her hips, adding to their 40 inches.

'No slimline,' called Giles from the sideboard.

Nikki gave a moue of displeasure and flicked her chestnut mane behind her shoulders. 'Mineral water then please.'

'Here we are,' said Giles, handing Nikki a glass. 'Now, fill me in, Martin. Is the housing market on the mend? The man here is our property tycoon,' he explained to Flora.

'Improving by the day,' said Martin.

As Munchkin chattered away about her marketing career, Flora longed to light up. Perhaps Jamie was right, it would do her good to be forced to consider other people. Was she getting set in her ways? How awful. She was 25 not 75.

She studied Jamie and Pete, arguing about which pistes they'd follow. The pair had met while they were ski bums during Jamie's gap year, where they had discovered the joys of drink, drugs and girls. Jamie had gone off to the States, Pete had hitched to Antibes and crewed on yachts for a few years before ending up in Antigua and then New York. When he had arrived in London, Jamie had put up some money for the bar.

'OK?' mouthed Jamie, then smiled.

She smiled back. When they had all arrived she had felt as if she were in the middle of the Sack of Rome, but now there was comparative calm. She was gradually orientating herself, but wasn't entirely at ease yet. They weren't that much older, but all seemed so much more confident and sorted and settled than she herself.

Munchkin was describing a recent business trip to New York, when she'd been upgraded to Concorde. Along with her effervescent jollity, she was also clearly very high-powered. Flora was overwhelmed; she was at the bottom of her career ladder and although she loved her job, her meagre salary was less than Munchkin's expense account.

Handsome Miranda was obviously an old hand at these sort of holidays. Flora was quite happy to let her take charge, in fact she felt as if she had no say in the matter. Miranda exuded so much natural authority, she was tempted to curtsey and call her ma'am.

Anna seemed interesting and had brought a huge stock of books. Perhaps she could loan her some for the hours on the balcony? She was definitely bright, and would know exactly what metaphysical meant.

Nikki was stunning, like Jem. It was unthinkable that she'd even whizz to the corner shop with bird's nest hair and old leggings. Her huge eyes and tip-tilted nose gave her face a sweetness that many glamorous women lacked. But her cool reserve, allied with those looks, made Flora feel gauche.

The chatter carried on around her. They all seemed easy enough to get on with, but the conversation was their territory and Flora was too shy to trespass upon it. The core four – Giles, Sam, Miranda and Munchkin – all seemed to know each other well and were talking about someone's party, underlining Flora's sense of being on the outside.

Feeling increasingly conspicuous in her silence, Flora wondered if she should go over and join Jamie and Pete. Then she ordered herself to try and make a bit more effort. After all, Martin was as much a stranger to them all as she was, and he had no difficulty joining in. He and Nikki made a striking couple; her doll-like delicacy enhancing his aura of commanding masculinity. He crackled with energy, making Jamie look languid and Pete seem positively catatonic.

'What are you staring at?' demanded Martin suddenly.

'Nothing. Sorry. I was miles away,' stammered Flora, blushing.

He stood in front of the sofa, assessing her and Miranda. 'So, who's who? Miranda, right. And you're, wait for it, Anna. No Flora. Flora. Yes? Who's engaged to Jamie?'

'Me,' said Flora.

Astonished, Nikki's lamplight eyes flashed to Flora's fingers, but her left hand was hidden.

Martin smiled. 'Congratulations. He and I went out about a month back, with Giles and Sam here. Great evening.' He leant forward, so she could feel his warm breath on her face. 'Your fiancé. Merchant wanker, isn't he?'

*   *   *

Alice struck the gong. The main lights were turned off, leaving just a glow from the fire and the candles on the table. Bottles of wine and baskets of hot bread were being brought in from the kitchen by Hetty.

Giles suggested Miranda organise the placement. 'Boy, girl, boy, girl,' counted Miranda. 'Nikki you're here, between Sam and Jamie.'

'Neah, ectually she's dine heah next to me,' cut in Martin, parodying Miranda's accent. 'Yah?'

'Fine.' Miranda was taken aback.

'Don't mind me.' He winked at her. 'Giles said your our resident bit of posh. How come he kept quiet about the rest of you?'

'What rest?'

He whispered in her ear. 'How absolutely gorgeous you are.' Smiling, he called, 'Pass the wine, Sam.'

As Martin filled her glass, Miranda told herself she shouldn't be feeling so absurdly flattered.

'Shall I be mother?' asked Munchkin, and started to ladle out steaming vegetable soup from a huge turreen. Delighted to be sitting next to Pete, she was hoping she could make up some lost ground for not being beside him in the Porsche. Flustered, she almost dropped a bowl, when their hands touched as he poured her some wine.

At the other end of the table, Flora asked Giles about his political career. Like the Duracell bunny banging his drum, he went on and on, giving her a countrywide tour of no-hope constituencies, marginal seats and boundary changes.

Hunched over his soup bowl, Martin asked Pete how long he'd had the Porsche.

'About a year.'

'Right, second hand. You can pick them up dirt cheap now, can't you? Jacked mine in, not much of a town car. All right for a bit of posing though.' He paused. 'If you're into that sort of bullshit. How's yours handle?'

'Great. Sticks to the road like superglue.'

'Hassle putting chains on. Can't be doing with it. That's why we brought mine, not Nikki's Mercedes.'

Pete stared at her, impressed. 'Mercedes? Sports? The 500? Nice one.'

Nikki was about to speak as Martin put his arm around her. He smiled at Sam who was gawping with envy. 'Dream to drive, isn't it, lover? Much smoother than any Porsche.'

Miranda's Polo had never had the same mesmerising effect on men. She reminded herself that cars were just a means of getting from A to B.

'Acceleration?' demanded Pete.

'Shit off a shovel.' Martin tore at some bread. 'If necessary. Grown out of all that foot to the floor, white knuckle ride malarky.'

'Glad someone has,' murmured Anna.

Catching her scowling at Pete, Martin laughed. 'Much nicer to relax and enjoy the ride. Took it nice and easy today, didn't we?' He put his arm round Nikki, showing off a bulging bicep. 'Precious cargo on board, Nikki here and Munchkin, of course.' Munchkin went pink with pleasure. 'Cooks like a dream. That cake. Booked myself in for dinner every night when we get back.'

Munchkin felt her allegiance swerving from Pete back to Martin.

'Get Flora a nice 500 as a wedding present, Jamie.' Martin slurped up the remains of his soup. 'You'll be back on the road soonish, won't you?'

Jamie scowled. 'Flora's happy with Freddy. Her ashtray-cum-dustbin on wheels. Aren't you, Flora?'

'Sorry?' She was almost panting from a sprint through every west country marginal.

'Want a Mercedes Sports?'

'No. Of course not.' She was puzzled. ' "Naff, noove and for flash old women." ' She was quoting what Jamie had once said. She saw him wince. 'Oh. Oh. Someone's got a Mercedes . . .' She was realising she'd made a hideous gaffe.

'Nikki,' said Martin.

'I didn't . . . er. Er.'

'Flora's not into cars,' said Pete, breaking the silence. 'Believed it when someone said to put sugar in the battery, didn't you angel? More soup, there, Munchkin?'

Martin and Nikki were clearly put out, and glared at the cringeing Flora. Scarlet faced she turned back to Giles. 'Where were we? Tiverton?'

Miranda summoned up her social cavalry to ride into the breech. She'd noticed Nikki had neither touched her soup, nor said a word so far. The situation must be remedied. 'Giles mentioned you're a model. Will we have seen you in *Vogue*?'

'Not recently,' said Nikki, feeling Martin's hand squeeze hers.

'Your face has to fit the moment, doesn't it, lover?' said Martin. 'Anorexic junkies are in. You're not.'

'Run across Zoe Janes?' asked Pete.

'Don't think so,' said Nikki.

'Lucky you.' He pulled a face.

'Nikki's between agents at the moment, aren't you?' said Martin.

'What sort of work do you do? Photographic?' asked Pete.

'It varies.'

'Page three?' demanded Sam excitedly, his brown eyes lighting up.

'No.' Nikki was shocked.

'Pity.' Sam sighed. ' 'Spose Anna will be glad to hear it. She and Imogen gave me such a hard time about the calendar on the fridge when they last came round.'

'Quite rightly,' said Anna.

'Wouldn't bother me,' shrugged Munchkin.

'Or me,' laughed Martin. 'Anytime. More wine there, Miranda?'

Nikki was relieved to be out of the spotlight. She glanced round the table at all the strange faces. Why had she come? She'd never be able to get away with this modelling business for a whole week. Why had Martin landed her in it? Modelling? The Mercedes?

Further down the table, Anna was telling Jamie about how she'd resigned from the Civil Service and started teacher training. She found him genial and easy to talk to. Insides still shrivelling from her appalling rudeness to Nikki, Flora was finding Giles a deafening struggle and lowered her voice almost to a whisper in the hope that he'd get the hint and turn down his volume.

The twins collected the soup bowls and returned with coq au vin and baked potatoes. Sam demanded more wine and three more bottles were opened.

In the kitchen, Alice peered anxiously round the door to the dining area. 'Hope that chicken's all right. It smelt a bit funny. God knows how long it's been in the freezer.'

'Don't worry.' Hetty was loading the dishwasher. 'They won't notice anyway. Not with the amount of wine they're knocking back. Did you see how much booze they've brought?'

'That guy Pete is soooo yummy. I'm in love. Think he's noticed me going red every time I look at him? Why did this huge zit have to break out?'

'It's not huge.'

'It is. Otherwise you wouldn't see it,' wailed Alice. 'That means he has. He'll never be unfaithful now. I can't believe that's his girlfriend. Lucky four-eyed cow.'

'It's not.'

'Really,' Alice shrieked. 'There's hope then.'

'She's sharing a room with Miranda, nice of her to remember the stockcubes, and he's in with that loud one, Miles.'

'Not Miles. Giles.'

'Whatever. Anyway, you can have Pete and I'll have Jamie. Anytime.'

'He's getting married soon.'

'So?' Hetty shrugged. 'Love, honour and betray. I can be his mistress. What's he doing with her? She's not that pretty, is she? She is? Oh. But she doesn't even ski.'

'Were they really doing it in the bath?' Alice sniffed. 'Shit, the apple crumble's burning.'

When the subject of work came up, Sam refilled his glass to overflowing. He sat in morose silence, while Munchkin told Anna about an avocado flavoured snackette she was helping to launch. Jamie and Giles were on finance. Further along, Pete and Martin were on about their companies, each trying to cap the other's bullishness.

Miranda, who explained to Nikki she was the Chairman's PA, said: 'We've just lost our place in the top 100, but Sir Graham is confident we'll be back by the third quarter.'

'Chairman's PA?' Sam raised an eyebrow. 'Typist who arranges plane tickets.'

Jamie's chit-chat about Japanese equities washed over Flora; he may as well have been talking Swahili. However, she kept her attention focussed on him. Still mortified with embarrassment by her tactlessness, she couldn't glance in the direction of Nikki or Martin. They were sitting too far away for her to apologise without drawing attention to herself and making it worse.

Martin put more butter on his potato. 'Hard exercise is the best form of relaxation, that's why skiing is a great holiday.'

Throughout dinner, Munchkin's head had swivelled between Martin and Pete like a spectator at Wimbledon, as she tried to decide who was the most attractive. 'Do you work out?'

Martin nodded. 'Every day.' He glanced at his biceps for confirmation.

'Still play at all?' asked Pete.

'Odd little charity match.'

'Never forget that goal against Arsenal,' said Sam. 'Fantastic. Goal of the season, wasn't it?'

'Yep.'

'Surprised you never went in for commentary,' said Munchkin.

'Was no money in it then,' said Martin. 'Won't say they didn't beg me. Wasn't interested. It was time to move on.'

'Ever consider coaching a team?' asked Anna.

'I wanted out.'

From the other end of the table, Giles let out a guffaw. 'Hey, Martin. Flora says she's never heard of you.'

There was a startled pause around the table. Flora froze. How could Giles be so tactless? She hadn't exactly said she'd never heard of him. Not in so many words. She'd just wanted Giles to fill her in. Quietly. Discreetly.

'This is Martin June. The Martin June,' continued Giles, pointing at Martin for Flora's benefit. 'One of the finest. Compared with Pele, George Best . . .'

Flora squirmed.

'Remember?' said Sam. 'The hat-trick against United. While back, though.'

'Sixteen years.'

'I was only nine then,' stammered Flora. 'And never into football.'

'Neither was I,' said Miranda. 'But we had a poster of you in the dorm, Martin. You even got us watching *Match of the Day*.'

Munchkin's eyes fell on the dish of potatoes. She mustn't have seconds. Must not. But she'd be getting a lot of exercise over the next week. Half a one, with a tiny bit of sauce wouldn't hurt and potatoes were so nutritious. Her fork reached out. 'Are we all skiing together tomorrow?'

'Hope so,' said Martin. 'Just point me at those black runs.'

Nikki and Munchkin protested that they weren't up to the more advanced pistes.

'Nonsense,' said Martin. 'We'll look after you. Won't we guys?'

Pete winked at Flora. 'Any heli-skiing in the area?'

'Ask the twins,' said Giles. 'Bit extravagant.'

Pete shrugged. 'Went in Zermatt, didn't we Jamie? One of the best days ever. Better than surfing, better than sex.'

'I adore Zermatt,' sighed Miranda. 'Lots of lovely runs. Chickened out of the Triffti though. So pretty there, no cars.'

'Like Murren.' Jamie smiled.

'Know it? Mummy and Daddy go there every year without fail. Done the Kandahar? Really? Mega impressive.'

According to Martin, Nikki loved Aspen. Giles and Miranda believed that Verbier took some beating, nice crowd there. Anna and Munchkin agreed that purpose built resorts had their advantages, less hiking to the lifts. Pete wondered if he'd need powder straps.

Flora sat in silence. Everyone else sounded so confident. They clearly couldn't wait for morning, like children on the eve of a birthday. Why was she alone in thinking that hurling yourself down a mountain on two pieces of fibreglass was at best ridiculous, at worst just plain terrifying?

'So, we'll aim for a nine-thirty start,' announced Giles. 'Sort out skis, boots and passes. All right with you, Flora? You're very quiet.'

She brought herself back from an icy ledge beside a drop down, down, down 200 feet. 'Sorry?'

'Leave at nine-thirty?'

'What for?'

'To ski, of course.'

'Ski? Oh, I'm not skiing,' she said blithely.

He was taken aback. 'Of course you are. You've skied before.'

'Years and years ago. And I always hated it.'

'Don't be silly,' he boomed. She tried not to squirm as he put an arm round her shoulder and squeezed. 'You're coming with us. You'll love it when you get going. Hubby'll look after you. Won't you, Jamie?'

Flora wondered if her hearing would be permanently impaired. 'I'm not skiing. It's not for me.'

As all eyes turned in her direction, she felt as if she were the Man Who in a Bateman cartoon.

Miranda was incredulous. 'You must. It's wonderful.'

Anna nodded. 'Exhilarating. You feel so alive.'

Munchkin joined in. 'Beautiful, when the weather's like this. Clear blue skies, dazzling white snow, the mountains . . .'

'I can get all that sitting on a balcony with a book and some hot chocolate,' insisted Flora.

'Ski school here is supposed to be marvellous,' said Giles. 'Join a class, polish up and come out with us later in the week. Besides, it's a good way of meeting people.'

Flora wanted to tell them that she knew enough people already. Everyone agreed she ought to give it a try, that she would get bored with a book after two minutes. She must have a go, for one day anyway. Learning's the hardest part. She felt like a pagan South Sea islander confronted by a bunch of zealous missionaries.

Pete winked at her. 'Stop pressurising poor Flora. It's up to her. How long were you in plaster for last time?'

Flora blushed. 'Weeks and weeks.'

'Poor you,' said Miranda. 'Leg?'

'Ankle, foot,' muttered Flora.

'But all the more reason to get back on your skis ASAP,' said Giles.

'Won't happen again.' 'Pilots after plane crashes, back in the cockpit straightaway.' 'Drivers after car smashes.' 'Lightning never strikes . . .' The chorus grew louder.

'I really don't want to ski,' protested Flora.

Jamie suspected she was about to lose her temper and tell them all to shut up. 'Stop making a fuss, angel, and just do it.'

'I'm not making a fuss . . .'

'Come on Jamie, fair's fair,' said Pete. 'She had a rough time.' Flora was grateful for one ally. 'Bad luck, sweetheart. No wonder you never touch tequila.'

Flora jumped with surprise and glared at Jamie.

'How old were you? Fifteen? Your parents must've been furious.' Pete's blue green eyes glinted with amusement. 'Flora sneaked out of a hotel one night to meet some guy in a bar, got blitzed on slammers and smashed her foot slipping over on the ice.'

Waves of mirth broke over Flora, as welcome as a bucket of cold scummy water. 'Jamie told you?' She glared at Pete.

'Sure.' He glanced at Jamie. 'Whoops. Have I just caught foot in mouth?'

'Thanks Jamie,' snarled Flora, provoking still more merriment. Jasper must've told him at the airport. Bloody Jasper. Bloody Jamie for telling Pete. And bloody Pete for showing her up in front of all these strangers.

'Well, you've definitely got to ski,' said Giles. 'Flora's got no excuse now, has she?'

Aghast, Flora realised she had forfeited any right to sympathy. She scraped back her chair.

'What are you doing?' asked Jamie.

'Going for a smoke.'

Flora slammed her bedroom door. Why the hell hadn't Jamie warned her that he knew about the whole sorry saga? Perhaps she should've owned up and asked him to keep it quiet. But even ten years on, it was so toe-curlingly embarrassing, she hated admitting it to herself. Besides, no spin could pretty it up.

'Oh, by the way, Jamie, I ended up unconscious in a gutter in

Davos. This German guy, who thought I was a cool chick of nineteen when he asked me out, had to find my parents and explain what happened. And they knew I hadn't blacked out from shock. I was sweating tequila for two days. As well as getting my leg plastered, I almost had my stomach pumped.'

She had wanted to give the episode a very deep burial. Now it had been resurrected. Bloody Jasper. Bloody Jamie. Bloody Pete.

She heard Munchkin's yell of 'Let's party' and the thud of a bass reverberated through the walls.

She went out onto the balcony, taking in deep breaths of Marlboro and freezing air, trying to calm herself down. Ice crust crunched under her feet. Far below in the valley, the lights of St Marie twinkled in the darkness. The moon was hidden by cloud behind Les Diables.

Bloody Jamie. Wasn't it enough that he was her future? Why should her past be his property too? Maybe she'd made everything too easy for him. Since he'd tapped on the cottage window that first Sunday of spring, her life had revolved around his.

Weariness stole over her as she imagined making the effort to be jolly and sociable over the next week. By the end, she'd fit in better, wouldn't she? She wouldn't feel like a diffident country bumpkin up in town for the day. This high octane, high earning, high living world was still so new. Alien. She'd begun to get to know it since meeting Jamie, but her own friends were completely different. Great artist he might be, but Fred Quince was a galaxy away from future MPs, models, peer's daughters and Concorde flights. Jem was a bit closer, but working for peanuts in a gallery and living at the wrong end of Ladbroke Grove, wouldn't count as hitting the jackpot in this company of gold cards, fast skiers and faster cars.

As the clouds moved, the mountain seemed to be moving too, closing in on the valley as if to crush and entomb everything in it. Shivering, she went inside, drawing the curtains against the blackness outside.

She didn't want to ski and didn't feel up to partying. She

wanted Jamie to herself. She wanted to spend tranquil evenings with him, snuggled up by a fire. In the summer, he had taken her to Provence where they had sunbathed, swam and made love. Delighting in their own company, they hadn't needed anyone else.

Remembering her gaffe over the Mercedes, Flora cringed inside. Pete's foot in mouth was catching, how could she have been so tactless? Sam or Giles might have laughed it off, but she sensed Martin was less forgiving. Why had she let it be known that she'd never heard of him? Actually, that wasn't strictly true. Jamie had mentioned something weeks earlier, but preoccupied by the wedding plans and thinking she'd never meet Martin, it had all washed over her.

Resolving to try and make amends, she returned to the sitting room.

Munchkin, Anna and Miranda were sitting round the fireside. The rest were grouped round Martin at the table, now strewn with empty bottles.

'Sorry about foot in mouth.' Pete held out his brandy glass. 'No hard feelings?'

'Course not.' Taking a sip, Flora decided she'd kill Jasper when she got home.

'Loan you Asterix.' He put his arm round her.

She snuggled into him. 'No need.'

'What's going on over there?' demanded Martin, grinning. 'Feeding Flora tequila? I'd watch those two, Jamie.'

Flora saw Jamie frown and hastily wriggled away from Pete. She wanted to protest against what Martin was implying. Wrongly implying. She and Pete could be stranded in an igloo in the North Pole together and nothing would happen. Ever. He was gorgeous, but 100 per cent out of bounds to her as she was to him. Unsettled by Martin's insinuation, she went and sat next to Jamie.

*　　*　　*

'Anyone want to hit town and explore?' asked Munchkin, hoping they didn't. She was delightfully snoozy after her two helpings of apple crumble.

'Typical,' said Giles fondly. 'Our party girl. Always tearing around. Actually, I vote we stay in tonight and make our own fun. Busy day tomorrow.'

'Not looking forward to sorting the skis,' said Martin. 'Always takes forever.'

'Thank God I brought mine,' yawned Jamie. 'Don't do hanging around.'

'Um. Should've brought mine. Heard the snow wasn't too clever and didn't want to ruin them.'

'What have you got?'

'Lazer 195s.'

Jamie raised an eyebrow. 'Bit long for you, aren't they? You're what, five ten?' Standing at over six feet, he could afford to be charitable.

Martin scowled. 'Got myself some new kit. Material developed for Polar exploration. Maximum warmth and movement without the bulk.'

'Sounds good.' Jamie yawned again. 'Jeans were fine today.'

'If you don't mind looking like you've wet yourself when you white out.'

'I don't white out.'

Martin turned to Flora. 'Doesn't he?'

'Wouldn't know.'

He stared at her. 'So you're not into skiing, not into football, not into cars, eh Flora? What are you into? Apart from tequila? And Jamie, of course.'

'Lots of things,' said Flora lamely. Her mind had gone blank. All she could think of was the Mercedes and how she'd forgotten who he was.

'Lots of things,' mimicked Martin, taking a gulp of brandy. 'Like what?'

He made her feel shy. Colouring, she wished she had an

interesting interest. Pete had flying, Anna had her music, Giles his politics. What did she have? Apart from her work, Jamie and her wedding? 'Not much I guess.' She smiled ruefully. 'Sorry, I didn't really know you were so famous. Why did you stop playing?'

Jamie kicked her under the table.

'Long story,' said Martin tersely, scowling at her. He turned to Giles. 'Well done, buddy. Thought the fax would blow up with the amount of bumf you were sending, but great organisation.'

Giles beamed. 'Be prepared et cetera. Don't want to be doing with asking Johnny Frog for directions and whatnot, bugger's bound to send you the wrong way.'

Pretending she needed to warm up, Flora escaped and stood in front of the fire. Obviously she'd caught a virulent dose of Pete's foot in mouth. Too late, she remembered Jamie telling her that Martin's career had been cut short by a car crash. He'd warned that even after all these years the subject was still sensitive and that Giles had put the word out that it was best not raised unless by Martin himself.

Yet again, Flora squirmed. Miranda, Anna and Munchkin were all talking Val d'Isere. Unable to join in, she caught sight of a Jackie Collins on the shelf and was tempted to start reading. It would be far more entertaining.

'Oh, let's see your ring,' said Munchkin. 'When's the big day? April?'

Flora shyly held out her hand for inspection.

'Lovely,' sighed Munchkin, her bosom heaving inside the dayglo sweatshirt. She turned to Miranda. 'But I always thought I'd go for something antique. Subtle and lowkey is more me. Sally, one of my best friends has something similar. Of course, one assumes it's a fake.'

'No good in a pawn shop then,' said Flora. Living on an

overdraft, she was convinced she was going to end her days in a workhouse.

'Don't you worry about the dreadful conditions in those diamond mines?' asked Anna, grey eyes full of concern.

'Not often,' confessed Flora faintly.

'Quite,' said Munchkin, dropping Flora's hand. 'I don't know if I'd be comfortable, knowing what goes on. It's like having a fur coat. My conscience wouldn't allow it. Anna's been telling us about the hostel she's been working in . . .'

'So sad,' cut in Miranda, not wanting to hear another lecture on homelessness, which had made her feel uncomfortable and guilty.

'Very,' agreed Munchkin. 'Still, we're on holiday. Can't do much about it from here.'

Anna guessed that she'd laid it on too thick. Why hadn't she explained that she had only volunteered because she'd been unable to face the festivities at home with her parents?

Miranda examined a lock of her immaculate bob for non-existent split ends. 'So, you'll have to leave your little local paper soon then, Flora. All those weddings and flower shows.'

'Carol services last week.' And a microlight crash and a murder trial and the latest installment of the bypass saga. And the secret plans to build a superstore, which would destroy the water meadows and the corn exchange. She was proud of that scoop, which had caused uproar locally and been the main feature on local TV news the following day.

'You must be excited at the thought of moving to London,' said Munchkin. 'I'm a city girl. It's so easy to vegetate in the country, isn't it?'

Flora had a pang at the thought of leaving Jaxley, the *Standard* and her cottage.

'Couldn't you commute?' asked Anna.

'Not really.' Jamie had spelt out the practicalities. The train was out, there was no bus and driving meant leaving around seven each morning and not returning until midnight some days. Anyway, as he pointed out, it was time to move on.

Miranda yawned. 'I'm pooped. Boring, but I'll have to toddle off to bed soon.'

Anna nodded. 'The drive was exhausting.'

'Fun though, being with Pete.' Munchkin was wistful.

'I'll swap on the way home.'

'You will?' Munchkin turned to Flora, who must know Pete well as he and Jamie were such good friends. She smiled sweetly. 'Poor you. Unable to come out with the rest of us. We were talking about it just now and agreed you must give it a go. Silly to come all this way and not ski, isn't it?'

Anna and Miranda nodded in agreement.

'I was so nervous when I first went,' continued Munchkin. 'Now there's no holding me back. Franz, the instructor in Val, said I was a natural. Of course, I'm a great believer in trying anything once. Giving it a go. Breaking the ice.'

'I'm more worried about breaking my neck,' muttered Flora.

'And ski school here is supposed to be marvellous,' said Munchkin. 'Who knows, if you try, you might be able to catch up with the rest of us by the end of the week.'

'Doubt it.'

'I'm not sure I'd care for ski school anymore. Bit too regimented. I suppose I'm just too much of an individual for my own good. But you'll have no problem.' Flora was bemused, but Munchkin swept on: 'I think she should have a bash, don't you Miranda?'

'Absolutely.'

'Otherwise, she'll get home and regret being so wet. Not that I'm saying you're wet, of course Flora,' added Munchkin hastily.

Anna gave Flora an encouraging smile. 'If you've had a bad experience, it can be off-putting. But have a go tomorrow. See how you get on.'

'Good idea,' said Miranda.

Flora looked at the trio of faces. She knew they all meant well, but they were relentless. She was fed up with the whole business. And she guessed she'd be subjected to the same badgering night after night, from them and Jamie and Pete and the rest. Give it a go. Have a bash. On and on and on. And deep down, though she hated to admit it, she was nettled by being judged wet.

'You girlies still on about men and shopping?' called Giles from the table.

'We're telling Flora she ought to ski,' said Munchkin.

'Of course she must,' the men chorused back.

'Silly for her to come all this way.'

'Take more of a risk crossing the road.'

They grew louder. Flora looked at Jamie in despair.

His eyes met hers. 'Do it for me,' he said softly.

In the hullaballoo, no one else had heard. At that moment they recaptured the earlier intimacy between them. Flora felt her resistance crumbling.

Slowly, she nodded her surrender. 'OK. I'll ski.'

'Promise?' asked Jamie.

Flora took a deep breath. 'Promise.'

Claps, whistles and cheers broke out. 'Super,' declared Giles. 'You'll have nothing to worry about with hubby around. You qualified as an instructor, didn't you Jamie?'

'Flora can go to ski school.'

'What? But you said . . .' Flora was bewildered. He'd promised he'd look after her.

'Far better idea for you to be in a class,' said Jamie. 'We'll sign you into ski school first thing tomorrow.'

Ski school? Flora's mood plummeted. She'd always been bottom of every single class, Jasper sneering that her woolly hat should have a big D for Dunce on it. Ski school meant hour after hour of humiliation in front of a dozen others.

There was no way she could backtrack now. Why had she given in?

As Flora became more lost in panicked thought, Miranda talked about her flat in Parson's Green which she shared with her sister,

Lally. 'Thankfully we're close to the Tube and it's not too bad for a fast black, though have you noticed it's always impossible to find a taxi when you're in evening dress?'

Anna wondered how she'd gone from a hostel for the homeless to Bellville Sassoon cream satin in less than 24 hours.

'Gosh, those men are noisy.' Miranda had to keep on repeating herself. 'Wonder if they'd like a game of Triv? No, probably not. Seem to be getting stuck in for a sesh.'

Laughter rang out. The table was more cluttered with glasses, bottles and cans. A gust of freezing air blew in as Jamie went to get more beers from the balcony.

'What do you call a woman?' asked Sam.

'Don't know. What do you call a woman? said Pete.

'Life support system for a cunt.'

The men guffawed. Flora gasped, outraged.

'What's up?' demanded Sam, as she glared at him.

'What do you think?'

'Oh God. Sense of humour failure over there guys.' Sam yawned ostentaciously. 'Bor-ing.'

Flora's green eyes were as cold as emeralds. 'Are you from the bottom of the swamp?'

'Angel,' warned Jamie, embarrassed.

'I'm not putting up with garbage like that.'

'Angel. It was only a joke.'

'Not a very funny one,' retorted Anna.

'Quite,' agreed Miranda.

'Well, we thought it was funny, didn't we guys?' said Martin. 'Get off those high horses, girls. Relax. We're on holiday.'

Torn between showing she was a good sport and sisterly solidarity, Munchkin kept quiet. Nikki was studying her French manicured fingernails.

Seeing that Miranda was not best pleased, Giles decided to step in. 'Sam, the ladies have a point. Bit strong.'

'OK, OK.' Sam looked Flora up and down. 'We'll find some cottonwool for their delicate female ears.'

'You can use it as a gag,' she muttered.

A little later, the women went to bed. They'd been up since six.

'I'll be along in a minute,' promised Jamie, when Flora kissed him. 'Big day for you tomorrow. Skiing for the first time in ten years.'

She winced. 'Don't remind me.'

Munchkin was anxious not to miss out on any fun. She was about to move to the table and sit next to Pete, then heard Nikki was going up. She decided she would too. If she stayed, she'd feel like a gatecrasher in a rugger club locker room. Besides, the whole week was in front of her and there'd be plenty of other opportunities to be with him.

Flora undressed, dumping her clothes on the armchair. Then knowing that she'd be nagged at by Jamie for being untidy, hung them up in the wardrobe. She went to the bathroom and began brushing her teeth. Miranda was right. The men were getting stuck in for a session.

Martin's voice rang through the thin wall. '. . . best rumpy you'll ever get. Not you, Jamie. Happily married man and all that.'

'Has its advantages, marriage.' That was Giles. 'Sex on tap.' Flora frowned, her brushing speeding up and yanked on the tap.

'Had this amazing threesome in Thailand.' Martin again. 'Only time I've ever paid for it. Only time I've worn a rubber, come to that. Girls are cheaper than a can of Coke. Know how to treat a man. None of this feminist crap.'

Gargling, Flora spluttered and almost choked.

'Marriage?' continued Martin. 'Ring on their finger, ring through your nose.'

Flora was coughing so hard she missed what came next. '. . . never get bored.' That was Jamie. Her smile grew broader, hearing him add how much he adored her.

'Feminism. Noticed the amazing thing about all these smart women?' asked Sam. 'So busy having it all, but they've got no idea when to cash in their stock. Wrong side of thirty and they're in a bear market. So suddenly there's no need to take anymore of this three dinners before you get to first base shit.'

Flora rinsed and spat, hard, into the basin.

Miranda spent almost half an hour getting ready for bed. After removing every scrap of make-up and cleaning her face, she applied cream from four different pots.

With a regime of soap, water and the occasional dab of Nivea, Anna watched her in astonishment from behind Dostoyevsky.

Guffaws rang out downstairs.

'Those men are pretty raucous.' Miranda slapped herself quickly a dozen times under the chin.

'Umm.'

'God, I'm getting a turkey neck.' Examining her face in a handmirror, she rubbed in more cream. 'Goes well with the crow's feet and the chicken skin arms. Don't smoke, though. Dreadfully ageing. How old's Flora?'

'Twenty-four, five.'

'Really? Quite young to be getting married, isn't it? A-mazing ring. Must've cost Jamie a fortune. Still, he's got one. She's certainly smartened up recently, used to look like a refugee from the Glastonbury Festival. Wouldn't have thought she was Jamie's scene at all. Pretty though. God, I look so old, no man will ever look at me.'

'Nonsense.' Anna sighed inwardly. 'Anyway you've got a man, haven't you? Charles? Imogen mentioned him.'

'Did she?' Miranda grimaced into the mirror. 'Anyone on the scene for you at the moment?'

'Not really.' They might be sharing a room, but there were some things Anna wanted to keep to herself.

Miranda took off her jeans and stood in front of the full length mirror on the wardrobe. She pulled up her top and pulled a face. 'Look at this massive stomach. I'm nowhere near the curse, so there's absolutely no excuse.' She peered at the glass. 'And I've tried and tried to shift this revolting cellulite. Nothing works. Hasn't Nikki got an a-mazing figure? So depressing. Not surprising, she hardly ate a thing at dinner. A model with a Mercedes, one could throw up with envy. Very quiet. Hardly a peep out of her all night.'

'Perhaps she was tired.' Anna hoped Miranda would get the hint.

'Can't believe he's *the* Martin June. Aged a bit since his pin-up days. Wasn't he dreamy. Awful thing that happened, it all came back at dinner. Still looks fit. Terribly hunky and broad.'

'Wide too,' muttered Anna.

'Pete. Hunk city.' Miranda was putting on more eye cream. 'And so nice. Sweet Pete. Commitment phob . . .'

Gales of laughter, followed by the crash of chairs overturning came up through the floor. 'Who's got the cards?' demanded Sam.

'Try the sideboard.'

Anna sighed.

'Found some.' Jamie's voice came up loud and clear. 'I'll deal. Don't look, Giles, for fuck's sake. Start again everyone. Up after three. Ace is high. One. Two. Three. Call, Martin.'

'What are they doing?' Anna was perplexed.

'Sounds like pisshead's poker. Let's hope they simmer down soon. It's well past midnight. Honestly, this place isn't very well sound-proofed is it?' Miranda put on an outsize T-shirt.

Anna switched off her bedside lamp. 'Don't mind me if you want to read.'

'Read?' Miranda sounded bewildered. 'Oh, no thanks. Night then. Sweet dreams.'

The darkness only intensified the noise from downstairs. 'Down in one' was joined by the stomp of feet.

'Well done that man,' cried Pete above the cheers. 'Your deal, Martin. How about some music?'

Nikki closed her bedroom door behind her and sighed a huge sigh of relief. One evening down. How many more to go? Six? Seven? So much for Martin's promise that the chalet would just be a base and they would go off and do their own thing. Back in London, she had pictured the two of them enjoying a succession of romantic dinners ending with a nightcap in a chic nightclub. Instead she'd had to endure a stodgy supper and hours of making her own fun, as that Giles had said. Fun? It had been about as much fun as getting her bikini line waxed.

She put on her cream silk wrap and tied back her hair. Hanging up her clothes, she hit her shin on the side of the bed and swore, which was unusual for her. The room was so small and pokey. Not enough space to swing a Hermès Kelly bag.

The unfamiliar surroundings, all those strangers and the noise had made her tense. All evening she'd been horribly disorientated. Fat lot of help Martin had been. Why had she agreed to this modelling story? Her instincts had told her to keep it simple and say that she was temping between jobs. No-one would've cared. And why did he have to go on about the Mercedes? It had just drawn attention to her, set her apart, especially from the other women. Anna rode a bicycle, about as far from a Mercedes as Mars. And as for that snotty bitch Flora . . .

Her eyes looked dull without their make-up. She needed a holiday. Needed to catch her breath, relax, take stock, work out her next move.

This wasn't a holiday. Someone would rumble her. Jack

Mancini, Martin's horrible journalist friend had rumbled her. If only he could be wiped away like her make-up.

If she hadn't met Jack, would she have owned up to Martin? Eventually, yes. She couldn't string him along indefinitely. Sooner or later the truth would've had to come out, but why not later? Much later. But Jack had frightened her so badly and in panic she'd confessed, hoping that Martin would protect her from him.

Why hadn't she booked herself into a health farm and let Martin go skiing on his own? She'd only known him for a few weeks. Surely she'd come too far to let lust control her like this?

Further along the corridor, Miranda thumped her pillow. If those bloody boys didn't pipe down soon, she'd give them a rocket. That idiotic game had finally stopped, but then the stereo was turned up. Finally, thankfully, Giles had the common sense to shut them all up. If only he hadn't had done it so loudly, just as she was dropping off.

'Pump up the volume, Sam,' called Martin. Sam obliged. Only too obviously.

'For God's sake,' muttered Anna, from the other end of the bedroom.

'You're awake too?'

'Am now.'

Miranda turned on the light. Both women squinted. 'Where's my shoe?' She was about to bash the floorboards, but suddenly the music died and the men's voices petered out.

'That fucking stereo might just as well be next to my fucking bed. Some of us are trying to sleep.' It was Flora.

'Hear, hear,' called Anna. Miranda's shoe applauded.

There was a loud wolf whistle. 'Nish legsh,' slurred Sam.

'Are you wearing anything under that rugger shirt, Mrs Naze?' called Martin.

'I'm not Mrs Naze yet. And at times like this I wonder if I want to be.'

A chorus of ooohs.

'Flora, angel, you don't mean that.' Jamie's voice was equally slurred.

'Come to bed soon,' pleaded Flora wearily. 'And meanwhile, can you keep the noise down all of you. Please.'

'We'll be very, very quiet. Quiet as mice,' called Pete. 'Nice mice. Nice mice, eh? I'm a poet.' He laughed. Miranda and Anna pulled faces. 'Just finish these drinks, OK, sweetheart?'

'Thank you.'

Downstairs the voices were hushed. 'Well done, Flora,' said Anna. 'Perhaps we can finally get some sleep.'

Miranda turned off the light and tried to settle. When had she last got a proper night's sleep? She stared up into the darkness.

Flora awakened with a start. For a second or two panic overwhelmed her. Where was she? This wasn't her bed, her bedroom. Where was she?

The thump, thump, thump of a bass seeped into her consciousness. She tried to block out it all out but the music and the voices grew louder the more awake she became.

'Not again.' Twice she had marched into the sitting room to ask them to quieten down. Twice they had promised they would. She may as well have saved her breath. And theirs. Somehow, two hours after going to bed, she had finally fallen asleep over her book despite the music, the drunken voices and even a singsong.

'Pump up the volume, Sam,' called Martin. They started to sing along.

A rush of exasperation forced her fully awake. There was no point in reasoning with them, they were all too pissed.

She tried to lose herself in her book. This wasn't the kind of evening that Jamie had promised her in London. He had painted a picture of cosy nights of chilling out, all of them gathered round a roaring fire, swapping books, playing games of Monopoly or Scrabble. He would take her to bed early, make love to her, talk about their future.

BANG!

Flora leapt out of bed, the ceiling was about to fall in on top of her, the floor collapse. Had a bomb gone off? Gas? She bolted towards the door.

Running into the sitting room she found the five men shrieking with laughter. Bent double, Sam and Giles were clutching one another.

'What the . . .'

Five pairs of bloodshot eyes turned towards her. 'Angel.' Jamie advanced unsteadily. 'Nice shurprish. Coming to give you a kish.'

Shaking herself free of him, she stomped to the stereo and turned it off. Angry hisses came from the fireplace. The surround and floor were wet. Among the doused logs, was the remains of a charred can of beer.

'Bet. Wager,' Sam was squinting. He hiccuped. 'How long to cook.'

Martin eyed her. 'What is under that rugger shirt?'

'Is everything all right down there?' called Munchkin from the top of the stairs. She remained out of sight, not wishing the men to catch her in thick specs and no make-up.

'Fine,' called Pete. 'Go back to bed.'

Jamie nodded. 'You too Flora. Back to sleep angel.'

'Sleep? Sleep? How the fuck do you expect anyone to sleep with this racket?'

She slammed the bedroom door behind her. The men looked at one another momentarily chastened.

'Lady's upset.' Sam hiccupped again.

Pete squinted at his watch. 'Shit. Past three. Must crash out.'

Jamie weaved his way into the bedroom. Flora was sitting up in bed smoking and trying to read. He crashed down beside her and buried his face in the pillow. 'Turn out the light and go to shleep. Love you sho much. Shouldn't shmoke in bed.'

'And you say you'll never get bored with me.' Flora ground out her cigarette. 'So why do you want a Boy's Own holiday?'

'Um . . . board . . . Seat on the board . . . Must play backgammon.' He kicked off his shoes, pulled the duvet over himself, reached past her and turned off the light.

Furiously, she yanked the duvet back and turned on the light. Jamie was already snoring.

CHAPTER TWO

Sunday

The sun was waking up, its rays beginning to stretch out across the valley. Another beautiful day was promised.

'What a mess.' Hetty yanked back the tartan curtains. Scores of empty cans and bottles lay on the mantelpiece, stereo and tables. Some had made their way under the sofa. A pile of butts from an overturned ashtray littered the rug. Spilt drink had soaked into the cushions. The room reeked of stale beer and cigars.

'Quick, open the windows,' said Alice in disgust. 'It stinks.' She righted two dining chairs. The floor was sticky underfoot. 'We'll have to do in here, then start on breakfast. Did the whole village come up here for a party?'

'Sounded like it.' Hetty scowled. 'I'm sure they let off fireworks.'

They made no effort to be quiet as they slung the rubbish into a sack and dragged the furniture across the tiles before sweeping.

After their clients had gone out, the houseproud twins would have to give the place yet another thorough clean, which would cut into their precious skiing time.

It was almost nine when Jamie woke up. Red, white and blue his eyes reflected his intense patriotism. They always watered at the sound of the national anthem, especially when it was played at the Stade de France.

He felt rough, dehydrated from the booze, his legs aching from the skiing. Getting up, he was careful not to disturb Flora. Which was more dumb? Getting pissed or pissing her off? He'd face her after a fortifying cup of tea.

'Morning James. How are we today?' Giles and the rest were gathered round the dining table having breakfast. Despite feeling ragged, they delighted in the view across the sunlit valley to the snowy peaks of Les Diables.

Giles sounded cheerful but looked dreadful, his guinea pig face bloated and blotchy. He was gratified by the exclamations of wonder. The chalet was much further out of the village than the brochure had led him to believe and he'd fretted there'd be grumbling. 'Where's the lady wife?'

'Morning everyone.' Jamie reached for the teapot. 'Flora? Sound asleep still.'

Pete caught his wince. 'Are we in the doghouse? She seemed a bit antsy last night. This morning rather.'

Giles decided he ought to eat something, despite feeling queasy. 'Definitely a bit miffed from what I can remember. Didn't keep you awake did we girlies?'

Munchkin decided to be a good sport, rather than a spoil-sport like Flora. 'Well, that almighty bang gave me a bit of a fright, but I dropped off straight away.' In fact, she had tossed and turned for hours disturbed by the revelry downstairs.

Despite eyes itchy with tiredness, neither Anna nor Miranda wanted to make a fuss. Nikki had slept like a log.

Jamie went into the kitchen. He apologised to the twins for any mess and thanked them for clearing it up. Except for Pete, no-one else had bothered and they appreciated it.

'Scrambled?' said a charmed Hetty.

'Couldn't rustle Flora up some coffee could you? asked Jamie.

'Of course. Sure you wouldn't like an omelette?'

'Smarmy git,' muttered Martin.

Miranda finished her muesli. The snow on Les Diables glinted in the sun. Suddenly she longed to get out into the fresh air after a day cooped up in the car and a night of broken sleep. 'Right. Who's the man with the plan? Giles?'

He cleared a space on the table and opened up a piste map. It showed St Marie encircled by peaks and was criss-crossed by different coloured lines. 'Well, first we must scoot down to the village, hire some skis and sort out passes. Now, do we want a week's pass or dailies? Mirandy and I were thinking of shooting off to Aubrisson, weren't we? Pity to waste the old funds.'

'Dailies might be worthwhile if anyone wants to skive off,' said Miranda.

'Slackers? Good God,' mocked Sam, longing to go back to bed. His head was pounding.

'Silly not to make the most of it,' said Munchkin.

'That's the spirit,' said Giles heartily. He pointed at the map. 'We're here. Just up from Les Pins. The chairlift goes up to La Croix, where there's a restaurant and another lift station. And what looks like another chairlift to here. What's that? La Bête.'

Jamie turned to Pete and pointed at a black run. 'Went there yesterday. Great moguls. You're going to love it.'

'Brilliant.' He blew smoke over the map. Miranda waved it away crossly. 'Sorry.' He gave her such a beautiful smile that she forgave him.

'As it's our first day, reckon we should take it pretty easy,' continued Giles. 'So, go into St Marie, sort everything out, go up to La Croix and give this nice long blue run a bash. Just to test the skis. Spot of lunch, then decide the form for this afternoon.'

'Morning.' Flora forced a smile.

She sat down wondering how on earth Miranda, Munchkin and Nikki had managed to put on full make-up. She couldn't muster the energy to drag a brush through her hair until after breakfast. With Fred staying at Billy's so often, she was used to living pretty much alone and pottering around for the first half hour of the day with her brain in neutral. The thought of sparkling socially within minutes of waking up was alarming. There wasn't even a paper to hide behind.

'Coffee,' said Alice, gazing at Pete and blushing. 'And scrambled eggs.'

'Thanks,' said Flora gratefully. She sipped in silence as the conversation washed around her. Ski resorts, mutual friends, work. They all seemed to be earning a fortune.

She wondered how the drunk, sexist Mr Hydes from last night had transformed themselves into these ambitious, successful Dr Jekylls. Could the Martin who was telling Pete about some Thames-side development be the same Martin? Could Giles the accountant and aspiring MP be the same Giles?

Jamie was once again James Naze Esq. Busily devouring his scrambled eggs, he squeezed her hand. As he smiled so lovingly at her, she wondered if she hadn't dreamt up the whole of the early hours.

'No bad staff, only bad bosses,' Martin was saying to Pete. 'Team building's the key.'

'Personnel bonding,' Munchkin nodded sagely. 'Team players determine a firm's success. These adventure days are a great way of bringing mavericks into the fold. We did a brilliant outward bound weekend in the Welsh mountains.'

Martin chortled. 'We got banned. They closed down one place after my lot ran riot there. Some fuss about trampling on a poxy plant.'

Flora looked up sharply. 'Where was this?'

'Place called Bluebell Wood,' said Martin, pouring himself more tea.

'Outside Jaxley?'

He nodded. 'Know it?'

'What fuss?' asked Munchkin.

'There we were minding our own business, having a nice day out, charging round the woods, letting off a bit of steam and suddenly these two hippies go ballistic. They'd spent the past fortnight hanging out among the trees, man, looking after this piece of vegetation. Complete headcases. Threatened to call the police and everything. Bound to have been on the local mushrooms.'

'And?' said Munchkin.

'And, well, we scarpered. Guy running the centre was well miffed. Said he'd lose his licence. I told him to calm down, deny it, nothing to do with us. Can you believe it, loads of aggro over a stupid plant. Haven't the carrot crunchers down there got anything better to worry about?'

'That stupid plant was an extremely rare orchid,' seethed Flora. 'Those hippies were botanists.' Surprised by the heat in her voice, everyone stared at her.

Martin laughed. 'Whoops.'

'Send them some flowers to say sorry,' suggested Sam. 'Orchids perhaps?'

Grinning, Martin turned to Flora. 'These hippies. Sorry botanists. Friends of yours? Interesting company you keep.'

'Contacts.' She had spent a glorious sunny afternoon interviewing them in the woods when they explained about the orchid's uniqueness. They'd been gentle and dedicated to their work. A few weeks later, when they told her about the destruction, they'd been heartbroken.

'Tell them to put up some signs next time,' said Martin.

'There were signs,' retorted Flora. 'That part of the wood is private land. You were trespassing. Besides, there won't be a next time. That orchid's gone forever.'

'Really?' Anna was dismayed.

'Oh well, history now.' Martin shrugged. 'That wood's going to be history soon too, isn't it? Some road's being built. About time too. Make a nice route to Oxford.'

'No-one wants the bypass,' snapped Flora.

Jamie winced; he knew all about the saga since Flora had been leaked the plans by someone in the County Council.

'I do.' Martin sounded as if that settled the matter.

'Why? To cut a few minutes off your journey time? Use the

motorway.' Flora glared at him, her normally pale face matching the heat in her voice. 'That is ancient woodland and now it's all going to be destroyed and covered in concrete because of some creeps of politicians in hock to the roads' lobby.'

Giles hurrumped. 'Any decisions by any ministry of any administration are judged on their merits.'

'Sure,' said Flora. 'Six lanes running alongside the water meadows, past a hermitage and almost through a Bronze Age burial site.'

'And once the road is built, there's going to be some nice opportunities for some housing estates,' said Martin.

'The road shouldn't be built,' snapped Flora.

'It's called progress.'

'Progress? Destroying one of the most beautiful . . .'

'Angel, off your soapbox,' muttered Jamie. 'We're on holiday now.'

Flora suddenly became conscious that she was being too strident in front of all these strangers. She took a deep breath. 'Sorry. But it's something I feel strongly about. Hundreds of millions are going to be spent on a road that no-one in Jaxley wants. It's got to be stopped.'

Anna nodded.

Martin leant back in his chair. 'So, Flora, how come you know so much about it, slumming it in your little ivory tower in Chelsea?'

'I live in Jaxley,' said Flora evenly.

Martin laughed. 'Ooo arr.' He put on a Somerset accent. 'A hick from the sticks.' He sniffed. 'Hey guys, thought I was hearing bullshit, didn't realise I was smelling it too. Hang on, Flora. What's that in your hair? There.' Her fingers began combing. 'Up a bit. Straw.'

His loud laugh rang out. Flora tried to join in the merriment, but having been made to look a twit by him, found it hard.

'So what do you do down in Jaxley?' asked Martin.

'Milkmaid,' replied Flora.

'Really?'

'Wind up,' said Pete. 'She works on the local paper.'

Martin's head swivelled in Flora's direction. Nikki choked on her low-fat cornflakes.

'Do you now? Journalist, eh?' Martin studied Flora with his narrow eyes, reminding her of a bird of prey. She had an unnerving feeling she was the prey. 'Giles, old boy, you should've told us there was a member of the Press here.'

'Oh, didn't you know? Flora's our Lois Lane, aren't you?' Giles put his arm round her shoulders and squeezed. 'Have to watch what we say in front of her.'

Flora smiled; it was an old comment.

'Won't we just,' said Martin softly, still staring at her. 'Run across Jack Mancini? Old mate of mine.' Flora noticed Nikki jump. 'Only scribbler I've got any time for. Works on the *Sunday Reporter*.'

She shook her head. 'Seen his by-line.'

'Not planning to stitch me up like some of your wanker colleagues, are you Flora?' Martin was icy.

'Of course not,' said Flora, taken aback. 'Why should I?'

'You journalists. God, the grief I've had. According to them, I've been an alcoholic, a poofter, a drug addict. My poor old mum lived under siege. I've had my fill of column inches, so don't even think of using me as copy. All right, Flora?'

'Fine.'

'Message clear enough for you?'

Every eye was on her. Flora took a sip of coffee. 'Ultra clear. And nice and loud as well.'

'Comprenday? Sure?'

'I think I can just about manage the small words.'

Giles smiled uneasily. 'Oh, I don't think young Flora here would betray any confidences. Would she Jamie?'

'She'd better not.' Martin's voice was grim. 'My experience tells me otherwise. Ever consider a nicer job, Flora, such as cleaning toilets?'

Flora bridled. 'Such as being a property developer and destroying the countryside?' Pete laughed. 'Ow.' Flora yelped as Jamie kicked her under the table.

'Touché,' said Anna. 'The Press is the fourth estate. It's got a valuable role in the defence . . .'

'Bollocks,' cut in Martin. 'I'll know who to blame, Flora.'

Bursting to tell him where he could shove his blame, Flora was silenced by another kick from Jamie. 'Don't worry,' he said to Martin. 'Flora's a trainee hack on a little local paper. She's not in the same league as people you know.'

Flora wanted to protest that she had finished her training, that the *Standard* was a brilliant local paper, but kept quiet.

'A hick hack,' said Martin. 'Well, I'm not being used to further her career. Understand, Flora?'

In the frozen silence, they stared at one another, until Flora gave him a nod of acquiescence.

'Fascinating. Must follow up the role of the Press some other time,' said Miranda smoothly, rearranging her hair band. 'Let's get cracking, shall we? Leave in twenty minutes?'

'Are you sure we can't change your mind and persuade you to come out with us, Flora old girl?' Giles' breath smelt of last night's beer.

'Fraid not.' She yawned.

'Tired?' asked Munchkin.

'Fresh air will soon put you right,' brayed Giles.

'Decent night's sleep would've helped,' scowled Flora. Her words hung in the air. Jamie gave her a 'don't start' look.

As the others began to leave the table, Flora got up abruptly and went onto the balcony. Still smarting from her exchange with Martin, she sipped her coffee and took deep breaths of the freezing air.

She stared across the valley, seeing nothing, oblivious to its beauty.

Zero hour. Crunch time. She was going to have to put on those clumsy red boots and pick up her skis. Why had she given in the night before? Stupid, stupid, stupid. Why had she allowed herself to be talked into this holiday? Her stomach was tight with apprehension, the mug trembled in her hand.

Upstairs, everyone was getting ready for a day on the slopes, stuffing pockets with essentials. Giles tucked some business cards into his jacket, Munchkin put blue eyeliner and scarlet lipstick into hers. Martin wondered if he should take his mobile, while Nikki changed outfits, then changed again. Sam counted his money, which seemed to have dwindled in his sock drawer overnight. Miranda stood in front of the mirror in pearls and her lilac and canary padded suit, wailing that she looked like the Michelin Man on acid. Anna wondered why Tom hadn't called.

Back at the table, Flora tried to swallow some croissant but her throat was constricted. She pushed away her plate with clammy hands. Jamie smiled at her encouragingly.

'We'll go and sort you out some lessons.'

Flora felt sick. Fear made her lash out. 'Nice friends you've got. Especially those sexist fuckwits. Especially Martin.'

'Angel. Don't go over the top. Not everyone has the same rosy view of newspapers as you do. Especially those who've been hounded by Fleet Street. Try and see things from his perspective.'

'You might have backed me up.'

'No need. You were able to manage on your own. You've both had your say and let's hope that's the end of it.' He sighed. 'We'll get a lift into the village and you'll probably be able to join a class this afternoon.'

'I don't want to ski.'

'What else are you going to do? You can't stay here all day.'

'Go to Siena. Go back to bed with you.' She reached over and kissed him.

Smiling, he ran his fingers through her hair. 'Flora, you're skiing. You promised you'd give it a try. Don't but. And don't be such a wimp.'

'I'm not a wimp. I'm shit scared and I'd rather be in bed with you than end up with my skis wrapped around a fir tree.' The clomp of heavy footsteps overhead was followed by the sound of Giles banging the bathroom door, ordering Pete to hurry up. 'Has he got a PA system down his throat instead of a voice box?'

Jamie sighed. 'Flora, I know you're nervous. But I'll look after you. Please just say you'll try. Just for one day. For me.' He kissed her cheek. 'If you hate it, get the train and go to Siena.'

'Or go back to bed with you.'

Miranda arrived, shaking her head. 'Honestly Jamie. What did you boys get up to last night? Sam's just taken three of my headache pills. You are naughty. Ruin you for skiing.'

'Best cure for a hangover.' He got up. 'Let's get ready. Come on Flora.'

She followed him across the room as if she were going to the gallows.

Munchkin came galloping down the stairs. She looked like a walking marshmallow in a powder pink one-piece with its motif of silvery snowflakes. 'What a gorgeous suit.' She touched Miranda's sleeve. 'You've got the height for it of course. So tall and elegant.'

Miranda preened delightedly. 'Oh this. Ancient now. Got it in Courcheval years ago. Warm though. That looks very cosy. Lovely colour. Aren't the flakes sweet?'

'I love bright colours. The consultant said I was definitely summer. All this black. So gloomy and ageing.'

'Slimming though.' Miranda worried if she weren't being tactless and moved on hurriedly. 'I was tempted to get something new, but I couldn't justify the expense. Not with Christmas and everything. People don't really notice anyway.'

'Well, skiing's hardly a catwalk. Main thing is to be warm.'

'Quite,' agreed Miranda.

Their mutual satisfaction in their good sense was dissolved as Nikki arrived looking like something out of a glossy magazine in a fitted scarlet jacket and matching skin tight ski pants. Both gawped with envy. Munchkin remembered her two helpings of apple crumble.

'Super outfit,' said Miranda, feeling like Henry VIII.

'Thanks.' Nikki smiled shyly. 'Ralph Lauren.'

It must have cost a fortune. Munchkin's only solace was that she looked better than Anna in her turquoise.

'Right, girls. Who wants a lift?' Martin ran down the stairs pulling on his gloves. Wearing a sludgy coloured one-piece, he looked askance at Pete in jeans and a fleece.

Longing to get Pete on his own, Munchkin was disappointed when he said he'd take Jamie and Flora.

'Coming with us, Munch?' said Giles. 'All set? Forgot, we're blocked in, aren't we?' He eyed Pete. 'One of the penalties of arriving first.'

Pete grinned. 'We'll meet you up at La Croix for lunch. Pissing around in the hire shop. One of the penalties of not having your own skis.'

'Come on Flora,' yelled Jamie.

'Coming.' In the bedroom, Flora checked that she had money, her pass and, most importantly, enough cigarettes. It was going to be a stressful day. Hands shaking, she tugged her hair back into a ponytail. Her face was paper white.

Outside, the sun was melting the ice crust. It crunched under their feet. Although the light was dazzling, the air was bitterly cold.

Flora watched in silence as Pete slotted three pairs of skis into the Porsche's rack. She wanted to throw up.

Stereo blaring, Ray-Bans on, Pete revved the engine and reversed down the drive into the road.

Giles got a mouthful of fumes and had a coughing fit.
'Flash git,' called out Sam.

The Porsche sped down along the winding road into St Marie.
On the balconies of the wooden shuttered chalets, people were
sitting in deckchairs enjoying the early morning sunshine.

'Beautiful day,' said Pete. 'We'll be baking when we get going.'

'Don't forget. Cold's the enemy, according to matey.' Jamie
pointed to the Range Rover up ahead.

'Should've told Martin where he could stuff his microfibred
suit. Still, if he wants to be a sad fag in a bag, his choice.' Pete
smiled and changed down a gear. 'Out of order, laying into Flora
like that.'

'He was hounded, remember,' said Jamie. 'You wouldn't,
would you? Probably surfing or screwing at the time.'

'Even so . . . How you doing in the back there, hick hack?'

'Fine.' Flora felt sick. They were passing the lift station at the
top of Les Pins. She caught sight of a skier tumbling out of
control on the piste. She swallowed hard. 'Actually, can you take
me back to the chalet?'

He laughed. 'Nope. Can't back out now. You're skiing,
sweets.'

The square was packed with cars. In the Range Rover, Miranda
spotted a couple getting into a Renault, which was parked near
the bus stop.

'Bit of luck,' said Martin. He pulled into the side of the road,
indicator winking, gear into reverse at the ready. 'Come on.' The
Renault hooted, the driver waving them forward. 'What's up
with him?' Behind them a queue of traffic was starting to form,
horns being blasted.

Anna peered out the back window. 'He wants you to go
forward. He can't get round.'

Martin slammed the gears into first. The Range Rover moved up, the Renault moved out and Pete's Porsche swung neatly into the empty space.

'Bastard,' screamed Martin, incandescent with rage.

'Not on,' said Miranda. 'Naughty.' Wagging her finger at Pete, she shook her head. He and Jamie grinned and waved back.

'You'd better move,' said Nikki through clenched teeth, hearing more hooting. 'We're holding everyone up.'

Martin glowered into his rear view mirror. With angry revving of the engine, the Range Rover shot forward.

On the fourth fruitless circuit of the square, the Range Rover passed Pete, Jamie and Flora heading for the ski school office.

'Not very friendly,' called out Anna through the open window.

'Who dares wins.' From the snowlined pavement, Pete grinned. Flora and Jamie giggled as an enraged Martin gave them all the finger.

They wove their way through the crowds. Pete put his arm round Flora. 'Hey, cheer up. You don't need lessons. Just come along with us.'

She shook her head. 'You're all so much better than me. I'd only hold you up. 'Spose I ought to be taught properly.'

'Jamie can teach you.'

Horrorstruck, Jamie glanced at Pete. 'Flora hasn't been on skis for years. Far better she's taught by a professional.'

Twenty minutes later Martin and his passengers trooped into the hire shop. Giles, Sam and Munchkin were trying on boots. Once again, the Beach Boys blared out.

'Excellent place,' bellowed Giles, parading up and down in some bright blue boots. 'Very good value. Amazing choice, got the rear entries I wanted. A One support, feel like they're sprayed on. Good shell, canting, firm cuff, inner's amazingly well padded. Do nicely,' he said to the bemused Carrot. 'Now what about some planks?'

As the others got their boots sorted out, Giles examined the rack of skis, proclaiming that he needed a good pair of all-terrain intermediates, about 195, suitable for hardpack and moguls.

He stood a ski on the floor and examined it. 'Lots of flex, so stable at speed. About the right side cut. What about torsion? Swing weight?' The Carrot looked blank. 'Bindings? Full spectrum release, of course. Din?'

Determined not to be outdone, Martin said he also needed 195s. The Carrot looked at him doubtfully. 'Too long for you. Better the 185s, unless you're an expert. How many weeks have you skied?'

'Enough,' retorted Martin, eyes narrowing. 'Look mate, I can take my business elsewhere.'

'OK. You try.' The Carrot shrugged. 'But you'll bring them back and change them tomorrow.' He'd seen enough customers whose egos demanded longer skis and stiffer boots than they could manage.

'Bar, bar, bar, bar, Barbara Ann,' sang Munchkin.

'Babar the elephant more like,' muttered Sam to Miranda, who tried not to giggle.

Munchkin blushed scarlet when the Carrot asked her how much she weighed. She fibbed.

Anna, served last, was unhappy with her boots. Should she get the next size up? She stuck with them, not wanting to hold everyone up.

Nikki had tried on three pairs, finally choosing those she'd put on first, which matched her outfits the best.

Over at the packed ski school office, Pete sorted out his pass. Jamie and Flora joined the queue to arrange her lessons. 'Must I?' she pleaded.

'Yes. You promised.'

'Tyrant.' Idly she glanced at the board above the counter, which set out the prices for lessons. She did a double take. The answer. She wasn't going within a centimetre of a ski school class. 'So, I have to ski. And I have to learn,' she said casually. Jamie nodded. 'And you won't teach me. So I have to have lessons. They're horribly expensive.'

He put his arm round her. 'I'm paying. Don't worry.'

'Sure?' She converted the francs into sterling and cheered up. Jamie was going to have to pay dearly for inflicting such torture on her. 'Right. How about at least two hours a day on my own with an instructor?'

'Good idea.' At least she was being a bit more positive. His smile died as his eyes followed her gaze to the notice board. He winced. 'Wouldn't you rather be in a ski school class? It's a brilliant way of meeting pe—'

'No.' She giggled. 'You pay, I stay.'

'Fine. You win.' On reflection, it was a cheap price to pay for getting Flora off his hands.

Her triumph was short-lived. 'But there must be someone,' she howled aghast. The clerk in half-moon spectacles had consulted her computer and said that regrettably no private instructors were available.

'What about a ski school class?' asked Jamie.

Thwarted, Flora stood sullen and silent as he explained that she wasn't a complete novice, but hadn't skied for many years. 'She doesn't need to be told how to put her skis on or hold her poles.'

'There's a place in an intermediate class at 1.30. That's all I can offer. Otherwise, we're fully booked. *Noël*. Christmas.'

'It's that or nothing.' Jamie turned to Flora. 'You promised you'd try.'

'Isn't there a chance of any cancellations?' she pleaded.

The clerk shrugged. 'You can come back in a few days and see. But I doubt it.'

'Join this class and we'll sort something out later.' Jamie was anxious for her to make a decison. If she were in a class, he'd have the chance to do some worry-free skiing. Behind them, a Scots voice urged them to get a move on. 'Angel. You promised.'

She hesistated for what seemed like an age. 'OK.'

Jamie booked her in for a week in the ski school class and handed over his credit card. Flora's stomach was knotted with nerves. One-to-one she could cope with, perhaps, maybe. But ski school? Memories of humiliation, a hat with a big D for Dunce on it, and the weatherbeaten gauleiters who'd shouted at her non-stop flooded back. She shuddered.

'Did you get all that?' Jamie interrupted her reverie.

'What? Yes of course.'

Pete pushed his way through to them, causing outraged grumbles from the Scot who thought he'd have to endure more delays. They went out into the street.

'I ought to take Flora to the nursery slopes for a couple of hours,' said Jamie. 'Meet you in the restaurant up at La Croix around half-one.'

'Suits me,' said Pete. 'I'll go out on my own. You had a headstart yesterday so I've got some catching up to do.'

They made their way back across the crowded square to the car. As Pete approached the Porsche, a group of teenage girls at the bus stop nudged one another. He pulled out his keyring and the car locks sprang up, provoking more nudging.

'Bonjour,' he said amiably.

Flora retrieved her skiboots from the back seat. Wincing, she put them on. Jamie unhooked her skis from the roof. 'I'll take these, you carry the poles,' he said. 'Catch you later, Pete.'

'Good luck Flora.' Surrounded by his new fanclub, Pete waved them off.

Flora and Jamie made their way through the streets towards the nursery slope. She was soon lagging behind Jamie like an Arab wife. Her route was dictated by her terror of slipping on rogue patches of ice in her smooth soled ski boots. She meandered across the pavements, into the road and back again. Heel, toe, heel, toe, she told herself, trying to get used to walking in her clumpy scarlet horrors. Although unclipped and loose at the shin, her feet and ankles felt as if they were held in a vice. Despite the chill air she was getting hot. Feeling uncomfortable and restricted in her bulky layers of clothing she stopped to unzip her jacket.

'What now?' called Jamie waiting at the roadside.

Flora dragged her eyes away from a mouth-watering display in a chocolatier's window.

The nursery slope was opposite the skating rink, at the foot of Les Pins. It was separated from the main piste by apartment blocks. Shrieking toddlers shuffled along elatedly on their skis.

Flora was comforted when she saw four groups of adults in the distance, lined up in rows and concentrating intently on the movements of the red-jacketed figures in front of them. At least she wasn't the only person more than three feet tall who couldn't ski.

Jamie set down the two pairs of skis side by side on the hard packed snow. 'Right. Put them on.'

Flora looked blank. 'How?'

'You must remember that much.'

'No.'

He rolled his eyes in disbelief and sighed. 'Scrape the snow off the bottom of your boots for a start. Now put your toe in here.' He pointed to the middle of the ski. 'Now put your weight back. That's it. Top of the class.' Flora felt the binding lock her boots onto the ski.

'And you can't remember how to take it off, can you?' said Jamie. 'Thought not. Push down the lock at the back with your pole. You can't do it with a cigarette in your hand. Give it to me. That's it.' She unclipped the back and her boot was loosened. 'Now do it again.' She put on and took off each ski four times before he was satisfied she'd got the hang of it. 'Now the poles.'

She put the straps through her wrists and automatically held them the right way. Perhaps her skiing would come back after all, like riding a bicycle? She was surprised by her sudden eagerness to find out. Twisting round awkwardly, she leant down and tried to fasten her boots properly. The back clip was stiff and refused to budge.

'Here.' Jamie knelt down. Clip. Clip. She pulled a face. The boots were now so tight around her shin, she was sure the circulation to her toes would be cut off.

Resting on her poles, she looked down at her red skis with distrust. They were now supposed to be a part of her, their path and movement determined by her. Would she be able to control them? Or, as she remembered, would they have a will of their own?

Zero hour had arrived.

As Jamie and Flora headed for the nursery slope, Pete made his way to the cable car station. He cut an impressive figure from his blond curls down to his multi-buckled boots. Unlike novices who were bundled up like badly wrapped parcels in thick jackets, pants and bobble hats, he moved easily in his jeans and fleece. The girls' telephone number was in his pocket. It was the 143rd pressed on him that year.

As Pete predicted, the rest spent far longer in the hireshop than they had intended. It was almost half-past eleven by the time they headed for the chairlift. Progress was slow. Wrongfooted by Nikki's Ralph Lauren, Miranda and Munchkin lingered in front of the skiwear shops, wondering if their budgets would stretch to something new.

Giles darted into anywhere that might sell the English papers demanding, '*Daily Telegraph* ici?'

'Shit. Look at that queue.' Sam pointed across the road to the lift station. Scores of people snaked round the building. 'We're coming up to lunchtime, supposed to be the quietest part of the day. It'll take hours.'

'Changeover yesterday,' said Anna. 'Everyone's probably doing the same as us and has been held up.'

Nikki complained that she was thirsty and Martin suggested they all stop for a drink in the café opposite. Still suffering dehydration after the night's boozing, Sam and Giles agreed. Both secretly calculated it would be cheaper to drink in the village than up in a mountain café.

Leaving their skis and poles in a rack, they all settled down around an outside table and ordered beers and coffees.

Giles sensed that Miranda and Anna weren't that happy at the further delay. 'You all right, girls? No point in having to queue for hours and getting miffed. By the time we've finished, it'll have thinned out. Cheer up. We're on holiday.'

Miranda smiled. He was perfectly right. She could hardly have set off on her own, that would be anti-social. Actually, it was nice just to sit in the sun and people-watch behind her dark glasses. Munchkin was saying that it always took a few days to settle in, relax and wind down, for you to realise how stressed out you've been. Miranda didn't need the few days to know how uptight she'd been.

Martin swallowed some beer and turned to Giles. 'You must've hacked off pretty boy Pete, pipping him at the post yesterday.'

'Think so?' Giles tried not to appear pleased.

'As I always say, it's the man not the machinery which counts.'

Giles beamed, feeling a surge of goodwill towards Martin. 'Didn't realise you once had a Porsche. Didn't get on with it?'

'OK up to a point. Impresses some birds, but never a client. Pisses them off, makes them feel you're making too much money out of them. Decided to knock the flash on the head, go for something a bit more low-profile.'

'Very wise.' Giles nodded sagely. 'Porsches were fine a few years back, but now they're a bit of a joke.'

Sam raised his eyebrows. 'You'd give your right testicle for one.'

Giles tried to ignore him. 'Any news on that deal, Martin?'

'Don't want to know.' Martin wagged his finger. 'I'm on holiday. No shop, right? Shall we make tracks?' As they stood up, he put his arm round Anna. 'See. Crowd's gone. No wait. Trust me.'

She wondered why she didn't.

Flora pushed her poles into the snow behind her and glided forward a few feet. Delighted she was still upright, she pushed again and moved across the white ground. Then, instinctively, she brought her ski tips together in front of her and leant forward with her knees bent. The back of her skis fanned out, so they were V-shaped. A snowplough. She halted.

'Why stop? You should feel your shin on the front of your boot. Bend your knees.'

The accent was different, but the words were familiar. She pulled a face. 'I'm not, not, not, on a parade ground. Don't shout.'

'Go over there.' Jamie raised his pole and pointed. 'Try and keep your weight on the bottom ski, lean further forward, with your arms higher up. Your skis ought to be parallel and about six inches apart.'

The ground seemed flat and it was difficult to get any momentum going. She crouched down and repeatedly dug her poles into the snow, knowing she looked ridiculous. She was supposed to be floating gracefully across the white like a swan, not getting stuck like some cartoon character.

'How are you meant to get anywhere if you're still in a

snowplough for God's sake? Look at the outside edge of your skis.'

Flora looked down. They were slightly raised. She flattened them down and they immediately moved off. Although she would never have believed it, there was a definite downwards gradient, which caused her to accelerate. Shakily, she gathered speed and was jolted as she went over a slight bump. Disconcerted she tried to slow down, but instead of coming to a snowplough stop, her left ski crossed over her right. The snow, which appeared so benign and soft, was iron hard — as her backside discovered when she crashed down onto it.

She sat up to see two smirking five-year-olds pointing at her and heard Jamie roaring with laughter in the distance. He came across, moving his skis as if he were ice skating. She'd always been useless at that too.

He towered over her, blocking out the sun. 'Well, what are you waiting for?'

'A bus? Godot? Christmas?'

'Get up, Flora.'

She couldn't. All around, toddlers were shuffling about on skis scarcely longer than a ruler. Flora felt like a hulking, clumsy Gulliver surrounded by curious and superior Lilliputians. Had they tied down her hair with their tiny ski poles? 'Jamie. Help. Please.'

'No. Get your skis parallel for a start, poles either side, dig in and use them.'

She got a quarter of the way up only to go down again, her backside landing on her skis.

Laughing, Jamie finally took her hand and hauled her up. Thank God someone else would be teaching her. It would be no mean task. They were at the bottom of a 20-foot slope, which screaming children were shooting down on brightly coloured toboggans.

'Now, angel. Go up to the top, come down and stop properly. Just remember to keep your weight forward. Please. That means bending your knees. Please.'

'How am I supposed to get up there?'

Jamie buried his face in his gloved hands. Flora really couldn't be this useless. Then again, Jasper had warned him. 'Herringbone. No. You'd better side step. Like this.' He turned sideways, dug the left edge of his skis into the snow and moved one, then the other. 'Kept your weight on the inside, towards the slope. Move it, you flatten the ski and slide. See.' Slowly, with perfect control, he slid sideways back to her. 'Off you go.'

It was hard work on the legs. When she at last reached the top, her face was red and she could feel a sheen of sweat on her nose. The sunlight was bright. She squinted down at him. 'Now what?'

'Ski down of course.' Jamie tried to stifle his impatience. He heard the church bell chime in the distance. The sooner she was off his hands the better. What the hell was she doing?

Jamie was to her left. Flora waited and waited until her path was clear of children, before she moved off in a snail-paced snowplough. Her thigh muscles trembled, but she reached the bottom upright. She smiled at him in triumph.

'What the hell are you doing over there? You're supposed to ski to me.'

'I can't remember how to turn.'

'Well, we'd better practise before you go up for your class, hadn't we?'

Flora was puzzled. 'Up? Go up where? My lesson's down here, isn't it?'

'I knew you weren't listening to that women in the ski school office. You're meeting the class up at La Croix.'

She was horror-struck. Up? She'd imagined a couple of hours in a class here on the nursery slope, practising gentle turns and stops like the groups in the distance. Up meant actual skiing, which would be way beyond her ability. She felt sick again. 'Up? And how do I get there?'

'Magic carpet? No, angel. Like everyone else. On the chairlift, of course.'

The chairlift? 'No, Jamie. No. No. No.' She seemed about to burst into tears. 'I hate them. They terrify me.'

'Don't be so silly. You've got to go higher up to get some decent snow.' Why was she looking as if she loathed him?

Flora remembered Davos and how the chairlift had suddenly stopped, leaving her and Jasper stranded above a piste in the freezing cold, swinging in the wind like a hanged man on a gibbet. Of course, he'd loved the novelty and delighted in her terror. 'The cable's very, very rusty and very, very thin. Just there. Look. It's about to break.' Her whimpers of fear had heightened his glee.

'. . . are you listening?'

'No. I mean yes.'

'So when you want to turn left, you snowplough, but you put all your weight on the left ski. Then, when you're round, you transfer it back to the centre and bring your skis together. Got it? Up you go.'

She trudged back up the slope again, preoccupied with her dread of the lesson and taking the chairlift. Jamie made her go up and down four times, then they went over to a pulley lift at the far side of the nursery slope which tugged them up the gentle incline. For the next hour, Flora skied down to the start umpteen times, before the pulley tugged her up to the top again. Her falls got fewer. At her elbow, Jamie barked instructions until he was satisfied she could safely snowplough, turn and stop.

'Brilliant. You see, you can do it. Just remember to try and bring your skis back parallel a bit sooner. It'll all come back to you by the end of the afternoon. You'll be amazed.'

'Sure.' Flora didn't care. Her immediate problem wasn't the skiing, it was getting to the skiing. She stared at the chairlift floating high above Les Pins piste.

'We'd better go.' Jamie put his arms round her and felt her shake. 'Nothing bad's ever going to happen to you. You're with me. I love you and I'm going to look after you.' Perhaps Siena had been a good idea after all.

She followed him across the slope towards the lift station. Flora had built up just enough confidence to take her eyes off her red ski tips. Up on the balconies, people sat round tables eating lunch in the sunshine. Cars drove along the road. Why wasn't she in one, being whisked away?

The lift station was ugly and concrete. Because it was lunchtime, few people were queueing. At the entrance, metal rails divided the queue into two lanes.

Jamie pointed. 'We go through here, up to the turnstile. Once the lot in front are safely on, a green light appears. Go through the turnstile, up to the blue line, then wait for the chair, coming round behind us. Sit down, lift the skis up and once we're clear of the shed, I'll put down the guard rail. Got that? Nothing to it. I'm right beside you. Off we go.'

Flora shuffled forward into the right-hand lane. Sheets of solid, dirty ice covered the ground under her skis, which slipped. 'Shit.'

She tried to snowplough stop, frantically grabbed the metal rail and, with its help, just about managed to stay upright. 'I'm going to break my fucking leg again.'

'Foot,' corrected Jamie. 'Dig in your poles. In front of you. They'll act as brakes.' It was worse than getting a frightened horse into the starting gates.

She edged up to the turnstile and rested her thighs on it. At least it was something solid to lean against. Hyperventilating, she peered into the dark lift shed. Ahead of her, a chic Italian couple were chattering away as the chair swung behind them. What should she do with her poles?

'Up to the blue line. Go,' ordered Jamie.

Flora pressed against the turnstile and scrambled towards the blue line, terrified that the chair would come round and knock her sideways. There was no traction on the ice, she wouldn't be able to stop.

'*Restez ici.*' Her arm was grabbed by the lift operator as she tried to snowplough and dig in her poles. Adrenaline was pumping through her. The clicks and whirrs of the machinery got louder, signalling that the chair was getting closer. She didn't dare look round, it took all her concentration to control her skis and prevent them sliding forward. She heard 'fuck' and from out of the corner of her eye, saw that someone had fallen.

'Jamie,' she screamed. 'Jamie.'

She felt a whack on the back of her legs and the operator shoved her down onto the chair. It started to move forward. She was jolted backwards into the seat, her skis and pole tips making a horrible scraping sound as they were dragged along the concrete floor of the lift shed. If they got stuck she'd be pulled out and end up under the chair.

'Jamie.' She screamed again. The operator yelled at her to '*levez les skis*'. She raised her legs, weighing a ton with their skis and boots, and clutched the side of the chair which lurched out of the gloom of the shed and into the blinding sunlight.

She looked down and wanted to throw up as she was carried higher and higher over the roofs and tops of fir trees.

'You bastard Jamie,' she sobbed, fear and fury struggling for the upper hand. Her boots and skis were lead heavy, their weight was going to pull her out of the seat any second. There was nothing between her and a seventy-foot drop. Closing her eyes, she clutched the metal side of the chair with her shaking hands and prayed.

In the chair behind, Jamie watched horrified. The stupid bitch hadn't pulled down the safety rail and wasn't sitting back properly. Why were her poles still strapped to her wrists?

Flora was being carried over a white expanse of piste. Apart from the sssh of skis cutting across the snow and the whirr of the wires as the chair was pulled up the mountainside, there was silence. The air was much colder and she longed to do up her ski jacket, but was too frightened to release her grip on the side bar. Her legs felt as if they were being stretched on a rack. It was a journey in hell, which she was certain would end with her freefalling through the air and smashing onto the piste below. She could see the headlines. BRITISH WOMAN IN SKI LIFT HORROR.

The wind carried voices towards her. A chair on its return journey to St Marie was approaching, two snowboarders lounging in it. 'Get them to stop the lift,' she screamed hysterically. 'What? What?' They were pointing above her head. 'Why?'

She glanced up. Anything was better than looking down. Of course. The safety rail. All she had to do was let go, reach up and tug.

Let go. She must let go.

Finally, she took a deep breath and pulled. The metal bar came down across her, entangling her poles and trapping her skis under the footrest. Swearing, she swung her legs out to the side and managed to rest them on top of it. She sat back, sniffing, shaking and exhausted.

Jamie heaved a huge sigh of relief. Next time she said she wanted to go to Siena, she could go. With his blessing.

Slightly calmed, Flora glanced around her. Over to the right were Les Diables, far below and behind her lay St Marie. The lift was approaching the wooden station at La Croix. What was she meant to do now? She hadn't a clue how to get off and pictured herself going up and down the mountain forever. Had Jamie said anything? Think. Think. She squinted at the Italians about 25 yards up ahead, who were pushing back the safety rail and lifting their skis as they disappeared into the gloom. Their poles were in their hands, not round their wrists. She knew there'd been something wrong with her poles.

The closer she came to the station, the more her composure ebbed away. As the chair entered the shed, dark after the dazzling sun and snow outside, Flora jerked back the safety rail and raised her skis.

It was no time for British phlegm.

'Help,' she yelled at the lift operator. The chair slowed down, she scrambled off, afraid she was going to be sent flying by it. Desperate to bolt for the exit, fifteen feet away down a gentle slope, she desperately shuffled forward, ankles and shins twisting inside her boots. The chair swung behind, catching her on the back of the legs, before it was grabbed by the operator. Almost losing her balance, she hurtled forward.

'Arrrgh.'

The Italians were directly in front of her, she was going to smash straight into them. In her panic, she dropped her poles. She aimed left and tried to snowplough, but couldn't, she was going too fast. Suddenly she was out in the bright sunshine, a kaleidoscope of ski jackets hitting her eyes as she slid across the back of someone's skis. She stopped the only way she knew; she threw herself to the ground.

'Jesus.' Winded and shocked, she lay on the snow and closed her eyes. Why couldn't the ground just open and swallow her up?

'Are you hurt?' The Italian was bending over her. She caught a whiff of Egoïste and found herself staring into one of the best looking faces she'd seen all year.

She shook her head and sat up, trying to recover her dignity and to ignore the gawps and mockery of the people around her. 'Sorry. Have I wrecked your skis?' Why did she have to make a fool of herself in front of someone so handsome?

'*Giovanni, andiamo.*' His companion sounded impatient.

'My skis are fine.' He smiled. 'Sure you are? Take care.'

As he left, Jamie arrived carrying her poles. 'Flora, angel, thank God you're all right.'

'All right? That was one of the worst experiences of my life. I could've been killed. Where were you? You promised you'd look after me.'

He was relieved she was suffering nothing more than bruised pride. 'I slipped, that's all. No big deal.' He held out his hand to help her up.

'You're not meant to fucking slip. You're meant to be fucking brilliant.'

Must she shout, people were staring. 'Flora, please calm down. You made it. Now let's get you up and we can go and have a drink before your lesson.'

She heaved herself up, brushed the snow off her and looked across to the Savoie, a large, two storey restaurant. Hundreds of people were sitting round the outside tables or sunbathing on deckchairs on the first floor terrace. Waitresses in black wove through the throng, carrying trays piled high with drinks and plates of food.

'No.' It was about fifty yards away and downhill. There was no way she could get there without making an exhibition of herself. She'd endured quite enough humiliation for one day. 'If I stay here, could you get me some water. Thanks.'

She shuffled over to a wooden bench on the side of the lift station. Her legs trembled beneath her. Exhausted, she took off her skis, unlocked the back of her boots and sank down. She lit a cigarette. So much for a holiday, she couldn't remember when she'd ever been so stressed out.

A tall woman, dressed in a pale blue jump suit emerged from the lift, long corn coloured hair streaming out behind her. She brought her skis smartly parallel, turned and stopped. She was tanned and perfectly made up. Flora hated her on sight. She knew she must look like dreadful, her face shiny, red and blotchy from crying, her hair scraped back into a tangled mess of a ponytail. She sniffed. Her nose was running, and as usual, she didn't have any tissues.

*   *   *

Jamie handed her a bottle of Evian, which she drank greedily. Hungry for lunch, skiers darted down the mountainside like a flock of starlings. They were fast, in control and graceful as they turned one way and then the other.

'Don't they look wonderful,' said Flora wistfully.

'You can do it. That's why you're having lessons.'

'Never.' She groaned. 'Lessons. More torture. Can't I skive off? Can't you write me a sick note or something?' Why couldn't she spend the afternoon in the sunshine on a balcony drinking hot chocolate and reading a book?

He looked at his watch. 'The class is meeting here any minute. You'd better get your skis on. Please don't look so miserable. It's supposed to be fun.'

Pete was having fun as he schussed down the piste towards the Savoie at breakneck speed. He sliced in front of a red-jacketed instructor who was being followed by a convoy of unsteady snowploughers. The music from his Walkman filled his ears and his blond curls were damp from almost two hours of non-stop skiing. He'd covered a lot of ground, been over some amazing bumps and had raced a Kiwi down a black run. As he glided to a graceful halt by the ski racks, heads turned in envy and admiration.

'Yoo hoo. Pete. Over here.' Munchkin stood up and waved.

Pressing through the throng, he made his way to the table she was sharing with Nikki and Martin. He sat down and ordered a beer. 'Where's the rest?'

Martin handed him a menu. 'Up there somewhere. These two wanted an early lunch and I said I'd keep them company.'

'You're the one who said you were starving,' retorted Nikki. 'I wanted to ski.' Taking out a compact, she applied some more sunscreen. It would've been nice sitting out in the sun with Martin, if only Munchkin hadn't decided to tag along.

'What's the snow like?' Martin held out his hand for a dollop of cream.

'Not too smart. Hardly anything there in places.'

Nikki frowned. 'Don't like the sound of that.'

Martin smiled indulgently. 'She's used to the best. All that powder in Aspen.'

'Aspen? Might go in March,' said Pete. 'Where did you stay?'

Nikki hesitated. 'With friends of friends'

Munchkin drained her glass. She was getting nicely whoosy, drinking *vin chaud* in the sunshine. Her guilt about wasting the morning was diminishing. She deserved to relax and the air was so clean, it was bound to be doing her good.

'You bunch of dossers.' Sam sat down, looking like a pixie in his scarlet woolly hat.

'Wash your mouth out.' Martin slapped him on the back. 'Here come the others. Better grab some chairs.'

Miranda's eyes were sparkling after the skiing. 'Phew. Quite hard going. J'ai faim. Manger everyone?'

'I feel as if my legs are going to give way,' said Anna.

'Come and collapse on me. Love girls on top.' Giles guffawed. His guinea pig face was already pink from the sun.

'Nikki likes it too.'

'Shut up Martin.' She didn't want the others to be privy to what went on in their bedroom.

Sam studied the menu. 'Cock monsewer for me, with extra frites.'

Anna gave him a withering look. He might be her best friend's brother, but he could be a bit of a prat. A few minutes later, she beckoned the waitress and gave their order in fluent French. The men agreed that foreigners should learn to speak English.

'Bit pricey, isn't it?' said Sam anxiously. How was his money going to last the week at this rate? No racing, No *Racing Post* and no bookies in St Marie.

'Exorbitant.' Giles peered at his omelette, which was tiny. 'Bread, bit of sweaty cheese and a few old potatoes.' He rarely went out to eat unless he could claim it on expenses.

'You're paying for the location,' said Anna.

'Want a job, sweetheart? Need you in sales.' Martin helped himself to Sam's frites. 'If you think this is expensive, try Switzerland. Had to take out a mortgage for a cup of coffee last time I was in St Moritz. Still, worth every penny, what with the polo and the Cresta. Incredible people, great skiing, terrific views of the Matterhorn.'

Munchkin sighed. It all sounded so glam.

'Not in St Moritz, surely?' said Miranda puzzled. 'Don't you mean Zermatt?'

Martin was blank. 'Course I do. Need a holiday, brain's packing up.'

Nikki saw Pete raise his eyebrows above his sunglasses, but couldn't read his expression. Admiring his long legs stretched out beside her, she wished Martin wasn't wearing his foul-coloured suit.

They ate heartily, shifting their chairs as people squeezed past. Bored children raced round, toddlers falling on the slippery decking and being cursed by the waitresses. The air was filled with the hum of multi-lingual chatter.

Giles got out his piste map. 'I for one have to find the old ski legs again, so personally don't want anything too hairy. Snow's actually a bit soupy, so I'm quite happy to leave the black runs to the experts this afternoon. Like Pete and Martin. And Mirandy of course. Puts me and Sam to shame. Brilliant for a girlie.'

Anna spluttered into her Coke.

Miranda beamed. 'Nonsense, Giles. We must all ski together and take it relatively easy. It's our first day, after all.'

Giles squinted at the map. 'I vote we take the chairlift over there again, but then press on further up, to what's this?, La Petite Col, via the funiculaire. That gives us a nice long gentle run back down to the village. Ah, James. Just in time.'

Jamie was swigging from a bottle of beer. Martin looked at his jeans for tell-tale signs of damp. There weren't any.

'Where's Flora?' asked Anna.

He waved up the piste. 'Having her lesson.'

'She joined ski school then. Well done her,' said Giles.

'Not quite moi, somehow,' whispered Munchkin to Martin. 'Still, each to their own.'

The moment Jamie had handed Flora over to Mirabelle the instructor, he had bolted for the lift, determined that his morning shouldn't be completely written off. Why was she in such a state? She couldn't be that scared, could she? It was too incredible to be believed. Jamie couldn't really remember when he hadn't been able to ski. Some of his happiest memories were of his prep school Easter holidays when he'd spent almost a month in Mürren going out from nine in the morning until it was almost dark. Skiing was one of life's joys. Flora could be very strange at times.

In three hours this will be over, thought Flora, waiting at Mirabelle's side for the class stragglers to turn up. She felt sick with apprehension again. Six foot tall, massive shoulders, cropped blonde hair, Mirabelle had been incredulous when Jamie explained that Flora was nervous.

'So why is she skiing then?' Her voice was scornful. She polished her mirrored sunglasses on the sleeve of her scarlet jacket and put them on.

'God only knows,' mumbled Flora unhelpfully.

'How often has she skied?' Mirabelle obviously regarded her as a halfwit and addressed all her questions to Jamie.

'Four times, well really three, but not for about ten years,' he said. 'Not that she seems to have ever made much progress.'

'Why's she with me then? She should be with the beginners.'

Flora felt even worse.

'I'll be off now,' said Jamie, squeezing her hand. 'Meet you over at the Savoie. OK?'

Flora watched him shoot over to the lift, waves of anxiety washing over her. She was an intermediate class imposter, she couldn't even turn or stop properly. Mirabelle made no attempt at conversation. Disconcerted by the sunglasses and forbidding expression, Flora could think of nothing to say.

A group trudged up from the Savoie carrying their skis.

'Hiya Mirabelle.' The voice was vaguely Scouse and belonged to a chubby faced twenty-year-old with spiky dyed blond hair and twinkling brown eyes. He turned to Flora and smiled. 'Are you joining the class? Great. The more the merrier. I'm Terry, by the way.'

'Flora.'

'This is Flora everyone.' Everyone nodded. She took in two middle aged couples and a woman who was wearing a silver jacket that made her look like a turkey ready for the oven. Hanging back were four adolescent boys, muttering what sounded like German. Remembering other Germans in other classes years earlier, Flora cringed inside.

Mirabelle looked at the sports watch on her powerful wrist. 'Terry, where are your friends?'

'Back there. They've decided to give it a miss this afternoon. Getting stuck into the *vin chaud* instead.'

'Lucky them,' muttered Flora.

Mirabelle was unamused. 'We go to the lift, then up. Practise what we learnt this morning. *Allez.*'

Flora was the last to move off. Despite the time she'd spent with Jamie going up and down the nursery slope, her skis and the sensation of travelling across the snow with them still felt alien. She was nervous, her body stiff with tension. The lift was only about 50 metres away, but by the time she was halfway to it, the others were already queueing. With so many skiers using the route, the little snow there was, was packed and icy. Instead of traversing with her skis parallel like everyone around her, Flora stuck to a faltering snowplough. Breathless and with trembling legs, she finally made it.

'How many times have you skied?' demanded Mirabelle. Not waiting for a reply she shook her head. 'Yay, yay, yay. Those ski school office idiots know jack sheet.'

'Jack shit,' corrected Flora.

Dozens of people were milling around the lift, young snowboarders cursed as they tried to queuebarge. The ski school and its pupils had priority over everyone else. Flora had no chance to psyche herself out of her fear as Mirabelle ushered her into an empty left-hand lane behind Terry and the Turkey. Before she knew it, she was putting her pass into the machine and found herself waiting at a turnstile shoulder to head with the amazonian Mirabelle. She knew any confession of the fear that was overwhelming her would fall on stone deaf ears. The turnstile was released and Flora was charging forward to the blue line.

'Carry your poles,' barked Mirabelle.

'Sorry,' said Flora abjectly, peering behind. The chair was approaching, her heart was pounding. It slowly swung round almost to a stop. Taking her cue from Mirabelle, she sat down and lifted her skis. They moved off.

Flora was stunned it was so easy. She reached in her pocket for her Marlboros to celebrate. 'Smoke?'

'No. And neither do you in my class.'

Stung, Flora found herself scowling in the mirrored lenses and looked down at the Savoie. She wished she was getting stuck into the *vin chaud*.

They spent the next ten minutes in silence as they were carried high over the trees and a mogul field. The sunlight bounced off the white peaks. If Flora hadn't been dreading the skiing, she might have enjoyed herself.

'Get ready.' Mirabelle pushed up the guard rail. The chair was slowing down on its approach to a wooden shed. '*A gauche*. Left.'

Too late. Flora had already scrambled off the chair and hared straight ahead, gathering speed until she collided with a row of hay bales. She landed on her skis as if she were playing musical bumps. Dutch, not German, she thought, as she heard the four teenagers laugh at her expense.

'Upsadaisy.' Terry held out his gloved hand. 'Are you OK, Flora?'

'Nothing broken.' Getting back upright, she rubbed her backside. It would be a mass of bruises by the end of the day.

Mirabelle was pursing her lips and shaking her head in disbelief. 'If we're all ready. Terry, Flora, over here please.'

'All right?' whispered one of the middle-aged women sympathetically. 'Getting off these lifts is always tricky. I'm Jenny by the way. Leonard, my husband.' He was grumpy-looking with dark over-lenses pinned to the bridge of his thick spectacles.

'Flora.' She smiled at the kind face under the hood of a paisley padded jacket.

'And that's Margaret and Neville.' They were wearing matching emerald green pompom hats. 'Our boys are in the junior class together. Staying in the St Julien?'

'No. In a chalet, somewhere over there.'

'If I can have everyone's attention,' thundered Mirabelle, glowering at Flora. Jenny looked sheepish and turned away. 'Remember the three points about the basic stem turn . . .'

Stemming? Flora was horrified. She could barely snow-plough. Why the hell was she in this class, it was way beyond her ability? She looked round for a means of escape. There wasn't one. There was nowhere to go apart from down the mountain-side. She felt sick again.

'. . . and remember, knees flexed at all times. *Allez.*'

Mirabelle pushed her poles into the ground and powered ahead, followed by Neville, Leonard and the Dutch. They traversed the piste, copying her as she raised her uphill ski, showing her weight was correctly balanced. Trying to get across the snow without falling, Flora didn't bother. Her eyes were fixed on her red ski tips. The Turkey was already about 15 yards ahead, silver jacket glinting in the sunshine.

Much further down the slope, Mirabelle had already turned

and was level with Flora. 'Flex your knees. Skis closer together,' she yelled.

Flora gritted her teeth. She must turn, otherwise she'd smash into the fir trees lining the piste. What had Jamie said? Into a snowplough, weight on the outside ski. Which ski? Right? No, left. She leant out to her left, like a keeling yacht. She knew it wasn't very stylish, but didn't care. The most important thing was to get round. She went round. The Turkey was already over on the other side of the piste, and about to turn again.

Flora's heart raced, her breathing was shallow and her body almost in a state of rigor mortis. As she was carried forward, she was aware of every little bump that she went over. Around her the landscape was like Narnia. As far as she was concerned, she was in the middle of hell.

Mirabelle had halted in the middle of the piste and was studying the class. 'Skis back parallel,' she bellowed. Flora wondered if she would start an avalanche. 'You, Flora, arms down. Skis parallel. Now turn.'

Confused by the orders, alarmed she was lagging so far behind the rest, disconcerted by a snowboarder darting in front of her, Flora turned too quickly and found her skis crossing out of control. 'Shit.' She tumbled and slid down the slope for about twenty feet before coming to a halt. 'Shit.'

Tears of misery and frustration pricked her eyes. In the distance an exasperated Mirabelle seemed to dance in front of her. 'Are you 'urt? Up. Up Up.'

Sniffing into her sleeve and brushing snow from her hair, Flora manoeuvred her skis back parallel and with the help of her poles, hauled herself upright. Why hadn't she been listening in the ski school office? Why hadn't she joined a beginners' class? The intense concentration, added to her lack of sleep was starting to catch up with her.

'*Allez*. Don't keep the class waiting.'

Flora moved forward gingerly, traversing to the scarlet figure standing out against the snow like a Monument to Victory.

Mirabelle was calling everyone to stop. 'Not you,' when Flora obediently slowed down. '*Allez, allez.*' She skied alongside her, calling out a non-stop torrent of commands.

Flora tried to relax her shoulders, keep her head up, poles down and flex her knees, but as she did one thing, she forgot the rest. Other skiers swept past, their movements fluid and easy, underlining her own incompetence. Her boots were biting into her shins and her fingers were frozen in their wet gloves. What time was it?

The class had stopped near a wooden building marked *Poste de Secours*. Flora ground to a juddering snowplough halt alongside the Turkey. A muttering Leonard had been watching her progress. He was given a warning sssh by Jenny. Flora knew he also thought she shouldn't be in the class, but she was slightly cheered up by Terry's wink of encouragement. Far, far below was the Savoie, customers milling around like multi-coloured ants.

'Not too bad, everyone,' said Mirabelle. 'Remember to plant the pole earlier in the turn. Now I want one of you to go down, do three stem turns and an uphill stop. The rest watch carefully. Neville.'

It wasn't a request. He skied away from them. Flora was envious, he was so controlled as he made a trio of turns and then neatly stopped by moving his skis up the slope. He waved back at them. From under her matching green pompom, Margaret beamed with pride and gave him a thumbs-up.

'Any comments?' asked Mirabelle.

'Great to me,' said Terry shrugging. 'Well done Nev,' he called.

'Pole in sooner,' piped up Leonard, earning himself a sour glance from Margaret. 'And knees lower on the approach.'

'Exactly.' Mirabelle nodded. 'Like this.' She squatted, her huge front thigh muscles bulged in their scarlet ski pants. The Dutch sighed in admiration. 'Another volunteer. Leonard.'

He set off at a much faster pace. All was well until he

approached Neville. He tried to stop, lost his balance and toppled onto his skis. Margaret smiled in satisfaction.

'What went wrong there?' demanded Mirabelle. 'Anyone.' Silence. 'Not enough body turn into the slope. Remember: angle your shoulders as well as your legs. Now we ski to the lift. Flora, you snowplough.'

Yet again, Flora found herself lagging behind the others. As the gap widened, she felt the humiliation of a long distance runner lapped by better athletes. As she snowploughed and occasionally traversed, her legs were jelly-like. Snowboarders and skiers zoomed by, inches from colliding with her, forcing her to come to an abrupt and frightened halt in the middle of the piste.

'Flora, round here. *A droîte.* Don't stop.' Assuming they'd be heading back towards the Savoie, Flora was surprised when Mirabelle raised her pole and pointed down a path towards another lift station. 'Bend your knees. Shoulders more downhill.'

Following Mirabelle, Flora tried to keep over to the right-hand side of the path, away from a sharp, snowy drop which plummeted down, down, down. She felt sick with fear and slowed down. The distance between the two widened and Mirabelle had to stop repeatedly. Her shouted commands grew more impatient.

Eventually she made it to the lift. The rest of the class were waiting. She smiled apologetically at them. Mirabelle was muttering to herself in French and staring at her with contempt.

'Well, I don't pay all this money to be kept hanging about,' snarled Leonard, ignoring Jenny's ssshing.

As she queued for the chairlift, Flora wanted to dig herself a snowhole, crawl into it and quietly die.

Approaching the turnstile, she found herself lined up with an elderly Frenchman, rather than Mirabelle, who whether by accident or design, was behind her. Flora decided it was design, but didn't care. The woman, Mirabête not Mirabelle, was a monster, as bad as every other instructor she remembered.

Slumping back in the chair, she squeezed her eyes tight shut to prevent tears of misery from falling. What time was it?

For the first time, she managed to ski off the lift without any mishaps. Terry's warm smile raised her spirits, but they sank again when Mirabête ordered her to tighten up her boots.

'How?' demanded Flora. Surely they were tight enough already?

Mirabête burst into mocking laughter. 'You must know how.'

'I don't,' snapped Flora, feeling every eye upon her.

She heard Leonard mutter, 'Good God.'

'Like this.' Terry bent down and twisted the dials at the back and side. 'All right?'

Mirabête launched into some complicated theory about pole planting. Flora switched off and looked around. Hectare upon hectare of white lay in every direction. Far above, a cable car glided across the blue sky towards a jagged peak.

'*Allez*,' shouted Mirabête.

Hastily, Flora began to traverse, realising the slope was impossibly steep. Well, it was for her. Streaking ahead, no one else was finding it a problem.

From somewhere behind her, she heard the rasping grate of a snowboard. She stopped, bracing herself for a collision. The board powered on. Looking round, she saw dozens of skiers and boarders who all seemed hell bent on slamming into her. She froze.

'Flora, ski. Never look back,' called Mirabête.

She was rooted to the spot. Mirabête's commands made her more agitated, like a nervous driver waiting at a busy junction who was being hooted at. Whimpering, she began to snow-plough.

'Bend your knees,' repeated Mirabête. As Flora drew level with her, she sighed heavily. 'Why are you in this class? It's too advanced for you.'

Flora wanted to agree, to explain, to apologise, but didn't get the chance. Once again, Mirabête skied beside her, hardly drawing breath as she ordered her to do this and that. Arriving beside the rest of the class, Flora knew there should be a big D for Dunce sewn on her hat.

'Sorry to keep you waiting. This always 'appens when something thinks too 'ighly of their ability,' announced Mirabête. 'Thinks the beginners' class is beneath them.'

Flora blushed scarlet. Everyone, even Terry, was staring at her as if she had a dose of the plague. Averting her eyes, she looked down at her ski tips, her face a picture of misery.

Still breathless, Flora found herself setting off yet again. Yet again, she was at the back of the class, yet again Mirabête yelled at her to do this, do that. Although she was nervous, her heart lurching as she went over the tiniest bump, she was able to inch her way down the mountainside without a fall. Her gloves were soaking from stress sweat, her legs were aching and her face was screwed up with fear and concentration, but she managed to remain upright. Just.

After twenty exhausting minutes she found herself near the path, where the class had peeled off towards the second chairlift. She lifted her eyes from her ski tips.

Where was the class? Nowhere. Far in the distance, she could see the Savoie. Dozens of people were scattered around across the snow, but there was no sign of Mirabête in her scarlet, the Turkey's silver or the green pompoms. She was alone, halfway up a mountainside with nothing but fir trees for company.

Not concentrating, she was jolted as her skis hit a rutted patch of ice, their edges grating. She crashed onto the snow. 'Pick yourself up, dust yourself down and start all over again,' she sang through clenched teeth.

Three minutes later she was down for the fourth time. 'Fuck, fuck, fuck,' she yelled, tearing the poles from her wrist and hurling them down the slope in frustrated rage and misery. All of her little confidence was shattered. Shivering with cold, scared and utterly weary, she just wanted to lie back on the snow.

At that moment she hated Jamie. It was his fault she was on this holiday, his fault that she was skiing again, or rather not, after all these years. She hated herself, for not trusting her gut feelings, for being so wet that she had let herself be bullied by him and everyone else in the chalet.

The cold ended her brooding. If she stayed put, she'd get hypothermia. She sniffed, wiped her eyes on her sleeve and looked down the mountain. The Savoie seemed a bit closer, that was something. All she had to do was get up, retrieve her poles and get there. To hell with Mirabête, the class and skiing. She'd had enough.

She took a deep breath and dug the inside edges of her skis into the snow. As she tried to struggle up, her skis slipped backwards and she found herself down again with a thump. 'Shit.' Why had she thrown away her poles? They were about six feet away. Whoever said a man's reach should exceed his grasp had never been skiing. There was nothing for it but to turn on her side and slither down to them.

With their help, she was finally vertical. Thank God. She lit a cigarette to celebrate and surveyed the slope, wondering if she'd ever be able to make it to the Savoie.

'Well, Flora. Nice to see you 'aving a little relaxation.' Mirabête skidded to a stop in front of her. She was furious.

'Relaxation?' Flora couldn't believe her ears.

'A rest.'

'Rest? I'm trying to get my breath back . . .'

'Breath back. Why are you smoking then?' They glared at one another. 'I've been searching the mountainside for you. Who are you, thinking you can stop the whole class?'

'I didn't mean to,' protested Flora, flooded by guilt. 'I couldn't keep up, it's not my fault, I . . .'

'Well, why join this class? It's for intermediates, not imbeciles. Imbeciles who pretend they can ski.'

Bitch. Flora was stung by the injustice. 'Listen, I didn't pretend I could ski. I didn't want to be in this class. The ski school put me in here. Don't worry, I won't be joining you tomorrow. In fact, I won't be with you for the rest of the afternoon. I'm not going to be screamed at by you for a moment longer. Go and bully someone else. *Allez* and don't forget to bend your fucking knees.'

Flora flung away her cigarette, dug her poles into the snow and skied off, leaving Mirabête open-mouthed.

Pete set a blistering pace, but couldn't shake off Jamie who was almost on the back of his skis as they tore down the gentle blue run. After twenty minutes they were back at the bubble lift. Both were panting, blond hair dark with sweat.

'Way to be,' grinned Pete, holding out a gloved hand which Jamie slapped.

'Way to be.'

A bit later, a breathless Miranda stopped beside them. 'You two really go for it.' Her voice was full of admiration. There was something about men who could ski well that was terribly attractive. She scanned the mountainside. 'Now, where are the others?'

Pete held up his pole. 'That's Giles, isn't it, up there? Arse out like Donald Duck. There's Sam, just about to turn. Whoops, looks painful. What's happened to Martin? Thought he'd be here by now.'

'Probably keeping an eye on Nikki and Munchkin,' said Jamie, thankful he'd dumped Flora in ski school.

They were talking Les Trois Vallees when Anna arrived, shortly after Giles. Controlled and steady, she was competent rather than flash. The tortoise to Sam's hare.

Pete nudged Jamie. They were bored with hanging around. 'How about it? Down to the village?'

'Fifty?'

'Done.'

They shot off, Pete slightly ahead. Shielding her eyes from the sunlight, Anna watched them. 'Impressive,' she sighed. 'Pete's faster, but Jamie's more stylish.' She pulled up the hood of her turquoise jacket. The sun was moving behind Les Diables, it was getting cold.

Ten minutes later, an angry Nikki stopped. She was followed by an exhausted Munchkin and Martin, whose face was thunderous. 'Sorry to keep you waiting,' he said. 'Nikki and I had a slight collision back there.'

'It was all your fault,' she spat. 'Look at this jacket. Covered in snow. It'll be ruined.'

'It's meant to get wet, it's a fucking ski jacket, stupid.'

'Don't call me stupid, stupid. You're the one whose skis are too long. That guy in the shop warned you.'

Miranda and the rest turned away in embarrassment, trying to ignore the shouting. 'Nice weather for it,' said Sam. 'And for skiing. How did you get on?'

'Fine.' Munchkin smiled brightly, not meeting his eye. She wondered if she could take the chairlift back down to St Marie. She had fallen nine times and resolved never again to drink *vins chauds* at lunchtime. At least the skiing had halted her fretting.

'I just couldn't get it together. Kept on going arse over tit.' Munchkin was comforted by how gloomy he sounded. At least she wasn't the only one.

Giles cleared his throat. 'Chilly willy standing here. Seems to be getting a bit misty down below. Shall we be off, chaps?'

'Good idea,' said Miranda wondering why Nikki and Martin had to be quite so loud in public. Not on. So embarrassing.

Jamie streaked ahead of Pete just past the Savoie, but was overtaken at the Les Pins chairlift. They tore between the nervous members of a ski school class, forcing a woman to stop and her fellow pupil to slam into the back of her. Pete managed to reach St Marie five yards ahead. They bent over double, resting on their poles, gasping for breath.

'Well done. Get you next time.' Jamie hawked and spat into the snow. He looked at his watch and frowned. 'Got to collect Flora. Meet you at that Igloo place on the square?'

'Sure. Fiveish?'

Jamie skied off to the chairlift, now deserted. Sitting back in the chair, he was glad of a chance to recover. A gentle mist was swirling round the buildings, softening their edges. It mingled with the steam rising from the huge outdoor pool on the outskirts of the village.

As he was carried higher, he found himself back in the sunshine. It was rush-hour on Les Pins piste, crowded with aching-limbed skiers who were looking forward to a hot bath after spending the day in the fresh air.

On the approach to La Croix, he noticed a prostrate figure on the snow directly under the chair's path. The khaki micro-fibre was unmistakable. Nikki was beside him. Perhaps Martin was testing the waterproofing on his wondersuit.

Jamie reached out and scooped up the snow lodged around his bindings. He packed it hard, aimed and threw. He peered down in delight to see Martin's furious face staring up, shaking the white from his hair. Direct hit. Jamie laughed gleefully.

'Bastard,' yelled Martin.

Flora made it to the Savoie without falling once. Still angry, she'd been so preoccupied by her exchange with Mirabête, she'd stopped worrying about her skiing and just got on with it.

Finding herself coming to a halt by the rack at the entrance to the restaurant, she looked back up the piste in amazement. She'd done it. However, she felt no sense of achievement, she was too fed up, tired and cold.

She slung her skis into the rack and unclipped the top of her boots. Just a few people were sitting outside, the air was now chill. On stiff legs she clomped inside and sank down onto a bench at a table next to the steamed up windows. Without bothering to look at the menu, she ordered a double expresso.

Her fingers and toes tingled as they slowly defrosted. The laughter and chatter and bustle swept over her. The clock above the bar said 3.30. Was that am or pm?

'Flora? What happened to you, girl?' It was Terry. Behind him Jenny, Margaret and their husbands ignored her and went to sit on the other side of the room.

'I quit.'

'Why?' His twinkling eyes were sympathetic. Ice from his boots melted into a pool of water as a shuddering Flora explained how she'd been put in the wrong class and was completely useless. 'And Mirabête-Mirabelle-and I didn't exactly hit it off.'

'Don't worry about her. Bark's worse than her bite. Just takes it all too seriously. Good teacher, mind. One of the best I've had.' He waved out the window to two men who were beckoning him.

Flora was incredulous. If Mirabête was one of the best . . .

Jamie arrived. The lesson should have gone well and Flora seemed to be making friends. Giles was right, ski school classes were a great way of meeting people. She'd be off his hands for the rest of the week. 'Hello angel.' He kissed her. 'Good day? How was it?'

'Tell you later. Terry, Jamie. Jamie, Terry. Where's the loo?'

It was upstairs, the steps as difficult for her weary legs as Everest. Seeing herself in the mirror, she hastily redid her ponytail. What a fright. She looked washed out without any make-up, washed off by all the tears she'd shed that day.

Jamie had ordered two *vins chauds*. He glowed with health and *joie de vivre* after his day. His blue eyes sparkled. Flora was tempted to check if he had grown a wagging tail and had a healthy cold nose. 'Terry was amazed you hadn't skied for so long. Said you did really well considering. Nice guy, isn't he?

'Very.'

'So?'

'So what?'

'So, was it fun? Where did you go? What did you do?'

'It was about as much fun as sticking needles in my eyes. What did I do? Got shouted at and fell over a lot. Where did I go? Out of my depth and onto my backside.'

'Oh come on, angel. First day. Things will improve tomorrow.'

'There's no tomorrow.'

Jamie became uneasy. 'What do you mean?'

'I argued with Mirabête and I walked out. Well, skied out. I'm not going back into that class. Ever. Anyway, doubt if she'd have me back.'

'Flora.' He was dumbfounded. What was he going to do with her for the rest of the week? For the next ten minutes, he pleaded with her to rejoin the class the following morning.

'I'm not going back to Mirabête's class. I'm not going into any class. These instructors are all the same. Bored, bullying sadists. Just like I remembered. Worse. Never again. No more. No way. No.'

Jamie's dream that Flora might prove such an enthusiastic convert that she'd be eager to ski down to St Marie turned to dust. She insisted they get the lift. There was a long queue, which he was tempted to barge. He didn't do waiting.

Recognising Flora and remembering her undignified exit that morning, the operator sniggered when he took their skis and rested them on the back of the chair.

The chair lurched out of the shed. Swallowing hard, Flora clutched the safety rail. The whole valley was laid out before them, lights from St Marie peeping though the mist. It was like being on a roller coaster. Why hadn't she skied down? Her knuckles whitened as her grip tightened on the rail.

Glancing at Flora, who seemed strangely rigid, Jamie wistfully recalled a passionate snogging session he'd once enjoyed on a lift in Kitzbühel with a pretty blonde deb. Happy days.

He looked at the mountains soaring skywards, their covering of snow glinting gold in the low sun. 'Beautiful view.'

'I feel sick.' Her vertigo was returning.

God Almighty, what was his holiday going to be like if she didn't go back to class tomorrow?

A quarter of an hour later back in St Marie, Flora realised her troubles were far from over. She must negotiate a flight of rickety metal steps to get back onto the road.

'Bit slippery and steep, so be careful,' warned Jamie. A pair of skis in his hand, he almost galloped down before bounding onto the tarmac 25 feet below. 'Hurry up.'

Flora inched towards the icy metal grating leading to the top step. She gripped the handrail. Two spotty youths pushed past her.

'Come on,' yelled Jamie, being hooted by a passing car.

She edged nearer to the top step. Underfoot was like an ice rink. If she slipped, her head would be smashed open, her nose ripped off by the metal. Her weeks in plaster came flooding back.

'I can't,' she called pathetically.

'Of course you can. Just turn sideways and take a step at a time.' His patience was wearing thin.

'I can't.' Her mental block about the steps was growing. She moved to one side to let people pass.

'Flora, just get down here now. There's no such word as can't.'

'There is. Can't. Can't. What's that, if it's not a word? A hippopotamus?'

Must she shout? Must she show him up in front of the whole

of France? 'Stop being such a bloody ninny and get down here. Now.'

'If I break my leg again, it's all your fault.'

'Foot. Now.'

Ice pure ice. No purchase at all. The soles of her boots were smooth. Hand tight on the rail, she climbed down like a slow crab, trying to ignore the complaints of the people behind her. It was horrible, like Kilimanjaro in reverse. When she finally made it, Jamie said a sarcastic well done.

They walked in silence towards the square. She was oblivious to the shops, traffic and crowds. Chairlifts, skiing, instructors, steps. Was there no end to the trials she must endure in one day? She felt frozen, suddenly starving, weary and her boots hurt. This was supposed to be a holiday, not a campaign with the French Foreign Legion. Why had she ignored her instincts which had told her to stay at home?

Jamie was forced to slow down to let her catch up. He should've let her stay at home. He was supposed to be on holiday, not acting as nursemaid.

They found the Igloo. Low-ceilinged, snug, it was crowded with boarders and skiers. Johnny Haliday was on the radio. Pete had just arrived and bagged a table. After ordering three *vins chauds*, Jamie sat and listened to Flora telling him about her lesson.

When all of the sweet Pete Aussie charm failed to persuade Flora to return to class, Jamie decided urgent action was needed. 'See you in a minute.'

He returned twenty minutes later, looking pleased with himself. He ruffled Flora's hair. 'Done it.'

'Done what?' Had he managed to change her flight?

'You don't have to go back to class.'

He *had* managed to change her flight. When could she leave? Tonight?

'You've got an instructor all to yourself,' said Jamie. 'Tomorrow at eleven o'clock. He's called Stefan and you're meeting him at La Croix.'

Pete whistled. 'Nice one, Flora.'

'But, but, but . . . I don't want to ski.' She looked at Jamie appalled. 'When did you arrange all this?'

'Just now at the ski school offices. What's wrong now? It's what you wanted this morning. Pure fluke that I was there, just as they got a cancellation.'

'Must've cost you a packet,' said Pete.

'Worth every centime.'

'But . . .' Flora was interrupted by Pete saying one-to-one was the best way to learn.

Didn't Jamie understand, she didn't want to ski? Ever. She had no more need to ski than she needed to parachute jump. Why couldn't she just be left on a balcony in the sunshine with some hot chocolate? Why couldn't she go home? This Stefan was going to be another monster like Mirabête. Besides, it didn't matter who was teaching her, she didn't want to learn.

She sighed and tried to switch in, but the two men were remember whenning past ski trips.

'Tell you who's not bad,' said Pete. 'Miranda.'

'Good style,' nodded Jamie.

'Good looking.'

'Hands off. She's almost engaged, isn't she.'

'Not my type,' yawned Pete, pushing his shaggy curls out of his eyes. 'Got a feeling Giles has the hots for her.'

Jamie finished his drink. 'Doesn't stand a chance. Can't see Miranda trading in Charlie Lyall for him. Or for anyone else. Let's go.'

It was dark. Mercury in the thermometers was plummeting to well below freezing. Anxious for the warmth and comfort of a fireside, the crowds hurried along the snowbanked pavements.

At the chalet, Flora dragged herself into the storeroom. She yanked off her boots and looked at them with loathing. Four inch stilettos would be like carpet slippers in comparison. She wiggled her toes, thinking this must be how the Victorians felt when they took off their corsets.

Slowly, she climbed the stairs to the sitting room, her socks leaving wet footprints.

Giles held out a plate of fruitcake. 'Hello Flora. You look bushed. Nice day?'

She picked up the biggest slice. 'Fine thanks.'

A fire was roaring away in the grate, tea things were scattered around the tables and gloves steamed as they dried out on the top of the radiators. With so many people, the room seemed cramped rather than cosy.

'Good lesson?' called Sam from the dining table.

'Just as I imagined.' She sank into an armchair, wanting to forget all about it. The lack of sleep was catching up with her. She could hear Miranda and Jamie in the kitchen, each praising the other's skiing. Perhaps he should marry someone like her. A brave goddess of the ski slopes, the sort who would always write thank you letters and make a picnic for a point-to-point.

Martin was on the sofa, briefcase at his feet, laptop on his knees and mobile phone at his mouth. He was leaving a long message for work, something about dropping by fifty kay, but don't let them go below half a meg. His loud voice dominated the room. 'Call me tomorrow and e-mail me a daily update.'

'Incredible, modern technology, isn't it?' said Munchkin to Flora. 'I've left everything behind. Powerbook, phone, pager, the lot. My assistant has the number here in case of emergencies, but I warned him, only emergencies.'

Flora thought of the scruffy notebook and Biros she used for work. Less high tech than no tech.

Martin smiled at Nikki beside him. 'Just leaving a message with my broker, then I'll be through.' He began punching the numbers.

'It's Sunday night and Bank Holiday tomorrow.' Sighing, she inspected her suntanned hands with their perfectly manicured nails.

'So? New York's open. Bill, Martin June. Those options you mentioned . . .'

Munchkin had recovered from her disastrous afternoon, which she blamed on too much *vin chaud*. 'Poor Flora. Exhausted, aren't you? Pity you couldn't come out with us. It was such fun. How was the instructor? Nice looking?'

'You know what they say about girlies and their ski instructors,' said Martin, winking at Munchkin.

'Clare, one of my best friends, ended up in bed with hers at Meribel. Said he was like a lollipop. Suntanned face, but white body.'

Nikki scowled and looked at the ceiling, wishing Munchkin would leave her and Martin alone for five minutes.

'Lovely ski pants, Nikki. Only you could wear them. So slim,' said Munchkin.

Nikki was unappeased.

'Ralph Lauren, aren't they?' said Flora, forcing herself to be sociable.

Nikki nodded. She was surprised Flora knew. With her disgraceful black sweater and old black ski pants, Nikki thought Flora a complete scruff. Pretty in that waif-like way, she conceded, but almost grungey. Her accessories could be a couple of tattoos and a dog on a string rather than lipstick and a decent handbag. Her hair needed a good brush.

She was reminded of a pair of turquoise eyes and a long leather coat. That night in the pub, Jack Mancini, Martin's horrible friend, had said his girlfriend never brushed her hair. Nikki shivered, recalling her visceral mistrust of him. He had seen through her at once, had sensed there was a good story somewhere. Would Flora? For now she was only working on some little, local paper. A hick hack. But that was how Jack had started out. Was Flora like him? She remembered being warned that anyone from the Press was scum, who would sell out their family, their friends, even their pet dog given half the chance.

Flora wondered why she should bother being sociable if all Nikki could do was stare at her as if she had a contagious disease.

Munchkin poured herself some more tea and cut her third slice of cherry cake. All tiny slices, she assured herself. 'I think you're being very sensible going into a class, Flora. There'd be nothing worse for the rest of us than being held back by a novice.'

Flora cringed inside, thinking how she'd held back the whole class that afternoon.

'I don't envy you having to go to classes, but I suppose we all had to do it. I'm so glad I've got past that stage. You probably don't mind being dictated to. What time do you start tomorrow?'

'Eleven, apparently.' Flora yawned.

'Eleven?' Munchkin was puzzled. 'That's very civilised for ski school.'

Standing beside the fireplace, Pete grinned. 'School's out forever, isn't it? Flora's got her own instructor.'

'If I hadn't left, I'd have been expelled.' Flora scowled.

'One-to-one,' said Munchkin. 'How much does it cost?'

'No idea.' Flora yawned again. 'Ask Jamie, he organised it.'

'Princess.' Pete tugged her ponytail affectionately. 'I'm going up for a shower.'

A private instructor. Munchkin was a mite deflated, as if Flora had somehow got one over on her.

At the table, Jamie was drawing diagrams on the back of a phone book as he explained different turns to Giles and Sam. 'Plant your pole here.'

Anna was telling Miranda about ski resorts in the former Eastern bloc, assuring her that the food in Bulgaria was plain but good.

'Interesting.' Miranda sounded sceptical. 'But I doubt if I could ever be unfaithful to France and Switzerland.'

Flora tried to stifle her yawns. All this chit-chat about skiing was worse than listening to golfers re-live a game hole by hole.

Sam called across the room. 'You should be listening to this Martin. Help you get down on your skis rather than your arse.'

Anna and Miranda tried not to smile.

'If I were you, I'd change them first thing tomorrow,' said Jamie.

'Why?' demanded Martin.

'Bit long for you, aren't they? Can't think what the guy in the hireshop was playing at.'

Sam sniggered. Remembering Martin in the shop, Anna and Miranda smirked.

'Sore subject,' said Sam. 'Sore bum as well, I bet.'

The two women giggled. Their amusement proved too much. Martin leapt up, his eyes blazing. 'Listen, your lordship, if I want your advice, I'll ask for it. Otherwise keep quiet and mind your own business. All right?'

His sudden aggression was like a tornado. Sensing trouble, the amusement faded from Miranda's face. Jamie was as taken aback as everyone else. 'Sure. Nothing to do with me . . .'

'No, it fucking isn't. I'm not one of your fucking squaddies.'

Flora wondered how Martin had got the scar on his cheekbone.

'You know best,' said Jamie appeasingly. 'No . . .'

Martin cut him short. He jabbed his finger in Jamie's direction. 'And don't think I've forgotten your little joke on the chairlift. Very funny, old chap. And nicking my parking space was another of your jolly larks, was it?' He was like a fierce guard dog, barking and snarling, trying to escape a leash. 'Yellow card. OK?'

The music died away and there was silence, heavy with awkwardness. Jamie raised an eyebrow, his face chilly with disdain. 'Not a red?'

Martin looked round the room, but apart from Jamie no one

would meet his eye. He suddenly turned on his heel and thumped down onto the sofa again. 'Wanker,' he muttered to Nikki.

Flora overheard him and felt even more uneasy.

Anna polished her glasses and Miranda got up to examine the books on the shelves. Nikki picked at the furballs on her sweater with her varnished nails. Desperately thinking of how to break the silence, Munchkin smiled brightly. 'More tea? Shall I make a fresh pot?'

'Good idea Munch,' said Giles. His white-lashed eyes were nervous. 'Where were we?'

'Music,' demanded Sam. 'Poles, Jamie.'

Under the cover of Simply Red, Giles lowered his voice. 'Apparently his staff called him Semtex. Always letting rip. I'll have a chat, smooth things out.'

'Don't bother,' said Jamie.

Unable to bear the stilted atmosphere, Flora went to her room. She closed the curtains against the darkness outside. Jamie had meant well, but she guessed that Martin was used to giving orders and disliked being told what to do.

Where was Jamie? For a man who said married life with her would never be boring, he was hardly eager for her company. She picked up the wedding file, but found it hard to concentrate because of the music pounding through the wall.

Hetty came in to clear away tea. 'Everyone had a good day?'

'Great thanks.' Anna was glad of the diversion. 'By the way, has anyone called for me?'

'No messages when we came back. Sorry.'

Helping Hetty stack the crockery, Miranda saw Anna's disappointment. 'Expecting a call?'

'Oh. Um.' She seemed confused. 'Someone's looking after my cats. I wanted to make sure they're all right. What's the code for England?'

The telephone was on the sideboard next to the dining table. Blushing, Anna smiled at Giles. 'Just leaving a message for Trotsky and Ortega.' He stared at her horrified. 'My cats.'

'They'll get it?'

'Probably out. When they're back, they'll ring and tell me Tom's taking good care of them.'

Was the woman deranged? 'Tom. Flatmate?'

'Lover.'

Giles was taken aback by her defiance. Married man? First boyfriend? Although she was a bit long in the tooth to be losing her cherry. God botherer perhaps. He'd check with Sam.

In a low voice, Nikki berated Martin for losing his temper. She sensed that Miranda, Anna and even Munchkin disapproved and their sympathies were with Jamie. There was an awkwardness in the air, which would only clear once he apologised.

Martin crossed to the table, caught Jamie's eye and smiled. 'Sorry I let rip mate. Had a bugger of a day, what with looking after the girls and everything. You're well ahead of me, dumping yours in ski school. Really sorry.'

'No problem.' Jamie was only too happy to accept the olive branch, especially after Sam's report on Martin's skiing. And if he'd been forced to look after Flora all day, he wouldn't be in the sunniest of moods either. 'Beer?'

'Good thinking.' Giles was relieved the pair of them were patching things up. If they fell out, the consequences would be disastrous. 'Sun's well over the yardarm. Mirandy, drink?'

'It's a bit early, but a gin ton would be nice.' It was dark after all, and a drink might help her relax.

* * *

Munchkin was swaying to the rhythm with her mug, tea splashed onto the tiles. 'Don't you love this song?'

Doesn't she know the word diet? Nikki admired her own neat, narrow hips and slim legs stretched out on the sofa. Her body was the result of a daily workout, frequent massages and ruthless self discipline at meal times.

Guessing Nikki's thoughts, Munchkin quickly pulled her jersey down over her hips as she pranced round in self-conscious abandon.

'Dancin'?'

'Askin'?' said Munchkin, heart beating as Martin began to jive with her.

He twirled her round a couple of times. Her leg caught the side of the sofa. She knew it would bruise, but didn't care as he leant her back almost to the floor. She could feel the huge muscles in his arm. He moved his face closer and stared into her eyes. 'Run away with me.'

What wonderful pewter eyes. An amazing contrast to his black hair, threaded with silver rather than merely greying. 'Munchkin, don't make me beg. Anywhere . . .' Such powerful arms. She imagined being pinned down by them as they embraced passionately, lying on white sand at the water's edge. *From Here to Eternity* had been on the box recently, it would be just like that . . . 'Skegness, Cleethorpes, your choice.' Laughing Martin pulled her up. Munchkin's dreams collapsed.

'Come on, Martin. Shower time.' Nikki stood up and held out her hand. She wasn't pleased.

'Together?'

'What else?'

Sam and Giles whooped as he was led upstairs. He turned back and winked. Watching him disappear, Munchkin felt depressed and very, very fat.

*　　*　　*

Nikki slammed their bedroom door. 'If you want to get off with that blob with the verbal runs, do it. But not in front of me.'

Martin was baffled. 'I don't. Besides, Munchkin's not a blob. She's just a bit plumpish. OK, so she talks a lot, but she's nice. Jolly.'

'If you fancy her, have her. I don't care.'

'Are you mad? I don't fancy her. I only fancy you.'

'I knew I never should've come on this holiday. You're after every woman in sight.'

'I'm not . . .'

'Oh no? I heard you last night coming on to that stuck up hairband. Telling her how gorgeous she is. And now Munchkin.'

'I don't . . .'

'Well, why say you wanted to run off with her then?'

'We were messing around. It was a joke.' He put his arms round her and pulled her towards him. She must really care to react like this. It was unbelievable she was jealous of Munchkin.

'Not a very funny joke. I knew it was a mistake to come here. Everyone prying, asking me about modelling. Why can't they mind their own business? They're as bad as your friend Jack.'

'Jack?' His stroking stopped abruptly. 'Have you been talking to him?'

'Of course not. Only in the pub that night.'

He had called Jack at the paper on Christmas Eve. Six figures would be a nice way for him and Nikki to start the New Year. It would just be a matter of persuading her. He'd have to choose his moment carefully. It wasn't just yet.

Below them, Flora was sprawled on the bed, trying to concentrate on kitchen catalogues, but distracted by music thumping, footsteps clomping and doors slamming. She'd even put on her jokey pink ear muffs, but they'd failed her. Didn't Munchkin ever pause for breath? Only, it seemed, when Miranda's Sloane tones announced it was time for a shower. Giles yelled that he'd like to be her soap. Creep.

Flora decided she must have been really, really wicked as there was no chance of any peace.

Miranda carefully applied some fresh make-up, spongeing on foundation to disguise the circles under her eyes.

Before her shower, she had heard uproarious laughter from Giles's room. Pete made her sit beside him on the bed while he showed her his Asterix annual. Then he'd been so sweet about her skiing.

Sweet Pete. Australia's greatest export. He had so much going for him, and hundreds of women going after him. But none of them were under the same roof for a week. Maybe her luck was changing.

As Miranda dried her hair, Anna arrived. She had lingered in the bathroom, the one place where there was any privacy. If only she had her own room. She was sick of the smell of Caleche and tired of Miranda's constant fretting about her appearance. Why hadn't the cats answered?

Giles stood in front of the wardrobe in a state of indecision. Should he wear a tie? Or was it a bit over the top? Would Mirandy appreciate the gesture? If only they'd been alone in the car yesterday, without Sam. Without Sam butting in and taking the mickey. If only she weren't almost engaged to Charlie. Still, he'd be invited to the wedding and there'd be all those house parties . . . He'd just have to make up his mind to be a good friend, an escort when Charlie was away on his horse business.

He combed back his string-coloured hair. Everything seemed to be going well, although there'd been that sticky moment with

Jamie and Martin at teatime. Still, all sorted. He pictured the invitations on his mantlepiece.

Flora was relieved to hear that Jamie and Martin had smoothed things out, but the episode had left her uneasy. A hairline crack in a dam, it seemed to herald possible trouble.

'He's intimidating,' she said.

'Nonsense.' Jamie played with her mane of hair. 'Sam explained that Martin didn't listen to the guys in the hire shop. I put my foot in it, hit a very raw nerve. Over now. Forget it.' He kissed her and picked up a leaflet. 'What's this?'

'Flooring. For the kitchen?'

Jamie pulled a face. 'Flora, angel, leave it. There's no rush.' He kissed her again. 'Worry about it when we get home.'

A few minutes later there was a thud as the wedding file fell off the bed.

'Isn't the table lovely,' said Munchkin to Anna. 'Candles give such a warm glow.' She felt good in her new powder blue cashmere sweater, bought in the pre-Christmas sales.

Miranda's efforts at placement were wasted. Nikki and Martin wouldn't be split up and Pete plonked himself next to Jamie. Giles sat next to her. She noticed his tie, thinking it a bit over the top, and Nikki's Hermès scarf.

Nikki had swaddled her neck to cover a lovebite Martin had given her during their frenzied pre-shower bout.

'I hope I'm not too stiff tomorrow.' Anna winced as she sat down.

'I was earlier, but Nikki soon sorted me out,' guffawed Martin. Nikki shot him a furious look and snatched her hand away from his.

'Why are we waiting, wh-y are we wait-ing?' said Sam beside Flora.

Hetty and Alice brought in a tureen of tomato soup and baskets of piping hot bread.

'Don't forget, you owe me fifty quid,' said Pete to Jamie.

'I'll get it back tomorrow.'

'Maybe Flora will beat us all by the end of the week,' said Sam. 'All those lessons. What's your instructor like? Hot to trot? You know what they say about girlies and their ski instructors. Eh? Eh?' He nudged Flora's arm, knocking soup off her spoon and onto the tartan cloth.

'Pass the wine someone,' called Martin from the other end of the table. 'We're dying of thirst up here.'

'Must have worked it up with all that incredible skiing you did today,' sniggered Sam.

'Watch it,' said Martin.

'Never seen anything quite like it.'

'Shut your face, you Irish short arse.' Martin chucked some bread at Sam.

Sam ducked. 'Missed. I might be short, but I'm perfectly formed.' He chose a missile from the breadbasket. 'And my hand eye coordination isn't . . .' He lobbed a slice and hit Martin directly on the nose '. . . bad. Gotcha.' He yelled in triumph.

'Right,' said Martin. Standing up, he threw three times in quick succession, missing Sam but getting Pete and Flora.

'Great,' she muttered, picking crumbs out of her hair.

Pete leapt to his feet, emptying the bread basket onto the table. He aimed at Martin. Direct hit. 'Howzat. Aussie rules.'

'Bastard,' shouted Martin.

Bread flew in every direction. Martin headbutted the slices, rocking the table. Soup slopped out of the bowls, the candles toppled over, a wine glass smashed to the floor. 'Boys, boys,' wailed Miranda, trying to make herself heard above the din. Pete dunked a crust into the soup and chucked. It missed Martin, but splattered against the far wall. 'Stop that Pete. At once. Sam, I said stop. Jamie. Stop it.'

Munchkin was laughing. 'Get him Martin. Get him.'

'Oh my God,' shrieked Nikki, as more soupy bread whizzed towards her. Screeching, worried about her Hermès scarf, she dived under the table.

'Destroy, destroy, destroy,' yelled Martin, hurling the last pieces within reach. His chair overturned. Another glass crashed to the tiles. Giles appealed for order. Anna backed into the sitting room, as Flora ducked for cover. Martin turned, and was scrabbling on the floor for more bread, when Jamie yelled 'Target.' He got Martin on the backside, Jackson Pollocking his jeans with soup. He and Pete whooped with delight and swapped a high five.

Munchkin cried, 'Take cover,' as Martin began another onslaught.

'What's going on?' Hetty stood at the kitchen door aghast. She noticed the wall. 'Quick, Al. Cloth.'

'Stop,' shouted Miranda ducking. Giles again appealed for order.

'Ceasefire,' yelled Munchkin, making a dash for the kitchen. As Sam and Pete threw, she screamed. Bread landed in the middle of her chest, splattering the powder blue with red, before it richocheted onto the floor. Peels of laughter rang out from the men.

'Bull's-eye,' yelled Pete.

Munchkin looked down at her sweater. Her new powder blue cashmere sweater.

'Oh shit. Munchkin. Sorry.' Realising she was upset, Pete was chastened. 'Sorry.'

'Sorry,' said Sam, laughing.

Frantically Munchkin swabbed at it with a napkin, which just left soggy shreds. Her new sweater.

'Are you all right?' asked Martin. She didn't seem happy.

'Fine.' She forced a smile. 'Better go up and change though.'

* * *

Apologising to the twins, Miranda got a cloth and a dustpan and brush. Grim-faced Hetty dabbed at the wall with a J-Cloth. Chairs and bottles were righted.

'Martin, your jeans,' exclaimed Nikki horrified.

He peered behind him. 'You bastards,' he exploded.

'Good shot Jamie,' laughed Pete.

'Second time he's got you today,' crowed Sam.

'Next time, I'll get him,' snarled Martin, stomping off upstairs.

Anna helped Miranda clean up the shattered glass. Her expression was as cold as her soup. 'This is appalling,' she rounded on Sam. 'How could you waste good food with so many people starving . . .' Behind her spectacles, her eyes were furious.

'Relax,' shrugged Sam. 'We're on holiday. Can't do much about it from here.'

'The overseas aid budget has shown an incremental . . .' began Giles.

'It's been cut,' snapped Anna.

'It has?' He looked startled. 'Well, charity does begin at home.'

Sam's eyes widened. 'Not that I've noticed, Rachman. I mean Giles.'

Miranda giggled.

Glaring at him, Giles continued, 'Of course, a trade not aid policy is the only sound long term objective. Welfare encourages dependency . . .'

Anna held out the dustpan to Flora, who was collecting up shards of broken glass. 'A famine relief policy from a man who looks as if he stores food for the winter in his cheeks.'

Martin changed out of his jeans, cursing Jamie. In the bathroom along the corridor, Munchkin was close to weeping as she scrubbed at the orange stain with a wet flannel. 'Bubbly not blubbery,' she muttered between clenched teeth. She filled the basin. The sweater would probably shrink, but it was ruined anyway.

'Stop.'

Munchkin was holding the sweater in mid-air as Nikki darted in.

'Leave it,' she ordered. Pouting slightly, she examined the stain, gently scratching at it with one of her immaculate finger-nails. 'No more water. Let it dry.'

'But . . .'

'You must take it to my dry cleaners. Soon have it as right as rain. Got port out of my cream Valentino.'

'Really?' Munchkin peered at the sweater. 'It's new. Brand new.'

'Cashmere.' Nikki studied the label. 'In the sale? Hold on.'

Half a minute later she returned. 'Have this.'

'I couldn't,' Munchkin gasped.

Nikki was holding an identical sweater. 'Go on. Please. I'm never going to wear it. One of those stupid impulse buys. Colour's all wrong for me. The lighting in that shop is some-thing shocking. Please. Silly to waste it.' It took her an age to persuade Munchkin the offer was genuine.

'This is really sweet of you,' said Munchkin. 'Let me pay.'

'Don't be silly. Give something to one of Anna's good causes if you like.'

Munchkin wondered what life would be like if she were as beautiful as Nikki. Her figure was shown off to perfection by her pink suede jeans and pink angora twinset. 'Where's your next assignment, anywhere glam?'

'Assignment?'

'Modelling.'

The light left Nikki's face. 'Not sure yet.'

Calm restored, everyone was tucking into Boeuf Bourgignon.

Pete apologised to Munchkin. 'It's fine,' she said. She had

changed into a sweat shirt with Party Animal emblazoned across it.

He pushed the hair out of his eyes. 'You're just saying that to be nice. Promise you'll send me the cleaning bill.'

'Done,' said Munchkin. The flash of duck egg blue and his obvious contrition made her heart melt. If he'd owned up to being a serial killer, she'd be able to forgive him.

Miranda warmed to Giles for staying out of it. In fact, he'd itched to join in, but as holiday organiser thought he should set an example. Besides, he could be liable for any damages and it might be difficult to get money out of the others.

Flora asked Sam how his search for a new job was going. 'I'll worry about that when I get back.' He yawned. 'Nice to have a sabbatical. Suppose the rest of your life will be a holiday once you're married. Landed a nice, big, rich fish, haven't you?' He gave her a shrewd glance. 'Don't blame you. I'd marry Jamie myself. Quite a catch, isn't he?'

'It wasn't like that . . .'

'Of course not. You just happened to fall in love where the money is. And you'll tell me that you'd still be with Jamie if he was skint.'

'I would be.'

'Sure.' Pulling a face, Sam poured himself more wine. 'I've been there, Flora. The chicks react differently when you're signing on rather than signing that nice gold credit card slip.'

'Maybe you know the wrong sort of,' Flora paused, 'chicks.'

'Tell me about it.' Sam glugged back his wine.

After dinner, Martin was restless. He decided to drive down into St Marie and explore the bars. 'Last one out of the chalet is a complete nance. Who wants a lift?'

Pleading tiredness, Anna and Miranda declined. Glancing at the cache of duty-free booze and hearing that Miranda was staying in, Giles said he'd give it a miss tonight. Anticipating a cosy early bed with Jamie, Flora shook her head.

'Sure?' he said, disappointed. 'Tired, aren't you, angel? I'd better stay and look after you, hadn't I?' She smiled.

'We'll let them do a recce for us,' said Giles. 'Plenty of nights left. Spot of backgammon, Jamie? Found a board earlier.'

'Great.'

Flora's heart sank.

'Party, party, party,' said Munchkin with all the enthusiasm she could muster. She was actually feeling shattered, but felt honour bound to go out. Anyway, it would give her another chance to talk to Pete. She ran upstairs to put on some more make-up.

Fetching her mink-lined parka from the wardrobe, Nikki spotted Martin's jeans steaming on the radiator and made him move them to the bathroom. Once again, he cursed Jamie.

'Come on,' shouted Sam.

As the five trooped out, their footsteps echoed on the stairs. The front door slammed. Voices and laughter could be heard from the drive, followed by a scream as Martin hit Nikki with a snowball.

'I don't know where they get their energy,' said Anna, stretching out on the sofa. Martin hooted and revved the engine. Music poured from the Range Rover, gradually fading as it drove away.

'That's better,' said Miranda, curling up in an armchair by the fire. 'Peace at last.' Hetty and Alice came in to clear the table. 'Thanks for another super dinner, you two. You do spoil us. Sorry about the food fight. Men will be boys.'

'That's all right,' said Alice sounding martyred. 'We'll cover the stain on the wall with a picture.' The twins returned to the kitchen for another good moan.

'Poor show,' said Giles, helping himself to Sam's brandy. He was pleased he was saving so much money by not buying it in some overpriced bar. 'Anyone?'

'No thanks,' yawned Flora, throwing more logs on the fire.

'It's all this fresh air,' said Miranda. 'Takes a bit of getting used to. Look at Anna, she's asleep already.'

'Not quite.' Anna smiled, but didn't open her eyes.

Flora sat in the other armchair and stretched out her legs towards the hearth. Instead of going through the wedding file on her lap, she watched the flickering flames, hearing only the crackle of logs and click of counters and dice.

There was no need for small talk. They smiled at each other companionably every few minutes, lost in their own thoughts.

'Lovely,' said Miranda. 'So cosy and peaceful. Fire's mesmerising isn't it?'

Giles got up. 'Well done, Jamie. Another? Must go and point Percy.'

As he disappeared, Jamie came over and squeezed Flora's hand.

Miranda stretched. 'Must toddle. Just know I'll be woken up the minute the others get back. Bound to put on that wretched music.'

'Don't.' Anna groaned. 'Last night. Thump, thump, thump. The floor was shaking. Then the explosion . . .'

'I was petrified,' said Miranda. 'Thank God you gave those silly buggers what for, Flora. Deaf ears, though. Too pissed to notice.' She looked at Jamie reproachfully. 'Honestly, you men are naughty. Teeny bit selfish of you.'

He was contrite. 'Sorry, Miranda.'

'Well, let's hope there's not a repeat performance tonight,' said Anna. 'I for one need a good night's sleep. Wish we could sabotage that stereo.'

'Throw it on the fire. With my blessing,' said Miranda.

'Bit drastic.' Anna sat up. 'Disconnect the speaker wires. Make them think twice.'

'Brilliant idea,' said Miranda.

Feeling guilty about the previous night, Jamie went over to the stereo and fiddled around with the back. Flora watched him uneasily. 'Job done,' he said cheerfully, going back to the table to set up the counters.

'Well done you mean,' said Miranda.

'Night Jamie,' said Flora sighing, her cosy early night with him vanishing. Jamie was more interested in the backgammon than he was in her. She stumbled to her room and collapsed into bed.

Flora was awakened just after three by Martin's booming voice coming from the sitting room. 'Hey guys. It's not working because the wires are out.'

'Well, put them back in again, shit for brains.' That was Sam. Jamie stirred beside her as the music started.

'Dunny,' slurred Pete, clomping towards the bedroom. He crashed into one wall and cannoned off it into another, before slamming the bathroom door. Flora groaned.

'Who's in the toilet? Hurry up.' It was Nikki, sounding drunk. She started hammering on the door.

'Come on Munchkin,' cried Martin. 'Now's our chance.'

Flora heard Munchkin scream. 'Put me down. Put me down.' Hysterical laughter was followed by a crash of furniture hitting the floor.

'Shut up,' murmured Jamie in his sleep.

'Pump up the volume,' yelled Sam. The music became louder.

'Sssshhh,' called Pete. 'Keep the noise down a bit. Everyone's asleep.'

'No they're bloody not,' hissed Flora. Angrily she turned on the light, put on her earmuffs and snatched up a book, hoping that Barbara Pym would have her usual soothing effect. For once she failed. Flora felt her body stiffening in rage.

Ten minutes later, she jumped out of bed, unable to bear the music, the shrieks and screams for a second longer. In the sitting room, Martin and Sam were trying to have a piggyback race, Nikki on Martin's shoulders. There was no sign of Pete. All the side tables were overturned. Slender Sam was unable to manage Munchkin and they crashed onto the floor, ending up in a tangle of arms and legs.

'Hello Flora.' Munchkin was giggling uncontrollably, her bosom shaking inside its Party Animal sweatshirt.

'Could you turn down the music please?' asked Flora icily. She watched Martin stagger across the room, Nikki giggling on his shoulders. Like Munchkin, she looked dishevelled.

'Hasn't Flora got great legs, Sam?' Martin crouched down, so that Nikki could reach the volume control. She turned it. The music became louder. All four laughed. 'Learn to lighten up, sweetheart. You're on holiday. Shouldn't go round spoiling the fun, should she Nikki?'

'No.' Nikki hiccupped.

'Go back to bed Flora,' said Sam. 'Unless you can be a . . .'

'Stop staring,' giggled Munchkin, hand across her chest.

'Party Animal,' continued Sam.

Flora turned down the music. There was a brief moment of silence before Martin turned it up again, louder than before. The process was repeated twice more, before Martin gently seized Flora's wrist. 'Stop it Flora.'

The other three echoed him. Flora was furious, but outnumbered. 'You win.'

'I always do.' Smiling, he let her go.

CHAPTER THREE

Monday

———◆◆◆◆———

Groggily, Flora squinted at the alarm clock. Eight-thirty. Why did she feel so unrefreshed? She'd gone to bed well before midnight. It came back to her. Being woken up, the horrible tussle with drunken Martin over the stereo. The memory brought her round faster than being thrown into an icy bath.

In the past two days, she'd endured sleep deprivation, noise torture and physical hardship. It was an SAS training ground, not her idea of a holiday. She'd had enough. Why stay a moment longer?

Jamie was in the bathroom. After pulling on her clothes, Flora swept into the sitting room. She could hear Giles in the kitchen, talking to the twins. At that moment his braying voice sounded more than usually irritating.

Turning her back to the kitchen, Flora leafed through the pages of the phone book, whose cover was defaced by Jamie's squiggles of explanation about pole planting. As she dialled, she saw an orange stain on the wall where the soup had landed the night before. 'Information, s'il vous plaît. Bonjour. Je voudrais aller today, er aujourdhui, au Siena. Siena en Italia.' What was the point of all those years of school French if she couldn't even book a train ticket? 'Siena. Près de Florence. Firenze. Siena not Vienna. Oh shit.' She slammed down the receiver and lit a cigarette.

Her eye caught the number of the airport on a list on the wall. She dialled. 'British Airways.'

'Morning Flora,' said Giles, his mouth full of croissant. 'Sleep well, I trust? Not thinking of leaving us, are you?'

She turned round, and realised Jamie was watching her. He seemed far from pleased. Flora dropped the receiver as if it were scalding her.

'Can we have some coffee please, Alice?' he called through to the kitchen. 'It might help Flora think straight. Put out that cigarette, it's disgusting first thing in the morning.'

Blushing, Flora stubbed it out.

'Something cropped up?' asked Giles.

'Excuse us,' said Jamie. 'Outside, Flora. Now.'

Despite the sunshine flooding the valley, it was bitterly cold on the balcony. The temperature matched Jamie's expression. 'What's going on?'

Flora leant over the wooden railings. 'Yesterday you said I could leave and that's what I was trying to do.'

'Why?'

She shrugged. 'Why? Isn't it obvious? I hate skiing and your friends aren't exactly my cup of Darjeeling.'

Fred Quince had warned her the chalet would be full of hearties of darkness. Why hadn't she listened and stayed in her peaceful little cottage?

'Shouldn't we have talked about it first?' snapped Jamie.

Flora turned her hand so the diamonds in her engagement ring caught the sun. 'Why? You didn't talk to me about coming here. Why should I talk to you about leaving?'

'Oh God, not that business again.' Jamie let out a long, exasperated sigh. 'Flora, look around you. It's beautiful. All this space, the view, the mountains. Don't you realise this is the first time in months I've been away properly? I have to get in that stinking tube most mornings, then work my guts out. I earn a lot, Flora, but boy, do I earn it. The bank owns me, so that you can play with your giant doll's house. The pressure I'm under to achieve, to perform. I need a holiday. Why do you want to fuck it up?'

As his words sank in, Flora bit her lip.

'Well, why?'

She was stricken by contrition. 'I wasn't thinking.' She told him what had happened in the middle of the night.

'So, they were having a bit of fun. Big deal. Instead of being so intolerant, why don't you make a bit more effort to get on with everyone?' His expression softened. 'Flora, I admit this set-up is far from ideal. We should've gone away on our own. But I was lazy. It was easy. Someone else did all the work. I just had to hand over the money. All I wanted was us to have a good time.'

'Us? Or did you want a Boy's Own holiday? Sometimes I think you'd rather be boozing with Pete and the rest or having food fights or playing backgammon than being with me.'

'Rubbish.'

'Come on. I must be a liability for you. Don't ski. Don't really fit in. Nagging you about the wedding and the house.'

'Flora, if you want to leave, we can. Pack our bags right now and go.' He suddenly seemed so dejected that Flora melted. She put her arms around him and burrowed under his sweater, feeling his warm skin. They hugged one another tightly. He kissed the tip of her nose and stared into her eyes. 'Stay? Yes? And you'll make an effort to be a bit jollier? Promise? Give the skiing your best shot? Swear?' She nodded. 'Good. My beautiful wife.' His arms tightened around her.

Hetty slammed a jug of orange juice onto the table. Yet again she and Al had been greeted by chaos. If the chalet got wrecked, they'd get the sack.

Giles jumped. He was nervous of the twins, having been given serious grief by them about the mess. Alarmingly, one of the side tables had been broken in the middle of the night.

Jamie waved a croissant-filled basket under Flora's nose. 'Have one. Need to feed you up for skiing.'

She was tempted to say fuck the skiing, but remembered her

promise. She tried to swallow some croissant, but her throat was constricted by fear. Her palms were clammy and her stomach knotted with nerves.

Munchkin sat down. For the briefest moment, Flora seemed to be staring at her Party Animal sweatshirt like a vegan confronted by a leopardskin coat, but then her expression changed and a bright good morning was joined by a dazzling smile.

'Fun out on the raz?' Giles passed Munchkin the teapot.

'Brilliant.' In fact, Munchkin wished she'd stayed at the chalet. The outing hadn't been a success. They'd ended up in Jimmy's, a bar where the average age was about eighteen. Sam had been overwhelmed by the Superbabedom, and had gone off to chat up some girls, who had gathered round Pete. She'd been left sitting with Martin and Nikki. The noise was so loud, talk was impossible, even if Nikki hadn't spent the whole time on Martin's lap whispering into his ear. Of course, Nikki hadn't meant to freeze her out on purpose, but Munchkin had felt a gooseberry. With no distractions, worry had hit her like a lead weight.

Sam, Miranda and Anna sat down. Miranda, who'd put on full make-up, was disappointed there was no sign of Pete.

'Good night?' asked Jamie.

'Yep. Jimmy's. Get down there, full of Überbabes,' said Sam. 'Gagging for some oh-la-la.'

Anna frowned and muttered to Flora, 'Was he made redundant or sacked?'

Giles moved the cereal boxes, spread out the piste map and tapped his mug with a teaspoon. 'Order, everyone please. Plans for today. Think we can be a bit more adventurous, agreed? Jamie and I have been working it out and how about taking the cable car up to La Pont. That's here, to the north.'

'East,' corrected Jamie, a map pedant from his Army days.

'Sorry, east. Anyway, we'll get a great view of the whole area on the way up. Then we can either follow this black or the red. How does that sound?'

'Super,' said Miranda. 'Definitely on.'

Sam sniggered. 'Must we know about your time of the month?'

'That's not funny,' snapped Miranda.

Martin arrived. 'Morning. God, my mouth's like an Abo's armpit.' He scraped his chair on the tiles and knocked the table. 'Tea, lover?'

Nikki nodded. Her head throbbed. She was wearing skin tight pale lemon ski pants and a thick cream sweater. Munchkin was struck dumb with envy.

'What a night.' Martin chuckled. 'Terrific. Can you believe it, Pete came back on the roof rack.'

After their exchange the previous night, Flora thought of another rack she'd like to see Martin on, but then remembered her promise to Jamie to make an effort. She watched Martin gobble down his breakfast with his usual fizz and energy. Told of the plans for the day, he complimented Giles on his organisation skills, 'if you were in the Army, you'd end up a five star general', and led the acclaim for Miranda's skiing, 'poetry in motion'.

As they finished breakfast, Giles cleared his throat. 'Er, sorry to be boring. The twins, er, are a bit, er, concerned about some trouble with a table. Seems one went for a burton last night. Broken. 'Fraid whoever's responsible will have to cough up.' Alice had also pointed out that seven glasses were smashed the night before.

'Nothing to do with us,' said Martin immediately. 'Anyway, only a cheap poxy thing. Probably making a fuss about nothing.'

'Accidents happen. High spirits and all that. But, quite frankly, I don't want to be lumbered with any bills,' persisted

Giles. 'Must have been one of you lot when you got back. It was fine when we went to bed, wasn't it, Mirandy?'

'Think so.' Miranda didn't want to get drawn into any unpleasantness.

'Probably the same person who tried to bugger up the stereo,' said Martin, digging his jammy knife into the butter.

'That was me,' said Jamie blithely. 'Not guilty when it comes to the table, though.'

'You, was it? Why did you want to do a thing like that?' He glanced at the others, then mimicked Jamie's drawl. 'Took us ages to get it sorted. Old chap.'

'Precisely,' Jamie poured himself more tea. 'Thought it might make you think twice about keeping everyone awake. Old chap.'

Martin's steely eyes flashed. 'Bit rich coming from you. This a lecture?'

'No.'

'Well, it fucking sounds like one and I don't like it. I've told you, I'm not one of your fucking squaddies, understand?' He jabbed his finger at Jamie. 'This is my holiday and I'm going to enjoy it any way I please. Love it or shove it. Got it?'

After an age-long pause, Jamie said: 'Got it.'

'Not too difficult for a double creamer to understand?'

'What?'

'You were in the Royals, weren't you? Also known as the double creamers. The whole regiment's rich and thick.'

'How interesting.' Jamie sounded bored.

Everyone else was silent, holding their breath as they looked at the pair like spectators at Wimbeldon.

There was an amused glint in Jamie's eyes. As if he were in a Swagger portrait, he looked down his aquiline nose. Flora guessed his cool disdain would be infuriating to Martin.

Jamie stood up. 'If you'll excuse me, I must go and get ready.'

His Guccied step was all the louder in the unusual quiet.

'Snotty bastard, who does he think he is?' Martin looked

round the table for support, his gaze falling on Flora. 'Royals, eh? Frightfully pukka, darling. Aren't they?'

'Are they?'

'Specialise in charm offensives and cocktail party survival.'

'Do they?'

'Never see any real action, far too busy poncing around in mess kit and playing polo.'

Flora glared at him. 'Let Jamie introduce you to some of the men who've been poncing around in Northern Ireland or the Gulf or Bosnia.'

Miranda and Giles exchanged uneasy glances. Anna read the label on the jam pot. Munchkin squirmed in her chair. 'More tea anyone?'

Martin ignored her. 'Your fiancé's got a real attitude problem.'

'If he has, which he hasn't, he's not the only one.' Remembering her promise to make an effort, but feeling herself about to lose her temper, Flora fled from the table.

As Martin justified himself to Nikki, the others tried to talk naturally, but sounded stilted. Miranda gamefully explained how long it took to boil an egg in different ski resorts. 'Depends on the attitude, I mean, altitude.' She wriggled.

'Snotty git,' continued Martin. 'It's not his chalet. If we want to listen to a bit of music, why should he or his bloody girlfriend stop us? All that fuss she made last night. Remember, Munchkin? Sam?'

Anna decided it was time to set the record straight. 'Actually, Miranda and I suggested the business with the stereo.'

'Our idea,' said Miranda. 'Nothing to do with Jamie.'

'We got a tad cheesed off with the noise on the first night,' said Anna. 'Knew you lot would get back and behave like a bunch of students in freshers' week. Oh, sorry Martin, Nikki, you wouldn't know anything about that, you never went to college, did you?'

Martin and Nikki were stunned by the rebuke from the mild-mannered Anna. 'I suppose we could've been a bit rowdy,' he said. 'We were? Sorry.'

A shame-faced Munchkin pleaded with Miranda. 'Sorry if we woke you up. About the table, Giles, I think it was me. Of course, I'll pay. Sorry, Anna.'

Hating scenes, Miranda was brisk. 'All over and done with. Let's close the subject. Giles, leave in half an hour?'

Flora found Jamie sitting on the balcony outside their room, flicking through the *Economist*. 'Martin. That monstrous jerk. Why are you at the top of his Jehad list?'

'He's on a short fuse, that's all.' Jamie yawned. 'Don't worry about it. He's only showing off in front of madam.'

Pete, in Timberlands, jeans and a huge dark green sweater strolled out and gave Flora a squeeze. He was munching a cheese-filled croissant. 'Come on Jamie, get ready. Got to win your money back. Nice room, didn't realise you had so much space. All set for your lesson?'

Flora tried to ignore the knot of fear in her stomach and remembered her promise to Jamie. She smiled. 'As much as I'll ever be. Better get my cigarettes.' It was going to be a stressful day.

Going into the deserted sitting room, she almost cannoned into Martin. Both looked as if the other were a bad smell.

'Can I ask you something?' said Martin. 'What's Jamie's problem? All that fuss about the stereo. All he had to do was ask nicely. No big deal, is it?'

After two nights interrupted sleep, Flora wasn't in her most forgiving mood. 'I asked nicely last night, if you remember. Didn't make much difference to you.'

'You didn't ask anything. You just marched in here and turned it off.'

'I did ask. You're not deaf as well, are you?'

The question hung in the air. Martin bridled. 'And I'm not

dumb either, if that's what you're thinking. Know something, Flora? You and Jamie are well matched.' He headed for the stairs.

Flora shrugged. At least someone thought so. She'd sometimes got the impression over the past few days that Jamie was beginning to have doubts.

Dressed for another day on the slopes, Munchkin came downstairs. In a state of suppressed excitement, she was bursting to mull over the exchange between Martin and Jamie. Anna and Miranda's bedroom door was firmly shut and she couldn't think of a pretext for barging in. Besides, she was nervous of them. Both seemed cross at being woken up. 'Sorry about last night, Flora.'

'Forget it.'

'Think we're all a bit hyper still. Still stressed, what with work and Christmas and everything.' She lowered her voice. 'I must admit I was surprised by Martin. Bit strong with Jamie, wasn't he?'

'That's their business,' hinted Flora.

'Well, personally I thought it was completely uncalled for. Martin should apologise. We all have to make an effort to get on.'

Flora remembered her promise. 'So, where are you skiing today?'

Giles was pleased to see them chatting. Things weren't going to plan, what with Martin at Jamie's throat, Flora wanting to leave and the twins being grumpy. Upstairs, Miranda and Anna had moaned to him about being woken up, urging him to have words, and Sam collared him about the damages, pointing out that he wasn't responsible for the glasses or the table and wasn't going to pay a penny. It was far from Happy Families. And his legs ached.

Upstairs, Nikki stood by the shoulder-high window and applied some blusher with a huge sable brush. Not even her flash mosturiser nor the eyebath could disguise the toll the drink had taken. Catching sight of Martin's reflection in her hand mirror, she frowned. 'All this fuss, because Jamie told you to change your skis. Well, he was right.'

Martin pulled on his khaki ski suit. 'That's got nothing to do with anything. I'm not being talked down to by some stuck-up prick.' He mimicked Jamie's drawl. ' "Got it?" Well, he's going to get my idea of a punch in the mouth if he's not careful.'

Nikki hurled the mirror onto the bed. 'Just leave it. Do you want to get everyone's backs up? It's hard enough for me here as it is, what with all these strangers and having to watch what I say all the time. Forget it, can't you? Otherwise take me home.'

Her outburst surprised them both, but his aggression was making her nervous. It reminded her that she had thrown her lot in with him, without knowing almost anything about him. Supposing she'd made a terrible mistake?

Outside in the corridor, Sam paused and cupped his ear. 'Lovers' tiff,' he said to Anna. She yanked his arm and pulled him away.

'Who's there?' demanded Martin, sensing they were being overheard.

'No one.' Nikki was impatient. 'It's just this place. You feel that everyone's on top of you.'

'Yes please.' Martin grinned, trying to cheer her up.

'That's not what I meant.' She failed to smile. 'Look at this room, so pokey and dark, no view to speak of. I don't see why I should be paying the same money as Jamie and Flora.' Her voice was peevish.

It made up his mind. 'Don't worry, I'm ahead of you. We're swapping halfway through the week. Now, come here and give me a kiss.'

The rest were out on the drive, getting asphyxiated by exhaust fumes from the Porsche, as they waited for Nikki and Martin.

'Come on,' yelled Pete, impatient at being blocked in.

Giles checked his oil, water and radiator, topping it up with anti-freeze. Munchkin and Sam started a sword fight with their poles. Miranda was telling Jamie again how mummy and daddy went to Mürren every year without fail.

Flora winced as her ski boots dug into her shins. She felt like a packhorse with her skis, poles, scarf, gloves, sunglasses, pass, money, sunscreen, lipsalve, cigarettes. And her black hat, which should have a big D for Dunce on it. She looked up to the balcony, wishing she could spend a day in the sunshine reading and drinking hot chocolate. Then she remembered her promise to Jamie.

Just as Giles had started hooting too, Martin came running outside. 'Sorry folks.' He backed the Range Rover into the road to let the others out. He and Nikki had been making love and he'd promised her they wouldn't leave until she had re-done her make-up.

'Coo-ee. Room for little me?' Munchkin knocked on the BMW's window. She was anxious not to be left behind to play gooseberry again and felt she ought to get back into Anna and Miranda's good books.

With bad grace, Giles pulled on the handbrake and got out to put her skis in the roof coffin.

'Meet you at the cable car,' called Martin.

Flora was hunched in the back of the Porsche. As Pete put his foot down, she felt glad of the crash barriers at the side of the road. There was an eighty foot drop down, down, down to the right. She fixed her eyes ahead and saw the onion dome of the church rising above the surrounding buildings. The car roared past dozens of people making their way to Les Pins lift, skis and poles over their shoulders, lips whitened with sunscreen.

Pete slowed down at Les Landais. 'Drop you off here?' He pressed open the window and stuck two fingers up at Giles, who had caught them up and was flashing his headlights and hooting.

Not wanting to have to make her way down the icy lane and across the worn piste to get to the lift, Flora said: 'Town please.'

The road twisted and turned down the mountainside and into St Marie. The streets were packed with people and cars. Incongruous among the skiers, an old woman dressed in black, was walking alongside the nursery slope carrying a wicker basket of groceries.

A dustcart pulled out and stopped, blocking the road. A furious Giles was forced to slam on his brakes. Hearing his demands to get out the way, the binmen smiled and worked more slowly.

Pete stopped near the entrance to the chairlift. 'Wonder what your instructor will be like?'

Flora was wondering the same thing. Surely not as bad as Mirabête?

'He'll be fine,' said Jamie, praying he would be.

'Bound to be awful with my luck.' Flora scowled, forgetting her promise. 'I always end up sitting next to the worst man in the room at any dinner or wedding. Remember Jonty's last week? I got lumbered with the one who markets dog food and you got the war photographer.' She scrambled out of the car. 'Thanks, Pete.'

'Hey, don't look so stressed. No-one's going to eat you,' he called, as she followed Jamie towards the lift. She turned and gave him a wan smile.

'You've got a good half hour, so you can go to the Savoie and have some coffee.' Jamie put her skis down on the snow. She stepped into them and he knelt down and clipped up the back of her boots. Dozens of people were milling round the lift. 'You can manage on your own, can't you?' She nodded, wishing she hadn't had breakfast, she felt so sick. 'I'll meet you up at the Savoie later. Off you go.'

As she watched the Porsche speed off, Flora was desolate. She had been abandoned. The unwanted runt of the litter. The lift's metal girders and steel cables glinted in the sunshine, which bounced off the white piste and snow-covered trees. She stared up and up, following the lift's path into the clear blue sky. The hardiest skiers were already finishing their first run of the day. Remembering yesterday's ordeal on the same chairlift, she wondered if she could skip her lesson.

'Poor Flora looks mis,' said Miranda, who had caught sight of her waiting at the back of the lift queue. 'Can't be much fun on one's own.'

'Seemed a touch ratty earlier,' said Giles. 'Any inkling of why she wants to leave?'

'Leave?' asked Anna.

'Phoned the airport and the station earlier. Everything's probably booked solid.'

'Really,' exclaimed Munchkin breathlessly. Her eyes lit up with this promising morsel of gossip to pick over. 'Perhaps the engagement's off.'

'Perhaps she's just fed up with not being able to sleep,' said Anna. 'I know I am.'

'Hear, hear,' said Miranda.

Munchkin squirmed in guilt.

During the long, cold wait for the cable car, Nikki and Martin arrived, causing grumbles as they squeezed through the queue.

'Bloody French,' said Sam. 'Who won the war while they were on their backsides collaborating?' He was shoved forward in the surge as the cable car swung into view over the roof tops.

'What a scrum,' said Miranda, trying to stand her ground. 'Sorry, Munchkin, was that your foot?'

'No, it was mine.' Anna's glasses were askew.

'Cosy, isn't it?' Giles was squeezed against Nikki. 'Stop pushing back there. Bastard French, never heard of queueing. Pity they didn't show the same spirit in the Ardennes.'

'No you don't matey.' Martin elbowed aside a snowboarder trying to push in during the scramble to get on board.

Munchkin envied Nikki, wishing she had someone to carry her skis for her. It was becoming more claustrophobic and she was anxious she might be left behind.

The door finally closed and the glass cage began its slow ascent towards the treeline.

'This is worse than the underground in the rush hour,' grumbled Nikki, who hadn't had to suffer it for several years. 'Everything's so much better organised in Aspen.'

'I wish your jackets weren't so bright,' said Sam to Miranda and Munchkin. 'They're hurting my eyes.' He belched loudly, getting looks of distaste from a party of chic middle aged Frenchwomen. 'Better out than in.'

'Better than the other end,' said Martin.

Anna grimaced and tried to remember Shelley's 'Mont Blanc'.

Above stark walls of rock, the snowy peaks reached out like fingers into the sapphire sky. The cabin was carried over a piste, its snow criss-crossed by the parallel tracks of the early risers. Far below, two boarders, bodies crouched low, jerseys almost to their knees, surfed across the white at spectacular speed.

The car entered the lift station and juddered to a stop. Outside, it seemed twenty degrees colder than in St Marie. The crisp air froze the lungs. Munchkin pulled on her knitted pink helmet, which she knew couldn't compete with Nikki's silver fox hat.

Giles scanned the slope around the lift station. There was no sign of Pete or Jamie. 'They seem to have pissed off. Suggest we go, it's brass monkeys up here.'

Pete and Jamie had leapt onto the earlier cable car just as the doors were closing. At the top they agreed they couldn't be bothered to hang around for the rest, who would only cramp their style. The snow was too inviting. From the lift, they skied along a central path, Pete with a cigarette glued to his lips. Rounding a bend, they halted.

'Bit more like it,' said Jamie delightedly. They were higher than the three peaks of Les Diables, far in the distance. Acre after acre of empty snow-carpeted mountainside stretched in front of them, before dropping down steeply to a fir plantation.

'The dog's,' grinned Pete, chucking away his cigarette and pointing his skis straight down. 'Hit it,' he yelled, speeding off.

They schussed faster and faster, their skis sliding left and right, leaving serpentine tracks in the snow. A freezing wind swept past them, watering their eyes already dazzled by the glare. Guiding their balance, their poles touched the snow so quickly it seemed it must be giving them an electric shock.

Jamie screamed for joy as the white ground flashed beneath his skis. The exhilaration was overwhelming. They raced on and on, tiny figures against the huge wall of mountain, so steep it appeared almost vertical.

Queueing for the chairlift, Flora told the people behind her to go ahead, hoping they thought her British manners, rather than her lack of bottle, was holding her back. She mentally rehearsed the procedure of getting safely onto the lift, praying there would be no repeat of her shaming, undignified performance the day before.

When the queue had thinned out, she shuffled forward on her skis and put her pass into the machine. The point of no return.

'Bloody ice.' She dug her poles in front of her and inched towards the turnstile. Her heart was pounding. At the green light she shot forward into the dank shed and found herself standing shoulder to shoulder with a freckle-faced girl who gave her a friendly smile.

The chair crept round towards them. Flora sat down with a thump and raised her skis as they were carried into the sunshine. The girl pulled the safety bar down. '*Schöne Aussicht, nicht war?* Beautiful view?'

'Beautiful.' Flora smiled happily, not believing it had been so easy. She relaxed and enjoyed the view which her terror had blinded her to only a day before.

A quarter of an hour later up at La Croix, she skied off smoothly enough before coming to a wobbly snowplough stop. Her confidence didn't extend to skiing to the Savoie, so she went across to the wooden bench, took off her skis and unclipped her boots. She sat warming her face in the sunshine and feeling smug at her victory over the chairlift. So, it was a bit silly to have spent 25 minutes psyching herself up, but who cared?

She lit a Marlboro and gazed idly towards the second lift on the other side of the piste. Among the dozens skiing past was an unmistakeable scarlet-suited, cropped haired blonde. Mirabête. Flora dropped her cigarette in fright. Mirabête leading her class across the snow like a guerilla general in charge of a rag-tag army. Praying she wouldn't be noticed, Flora tried to shrink into the bench.

Despite her promise to Jamie, Flora wanted to flee. What was this Stefan going to be like? Her stomach knotted with apprehension as she thought of the hours of torture ahead of her.

An instructor with an Ecole de Ski jacket stood about twenty feet away from her. He was four feet tall, completely bald and the wrong side of sixty. Flora could tell he was a humourless crosspatch. Stefan. Her heart sank.

'*Excusez-moi.*' She jumped. The voice was husky, heavily accented. She shielded her eyes from the sun, unable to see properly. 'Are you Flora?'

She nodded, puzzled. The stranger towered over her. Her eyes were watering, his hidden behind dark glasses. He smiled a slow, lazy smile. She took in a mass of shoulder-length black hair pulled back in a ponytail, Slavic cheekbones and the long, lean body of an athlete. He reminded her vaguely of her ex, Lorenzo, except this man was far, far, better looking.

'Stefan.'

She glanced at the bald dwarf. 'You're Stefan? You can't be.'

He laughed. 'I am. I promise. See.' He undid the red Ecole de

Ski jacket knotted round his waist. His thick black sweater was as shabby as her own. 'You're Flora, I hope?'

'Yes.'

'Good.' He smiled another slow, lazy smile. 'So, unless you prefer Jacques to me, I'm going to teach you to ski.'

'You are?' said Flora faintly. She gazed up at him, feeling breathless. 'You can try. I can't really ski at all, in fact I'm useless and nervous and I get vertigo going up a stepladder and . . .' She knew she was gabbling, though not really aware of what she was saying. Deliberate designer stubble, or couldn't be bothered to shave? What were his eyes like behind those glasses? 'Have you got a lot of patience?'

'Enough.' He watched her scrambling up and yanking shut her boots. 'No rush. Where are your sunglasses? You don't want to get snowblind.'

'I won't. I'm not really into cocaine.' She clapped her hand over her mouth. What was she saying?

Stefan grinned. 'This is going to be an interesting lesson. *Allez*. To the lift. Then we can have a nice rest in the sun before you show me what you can do.'

Jamie and Pete skied on and on, drunk on the speed carrying them down the mountain. They skirted round a wood and hurtled towards the enticing ripples of a mogul field. They jumped and turned like surfers as they raced across the white hillocks of snow and ice. Neither eased off, although it was gruelling work and they thought they'd smash a ski.

'Way to be,' yelled Pete as he sped down a wooden jump before launching himself into the air.

'Way to be.' Jamie opened and closed his skis before he landed with a thump on the snow.

Half an hour later they arrived on a busy main piste leading to the top of Le Toit. They were finally forced to ease off, and drew to a breathless halt outside a bar.

'Brilliant,' gasped Pete. He coughed and spat into the snow. 'Got to quit smoking.'

'Best yet,' panted Jamie, wiping the sweat from his forehead. 'Thanks.' Grinning, they swapped a high five.

'Where next?'

'Not here. Leads down to La Croix. Done that.'

Still breathless, Pete pulled Giles' photocopied piste map from out of his back pocket. 'If we take the drag-lift which should be over there somewhere, we get back to the other side of the woods. Go on from there and stop for a drink?'

'Sure. Got some catching up to do. Should've come out last night.'

'But you had to look after Flora.' Pete grinned. 'Taste of things to come. And soon there might be lots of little Flora and Jamies running around. What would they be? Flamies?'

'Expensive.' Jamie groaned. 'I worked it out the other day and if we had four that would be a new Porsche in school fees. Every year. Not including the nannies and the holidays and my little ponies.' He drew a figure in the snow with his pole. 'This is me.'

Pete looked down at the hanged man and laughed.

'I could feel the noose of responsibility tightening. It's enough having to think about Flora sometimes.'

'Come on. You love Flora. You're more in love with her than you've been with anyone, ever.'

'Sure, I am. And no one, ever, can help me so much to get that seat on the board.'

'As you said the other night.' Pete frowned. 'Don't be such a cynical shit, Jamie. Besides, she can't. Not from what she told me. Her side cut all connections with Rosehagens. Cut the connection, cut the surname. Remember, mate, you're marrying Flora Rose.'

'My beautiful wife,' said Jamie.

*   *   *

At the top of La Pont, Miranda was leading everyone along the path that led from the cable car. It was narrow, with a rock wall on one side and a drop on the other. Progress was slow. The path was crowded with skiers, the snow was worn thin with icy patches. Forced to snowplough, their leg muscles burned after a few minutes.

Munchkin tried to stick close to the wall and to copy Miranda's graceful movements. But as she progressed, she felt the back of her skis getting wider and wider apart until she was almost doing the splits. She was given a welcome chance to stop when Sam and Anna came down in a heap, after she accidentally went over the back of his skis as he tried to cut in ahead of her.

Further on, the path forked. One way branched off to the precipitous black run that Jamie and Pete had taken. Miranda insisted they should take the easier route.

Anna agreed. 'Looks far too difficult for me.'

Munchkin almost fainted when she saw the drop. She needed a parachute not a pair of skis.

'Come on girlies,' urged Giles. 'It's not that bad.'

'No way. Not in a million years.' Nikki was adamant and shook her head so vigorously the fox seemed to be coming to life again.

'Piece of piss,' agreed Sam. 'Isn't it, Martin?' Martin nodded.

Miranda was getting impatient. Someone must take charge. 'You boys do as you please, but we're going down there. Come on ladies.'

'OK. You win,' said Martin.

All three men were glad to be overruled.

'You see. No problem. Why say you can't ski?' demanded Stefan. 'You're supple and have very good balance.'

Flora stopped beside him and smiled. They were almost at the Savoie, having skied down the piste she'd found such a trial the day before. She hadn't fallen once.

'Thanks.' Biting off her glove, she took one of the cigarettes he offered. It was all so different from yesterday, so different from every other lesson, from every time she'd got on skis. Stefan was so laid back, hadn't shouted once. 'I can't ski. Not properly.'

'If you can snowplough, you can ski.'

Weaving across the snow, skiers threatened to collide with them, but turned away just at the last moment. Flora watched them enviously. 'That's skiing properly. Parallel turns.'

'Easy.' He shrugged. 'First, you must have the basics.' He crouched down, clasped his hand round the back of her knee and pulled gently. 'Forward. All the time. Not just when you remember. But loose. Yes?' He looked up at her.

Huge green eyes, slanting up at the corners. Greengage green. Mesmerising. 'Yes.'

He stood up and pushed her shoulders down. 'Too tense. Relaxed. Yes?'

How tall, six one, six two? 'Yes.'

'Arms like this. You're not in a boxing match.'

Three earrings in a row. If anyone bit into his ear . . . 'Yes. I mean no. No I'm not.' The diamonds in her engagement ring glittered as they caught the sun. Flora told herself to concentrate.

He smiled his slow, lazy smile. 'How far did you get when you learnt to ski?'

She frowned. 'Stemming, I think. But that was years ago.'

'Today we'll stem again. After another nice rest on the lift.' He threw away his cigarette. '*Allez.* Weight on your bottom ski. And Flora . . .'

'What?'

'Remember to flex your knees, eh? Please.'

The seven finally reached the open piste. Far below them over to the left was a mass of fir trees. Miranda, Giles and Sam shot off like rival drivers at a green traffic light.

Munchkin was apprehensive. The slope was almost as steep

as the one the men had wanted to ski earlier. Between her and the trees there seemed to be a sheer drop.

Half an hour later, Munchkin was close to tears and cursing herself for the late, boozy night before. She anxiously scanned the slope, feeling like a Chinese daughter left on a mountainside to perish. Uncoordinated, she'd spent more time on her backside than on her skis.

The piste was so steep, so endless, and as she was realising, far beyond her ability. Why hadn't she booked herself into ski school? Two weeks skiing in three years was not enough to manage a difficult red run. There was no sign of Miranda or her two disciples, but far below a turquoise figure had stopped. Anna?

It was Anna. Comforted, Munchkin wearily clambered back onto her skis and started a shaky traverse. Her legs were so tired she could barely move them into a snowplough. She dreaded every turn, when her skis pointed straight downhill, gained speed and threatened to go out of control again. If she hadn't been so anxious about being left behind, she'd have recognised she was in a vicious circle. Every time she fell, she lost a little confidence, which made her tense up and more liable to fall. Again.

Her eyes left her ski tips and she saw a khaki suit and a furry hat over the far side of the piste. She relaxed slightly, then two skiers yelling in Italian whizzed past her with millimetres to spare. Disconcerted, she tried to stop, but hit a treacherous patch of ice. She crashed down, then slid on her side like a pink toboggan.

Far below, Anna prayed.

Trees, snow, sky, skiers all flashed past Munchkin as she hurtled down and down. She screamed in terror. One of her poles was dragged from her wrist. Finally, as the slope flattened out, she managed to dig in the edges of her skis into the snow, and come to a halt. Shocked and shaking, she burst into hysterical tears.

'Munchkin.' Someone was calling her urgently. 'Munchkin.'

She could've been killed. Why hadn't her skis come off? There must be something wrong with the bindings. She could've had her legs smashed. 'Munchkin, are you all right?'

Teeth chattering, she sat up. Through her prism of tears, she could make out someone skiing towards her. Why, oh, why wasn't she in a class?

'I'm coming.'

It was Martin, coming across the piste. Behind him, a boarder appeared out of nowhere. He was skimming over the snow, baggy-trousered backside almost touching the ground, the pompom on his stripey Wee Willie Winkie hat bouncing against his outstretched arms.

Making his way over to Munchkin, Martin was determined to prove to Nikki that he could ski. During the previous half hour, her doubts about his ability had become increasingly vociferous. He attempted an unnecessary parallel turn.

It took him straight into the path of the boarder.

Gasping, Munchkin had to look away as the snowboard scraped over the back of the skis. Martin crashed to the ground to the sound of furious swearing with a Kiwi accent. The boarder wobbled but somehow remained upright. While giving Martin the finger, he continued gliding across at breakneck speed down to the piste, pursued by shouts of apoplectic wrath.

After sliding almost twenty feet and losing his right ski, Martin came to a halt. 'Fucking piece of shit.'

Nikki, who been frozen with anxiety, relaxed. If Martin could shout like that, he wasn't seriously hurt.

Banging his fist into the snow in rage, Martin turned round to see where his ski had disappeared. A skier brushed within a few inches of him. 'Watch out, you bastard,' he yelled, snatching back his fingers and leaning back in surprise.

The skier arced neatly in front of him and came to a perfect uphill stop. Martin's ski was chucked down onto the snow beside him.

'Got it, old chap?' drawled Jamie.

'Thanks.'

'Don't have to call the blood wagon, do we?'

'No. Listen, about this morning. Sorry. No hard feelings . . .'

Jamie paid no attention and skied off towards Munchkin, collecting her pole on the way. He crouched down beside her. 'Nasty fall. Nothing broken, is there?'

'No.' Her voice was thick with tears. 'Don't think so.'

'Come on then. Upsadaisy. Here's your pole.'

'I can't.' She surveyed the piste in despair. 'I can't.'

'I'll be with you. We'll take it very gently.' Jamie held out his gloved hand. 'It's only a few hundred yards and you've done the most difficult bit.'

'No.' There was a fresh outbreak of weeping.

Jamie sighed. She was worse than Flora. 'Sorry, but you've got no choice. You can't stay here. Now come on.' He took her hand and pulled her to her feet. He knew she was in shock, but she must move.

Munchkin was trembling. Sniffing heavily, she took her poles. He was right, the lift wasn't so far. But her legs were like jelly and seemed about to collapse under her. 'I can't.'

'You can. Just snowplough. Nice and easy. That's it.' He coaxed her into moving a few feet, before her skis almost crossed again.

She stopped in panic. 'I can't.'

'You can.' Jamie sounded one hundred per cent certain. 'Weight forward and keep your skis together like this.' Skiing backwards in a reverse snowplough, poles under one arm, he bent in front of her and held the tips of her skis together. They inched across the piste, Munchkin letting out hiccupping sobs, her shoulders heaving.

Standing beside Anna near the lift, Nikki watched their faltering progress. Her expression darkened as she caught sight of Martin making his way towards her. He had given the impression back in London that he was an expert. All right, maybe it was down to his skis, but if he had to loan his own to a mate, why hadn't he hired ones that suited him? And why did he have to wear that yucky-coloured suit? So unhip, so uncool, so sad.

'You took your time,' she said, when he finally arrived.

He glared at her. 'Thank you for all your concern. That bastard boarder could've broken my leg. What the fuck was he playing at, going straight over my skis?'

'Well, he would've missed them if they weren't so long,' snapped Nikki. 'Why did you suddenly decide to turn, anyway?'

'I was going to check on Munchkin, you stupid bitch.'

'Seems Jamie beat you to it.'

'They've stopped again.' Anna squinted in the sunlight. 'What's going on up there?'

Munchkin had managed to keep her balance as she turned, but her misery and fear caused her to shed more tears. The lift seemed no closer. Aware of the dozens of skiers and boarders zooming past, she felt even more useless. She traversed the piste, was just about to turn, but flunked it and stopped. 'I can't do it. I just can't.'

Jamie failed to persuade her that she could. He rolled his eyes in impatience. Munchkin could hardly ski any better than Flora, who would quit smoking and chocolate rather than attempt this sort of run. Her sobs got louder. He looked at her helplessly, unable to cope with weeping women at the best of times, let alone halfway up a snowy mountain.

'My nerve's gone completely. Sorry. Sorry . . .'

'Would you prefer to walk down to the lift? I'll take your skis.'

'Would you?' She unclipped her skis and gratefully handed them over, giving him the benefit of her blotchy face and snotty nose as she tried to smile. 'Thanks Jamie.'

Slinging her skis and his own poles over his shoulder, he made his way down to Nikki, Anna and Martin in a series of elegant parallel turns, his body almost motionless. He came to a long, controlled uphill stop, raising a perfect arc of snow out behind him. It showered Martin, who angrily swiped it off his jacket.

'Tricky run. Far too icy and patchy in places.' Jamie stabbed Munchkin's skis into the ground.

Nikki nodded. 'That's just what I was saying, isn't it Anna? Nothing like the powder in Aspen.'

Both men eyed her with disfavour. Martin didn't like being reminded of her past; Jamie wondering how any decent women could possibly choose Martin as a boyfriend.

'I could do with a drink,' said Jamie. 'Anyone else? Anna?'

'Good idea.'

The La Pont bar across the piste looked very inviting. It was bustling with sunbathing customers, trying to rid themselves of their midwinter pallor.

It had been a trying morning for Anna. She had let Miranda, Giles and Sam race off, but then had felt obliged to keep stopping to wait for the other three, which had prevented her from getting into a rhythm. When Munchkin fell so terribly, she had been horrified by her own helplessness and overjoyed to see Jamie turn up, more welcome than a black cab for hire on a cold, rainy night.

'You two go on. We'll wait for Munchkin,' said Martin, motivated less by altruism than the desire to rid himself of Jamie.

Nikki resented his 'we'. Why did she have to hang around in the freezing cold waiting for that lump of lard? She watched Anna and Jamie ski off chatting amicably and turned to Martin. 'What's going on? You can't ski any more than Munchkin can.'

He glared at her. 'You're not much better yourself, you tart.'

'Tart? I'm not a tart, how dare you?' she squawked, drawing 'oohs' from a group of Dorset young farmers standing nearby.

'Aren't you? What would you put in your CV then? Brain surgeon?'

'Oh piss off . . .' Their voices grew louder, their faces uglier, their words more bitter until they lapsed into hostile silence.

'Hi,' called Munchkin, waving her ski poles. Walking had been almost as tough as skiing. She knew her face was tearstained, her make-up had run, but didn't care; it was such a relief to be alive and unhurt.

Martin turned wearily to Nikki. 'Look, lover, let's not argue. Please. Of course you're not a tart. Sorry. It's been a pig of a morning. That boarder was too close for comfort.'

Surprised by his admission, her resentment thawed.

He put his arm round her. They watched some children race to the restaurant. They were probably no more than seven years old, but they skied with utter confidence. 'Hoopla,' yelled one, edging in front of the rest. They were loving every second.

'Listen,' said Martin. 'How about going back into St Marie and booking some lessons? We could all probably do with a quick refresher.'

Munchkin nodded. 'If the snow was better, it wouldn't be such a problem. That's why we're finding it so tough. Need a completely different technique in these conditions.'

'Quite. We've all been caught out,' agreed Martin. 'You can practically see the grass in some places.'

'It's so different in the States,' said Nikki. 'You must both try Aspen, you'd love it.'

'Neil, one of my best friends, was in Mammoth last year,' said Munchkin. 'Swears he'll never bother with Europe again. Everything's so much better organised apparently, sounded fantastic.'

'It is,' said Nikki. 'All that cheap Ralph Lauren. Stunning people everywhere, so many film stars. I almost shared a gondola with Robert Redf—'

'Make a move, shall we,' ordered Martin abruptly.

'Are we skiing down?' Munchkin was anxious, dreading the prospect of putting her skis on again.

'Lift,' said Martin firmly.

The lift carried three to a chair. Martin held Nikki's hand. Delighted to sit down, Munchkin tactfully turned away to admire the view when they kissed. 'You don't mind me tagging along with you for lessons?' she asked when they broke apart.

'Of course not,' fibbed Nikki.

'Let's hope we can get some. Flora said they were fully booked.'

'What does she know? Jamie organised it. Running after her like a blue-arsed fly.' Martin was dismissive. 'Perhaps we can have hers; she's trying to go home.'

'Did Giles tell you as well?' Munchkin cheered up at the chance of a gossip.

'Heard her whining out on the balcony this morning. Jamie, why did you bring me here? Your friends aren't exactly my cup of Darjeeling. Bunch of sexists.' The two girls laughed at his accurate mimicry of a pissed off Flora.

'She called the airport, station, everything,' said Munchkin. 'Booked solid. She doesn't seemed to want to join in, does she? Very reserved. Shy. On a holiday like this, you must be prepared to muck in.'

'Lady Muck, more like,' said Martin. 'So effing superior, she and her know-it-all boyfriend are well suited. Fuss they've made about a bit of music.'

Munchkin grew uncomfortable. She liked Jamie and knew that Miranda and Anna were definitely on his side. 'Oh, Jamie's sweet when you get to know him.'

'He should be, with all that toffee in his nose,' said Nikki.

It was almost lunchtime when they finally reached St Marie. Martin swallowed his pride and went back to the hireshop. He had to bite his tongue when the Carrot said, 'I told you so,' smirking as he handed him a shorter pair of skis.

'*Non*. Full.' In the ski school offices, the clerk peered over her half moon spectacles and shook her head. 'Completely full.'

'We'll pay extra,' pressed Martin.

'No private instructors are available all week.'

'What about ski school?' wailed Munchkin.

'*Je regrette* . . .'

Despondent, they trooped out onto the pavement. 'That's that then,' said Nikki.

'Perhaps there'll be a cancellation,' said Martin gloomily. 'They've got our number.'

'I know, let's ask Flora,' suggested Munchkin. 'She won't mind us joining up with her. Anyway, Jamie'll be glad to share the expense, I bet. Did you see those prices?'

Martin scowled.

'Come on,' shivered Nikki. 'I'm cold. Let's go and have lunch.'

With the village's restaurants packed, Martin suggested they go back up to the Savoie. Nikki was finally persuaded, after complaining she was fed up with walking around in her ski boots and that the lift was miles away.

'It's about three minutes,' said Martin.

Delighted at not having to ski for a few hours, Munchkin's spirits rose. She might not have done much skiing, but she was making good use of her pass. If only she had a man to carry her skis for her, like Nikki. 'You never know, there might be a cancellation.'

'Doubt it, it's high season,' said Nikki. 'How stupid to run out of instructors. It would never happen in Aspen. And you don't have to wait ages for a lift there, either.'

Up at La Croix, Martin came to a sudden halt on the short run across to the Savoie. He burst out laughing. In front of him a skier had wobbled coming out of a turn, crossed skis and lost it. The ground was almost flat.

'Not hurt are you?' He guffawed and turned to Nikki and Munchkin. 'That would be a shame.'

Sitting up, Flora let out a long breath. She was furious with herself. She'd managed to ski perfectly for the past half hour. Why did she literally have to let herself down just then? 'Hello.' She sounded wan.

'Pride before fall, eh?' gloated Martin, not offering to help her up.

Neither Munchkin nor Nikki were sympathetic. They were trying not to smirk. 'Poor Flora,' clucked Munchkin. 'Still, all part of the learning curve.'

Patronising fatarse, thought Flora, trying to struggle up.

'Come on. All the tables will be gone soon.' Nikki sounded impatient.

'Pity you can't join us, Flora,' sneered Martin. 'Next time, I'd try walking to lunch if I were you.' Nikki and Munchkin giggled.

Flora scowled up at him, and was trying to think of a crushing reply, when a shadow fell across her. Her hand was firmly gripped and she was hauled back onto her feet. 'Thanks.' She was extremely grateful. 'Stefan, meet Martin, Nikki and Munchkin.'

Stefan turned round.

Nikki's jaw dropped in wonder, then she hastily smiled her most seductive smile. 'Nikki.' Getting a table at the Savoie was no longer so pressing. Flora might be on her bum, but obviously knew how to land on her feet. He was gorgeous. No wonder she had fallen over, how could she concentrate if she had to follow that body and those legs down the mountainside?

Munchkin gawped, whipped off her pink knitted helmet and ran her fingers through her hair. 'Munchkin. Enjoying your lesson, Flora?' she asked, not tearing her eyes from him. He was more like a rock star than a ski instructor.

'Um. I've got a good teacher.' Flora smiled. 'When he stops telling me to flex my knees.'

'Good pupil,' he smiled back. 'When she stops complaining.'

'We'll be over at the Savoie if you both want to join us for lunch,' said Munchkin, emphasising the 'both'. Why hadn't she booked herself some lessons?

'Thank you,' said Stefan. 'But we must work. *Allez.*' Flora groaned and pulled a face. He laughed. 'See. Complains non-stop.'

'We've noticed,' said Martin dryly.

Nikki watched them disappear. 'We'll ask Flora about sharing.'

'She won't mind,' said Munchkin. 'The more the merrier.'

Setting off down the slope, Flora felt three pairs of eyes boring into her back. Concentrate. Lean forward, weight on the bottom ski, head up, shoulders slightly turned. Arms loose, not waving about like a windmill. Skis about six inches apart and absolutely parallel. Got to get it right this time. She followed Stefan's turn. She pushed out her left ski, shifted her weight, planted her pole and turned round it, bringing her skis back parallel. Traversing the piste, she turned the other way, then again.

Her three perfect stems were rewarded with a huge grin from Stefan as she skidded to a halt beside him.

'You've got it. No problem.'

'Had no choice,' said Flora. 'I wasn't going to give that creep the satisfaction of seeing me falling flat on my face again.'

'*Allez.* Faster this time.'

Luckily, Flora was well out of sight when she turned again far too quickly and plunged headfirst into the only snowdrift on La Croix. 'Listen Stefan,' she spat snow out of her mouth, 'I don't want to ski fast, I don't want to be daring or bother with black runs. Let's just aim for me looking good fifty metres either side of a restaurant.'

Laughing, he pulled her up. 'Or in front of your friends.'

'Or that.' She paused. 'Except they're not my friends.'

He took a Marlboro she offered. 'Friends of your rich husband's?'

She realised he was looking at her ring. 'Jamie's very generous.'

'And rich.'

'I guess.' Flora shrugged, hating discussing it. 'Besides, he's not my husband until April.'

'He's not?' Stefan smiled another of his slow, lazy smiles.

'Wake up, Sam.' Miranda nudged him and he let out a large snore. 'Up sticks.'

Anna obediently put on her gloves, although she was enjoying the ambience and was in no rush to leave.

After downing a quick Pepsi, she and Jamie had jumped into their skis and onto a drag lift. They'd spent an hour skiing round the other side of the mountain. He was considerate, never racing ahead and guiding her through a mogul field she'd been nervous of tackling. Being with him increased her confidence and she'd ended the morning on a high.

The Paradise Café was packed. There'd been a frustrating wait at the self service counter, where they'd met up with Miranda, Giles and Sam. They'd managed to bag an outside table on the terrace overhanging the mountain, with a stunning view of the sun-filled valley far below. A pale moon was rising.

Instead of admiring the scenery, Giles had complained that his spag bog was overpriced and stone cold. Miranda had stalked off to complain to the manager about the state of the loos.

Sam came to life after Jamie flicked some spilt beer at his nose.

'Up sticks,' repeated Miranda. 'Piste map, Giles.'

'Bossy boots,' grumbled Sam.

Groggy from his nap, he found himself struggling to keep up with the rest as they skied their way back to Le Toit.

*   *   *

Jamie looked at his watch and decided that Flora probably wanted a rest in the sunshine after her lesson. He peeled off towards La Bête and the mogul fields.

Flora stood beside the Savoie's ski rack. She frowned as Stefan drew a hairpin in the snow with his pole. 'Here, yes? Just before the turn. You always leave it too late.'

'I can do it all in my head, but my skis seem to have a mind of their own too.' She was downcast.

'Two days in ten years? What do you expect?' He laughed. 'You've done well today. Hey, Flora.' She looked up into his greengage eyes. 'You're tired. Forget all these people in your chalet. Get some sleep tonight and dream beautiful dreams.'

Flora was uneasy that she'd bitched to Stefan about Martin and the others on one of their long rides on a chairlift. She'd found him too receptive an audience; he had listened and laughed and been understanding in all the right places. He'd said the English should find something better to do than drink at bedtime and then smiled his slow, lazy smile. 'Dream about what? Perfect parallel turns?'

He tutted. 'Something a little more interesting.'

'Surely there's nothing more interesting for a ski instructor?'

'But I'm not a typical ski instructor. Am I?'

'No.' She smiled, congratulating herself on her good fortune. 'No. You're nothing like any of them.' There'd been no pressure to keep up with a dozen in a class, no big D for Dunce, no shame in falling over. She'd wanted to get it right, and when she did, had felt triumphant. She had marvelled at the sensation of gliding across the snow, the sun on her face. For the first time in her life, Flora could understand why skiing was addictive.

Stefan looked at his watch. 'Are you hungry?'

'Starving.'

'Let's have some lunch then. Or do you have to go?'

'Er . . .' Flora wondered what Jamie would say about finding her with Stefan. But why shouldn't she have lunch with him? It was hardly a clandestine assignation, was it? 'Sure.'

Flora followed him past the benches crowded with people, aware of women glancing up at him. He found a table. A waitress darted over with a menu and stood gawping at him while they decided.

Martin peered down from the Savoie's first floor balcony. 'Look very cosy, don't they? Wonder what his Lordship will make of it?'

Nikki looked up from her compact, following his gaze. 'Notice, he gets served immediately.' They'd had to wait almost twenty minutes before placing their order. She pouted, put on more lipstick and adjusted her silver fox hat.

'Let's go,' snapped Martin. 'Ready, Munchkin?'

'Perhaps we ought to talk to Flora about sharing her lessons,' suggested Munchkin, desperately wanting an excuse to talk to Stefan. She stood up, deciding to dispense with her pink knitted helmet and ran her fingers through her hair to tidy it.

'Later,' said Martin.

Munchkin followed him down the stairs reluctantly.

'Where are you going?' demanded Martin at the bottom. 'The skis are this way.'

'So they are.' Munchkin laughed airily. She went into reverse, towards the rack and away from the tables. She'd talk to Flora later. Surely Flora wouldn't object? It would be a bit greedy to keep Stefan all to herself. Anyway, she had Jamie.

Flora felt self-conscious sitting opposite Stefan. The fear of skiing that had made her stomach tighten had been replaced by a weird excitement. She found it hard to eat her croque monsieur and even harder to meet his green eyes. If she did, she would turn away.

On the piste, a woman sped past them, graceful and athletic. Flora watched her. 'If only I could ski.'

'You can.'

'Ski well. Parallel turns.'

'If you want to ski parallel, you must ski faster. Like her. Very good style.'

'Impossible.' She became more disheartened watching a group of children wearing crash helmets following their instructor. Was she the only person in the world older than five who needed lessons?

'Anything's possible if you want it enough.' He leant forward. 'You've just got to know what you want.'

'Do you? Know what you want?'

'I thought I did. Until recently. Marie-France says I lack focus.'

'Is she a sculptor too?' Earlier, Flora had asked him what he did off-season, expecting him to say he taught water skiing. She'd been intrigued when he told her. He'd grown up in Annecy, so he'd skied every winter since he'd been able to walk. He'd qualified as an instructor, needed some fast, easy money for materials, so it had seemed logical that he should teach for the season.

'Marie-France? She's training as an architect in Paris. Are you English?'

'More that than anything else.'

'Don't look it. Wrong colouring. Green eyes, dark hair.'

'Like you.' Flora was immediately troubled. Of course, she couldn't fail to notice, but should she make it so obvious she'd noticed? 'Stefan? That a French name?'

'My mother's Czech. Still upset that I'm not a surgeon like her.'

Czech? That explained the cheekbones. '*Dve piva.*'

He was surprised. 'Where did you learn that?'

'Prague.' Suddenly, they were transported from the slopes to their favourite city, comparing bars, galleries, churches, sights seen . . .

Flora jumped, feeling an arm on her shoulder. 'Jamie. You gave me a shock.'

'Hello, angel. Good lesson? You must be Stefan. Jamie Naze.' Smiling, Jamie shook hands. He pulled up a chair and kept a proprietorial hand on hers while asking Stefan about her progress, the snow conditions and off-piste areas. 'Like a drink?'

Stefan declined and put on his sunglasses. '*A demain.*'

'*A demain,*' said Flora.

They watched him ski off, weaving his way through the other skiers. 'Seems nice,' said Jamie.

'He is.'

The afternoon slipped away, the sun moving towards Les Diables, mist beginning to creep around St Marie. After getting Flora a hot chocolate, Jamie disappeared again, unable to resist the call of his skis.

Pete was in a bar over the other side of the valley. He was sitting with a pair of hard drinking divorcees from Fulham, who'd dumped their children in ski school. He ordered a third bottle of wine.

Miranda wondered where he was. 'We'll take the what-a-drag-lift and ski the other side of La Toit.'

'Yes superma'am,' said Sam.

'Did you learn anything today?' demanded Jamie.

'Yes. That I'm really glad you're not teaching me.'

An hour later and halfway down to Les Pins, Flora had reverted to a faltering snowplough. All the progress she'd made in her lesson was forgotten. Waiting for Jamie, her body had stiffened up. When she'd put on her skis, she could hardly move her aching limbs. The sun was disappearing and the air was suddenly much colder, making it difficult for her to loosen up. She was exhausted.

Further down the slope, Jamie stopped for the eighth time to let Flora catch up. Why had she stopped again? 'Come on. Don't be such a wimp.'

'I enjoy being a wimp. Wimps have a highly developed sense of self preservation.' The snow was thin, icy and badly churned after a day being carved by countless pairs of skis. Far below, thousands of lights were coming on in St Marie. Overhead, the chairlift whirred from one metal girder to the next. Why hadn't she taken it? Les Pins seemed no nearer than when she had started out.

Stefan would've despaired if he'd witnessed her technique right now. Jamie witnessed it, despaired and wondered why he was shelling out so much for lessons. Instead of belting straight down like any normal person, Flora insisted on inching across the piste almost horizontally and then turning at a speed which would have shamed a tortoise. Yelling at her to hurry up was useless; she'd just come to a complete stop and yell back.

She had no chance to marvel at the beauty of the sunset, her eyes were fixed on the ground trying to plot her path and avoid the dark patches of ice.

At last, they were near the lift station at Les Pins. About fifty metres of piste separated Flora from the lane leading to the road. The little snow that was left was packed down and rock hard.

Suddenly, she heard a horrible scraping behind her as a boarder lost control and slithered down on his side. He was heading straight for her. Convinced she'd be knocked flying, Flora panicked, shuffled her skis round and hurtled off to her left as if the hounds of hell were at her heels. In her haste, she lost her balance, crashed down and was propelled forward towards the lane.

She stopped on the edge of the piste in a mush of watery snow, her poles tangled in her skis. Wet was seeping through her skipants and had drenched the end of her ponytail.

'For God's sake, Flora, what was all that about?' Having taken off his skis, Jamie bounded over a mound of snow and held out his hand.

'He was aiming straight at me.'

'He was miles from you. Why are you so jumpy? Look over there. Kids of four are able to ski this. Why can't you? Jasper's right, you're pathetic.'

'I'm not pathetic, I'm scared. Why don't you just leave me alone.' Ignoring his hand, she struggled onto her feet.

'Fine.' He shrugged and stalked off.

Flora loosened her bindings, unclipped her boots and picked up her skis. She clambered over the mound of snow and into the lane leading to the road. The surface was rutted with ice. Remembering Davos, Flora leapt from one patch of snow to another to avoid it. Walking nonchalantly up ahead, Jamie could've been in Bond Street.

They were almost at the road when they saw the Range Rover speeding past.

'Great,' snapped Jamie. 'If you hadn't been pissing around, we could've got a lift.'

'Who wants a lift with him?' retorted Flora.

'I did, actually. Do I have to remind you again that you're sharing a chalet with these people and you have to make a bit of effort to be nice.'

'Why? Haven't noticed Martin making much of an effort with me. The hick hack.'

'Quits then. Serves you right for being so bloody rude about Nikki's Mercedes that first night.'

'I didn't mean to be,' exploded Flora. 'Besides, I was quoting you.'

'Obviously, tact isn't part of your extensive vocabulary. Now, you promised you wouldn't fuck up my holiday, so kindly try and be the sweet, charming girl I know you can be.'

'Why are you sticking up for Martin? He's been horrible to you. Why put up with it?'

'Do I?' Jamie stared at her. 'Sometimes Flora, the smartest thing to do is nothing. Wait. Then act. Learn to fish, you'll learn a lot.'

* * *

Hetty had said it was a five minute walk from Les Pins to the chalet. The five minutes had obviously been done by Linford Christie on one of his record breaking days. After yanking off her boots, an exhausted Flora limped up into the sitting room.

From the dining table, where he was tapping into his laptop, Martin glanced up. 'Flora. What a nice surprise. Thought you'd be in Vienna by now.'

She felt her insides shrivel up. She looked vaguely in his direction, but lacked the guts to meet his steel eyes. 'Siena, actually.' She smiled brightly, bitterly regretting her earlier deaf-dumb jibe. How did he know about her wanting to leave?

Pete leapt up from the sofa. He was reeling after sharing five bottles of wine with the divorcees, who had staggered onto a lift blowing kisses at him. 'How was the lesson? Good? You're joking. You enjoyed it? Great.' He gave her a bear hug.

Nervous of Martin, Flora hugged him back with all her might as if he were a security blanket.

Munchkin watched them with a pang, regretting that Flora had arrived and interrupted her tête-a-tête with Pete, who was just as pretty when he was pizzled.

'Good teacher?'

'Patient, unlike some,' said Flora, thinking of her trip down to Les Pins with Jamie.

'They have to be, don't they?' said Munchkin. 'Though it must be incredibly boring for them.' She smiled archly. 'Stefan's rather attractive, isn't he?'

'Is he?' Flora was guarded. She was aware of Jamie in the kitchen, wheedling a sandwich out of the twins. Alice was telling him that a packet had arrived for him in that morning's mail.

'Oh yes. Very attractive,' said Munchkin. 'Nikki and I both thought so, didn't we?' She glanced at her for support.

Sitting beside Martin, Nikki winced guiltily. Martin looked up from his screen to glare at her.

'What does he do off-season?' asked Munchkin. 'Franz in Val taught hang-gliding.'

'Stefan? He's a sculptor,' said Flora.

Martin laughed mirthlessly. 'That accounts for the earrings then. Don't waste your time, lover. Arty-farty, not for you.' He patted Nikki's hand, smiling at Flora. 'Sculptor, eh? Giles mentioned you live with an artist. This Stefan might be right up your alley. If I were Jamie, I'd watch out.'

Flora suddenly understood why Martin had a scar across his cheekbone. If anything had been to hand, she would've been tempted to do something to give him another.

'Stop trying to shit stir,' mumbled Pete, his grip round Flora tightening. 'Waste of time. Flora and Jamie are a perfect match.'

Martin bared his teeth. 'Just as I told you, Flora.'

Nikki wondered when he had told her. Munchkin realised there was a tension between Martin and Flora that threatened to develop into the most almighty row. She longed to mull the situation over with someone.

When Pete wandered off to find Jamie, Flora's instinct was to bolt to her room. She picked the cherries out of her slice of cake, gazing out at Les Diables, but was aware of little else but Martin. He had unzipped his suit, revealing a black T-shirt underneath. His neck was like a tree trunk, even the fingers stabbing at the keyboard seemed to have done weight training. He dominated the room so entirely that even the air she breathed seemed to belong to him.

Just as Flora was deciding she could bear it no longer, Munchkin began to tell her about their fruitless search for a guide. Flora tried to listen and tried not to yawn. She was tired after the skiing and her broken night. Broken by the three of them.

'. . . and so, Flora, we were wondering if we could team up with you? Share the expense and all that?'

Flora was alarmed. Not a chance. Not with them. Not with Martin, especially not with Martin. In her panic she gabbled. 'I'm not sure that would be such a good idea you saw me today flat on my face the whole lesson was like that I'd only hold you all back which would be very boring for you very, very boring as you pointed out.'

'Did I quite mean boring . . . ?' said Munchkin

'You did. It would be. You were right.' Flora was emphatic.

'Oh. Well. If you feel like a break one day or want to split the hours, just to let you know we'll have them in your place.'

'How kind.' Flora smiled. 'I'll let you know. Perhaps there'll be a cancellation.'

'Unlikely. Everything's fully booked.'

'What about ski school classes?'

'Those too.'

'Oh. *Tant pis.* But ski school wasn't quite you, was it? Now, if you'll excuse me, I must go and catch up on some sleep before dinner.' Despite her promise to Jamie, Flora just couldn't resist sticking the knife in.

Nikki's jaw dropped. Had Flora told Munchkin to piss off?

'Flora might change her mind later in the week,' Munchkin shrugged. She had recovered some of her nerve during the afternoon, but knew her technique was wanting.

'Forget it,' said Martin, turning up the volume on the stereo. He'd acquitted himself far better on his shorter skis, only knocking into one child and falling nine times. 'Who needs lessons anyway?'

'I do,' said Nikki darkly. And so did he. 'It's the only way to get any better. You can't just go out, ski and hope to improve. Everyone in Aspen goes to ski clinic, no matter how good they are.' Why couldn't Martin get things organised for her? Not only was Flora having lessons with the gorgeous Stefan, she also had the best bedroom. Her own clothes were getting ruined; she'd soon be reduced to wearing Issy Miyake. 'When are you going to talk to Jamie about swapping rooms?' she hissed.

'What's this?' demanded Munchkin, drawing the tartan curtains.

Frowning at Munchkin's back, Nikki wanted to say, none of your business. 'Martin, it's only fair.'

'Might be tricky,' hissed back Martin, not relishing a refusal. 'It's no big deal, is it? We're only in there to sleep.'

Nikki pouted, flicking minute cake crumbs from her ski-pants. 'I'm sure he'll understand. Once you've got this stupid business about this morning cleared up. I've told you already, sort it out.'

Munchkin nodded sagely. 'Good idea. We've all got to get on, haven't we?'

Nikki let out a long, deep breath through clenched teeth. Why couldn't Munchkin leave them alone, shut up and stop poking her long nose in where it wasn't wanted? She stood up abruptly and attacked a burning log with a poker, causing a flash of sparks.

Jamie arrived from the kitchen, calling over his shoulder that he'd have to ski with the twins one day and pick up a few tips. He disappeared for a few minutes and came back from the storeroom with a basket full of logs. 'How was this afternoon? You recovered, Munchkin?'

'Yes thanks. You've caught the sun, haven't you?' His hair seemed blonder. 'Can we go through pole planting sometime when you have a minute?'

'Sure. After the game?' He began setting out the back-gammon counters.

Nikki nudged Martin, who got up reluctantly. 'Jamie? Word. Sorry about having a go at breakfast. Unforgivable. Should've clocked me one to shut me up. Blinding hangover. In fact, I reckon I was a bit pissed.'

'No problem. Long forgotten.'

'By the way, took your advice. Changed my skis at lunchtime. I tell you, different class. The guy in the shop obviously didn't have a clue what he was on about. So much better.'

'Great.' Jamie sounded pleased. 'By the way, got to get a new car when I'm back on the road. What's the Range Rover like?'

As Martin went through its merits, Nikki pouted on the sofa, mentally urging him to bring up the subject of the room. 'Fancy a test drive?' Martin held out the keys.

'Thanks. Bit risky. Don't have a licence, remember.'

'Details,' said Martin. 'Anytime. Say the word.'

Pete scraped back a chair and demanded how much a point. 'Hundred francs?'

'That bar of yours is doing too well. Fifty.'

'Come off it, you owe me fifty quid. You've got to win it back so you can carrying on spoiling Flora. Seventy-five.'

Miranda and Anna arrived at six-thirty and headed upstairs. While Miranda was in the shower, Anna lay on her bed, marvelling at all the creams and cosmetics covering the dressing table. Just as well she didn't wear make-up, she'd have to book mirror time.

'Good book?' said Miranda, sitting on the stool and opening up her manicure bag. Nodding, Anna held it up. '*The Female Eunuch*,' said Miranda, taken aback. 'Oh. The feminist jobbie. Interesting?'

'Um. Do borrow it.'

'Thanks. Later in the week perhaps. You do look pooped.'

'I am.' Anna yawned.

'Perhaps it's the altitude.'

'Or the attitude,' muttered Anna.

'We're quite high here, aren't we?' Music came up through the floor, followed by the stamping of feet and squealing from Nikki. Miranda began cleaning off her nail varnish. 'Chalets are always like this, aren't they?'

'They are?'

'Madhouses.' The music got louder. 'Still, all part of the fun, I suppose. Last time I was in Verbier the police turned up three times.' She was interrupted by screaming, then the sound of footsteps running on the stairs, with a second, heavier tread in pursuit. 'Once, Johnny, my bro, and his chums had to pay out more in damages than they did for the holiday. They trashed their chalet. Naughty things. Still, boys will be boys.'

Seeing Miranda's indulgent smile, Anna wanted to hit her over the head with *The Female Eunuch*.

Outside, Martin was chasing a shrieking Nikki along the corridor. 'Come here you' from Martin was followed by prolonged squeals then a door being slammed. Anna sighed in exasperation.

'All been pretty typical so far.' Miranda picked up an emery board. 'Entre nous, the bread chucking business is a bit of a yawn. Still, no one's drunk a pint of you know what. Yet.'

'No, I don't know. What?'

'Pee. That's happened before now. Quite revolting.' Miranda shuddered.

Behind her spectacles, Anna's eyes widened in astonishment. 'You tolerate that sort of thing?'

'Well, you know what boys are like. I'm not saying I like it, but there's not much one can do about it, is there?' Miranda rubbed in cream with a handwashing motion and put the signet ring back on her little finger. 'One's just got to put up with it and hope they grow up.'

Anna's jaw dropped. 'I'm sorry, one doesn't have to put up with it.' Her face was growing heated. 'These men, boys, who you know. They're probably an expensively educated bunch of over-privileged public school hoorays, aren't they? You wouldn't tolerate a house being smashed up by yobs from some sink comprehensive. Or would you?'

Snatching her towel, Anna headed for the bathroom.

Munchkin's powder blue sweater was finally dry, but the orange stain was still visible. It didn't matter much that Nikki had given her a replacement; the ruin of the original made her depressed. She repeated 'bubbly not blubbery' like a mantra.

Coming out of the bathroom, she'd heard Miranda and Anna murmuring from behind their closed bedroom door and been stricken by envy. They were obviously getting on well. She was nervous of their reaction if she barged in on them. Both had been decidedly cool to her that morning and had spent the day together, which must have cemented their friendship.

If only she had stayed in the night before. She would have got to know them better and now wouldn't be feeling such an outcast. She wouldn't have got wrecked and smashed the side table. Allying herself so firmly to Nikki and Martin was a mistake; they were a couple, they didn't want her hanging around all the time.

Getting wrecked had stopped the worry, but it always returned. Like a horrible shadow, the more frenziedly she played the party animal, the worse it was when she had to return to her lonely lair.

Sam said they were mates. Mates talked, didn't they? Perhaps she should confide in him.

In his room, Sam sat on his bed and counted out his francs with growing dismay. That's all that was left? He recounted and searched through every pocket of all his clothes. Nothing. Why had he spent so much last night? At this rate, he'd be cleaned out by Thursday. Why had he cut up his credit cards?

Who could he scrounge from? Not Giles, stingy git. He wouldn't lend anyone the pickings from his nose. Pete. Jamie. Martin. Well, take your pick. They were loaded. Successful. Everything he wasn't.

He stared up at the ceiling. This holiday was an expensive mistake. Giles was right, he should be in London searching for another job. He'd needed to get away so badly. Most of the past two months had been spent staring at the television, his sense of worthlessness growing stronger as his confidence dwindled away.

A headhunter unable to find work. What use would he ever be to anyone?

Curled up in her armchair, Flora tried to lose herself in the wedding file. She failed.

First the music, then Giles had arrived back blaring his horn, then, egged on by Munchkin, a hollering Martin had chased a screeching Nikki round the sitting room. Studying menus from a catering company, Flora had turned the page so violently, she'd ripped it. If only Party Animals were an extinct species.

There was no way in a million years she was going to share her lessons with those three.

She began to stretch out. Perhaps she ought to be working to make her mind and soul more flexible? Live and let live. It was only Monday. There were days and days of the holiday left and she'd promised Jamie she'd try and make the best of it.

She wondered how she could make the best of things with Martin. Apart from shutting herself away to avoid him. From that very first night, she'd been a novice pianist sitting down to play a duet with a maestro. She'd constantly hit the wrong notes at the wrong tempo, she'd been too flat or too sharp. The result had been jarring discord. Her initial mistake over Nikki's car, not knowing who he was, his reaction to her job, last night's struggle over the stereo, and the suggestion he was dumb. A big cringeworthy mistake.

And it was only Monday.

Yawning, she picked up her wedding file again without much enthusiasm. Stefan was right; what she needed was a good night's sleep. She drifted back to the hours she'd spent with him and turned the pages unread.

She gave a guilty start and told herself to stop thinking such thoughts. What if Jamie had been reading her mind? God. She got up to shower, vowing to make an extra effort to look nice for him.

In the upstairs corridor, Sam and Martin had started a water fight with the bathroom mugs, Miranda's bath sponge and Nikki's loofah. Munchkin was refereeing with her avalanche whistle.

'Next time, can we have a week in a leper colony,' said Flora.

'What?' Because of a particularly ear-shattering blast, Jamie missed the comment.

She kept quiet. He needed a holiday, not her giving him grief. She began putting on some make-up.

Lying on his stomach on the bed, he brought out a small packet from his back pocket. 'How about a Range Rover? Celebrate me being back on the road?' Her back to him, he missed her scowl.

Jamie's drink-drive ban had resulted in a monster row. She'd gone ballistic, threatening to call off the engagement. Sometimes when she drove him to and from parties, she'd wonder if he hadn't lost his licence on purpose to make her act as chauffeur.

'You won't be back on the road for ten months,' pointed out Flora with as much casualness as she could muster. 'So what's the point in getting a new car?'

'You can have it. Martin says he'll put me in touch with this bloke who got him a deal.'

'Martin said that? You've kissed and made up?'

'Sure.' Jamie looked surprised. 'I'd forgotten all about it. He's on a short fuse and was hungover, that's all. Knows a lot about the car business, he's put Pete onto some place that can service the Porsche half price.'

'He has?' Flora's heart sank. Her view of Martin was obviously warped and mistaken. In the mirror she saw Jamie's reflection. Jamie unwrapping a packet. She froze, praying it wasn't. 'What's that?'

'A late Christmas present from someone at work. Charlie by name and,' smiling, Jamie paused, pulling out a plastic packet and holding it up to the light, 'Charlie's his game. Not Miranda's Charlie. Nice couple of grammes of Colombia's finest. And he's chucked in some grass. Generous boy.'

Flora fled.

The twins were in the kitchen, peering anxiously up at the ceiling. 'What's wrong?' asked Flora.

Scouring a dirty saucepan at the sink, Alice scowled. 'Just praying that none of that water will come through.'

Flora caught a mutter of 'bunch of prats'.

Hetty frowned at her twin. 'Gosh, Flora you look nice.' She checked the lasagne in the oven. 'Jamie said you've got some solo lessons. That's great. He? She? Nice?'

'He. Very nice.'

Hetty grinned. 'Nice looking?' She laughed. 'You're blushing. Gorgeous? Come on, fess, we won't tell. Will we, Al?'

'As gorgeous as Pete?' asked Alice.

'Different.' Despite her anger, Flora managed to smile. Earlier she'd planned to ask the twins for their Sachertorte recipe. Suddenly, she'd changed her mind.

'You look nice, Flora,' said Munchkin by the drinks tray. She frowned. The tatty strips of multi-coloured string around Flora's twig-like wrist looked out of place against her jet embroidered black cardigan, long silk skirt and black velvet slippers. 'What's that?'

'Friendship band,' said Flora. Fred Quince had given it to her. She wished she could talk to him now.

'Nice skirt,' said Munchkin. 'Didn't realise you were so slim. I never wear skirts except to the office. Pear-shaped, me. Can't change. Tried everything, diet, exercise, massage, creams.'

'Speed? Jem used to swear by it,' said Flora, then wished she hadn't. Just then, drugs were her least favourite subject.

Puzzled, Munchkin remembered driving her Golf, Humpty, over Battersea Bridge, being stopped by the police and given a horrible talking to for doing 48mph. Would shame have burnt off the calories? 'I've just got to accept the way I am. Good, old child-bearing hips. If I ever find a father for any children.' She looked into the fire, utterly forlorn.

Flora suddenly felt very sorry.

At the sideboard, Giles was doing a stocktake of the booze. A bottle of gin, two of vodka and, unbelievably almost a bottle of cherry brandy, had gone. It must have been drunk last night. He picked up the honesty book and frowned. Everyone was supposed to write down any drink supplied by the twins. He was the only one to have bothered. He'd have to have words. First, he'd better go up and check that Martin and Sam were mopping the floors.

One by one the rest trooped down, sniffing the air like Bisto Kids as the smell of warming bread grew stronger. Flora listened in as Munchkin, Miranda and Nikki compared their favourite restaurants, all in London's better postal districts where the paparazzi monitored the comings and goings of royalty and film stars. Their health clubs sounded exactly the same.

Feeling like a country bumpkin, Flora wondered if Martin hadn't been right in making her check her hair for straw. Jaxley's Chinese takeaway and the leisure centre hardly measured up.

Talking nightclubs, Martin offered to fix Giles a membership of his place.

Giles' guinea pig face lit up. Now, that would be something serious to let drop at work. 'Could you? Isn't there a massive waiting list?'

'Not for us.'

Somehow, the honesty book was no longer such a pressing issue. Neither did Giles feel inclined to take Martin to task over the water fight, despite his promise to Anna. She had protested that the upstairs corridor resembled the Mississippi. These girlies did exaggerate. 'Membership, eh? You could sort it? Great.' It confirmed that organising the holiday would pay dividends.

'Would you be interested, Anna?' asked Martin.

She laughed, showing off her beautiful teeth. 'Nightclubs aren't really for me, even if I had the clothes or the money. A student grant or a teacher's salary doesn't really stretch very far.' She added gently, without rancour: 'Not everyone is well off, you know.'

Startled, Flora offered up three silent cheers. At that moment, she could have showered Anna with rose petals, put garlands round her neck, kissed the hem of her leggings. At last, at last, at last, a dose of real life.

Giles puffed out his chest. 'The Party's new funding formulae for teaching staff . . .'

'I know the reality. You don't,' Anna cut him off. 'I'm not going to be swayed by one of your political broadcasts.'

Miranda was sipping her gin ton. 'I saw her once in Beauchamp Place. She looked amazing. Simply stunning. But six ghastly photographers chasing her.'

'Dreadful business,' said Munchkin. 'Being hounded like that.'

'It is,' said Martin grimly. 'Years ago now, but I'll never forget it. Phoning in the middle of the night, doorstepping at six in the morning. Scum.'

'The Press has a lot to answer for,' declared Miranda. 'Destroying people's lives, making up terrible stories.' She clutched her string of pearls, as if it were a cross to ward off vampires.

'Perhaps Flora can answer for them,' suggested Martin.

Feeling all eyes upon her, Flora swallowed hard. 'Stories aren't made up. The level of accuracy aimed for is 100 per cent.'

There was general disbelief. 'Think of all the millions of words printed each week and how often is there a correction, let alone a libel action?'

'Bollocks,' said Martin. 'I've been there, Flora. And if I'm there again, I'll know who's responsible. Remember.'

'Oh, Flora wouldn't . . .' began Giles.

'Yellow card. A warning.'

Flora had had enough. Her promise to Jamie was jettisoned. 'Look, I don't know why you're so worried. I work on a local paper. Hick hack. Remember? And even if I were on a national, so? You might have been newsworthy once, but not any more. Surely? Otherwise I'd have heard of you, wouldn't I? At work, I have to read all the papers every day. I've never seen your name once.'

There was a frozen silence. Martin glared at Flora as if she were a mosquito he'd like to swat. Hard.

'Everyone's heard of Martin June,' said Giles.

'Maybe Flora's just ignorant,' snapped Martin.

'It might sound strange, but I'm a different generation from all of you.' She sighed. 'Sorry.'

Sitting beside Flora on the sofa, Anna smiled. 'I'd never heard of him either,' she whispered.

Jamie and Pete were invigorated by a power snooze. Eyeing Jamie sourly, Flora hoped that was all they were invigorated by.

'The room,' hissed Nikki, out of the corner of her mouth. Feeling the pressure of her foot on his own, Martin offered to get Jamie a beer.

Nikki stood mutely at Martin's side, as he and Jamie talked business. She increased the pressure on his foot.

He could no longer ignore it. If she was to fall in with his plans for her, she must be kept happy. 'How's your room?'

'Fine.' Jamie shrugged. 'Don't notice it much. Just a place for sleeping in, isn't it?'

'There we agree,' said Martin. 'It's just young Nikki here needs a bit more space for all her clobber.'

'Use one of our wardrobes if you like. We've got tons spare.'

'You've also got a view and a balcony.' Nikki sounded aggrieved. 'It doesn't seem right that we're paying the same money as you and you should have such a nice room and ours is so pokey and nasty.'

Martin sighed. 'It's cosy, lover. But I'm sure, Jamie, you realise the lady here does have a point. Wondering if we couldn't do a swap with you halfway through the week? Fair's fair and all that.'

Jamie's slow blink belied his quick thinking. He smiled his most urbane smile. 'Shouldn't be any problem at all. I'll just square things with Flora.' The gong sounded. 'After dinner.'

In the kitchen there was speculation about which food would be chucked or furniture broken that night. Thank God, the twins agreed, the upstairs corridor wasn't carpeted. They suddenly missed the two boring dentists and their dreary wives and food-faddy children who'd stayed at the chalet the week before.

As Flora was en route to the table, she heard Martin call her name. He was smiling and sounded friendly. Perhaps he was offering an olive branch, he'd agree that yes, they'd definitely got off on the wrong foot, but let's put it all behind us.

In cream cashmere, expensive jewellery and a suntan, Nikki was intimidatingly gorgeous. Martin's tan suited his colouring. Healthy, rich, glossy they could've been posing in an upmarket lifestyle feature. Flora was glad she'd bothered to make an effort.

'Martin?' Flora smiled.

'We've just been having a chat with Jamie about the room situation.'

'Really?' What room situation?

'He's agreed that it's not on we should be paying the same money considering the difference.'

'Ours is so grim and pokey,' butted in Nikki.

Martin interrupted her. 'And perhaps the best solution is to swap halfway through the week. Fair's fair and all that.'

'Um . . .' Flora wondered what the hell Jamie was playing at. Why hadn't he discussed it with her first?

'So, we'll shift our stuff tomorrow morning. OK. That's sorted, then.'

Flora was feeling like she was being run over by a steamroller.

'Good,' said Nikki, noticeably buoyed. 'It'll take about two seconds to move your things, won't it, Flora? Didn't bring much, did you? Must be lovely to have clothes you don't have to look after. Though, nice skirt. Oo, love the cardi.'

'First thing tomorrow, it is then,' said Martin.

'It isn't.' Why couldn't Jamie be bothered to talk things through with her? How dare he?

'But you said . . .' Martin glared at her.

'I didn't. You assumed.'

'You won't swap?' Nikki was furious. She turned to Martin. 'Typical. I knew she wouldn't.'

'I can't believe you're being so fucking unreasonable,' hissed Martin.

'Dinner's ready you lot,' called Giles. Flora marched off to the table. 'Where's Sam got to?'

'Here.' He sounded heavy-hearted.

'Where have you been?'

'Outer Mongolia,' he snapped.

'Bit anti-social.'

'I just wanted a bit of space. All right?'

Flora plonked herself down beside Jamie, upsetting Miranda's placement.

'You're meant to be down there, next to Martin,' she reproved.

'Sorry ma'am, I mean Miranda.' Flora forked up a slice of ham from a wooden platter. She'd like to see Martin's head on it.

Nikki was fuming. 'There's no way she's going to give in,' she hissed. 'It's so unfair. Talk to Giles. He'll sort it out.'

'The only way that bitch is going to be sorted is with a big slap.' Martin scowled. 'I'll work on Jamie. Promise.'

Miranda turned to Pete. 'We must all meet up back in London and have a get together.'

'All?' Pushing the hair out of his eyes, he smiled. 'Need to get you on your own for a chat sometime. Wine?'

'Thanks.' Miranda was bewildered. What did he mean? He really was gorgeous. Tall, blond and handsome. And so sweet. Sweet Pete, Australia's greatest export.

'Nice watch, Pete,' said Munchkin on his other side. 'What make?'

Wine bottles emptied, the lasagne was eaten, the candles burnt lower and the voices became louder. Flora sat in lonely silence, trying to avoid looking at Nikki and Martin, needing to talk to Jamie. Fearing she might give him grief over the stash, Jamie kept his attention fixed on Anna.

Giles felt a pang. Pete and Mirandy seemed to be getting on well. Far too well. Was he making a play for her? Surely not. She was almost engaged and even Pete the playboy must have some scruples. Why had he bothered with a stupid tie if all Pete could do was change sweatshirts? Not that Mirandy seemed to object. She seemed fascinated by his Breitling, now on her sturdy wrist. Thankfully Munchkin kept on butting in.

'Both come flying? Sure. Anytime,' Pete was saying.

'Wow,' said Miranda. 'The airfield's just down the road from mummy and daddy's. You must pop in for a drink whenever you're around.'

Giles felt a tightening in his guts. Never in the two years he'd known her, had she invited him to meet her parents.

'Let's set a date,' said Munchkin eagerly. 'I've got to go to the States in the New Year, but we can work something out.'

'Another business trip?' Pete was impressed. 'You're in demand, aren't you? Whenever. I practically drive past your place, so I can give you a lift.'

'Can you?' Munchkin's eyes lit up. 'Drop in anytime you're passing. Promise.'

After dinner Jamie and Pete set up the backgammon board. Pete demanded best of three. 'Pity we can't play for Miranda.'

'If only.' Jamie winked at her.

Sitting beside her on the sofa, Giles noticed Miranda was so pleased she was almost purring.

Munchkin felt put out. She knew the two men were kidding, but why couldn't they kid about her? Miranda was almost engaged.

Pete lit a cigarette. 'Double you.'

'I'll play the winner,' announced Martin from the fireside.

'Redoubled,' said Jamie.

Munchkin ambled across to the dining table and peered at the board. 'Remind me, what does that mean?'

'That when Pete loses, he'll have to cough up at least 300 francs,' said Jamie breathing on the dice.

'Double four. You jammy bastard,' exclaimed Pete, pouring out two more huge brandies.

Sam and Munchkin began a half-hearted jive near the stairs. They almost knocked over the Christmas tree before they gave up. Miranda kept on glancing at Pete, who was frowning in concentration and pushing the hair out of his eyes. He reminded her of a sheepdog puppy. Twenty minutes ticked past and Jamie won back the money he'd lost in the ski race.

'Not my night.' Pete scraped back his chair. 'Well done mate. Who wants to come out later?'

Miranda hesitated. She was shattered. And it wouldn't do to appear too eager. 'Perhaps.'

'Possibly,' piped up Giles, determined to keep an eye on Mirandy.

'You two finished?' said Martin. 'Right, so it's me and Jamie. How much?'

'Twenty five francs?' suggested Jamie.

'Come off it.' Martin scoffed. 'Big boys rules, old chap. Two fifty.' He stared at Jamie steadily. 'And the bedroom.'

Nikki and Flora froze. In the background, Sam whistled. 'Monster stakes.'

There was a pause.

'Fine,' said Jamie at last.

Martin started, immediately throwing a double five. Jamie a one and a two. His next few throws were just as bad. Nikki went and sat next to Martin. Flora knew she was willing him to win, as much as she herself was urging on Jamie. Monster stakes indeed.

'Six and five, Martin. Nice,' said Sam, offering them some more brandy.

'Double you,' said Martin, after Jamie threw a two and a three.

Flora pictured herself throwing her clothes into her bag and meeting a triumphant Nikki on the stairs.

Jamie hadn't made much progress. His red counters were mostly on Martin's side of the board, including two on Martin's home base, now getting crowded with white. He peered at the board and frowned. 'Redoubled.'

Martin scoffed.

'Blimey,' said Sam.

Flora winced. Jamie was mad, he was going to be gammoned at this rate. Martin had begun to take off his counters, leapfrogging over Jamie's pair stuck in the corner. With only a few counters left, Martin grinned, sniffing victory. He threw his dice. Six and five.

'You can't do that,' hissed Nikki. 'It's blocked. You've got to take them off.'

Martin's smile vanished, realising that two of his counters were suddenly vulnerable, so close to home.

Jamie threw.

'Bloody hell, lucky or what?' said Sam. Jamie snatched up one of Martin's counters.

'There's no point in shaking,' said Nikki. 'You can't get on.'

Every point on Jamie's home base was blocked by a pair of red counters.

'Can you believe this man?' exclaimed Sam, as Jamie threw a four and a one, which allowed him to capture another of the white singletons.

Martin and Nikki watched impotently as Jamie made his way round the board and started taking off his red counters. When two double fives were thrown in succession, Martin ground his teeth.

'Can you believe this man?'

As Jamie removed four reds, Martin could not.

'Unlucky,' said Sam. Martin's dice showed a six and a one. He had failed to get back on the board. He was left with four white counters at the game's end.

'Phew,' said Jamie. 'Close.' Too close for comfort, thought Flora. 'Thought you had me there. Another?'

It was hard to tell whether Nikki or Martin was the most enraged.

'No,' snarled Martin, grabbing her hand. 'Bedtime. Night everyone.'

'Poor old Martin, 1,000 francs,' sniggered Sam. 'And the bedroom, whatever that means. The drinks are on you, Jamie. Who's coming? To the village, of course.'

Anna shook her head.

'Not me,' said Munchkin. Not even Pete's charms could lessen her weariness.

Wrapped up against the cold outside, the twins wished everyone goodnight. Pete smiled and asked if there were any chance of a lift.

'Sure,' said Alice, blushing. 'Can't guarantee to bring you back though.'

'Great,' said Pete. 'Jamie, you coming? We can go and play pool.'

'Can we?' Jamie asked Flora, ruffling her hair.

'You go,' said Flora. 'Think twice about you know who. Please, Jamie.'

'Who?' said Pete.

'Charlie,' replied Jamie in a low voice.

'You're joking.'

Miranda looked up sharply. She decided to stay put. It looked like a boys' night.

'Don't get wrecked, Jamie,' pleaded Flora, as he kissed her before running out into the night. 'And don't make too much racket when you get back.'

'Enjoy your knitting, girlies,' said Sam.

Downstairs, the front door slammed. The chalet seemed calmer, less cramped. Anna turned down the stereo, went to the window and stared out at Les Diables, lit up by the moon.

'It's awful being a party pooper,' yawned Munchkin. 'The men must think we're very boring.'

'Who cares what they think?' said Anna. 'Brandy?' She poured out four. Handing a glass to Miranda, she lowered her voice. 'About what I said earlier. In the room? It was a bit strong. Sorry.'

'Don't be,' said Miranda, as quietly. '*Entre nous*, after that water fight,' she scowled slightly at Munchkin, 'I can see your point.'

Munchkin crossed her legs, so they appeared slimmer. She fixed her eyes on Flora. 'So, you must see a lot of Pete, him and Jamie being best friends. Surprised he hasn't got a girlfriend.'

Miranda's ears pricked up.

'He took a hell of a knock,' said Flora. 'Still getting over it.'

'Awful for him,' clucked Munchkin. 'He found her, didn't he?'

'From what Jamie's told me. Yes.'

'She was always unbalanced, according to Giles,' said Munchkin. 'No one can really blame Pete, can they?'

'What did you make of her?' Miranda looked for split ends.

'Caro? I never met her.' Flora felt uncomfortable. 'It all happened before I knew Jamie.'

'Incredibly good-looking, modelly, gamine,' said Miranda. Munchkin sucked in her cheeks. 'But one knew there wasn't something quite right.'

'Quite,' said Munchkin. 'It wasn't Pete's fault. Though people will gossip.'

Wanting to change the subject, Flora picked up the book lying on a side table. 'Yours?' she asked Anna.

'*The Female Eunuch*,' Munchkin peered across. 'Not much call for that stuff now, is there? All equal now, aren't we? Equal pay, equal rights. Celebrate our differences, that's what I say.'

'Can I borrow it sometime?' asked Flora.

Anna smiled. 'Swap you for Dorothy Parker.'

'Wouldn't have thought feminism was quite you, Flora,' said Munchkin. 'Giving everything up to marry your good old-fashioned breadwinner. Still, each to their own.' Flora stared at her open-mouthed. 'And Jamie's a serious catch, isn't he?'

'Who's making the wedding dress?' asked Miranda.

Flora went to bed, leaving her clothes piled on a chair. Catching sight of her ski pass on the dressing table, she remembered Stefan's low voice telling her to dream beautiful dreams.

After what seemed only minutes, Flora half-opened her eyes. Mole-like, she squinted. She made out a figure at the side of the bed. 'Jamie?' she murmured.

'Sssh, sleep . . . Fuck,' There was a crash as he tripped.

'Jesus, what's going on?' Flora sat up, turned on the bedside light and found him sprawled on the rug. It was three thirty.

'Hello, angel. My beautiful wife.' He peered up at her, blond hair tousled, eyes glazed. 'Know something? Really love you.' He hiccuped. 'Come and give me a hug.'

Flora sighed. He was wrecked. Her eyes, still sleepy, widened in alarm. 'What's happened to your hand?'

'Fell over. Hurt my paw.'

'Let me see.' Blood had seeped through the white hand-kerchief he'd wrapped around it. 'When did this happen?'

'Just now. Walking back.' He collapsed beside her on the bed. 'S'nothing. Fell over on Les Pins, that's all. Bloody dark.' He pulled a pillow over his head to shield his eyes from the light.

Flora snatched it away. 'You walked up a mountainside?'

'Shortcut.'

'Are you completely mad? How much of that stuff have you taken? Where are the others?'

'Dunno.'

She was now fully awake and exasperated. His breath reeked of booze. 'Come on. Up.'

'Leave me alone,' he protested, as she tugged him to his feet. 'Where are we going?'

She dragged him into the kitchen. The tiled floor was freezing under her bare feet. They winced as the fluorescent light flashed into life overhead. Taking his hand, she thrust it under the tap. Above the gush of water he told her he loved her so much.

'How much went up your nose tonight?' She searched through the cupboards.

'Quick tiny toot.' He sniffed. 'Hours ago. Love you so much.'

The first aid kit was under the sink. She swabbed some kitchen roll with disinfectant.

'Ouch. Stings,' said Jamie.

'The booze will kill you first.' She sighed. 'The bleeding's stopped. You won't need stitches. How can you be so stupid?' She stuck down a plaster. Footsteps yomped up the stairs, along with a chorus of drunken ssshes and muffled guffaws. 'Hello, you lot.' Flora eyed Sam, Giles and Pete as they trooped into the kitchen. They were as gone as Jamie.

'What the fuck happened to you?' slurred Pete. 'Thought I'd lost my best mate ever forever.' He staggered over to Jamie and put an arm round his shoulders. 'Ever forever, that's good.' He squinted and beamed in delight. 'I should be a poet.'

'A poet,' agreed Jamie, slapping his back. 'Lovely.'

'Missed your voc, voc, forget it,' hiccuped Sam.

'Girls are poets. Call me sweet Pete. Flora, you call me sweet Pete, don't you?' Flora rolled her eyes at the ceiling.

Jamie reeled round, hanging on to Pete. 'Poetry. Wait. Sssh, I'm thinking . . . wait . . . "The sand of the desert is sodden red, Red with the wreck of a square that's broke, The Gatling's jammed and the Colonel dead . . .' How does the rest of it go? Come on. Giles?'

Flora headed for the door, unable to cope with a drunken Jamie reciting Newbolt at four in the morning. Giles caught her sleeve and put his arm round her, hugging her close to him. 'Can't go. Party's just starting.' His breath stank.

'Giles. How does it go? "The Gatling's jammed . . . The Gatling's jammed and the Colonel's dead, And the regiment blind with dust and smoke",' Jamie crowed gleefully. 'Aren't I good? Learnt it at prep school. How does the rest of it go? Sam. Pete. Someone must know,' he bellowed.

'Sssh,' hissed Flora, struggling to break free of Giles.

'Munchies,' said Sam, rooting through the cupboards.

'The more it snows, tiddly pom,' said Pete, clinging onto Jamie and wheeling him round. 'Tiddly poms, that's what you are.' They began to laugh.

'Sssh.'

Giles squeezed Flora more tightly. 'May I say, Flora. Can I call you Flora? May I say, that you're one of the most finest looking girlies I know. If you wasn't going to marry Jamie. Not that I've got anything against him. Fine man, James. Don't look away now.' She'd averted her head, asphyxiated by his breath. 'Luke at me . . .' As he rambled on and on, Flora wondered why Giles was bothering to put on a thick Lancashire accent. She tried to bolt.

'Never mind the munchies, Sam. Get the beer out,' called Pete.

Sam got a six pack out of the fridge. 'Let's play the flour game.'

' "And the regiment blind with dust and smoke",' slurred Jamie, taking a beer bottle. 'Let's skin up something that will give us the munchies. Where's my Rizlas? Flour game. Lovely idea. Giles, bowl. Sam, flour.' He patted Pete's shoulder and grabbed Flora. 'Angel, love you so much, we played pool and I won. Beat the lot of them.' He smiled inanely. 'Where are you going?'

'Bed,' hissed Flora. 'I am very cold and very tired.'

Jamie held her like a vice. 'No, you're not. Party's just starting. Isn't my wife beautiful, everyone?'

'Let me go.'

'Cherry cake.' Sam opened a tin. He got it out, put it on the counter and rummaged through the drawers making a clatter. 'Got one.' He brandished a knife and started to hack into the cake. It split apart, one half landing in the sink, the other on the floor. 'Whoops.'

'Never mind,' said Pete, searching under the sink. 'Where's the flour?'

'Here.' Giles held up a leaking bag. Flour went everywhere.

'Where?' Pete spun round and trod on the cake. 'Now. Apple.'

'Sssh.' Flora wriggled free of Jamie. She ran out of the kitchen and back to bed. There was no point in trying to get them to quieten down, they were too far gone.

She rubbed her feet together trying to warm them up. For the next twenty minutes, laughter, shouting and sudden violent coughing sounded from the kitchen. She tried to read, getting crosser and crosser. Just when she was thinking of castrating them all with the carving knife, Jamie appeared in the doorway. His face, hair and clothes were covered in flour. After declaring he loved her so much, he collapsed onto the bed, reached across to turn out the light and was snoring within seconds.

Flora lay fuming in the dark.

CHAPTER FOUR

Tuesday

The sound of serial vomiting woke Flora up. It was coming from the bathroom next door. Beside her, Jamie snuffled, turned on his side and resumed his heavy snoring. Flour encrusted his hair, his face and the pillow. Flora felt a rush of rage. She'd always dreamt she'd be swept away by a cross between Mr Darcy and Max de Winter. Now it seemed she was about to marry Just William or Dennis the Menace.

Her eyes felt sandblasted, her body beaten up. Pulling on a huge sweater and a pair of socks over her pyjamas, she headed for the kitchen. Coffee. Preferably intravenously. She hadn't got the energy to lift a mug. Passing the bathroom, she heard more puking coming from Giles. She shuddered.

'Morning,' said Hetty sourly. Well scrubbed and wide awake, the twins made Flora acutely aware of her early morning breath and last night's make-up.

Alice muttered an equally churlish greeting and carried on unloading the dishwasher. 'Coffee, I suppose.'

'If it's no trouble. Thanks.' Flora sensed something was very wrong.

Hetty turned on the kettle. 'Er, Flora? When we came up this morning we found the kitchen in a terrible state. At first we thought it must be burglars. Someone had gone through all the cupboards and drawers, there was flour everywhere and broken glass . . .'

'And my cherry cake,' cut in Alice darkly.

'And Al's cake had been stamped on. Had to throw it away. Maybe we should've said something earlier, but we like clients to tell us in advance if they want to use the kitchen. Of course, people raid the fridge sometimes. We like to keep track, so we know exactly what to shop for. It makes it difficult if things are moved or used up, you see.'

'I do see.' Flora squirmed guiltily as if she were to blame.

'It took us half an hour to clean up,' hissed Alice, face in the dishwasher.

Hetty filled up the cafetière. 'We wondered if you could have a word with Pete and Jamie for us.'

'I heard them,' snapped Alice. 'Running round like loonies. That's the third night in a row we've been woken up.'

'I'm really sorry if they've put you out,' grovelled Flora, grabbing the cafetière and backing out of the kitchen. The twins' niceness made their displeasure harder to bear. 'I'll talk to them. Promise.'

Thankfully, Giles had failed to pebbledash the bathroom. While her coffee cooled, Flora had a quick shower, brushed her teeth and went into the bedroom to dress. Jamie lay sprawled across the bed, still in his clothes.

Flora stared for a moment, then was suddenly unable to bear the sight of him. She dressed, dragging her shabby black sweater over her head and then, diving to the floor, she yanked her biker boots out from under the bed and put them on.

It was another beautiful day, the light crystalline.

Flora sat at the dining table munching on a croissant and staring out at the snowy peaks of Les Diables. It was impossible not to overhear the twins in the kitchen, cataloguing their complaints about Jamie and Pete. As each fresh outrage was recounted, Flora cringed with shame. She tried to concentrate on Dorothy Parker.

At the sound of footsteps on the stairs, she turned round to see Martin approaching. Nikki was looking ravishing in silver-grey leggings and a matching sweater. 'Morning.' She smiled, trying to make an effort.

Both looked at her with dislike and remained silent. Crushed, Flora's eyes went back to her book. She tried harder than ever to concentrate, but could sense a horrible tension. She turned a page. The silence grew louder. She wished the stereo were playing at full blast. When Nikki began to complain about how tired she was, Flora guessed the words were directed at her.

Flora reached across for another croissant and found Martin staring at her, his eyes flinty. 'Hope your boyfriend realises he woke us up last night. Rich of him, after all that fuss he made about the stereo. Have a word, will you?'

Nikki looked suitably martyred.

Resentment surged inside Flora. She wasn't Jamie's keeper. First the twins and now Martin.

'Just be a good girl and pass the message on, Flora. Or is it too much to ask?'

Flora took a deep breath. They were stuck under the same roof until Saturday; she'd better try and get on with them. 'Of course it's not. I'll tell him.'

'Good,' said Nikki. 'I don't want another broken night because of Jamie, thank you very much. He acts like he owns the place.'

'Flora and he are well matched,' said Martin. 'I heard you, Flora. In the kitchen. In fact you,' he pointed his knife at her, 'you woke me up.'

Guilt washed over Flora. 'I'm sorry, but I was trying to find the first aid box. Jamie had hurt his . . .'

'Plaster in there? Should've used it as a gag,' growled Martin.

'I'm really sorry if we woke you up.'

'I think he owes Nikki a big apology.'

Flora was tempted to say what about Sam and Pete and Giles, but kept her mouth shut. The pair had every right to feel aggrieved. In fact, she could sympathise with them. 'I'll talk to Jamie. As I said, I'm sorry.' She hadn't been that loud, had she?

'Think you owe us after the way you two behaved last night,' said Martin. 'Waking up the whole house.'

'Too right.' Nikki nodded.

'I tried to be quiet . . .'

'Uh.' Nikki was dismissive. 'Really . . .'

Martin sshed her. 'Let's put all this bother behind us, eh?' He sounded so friendly, Flora was wrong-footed. 'By the way, any more thoughts about this room business? We can swap over after breakfast.'

She blinked in surprise.

'You owe us,' chimed in Nikki. 'After the way you carried on last night.'

'I didn't make that much noise . . .'

'Like Concorde doesn't make much noise . . .'

'Only take five minutes,' said Martin.

As Nikki repeated she owed them one, Flora stared down at the boots at the end of her outstretched legs. Old friends. Suddenly she knew for certain she hadn't been that loud. She was almost amused. The conniving creeps. 'Wasn't this room business settled by your backgammon game?'

'Nothing's cast in concrete, is it?' said Martin. 'Only take five minutes.'

'You owe us one,' said Nikki.

'No I don't,' said Flora casually. 'If I woke you up, which I didn't, we're quits.'

'You're not swapping then?' Martin glared at her. 'You've got to. Come on, fair's fair.'

'Told you it wouldn't work,' hissed Nikki. 'Nothing will change her mind.'

'That's because this particular hick hack is the most selfish, petty, unreasonable bitch that ever walked the earth.' He was furious. 'Know something, Flora, everyone in the chalet wishes you'd got on that plane yesterday. And taken that boyfriend of yours with you.'

Flora flinched as if she'd been slapped. Everyone in the chalet? She'd made herself that hated? They'd all been talking about her . . .

'I would've bought you a ticket,' hissed Martin. 'I don't like being called dumb or having my girlfriend and her car slagged off by some scruffy little scrubber from the backarse of nowhere. A hick hack who's completely up herself because she's landed a toff. Well, we all know why Jamie's marrying you.'

Flora felt herself crumbling. Nikki was studying her as impassively as a beautiful china doll. Wave after wave of desolation washed over her.

'Ticket to Tasmania suit you, Flora? One way?'

'Very generous of you.' Flora's voice was cracking, she was close to tears. 'Give the money to Jamie. You owe him. Thousand francs, wasn't it?' Martin's eyes narrowed. 'Bet you'll try and get out of that one too.'

'I'll give Jamie his money later.'

'Sure,' taunted Flora, standing up. She must go, quickly, deny them the pleasure of seeing her breaking down. 'Double you.'

'After breakfast.'

'Redoubled.' Flora turned on her heel.

'Wait,' called out Nikki. She brought out a wad of notes and counted them. 'Here you are, Flora.' She threw a bundle across the table. 'Take it. And shut up.'

Snatching up the thousand francs, Flora fled. Blinded by tears, she knocked into Anna.

Puzzled, Anna sat down. 'Is Flora all right?' She shook some cornflakes into a bowl. 'Seems a bit unhappy.'

Giles swilled tea around his gums. 'We had a bit of a late one last night. She had to be Florence Nightingale for Jamie.'

'Florence Nightingale?' Martin was incredulous. 'Nurse Ratched, more like.'

'Nurse who?' Giles's head was pounding.

'The one in *One Flew over the Cuckoo's Nest*,' said Anna.

'The bitch,' said Nikki.

Watching Anna tuck into her cornflakes made Giles feel queasy again. Not even the sight of Mirandy, looking unusually glamorous, could prevent him from dashing from the table.

Hearing violent retching from the bathroom, Anna smiled in satisfaction. 'Serves him right.' Another broken night, this time broken by the four men.

Miranda pulled a face. 'They are the absolute limit. Sam looks like death. Just asked me for more headache pills, then collapsed back into bed. No skiing for him this morning. Waste. We're so lucky with the weather. Has Pete surfaced yet?'

At the sound of footsteps on the stairs she looked round eagerly, but was disappointed.

Munchkin eased herself into a chair. 'I just saw him coming out of the bathroom looking very sorry for himself. Morning everyone.' Bumping into Pete first thing was a mixed blessing. As nice as it was to be in such close proximity to him, he might catch her when she was looking far from her best. At least she'd managed to whip off her glasses in time. Not that he'd been able to register much this particular morning.

Her arms ached so much she could hardly lift the teapot. Why hadn't she stuck to her resolution and gone to the gym? 'What on earth did they get up to last night?'

Hetty arrived with another basket of croissants. Noticing she seemed glum, Anna asked what was the matter. Hetty told them about the havoc in the kitchen and was rewarded by tuts, 'poor yous' and profuse apologies from Miranda and Martin.

'Flour everywhere,' she said. 'Scrambled eggs, Anna?'

'If it's no trouble.'

'That's well out of order,' said Martin piously, when Hetty had left them. 'They have a hard enough job as it is.'

'Quite,' nodded Munchkin. 'I must say, the boys were on the rowdy side last night. I know they were all pizzled, but they should have more consideration.'

Anna and Miranda were astonished. 'Pot and kettle,' mouthed Miranda.

'Some of us were trying to sleep,' scowled Nikki. 'I don't want to hear some stupid poem about jam at four in the morning.'

'Jamie was loud, wasn't he?' said Munchkin. 'Well, they all were.'

'Especially Jamie,' said Martin.

'Done now.' Anna sighed. 'Never mind them. What's the plan for today? Any ideas?'

'Martin and I are going into St Marie to look around the shops this morning,' said Nikki. She was determined to escape from Munchkin. 'We'll meet up with you later.'

Miranda thought quickly. Things had started to look rather promising with Pete, but he hadn't gone to bed until well past four and he'd probably need to sleep in and sleep it off. She couldn't hang around the chalet waiting for him. Better to go skiing with Anna. But they couldn't abandon Munchkin, could they? But Munchkin wasn't up to the more taxing runs.

'The three of us can go up to Le Toit again,' said Miranda. 'It's not very adventurous, but it'll give us all a chance to polish up. Then link up for lunch. OK with you?'

Munchkin was touched. It was nice of Miranda to be so considerate and include her.

'We should ring the ski school and see if there are any cancellations,' said Nikki. She turned to Anna and Miranda. 'Tried to sort out some lessons yesterday but they're all booked. It would never happen in Aspen.'

'Couldn't you team up with Flora?' asked Anna. 'Share the expense?'

Nikki shook her head. 'No way.'

'We're at such a different level,' said Munchkin.

'We'd only be in the way of a beautiful friendship,' added Martin.

'What?' Miranda was intrigued.

'Nuff said.'

Flora wished she'd left the money alone. She threw it on the dressing table, feeling cheapened. Jamie stirred, rolled onto his back and continued snoring. Longing to catch up on some sleep, she couldn't as he was sprawled out across the entire bed, denying her any mattress. They could have fifty, sixty years together, decades of him sharing her life, sharing her bed.

Desperate for fresh air, she went out onto the balcony.

She stared out across the valley, lost in her thoughts, oblivious to the cold. She heard laughter as people trooped down the road towards the lift station. Why couldn't she be like them? So carefree and happy. She was only miserable because she was tired. Tired and tense. She must lighten up and think positive.

She thought hard and couldn't come up with anything positive.

'Aren't you cold?' Anna was calling up from the drive.

'No . . . yes.' Flora sniffed, hastily wiping her eyes on her sleeve. Her teeth were chattering. She realised she was freezing.

'Beautiful day, isn't it? What time's your lesson?'

'Half-one.' Did Anna really want her to leave? Had she made herself that hateful? 'Where are you off to?'

'Le Toit. Come along with us.'

'Thanks.' Flora shook her head. 'But no. I'd only hold you back.'

'Sit in the sunshine on a balcony and read and drink hot chocolate.' Anna smiled. 'Don't blame you. If you want any books, there's stacks in my room. Borrow away.'

'Morning Flora,' called Miranda. 'How's Jamie? Under the weather?'

'Still asleep.'

'Heard about the kitchen? Havoc. You must keep him under better control when you're married. Shorter rein required. Tighten your stirrups.'

'I'll try.' For God's sake, she wasn't marrying a horse.

'Do,' urged Munchkin, bustling out. 'Heard about the kitchen? The twins are upset. Understandably. Have a word with Jamie. It's not really on, is it?'

'No.' Flora sighed. Why did they think it was her fault? She wasn't Jamie's keeper.

'It's not really on,' repeated Munchkin.

To Flora, she sounded revoltingly self-righteous. 'No. It's not on. But smashing tables is, I suppose.'

Filled with indignation, Munchkin watched Flora storm back inside.

'Come on, girlies, in you get,' said Martin. 'Chop chop. Now where's Nikki got to?'

Munchkin appealed to Anna and Miranda. 'I didn't mean to break the table. It was an accident. I told Giles I'd pay for it. I can't see what that's got to do with anything.'

Her mutterings were drowned by the music Martin was scraping the windscreen to.

They had to wait for another ten minutes, Martin hooting with increasing urgency, before Nikki finally sauntered out in her Ralph Lauren, unrepentant about the delay.

'What kept you?' demanded Martin as she climbed into the passenger seat.

'I couldn't find my pass. That room is so dark and pokey.' She pouted and turned round to the back seat. 'Do you think it's fair that Flora and Jamie are paying the same money as all of us? Have you seen their room? It's massive, they've got all that wardrobe space and a balcony . . .'

'Well, now you mention it . . .' said Munchkin.

She was interrupted by Miranda, who spotted trouble. She had stayed in enough chalets to know that this sort of grumbling must be nipped in the bud. 'Giles did explain. First come first served. We all agreed in London.'

'But . . .' said Nikki.

'We all agreed in London.' Miranda's patrician authority asserted itself.

'Well, I . . .'

'Surely the backgammon game settled things pretty conclusively?' said Anna.

In the rearview mirror, Martin saw Munchkin nodding in agreement. The cause was lost as far as that trio was concerned. Nikki was about to whinge, but he cut her short. 'The room would be fine, if your stuff wasn't cluttering it up. Why did you bring so much, for crying out loud?'

'I didn't.'

'Four handbags . . .' As he and Nikki began to bicker, Anna wished she had walked.

Flora dragged herself back to the sitting room to fetch her book. Sweeping the floor, Hetty looked at her in surprise. Had Flora been crying? 'We're going into the village. It's market day and we're collecting the video from the menders. Would you like a lift anywhere?'

'Thanks. Yes.' Flora was grateful. 'What time?'

'Twenty minutes or so. Al's just doing a stock take.'

'Great.' She'd wander round St Marie, then go up to the Savoie and sit in the sun before her lesson. A note was propped up on the table. '*Dear wasters,*' she read. '*The good girlies have hit the slopes. Will be in Café Le Toit from one onwards. See you later??? Miranda.*'

Flora gathered up her stuff for the day and peered into the bedroom mirror. The bright sunshine was unforgiving. She looked dreadful. Puffy-eyed, even paler than usual. Urgent action was called for; on with the slap.

Jamie sat up and groaned. His blond hair was tousled, embedded with flour. As he caught sight of the white powder covering his clothes he yelped in alarm.

'Don't worry. It's only flour,' said Flora dryly.

'Morning angel,' he croaked, trying to smile. 'How are you?'

'How do you think?'

Her face was reflected in the mirror. She looked as she sounded. Extremely pissed off. Oh God. His head throbbed. His hand was tender. He saw the plaster, then more of the flour, then it started to come back to him. His head throbbed even harder. 'Come and give me a hug,' he pleaded pathetically.

Flora carried on putting on her mascara. 'You want a Boy's Own holiday, so get Pete or Sam or Giles to give you a hug.'

'I think I'm going to die.' He lay back on the pillows and closed his eyes.

'Good. It will save me the trouble of getting married only to get a divorce.'

Alarmed, he sat up again. 'You don't mean that.'

'Don't I? By the way, there's your backgammon money.' Flora pointed to the wad of notes. 'I never, ever thought I'd go on another skiing holiday. I never, ever thought that if I went on another skiing holiday, the skiing would be the best thing about it.'

Jamie squeezed his eyes tight shut, trying to think. 'But you hate skiing.'

'Precisely.'

'Never mind him, just move,' shouted Martin at a Renault, which had stopped at a pedestrian crossing. Being market day, St Marie was packed, the traffic at a standstill.

'Stop moaning, will you?' Nikki smiled a surreptitious smile back at two Frenchmen walking past who had just wolf-whistled in admiration.

'Don't flatter yourself that you're anything special.' Martin had caught her out the corner of his eye. 'Frogs are always leching.'

She wished the other three were still in the car. 'God, Martin, you're a right misery guts today. What's got into you?'

'Nothing.' Before breakfast Nikki had moaned about the bedroom. Again. Then gone on about the backgammon. Again. Then, calling work, he'd only got a voicemail, so the lazy buggers were taking it easy while he was away. And his strategy had failed. Not only had that bitch Flora refused to budge, but she'd waltzed off with a thousand francs.

Nikki pulled round the rearview mirror to check her mink headband was in place. 'We must go in there.' She'd caught sight of a pair of pink suede gauntlets in a shop window. She was itching to use her credit card.

Martin blasted the horn again. 'Haven't you got enough clothes and stuff? It's not as if you wear a quarter of it.'

'So?'

'So, it's a waste.'

'So, it's none of your business. It's my money. At least I spend it on something worthwhile instead of stupid games of back-gammon. That reminds me, you owe me a thousand francs.'

'No one asked you to interfere. Jamie would've forgotten all about it, the state he's in. And even if he'd remembered, he'd never expect me to cough up.'

'Like he'd forget about the bedroom, I suppose?'

'Shut it, will you? On and on and on since last night. I was unlucky, that's all.'

'Monster stakes.' She imitated Sam. 'Well, next time you have to show off, show off with something that doesn't involve me. How could you? And so much for your great plan with Flora. Stubborn cow.'

He blasted the horn again. 'Come on.'

'Stop that, for God's sake. It's not as if we can move, is it?'

'Just shut up.'

They lapsed into an angry silence, the car thick with tension.

Both glowered out of their windows. The road and pavements were thronged with people, wrapped up against the chill like polar explorers.

A loud thud came from behind them.

'Pardon.' A French teenager had whacked a rear window with the back end of the skis over her shoulder as she had turned round. She winced, then called an apology.

'You stupid fucking bitch,' yelled Martin. The girl and her friends stared at him in shock.

'Martin,' protested Nikki.

'Next time you try and break my window, I'll break your fucking neck.'

'It was an accident,' hissed Nikki. 'You can't go round threatening people like that. God, what's got into you today?'

'The stupid cow should look where she's going. Come on.' He hooted at the Renault again.

'Just calm down. Please.' She couldn't take much more of this. 'Look, let's not bother with the shops. Go skiing instead?' Perhaps some exercise would get rid of his foul temper. She wished Munchkin was with them, he'd behave better in front of her.

'Make up your mind, will you?' They inched forward about a foot, then had to stop again. 'You're the one who wanted to go shopping. Flash the cash on stupid tat. Still, it's your money.'

'Too right it is.'

'And we all know where it came from, don't we?'

'Shut up.'

'Why? Whore. Can't take the truth. No you don't. You're staying here.' As she tried to yank open the door, he reached across and grabbed her wrist. 'Whore.'

'Let me go,' she screamed, twisting round, trying to break free. 'Let me go.' Passers-by were staring into the car. 'Let me go.' With her free hand, she managed to hit him round the head and pulled out a great chunk of hair.

'Ow, you bitch.'

Nikki fumbled with the handle, kicked open the door and jumped out. Slipping and sliding along the pavement, she disappeared into the crowd.

Jamie shuffled into the kitchen and found Pete wearing sunglasses, dropping Alka Seltzer into a glass.

'How many?' Pete held out the tube. 'Three?' His voice was croaky, his blond curls matted with flour.

Jamie nodded, downed the fizzy water in one and shivered. 'Yuk. Tea?'

Sam arrived, eyes half shut. 'Glad I'm not the only one suffering. Hurry up and boil,' he ordered the kettle.

'What happened to you lot after pool?' asked Jamie.

Pete took off his sunglasses, his eyes looked poached. 'Went to a club. Thought you'd be there.'

'Looked for you everywhere. Had to walk back. No taxis.'

'Walk? You're barmy.' Sam cleared his throat and spat into the sink. 'Should've come clubbing. Superbabes. Met a nice little one called Murielle, meeting her and her mate later. Pete got off with two, one at either end of the room. Luckily it was packed.'

'I did?' Pete grinned. 'So Flora's the only one who wasn't pleased to see me last night.'

'Don't.' Jamie groaned. 'I'm really in the doghouse. Again. In fact, this time I think she wants to get me put down.'

'It looks like it's already happened.' Sam's hands were shaking so much the milk missed the cups and splashed onto the counter. 'Shit, I've got to go back to bed. Catch you later.'

'Nice to have someone to nurse you at four in the morning,' said Pete wistfully. 'Was she cross?'

'Earlier? Grief city.' Jamie shuddered. 'Thank God I was still anaesthetised. Ski?'

'Ski.'

*   *   *

At Le Toit, Munchkin and Miranda skied off the lift, arcing round the side of the station where they waited for Anna.

While Munchkin yacked on about how Ant, one of her best friends was going cross-country skiing in Norway, Miranda traced the letter P in the snow with her pole. Then, appalled by what she'd done, quickly changed it to a B before scrubbing it out.

'Those boarders are terrifying,' said Munchkin, watching three of them gathering speed and heading off down the slope.

'Absolutely. Half of them don't know what they're doing, they white out all the time and they look so scruffy.'

'Over here, Johnny,' cried a voice.

Like a dog hearing a familiar whistle, Miranda swivelled round and saw two cropped haircuts showing off ears, collars and clean cut features. Must be Army. Nice.

Munchkin followed Miranda's gaze. 'Anna.' She was un-necessarily loud, hoping to attract the attention of the pair. *An Officer and a Gentleman* was one of her favourite films. If not quite in Richard Gere's league, the two were tall, fit and promising.

'Just a sec.' As Anna arrived, Miranda got out her piste map, playing for time. The pair were standing a few feet away, planning their route. She hoped they'd think she was lost and offer assistance.

Munchkin had whipped off her pink helmet and had a smile ready for when they looked in her direction.

The pair disappeared down the piste. 'They looked nice,' sighed Miranda.

'Um,' agreed Munchkin, equally disappointed. 'Your type, Anna?'

'Not really.'

A scarlet figure skied slowly past them and stopped, waiting for a fat, nervous-looking couple to catch up. Munchkin gave him a huge smile. Puzzled, he sketched one back, before shouting something encouraging in German.

'Munchkin. You're awful.' Miranda giggled. 'Trying to pick

up every man who goes past. Can't blame you though. Talk about bum on legs.'

'That's Stefan,' hissed Munchkin. 'You know. Flora's instructor.'

'You're joking.' Miranda gasped. 'Lucky Flora.' She peered round Anna's shoulder to have a gawp. 'Look at the body. Yum yum. No wonder she didn't want to share her lessons.'

'Looks kind of wild, doesn't he?' muttered Munchkin. 'Apparently he's arty farty. A sculptor or something.'

'I wouldn't mind him teaching me a thing or two,' said Miranda, admiring Stefan's profile as he disappeared from view. 'Full on gorgeous. Wakey, wakey.'

Feeling a nudge, Anna opened her eyes and blinked. She had turned her face up to the sun. The warmth and dazzle was blissful after the grey gloom of the English winter. 'Ready?'

They enjoyed their morning. Instead of having to keep up with the furious pace set by the men, they could travel at their own unmacho speed. They took frequent stops to admire the views across the valley to Les Diables or down into St Marie.

For Munchkin, the pressure of being left behind was off. Anna and Miranda were considerate and encouraging. She relaxed and as a result, skied far better. Her nerve, lost the day before, returned.

Rather than fixing her eyes on her ski tips, she was able to look round, hoping to see Stefan or the two Army officers.

Wearing huge Jackie Onassis-style sunglasses, Nikki went into a café. She headed for the darkest corner and sat with her back to the room. Not looking at the waiter, she whispered for a coffee.

Now what?

Despair rose in her. Here she was, in the middle of France, having thrown her lot in with someone she hardly knew. She had no home, no job and no income.

Now what?

Why had she ever told him?

Whore. Tart. Well, what *could* she put on her CV to cover the past 18 months? Chairman's PA, like Miranda? The hairband would look down her nose and sniff: 'PA? Rarely? Entre nous, tart.'

She was now feeling as bleak as she'd felt in the summer when it had all begun to pall. When the flat had become a prison, and the Mercedes a black maria and David Thone her jailer.

David Thone? Yes. Sir David Thone. That's right, Chairman of Thone Corp, field marshal of industry, the Prime Minister's golfing partner, Britain's leading businessman. Philanthropist, devout church-goer and devoted family man. Even Martin June, former footballing hero had been impressed when she'd finally admitted it. Gobsmacked, but impressed.

The first year was exciting. The novelty of the private jet and the chauffeur driven Daimler and the trips to Aspen made up for their 30–year age gap. Her flat, the Mercedes and her lavish pocket money blinded her to their eight stone weight difference. She could even put up with his funny ways in the sex department, spellbound by his confidences about the PM and his appearances on the telly.

For a year she believed he'd leave Marjory the Dreadnought, his do-gooding wife and she'd hit the jackpot as the second Lady Thone.

Fat chance.

Longing for a peerage, mindful of his shareholders, David Thone would never court a scandal. He was paranoid about the Press, and had impressed on her the need to be discreet.

She'd been discreet, all right. And how. No one knew. Not that there'd been many to tell. Apart from Aunt Patsy in Worthing, she'd had little contact with her family since leaving the grim council estate where she'd grown up. In London, she'd always drifted in and out of circles of people, abandoning those she'd met on the lowlier rungs as she'd climbed up the social ladder.

No one knew. Then she'd told Martin. A little over a week ago.

It had been like going to Confession, the pub a church, Martin her priest. She hadn't expected it, but he'd given her Absolution. She'd been waiting for him to be repulsed by the whole sordid business that was her life; to say Nikki, love, you're bad news, I'm off.

Instead he'd insisted she move in with him and come away skiing.

Was Martin now regretting his decision to play the white knight? Probably. How could she tell? She hardly knew him.

She'd met him six weeks ago in a wine bar round the corner from the flat. She was being pestered by a pair of prats. Martin had strode up. 'So, you've met the girlfriend? Champagne darling? Boys, hop it.'

They hadn't argued with him. Few would. The Hugo Boss suit couldn't disguise the brute strength. She was delighted when he asked if he could join her. Most men found her too intimidating to chat up. Those who did, sober, were usually supremely confident with a lot going for them. Martin had a lot going for him, she knew, when she realised who he was. She hadn't clicked at first. The face was familiar, but was slimmed down and lined compared with the one that had been so famous all those years ago.

She'd agreed to meet him for lunch. For the first time in ages, she'd had something to do other than idling away her mornings in the gym, afternoons in the shops and evenings waiting. She had someone to wear her beautiful clothes for.

They'd had lunch, then dinner, then another dinner, before she'd spent the night at his house in Wimbledon. By the end of the third week, she was staying with him almost every night. David Thone was in the Far East.

She thought he'd accepted her story that he couldn't visit the flat until the builders had moved out, and it was better to contact her through her answering service. No, she didn't have a mobile, you didn't know who was listening in. Her home phone? Playing up, builders' fault. Job? Between them. Mercedes? An aunt had left her some money.

She thought he'd swallowed the lot. 'Just promise me you're not married and you don't have a live-in boyfriend with a meat cleaver, who's going to get heavy.' For weeks, he seemed content enough.

She'd managed to stall him, until that Monday night. Just over a week ago.

They'd met in a pub of all places. In Soho. She'd always hated pubs. It was packed with office workers. Somehow, they'd managed to get a corner table. Martin apologised for the scrum, but said that Jack had insisted on meeting him there. By the bar, a group of salesmen were singing 'Silent Night'.

A short guy with a greasy little blond ponytail had appeared out of nowhere. He was wearing a black leather coat which reached almost down to his ankles. 'Hello Mart. Good to see you man. You must be the lovely Nicola. Hasn't old Mart done well for himself? Jack Mancini.'

He had looked her slowly up and down with his huge cold turquoise eyes. She'd immediately felt uncomfortable, wondering if he were trying to guess the colour of her knickers.

As he was grabbing a chair, his pager bleeped. 'Fuck it.' He'd read the message and frowned. 'Bloody lawyers, quibble, quibble, quibble.'

Martin had offered him his mobile.

'Nah, it can wait. Listen man, I've got to shoot off soonish, so tell me your news.' Jack had turned to her. 'Go and get some drinks, darling. Scotch for me. Straight. Make mine a double double, it's been a long day.' He'd handed her £50 from a wad of notes and told her to get a receipt.

Martin had leapt up, saying he'd go, but Jack had insisted that Nicola here was closer to the bar. 'Don't mind, do you, sweetheart? We've got some catching up to do.'

She'd asked herself why Martin was so in awe of this grubby

rat-featured midget. Pushing her way to the bar, she was worried that someone would spill beer over her red jacket, but more worried about Jack. He smiled in a way which hinted he knew all her secrets. She'd stood in the crush, trying to remember what he did for a living. Pornographer? Child molester? Then she knew.

She'd sat in silence while Jack related some story about a lord, a dinner party and some botty basher. Jack had passed out head first into the roast tatties because of some dodgy sulphate. 'I came to just as his earlship was about to give me the kiss of life. Frightful business. Then we had to sit through all these vids, disgusting, before his nibs got down to business. Heard him out, saw the colour of his money, made our excuses and left. Job done. Government minister in rent boy shocker, blah, blah blah. Read it yesterday, did you? He's resigning Wednesday, according to my sources.'

She'd made the mistake of blurting out: 'I thought these stories were all made up.'

Jack had stared at her with those cold eyes. 'Did you? Well, they're not. I work fucking hard.' He'd pretended to smile, showing off greenish teeth. 'Tell me, what line are you in?'

Martin had said something about her being a lady of leisure just at the moment.

'Isn't that nice? Private means, eh? Lucky lady. I can't see you driving that Mercedes of yours down to sign on. Is there a dole office in Knightsbridge?'

At that moment she could've murdered Martin for opening his big mouth about her business. Beating a retreat, saying he'd get some more drinks, Martin had urged Jack to tell her about Klosters and that time he was chasing the royals. She'd been left to fend for herself.

'Nice guy, Mart. Wouldn't want anyone to upset him. Lovely jacket, Nicola. Armani. Scarlet, like all the best women. What does your old man do?' She'd nearly jumped out of her skin. 'Old man, husband.' Then he'd grabbed her left hand and examined it. 'No, you're not married, are you? My suspicious mind.'

The green teeth were bared again. 'Can I tell you something, just between ourselves?' He'd leant forward, those cold, weird eyes boring into her. 'You don't strike me as a private means sort of person. Too well dressed, wrong sort of car, wrong address, you don't smoke Camels and you brush your hair. I know about these things. Milly, the girlfriend, is on the trustafarian side, you see.'

He'd drained his glass and winked at her. In the background, the salesmen were singing 'Oh Come All Ye Faithful'. 'Apt, eh? You're a woman of intrigue and mystery, Nicola. I like that. Martin does too. He's very excited about your answering service. So am I. But I'm a teensy weensy bit more curious than dear old Matt. If I were a betting man, which I am, I'd say you have, how shall I put it? A benefactor. Or benefactors. Careful, don't spill your drink, mineral water's a terrible price these days.'

She'd half stood up, but he'd pushed her back in her seat. He waved at Martin, before turning back to her. 'Dear old Mart. Such an innocent. Great story that, national hero cut down in his prime. History now, eh? Not cheap to run, are you? That handbag costs almost a grand. So this benefactor, if there's only the one, must be rolling in it. I wonder what else he is?

'I love a puzzle. So does my editor. We pay an awful lot if people ever want to solve little riddles for us.' Jack had leant back and smiled. 'Just a thought. Thanks, man.' He'd stood up, taken the glass of whisky from Martin and swallowed it in one. 'Seasons greetings and all that. Nice to meet you, Nicola. Enjoyed our little chat. Better be off. Got to go and see a man about some drugs.'

While Martin saw Jack into a cab, she'd been left with her panic. Her first impulse was to run, but there was nowhere to go. When Martin came back saying Jack was very perceptive, had her spot on, she'd felt sick. 'Don't look so worried. All he said was that you're as sweet as you're beautiful. What's wrong?'

For the next few minutes she'd denied there was anything wrong, then the button that she was twisting in her nervousness, came off her jacket. She'd told Martin she had to stop seeing him.

'Why?'

'Because . . .' She was almost crying.

He'd laid his hand on hers. His voice was gentle. 'Who is he? Nikki, love, I'm not stupid. All this business with the builders and the phone. Isn't it time you told me what the hell is going on?'

And so she had told him.

After she finished, Martin had just sat there in silence. The pub was emptying. 'You've got to get out. Come and stay with me.' She'd needed persuading he was serious, that he still wanted to be with her. 'I do. Trust me.'

The next day, as she was packing up her stuff, he'd called to ask her to go skiing. Preoccupied, she'd said yes without thinking.

Her coffee was stone cold. The holiday was a huge mistake. She was having to watch herself every time she opened her mouth. These weren't her sort of people, too normal, too straight. God knows how they'd react if they knew the truth. Why hadn't Martin played it low key, instead of going on about modelling and the Mercedes?

He had a fixation about that car. After they'd loaded her stuff into the Range Rover, he'd been put out when she climbed into the passenger seat. 'What about the Mercedes?' What about it? An hour before she'd sent the keys to the car and the flat back to David Thone.

The waiter took away her coffee cup. Now what? If Martin changed his mind about her, then what? Was she vulnerable. Homeless, jobless. She had quite a bit put by, but not enough to finance her lifestyle for very long. It would be back to bedsits and temping.

In many ways, Martin was ideal. She might even allow herself to fall for him. He had money, looks and a strong will. She'd always wanted to marry an old-fashioned millionaire. Even on the course at the local tech all those years ago, she'd known secretarial work wasn't for her. She'd known that she'd make a better career out of her looks than in any office. The Wallets had always gone for her, picking up her bills and giving her presents. Martin was a Wallet, but one that suited her down to the ground.

If only she had some serious money of her own. A girl needed security.

'Nikki. There you are. Thank God. I've been searching the whole village.'

'Hello, Martin.'

Munchkin juddered to a snowplough stop at the end of a path which went alongside a wood. 'I wish I could ski as well as you.'

'Just practice, isn't it?' Anna breathed deeply and sniffed. 'Pine. Wonderful smell . . . Watch out.' She glared at a snowboarder, Walkman clamped to his ears who had brushed within feet of them.

'Turd,' yelled Miranda, then smiled sheepishly. 'Horrible little oik. Anyone?' She held out some lipsalve.

Anna shared out a bar of chocolate between them.

'Delicious,' said Munchkin. 'Straight to the hips, but delicious.'

'Sex substitute,' said Anna.

'Nine of ten times, I'd rather have a Toblerone,' said Munchkin gloomily.

'Surely not,' said Miranda. 'Kit Kat, everytime.'

They pressed on, skiing one piste before taking a lift to another. The sun climbed higher in the cloudless sky. Exhilarated, they delighted in the cold, clean air and the warm sun on their faces. Although they only covered the wrinklies' runs, Miranda was content to take it easy for Munchkin's sake.

They headed towards La Croix. It was suddenly much busier. Skiers flew past in all directions. The snow was thinner, in some places reduced to little more than a thin crust of ice. Getting tired, Munchkin fell several times. Her newly-won confidence was beginning to evaporate. She slowly made her way to the lift station where the other two were waiting.

'That final bit was horrid,' sympathised Miranda.

'If you two want to go on, do. Please,' said Munchkin. The snow was even worse on Les Pins. 'I'll have a coffee and meet you up at La Toit later. I know it's skiving, but I don't want to overdo it.'

'Skiving? Rubbish. You're on holiday,' said Anna. 'Have a nice doss on the balcony and we'll see you up there in an hour or so.'

Munchkin dumped her skis in the rack and clomped up the stairs to the Savoie's first floor balcony. It was too early for the lunchtime rush and there were few people about. She settled down on a lounger and ordered some coffee. The sun beat down and she felt wonderfully drowsy and relaxed.

Munchkin missed Flora, who was sitting at a slope-side table, alternatively engrossed in Dorothy Parker or despairing over the Jumbo crossword she'd torn out of *The Times*. A cup of hot chocolate and a packet of Marlboro were at her elbow.

Unable to face hiking around the crowded streets with her skis and in her skiboots, Flora had changed her mind and headed straight for the lift and La Croix. Sucking the top of her biro, she tried to work out 48 down. Isolation. Something isolation. What? Solitary? No. Splendid. Splendid isolation. It was exactly how she'd enjoyed wiling away the last hour. Completely alone.

Whenever she thought of Jamie, anger boiled up inside her. How could he get so drunk, then wake her up to nurse him, only to play stupid games with flour? He'd promised her he'd never touch cocaine again, which only scrambled his reactions to booze. If £100 worth hadn't been snorted up his nose, he'd have realised he was way over the limit and in no state to drive the night he'd lost his licence. Was he arrogant or simply stupid to get Class A drugs mailed to him?

They were getting married in April, it was only weeks away. They would be together until death did they part. The rest of her life . . . Oh God. Flora felt panic rising in her. Marriage was one of the biggest decisions anyone would ever make. Had she got it right?

Her life had turned topsy-turvy and revolved around him ever since that first Sunday of spring when he'd turned up at the cottage. He was spending the weekend with his godfather, the local squire Bill Blest, who was her landlord. Jamie was taking two aged black labradors for a walk. After introducing himself, he'd asked her if she'd like to come to church. She must, she'd protect him from the rector, who was always trying to make a pass at him. Flora, who never went to church except for weddings, found herself saying yes to the handsome stranger in the battered tweed jacket.

Jamie had tried to sneak the dogs in too, much to the congregation's disapproval.

'All God's creatures,' he'd told the church warden, before tying them up outside. As the first hymn was sung, the dogs could be heard howling in chorus, provoking giggles from her which had lasted throughout the sermon. Afterwards, Jamie had taken her to the village pub and ordered Bloody Marys, before insisting that she must come to lunch at the Blests.

She had gone reluctantly and it had been a disaster. Lady Blest had been icily furious and clearly unhappy by Jamie's lateness and Flora's unexpected arrival. Not only had he kept everyone waiting, but the cruise-liner-long dining table had to be re-laid. Flora had escaped as early as possible, convinced that she was going to be househunting yet again.

Jamie had laughed off her anxiety. He had driven down from London the following evening and taken her out to dinner. Used to arty and stony-broke boyfriends, Flora had been unprepared for the enchantment of being spoilt. As spring turned to summer, the cottage was full of flowers and bottles of champagne. Like the Marx brothers, Jamie gave her days at the races and nights at the opera. He'd unlocked the door to a magical, sunlit world, infecting her with his *joie de vivre*.

Thinking of Jamie, Flora unfailingly thought of those hot, sunny days and ice cold Pimms, of picnics and polo and parties and punting. Of laughing as they drove along country lanes in his Austin Healey, wildflowers lacing the hedgerows and ditches. Of stopping to make love in fields.

It had taken Flora a few months to believe that he was really interested in her. She'd been surprised. Jem had been stunned. 'How can you of all people land him? Brilliant H M.' Husband Material. At the time Flora had laughed it off, but gradually it dawned on her that Jamie might want to get married. When he produced a ring flashing with diamonds and proposed to her on her birthday in October after the six most joyous months of her life, she'd accepted.

When she saw the announcement of their engagement printed in the paper, she had suddenly been hit by the enormity of her decision. She loved Jamie but did she know him well enough to spend forever with him? Weekends and trips away and holidays together were hardly the same thing as the daily domestic grind. Her unease that frosty morning was the same she'd felt briefly en route to the pub from the church when he'd told her he worked at Rosehagens.

Had she got it right? Flora stared at the piste, now crowded with skiers. Of course, she had. She loved Jamie, he was wonderful. Everyone said so. He was good-looking, charming, out-going and bright. He was a good sportsman, with a brilliant job and a wonderful future. And he was rich.

But. But. But. The Jamie who thought life was a non-stop party was also the Jamie who ended up in police cells, who was banned from driving. The Jamie who was so self-assured because of his background and education, was also so arrogant that he thought himself above the law. The Jamie who was a brilliant skier, ended up taking her on skiing holidays with people like Martin. The Jamie who she was told was such an eligible catch was the Jamie who knew it too.

As Jamie's wife, she'd never have to worry about money again. He earned a fortune and there was his income from all those mysterious trusts and the mortgage-free house in Chelsea. The house he'd given her carte blanche to redecorate. How much had she allowed herself to be remodelled by him ever since he had turned up at the cottage that first Sunday of spring?

Why had Jamie chosen her? Had she just happened to be with him at the time he decided it was time to settle down? Had Jamie thought, Flora will do, the raw material is there, she's young enough, she'll learn? Get her into some decent clothes and onto that cooking course. Was Jamie thinking that Flora will fit in with me and whatever I want to do? She'll give up her job and move to London for me. She'll smarten up for me and adopt my attitudes, parrot what I say. Was Jamie thinking, I can even make Flora go skiing, so she'll come into line in every other way? Was Jamie thinking that Julius Rosehagen might never have set eyes on his distant cousin, but perhaps one day things might change? Getting married to anyone will advance my career, it reflects gravitas, but marrying Flora Rosehagen might one day reap huge rewards. Was Jamie thinking, I can lead a Boy's Own life with sex on tap?

Lighting another cigarette, Flora decided she must talk to Jamie so he could put her mind at rest. But how could they talk in the chalet? Everytime she walked in there she felt tense, but after her exchange with Nikki and Martin earlier, things would be even worse. Perhaps she should persuade Jamie to swap rooms.

Someone was standing very close, blocking out her sun. Couldn't she be left in peace? Irritated, she glanced up.

'Hello.' She broke into a huge smile.

'Can I join you?'

'Of course,' she put aside the crossword.

Suddenly, waitresses seemed to be swarming to the table. Stefan ordered two hot chocolates. 'So, did you dream your beautiful dreams of perfect parallel turns?' He smiled his slow, lazy smile. 'How's everyone in the chalet?'

'Don't ask. How were your Germans?'

'Nervous, slow, complaining all the time.'

'Like me then.'

He laughed. 'You're not fat and fifty. They wanted to finish early. *Gott sei Dank.*'

'Do you really want to teach skiing?'

Stefan looked at her sharply. 'You're asking me what I've been asking myself the past three weeks.'

'Why are you doing it?'

'Do you really want to know?' She nodded. He started to explain that it had seemed a good idea back in Paris. He'd wanted to escape since October when a show of his had been slated by the critics. Since then, he'd suffered a crisis of confidence and his funds were dwindling into non-existence. Having fled Paris, he wished he were back there. 'Marie-France says I should confront my demons, instead of trying to run away from them.'

'A friend of mine had a similar crisis. Block. He ran. Got cured,' said Flora.

'And he's a sculptor too?' Stefan sounded sceptical.

'An artist. My former tutor at Art College. In fact, my only tutor. After seeing his work, I realised I could never compete. I changed course. Did Art History instead. He hated teaching too.'

'Not much of a teacher if he couldn't encourage you,' said Stefan.

'No. But a brilliant artist.' Flora smiled, looking at her frayed bracelet.

'Really?' Stefan sounded even more doubtful. 'Successful?'

'Getting there. His last show sold out. Fred Quince.'

'Fred Quince?' Stefan looked stunned. 'He had a show in Paris in the spring.'

'You saw it? Liked it? Loved it? Really?' Flora was delighted.

From that moment, they talked and talked, pausing only to light their cigarettes, oblivious to the bustle and chatter around them, not hearing the whoosh of skis or the occasional cry as someone took a tumble on the piste.

He told her about his work in steel and glass, how he'd won countless prizes, had been commissioned but the work had dried up as his self-doubt had grown. She told him about her job, the cottage and how she'd met Jamie.

'And you'll get married and live happily ever after,' said Stefan.

'Of course.'

Stefan frowned. 'Where's he now?'

She looked up at the tree-lined piste stretching up into the distance. 'Skiing somewhere, I guess.' She began to doodle on her crossword.

'You guess?' asked Stefan quietly.

'Jamie loves skiing.' She shrugged.

'You're sure about getting married?'

'Of course. I'm pissed off with him right now for being such a twit last night and for bringing me on this holiday, that's all. We'll be fine when we get home.' Not wanting to pursue the subject, Flora abruptly turned away. The Savoie was packed, all the tables were now taken. Had an hour really passed? She'd been so wrapped up in talking to Stefan she hadn't noticed.

'Lunch? We'd better order. Stefan?' He was leaning across the table. Why was he staring at her? Growing flustered under his scrutiny, she tried to think of something to say to break the silence. 'Jamie made me ski down Les Pins yesterday it was so horrible I forgot everything you'd taught me I only managed to snowplough when I was actually on my feet which wasn't very often . . .' She knew she was gabbling and that she was going from pink to scarlet to puce as she became more self-conscious. '. . . And then I had to walk . . .' her voice trailed off. Seconds ticked past and she couldn't take her eyes from his. 'Stefan, didn't anyone ever tell you it was rude to stare?'

'Yes.' He smiled his slow, lazy smile, his eyes still fixed on hers. 'Didn't anyone ever tell you the same thing, Flora?'

'Yes.' Greengages, definitely. It was like a grown-up version of flinch, the game she'd played as a small child with her friends to see who would be the first to blink. But none of her friends had ever been so spellbinding. 'Are you trying to hypnotise me?'

'I don't think so. Are you trying to hypnotise me?'

'I don't think so. Stop it,' whispered Flora.

'I can't. You stop first.'

'*Vous mangez?*' demanded the waitress for the third time, just as Flora was wondering how raw his stubble would feel. Saved by the mam'zelle. She gave a start of alarm and ordered herself to banish all such speculation from her mind.

On the Savoie's terrace, Munchkin shook herself out of her doze and sat up in panic. Despite the rush and chatter around her, she had drifted off in the sun. It was past one. She'd better hurry or she'd miss Miranda and Anna up at La Toit.

'*Moment,*' cried a waitress buckling under the weight of a tray of drinks, when Munchkin asked if she could pay. The Savoie was packed, but at least there wasn't a queue for the chairlift. Would she able to find her skis among the dozens lying propped up against the rack?

She peered down, trying to see them. In the throng sitting around the tables below, her eye was caught by a scarlet jacket and a mass of black hair in a ponytail. Her spirits soared. Was he heartbreaking. Such a beautiful profile with that straight nose and those cheekbones. And he was alone. What an opportunity. She'd introduce herself again and ask about lessons.

Congratulating herself on her good fortune, Munchkin looked round for a waitress. 'Come on,' she murmured impatiently.

Suddenly there was a cheering-up glut of fanciable men about. Martin and Jamie were bagged, unfortunately, but there was Pete, who'd been so sweet the night before. Going flying with him was a huge something to look forward to. Miranda wouldn't go, she'd be off with Charlie. And now, sitting only yards away was the panther-like Stefan. Pete and Stefan. A delicious contrast. It was like opening a box of chocolate truffles and trying to decide which one to have first.

The waitress came back, only to complain she didn't have enough change and then disappeared again. Checking to make sure Stefan hadn't moved, Munchkin peered down. Someone had joined him. Her spirits plummeted. And that someone, she realised, was Flora.

Puzzled, Munchkin stared. A relaxed, happy Flora, whose smile for once seemed genuine. A Flora whose stiff, wary reserve had melted away. A giggling Flora, who was trying to sneak Stefan's chips, while he laughed and held his plate out of her reach. A carefree Flora, who for once looked as if she were having a good time.

'Ow.' Flora screamed. The people around her turned to look. Stefan's knife had cut into the back of her hand.

Craning her neck to see what was going on, Munchkin pulled a face. How typical of her to make a fuss. He probably hadn't even drawn blood. Flora was sucking her hand, in between saying something to a clearly contrite Stefan. She was shaking her head, he was being insistent about something.

Munchkin watched Stefan reach across and gently take hold of Flora's wrist. Finally, she relaxed her arm and surrendered to his grasp. Frowning, he dipped his napkin into his water glass, then dabbed at the cut one-handed. Despite Munchkin's silent urging from the balcony, his other didn't release Flora's. Instead he turned it one way and then the other, studying it. Munchkin told herself that he was a sculptor and Flora had beautiful hands. Why didn't he let her go? What was he saying as he stared at her so intensely? Munchkin wished she could lipread. Whatever the words were, Flora seemed spellbound, unable to tear her eyes from his, even when someone knocked against her chair.

Flora couldn't be after Stefan, could she? No. Ridiculous. She was getting married to Jamie any minute now. Surely Stefan couldn't be after Flora? Never. Not in a million years. But something strange was going on.

The waitress returned with the change. Munchkin didn't bother to check it as she peered down. They were continuing to stare at one another, transfixed, lost in their own world. His hand was still round hers. He began to stroke each of her fingers one by one, smiling a reply to her protests. Flora fell silent, clearly mesmerised by him. And it was becoming dismayingly apparent to Munchkin that Stefan might be equally entranced by her.

Smiling his slow, lazy smile, Stefan said something, then raised Flora's hand to his mouth. He seemed to bite into her fingers, then as Flora tried to snatch her hand back, his grip tightened. Munchkin's jaw dropped in disbelief as she watched him kiss each of Flora's fingertips. She saw Flora shiver, briefly close her eyes and entwine her fingers in his. The diamonds in her engagement ring glittered in the sunshine.

What were they saying now? From their expressions, Munchkin guessed it had nothing to do with the finer points of snowplough turns.

Another instructor arrived, slapped Stefan on the back and the hands broke apart as if they were scalding each other. Flora's face was suddenly instructor-jacket red.

Munchkin sat back, relishing Flora's discomfort. There was no mistaking what was going on there, and in full public view. No wonder Flora hadn't wanted to share her lessons.

'Thank God I'm on the windward side,' said Sam. Giles was throwing up over the side of the chairlift. 'Dear oh dear.' He grimaced. 'Try and aim for the trees and not the people.'

Giles sank back, closed his eyes and wiped his mouth with a tissue. 'I think that's finally it.'

'You look in need of a drink.'

'Don't,' groaned Giles.

'A couple of Bloody Marys and a monster fry-up dripping in grease.'

'Piss off.' The swinging chairlift was making Giles feel queasy again.

'Get it together this afternoon. We're meeting Murielle and her mate, remember.'

'Who's Murielle?'

'The babe in the club.'

Giles tried to remember. 'She wasn't the one with the face like a pepperoni pizza?'

'That was the mate.'

'Thanks. I get lumbered with her.'

'Only joking. Anyway, they're both really nice.' He sighed. 'If they bother turning up. Just make sure you get hold of some mints.'

Bursting to pass on the incredible news, Munchkin scampered off the lift up at La Toit and sprinted through Café Neige. Infuriatingly, it had to keep. Jamie and Pete were there, gobbling up sausages smothered in tomato ketchup.

'Hello. How was the Savoie?' asked Miranda. Under the blue mascara, her eyes were a tad glazed. Pete had persuaded her to try a hot chocolate laced with cognac on top of two *vins chauds*. 'Not too lonely?'

'No. Had a nice time people-watching.' Munchkin sat down on the bench next to Anna and Jamie.

'Was Flora there?' Jamie peeled back his plaster and studied his hand with bloodshot eyes. 'Ouch.'

'Didn't see her,' said Munchkin warily. 'Heavy night?'

'Obese,' sighed Pete. 'Didn't wake you up as well, did we?

Already been read the riot act by these two. We've got to go and grovel to the twins. I told Miranda to give me a good spanking but she refused.'

'I remember we tried to be very quiet,' pleaded Jamie.

'What good boys you are,' said Anna dryly. 'Gold stars? A medal?'

'The George Cross after I've faced Flora.' He was gloomy.

'Courage beyond the call of duty,' sympathised Pete. 'Rather you than me.' He winked at Miranda. 'Another? Go on . . .'

'Well . . .' She wished she'd brought some powder, her cheeks were burning from the booze. Sweet Pete. He'd insisted on paying for lunch to make up for disturbing her sleep. Admittedly he'd paid for Anna's too. But with quite as much solicitude? She must think of a way of getting him on his own.

'Must get some postcards,' said Anna, noticing a couple at the next table writing theirs.

'Oh God. Granny. Mustn't forget this time.' Jamie sighed. 'By the way Miranda, you must give me Charlie's numbers sometime. Nice to get in touch after all these years.'

'Of course.'

'We must all meet up when we get back. Have dinner or something.'

'That would be lovely. He's away quite a bit over the next few months.'

'Poor Miranda,' clucked Munchkin. 'Still, absence makes the heart grow fonder.' She was glad Pete was being given a reminder that Miranda was attached. 'Now, when are we going flying?' Pete was bemused. 'Remember, last night, you promised . . .'

Irritated, Miranda knew that the spell between her and Pete was broken as Munchkin hijacked the conversation. Munchkin's advice to Pete to rub lemon juice into his hair to make it blonder, was followed by a vigorous protest that she didn't dye her own, then a casual inquiry if Miranda did.

Miranda managed a fast conversational tack to skiing off-piste.

Munchkin sat in silence as Pete and Miranda prattled away. Off piste? She could barely manage on piste. Why hadn't she booked herself into ski school first thing?

Finishing an ice-cream, Jamie took out his map. He felt almost restored after the food, a quick toot and five Pepsis. He and Pete would take the cable car and then join the drag-lift to La Chevre, one of the highest points in the area. However, suddenly it seemed that Pete might have other plans. Miranda was offering to race him down to La Croix, an offer he was laughing at.

'Frightened you'll lose?' Miranda smiled. 'Thought you Aussie men were men.'

'You're on. How much?'

'Say, 100 francs?'

'No. Let's say I name my price when I win.' Pete grinned wickedly. 'Not money. Something else . . .'

He didn't mean . . . She blushed. While congratulating herself at her successful ploy to get him on his own, she had an uneasy feeling that things were moving too fast. 'What?'

'You can name yours if you win. Have we a deal?'

They shook hands. He hoped she could iron.

While Stefan finished his lunch and talked in French to his colleague, Flora sat in bemused silence. They collected their skis from the rack and he told her they'd take the button lift in the direction of La Bête. As she followed him across the piste, she was lost in thought. Nothing much had happened. They'd just been fooling around, Stefan telling her that someone would bite off her finger for her engagement ring. Nothing to be taken too seriously, surely?

But. But. But. A line had been crossed. She'd gone further than was wise. How could she explain holding hands and staring into the eyes of a beautiful stranger? Get out of that. Anyone could have seen her. At least Miranda and co were safely up at La Toit. Supposing Jamie had been watching? She'd been so engrossed, so carried away, would she have known he was here? She hadn't thought about him once. He could've been sitting at the next table. Shit.

Appalled by her own imprudence, Flora skied on autopilot before skidding to a halt beside Stefan at the lift. He was bound to flirt with all his female pupils, it came with the job. Even if he knew of Fred Quince, this sculptor business was probably bullshit. If he were that good, he wouldn't be in St Marie, would he? It was bullshit and she'd been dumb enough to fall for it. How had she allowed herself to be swept away, even for a few moments, by a bit of flattery? Dumb.

'And?' Her voice was cold, her expression colder, she refused to meet his eyes. Mentally she was shutting him out as if she'd built a wall of ice around herself.

'And. We go up. You know what to do?' He sounded businesslike.

She nodded, scowling at the lift's path stretching up the mountainside. Queue, wait for the lift operator to hand over the metal button welded to a long metal pole which was attached to the wire cables. When the cable was taut, it would pull her forward. Sit on the button and hang onto the pole.

'I'll be behind you,' said Stefan. 'Flex your knees.'

All Flora's concentration was needed to hold onto the pole and keep her skis in the deep parallel tracks made by earlier skiers. The cable, linked to a pulley about thirty feet overhead, was meant to be at 45 degrees. Instead it kept slackening off and she was slowed almost to a standstill. Then there would be an alarming burst of speed and she'd be jolted forward, her arms yanked out of their sockets. Her backside was becoming frozen solid from the metal button and the front of her thighs numb from bending her knees.

After an interminable quarter of an hour, she finally saw the wooden hut where the operator sheltered. Thank God, the end was finally in sight. Before she realised what was happening, her skis took her over a series of bumps on the approach. She was shaken as if she were in a liquidizer and her left ski crossed over the right. She fought to regain control of them and of her balance as she was pulled alongside the hut.

'Let go,' yelled the operator.

Flora let go. The button shot high above her head, while her skis battled with one another at her feet. She found herself hurtling down the exit slope like a pinball hit by a flipper, before she crashed into a haybale.

She swore loudly. 'It's not funny,' she raged at Stefan standing above her holding her poles and hat which should have had a big D for Dunce on it.

Still grinning, he pulled her up onto her feet. She brushed away the snow on her ski pants. 'Flora, today I'm going to work you hard. Stem turns, side stepping and stopping, which you need to practise. So concentrate. And. And no complaining. *Allez.*' He skated off, zipping up his jacket.

As she scrambled after him, Flora pulled a face and stuck out her tongue at his back. Other skiers raced past her.

Knees bent, weight on the lower ski, head up, arms relaxed, shoulders turned downhill, she repeated to herself. It would never come automatically, why was she bothering? She hated skiing and she was far too old and clumsy to learn now. It was easy for children, who were closer to the ground and as supple as Bendy Toys. They didn't worry about looking silly and un-dignified. Why hadn't she stuck to drinking hot chocolate on a balcony or, far better, margaritas on a beach?

She followed him down the piste, traversing and turning, traversing and turning. After ten minutes he stopped, watching her as she came towards him. Instead of a snowplough, she tried to copy him by keeping her skis parallel, and bending her knees still further before turning uphill. She felt the back of her skis slide across the snow and then stop.

Stefan smiled. 'Very good. Top of the class.'

She beamed in delight. She'd actually done a proper stop. Well, almost. No more soppy snowploughs . . .

'Are you listening?' He sounded irritated.

'Yes. You want me to sideslip. I can't see why. I can do it. Easy peasy.' She was standing sideways to the slope, with her weight on the inside edge of her skis. She flattened them down and slid away from him. 'Bye . . .'

The smile was wiped off her face as she gathered speed, lost control and landed on the snow with a thump.

Stefan laughed. 'Hubris followed by nemesis.'

'There's no need to gloat.' Flora tried to struggle back up but her skis kept on sliding away beneath her. She felt like a clown in a circus. Another instructor being followed by three supercilious children skied past. They all looked at her smugly. The instructor called out something to Stefan, who laughed again.

'You're going to learn to ski. And learn to listen,' said Stefan, when she was finally vertical.

Slow down, Jamie told himself. Ease off the throttle.

The run from La Chevre would've been challenging if he were on his best form, but after the excesses of the previous night, it was scary. He was uncoordinated, his reactions numbed and not being helped by the intense cold on the north-facing slope.

His skis slicing through the thick snow felt about a metre too long, and the gradient was getting steeper by the second.

He was utterly alone. A shiver of fear ran through him. There was no one, just him. A tiny blue speck on the side of this vast mountain. He was filled with longing to see other people. Above all, he wanted to see Flora. His beautiful wife.

Sam nudged Giles as a peroxide blonde sauntered past their table, the roots of her hair as black as her tight plastic trousers. 'Bow wow wow wow wow.' He swivelled round following her progress, his tongue hanging out. 'I love you. Come back.'

Anna sighed.

'Where was I?' Giles was put out. 'The Party must keep its nerve. The ordinary voter won't stick in-fighting.'

'Put a sock in it,' yawned Sam. 'We ought to get some skiing in. And don't forget the mints for the babes.'

'Oh. What babes?' asked Munchkin.

Sam shrugged. 'Babes from the club last night. Meeting us later.'

'Have fun.' Great. Sam and Giles pairing off with some babes. Two couples in the chalet already. And then Miranda zooming off with Pete. And Miranda seeming to hint that she was interested in a bit more than Pete's prowess on black runs, even if she were almost engaged.

For a split second, Munchkin was tempted to divulge the intriguing scene she had witnessed from the balcony. No, girls' talk. The men would blab and it would get straight back to Jamie, who'd probably kill the messenger. It could keep.

For once, Sam was glad that Giles was so nit-picking about the bill. His funds were getting so low, he'd only had a Pepsi.

'Oh Martin, they're gorgeous.' Nikki smiled in rapture and kissed him on the cheek. 'My turn.' In exchange for the most expensive pair of skis in the shop, she bought him a pair of boots. And then some for herself. If they were going to Gstaad in March as he promised, she needed her own equipment.

Peace had been restored and there was a new closeness between them. They'd spent the remainder of the morning going around the shops where Nikki's expensive chic assured them of a warm welcome. She bought the pink gauntlets and then some in emerald. She longed to persuade Martin to get out of that yukky suit and into some new skiing clothes but hadn't liked to push things too far.

After ambling round the town, they'd shared a pizza in a restaurant near the square. On their way to the chairlift, Nikki slipped her arm through his. Her new skis, slung over his shoulder were matt black and a perfect match for her Ralph Lauren.

'Thank you lover,' Martin stopped and squeezed her. 'These boots are like slippers.' As she nuzzled closer, lust swept through him. 'Let's go back to the chalet.'

'No, later,' she giggled. 'Ski first.'

They were across the road from the lift station. Scores of people were waiting. He frowned. 'What's up? Not usually this bad.'

The lift had been stopped for almost fifteen minutes. No one knew why. Those in the queue were growing restless, fed up with being kept hanging around in the cold.

'Never happen in Aspen.' Nikki pouted.

Some of Martin's good humour began to evaporate.

At the head of the queue, people were demanding when or if the lift would ever start. The operator merely shrugged in reply. Some were giving up and angrily stomping off.

'I hate waiting,' said Martin. 'Let's go.'

As the lift machinery suddenly clattered into action, cheers broke out. The crowd began shuffling forward as best they could on the ice, trying not to jostle or push one another too much as they moved towards the turnstile.

Martin and Nikki squeezed ahead of an elderly French couple. The wife almost overbalanced. Two angel-faced Italian children managed to wriggle themselves through the scrum and take their places eight couples ahead of Martin, who swore at them. A hefty German, breathless and sweating from skiing down Les Pins, skidded to a halt beside them. After weighing up his chances, he reluctantly made his way to the back.

Martin, who'd been watching him, relaxed. 'Come on Nikki.' He inched forward, his skis wide apart, making sure that no one would get in front of him.

'I'm stuck,' she snapped. The elderly Frenchman's ski was on the back of hers. 'Get off can't you?'

'*Pardon.*' He lifted his ski and smiled in apology.

She slid forward to Martin, who put a protective arm around her shoulders. With people pressing all around her, she was starting to feel claustrophobic. Thankfully, they'd almost reached the point where they could start filing into the two lanes. 'They've got queue marshals in Aspen.' She tried to inch forward, but once again her precious new skis were trapped under the Frenchman's. 'He'll scratch them,' she squawked. 'Get off. Leave me alone, can't you?'

Martin turned round and glared at the Frenchman. 'You heard the lady, buster, now back off.'

'*Pardon, mais . . .*'

'Never mind pardon. Just get off her skis.'

Bouffant grey hair under the hood of her cherry suit, the wife bristled with indignation at Martin's belligerence. '*C'est pas . . .*'

Distracted by the couple, Martin didn't realise that the people ahead of him were moving forward. A snowboarder in his late teens, who had just finished scooting down Les Pins, saw the gap and darted into it.

'Oi, you. You.' Martin prodded the boarder's leg with his ski pole. 'Yes, you. Where are you going?'

'Up the lift.' The boarder was Australian and wore a scarf tied pirate style round his lanky shoulder-length hair.

'No you're not. Not in front of me. Back.' The boarder shrugged and resolutely stared ahead. 'Now. Are you deaf? Get back.' The boarder ignored him. 'Back.' Martin tried to elbow him aside.

'Piss off.' The boarder stood his ground.

'Back.' Martin gave a shove.

'Who d'you think you're pushing, mate?' The boarder shoved Martin.

Martin jammed an elbow into the boarder's ribs. 'Just fuck off out of my way.'

'Piss off.' He pushed Martin, who cannoned into Nikki. Both just managed to keep their balance.

'You little . . .' Incandescent with rage, Martin raised his fist and punched.

The boarder toppled backwards.

The crowd stood stockstill, murmuring in dismay.

'Jesus.' The boarder was sprawled on the snow, his face twisted by pain, eyes watering as blood started to gush from his nose. He shook his head. 'You bastard.' Mustering his strength, he suddenly leapt up, sprang at Martin and punched back. Martin was knocked down onto Nikki's skis. She screamed. All around, people were shuffling backwards in alarm on the icy ground.

Still dizzy with the force of Martin's punch, the boarder staggered towards the metal railings. Winded, he clung to them bent over double. Martin tore off his skis, picked himself up and with a yell, ran at the boarder, who was brought down onto the hardpacked snow with a rugby tackle. They wrestled, fists trying to connect. Nikki was screaming at them to stop, two ski school instructors were racing over and the rest of the queue were watching in appalled fascination, backing away as the pair drew closer. Martin, who was by far the stronger, had managed to pin the boarder under him. Just as he bunched his fist, the instructors grabbed him under his arms and began to tug, prising him away. The boarder found himself being yanked across the snow and out of reach by two burly brothers.

'Tim. Calm down, will you?'

Separated and hauled onto their feet, Martin and the boarder glared at one another with loathing. Both were trying to struggle free from the arms that restrained them. The boarder was gasping, his face bloodied.

'What the fuck is going on here?' demanded one of the boarder's captors, who stood at six feet four and had flaming red hair and freckles. 'Calm down.' His grip tightened.

'This Pommy piece of shit had a go at me, the bastard,' he gasped.

'What did you call me?' Martin tried to lunge. 'You're dead meat.'

The ski instructors ordered him to keep quiet.

'Piece of shit,' taunted the boarder.

'That's enough,' ordered the beefy Aussie, as he and his brother dragged the boarder further away from Martin. 'Both of you.'

'Fucking Aussie scum. All three of you,' jeered Martin, trying to struggle free from the instructors. 'Get off me, you arseholes. Ow.' His eyes watered as his arm was twisted into a half-nelson. Someone in the crowd whistled their approval. 'Scum,' he yelled defiantly.

The brothers' faces darkened. The first stepped forward, advancing on Martin.

Nikki whimpered, he was at least half a foot taller and twice as broad as Martin.

'Listen mate. We're taking Tim to get cleaned up. Now you watch your mouth. Right?' There was a pause while he stared at Martin. 'I said, right?' Martin's eyes narrowed as he recognised defeat. He nodded. 'Take care of this creep.' The instructors smiled grimly. 'Come on you guys, let's find a beer.'

Muttering, looking over his shoulder at Martin, the boarder was led away by the two giants. Blood was still pouring from his nose.

'Well, rarely,' said a Sloane woman behind Nikki. 'This sort of display makes one ashamed to be English. The travel people swore this was a yob-free zone. They promised, no lager louts.'

Nikki blushed crimson at the tone of withering scorn. The crowd were murmuring their disapproval, glancing at her as they re-grouped. Martin, clearly furious, was being lectured by the two instructors who were threatening to call the police. Unable to meet anyone's eyes, she decided to join Martin. She pushed forward. Something was wrong. She pushed again and found herself down on the snow, as her boots came away from the skis.

'Shit,' she sobbed in humiliation. Gleeful giggles filled her ears. She scrambled to her feet and snatched up her skis to a chorus of catcalls and mocking jeers from the crowd.

During the fracas, the French couple had used their poles to release her bindings.

Miranda had enjoyed the most exhilarating ski of her holiday. The *vins chauds* and choccy cognacs seemed to add wings to her skis. Caution was thrown to the icy wind streaming through her hair. She managed to keep up with Pete, and at one point had actually powered ahead, screaming with joy as she swept past him. But halfway to La Croix, she had eased off. The piste was crowded. Even in her dazed condition, she was mindful of the mountain code. Pete, of course, kept up his furious speed, careering past everyone with just inches to spare.

'Well done.' He grinned as she skidded to a halt beside him at the chairlift. 'Great style you've got there. But I win my bet.'

Miranda blushed. 'Er, what exactly have you won?'

'Later.'

While Pete had a cigarette, Miranda tried to work out where they should go next. They'd take the chairlift so they wouldn't be separated and they must try and avoid Giles and the rest of the gang. She never realised how delightful it would feel to be with a man at whom other women stared.

Deciding to go over towards La Chevre, they joined the queue for the chairlift. As they were carried above the piste, Pete asked her about Charlie.

'He's away for months.' She shrugged.

'Absence makes the heart grow fonder, according to Munchkin.'

'Umm. To be honest, things have been a bit strained between him and me recently.'

'Sorry to hear that,' said Pete softly.

'It's, er . . . The thing is . . .' She took a deep breath. 'Can we change the subject?'

'No worries. Listen if you ever need an ear to bash, or

shoulder to cry on, here's one,' he said, putting his arm round her and pulling her towards him.

'Lovely,' she murmured, snuggling down into his chest. He was deliciously broad and strong. She peeked up at him, and he smiled down at her, holding her still tighter, resting his head on top of hers.

They were carried higher and higher. She could just feel his heart beating. With an eyeful of blue jersey and a mouthful of wool, she wondered if he'd ever, ever make a move, or was this closeness purely fraternal?

A few moments later, she was glad they'd grabbed a handful of mints on their way out of the restaurant. It was a far from ideal venue for passion. Miranda had her head jammed against the metal chair back and her skis clamped to her feet. She was uncomfortable but didn't care. All she wanted was Pete. More and more and more of him.

'Shit.' Pete broke away from her abruptly. One of his poles plummeted through the air and landed on the piste far below.

'Quick, quick, we need some ice.'

In the kitchen, Hetty was surprised that the normally cool Nikki sounded so panicked. 'Has someone had a fall?'

'Plastic bag? Martin's been attacked by this awful Australian in the chairlift queue.'

'No.' Hetty was aghast. 'What happened?'

'This guy was trying to push in and Martin asked him not to and then the guy just hit out. It was horrible.'

'Poor you,' clucked Hetty to Martin as he walked in. His left eye was swelling up. He opened the fridge door and peered inside. 'Got any steak?'

'Ice is the best we can do, I'm afraid.' She was apologetic. 'But the video's fixed and Al's made a lovely chocolate cake for tea.'

Delighting in the chance to play nurse, Nikki made Martin stretch out on the sofa as she fussed around lighting the fire and making him tea. With everyone else still out skiing, the chalet was tranquil. She half-closed the tartan curtains against the waning sun so they could get a better picture and settled down next to Martin just as the film started.

If only they had gone away on their own. It was really lovely to have the chalet to themselves. No problems with watching what she was saying, with bedrooms . . .

A car pulled up outside.

After retrieving his pole which had been moved to the side of the piste, Pete asked Miranda if she would mind if they called it a day. He was knackered.

Miranda didn't mind one bit. It was still early, no one else would be back at the chalet for ages and she'd have him to herself. She pictured them curling up together in front of the fire or sitting out on the balcony, watching the sun set. She'd be able to open up to him, put the record straight.

When the Porsche pulled into the drive and she saw the Range Rover, her heart sank.

An explosion followed by a volley of machine-gunfire greeted Pete and Miranda. Martin was watching a Rambo video, his feet almost in the chocolate cake on the coffee table. Nikki was holding a plastic bag and a flannel to his eye. They asked what had happened.

Waving Nikki away, Martin turned down the volume with the remote. 'There we were, minding our own business, being thoroughly British and queueing, when this bastard boarder just steams in ahead of us. I asked him if he minded waiting his turn like everyone else and the shit just turns round and clocks me.'

'No,' exclaimed Pete and Miranda.

'Never happen in Aspen, they've got line marshals,' said Nikki.

'German? French? Italian?' asked Miranda.

'Aussie,' said Martin. 'In the blood. Nation of convicts.'

'Er, if you don't mind,' said Pete.

'Forgot. Sorry, mate,' Martin was unabashed. 'Anyway, gave him a right pasting.' His eyes swivelled back to the screen. 'Come on, my son,' he yelled at Stallone, who was about to blow away more Viet Cong. 'Brilliant.'

'Horrible,' shuddered Nikki, 'never happen in Aspen.'

'Then,' continued Martin, 'then his two mates turned up and started having a go as well, if you please. No? No probs, you mean.' Martin grinned. 'Decked one, he spat out a tooth. Should've picked it up as a souvenir, made a nice earring for Nikki. After that, the other two fucked off.'

'You were very brave,' said Nikki ruffling his hair. Why must he exaggerate? She thought hard about her beautiful new skis. 'Just like Rocky.'

'Rambo, stupid.' Martin pulled a face.

Nikki looked hurt. There was an awkward silence, broken by Pete saying he was going up for a shower.

A few minutes later Miranda casually announced she must tidy her room. Nikki wondered why the hairband looked so pink in the face.

Upstairs, Miranda was about to enter her room, when she heard the pad of footsteps behind her. She went from pink to scarlet as she saw Pete with nothing but a bathtowel wrapped pharoah-like around his waist, water streaking from his blond ringlets down his shoulders and onto his chest. Had the statue of David come to life? One hundred per cent pure Aussie beefcake. As she gazed and gazed, she decided to hell with skiing, she was going straight to Sydney.

'Thank you for a . . .' Miranda's words were smothered as he pulled her towards him, kissed her and started dragging her into the room. They fell onto her narrow bed and then crashed down onto the floor as the sound of gunfire filled the chalet.

✳   ✳   ✳

It was almost half-past five when a weary Flora followed Stefan into Jimmy's, barely able to put one lead heavy boot in front of another. She sat down gratefully at the corner table. He had delivered his promise to work her hard, making her ski run after run and then down Les Pins. He paid no attention to her complaints about being cold, her aching legs or her exhaustion.

Her mind full of technique, of stemming and stopping, she hadn't had much chance to reflect on what had happened at the Savoie. Looking back, it had only been a little harmless flirting that both of them could forget all about. Throughout the afternoon, he had treated her like any other pupil. He'd even refused, with an incredulous laugh, to carry her skis.

Scarcely gathering the energy to take off her gloves and jacket, she waited for him to return with her drink. The place was almost empty. Around the other side of the bar, three blokes were setting up balls on the pool table. The television on the wall was tuned to MTV and Tina Turner sang from the juke box.

Flora watched Stefan joking with the barmaid. There was no doubt about it, he was devastating. Out of bounds, forbidden, but devastating. Anything that had happened at the Savoie, if anything had and she'd probably misread the situation, was nonsense. He was in love with Marie-France, she was in love with Jamie.

She was suddenly glad she'd dismissed her reservations about his offer of a drink, even if she didn't have a clue how she was going to get back to the chalet. And why should she go back? For Jamie, for whom she was just a nursemaid when he wasn't skiing or enjoying his Boy's Own holiday? All out war with Martin and Nikki? Awful music? Food fights? Water fights? Stefan's company was far more interesting than all that tedious chit-chat about skiing or house prices.

He put a huge glass of whisky in front of her. 'You deserve it. Worked hard, skied well. Not too much complaining.'

Flora laughed. As he smiled his slow, lazy smile she reminded herself that he was out of bounds. If she weren't with Jamie and if he weren't with Marie-France . . . Their eyes met. She wondered what he was thinking. If? No. To him, she was just someone more amusing to teach than some old, fat Germans.

'What's on your mind?' he asked. 'Were we thinking the same? I wonder.'

'I wonder.' She sipped slowly, telling herself not to blush. 'Nice whisky . . . Oh no, I don't believe it.' Alarmed, she tried to disappear into the chair.

'What's wrong?' Stefan turned round towards the door.

'Too late,' hissed Flora. She forced a smile. 'Hello, Giles. Had a good day?'

'Flora, almost missed you hiding away in the corner here. Superb day thanks. Bit of a late start, ha ha.' He sat down. 'You don't mind if we join you. Mine's a demi,' he called across to Sam at the bar. 'Pity they don't do a decent pint of Directors. Proper ale. You must be the famous Stefan. Giles Thomas.' He held out his hand.

'You're also staying at the chalet?' asked Stefan.

'Correct. In fact, just dropped hubby off, Flora. Bumped into him at La Croix, well Munchkin did, literally. You've met Jamie, Stefan? What a skier. A-mazing. Heiss Scheiss. Really knows how to melt a mountain.'

Putting down two beers, Sam winked at Flora. 'Not interrupting anything, are we?'

'Stefan, Sam. Sam, Stefan,' said Flora frostily. So much for escaping from the chalet. She listened as they badgered him for tips. After comparing Verbier and Meribel, Giles went into some long theory about pole planting.

Stefan swallowed yawns. 'It's difficult for you English. You only ski about a fortnight a year in a good year.'

'Tell me,' Sam leant forward, 'which boots would you recommend?'

Flora groaned inwardly. She slumped in silence, playing with the ends of her hair and watching the TV. She may as well have been non-existent. Suddenly, two girls appeared, shyly hovering near the table. What did they want? Stefan's views on Courch-eval?

Sam sprang up and introduced Murielle and Hélène.

'Budge up Flora,' ordered Giles.

Flora scraped her chair closer to Stefan's. Her plans for a quiet drink had definitely gone awry. She glanced at the two girls. Sweet-faced jailbait with puppy fat, and by the look of it, about to become fully paid-up members of the Stefan fan club. Chattering away in French and giggling, they hardly bothered to thank Sam when he returned from the bar with their *vins chauds*.

While answering Giles's questions about her lesson, Flora listened in, trying to translate what the girls and Stefan were saying. Her pique grew. They were inviting him to supper later in the week at their apartment. Cheek. Why was she bothering to come for a drink with him, if all he was interested in was being chatted up by schoolgirls?

'Another, Flora?' Giles stood up.

'No thanks. I should be getting back to Jamie,' she said pointedly. 'Where can I find a cab?'

'Oh, have another drink,' said Sam. 'Special day. Giles offering a round. Beer, Stefan?'

'Thank you.' His eyes met hers. 'Don't go. Please.'

So, he'd realised she was still there. 'Whisky. Thanks.'

Flora immediately regretted her decision when Sam got out his map, demanding to know where the best off-piste terrain could be found. Stefan pointed out one area, up by La Bête, but the girls disagreed. On and on they went, seeming to know every snowflake on every mogul.

Just as Flora was deciding to get out Dorothy Parker, a hand brushed against hers under the table. Instinctively, unthinkingly, she pulled away, but felt his touch again, and realised it was deliberate. She caught her breath and looked at Stefan, who was sitting almost shoulder to shoulder with her but he was talking to the others. His long fingers started to explore hers. A shiver of desire rippled through her. Giles put their drinks in front of them and Flora took a slug. As the hands coiled and uncoiled, their fingers snaking round, they occasionally glanced at one another. Their expressions were dead, their eyes searching.

Flora felt giddy. Sam was talking about the flour game, but all she was aware of was the warmth of Stefan's touch and the way he sometimes clasped her hand as if he never wanted to let her go. Was desire written all over her face? She could almost feel the pupils in her eyes dilating with lust. He was translating something for Sam as he tightened his grip. They stared at one another before he relaxed and began tracing with his fingers. She wanted him so much . . .

Flora snatched her hand away. What was she thinking of? She must be mad. How could she play such a dangerous game, especially under the noses of Giles and Sam? She jumped up and fled.

'Watch it,' called out one of the pool players as she almost ran into him. Broad-shouldered with flaming red hair and freckles, he towered over her.

'Sorry.'

'American?'

'English.'

He screwed up his good-natured face in disgust and turned to the other two. 'Hear that? English.' They made being sick noises.

To wind them up, Flora asked if they were Kiwis.

'Kiwis? Wash your mouth out, you get worse. Australian.' He smiled. 'English aren't exactly flavour of the moment round here.'

'Why not?' Flora tarried, needing time to get back to reality.

He took a gulp of beer. 'One of your countrymen, and let's stress the first syllable there, had a go at Tim this afternoon.' He pointed to his lanky-haired friend who was cueing up. 'Pom was probably crabby about the Ashes.'

'Ouch.' Flora saw Tim's nose was bruised and swollen. 'What happened?'

'Whinger in the chairlift queue was like, distracted. I jumped in ahead. He didn't appreciate it. Got antsy, pushed, I pushed back, he thumped me.'

'Then Bob and I arrived like the cavalry and he backed off.'

'How uncivilised.' Flora frowned. Chairlift queues were bad enough, without having a ruck.

'Uncivilised.' The giant mimicked her accent. 'Just one of those things. Want to shoot some pool?'

'No thanks. I've got to go.'

'See you round, yeah?' He smiled. 'What's your name? Flora. Right, I'll remember that. Bob, my brother, Tim you know and I'm Dooley. Next time you're in here, we'll shout you a beer.'

She pushed her way through a door marked *Toilettes*. Inside was a wash basin, and two cubicles off to the right. As hot water ran over her hands, she looked in the mirror.

Her expression froze as she saw Stefan's reflection in the glass. Leaning against the door he was watching her with his green eyes. She swallowed hard and stammered something about getting back to the chalet. Unable to tear away her gaze, she didn't notice that the sleeves of her sweater were getting soaked.

'How's your hand?'

Flora looked down and saw a trace of red where the knife had cut her earlier that afternoon. 'Fine. Won't scar.'

'Let me see. Please.'

'I must go.'

'Please.'

She turned round and held out her hand to him. 'See. It's fine.' As he took it, he slowly drew her towards him, then yanked her outside and along a dark passageway towards an emergency exit at the back of the building. It was all so fast she didn't realise what was happening.

'Stefan, what . . . ?'

Minutes later they broke apart. Her lips felt bruised, her face and throat rubbed raw from his stubble, wet from his mouth. They gazed at each other in shock and wonder.

He smiled his slow, lazy smile and said something in French. 'I was asking if you're the world's best kisser.'

Flora smiled. She was dazed, floating. 'I can't be. You are.'

'Beautiful,' he whispered, tracing round her face with his fingertips. 'I can't let you get married.' Suddenly, his expression hardened. 'You'd better go. Your friends are waiting.'

Shellshocked, she nodded. After one final look, she dragged herself away and stumbled back to Giles and Sam. The bar was busier, the tables were filling up. The Australians had disappeared, Murielle and Hélène had gone.

'About to send a search party,' said Giles, draining his beer. 'Stefan's gone.'

'He has?' Flora smiled dreamily.

Twenty minutes later, Flora crept into the storeroom. During the drive back to the chalet, her elation had evaporated. A sickening guilt overwhelmed her. Easing off her boots, she heard Jamie asking had they seen Flora and Sam saying they'd given her a lift and she was around somewhere.

Crushed by shame, she sank down onto the floor.

Why had she done it? Why hadn't she come straight back to the chalet? Lunchtime had been a warning, but she'd refused to heed it. Harmless flirtation? There was no such thing, not with a man she was as attracted to as Stefan, an attraction that had hit her like a blow the very first second she'd seen him. An attraction that she'd like to think would just go away if she ignored it, but which she carried around with her the way she carried around her heartbeat.

Her face felt raw, as if Stefan had branded her with a reminder of her weakness and her folly and her betrayal of Jamie. Jamie who she was marrying in a few weeks, Jamie who she'd spend forever with, Jamie who she loved.

He was bound to guess, he knew her so well. She could offer

him no defence, no excuses. It would finish them. 'Flora? Her. Yes, we were engaged once, but luckily I found out in time what a disloyal, cheap slut she was.'

Feeling sicker, Flora longed to hide herself away in the darkest corner and stay there all night. Or better still, run away.

'Flora. Flora?'

Jamie. Her heart pounded. 'Down here. Won't be a minute.' She'd have to face him, have to own up and let him tell her it was all over.

Taking a deep breath, she got to her feet, climbing the stairs as if en route to the noose. Their bedroom door was ajar. Jamie was sprawled in an armchair, reading the *Economist*. Once again, he was James Naze Esq, the astute banker with an imperial profile, not Jamie the drunk, the cokehead who played stupid flour games at four o'clock in the morning.

'Just getting a drink.' Flora rushed past, her voice sounded strange as if her conscience were strangling her vocal cords.

Sam was standing in front of the roaring fire. 'Jamie knows you're back?'

'Still not graced Vienna with your delightful presence?' The voice was mocking.

In her dazed state, Flora had failed to take in Martin and Nikki sitting on the sofa. She jumped. The argument at breakfast began to flood back. A scruffy little scrubber from the backarse of nowhere. The hick hack who's completely up herself because she's landed a toff. Her insides shrivelled.

'No, Flora's still with us.' Nikki pouted, flicking her sleek chestnut mane over her shoulders, showing off her Tiffany bangles.

'Jolly good.' Martin sounded hearty, but fixed her with a granite stare. 'Oh dear, we seem to have caught the sun, Flora. Not too painful, I hope?'

Flora felt herself stiffen, like a cat whose fur stands on end when its territory is invaded. She wondered why Martin looked as if he were getting a black eye.

'Carry on, Martin,' urged Giles, over by the sideboard. 'Then what happened? Whisky, Flora?'

'Well, I told them it wasn't on and they just laid into me.'

'It was horrible, never happen in Aspen.' Nikki shuddered.

'And then what?' demanded Sam.

Flora wished Giles would hurry up pouring her drink.

'And then I gave them what for. Toerags.'

'All of them?' Giles whistled. 'Rather you than me, old chap.'

'All right, so I took a bit of a shiner, but it was worth it,' continued Martin. 'Put the wankers in their place. Tooth out, blood all over the snow, the works.'

'They're probably all in hospital, feeling very sorry for themselves.'

'Thanks Giles.' Flora snatched her whisky and almost ran across the room.

'Yep.' Martin sounded pleased with himself. 'Taught them a lesson they won't forget in a hurry.'

Flora took a huge gulp of whisky, braced herself and went into the bedroom.

'Hello angel,' Jamie broke into a smile. 'You're back late. I'm so sorry about last night.'

'This morning. How's the hand?'

'This morning. Fine. Say you forgive me.'

'You forgive me,' parroted Flora. As he put aside the *Economist*, preparing to move towards her, she panicked. She grabbed a towel, gabbled something about the hot water and ran.

She slammed the bathroom door and locked it with fumbling fingers, her heart thumping.

She looked in the mirror, expecting to see the word 'guilty' tattooed across her forehead. After brushing her teeth until her gums bled, she shampooed her hair three times and scrubbed her neck with a nail brush. As the shower water cascaded over her, she wished she could scour her conscience, and wipe Stefan from her memory.

Her prayers that Jamie might have gone to play backgammon, even the flour game, were unanswered. She had lingered in the bathroom for as long as possible, but there he was, still reading the *Economist*.

'How was the lesson?'

'Hard work.' Her face was red because of sunburn and the shower, wasn't it? Hands trembling she reached for her foundation. At least the mirror would give her an excuse not to look at Jamie. 'Lots of uphill stops and stems. Can't lift the ski during a turn.'

Jamie frowned. 'What happened to your hand?'

'This? Oh, er, Stefan caught me with his knife when I was trying to sneak some of his chips.' The layer of foundation failed to disguise her blush.

'At lunchtime? Where?'

'The Savoie.'

'I thought you might be there. Busy was it? You and Munchkin must have missed one another. She said she hadn't seen you.'

'Munchkin was there?' Flora felt dizzy.

Jamie put aside the *Economist*. 'Can you tell me what on earth you're up to please?' He sounded as if she were an office junior who had caused the bank's computer to crash.

Flora jumped. 'Sorry?' How did he know? Giles or Sam must have seen her with Stefan and told him. The room started to spin.

'Taking that money off Martin. He asked if we'd enjoyed ourselves with his cash. I wondered where all those francs came from.'

Her dizziness began to subside. 'I told you. This morning.'

'It didn't actually register.'

'Surprise, surprise,' mumbled Flora.

'So you played debt collector. Why? I was the one playing backgammon. My game, my money. You shouldn't interfere. It was very embarrassing, especially just after Martin let me drive the Range Rover.'

'You've been driving? But . . .'

'Don't start. Why did you get involved? It's just the sort of thing to cause bad blood. I offered Martin the money back, but he wouldn't hear of it.' His blue eyes were glacial. 'Quite frankly Flora, you've put me in a highly invidious position.'

'But Nikki gave me the money,' protested Flora. 'Anyway, what about the room? Are we swapping or something?'

'Of course not. I'm not going into that pokey little dump.' Jamie sighed. 'Money's different. It causes more ill feeling than anything else.'

'There's already ill feeling between me and Martin,' said Flora. 'You just haven't noticed.'

'Nonsense. Stop exaggerating. Anyway, why have you got a problem? No one else has.'

'He's not foul to anyone else . . .' protested Flora.

'And when's he been so foul to you?'

'Always. All the time. Slagging me off, slagging my job off.'

'He was given an awful time by the Press. His career was finished. Gone. And still they hounded him.'

'That was years ago . . .'

'So? He didn't need that on top of everything else. How would you like it? Someone almost dies because of you, your life's changed forever, you're cracking up and still you're chased day and night by those scummy reporters.'

'Is that what happened?'

'I told you back in London. If you'd bothered to listen, you might be a bit less selfish and a bit more sensitive.' Flora flinched. 'And Flora, you might begin to understand why he's wary about anyone from the media.'

'A hick hack on the Jaxley *Standard* is hardly the media.' She sighed. 'And no, it still doesn't explain why he's so foul to me.'

'When's he been so foul to you?'

'Sunday night, last night, today at breakfast.'

Jamie was close to losing his cool. 'It's hardly surprising if you take a thousand francs off him.'

'I didn't. Nikki gave it to me.'

'Whatever. It's hardly endearing, is it? Anyway, you're usually grumpy first thing.'

Flora scowled. 'If you'd been in any fit state to be up, you'd have been there this morning and seen how he and Nikki had the whole thing worked out . . .'

'Worked out?' Jamie brushed some fluff off his Guccis. 'Don't be so ridiculous. Make an effort. Nikki is perfectly charming, even if she does go on about Aspen.'

'Charming?'

'The poor girl's had the most terrible afternoon. Martin got attacked by three Aussies in a chairlift queue.'

Flora clicked. 'He didn't.'

Jamie stared at her. 'How do you know?'

'I met them just now.' Her heart began pounding again. 'At Jimmy's. I was having a drink with Stefan.'

'Avant and après ski? You're getting friendly.'

Flora's blush was hidden by the black sweater she was pulling over her head. 'What's that supposed to mean? Giles and Sam were there too.'

'Calm down,' said Jamie. 'So you got chatting to the three musketeers. From what Martin said they should all be in intensive care.'

'One was clouted on the nose. He and Martin had a ruck, before the other two pitched up. Martin backed off. End.'

'Sounds a bit more like it,' said Jamie. 'Does Martin know you ran into them? Good. Keep it that way. There's no point in stirring up trouble.'

'There's trouble between Martin and Nikki and me anyway.'

Sighing impatiently, Jamie got to his feet. 'Nikki is charming and . . .

'Her only charm is her looks.'

'Well, she knows how to make the best of them. Perhaps you could learn something from her and dump those fucking biker boots and wear a decent sweater. I thought you'd grown out of all that.'

'Like you've grown out of taking drugs,' hissed Flora. 'You promised . . .'

'Not that again. Ask yourself, Flora, why it is that everyone else gets on with Martin perfectly well? Why is it that you're so different? Remember, you promised me you'd make an effort and not fuck up my holiday.'

'And you promised me you wouldn't do any more coke. Jamie . . .' She had to talk to him. As he stalked out, Flora hung her head in despair.

Miranda glowed with contentment as she finished drying her hair. Sweet Pete. So gorgeous, with the most beautiful body she'd ever known. And he knew exactly what to do with it – unlike some.

Sweet Pete. As they'd snuggled up together afterwards, his honeyed words had acted like a balm. Had he really murmured that she was just the woman he needed? He'd been so sensitive too. 'Your situation is, er, delicate,' he'd said, kissing her on the shoulder. 'I'm not into rocking boats. Our secret. Promise.'

Just at that moment, they'd heard Anna and Munchkin arriving and he'd bolted out of the room. Bad timing. A few seconds later and she'd have had the chance to explain her situation. Still, she'd be able to set the record straight very, very soon.

Could she and Pete get away with not being found out? Like her, he couldn't face the general piss-taking that would inevitably follow if everyone else in the chalet found out about them. She could imagine Sam and Martin's reaction. Ideally, they could all work it out for themselves when she got into the Porsche for the journey home.

Anna returned from the shower. Miranda stared at her as if for the first time. 'You've got a-mazing bone structure.'

'Have I?' Anna smiled shyly.

There was a knock at the door. 'Pretty please, my hairdryer's playing up. Can I borrow yours?' Munchkin sat on the edge of Miranda's bed and seemed in no hurry to leave. 'Did Martin tell you what happened? Dreadful business.'

'Pete thinks all this about taking on three of them is rubbish.' Able to say his name, Miranda smiled.

'Really? Oh. Poor Nikki though, must've been terrifying for her.'

'Her new skis must help ease the pain.' Anna rubbed her cropped hair with a towel. She'd been bored stiff when Martin showed them off to her, repeating verbatim what the salesman had said.

'What a lovely present.' Munchkin sighed. 'Must be nice to have a boyfriend who spoils you that much. Charlie good at gifts? Who won the race?'

'Pete.' Another smile. 'Brilliant style, terribly athletic.'

'Speaking of skiers . . .' Munchkin looked furtively round the room and lowered her voice. 'I saw something rather intriguing today.'

'What?' The other two were curious.

'Well . . .' Munchkin got up to check the door was closed. 'Strictly entre nous . . .' Miranda nodded impatiently. 'A certain person not a million miles away was getting on extremely well with their ski instructor.'

'Flora?' Anna frowned. 'And that guy we saw this morning?' Munchkin nodded.

'Extremely well?' asked Miranda.

'Extremely well,' repeated Munchkin.

'Getting on or getting off?' demanded Miranda. Munchkin squirmed excitedly. 'No,' breathed Miranda. 'You're joking.'

'When?' Anna quite forgot her scruples about tittle-tattle.

'At the Savoie at lunchtime,' hissed Munchkin. 'I was upstairs on the terrace and they were sitting below me. Didn't have a clue I was there.'

'Go on,' urged the other two.

'They sat there gazing into each other's eyes for simply hours, murmuring sweet nothings. Transfixed by lust, obviously. Body language. It never lies. And then I don't know how it happened but while he was eating he caught her hand with his knife. Of course, she had to make a fuss, you know what she's like. And then he sort of grabbed her and started kissing her . . .'

'No,' gasped Miranda and Anna.

'Truth, I swear.'

'And?' demanded Miranda.

'I had to meet you up at La Toit. But, let's face it, Stefan's bound to live in the village and I bet you pound to a penny Flora didn't ski this afternoon. They probably sneaked back to his place.'

Anna was unconvinced. 'You can't be sure.'

'You should've seen them,' said Munchkin emphatically. 'Body language. It never lies.'

'No wonder Flora got so shirty about you sharing her lessons,' said Miranda.

'Exactly.' Munchkin was triumphant. 'You should've seen them. Pure lust.'

'God. I wonder what Pete will make of it?' said Miranda.

'No.' Munchkin was alarmed. 'You mustn't breathe a word. Girls' talk. He'll tell Jamie, they're best friends. You know what men are like, such big mouths. Promise you won't say anything.'

'Of course I wouldn't. Can you imagine the rumpus? Quite ruin the holiday. Poor Jamie, though,' clucked Miranda. 'When are they getting married?'

'April,' said Anna.

'Meant to be anyway.' Munchkin picked up an emery board. 'You won't say anything, will you, Anna?'

'No, Munchkin, I won't. It's not my business.'

Towel over his shoulder, Giles popped his head round the bathroom door. Pete was shaving and chatting to Sam, who was perched on the edge of the bath.

'Budge up.' Giles took a swig of Sam's beer. 'Well, Murielle and Hélène weren't much cop. Took those drinks off us and scarpered without so much as a thank you.'

'Win some, lose a lot.' Sam shrugged. 'They were more interested in bloody Stefan. As soon as I said I was out of work, they went off me like a bucket of prawns in a heatwave.'

'Why tell them?' asked Giles. 'Laid it on a bit thick, didn't you? Girlies came out for a drink, not a lecture on the evils of unemployment. Anyway, thought you were having the time of your life these past few months.'

'Sure.' Sam yanked at the bathtap.

'Turn it off.' Getting splashed, Giles leapt up. Settling down, he swigged again. 'Just had another rocket from the twins. Must try and lay off the booze, hardly managed a run all day. Get much powder hounding in this afternoon, Pete?'

'A bit.' Pete sounded uneasy.

'Tame any mountains?'

'A few.'

'After the race Pete, eh?' Sam cocked his head. 'Bet you explored all sorts of peaks and valleys.'

'Went off-piste, did you?' Giles was puzzled.

Sam roared. 'You did, Pete didn't you?'

'Ow.' Pete nicked his neck.

'You did.' Sam whooped in triumph.

Pete threw down his razor. 'Shut it, Sam.'

Giles was admiringly envious. 'You're such a randy bastard.

Surprised it hasn't dropped off through wear and tear. Who was the lucky lady? One of the birds in the club last night?'

'Mirandy bastard, you mean.' Sam winked.

'Shut up.' Rattled, Pete peered along the corridor.

'What?' The penny was dropping, Giles was feeling sick. 'You? And Miranda? You're joking.'

'Keep your voice down,' snapped Pete, closing the bathroom door. He pushed his hair out of his eyes and smiled beseechingly. 'Listen, let's keep this one quiet. Can we? Please.'

Giles stared at Pete in disbelief and wanted to smash his face down into the basin and break his nose again. How could she? With Pete? Charlie he was used to, he could cope with, but Pete?

'Gobbler?' asked Sam chortling.

'Fuck right off.'

'Only asking.' Sam took another swig. 'Had this temp at the office. Lucy. Juicy Lucy. Huge jugs. Gagging for it, well to start with anyway. Then she got shy on me. Really offended when I tried to get her to gobble it. Kept on saying she's not that sort of girl. Had her knickers round her ankles at the time, so bit strange. Wasn't it?'

'Bit.' Giles tried to grin back.

Pete rinsed his face. Miranda would go ballistic if she found out he'd blabbed. Understandably. She wanted to keep it quiet because of Charlie. After all, they were almost engaged. Sam knowing was like Radio Free Europe knowing. Shit.

'Natural blonde?' asked Sam. 'Collars and cuffs match, do they?' He sniggered, then realised Pete was about to lose his cool. 'Hardly any of them are, are they?'

'Munchkin is,' said Pete, glad to move on from Miranda.

'How do you know?' demanded Sam.

'Not from experience. She was telling me at lunchtime. Listen Sam, if you breathe a fucking word about me and Miranda, I'll fucking murder you.'

Sam was startled. Pete was usually so laid-back. 'Sure, I won't . . .'

'Head-hunters need to be discreet, don't they? So start practising for your next job. If you ever get one.'

'I won't breathe a word. Swear,' said Sam, looking as if he'd been slapped.

'This is one situation I'm not having you taking the piss out of.'

'I won't . . .'

'Good. By the way, watch out for the shower. The hot water's going.'

While Giles was in the shower, a glum-faced Sam knocked on Pete's bedroom door. 'Pete? Can I have a word?'

'Sure.' Pete looked up from Asterix.

'Want to set your mind at rest. I'm not that much of a prick.' He sank onto the edge of Giles's bed and stared at his shoes. 'Despite what everyone thinks.'

'What's up?'

'Jobless, penniless, loveless, homeless.'

'Need a loan? Pay it back whenever,' said Pete.

'Prefer a future, actually.'

'Bad time of year to be looking for work,' suggested Pete.

'Bad time, full stop. The whole world at office Christmas dos, while I'm stuck at home feeling useless. Know something? I look forward to *Neighbours* at lunchtime. Gives me something to get up for.'

Pete was bewildered. 'But you're always so upbeat.'

'Everyone loves a bull market. Ask Jamie. What should I do? Own up to being a complete fucking failure? Tried it tonight with those chicks. Ran a mile.'

'Wrong sort of chicks, then.'

Sam shook his head. 'Gospel according to pretty boy Pete, the playboy with the Porsche.' He sighed. 'You're on top of the mountain, I'm back on the nursery slope with all the other losers.'

Lost for words, Pete's heart went out to the forlorn figure opposite.

Sam screwed up his face. 'A man's judged by his job. Without one, you're nothing. Even on holiday.'

Half an hour later, Sam went downstairs, feeling a bit more cheerful. Pete hadn't scoffed, instead he'd been constructive. He'd loaned him some money, advised him to talk to Jamie and promised to put the word out at his bar in Cheapside.

'Hi,' he said to Munchkin.

'Hi.' She smiled awkwardly. 'How were your babes?'

'Dull. Too young. Nothing to say for themselves.'

'Oh.' There was a long pause, then they both started to speak. 'You first. Age before beauty,' she tried to sound light-hearted.

'I've been er . . . About what happened.' Sam heard footsteps on the stairs. 'Later, eh?'

Flora hid herself away in her bedroom. She slumped in the armchair, chain-smoking, feeling sick with nerves. Her wedding file, unopened, seemed to be screaming 'traitor'. What should she do? Tell Jamie everything, call off the wedding and flee into the night?

Music and voices came through from the sitting room, everything was carrying on just the same. In the mirror, she looked just the same. Only she knew of the guilt and confusion that was tearing her apart.

Arriving for dinner at the last moment, Flora sat as far away from Martin as possible. As soon as she caught sight of him, her fur stood on end.

'About to invade Poland?' said Pete, grinning at her biker boots.

'Or Glastonbury?' said Miranda.

Jamie scowled. Why couldn't Flora bother to make some sort of effort to look respectable? And why couldn't she get rid of that tatty piece of rag round her wrist?

Giles sat between Miranda and Flora. He had spent an hour lying on his bed, jealousy gnawing into his entrails. How could she? Miranda, almost engaged to Charlie, Miranda, his goddess, had turned out to be like all the rest of them. A pushover for a legover from Pete. And the slut was almost engaged.

His white-lashed eyes were dull, his jowls more than usually pronounced in his inanimate face. Trying to swallow the soup, he wished he'd stayed upstairs. A sparkling Miranda began talking about safe seats, but she was half-hearted because she kept on glancing at Pete, a new softness in her expression. He caught him winking at her.

Pete and Jamie were deciding whether they should go to Aubrisson, a resort about forty miles away.

'Tomorrow? We could all go,' said Martin. 'I can squeeze six into the Range Rover.'

Nikki smiled. 'Oh, let's. There are supposed to be some great shops there. And I can try out my new skis.' She turned to Sam. 'Have you seen them? Martin bought them for me today. Wasn't that darling of him?'

'Bargain. Guy in the shop gave me a deal. And you should see our boots,' gloated Martin. 'The dog's.'

Pete offered round some bread. 'It would be what? An hour's drive? So early start. Want to come, Flora?'

'Sorry?' She was miles away.

'Aubrisson. Tomorrow.'

'Got a lesson.'

'Such a dedicated pupil,' said Munchkin. 'We saw Stefan today, up near La Toit. Didn't we, Anna?'

Anna ummed. Why was Munchkin stirring it?

'Really?' Flora's cheeks grew hotter, she hoped it didn't show in the candlelight. Had Munchkin seen her and Stefan at the Savoie?

'You must be making terrific progress,' said Munchkin. 'Three hours a day.'

'Must say, I thought Stefan was a decent sort of chap.' Giles refilled his glass for the third time. 'Despite the earrings.' He turned to Jamie. 'Met him down at Jimmy's.'

'Nice guy, isn't he?' said Jamie, spooning up the remains of his soup.

'Didn't break up your little party, did we, Flora?' asked Giles.

'Of course not,' snapped Flora, cheeks burning like a furnace.

Munchkin and Miranda exchanged the minutest of glances.

'I'd watch out Jamie,' continued Giles. 'You know what they say about ski instructors. Randy bastards to a man . . . Bloody hell.' He leapt up as the contents of Flora's overturned wineglass seeped over the tablecloth and towards his lap.

'Sorry.' Flora mopped up the wine with her napkin. Accident or design? She couldn't tell, she was so jumpy.

Munchkin sat back satisfied. A prosecuting counsel, she looked at the jury of Miranda and Anna, as if to say 'I rest my case'. Flora's guilt was transparent for all to see, except for poor Jamie, of course, chatting away to Pete about Aubrisson. Perhaps there would be another highly eligible man in the chalet before the end of the holiday?

'Poor baby,' said Nikki, frowning at Martin's eye. 'Sure we shouldn't get you to the doctor's?' She squeezed his arm, showing off her bangles. 'Thugs. I could kill them. It was awful,' she turned to Anna. 'There they were, barging all these children.'

Jamie gave Flora a 'don't start' look.

'Leave it, Nikki,' ordered Martin.

'You were the only one who stood up to them.'

'Leave it.'

Giles raised his glass. 'Just like to say, well done that man. Snowboarders are bad enough, but Australians. God. Nation of convicts.'

'Oh come on,' protested Pete.

'Who do they think they are? Dumping Her Majesty indeed, after all she's done for them. Marvellous woman. They're lucky to have her. Bloody Aussies, always whingeing on about doing more than their share at Gallipoli . . .'

'What . . .' exploded Pete.

'Good for you, Martin, sorting a few of them out, showing them who's still boss.'

'Oh hear, hear,' mocked Sam. 'Heard the cricket latest, Giles?'

'Details,' declared Giles. 'England is still the finest country in the world. Isn't she, Jamie?'

'Uh?'

Sam started humming 'Rule Britannia', then suddenly switched to a booming but tuneless 'Jerusalem'. The other four men joined in, trying to outdo each other on the decibels. Suddenly, they were in the grandstand at Twickenham. The only one who knew all the words, Jamie finished off to applause and foot stamping.

'We'll sort these wankers out for you, Martin,' slurred Giles. 'Aussie scum.' Suddenly, he leapt to his feet, pulled down his cords, showing off his Union Jack boxer shorts. He tugged them down, turned round and stuck out his backside at the table. Munchkin and Nikki shrieked like hyenas. 'Kiss this Australia.'

'And this.'

'And this.' Martin and Sam followed gleefully.

'No fucking way,' laughed Pete; Nikki and Munchkin were shrieking hysterically. Wondering what all the commotion was about, Hetty and Alice came out of the kitchen, only to take one look at the three bared bottoms before retreating in horror. Munchkin was laughing so hard, she nearly fell off her chair.

'Siena, next time, I promise,' giggled Jamie, seeing Flora's lip curl in distaste.

'I should be there now,' Throwing aside her napkin, she got to her feet.

'What's up?' asked Giles beside her, pulling up his boxers.

'Not you mate,' laughed Martin. 'Not sitting where you are.'

'Not enjoying the show?' Giles buttoned his fly.

'Exterminate, exterminate, sense of humour failure,' said Sam in a Dalek voice.

'Some people just don't know when to lighten up,' muttered Nikki.

'Stepford Wife,' muttered Flora, turning on her heel.

Anna watched her stride off. Behind her spectacles her eyes were icy. 'Thank you for ruining our dinner you three.'

'Not you as well.' Sam grimaced. 'It was only a bit of fun.'

'No wonder you need big cars. Compensates for massive inadequacies in other areas.' Anna's voice was as bland as her expression. As her words sank in, everyone looked at her in astonishment. 'Could you pass the butter please, Miranda?'

'Hear, hear,' said Miranda. 'Good for you Anna. We don't want to see your hairy bums, thank you.'

'Wanted to see Pete's this afternoon, though, didn't you?' said Giles tucking in his shirt.

Miranda turned crimson as everyone cottoned on to what he meant.

Anna frowned. Munchkin's jaw dropped. Miranda and Pete? This afternoon?

Pete pushed his hair out of his eyes and froze.

'Way hay.' A delighted grin spread across Martin's face. 'Nikki and I thought we heard a bit of the old rumpy pumpy going on. Creak of bedsprings. Afternoon delight, eh, Miranda?'

'Shut up, Martin,' giggled Nikki.

'Yes. Shut up, Martin,' snarled Miranda.

'Don't know what you're on about, do we Miranda?' said Pete, seeing the anguish on her face. 'If only. But alas. Not my lucky day.'

'That's not what you told us,' said Giles. There was a sudden silence. Miranda stared at him in shock. 'Haven't put my foot in it, have I?'

'What?' she was incredulous. 'What did you just say?'

'More wine anyone?' said Pete desperately.

'Roll in the way hay,' chortled Martin. Munchkin snorted as she tried to suppress a giggle. 'While the cat's away, the mice will way hay.'

'Be quiet,' growled Jamie.

'You promised,' whispered Miranda, staring at Pete.

'I . . .'

'You promised. You're an absolute shit.' Miranda stood up, knocking over her glass.

'Don't worry, Miranda,' said Martin. 'We won't tell the boyfriend. Will we guys? By the way, Giles, what's his number again?' Sam laughed. 'Only joking Miranda. Whatsisname, Charlie, will never know.'

'Souls of discretion,' agreed Giles.

'Shut up,' said Jamie and Pete in unison.

'Bum's, I mean, mum's the word.' Sam laughed louder.

'Sam . . .' Pete was furious.

'Doesn't matter, Pete.' Miranda stared at him, her eyes filling with tears. 'Charlie wouldn't care. Charlie finished with me weeks ago.'

There was a long pause.

'But you're practically engaged,' spluttered Giles.

Miranda heaved a sob. 'Charlie's engaged, you mean.'

She fled from the table. The long, stunned silence was broken as a door slammed overhead.

Flora was curled up in the bedroom armchair. Jamie came in to tell her off for being anti-social.

'I don't want to socialise with your friends,' she snapped, not looking up from *Excellent Women*.

'For God's sake, it was harmless. A bit of fun. Nikki's right. Learn to lighten up.'

As he stomped back to the sitting room, Flora threw aside Barbara Pym. In all the scores of leaflets and lists in the wedding file, why was there no advice about being dragged on a week's holiday with a bunch of strangers? Why was there no guidance on how to resist a Franco-Czech with a low voice and a slow smile and the most mesmerising pair of green eyes? Why was there no help being offered about what she should do next?

Half an hour later, Jamie arrived with the backgammon

board and told her about Miranda. Music was blasting through the wall. 'Pete's gone to try and talk to her again. She's not very happy.'

'Everyone's been going on about Charlie, haven't they?'

Jamie winced. 'I even asked her for his number today. Suggested we should all go out.'

'And me. Talking about the wedding . . .' Flora cringed. 'She must've thought her nose was being rubbed in it.'

Sitting on the bed, Jamie set up the counters, then began rolling a joint. 'When I heard about her and Pete, I guessed something was up. Miranda's not the sort to play away.' Flora froze. The bedroom wall shook as something crashed against it on the sitting room side. Jamie frowned. 'What's going on in there?'

Pete arrived. For once there was no sunshine in his face, no warmth in his green-blue eyes. He slumped dejectedly onto the bed. 'She doesn't want to know. She's crying and crying and furious with me.'

'You can't blame her,' said Jamie.

'Bloody Giles.'

'Why tell him, dumbo?'

'I didn't,' protested Pete. 'Bloody Sam guessed something was up. I was so busy worrying about him, I didn't think about Giles. How could he be so fucking tactless? Pissed, I suppose.' There was another crash against the wall. 'Sam and Munchkin are trying to dance, but they're so wrecked they keep falling over. God, why do I have such bad luck with women?'

Flora was amazed. 'You don't. You've got hundreds queueing up.'

'Not counting the two from last night.' Jamie tore up Flora's cigarette packet for a roach.

Sam, Munchkin and Giles began to sing 'Teddy Bears' Picnic'.

'What a racket.' Pete got up and paced, then stroked Flora's hair. 'Is my love life always going to be such a disaster? What am I to do?

'Learn to keep your mouth shut?' suggested Flora, squeezing his hand.

'Not what Miranda said this afternoon. Joke. Bad joke.' He wrinkled up his crooked nose. 'What a fucking mess. She kept on and on about me ruining her holiday.'

'Thought you would've made her holiday, actually,' grinned Jamie. 'Shake to start.'

Pete sat down on the bed. 'Shall I go to a hotel? Makes it really awkward for everyone if Miranda's grump city with me.'

'She'll calm down,' said Jamie. 'And she'll forgive you, you'll see. My start.' He moved his counters. 'So what's your next move?'

'Three and a four? This of course. With Miranda you mean? God knows. Why did I do it? She was a mate and now it's all messed up.' The stereo was turned up, bass shaking through the walls. 'Why can't they turn down that bloody music?'

There was an almighty bang and suddenly the bedroom was plunged into darkness. In the sudden hush, Jamie cursed. 'What the hell is going on out there?'

Sam had missed Munchkin's hand as she spun round. She'd lost her footing, skidded into the Christmas tree which had toppled over and crashed onto the floor with a flash from the fairy lights.

A cry of outrage came from the kitchen, where Alice was trying to load the dishwasher.

'Where's the fuse box?' called Anna from the sitting room.

As Jamie got up, the counters slid off the backgammon board.

'Torch?' Anna asked Hetty, then went downstairs to check the fuses.

'Lighter?' Jamie asked Flora, then lit up his joint. He and Pete puffed away in the dark.

When the lights were finally restored, Pete saw the counters strewn across the bed. 'Will you two come out? I can't stand it here. Let's go and play pool.'

*   *   *

Martin decided that he also wanted to go out and offered the others a lift. In the Range Rover, he adjusted the bass on the stereo before reversing onto the road. 'Well, who'd have thought it? Pretty boy Pete and Miranda,' he said as they sped down towards the twinkling lights of St Marie.

Munchkin poked her head between the front seats. 'He treats women very badly. Look what happened with his ex. Loves them and leaves them, you were saying, Giles, weren't you?' She swallowed a hiccup.

'Fucks them and forgets them you mean,' said Giles.

Martin grinned. 'I'd never have guessed Mirandy was up for a bit of rumpy.'

'Slapper,' muttered Giles.

'She's not the only one,' said Munchkin, the gin and the wine getting the better of her. 'Is she, Anna?'

'What do you mean?' said Martin intrigued.

'Come on, spit it out,' said Sam.

'Is she, Anna?' said Munchkin.

'Don't,' said Anna.

'Do, Munchkin,' said Nikki. 'You can't leave us in suspense like this.'

Revelling in being the centre of attention, Munchkin brushed aside Anna's hissed don'ts. 'Promise not to breathe a word to Jamie or Pete. Well, strictly entre nous, someone was seen getting very friendly with their ski instructor today.'

She was rewarded by a collective oh.

'Flora? How friendly?' demanded Nikki breathlessly. 'Turn down the stereo, Martin, and keep your eyes on the road, for God's sake.'

'Munchkin,' warned Anna. 'Don't.'

'Munchkin,' pleaded Nikki. 'Do.'

Munchkin lowered her voice. 'I saw them in the Savoie at lunchtime . . .'

'And?' said Nikki, turning down the stereo.

'Munchkin,' hissed Anna between clenched teeth.

'Tongues practically down each other's throats,' whispered Munchkin. 'Holding hands, whispering sweet nothings . . .'

'No,' screamed Nikki amid the gasps.

Martin hooted the horn in delight. 'Well, well, well. Wonder what his Lordship will say? Hey guys, this brings a whole new meaning to the phrase sloping off.'

'Swear you won't tell Jamie or Pete,' pleaded Munchkin.

'Knew it,' said Giles. 'As soon as I saw them in the bar earlier, tucked away in the darkest corner.'

'No wonder Flora didn't look pleased to see us.' Sam whistled.

'The thing is,' said Munchkin out of the corner of her mouth, 'had they actually been skiing? Don't Munchkin me like that, Anna. It's a perfectly legitimate question.'

'No wonder Flora wants to keep her lessons to herself,' said Nikki. 'If she's actually been having any.'

Anna buried her face in her hands.

'Bet she hasn't,' said Munchkin. 'He's bound to have a place in the village. Did you see her at dinner? Guilt written all over her face.'

'Definitely shifty,' nodded Nikki. 'And now we know why.'

'Gotcha.' Martin was triumphant.

St Marie was busy, the icy pavements crowded with people going from bar to bar on the lookout for action. Parking the Porsche outside Jimmy's, Pete drew envious glances from a group of teenage boys.

As Flora pushed her way through the door, 'Waiting for my Man' was playing on the jukebox. A group of girls were hanging round the bar, pretending to chat, but restlessly glancing round for the talent. She saw two of them nudge each other as Jamie and Pete approached.

Pete squeezed in beside them. 'Beer, Jamie?'

Flora was almost lifted off her feet in the scrum, the floor under her biker boots was sticky with spilt drinks. Jamie was pushing his way to the pool table, where he put down a ten franc piece. As five pairs of eyes hit on Pete, then her, Flora knew the girls were wondering if they were together.

'Your charms are working their usual magic,' she teased as he handed her a drink.

'The redhead's stunning.' A mass of pre-Raphaelite curls snaked down a slender back. Pete yawned. 'Not interested. Off women. Rather play pool.'

'Safer,' agreed Flora.

Followed like the Pied Piper, Martin arrived, shoving his way through the throng. He asked Pete what he was drinking. His steely eyes briefly met Flora's before she turned her back on him. His mocking smile seemed to be at her expense.

'We're on,' yelled Jamie from the pool table.

Pete hurried off to join him.

'Hey, Flora. Know something?'

She felt a hand on her arm, turned round and found Martin's smiling face inches from her own. He looked friendly. He pulled her closer to him so his mouth was level with her ear.

His smile grew broader. 'You're the biggest cunt I've ever met in my life.'

Flora froze with shock.

'And what's Jamie going to say when he finds out, eh? Gotcha, sweetheart.'

Ignoring Giles who was moaning about the crush, Flora made her escape.

'OK, angel?' called Jamie as she stumbled past the pool table in a daze.

'Fine.' She wasn't fine at all. Had anyone ever before revealed such naked loathing of her? She was shaken by the depths of Martin's raw malevolence. What was the good of bleating to Jamie about it? He'd say Martin was joking and that she should make a bit more effort, not be fucking up his holiday. And what had Jamie got to find out? She went over to the jukebox and gazed and gazed at the song titles.

Across the other side of the bar, Sam had bagged a table. Munchkin sat down next to him, determined to talk.

Nikki sat down, eyeing her surroundings with disfavour. She was feeling very out of place in her mink parka, new gloves and Chanel bag. Her suede Guccis had already been splashed with beer and she could hardly breathe through all the smoke. It was so hot, even the walls seemed to be sweating.

What the hell were they doing in here? There must be somewhere chicer to go. Next time, Martin had better stick to his promise and take her to somewhere like St Moritz. 'What a racket,' she wailed.

Giles and Martin started to play spoof.

'Yes,' roared Jamie, potting the black and lifting his arms in triumph.

Over by the jukebox, Flora wished she had stayed at the chalet. Coming back here only made her think of Stefan, the touch of his hand, his green eyes, her desire, her madness. Anyone could have seen her in the passageway, she wouldn't have noticed. She'd been aware of nothing, cared about no-one, except him. What had Jamie got to find out? Shivering with nerves, needing another drink, Flora made her way to the bar. She caught sight of Martin and felt worse.

'Isn't this a bit uncivilised for you?' a voice mocked.

Flora craned her neck up at a good-natured freckled face and a wide grin.

'Shout you a beer?' offered Dooley.

'My shout,' said Flora.

'So, who are you here with?'

'Jamie. He's over there playing pool with a friend of ours.'

'Jamie. Boyfriend? The Aussie guy?'

'Jamie. Husband soon. English.'

'Thought you'd be too young to be getting married,' said Dooley. 'Still, me and Bob and Tim can be your toyboys. Great boots.'

Out of the corner of her eye, Flora could see Martin standing directly opposite her across the other side of the horseshoe bar. Had he seen her? She tried to hide behind Dooley.

'You won't get served like that, Flora.' He turned round to the barman. 'When you're ready. Oh no, look what the cat's sicked up.' Flora didn't want to look. 'See over there? That's the guy Tim had the bother with. Piece of shit.'

'Martin,' sighed Flora.

'You know him?'

'We're staying in the same chalet. Took on all three of you, didn't he? Blood and guts over the snow. You're all in hospital now.'

The giant laughed. 'Wanker. The guy's all mouth.' He suddenly looked concerned. 'Listen, Flora, we don't want any trouble. Your husband and his mate aren't feeling sore on his behalf, are they?'

'No. Promise you. Don't worry.'

'You're not going to be very popular, fratting with the enemy.'

'I'm not anyway.' She peeped round to see Martin muttering to an outraged Nikki, fingers tensed round his glass, expression like a thundercloud. Just then, Bob and Tim arrived, kissing her on both cheeks. 'My shout,' said Flora. Might as well be hanged for a sheep as a lamb.

Cocking his head towards Martin, Dooley muttered that trouble was over the other side of the bar.

'Well, let trouble come to us,' jeered Bob. 'And trouble's mate.'

Flora peeped again. Giles was standing beside Nikki, who clearly had something urgent to tell him. He was nodding, mouthing 'where? where?' his guinea pig face indignant. His expression changed to visible alarm at the sight of Bob and Dooley, and suddenly he was backing away.

'Trouble's staying at Flora's chalet,' said Dooley.

'Great taste you've got,' scoffed Tim. His nose had doubled in size.

'He's about as fond of me as he is of you,' she scowled.

Tim grinned. 'You're all right then. Party up the road. Coming along?'

'She can't. She's a married woman and her husband's over there,' said Dooley. 'Do you spend all day with him? No? Want to meet up tomorrow, come powder surfing?'

'Sorry, I've got a lesson.' She was taken aback by their laughter.

'On skis? You what? And lessons? Can't you skip class or will teacher get cross?' Tim mocked. 'You should be surfing, sweets, not skiing. That's for wrinklies.'

Dooley downed his beer in one gulp. 'Party. See you round, Flora. You're good news. Real pity you're getting married, you know.'

Kissing her goodbye, they headed for the door.

Jamie pressed his way towards her. 'So. Those were the three musketeers. Great tact you showed there, Flora. Well done, angel.' His sarcasm was withering. 'Martin is not very happy. Told Pete you're a Judas.'

'How much would thirty pieces of silver be in francs? More than the backgammon money? What did Pete say?'

'He's outside sharing a spliff with them, talking surfing. Aussie solidarity.'

'So I'm a Judas, but Pete isn't. Great.'

'It's different.' Jamie sighed. 'Flora, people are beginning to notice your animosity towards Martin. It's making them uncomfortable. We're all on holiday and here to enjoy ourselves. Now, I don't want the pair of you at each other's throats and spoiling things. You promised you'd make an effort. Don't sulk. At least say you'll try. Please.'

Flora looked up at him. He seemed so removed from her, so far away. Whose fault? Hers, Stefan's, his? Here was the man she was meant to be spending forever with. 'Jamie, we've got to talk.'

'We are talking. Hello, Anna, having fun?'

'Bit loud in here, isn't it?' She smiled wickedly. 'So who were those blokes you were talking to, Flora?'

'Just some guys I met earlier.'

'Martin's certain they're the three who had a go at him this afternoon.'

'Really?' said Flora, all innocence. Jamie rolled his eyes ceilingwards.

'As I said to him, they couldn't be. After all, from what he said, his three are all meant to be in hospital.' Anna winked. 'And your three didn't have any missing teeth or broken bones, did they? Perhaps that punch has affected Martin's memory. I advised him to get along to the doctor, he might be concussed.'

'You idiot.' Nikki's squawk could be heard above the hubbub. 'Ruined. Do you know how much this cost?' She pushed through the crowd, wiping her wet sleeve with a handkerchief, a pleading Martin in her wake.

Outside, she almost ran, skidding along the pavements. She was beside herself with rage. Martin had spilled almost a demi of beer over her jacket. 'Where's the car?' she screamed. 'I'm going back to the chalet.'

'Just calm down. It was an accident.'

'Give me the keys. I want to go back.'

'What about the others?'

'Fuck the others,' she exploded. Two passers-by stared at her. 'That's all you care about. Showing off to them. What about me? Having to sit around and listen to your bullshit. Your fight. What about that? You look a right wanker. Everyone knows it's not true. Even Anna, taking the mickey like that. You can't fight. You can't ski. You can't even play backgammon. What can you do, apart from pulling your fucking trousers down?'

'Shut up, you stupid bitch.' Martin's contrition evaporated.

'Typical, always putting me down. Jamie and Pete would never speak like that.'

'Perhaps you'd prefer to be with them. One who's so full of himself he shits ego and shags everything in sight, and the other who's a snotty git whose girlfriend's having it off behind his back. Poor bastard. Waking up to that every morning. I'd rather stick a rat up my arse.'

'You're just pissed off because Flora's got one over on you. She knows all about your so-called fight. And you promised you'd make her swap rooms. And what happened? She walks off with a thousand francs. How did that happen, clever clogs?'

'You paid, remember.'

'You still owe me, remember.'

Miranda crept downstairs, cut a huge slice of chocolate cake and poured herself a quadruple brandy. Her eyes were so puffy from crying she could hardly see out of them.

How could she have been so stupid as to end up in bed with Pete? And to trust him to be discreet? They might just as well have done it on the dining table in front of everyone else. Shooting his mouth off wasn't that important, breaking his promise was.

Trusting Pete to respect her was as stupid as fantasising about becoming Mrs Charles Lyall. As stupid as spending hours imagining her future in the beautiful Palladian house surrounded by Capability Brown parkland that would be Charlie's one day. That little bitch Emma wouldn't have a clue how to run a place like that.

Staring into the fire, she gulped some brandy. She'd managed to get through the past four days without crying once. It had been the first time in over a month that she hadn't wept. Ever since that awful Saturday morning back in November when Charlie told her it was all over.

She'd been just about to leave the flat when he called. They'd planned to meet at his cottage on the Berkshire Downs, before going to the Hennessy meeting just down the road in Newbury.

She was wearing a new navy wool suit. The day before in the hairdressers, she'd boned up on all the runners and riders in the big race, so that she'd have something intelligent to say to Charlie's cronies. As a bloodstock agent, he always seemed to know half the people at the races. She'd refused to admit to herself that racing actually bored her. All the horses looked the same, the bookies were intimidating and, as she had no binoculars, she never saw much anyway.

'I'm just leaving,' she'd said, 'so I'll be with you around eleven. Sweetpea is twenty to one in the paper. Must be worth an each way.' Sweetpea had stuck in her mind, because it was a nice name.

'Fucking donkey,' came Charlie's crushing reply. 'Don't waste your money.'

She'd assumed he sounded tetchy because he'd had a big bet. 'Don't worry. I won't be late this time.'

Then he'd told her not to bother coming down. Tears fell as she remembered how Charlie had said he was very sorry but it wasn't going to work out between them. It wasn't her fault, she was a great girl, but it wasn't right. No, there was no point in coming down to the cottage, there was nothing to talk about. She was a great girl, she'd find someone else in next to no time. He'd always remember her fondly. Had some fun, hadn't they? She couldn't expect him to answer that. Please. Why was she making things so difficult? Yes, he'd met someone else. Emma. Yes, that Emma from Goodwood. They'd met again at the Newmarket Sales and something had just clicked. It wasn't his fault. Nothing like this had ever happened before. He was so sorry. He'd tried to tell her weeks ago, but it hadn't been easy, because he guessed, she was, well, keen.

'Keen? Charlie, you know I love you.'

God, he felt such a bastard. He knew she'd be upset. Please stop crying. He guessed there was something else she ought to know. It was only fair she heard it from him. 'I'm going to ask Emma to marry me.'

As the full impact of his words had hit her, she'd dropped the receiver, rushed to the bathroom and thrown up. When she went back, the line was dead and Charlie had gone.

Miranda had more brandy, swallowing it with her sobs.

That Saturday had been the worst day of her life. She'd stayed by the phone, praying that Charlie would call back, say he was joking. Except to take off her new suit and chuck it in the bin, she hadn't moved. She'd turned on the racing, hoping to see Charlie and caught the tail end of an interview with a delighted winning owner. A spoilt bitch of 21 with waist length blonde hair and a massive trust fund. Emma. She'd thrown up again.

Since then, she'd turned into a recluse, too terrified to go out in case she broke down. Unable to accept that Charlie had dumped her, hoping he'd change his mind, she'd told everyone he was abroad, which thankfully had been true.

She thought about him all the time, far more than when they'd actually been supposedly together. The Charlie with whom she had little in common, the Charlie who'd never said he loved her, didn't exist. Neither did the bastard who was so gutless that he'd finished with her over the phone. Instead, an idealised Charlie haunted her, one who was more handsome and caring and attentive than the real Charlie had ever been. The real Charlie she'd only seen about one weekend in three, when she went to stay at his damp cottage where she had to change the sheets.

Since then, every morning at work she'd forced herself to read the Forthcoming Marriages column in *The Times* and the *Telegraph*, her back and neck tightening with stress. How everyone would outwardly pity her but inwardly gloat when they saw pictures of his wedding in *Tatler*.

It should have been her wedding too.

Staring into the fire, she howled in anguish. Would the pain never stop? Would the hurt never go away? Sometimes she thought she'd go mad with grief and bitterness and jealousy.

She'd only agreed to this holiday because she'd thought a show of independence might goad Charlie into saying he loved her. And he'd never done that. Not once. Then she'd told herself that a week away would allow her to come to terms with things, that she'd finally be able to admit to herself and to everyone else it was over.

And here she was. In a worse state than when she'd left.

Pete told Jamie the three Aussies had invited him, Agnes and her friends to a party. 'Coming?' he shouted above the music.

'No. Who's Agnes?' Jamie grinned as Pete pointed to the stunning redhead standing by the door.

'Then there were six,' said Anna, when the rest of them found themselves out on the icy pavement a little later.

'Bit much, Martin pissing off like that,' grumbled Giles. Flora was relieved he had. 'Who was Pete's new popsy?'

'That stunning redhead?' said Jamie. 'Agnes.'

'What are we going to do?' wailed Munchkin, feeling decidedly pizzled. 'I'm freezing.'

Sam, equally pizzled, hugged her to try and warm her up and they almost ended up crashing down into the gutter.

'Bring back memories, Flora?' said Giles.

She shivered, breath swirling round her face in a white stream. 'Aren't there any taxis?'

'Can't recall where we got one from last night,' said Giles. 'Can you, Sam?'

'No chance.'

Anna stamped her feet and sighed. 'You two are completely useless.'

'I'll ask these guys,' said Jamie, seeing two men approach. 'Excusez moi . . . Stefan? Hello. We met yesterday.'

Flora spun round in surprise and saw Stefan shaking hands with Jamie, who was making introductions. 'Gather you met Sam and Giles earlier.' She hung back.

Stefan introduced Claude. '. . . and Flora, you already know,' he said, meeting her eyes. She hastily looked away.

'Of course. How was your lesson?' asked Claude, the instructor who'd joined them at the Savoie at lunchtime.

'Fine.' She noticed Munchkin and Sam nudging one another. Nervous, guilt ridden, unable to stand the sight of Jamie and Stefan standing side by side, she felt sick and sounded curt.

The church bell began to strike twelve, but it was drowned out by the sound of a van, which stopped beside them.

'Bit of luck,' said Giles. 'Hello twins. Sisters of mercy.'

Flora scrambled inside the Camper, while Jamie asked Claude about Aubrisson. She kept her gaze resolutely on Jamie as the others piled in around her. It was only when the Camper pulled away, that she allowed herself the smallest of glances at Stefan. He was staring back at her, with no sign of his usual slow, lazy smile.

CHAPTER FIVE

Wednesday

———◆◇◆———

Munchkin let out such a loud snore that she woke herself up. Her head pounded and her mouth was as dry as a desert. It was so hot. The sheets were clammy. Groaning, she tried to force herself back to sleep. Feeling a hairy leg making hers feel itchy, a thought groped its way through the fog of her hangover. She was not alone.

Sam.

She knew she was going to be sick. Crushed up against the wall, she had to clamber over him. Snatching up her wrap and her glasses, she ran to the bathroom.

She made it. Just. Dizzy, she grabbed the washbasin. The white tiled floor, freezing her feet, was suddenly inviting. She could die there quite happily. She tried to focus on the mirror. Her make-up was raddled, her eyes so small and bloodshot they hardly existed. It wasn't a pretty sight. She ate some toothpaste, then scooped up a handful of water. Her stomach heaved.

Oh no. Not again.

All the alcohol in her system failed to numb the pain. Clutching the towel rail, she lowered herself to the floor and slumped against the wall. What had happened during the past twelve hours that had ended up with Sam in her bed? Again.

She must get herself together, she must talk to him. Urgently.

A weariness stole over her. For days, she'd been pretending.

She'd been running and running, a demented hamster on a wheel. Running and running. Skiing, drinking, playing the bubbly never blubbery party animal.

She was ready to wave the white flag and admit defeat. It was time to surrender.

She was pregnant. She knew she was pregnant. She couldn't be, could she? Panic overwhelmed her. Something that was supposed to be so joyful had caused her so much torture. What was she going to do?

Kate Williams, 34, company director, go-getting professional, knew exactly what to do. She was a woman with the right to choose and the money to pay to make that choice easy. Trip to a clinic, day off work. Safe, quick, clean, easier than having a tooth out.

Munchkin Williams, soon to be the wrong end of her thirties, was racked by doubts. This thing inside her was smaller than a tooth at the moment, but it would grow into something she'd yearned for more than anything. It might be her last chance.

What would she tell him or her? You're the result of a drunken one-night-stand between me and a nice but hopeless Irishman, Sam Shaughnessy. The loser from Limerick. A one-night-stand that had happened after a party fell flat and the two of us had gone for a pizza and got smashed. And that morning after the night before, the pair of us were mortified with embarrassment.

She was under no illusions that Sam had suddenly found her devastatingly attractive. They'd got pissed, she'd been available. Few men passed up the chance of an easy lay.

A single mother. How would she cope? Millions of women did; widowed, divorced they had no choice. They just got on with it. But it was different making a conscious decision to do without a man from day one. Supposing it was a boy? What good would she be at kicking a football? Even if she could continue her career, be the provider, could she manage without the father's moral support?

A single mother. Listen to Giles. Single mothers were either feckless scroungers-off-the-hardworking-taxpayer or selfish have-it-alls, such harridans that no decent man wanted them.

Munchkin began to weep. She wanted a baby so much. She wanted babies, but in a traditional set-up. With a husband who'd be there with her, who wanted a family with her. Had she the right to deny her child any chance of family life?

She was not pregnant. Could not be. But she was two days late. But only two days. Worry was causing the delay, wasn't it? Her body felt weird, heavy. Perhaps she was getting the curse after all.

She was pregnant. She'd known she'd taken a risk. Why hadn't she postponed her trip to Birmingham and gone to get the morning-after pill?

Exhausted by despair, she got slowly to her feet and crept back to her room for her sponge bag. Sam was sprawled across the bed. The room stank. She opened the steamed-up windows. Her alarm clock showed it was quarter to seven.

Sam was lying on his back, whistling and grunting. She studied him with fondness. He was always so cheerful. Even after losing his job, he'd always been ready with a wisecrack, up for having a laugh, cheering everyone up. His hands were strangely beautiful, she hadn't noticed them before.

Later. She'd talk to him later, when she could think a bit straighter. After some tea, a shower, some painkillers.

Of course, when she told him, he'd think she was trapping him. A heavy price for him to pay for a night's sex. He'd hate her for it. Suddenly, she wanted him out of the way.

'Sam,' she hissed, nudging him. 'Wake up.' She braced herself for his embarrassment covered up by some sort of joke, before he bolted for the door.

He sat up, squinting. 'Morning. That the time?'

'You'd better go.'

'Why? Come back in here and let's go back to sleep.' He

pulled her to him, kissed her on the nose and holding her hand, fell asleep again almost at once.

A couple of hours later, Nikki watched Martin get dressed, admiring the muscles in his back. They'd had a glorious reconciliation after their row outside the bar. She smiled in contentment at the memory.

He'd explained he'd been uptight because of some deal, a development on the Thames. And, frankly, Nikki love, thinking about her and David Thone together got to him. Call him a prat, but he was jealous. OK, it was history. But he wasn't too impressed by the way she'd been treated. Well, the dirty old git should've at least given her the flat and the car after all that weird sex stuff she'd had to put up with. Perhaps it was harmless enough, funny even, but weird. Come on, hardly normal was it? In fact, if he ever met Thone he'd punch his lights out. And if he were her, he'd pay Thone back. How? Go to the papers. They'd pay a fortune for a story like hers

Nikki rolled onto her stomach and pulled the duvet round her. 'Martin, you know what you were saying last night? About the papers?'

'What about them?' He pulled on a T-shirt.

'How much is a fortune?'

He shrugged. 'High five figures, closer to six.'

'You're joking.' She sat up astounded. 'How do you know?'

'I've had experience, don't forget. Know my way round. Why? Interested?'

High five figures, closer to six? 'Just curious.'

Miranda was drained. She dressed on auto-pilot, eyelids so swollen she could hardly open them. Downstairs, Giles was braying something with his usual heartiness. Dreading having to face them all, she longed to escape. Martin and Sam would doubtless make some crack about Pete.

She bathed her eyes and reached for her make-up. Warpaint. She was going to go into battle to win back the self respect she'd lost after making such an idiot of herself in front of everyone the night before.

Pete. Only yesterday, she'd been on cloud nine, congratulating herself on finding a gorgeous new man to get over Charlie. She'd even imagined them turning up arm-in-arm to cousin Fiona's wedding in May, him looking divine in a morning coat.

She'd thought Pete would heal her wounds. Instead he'd reopened them.

She'd have to confront him, if only to ask him how they were going to get through the next few days under the same roof. A sudden shyness struck her. Pete the commitment phobe had thought nothing of going to bed with her when he thought she was almost engaged. Pete the commitment phobe would now see her as yet another predator trying to ensnare him. Better get it over with and confront him.

As she crept along the passageway to his room, her awkwardness grew. Knocking on his door, she was tempted to bolt, but told herself she had every right to talk to him. No answer. She knocked again and opened the door.

No Pete. She peered out the window. No Porsche.

So, he'd already left for Aubrisson without a second thought about her. Obviously she was just another one to chalk up, another one who'd fallen for the sweet Pete charm. Another pair of tits on the wall.

With her lesson starting at lunchtime, Flora was lying in bed planning a lazy morning on a balcony reading in the sunshine and drinking hot chocolate.

As she tried to shut out the clatter from the kitchen, in the room directly overhead Martin and Nikki got up and stomped around. They sounded like an army on the march.

'No Martin. Don't,' shrieked Nikki.

Flora pulled the pillow over her head and tried to read. Her eyes scanned the lines and the pages turned, but she wasn't taking in a word. The thumps and thuds intruding on her were an unwelcome reminder of Martin's malevolence. It had been bad enough even before she'd talked to the Australians. He'd be out for her blood this morning. She'd keep out of his way until he'd gone. What had Jamie got to find out about?

Stefan?

She began to reconstruct every second of her time with him. How he'd looked, what he'd said as his green eyes stared into her own. How he couldn't allow her to get married. Did he really want her so much? When could they . . . ?

Stop. This was so wrong. What happened yesterday must be erased from her memory, deleted, as if it had never happened. The only man for her was Jamie. She loved Jamie, she was going to marry him. Since she'd met him, she'd never once thought about anyone else, her loyalty to Jamie was absolute.

How could she've been so weak? Betrayed Jamie's trust? A few minutes of pleasure with Stefan weren't worth the pain she'd cause Jamie if he found out. Why had she surrendered to temptation? Was a beautiful face worth all this confusion? There was only one thing for it, she must own up. Tell Jamie and take the consequences.

'Morning angel.' Jamie leant over to kiss her. 'I love waking up next to you.'

He bounded over to the window and pulled back the curtains. He was the only person she'd ever met who greeted the day as if he were starring in a cornflakes commercial.

The thud of footsteps came from overhead. Flora winced.

'Next time we'll go away on our own. Promise,' said Jamie.

'As next time will be our honeymoon, I hope we will be on our own.'

He got dressed and opened the balcony doors. 'Weather might be changing. Maybe there'll be some snow. Hetty said it was forecast.'

'Great,' said Flora flatly. She didn't want to think about snow and skiing. Or skiing lessons.

Jamie had had enough. 'For fuck's sake, Flora, why the hell can't you cheer up? You're in a beautiful place, you're skiing again. You're lucky. Privileged. There are thousands of people who'd love to swap with you.'

He yanked back the duvet and pulled her from the bed, tugging her out onto the balcony. 'I know you're useless at maths, but start learning to count your blessings.'

She tried to struggle free of him. 'Beautiful place. Yes. But people make the difference, Jamie.'

'And what's so wrong with the people here? Think of the nutters you know. Jem. Can't decide whether she's Lucretia Borgia or the Virgin Mary. Quince the Mince, that screamer, out cottaging every night . . .'

'He is not. Fred's a brilliant . . .'

'He's a nutcase as well as a fruit.'

'He's not. He predicted this place would be full of Guernsey sweaters proclaiming they're party animals.' She wrenched herself free of him. 'The hearties of darkness.'

'Live and let live,' yelled Jamie. 'Learn to lighten up. Make a fucking effort. You should eat more. You'd be less ratty.'

What had possessed him to drag her off skiing? Next time, he'd have a Boy's Own week and she could go away with Jem.

Martin was on his mobile and tapping into his laptop, while munching a croissant. Beside him, Nikki was exclaiming that luckily her eye showed only a tiny bit of swelling. Her pristine white sweater highlighted her deepening tan.

Miranda had isolated herself behind an old magazine. Seeing

her, Jamie disappeared. He returned a few minutes later with three snowdrops in a tiny glass and put them beside her plate.

'Sorry about Charlie,' he murmured. 'If you've got a decade, I'll fill you in on what a shit he was at school.'

'Thanks,' croaked Miranda in a whisper. Touched, she was afraid she was about to break down again. 'Sweet of you.'

'James? Surprised to see you,' said Giles. 'Thought you'd gone off to Aubrisson with Pete.'

'We decided against it last night. Couldn't be fagged.'

'Hasn't Pete gone?'

'Doubt it.' Jamie was puzzled. 'He's still asleep, isn't he?'

'The Porsche isn't here,' said Miranda casually.

'It's not?' Although it was early, Jamie thought quickly, then banished all thought of stunning redheads from his mind. 'Perhaps he's gone down to get his skis waxed, mentioned something about it yesterday. Hope he's remembered to take mine.'

'Didn't hear him come back last night,' said Giles. 'Perhaps he struck lucky with that gorgeous bit of Frog totty. You remember, the one with the red hair.'

Miranda froze.

'Doubt it,' said Jamie, seeing the fleeting anguish on Miranda's face and not wanting to land Pete in it. 'Went off to some party with those Aussies.'

Nikki and Martin glared.

Cursing Giles, desperate to change the subject, Jamie turned to Nikki. 'Are you two still planning to go to Aubrisson?'

'Maybe,' said Martin, stabbing at his laptop keyboard.

'Good place to try out the new skis, Nikki,' said Jamie. 'What make are they again?'

'Ros . . .'

'Aubrisson, eh,' interrupted Martin, eyes on the screen. 'If I were you, I'd stick around in St Marie and keep an eye on your wife.'

Nikki's tea went down the wrong way. Anna and Miranda

exchanged glances. Giles grew uneasy, remembering what Munchkin had said about Flora and that Stefan chappie. Just then he heard a car. 'Ah-ha. Must be Pete.'

Jamie leapt to his feet, muttering about his skis. He intercepted Pete who was running up the stairs two at a time. Putting his fingers to his lips, he whispered, 'Miranda's up. Told her you probably went into town early to get your skis waxed.'

'How is she?'

'Low, I guess. Sort things out, will you?' He studied Pete, then broke into a smile. 'You look knackered.'

'I am.' He yawned.

'She was gorgeous.' Jamie grinned. 'But a bit much even for you, isn't it? Two in one day.'

'Nothing happened,' hissed Pete, unusually agitated.

'Nothing?' Jamie sounded sceptical

'Nothing.' Pete pushed his hair out of his eyes. 'Went to the party. Agnes and her friends are staying in the same apartment block. I got stoned, too off my face to drive, so crashed on their sofa.'

As Pete walked past the dining table on his way to the kitchen, he gently squeezed Miranda's shoulder. She looked a bit ragged, but not bad considering. 'Can we talk a bit later?' he whispered.

'Of course.' Miranda noted with suspicion that he was wearing the same clothes as the night before.

'Are you OK, Anna?' said Nikki. 'You're very quiet this morning.'

'Fine.' Anna forced a smile. 'So are we going to Aubrisson?'

'Let's, Martin,' pleaded Nikki. 'The snow's supposed to be better and there's some great shops there.'

'For you, lover, anything.' He was rewarded by a huge smile. 'What about you Giles?'

'Absolutely. Make a nice change. Is the offer of a lift still on?' He didn't want to drive, or have to fuss about making everyone divvy up for petrol. 'Great. Miranda?'

'Maybe.'

'We'd better get a move on then.' Martin was businesslike. 'Pete, when are you planning to leave? Pete?'

Under his tousled hair, Pete's blue-green eyes were vague. 'Leave? Saturday.'

'For Aubrisson.'

'I'll pass. Too much effort.' He yawned. 'Probably go to La Chevre with Jamie.'

'Bet your trouble is too much bed and not enough sleep,' Martin winked at Giles. 'Tired you out, has she?'

Pete glanced uneasily at Miranda. 'That's not funny. And not true.'

Miranda stood up abruptly, wanting to escape the unthinkable, wanting to escape from Pete. He hadn't, had he? She felt sick. 'I'd better get ready.'

'Where's Sam and Munchkin got to?' asked Martin.

'You might well ask.' Giles sniggered. 'Bed probably.'

'What? Together?' Martin's eyebrows shot up. 'Humpty Dumpty, rumpy pumpy? Making the beast with two backs?' He nudged Nikki.

'Be quiet, Martin,' she frowned. 'I think it's nice. Bit of holiday romance. Must be something in the water, what with them and you tw . . .' She stopped herself.

Miranda was halfway across the room and heard Nikki's, then Martin's laugh ringing out. Giles pushed past, yelling 'snog patrol'.

Safely back in her bedroom, Miranda bit the inside of her cheek. She was not going to be feeble, she was not going to cry. Despite Jamie's pathetic efforts to cover for him, she had the most awful suspicion that Pete had spent the night with someone else. Impossible. He wasn't that much of a bastard. Was he? He was enough of a bastard to promise one thing and do another. Pretty boy Pete, the playboy with the Porsche. He'd probably said all those same sweet things to all those hundreds of other women.

'I'll come back in a minute.' Ever tactful, Anna hovered.

'It's all right.' While Anna grabbed her jacket and money, Miranda turned her back and dabbed at her eyes, then hid them behind sunglasses. She could hear Martin at the foot of the stairs, shouting at Nikki to hurry.

'Miranda?' The voice was tentative.

Pete was standing at the door. Anna hurried away.

'I'm really, really sorry about you and Charlie.'

His sincerity reminded her of his honeyed sweetness the previous afternoon.

'About last night,' continued Pete. 'I didn't mean it to become public, er, the thing is, um, Sam . . .'

'Done now,' whispered Miranda. 'By the way, have you really been into town to get your skis waxed?'

Pete pushed the hair out of his eyes. 'No. If you'll let me explain . . .'

'Time to make a move,' Giles's guinea pig face popped round the door. 'We should be there by eleven at the latest.' His white lashed eyes darted between the pair of them. 'Load up Mirandy, Anna's already in the car.'

'Beat it, can't you?' growled Pete, exasperated. As Giles withdrew in a huff, Martin repeated his call to hurry up. 'Where was I?'

'More to the point, where did you spend the night?'

'Let me explain. I went to this party and . . .'

'Come on Miranda.' Nikki's huge brown eyes sparkled. 'Isn't this exciting? Somewhere new.'

Pete pulled a face. 'I went to this party and . . .'

'It will keep until later,' cut in Miranda. The Gods were clearly against her. Why did Nikki have to be punctual on this morning of all mornings? 'I'd better go.'

'Have a good time.'

'Thank you.'

Feeling wretched, Pete watched her stride along the passage-way, head held high. He knew she'd been crying. She had guts though. Most women would've crumbled for months after being dumped as she'd been dumped. Instead she'd carried on, come away, kept her stiff upper lip stiff, her head up and her heartbreak to herself. No one had guessed anything was up.

He felt even more rotten. Not even Jamie believed how he'd spent the night.

Keen to ski the other side of the valley, Jamie returned to the bedroom to grab his jacket and pass. Flora was out on the balcony, huddled under the duvet, reading.

'Have some breakfast, it'll cheer you up. Let's meet at the Savoie around half-twelve,' said Jamie. 'Whatever's got into you recently, try and deal with it by then. Please.' He kissed the top of her head. 'It's getting very boring.'

'Thought you'd never be bored with me,' muttered Flora, turning the page.

She sighed as he walked out. If only he understood why she was hiding herself away. If she tried to explain, he'd only be dismissive, tell her she was being paranoid, tell her to make an effort and not fuck up his holiday.

Voices came up from the drive, then the Range Rover's engine revved up. Safe now to get some breakfast. How ridiculous to have to hide herself away. Ridiculous that she was too gutless and shy to confront Martin. The air didn't belong to him, no matter if that was how he made her feel. She wasn't a trespasser. But it must be better to keep out of his way than to have a massive row with him, spoiling things for everyone else.

Flora went to the kitchen and made herself some coffee. Hetty and Alice were upstairs cleaning the bathrooms. She sat at the dining table and stared across the valley.

Was this what she had to look forward to in the coming decades of life with Jamie? Being dragged from one bunch of people to the next, always feeling so out of place? Why couldn't she be like him, breezing through life, being sociable, seeing the best in everyone and making the best of every situation? Light, sparkling, a good mixer, Jamie was tonic water. Compared to him, she often felt like a dose of cod liver oil.

Was Fred right to have his doubts about them? 'Darling, are you quite, quite sure?' he'd trilled, when she told him about her engagement. 'Lovely ring, you lucky, lucky thing. Not rocks, mountains. I'll come and bite off your finger in the middle of the night. Quite, quite sure? Of course, he's so very pukka and a dish in the upright Empire-building way, but he'll be dragging you up and down a grouse moor before you can say the fourth of June.'

'Twelfth of August.'

'Flora, exactly. Is it really you? Now Lorenzo . . .'

'Lorenzo's history . . .'

'Shame. My favourite.'

'You were after him.'

'Who wasn't, Flora, who wasn't? Mad, bad and thrilling to know . . .'

'That bastard broke my heart. And he'll end up shot or in prison.'

Lorenzo had been packed away in a trunk called 'youth', along with the phone being cut off, the fridge empty apart from a bottle of vodka buried in frost, and seedy clubs. Her biker boots should be in there too.

And Stefan? Shouldn't he be locked away in there as well?

She stared down at her engagement ring. It would soon be joined by a thin gold band. How could she have jeopardised her future with Jamie for him? She'd met him two days ago, she knew nothing about him, apart from the fact that he was a penniless ski instructor with a girlfriend called Marie France.

She'd risked everything, could have thrown it all away, for the sake of a stranger?

'Penny for them.'

Flora looked up and saw Munchkin in her wrap and heavy spectacles, looking decidedly hungover. 'How about a franc?'

'You seem low. Anything wrong?'

'No, I'm fine. Really.' Flora managed a smile.

Munchkin stacked the four remaining croissants onto a plate. As if reading Flora's mind, she said hastily, 'Not all for me. Sam's starving. Jamie about?'

'Skiing.'

'No lesson?'

'Later.' Flora picked up the cafetière.

'With Stefan? Very attractive, isn't he?'

Flora tried to sound emphatic. 'Not my type.'

'Local? Lives in St Marie?'

'Somewhere.' Coffee was suddenly spilling all over the table.

'I'll get a cloth.' Munchkin headed to the kitchen with a smirk. Guilty as hell.

Anna closed her eyes as Martin screeched the Range Rover around another hairpin bend and hurtled towards the car up ahead. He came within inches of it, then had to brake, sharply. The skis and poles clattered in the back.

'Move over,' he yelled, flashing his lights at the Citroen, overtaking it and scowling at the driver.

Anna gripped the side of the seat in anxiety for the fifth time, and they were only just outside St Marie. This was as hideous as driving with Pete.

Nikki sang along to the music, on full blast as usual. 'What a view. We're right on the other side of the valley. Where's the chalet?'

Miranda stared out stony-faced. She should've stayed behind and had things out with Pete. He couldn't have spent the night with anyone else, could he? Surely Martin had been making one of his typically crude jokes? But why had Jamie tried to cover for him? And what had Giles meant about gorgeous Frog totty?

Giles wondered why they were shooting off. It had seemed a good idea last night, but actually it was a bit of a fag in the cold light of day. And it would be expensive. He glanced at Miranda, who was clearly very pissed off. Perhaps he shouldn't have stuck in his paddle at dinner. On the other hand, he was doing her a favour in the long run. Pete loved them and left them all. But you had to hand it to him, two in one day was going some.

The car sped on, down the twisting road cut out of the mountainside and towards the next valley. The buildings, huddled close together as if for warmth in St Marie, became more spread out. Soon there was nothing but grey rockface and green forest, impenetrable by the sun.

Giles sniffed. Frowning, he sniffed again. There was definitely an acrid smell coming from somewhere. 'Is something burning?' he called above the noise of the music. 'Martin?'

'Something burning?' repeated Giles, just as wisps of steam started to appear from under the bonnet.

'Shit.' Martin pulled to the side of the road and braked violently. The needle on the temperature gauge was on red. 'Open the bonnet, Nikki. Quickly.'

'How?'

'The catch. Not there. Let me.' He shoved her aside. 'Bloody women.'

Anna pulled a face.

Steam was pouring out in front of the windscreen. Giles and Martin jumped out, lifted up the bonnet and peered at the engine. They were copied by the three women, who were clueless about what they were supposed to be looking for.

'Shit.' Martin was furious.

'Looks like a cracked radiator, old man,' said Giles. 'Did you put in enough anti-freeze?'

'Of course.' Martin was indignant. Nikki stared at him tight-lipped. 'I did.'

'Umm,' said Giles doubtfully.

'What are we going to do?' wailed Nikki. 'It's freezing.'

'Call a garage. There must be one in St Marie,' said Martin.

'The twins will know,' suggested Anna. 'We need a phone.'

'Good idea,' said Nikki. 'Martin, mobile.'

'It's back at the chalet.'

'What?' she screeched.

Surrounded by a dense tangle of green forest, they looked round helplessly. Far, far above the mass of fir trees, the three peaks of Les Diables towered above them, soaring up into the pale blue sky. There were no buildings, no people, no sound of birdsong. Nothing.

'Did we pass a call box?' asked Anna.

No one could remember.

'We'd better head back to St Marie,' said Martin.

'If the car's all right to drive, why don't we carry on to Aubrisson?' demanded Nikki.

'We're going to walk,' hissed Martin.

'Walk?' She was aghast. 'It's miles. My Gucci's will be ruined.'

'Well, stay here and freeze.'

'What about the skis?' said Giles. 'Someone might nick them.'

'Leave them,' said Martin. 'They're insured.'

'We could always *langlauf*,' said Anna, trying to be cheerful.

'It's uphill all the way and there's no snow,' snapped Nikki.

Martin took charge. 'There's no choice. We've got to walk. It's what? Four miles, max. Should do it in under an hour. Used to do 10 miles in a morning in the old days, with a pack on the back.'

'There might be a bus,' said Anna, zipping up her turquoise jacket.

'That would be brilliant.' Having not used public transport for two years, Nikki was suddenly a convert.

Eager to show off how fit he was, Martin set off at a furious pace, telling Giles about his daily work-out regime. Giles had to gasp his replies. He stopped frequently to get his breath back, although he pretended he was allowing the women to catch up.

'. . . followed by twenty reps on the bench press.'

'Instead of doing weights, you should carry Nikki,' panted Giles. He could hear her grumbling in the distance about how her feet hurt and how thirsty she was.

'Eat some snow then,' called Martin.

They trudged on for another half an hour. Few cars went by and those that did ignored Anna's upturned thumb. The road became steeper as it wound its way round the mountainside. Their spirits lifted when they saw a bus shelter, only to sink again when they discovered that the timetable had been torn out. It was pointless waiting. Five minutes later, they had to leap to the side of the road, hearing an angry blast of a horn. Nikki could've wept, seeing a dirty blue bus speeding past them.

Anna started to sing 'Lost in France'.

'We may as well be lost in space,' growled Nikki. 'I could kill Martin, look at this place. Nothing. I never want to see another tree in my life.' She tore off her silver fox hat and felt her sweat-damp scalp. 'I can't wait to get back and wash my hair.'

'Vain, whingeing cow,' muttered Miranda, shivering.

Out of the sunshine, it was bitterly cold.

'Come on girls, bit more effort,' yelled Martin. 'Can't be far now.'

Forty minutes later, just as Nikki was reaching breaking point, Giles turned round and pointed triumphantly at a roadsign. 'St Marie,' he called back.

'Thank God,' muttered Miranda through clenched teeth.

Even Anna was surly.

'Drink first, car later,' said Martin, seeing a café beyond the fire station. He turned to Nikki. 'Well done, lover. You made it. Not bad for someone whose idea of a walk is going round Harvey Nichols.'

She glared at him. 'It's not funny. It's all your fault. I don't remember you putting in any anti-freeze. Can't you get anything right?'

'Just shut the fuck up, can't you?'

'No I can't . . .'

Rolling her eyes in exasperation, Anna gestured to Miranda and Giles to cross the road to the café.

'. . . Two days messed up down to you . . .'

The café was dark and deserted. In English, Giles asked for a glass of water, insisting it should be tap. The patronne, unsmiling and rotund, told him to leave.

'*Madame, cinq cafés au lait,*' cut in Anna. 'For God's sake Giles, stop being so stingy can't you? *Et deux grandes bouteilles d'eau. Notre voiture est en panne . . .*'

'What's that?' Giles tried to translate the pair's rapid speech.

'Her son runs a garage. She's going to ring him now.'

Giles glugged back his water. 'That'll cost Martin. Still, not our problem, eh?'

The patronne returned and told Anna that her son would meet them there and drive them to the Range Rover.

They sat down in relief and were joined a few minutes later by a scowling Nikki and Martin. Worn out by the hike, no one felt much like talking. Miranda picked up a paper at the next table and hid herself behind it. Finishing his coffee, Martin got up to play pinball.

Giles looked at his watch. 'Should we grab some grub? Don't want to waste the afternoon. Mirandy?'

'Not hungry,' came a voice behind the paper.

'Sure? You hardly had any breakfast.'

'On a diet for Pete?' piped up Martin, as his second ball rolled through the flippers.

Miranda lowered the paper. 'Of course not.'

'Sure? You're blushing. Isn't she, Giles?'

Nikki shot Martin a warning look. 'Shut up.' She patted Miranda's arm. 'Ignore them. They're only trying to be funny.'

'Can't anyone mind their own business?' Swallowing hard,

Miranda buried herself behind the paper. Hearing sniffing, the four looked at one another uneasily. Suddenly Miranda rushed to the door.

As Giles raised his voice and asked in English for the menu, Anna slipped outside. She found Miranda sitting on a bench in the bus shelter across the road, blowing her nose.

'Anything I can do?' Behind her glasses, Anna's grey eyes were concerned. She sat down.

Miranda shook her head.

'I was so sorry to hear about you and Charlie.'

'Not as sorry as me.' Miranda sounded bitter. She stared out at the road. 'Not as sorry as my mother will be. She thinks he's perfect. Perfect background, perfect bank balance, perfect house, perfect husband material. Sure. He'll make a perfect husband for the very young, very pretty, very rich Emma.'

Anna delved in her pocket and handed Miranda a tissue.

'Sorry. Thanks.' She wiped away her tears. 'Christmas was hell. Mummy going on and on about it being time that Charlie made up his mind. Proposed. I didn't have the guts to admit he's dumped me.' Her voice cracked. 'For the last month, I've had the excuse that he's away. I know I should've owned up straight away, but I've felt so low and worthless and rejected. And I was hoping he'd change his mind.'

Anna watched helplessly as Miranda began crying her heart out.

Finally, the howling gave way to hiccuping. 'I thought this holiday might give me a chance to come to terms with things,' Miranda sniffed hard. 'What a joke. Wish I'd stayed at home.'

A bus arrived. As the passengers stepped off, Miranda pulled up her collar and hunched over to avoid their eyes. 'God, I'm being pathetic. This business with Pete . . . I believed he was a nice guy, apart from everything else he's got going for him. You see, he promised he'd keep it quiet. And then he ran off and told everyone. It's trivial, I know. They would've found out anyway. It's just that I felt so let down. Again. That's why I made that dreadful scene at dinner. Sorry. Pathetic of me to overreact like that.'

'Nonsense,' said Anna. 'You didn't.'

'I couldn't face everyone taking the piss and spoiling things.'

'Don't blame you.'

'I wish I'd never come on this bloody holiday.'

'If I had the money, I'd have left days ago.'

'You would?' Miranda was astonished.

'Odd man out, that's me. Odd woman out, rather. Yet again.' Sighing heavily, Anna focussed on the sky. 'This morning at breakfast, I thought why can't I just be like everyone else?'

'Why would you want to be?' Miranda scowled.

Anna bit her lip. 'It would just be easier, that's all.'

'Like who? Me? The yomping, bossy bit of posh turned snivelling wreck? Not so sweet Pete? Martin, Giles and Sam?'

'Insufferable gits,' muttered Anna. Miranda actually smiled. 'Sorry, shouldn't bitch, but I find them impossible sometimes. Correction, most of the time.'

'Food fights, water fights, loud music, pulling down their trousers . . .' Miranda pulled a face.

'I keep on reminding myself that everyone's on holiday. They're out for a good time. It's not for me to spoil their fun. But I've hated almost every single minute of it.'

Miranda was taken aback by Anna's dejection. 'I'm sorry.'

'Don't worry.' Again she looked up at the sky, as if she were hoping for some sort of message. 'Life's been a bit mixed up over the past few months. Leaving my job, being a student again and . . .' She hesitated. 'Doesn't matter.'

An elderly man arrived, and they squeezed along the bench to let him sit down.

'I was really looking forward to this week,' continued Anna. 'I imagined skiing all day, relaxing in the evenings, then quality sleep. Instead I feel as if I'm in the middle of a war zone. I'm more exhausted than we left. I've never felt so out of place, so out-numbered. My fault, I suppose. Typical Anna, permanent sense of humour failure, boring, heavy, never seeing the joke or learning to lighten up. No one else seems to mind all that hideous horseplay, in fact they're having the time of their lives.'

'Well, I mind. So, you're not alone.' Miranda sniffed. 'And actually you're not the least bit boring.'

'Oh no? I haven't got a flash car, or a brilliant career or megabucks . . .'

'And I have? I hate my job. Chairman's PA. Huh. Typist who arranges plane tickets as Sam said.'

'Unkind.'

'True.' Miranda was despairing. 'Since I met Charlie in April, I've lived from weekend to weekend. Everything else was on hold, because deep down I was thinking . . .' She shook her head. 'How dumb can you get?'

Anna's teeth began to chatter. She noticed Miranda shivering. 'Let's have something to eat and go skiing.'

'Therapy.' Miranda nodded and clambered to her feet. 'Thanks, Anna. Letting me whinge on and on. Sorry to ask, but was Pete with anyone in the bar last night?'

Anna hesitated. 'Jamie. They were playing pool.'

'No redheads?'

'Couldn't see. It was packed.'

Flora had cadged a lift with Pete, after he had a post-breakfast power snooze. Up at the Savoie, they were joined by Jamie. The three of them lay stretched out on the upstairs terrace, soaking up the sun.

A morning's hard skiing had drained Jamie, wiping away his previous irritation with Flora.

A morning's hard thinking had, she hoped, given Flora new resolve. Stefan was packed away in the trunk called youth. Her future was with Jamie.

'The life,' smiled Pete. 'Sun, skiing, beer. What more does a man need?'

'Sex,' yawned Jamie. 'Surprised you of all people left that one out. 'Money. Drugs.'

Watching a couple paralleling their way down from La Toit, Flora counted off on her fingers. 'A brilliant mind, wit, charm, ambition, savoir faire, looks. And a huge dick.'

Both men opened their eyes. 'Thought size didn't matter,' said Pete.

'Who told you that? Martin? He's probably got one the size of a radish, that's why he behaves like he does.'

Pete nudged her. 'Didn't you see it last night at dinner.'

'Missed that treat.' Flora scowled.

'Oh come on, things just got a bit out of hand,' said Jamie.

'In hand and they'd have been having a wank.'

'Flora, please,' protested Jamie. 'It was only a bit of fun.'

'Wonder how they're getting on in Aubrisson,' Pete yawned so hard he showed his tonsils.

'Good luck to them. Far too much effort,' said Jamie.

'Nice to get away from them all. Remind me never to get pissed again and book myself onto a holiday,' said Pete. Jamie shot Flora a 'don't start' look. 'If I had someone like you Flora, I wouldn't do such dumb things.'

'Thanks,' said Jamie.

Pete offered Flora a ciggie. An Amazonian blonde in a yellow ski suit sauntered over and asked him for a light. 'What am I going to do about Mirandy? Another dumb thing.'

'Miranda's not that stupid,' said Jamie.

'I didn't mean that. Going to bed with her was dumb. First off, she was meant to be engaged, so what sort of shit am I to trepass? Then she was a mate.' He sighed. 'I've got to start using my brains instead of my dick. Oh God, what am I going to do?'

'Kiss and make up,' suggested Jamie.

'If only.' He sounded rueful. 'I tried to explain but she wouldn't listen. Now she thinks something's going on with Agnes.'

'Well, you did spend the night at her place,' said Jamie.

'Nothing happened,' said Pete, irritated. 'More complications. Why did Giles have to land me in it last night? I thought accountants were meant to be discreet. It wasn't deliberate, was it? You said he was after Miranda.'

'He was pissed.'

'True.' Pete dragged heavily on his Marlboro. 'Sam. The Miss bloody Marple of the chalet.' He blew a smoke ring. 'Anyway he and Munchkin have got it together. Punishing the mattress earlier. Should cheer him up. He's really hacked off, you know, about being out of work.'

'But he's always so upbeat.' Jamie was surprised. 'Brave face? Fits. Silly little bugger should've mentioned something. The bank might be looking for human resources people. I'll have a chat.'

Flora looked at Jamie's watch, stood up reluctantly and stretched. 'Saltmine time.' She kissed his forehead, now turning brown.

'Meet you back here, angel.'

Jamie watched her as she collected her skis from the rack, slung them over her shoulder and made her way across the snow to the chairlift. He could easily see Stefan in his scarlet suit, that mess of a ponytail between his shoulders. Flora turned back to wave. Jamie waved back. She threw her skis down onto the snow and stood in them, then reached round to the back of her boots.

Jamie could just about see her pulling a face, then saying something to Stefan, who stooped down to clip them up. Seeing Flora's arm resting on Stefan's shoulder, Jamie felt profound disquiet. What had Martin meant about keeping an eye on Flora?

With every step she took towards Stefan, Flora grew more nervous. She sensed Jamie was watching her from the Savoie balcony. Suddenly, she longed to be back at his side; his love and care and familiarity wrapped around her like a comforter, protecting her from her confusion.

'Hello,' she sounded distant.

He smiled his slow, lazy smile, studying her intently. '*Ca va?*'

'Yes. Thank you.' Not meeting his eyes, she threw her skis down on the snow, then turned back to wave to Jamie. 'So. Where are we going today?' Rarely had she felt more awkward.

'Higher. Better snow. Better sun.' He raised his ski pole beyond La Toit. Far down in the valley, mist was edging round St Marie. 'We'll escape your rich husband.'

She looked up sharply. 'I don't want to escape him.' She wanted to tell Stefan that what had happened in Jimmy's last night had been a huge, horrible mistake. She tried to fasten her ski boots but as usual the clips failed to budge.

'Let me.' He crouched down. Almost over-balancing, she instinctively steadied herself, grabbing his shoulder. '*Allez.*'

She followed him across the piste, struggling to copy his skating style. Her skis kept on getting stuck as if they were in treacle, rather than on snow. Anxious to keep her distance, at the chairlift Flora scooted ahead of Stefan and lined up next to a woman who was rather depressingly a double for Catherine Deneuve.

As the lift began to take them high above the piste, Flora pulled down the safety bar. She laughed. Something she'd thought of as an ordeal only a few days earlier had become second nature.

Below, a lone skier glided effortlessly across the snow. Suddenly Flora longed to be able to ski well. She forgot Jamie, forgot Stefan, forgot all the frictions at the chalet and the emotional turmoil inside her as she was filled with the longing to be able to parallel.

'Where now?' she asked, when they reached the top.

'The cable car.'

Flora looked up hundreds of feet at the cabin which seemed to be floating in the sky. She swallowed hard. Some of her new-found enthusiasm began to ebb. 'Must we?'

Stefan was puzzled. 'Yes. *Allez.*'

*   *   *

There was a long, dismal wait in the café for the tow-truck to return with the Range Rover, Martin, Anna and the skis.

'Twins' night off tonight,' said Giles.

Brooding, but pretending to brush up her almost non-existent French by reading the paper, Miranda picked at her food. She must talk to Pete. On the pretext of asking the twins about where to eat that night, Miranda telephoned the chalet. She got the answering machine.

'No luck?' asked Giles. 'We might as well go to Les Landais.'

No Pete. Miranda slumped down. 'They must all be skiing.'

'Lucky them,' scowled Nikki. 'What a waste of a day.'

Flora's new found enthusiasm vanished completely when she entered the cable car. She was tempted to bolt straight out. The glass cabin was empty apart from two boisterous young boys and their instructor who began talking to Stefan.

She stiffened when the car suddenly lurched, moved slowly out of the lift station and began its ascent.

The boys aged about eight, started to play tag, ignoring their instructor's half-hearted appeals to calm down. It had been a trying morning for him and he'd almost given up trying to make them behave. As they chased each other around more furiously, weaving between the two men, their shouting and laughter became louder.

Flora peered down, down, down. Far below, tiny figures were skiing along a path. The mountain towered above them, its jagged fingers reaching up.

She felt a familiar sickening giddiness. The ground seemed to be coming up towards her, she was heading down as if dragged by a magnet. The floor was tilting.

Vertigo.

Her heart pounded and her breathing came faster and shallower. She knew she was going to tumble down, down, down onto the grey rockface below. Closing her eyes, she clutched the metal bar that ran round the windows. One of the boys crashed into her, jolting her backwards.

'Hey, hey, hey, *arrêtes*,' called the instructor, hearing Flora's gasp. The boys smiled impishly and giggled. She wanted to whack them with her ski poles.

She cut off the instructor's apologies with a nod and turned away. Panic was overwhelming her. She tried to calm her breathing and to stare upwards into the sky. She kept telling herself she was safe, only to be overcome by blind fear. The giddiness and the sensation of falling refused to go away.

The lift stopped suddenly. Silence fell, broken only by the wind and the eerie creaking of the cable overhead. The boys looked round wide-eyed. Flora's grip on the metal bar tightened. There was a drop of hundreds of feet and only a thin strip of metal floor between her and the hard white ground. She was going to be dragged out, then she'd crash down, down, down, freefalling through the air. The whole world was tilting.

The creaking grew louder.

The cable was breaking. The floor was cracking open under her feet. The ground was coming up towards her, she was plunging down, down. She closed her eyes. 'Why have we stopped?'

Stefan reluctantly broke off from his colleague's account of his Olympic trial. 'It's always happening. Relax. Enjoy the view.'

Flora peered down and then quickly turned her head away. She felt sick. Clammy inside their gloves, her hands gripped the bar. The cabin lurched to the left in a sudden gust of wind making the cable creak more loudly. The two boys squealed in delight and rushed from one side of the cabin to the other trying to make it rock.

'The door, mademoiselle?' asked the instructor laughing. 'In high wind you sometimes have to open them.' He reached towards a metal handle.

'Don't,' screamed Flora. 'Please.'

Now bored and yearning to ski, the boys started a sword fight with their poles.

'*Arrêtez. Taissez vous*,' ordered the instructor, marching across to them and seizing their poles.

Hearing Stefan ask if she were ill, Flora shook her head. She peeled open her screwed-tight eyes to find him standing in front of her, his lean face level with hers. 'Vertigo,' she gasped.

'Sssssh, I've got you.' He put his arms around her and pulled her to him. 'I've got you. Sssssh.'

'Hate heights.' Shaking, she rested her head on his chest. 'Sssssh.'

At the other end of the cabin the boys were being told off in furious French. Wrapped round her, Stefan's arms were like a lifejacket. She could feel his fingers, the stubble on his jaw against her forehead and his warm breath in her hair. Instinctively she drew closer to him, then closer still.

The machinery clattered into life and the cabin moved upwards. Flora dared herself to peer down. 'Oh God.' The floor under her feet tilted and the snowy ground rushed towards her. Feeling giddy, she buried herself against Stefan, holding onto him as if her life depended on it.

'Better now?' asked Stefan.

Flora looked round to see they were in the lift station. The cable car had stopped.

'Vertigo,' she stammered, hastily extricating herself from his arms. 'Sorry. If I'd been able to let go, I'd have written my last will and testament in the condensation on the window. Sorry.'

'Don't be.' He smiled his slow, lazy smile.

Gazing up into the green lake of his eyes, Flora caught her breath, then quickly looked away.

Outside, the icy air froze their lungs. One of the highest points in the area, it felt like being on the roof of the world.

Flora tapped the snow from the bottom of her boots and was in her bindings ready to go. Stefan was saying farewell to his intrigued colleague, who kept glancing in her direction. She gazed across at the distant snowy peaks which surrounded them.

'So. You want to ski today,' said Stefan. 'Good. Keep your shoulders turned and bend your knees.'

Martin blanched when he was handed the bill by the mechanic in the garage. At least they took plastic and he'd be able to claim on insurance. Or would he? Nikki was sitting on a foam-leaking chair in the glassed-off office. She was flicking through a battered auto magazine, looking fed up. Would she come up with the goods for Jack?

Nikki took out her compact and applied some more lipstick. Five figures closer to six. It was a hell of a lot of temping. If she sold her story, and let's face it, it was a huge story, she'd be buying her independence. It would go a long way towards a nice little flat she could rent out. A bolt-hole if things didn't work out with Martin. A girl needed a bit of her own security.

The more she thought about it, the more appealing the idea was. The only drawback was having to deal with Jack Mancini.

Flora began to traverse the white field. It was almost empty. Glancing behind him, Stefan nodded his approval. He had no need to tell her to bend her knees properly or to lean forward, she could feel she was doing it right. The top of her boots were almost sawing into her shins. Approaching a turn she talked herself through it. Bend further, plant the pole as the downhill ski moves out, then bring both skis back together.

As they sped on with her executing perfect stem after perfect stem, her satisfaction warmed her more than any sauna.

Breathless and smiling in triumph, she glided to a halt beside him.

'Excellent.' He gave a little bow. 'The snow is better.'

'Maybe I'm getting better too.'

'Maybe.'

As she returned his slow, lazy smile, her awkwardness vanished.

Flora's joy was shortlived. They skied along a jagged path, then came to a stretch of piste that seemed to be sheer cliff face. Seeing the ground plunge steeply towards some trees in the distance, she felt as if she were on a high diving board.

'Relax. Keep your weight on your downhill ski and your shoulders turned,' called Stefan.

Relax? She was stiff with fear. She no longer cared about her technique, she just wanted to get down in one piece. Inching along, she automatically returned to doing snowplough turns, stopping for frequent rests, trying to stifle her pathetic whimpering.

Other skiers zoomed past in flashes of fluorescent colour. An American voice cried out, 'Melt this motherfucker'.

Finally she made it to the trees. Was it getting foggy? Breathing more easily, she followed Stefan and found herself on another path.

Too late, she realised it was narrow, steep and icebound, with a drop down, down, down about eighty feet to the right. She stopped stockstill and shook her head, with the obstinacy of a dog confronted by a hated bath.

'I can't,' she called, her eyes fixed on the edge. Up, or rather down ahead, Stefan had stopped and was waiting for her. 'I can't.'

'Flora, know something?' he called back. 'You must.'

'Isn't there another way?' she cried in desperation.

'Not for you. Too difficult. Do you want to walk back up to the cable car?' Was he mad? Walk up? She'd need Sherpas and base camps and oxygen. 'It's easy,' called Stefan. 'You'll do it no problem.'

Reasoning there was no choice, Flora took a deep breath. She manoeuvred her skis horizontal to the slope so that she could sideslip. She got as far over to the left as she could, huddling against the rock wall as if she wanted to take cover from snipers and began to slide inch by inch down towards Stefan. She kept on stopping, imagining her skis going out of control and hurtling themselves and her over the edge. Her pulse went nuclear.

'No problem,' Stefan called encouragingly.

She got to within a few ski lengths of him. Thinking she was safe, she relaxed her concentration. Suddenly she found herself being carried towards the edge of the path. The drop down, down, down eighty feet was getting closer.

Flora cried out in terror. She twisted, instinct taking over and jammed her poles and her ski edges into the ground, somehow managing to stop and stay upright. Adrenaline pumped through her. The front of her skis were far too close to the drop.

Her legs trembled and she took several deep breaths, trying to calm down. Her heart was beating so fast she could feel the pulse in her throat. Livid, she stared at Stefan. Did he seem shaken too? The bastard was trying to get her killed. 'Don't even think of saying an inch is as good as a mile.'

'How about a centimetre is as good as a kilometre?' he tried to joke. 'You're doing fine. Just a little further. *Allez, lentement.*'

'I can't.'

'What do you want right now?'

'What?'

'Imagine I'm everything you've ever wanted. All you have to do is ski to me and you'll get it.'

In spite of herself, Flora laughed. She pushed backwards on shaking legs so that once again she was over to the left. At least there was no one else on the path to distract her. Sliding at a snail's pace, stopping every few inches, she finally reached Stefan.

'You see. You can ski a black run. An easy one.'

'Easy?' Flora looked back. 'Besides, that wasn't skiing. It was survival.' Wisps of mist swirled around them. 'Is it getting foggy?'

'Probably. Lower down.' He passed her his cigarette.

'You won't get us lost, will you?'

'So, you don't want to be stuck on a mountainside all night. Not even with me.'

Flora blushed and peered over to the right. 'Not even with you,' she said lightly. 'The view might be quite picturesque in summer. Bosky. Nature at its most sublime. Mossy rocks, dappled sunlight, arcadian grottoes . . .' Must she talk such complete twaddle?

'Another night then?' Reaching out, he gently took off her sunglasses, searching her eyes with his.

Her resolve to keep her distance, not to surrender to temptation, melted away. She longed to bury her hands in his hair, to feel his arms around her again, to lose herself completely, to say yes, here, right now, down on the snow . . .

'Another night,' he repeated.

Mesmerised, Flora felt desire burn through her.

'Not in St Marie. I got a call this morning and decided on the perfect place to see you again.'

'Where?' she whispered.

'Amsterdam. I want to take you to a gallery and show you some wonderful sculpture.'

'Whose?'

'Mine. Will you be there? Late February?'

Flora gasped, her head spinning. February meant he thought they had a future. Images ran through her mind; canals, cafés, Rembrandts, walking arm in arm with him along misty towpaths, drinking schnapps, Stefan keeping her warm, it would be so cold in February, February, six weeks before her wedding . . . Jamie.

'You're shivering.' He handed her back her glasses. '*Allez*. The hardest part is over. Just beyond the next bend, we'll find some wonderful snow.'

Flora moved off, all thoughts of the drop forgotten. Amsterdam? Was he serious? He couldn't be. Admittedly, they weren't bad lines, but doubtless they were from a well-worn script. He must've said them hundreds of times before, probably to every woman who came his way. She'd been almost lulled into believing him, he'd sounded so sincere as he gazed at her with those mesmerising green eyes.

She told herself to wise up. Stefan might be beautiful, but he was just another bullshitter trying it on with everyone he met. Women falling for their teachers was one of the oldest stories in the book. He wasn't Abelard, she wasn't Eloise. Stefan was a ski bum and she should know better. Why had she thought, even for a split second, that meeting him in Amsterdam might be possible? She was about to get married and live happily ever after.

'Not far,' called Stefan ahead of her. 'The hardest part is over.'

'Promise?' She began to snowplough. The ground was flattening out but was still icy. A deafening silence was echoing off the rocks. Why was it so deserted?

A horrible grating sound was followed by a shout of dismay. She slammed into a stop and froze, rooted to the spot as a snowboarder hurtled by, zig-zagging in front of her with inches to spare.

'Be care . . .,' called Flora. She watched as he careered over to the left. Just as she was sensing something was wrong, he hit a patch of ice and cannoned into a rock then ricochetted into the air. He half somersaulted before crash-landing onto the concrete-hard snow.

'Stefan. Stop.' The boarder was lying in the middle of the path. 'Stefan.' Flora edged towards him. Blood was seeping onto the snow from a gash on the boy's forehead. His leg was bent awkwardly. 'Jesus.'

Stefan bent over him and winced. Unzipping his jacket, he gently placed it over the boarder. 'Your jacket. He must be kept warm. Give me your skis.'

She gazed helplessly at the unconscious figure. Under the layers of baggy clothes, he was so slight. In his teens, he was trying to grow a goatee beard. He was still breathing, but his mop of blond curls was matted by blood. His leg was horribly twisted, like a doll's bent out of shape. It must be broken, probably several times.

Stefan powered up the path with Flora's skis, digging them into the snow, making a St Andrew's cross. 'Stay here. When anyone stops, they mustn't touch him. I'll be back as fast as I can.'

Flora watched as Stefan sped down the path, round the bend and disappeared.

Hetty and Alice were in Café Neige drinking hot chocolate with a crowd of other chalet girls.

Hetty's jaw dropped. 'Yours offer to do the washing up? Never. Hear that, Al? Scrabble and bed by eleven? Oh, bliss. Ours are ancient too, but half of them are prats. No, no patters or pinchers. Prats. They're all too busy bonking each other. Mi-rara-randa, bossy Sloaney, ended up with Pete yesterday after-noon, that utterly dreamy Aussie Al was going on about earlier. Then he spent the night with a bit of Frog totty. Shame.'

The minutes dragged past and Flora became more frantic. The mist was thickening. Where was everyone? Where was Stefan? What if he got lost? What should she do? The jagged rock wall towered above her, reinforcing her isolation.

'Please be all right,' she begged the boarder. She was shivering, her teeth chattering with cold. 'Please.' She leant over him to check he was still breathing. The bleeding had stopped. Should she test his pulse or something? Where was everyone? To give herself something to do, she edged down the icy slope to retrieve his snowboard and knitted Rasta hat.

'Come on, Stefan. Where are you?' Flora hated herself for not being one of those capable, practical people who knew exactly what to do in a crisis. Someone who knew about first aid, about bleeding and shock and concussion. Someone who knew how to make a splint out of a ski pole. Someone selfless, kind, noble, whose mind would never be crossed by the tempting thought of snatching their jacket from an injured boarder to keep themselves warm. She was a monster. Why was she so useless?

'Stefan.'

Munchkin pulled back one of her bedroom curtains and squinted. She wiped away the fug from inside the windows with the sleeve of her wrap. The light hurt her eyes. 'It's quite misty out there.'

'You don't want to ski, do you?' asked Sam.

'Um,' she hesitated, hating being thought of as lazy. But it was so warm and cosy inside.

'Please don't be a snow queen like Miranda. Come back to bed.'

Thinking that her blood must be turning to ice in her veins, Flora circled her arms, trying to keep the circulation going. Where was everyone? There was no sign of life anywhere. The boarder was as still as a mummy. Pacing the path, she almost slipped in her smooth soled boots. If anything happened to Stefan, no one would know about the boarder or her.

Mentally she ticked off the minutes, comforting herself that each one brought help that bit sooner. Should she put the hat on the boarder's head? No, mustn't touch him. But supposing he got hypothermia?

'Oh God,' she called out helplessly.

Waiting in the queue for the drag-lift, Jamie reminded Pete to organise his stag night.

'Night?' scoffed Pete. 'Weekend if you don't mind.'

'Where?'

'Verbier.'

It was the loneliest, most anxious time of Flora's life. Her panic grew, the colder she became. Where the hell was Stefan? Where the hell was anyone? It was as if the end of the world had been and gone. Should she retrieve her skis and try to get help?

'Don't die, don't die,' she pleaded, half covering his head with his hat. Shivering, her eyes were fixed on him, making sure he was still breathing. Where was anyone?

Her hope was almost on empty, when the silence was broken by a roar overhead. She looked up to see a helicopter with a red cross painted on its side circling above. The force of its blades was scattering the snow from the rockface and the trees. She shielded her eyes. It started to descend before it disappeared out of sight.

'You're going to be all right.' Crouching down, she whispered to the boarder. 'Thank God.'

When she saw Stefan tearing round the bend followed by two men dragging a high-sided metal stretcher, she burst into tears.

'It's concussion, isn't it? Nothing worse?' asked Flora.

Grim-faced, they examined the boarder, muttering to one another.

She tried to do up her jacket but her fingers were so numb, she couldn't make the zip connect. 'Nothing worse?'

'Let's hope so. His leg is broken twice, maybe three times. Here.' Stefan bent down to fasten her jacket. 'The path was closed just behind us. Too dangerous. Has the ski patrol been down here? What?' He exploded. 'No? Flora, are you sure? Lazy bastards.' He said something in French to the paramedics. 'I'll have to complain officially. The boy's lucky that you go so slowly and the pilot was prepared to go up.'

They watched the boarder being gently lifted onto the stretcher and wrapped in blankets before being strapped down. He groaned in agony, opened his eyes in bewilderment and passed out again. Flora tucked his hat under one of the canvas straps as the two paramedics said something to Stefan. They each picked up one of the two front arms of the stretcher, now a sledge, and skied off round the bend.

Less than a minute later there was a roar, before the helicopter hovered over the trees and disappeared.

'You're in shock.' said Stefan. 'Ski. You must get warm.'

She was drained and frozen to the marrow. 'Wouldn't have minded cadging a lift.'

'There's a place we can stop for a drink just a few minutes away.'

Rounding the bend in an unsteady snowplough, she saw the roof of a wooden hut far below. She was stiff and shaking, unable to lose the image of the boarder somersaulting through the air. Frightened she'd lose control of her skis, as soon as she gathered any sort of speed, she stopped abruptly.

'Got the fear,' she said dejectedly. Skier after skier powered ahead of them down the piste and into the distance.

'Not surprising.' Stefan skied alongside her, snowploughing at her pace. 'I'll look after you, you're safe.'

The hut was tiny, with a counter and a few tables. A group of American students were talking excitedly about seeing the helicopter. Flora went straight to the wood-burning stove and held out her frozen hands. The boarder must have arrived at the hospital by now, and she hoped was being given something to ease the pain.

Stefan handed her a huge mug of hot chocolate topped by a layer of cream and a large glass of brandy.

'Thanks.' Outside the windows was a treelined path. She'd have to go down that soon. It was exhaustingly scary just thinking about it.

She stared outside, sitting in silence, sipping. The brandy was rough, but effective. Her toes and fingers tingled as they defrosted. She nodded when he offered her another. 'Please. Dutch courage.'

At the counter Stefan was being asked by an American if he knew why the helicopter had gone up. He followed Stefan back to the table, held out his hand to Flora and introduced himself as Foster from Michigan. Did they mind if he joined them?

A walking advertisement for the marvels of American dentistry, Foster said that Europe was neat, especially London, England, but then lectured them on why they should try the skiing back home. When Stefan offered him a cigarette, he looked at them horrorstruck as if they were junkies about to shoot up.

Flora gazed out the window, Foster's tour of North American ski resorts washing over her. Whistler, Jackson's Hole, Calgary, Breckenridge. Occasionally, she caught Stefan's eye and smiled. As a delightful lethargy took hold of her, she felt at peace with the world again.

Helped along by the two large brandies, her body relaxed and her mind started to drift. She studied Stefan, his long, lean body stretching out in the chair, and began to wonder what that body was like under the layers of clothes, and then knew for sure that it would be as wonderful as his dangerously beautiful face. She tried to remember how his muscles had felt when he'd held her in the cable car. If they'd been alone, would they have pulled each other down onto that hard metal floor? Probably. Definitely.

As she smiled to herself, she caught him staring at her as if he read her thoughts. Hastily, she forced herself to concentrate on Foster, who was now somewhere in Utah.

Warm, her spirits restored after the brandies, Flora put on her skis and followed Stefan along the path. She gasped in wonder when she saw a huge expanse of snow laid out like a massive cloth for a giant's picnic. 'It's beautiful.'

Stefan grinned at her delight. 'You must go fast to keep warm. Good snow. No people. No excuses. *Allez.*'

She pushed off with her poles, at first skiing tentatively while she tested her nerve. Then she seemed to go up a gear and Stefan was yelling at her to get lower. She crouched down so that she was almost sitting and was swept along faster and faster. Up ahead he roared his approval and shouted at her to turn not stop. She did it automatically, barely slowing down before she raced forward again, hurtling past other skiers.

Suddenly she was lost to speed, with no time to think, only to do. The wind streamed past her as she traversed and turned, traversed and turned, her skis carrying her across bumps and ruts which only added to the thrill. It was so exhilarating, she never wanted to stop.

All too soon, they were back at La Toit. Reluctantly, she slid to a halt, resting on her poles to get her breath back. Below in the distance was the Savoie.

'That was wonderful. Thank you.'

'If you remember to flex your knees, tomorrow we'll start to parallel. We'll have an extra hour because of all the stops today.'

'Parallel?' She was going to parallel. She was going to ski properly. Making her way down the piste, Flora bent her knees as if she were Groucho Marx.

At the Savoie, only a few hardy souls were sitting at the outside tables. Everyone else was sheltering from the cold.

'You're skiing well.' He smiled.

She laughed. 'Dutch courage.'

'Dutch courage?'

'Brandy.' Flora realised she'd probably drunk far too much of it.

'Dutch courage. Will I see you in Amsterdam?'

She was lulled into a moment's delight as she pictured the days and nights they could spend together, making love again and again and again. Her smile vanished, her elation died. 'Stefan, I'm about to get married and you have a girlfriend. Remember?'

'You were about to get married and I had a girlfriend last night. Remember?'

She blushed. 'Last night was a mistake.'

He lit a cigarette and blew the smoke out slowly, watching her like a predator. 'Was it?'

'Yes.' She was vehement. She told herself that she was just ego fodder for him. He had Marie-France and doubtless countless others. Her future was with Jamie. 'Stefan, stop this. It's all nonsense, isn't it? Sweet, but nonsense.' He raised an eyebrow. 'Go and find a more receptive audience. You won't have any problem. They're queueing up, aren't they?'

'You're the one who's talking nonsense. You are the receptive audience. You've been thinking what it would be like to make love with me. Look at me. You have. Yes?'

How could she have made it so obvious? She was furious with herself and with him. 'Have I? You're so sure of yourself, aren't you?'

'After last night, yes.'

'Last night was a mistake. I've told you. It's not going to be repeated. You're being paid to teach me to ski. I don't sleep with the staff.'

His green eyes narrowed as he grabbed her wrist. His grip was a tourniquet. 'For someone who is beautiful, you can be very ugly.'

'I'm sorry.' She was filled with remorse. 'That was a horrible thing to say. Unforgiveable.'

He yanked her towards him. 'Do you think I want to teach spoilt children like you how to ski? Have you any idea how boring it is? Imagine it. Or did you think you were something different?'

'If it's so boring, why are you doing it? Leave. If you're really a sculptor, fuck off back to Paris and do some proper work.'

'I'll go back to Paris and what will you do? Go back to your rich boyfriend and live happily ever after? He won't make you happy, Flora.'

'Jamie will. He does,' she protested.

'Who's talking sweet nonsense now?'

'I'm not.'

'Last night. Remember it. You wanted me, Flora, and you still want me.' She hung her head, hating him for saying it. 'And you still believe you'll marry your rich prince charming and live happily ever after. You are so wrong.'

'Stop this,' pleaded Flora. 'I'm getting married in April.' She told herself to say au revoir and walk away.

'Don't run away.'

'I'm not. Well, I am. I must.'

'Why must?'

She stared up at him in despair. 'Because, because I've been weak and stupid and almost destroyed everything because of you.'

'Destroyed what? Your future with your nice, rich Englishman? He's not right for you.'

'He is. I love him.'

Stefan shook his head. 'No. If you were in love with Jamie, you wouldn't have thought twice about me. Wake up Flora. You're supposed to be getting married in April and you want to make love to me.'

'No.'

'You do. Why deny it? Jamie's money is going to make a nice cushion for you to idle your life away on. One day you'll look back and realise you've been smothered. You, your dreams, your hopes, your life all wasted.'

'Stop it,' whispered Flora.

'All that poetry in your soul gone. Squandered. On what? Cooking courses.'

'Stop.' She squeezed her eyes tight shut.

'You're braver than you know. Jamie will keep you docile. Timid.'

'Stop.'

'I'm going to help make you brave. I'm your salvation.'

'My what? I don't know you. You come along, you question, question . . .' She could hardly get the words out. 'Stop it, Stefan, I can't take this. It's got nothing to do with you.' Flora began to see red. 'You're not a marriage counsellor, you're a ski instructor, remember. You're not even a sculptor, are you?'

'Yes.'

'You're not. There's no exhibition in Amsterdam. You remind me of all those waiters who say they're actors. Actors act, waiters wait tables. Sculptors sculpt, not teach fucking skiing. Sort out your own life, before you start judging mine.'

Stefan's grip on her arm tightened. 'You won't have a life soon, you'll just be Jamie's wife. Think of what you've told me about him. He doesn't like your friends, your job, your clothes. He's trying to change you and you're so lazy and lacking in self belief that you're letting it happen.'

'That's enough.' She jerked free of him. 'Isn't it time you fucked off and found your next pupil, mister ski teacher? At least Jamie is successful. What were you told about your sculpture? Don't give up the day job? Well, it seems that you listened.'

He flinched, his eyes were as cold and hard as emeralds. 'Goodbye, Flora.'

Munchkin had made cheese omelettes and a stack of toast as Sam lit the sitting room fire.

'You're a brilliant cook,' he sighed. The omelette was perfect.

'Way to a man's heart,' she said without thinking, then squirmed in embarrassment. 'Sure you don't want to ski? I mean, I don't want to force you, don't feel as if you have to hang around for my sake.'

'I want to hang around if you want to hang around,' said Sam gently.

'I don't want to put you under any pressure . . .'

'Munchkin, you're not. This has been the best day in ages.'

'It has?' He was just being nice, wasn't he? 'Sam. Er . . .'

'Out with it.'

'It's difficult.' She fiddled with the pepper pot. 'Look, we've had a bit of fun, haven't we? Nothing too serious. I mean the last thing we want to do is to get heavy about things.'

'Ding ding. Warning. Dee and Em coming up.' He saw her puzzlement. 'Deep and Meaningful.'

'Oh.'

Sam shrugged. 'You're about to tell me, Sam you're a great guy, we've had a bit of fun, but let's not spoil a nice friendship. That's fine.'

Munchkin wondered how it was that only half an hour ago they'd been so close and now there was a chasm the size of the Grand Canyon between them. 'Let's be realistic. You're not . . .'

'No, I'm not anything.' His expression was bleak. 'I'm out of work, I'm Giles's lodger, I'm 32, I'm broke and I'm a midget. I'm certainly not the right sort of partner for a successful woman with so much going for her like you.'

Munchkin was stunned. 'I was about to say that you're not interested in me.'

'What gave you that idea?'

'You did. That morning in my flat. After—'

'Excuse me,' exclaimed Sam. 'You were the one who said no worries, nice but a one-off. Remember? And you could hardly even be bothered to say that, you were so busy checking your E-mails and calling work and getting ready to go to Birmingham. It's like, thanks Sam, you can piss off now. Wham, bam, thank you man.'

'But—'

'You brought new meaning to the term service industry.'

'Sam.' Munchkin smiled ruefully. 'Sam. Sam. I thought you

thought that night was a big mistake. I'm not a babe. I'm 34 and I'm size fourteen on a good day and . . .'

'Come here.'

Jamie found Flora inside the Savoie staring into space, oblivious to all the hullaballoo around her.

'Sorry I'm late, angel. More chocolate? How was your lesson?'

'Awful. Got vertigo in a cable car, almost skied over a precipice and a boarder wiped out in front of me.'

'Badly? Blood wagon?'

'Leg smashed. Unconscious.'

'We saw the helicopter. Don't worry, he'll be fine. The doctors are used to it.' He squeezed her hand, she seemed very low and distracted. 'I've just taken another fifty quid off Pete. Found a new lot of bumps. Best afternoon so far, hardly anyone around.'

'Um.' Flora told herself to pay attention. 'So, where's Pete?'

'He ran into Agnes and her friends, the redhead from last night. Gone into town with them. He's meeting us later in Les Landais. It's the twins' night off.'

'Is everyone going to be there?' Flora was alarmed, she couldn't face Martin on top of everything else.

'Of course.'

'Jamie, can't we go out on our own? We really need to spend some time together, sort things out.'

'There's nothing to sort out, is there?' He leant over and kissed her cheek. 'What's wrong?'

Where could she begin? 'Nothing. It would just be nice to be together, that's all.'

'We are together.'

'Are we?' She sighed. 'This holiday just seems to focus on how we're so different. You're so happy-go-lucky, take life as it comes.'

'You always said that's why you love me.' He smiled.

'Yes. That's why I love you.' She stirred her hot chocolate. 'I suppose I hoped all that confidence and joie de vivre would rub off on me.'

'Flora. You love me. I love you. Whatever is the problem?' He seized on her long silence. 'You see. Nothing.'

Was he right? The strain of being at the chalet, the lack of sleep, the gruelling skiing was making her lose her sense of proportion. All that and prenuptial nerves. Once safely home, surely her doubts would fade along with her memories of Stefan?

'You're too introspective sometimes.' He sniffed. 'Have you been drinking?'

'Dutch courage.' The evaporation of her brandy-fuelled euphoria would explain why she felt so miserable, wouldn't it? That and everything else that had happened during the afternoon. Rowing with Stefan had nothing to do with it. He was an irrelevance. In a few weeks time, she'd be married to Jamie. Jamie was the one who mattered.

'Jamie, I really don't want to go out with hundreds of other people. I need a break from everyone in the chalet.'

Seeing a waitress, he mimed a scribble. 'We've been through all this hundreds of times. It's getting boring, Flora. I'm going to dinner tonight and I'm taking you with me. I can't see why you're making such a fuss. We'll get the lift. It's getting foggy.'

Far below, St Marie was just a yellowish haze from its streetlights. As they were carried down, they could hear voices and the whoosh of skis on snow. Skiers came into view, then were swallowed up by the mist. Flora rested her head on Jamie's shoulder, seeking comfort from her confusion.

At Les Pins they got off the lift and walked the short distance across the icy piste to the lane. Up ahead Jamie was yelling at her to stamp her feet down hard. Flora stamped and lost her footing, crashing down, four ski poles clattering around her. Swearing in fury, she got up, then immediately went down.

'I'm going to break my leg again.'

'Foot,' corrected Jamie.

Determined not to risk another tumble, she began crawling on her hands and knees.

Watching from the side, Jamie roared with laughter. 'For God's sake, Flora, get up. You look ridiculous.'

'Don't care. Done it.' She held out her hand and he hauled her up.

Every uphill step on the road back to the chalet was agony. With her boots gnawing into her shins, her knees bruised, and damp seeping through her long johns, Flora thought she'd never make it.

Jamie paused at the front door of the chalet and wheeled round, almost hitting her with the two pairs of skis on his shoulder. 'This is really good for you,' he said thoughtfully.

'What do you mean?'

'Taking risks you'd never normally take . . .'

'Risks like catching pneumonia?'

'Conquering fear. It's character building.'

'My character is fully built, in case you hadn't noticed.'

Jamie rolled his eyes. 'Come on, admit it. It's fun. You're enjoying your lessons . . .'

'Lessons? Fun?' Flora exploded. 'Skiing is just masochism for the monied middle classes. We could be sitting in ninety-degree sunshine on a Caribbean beach. But no. Not us. You wanted to ski, so we're skiing.'

'I thought you were enjoying your lessons. Stefan seems like a nice . . .'

'Why are you going on about the lessons?'

'I'm not.'

'You are.' Filled with furious despair, she threw her poles at the wall and stormed inside.

Sighing, Jamie stooped to pick them up. Perhaps he should've had a Boy's Own week after all. Flora would calm down after they were married, wouldn't she? Perhaps he should've proposed to docile Ginny, who loved skiing as much as she adored him. She would've asked for nothing more than an account at the

General Trading Company and she could turn out Beef Wellington in minutes.

Why Flora? Flora was like the girl with the curl in the middle of her forehead. When she was good, she was very, very good. He hadn't expected her to be that good the morning he'd turned up at the cottage. Bill Blest had told him he'd rented the place to an artist who was away a lot and a sweet girl who worked on the local paper. He'd been surprised. Pompous Bill had always been finickity and the pair had sounded unlikely tenants. To help secure the place, Fred Quince never quite as silly as he pretended, had told his prospective landlord about Flora's distant connection with Rosehagens.

Of course, he'd fallen in love with Flora Rose. His beautiful wife. But he'd let it be known in strictest confidence to the bank's biggest gossips just who his beautiful wife was. Word had got round as he knew it would.

'Heard you're betrothed to one of the rebels,' God, or rather chairman Julius Rosehagen had said one morning in the lift. God never spoke to anyone. 'Feckless and headstrong like her great-grandfather is she? My youngest uncle. Although you've probably worked that one out.' A shrewd stare. 'Interesting. We'll talk soon, young man. Heard impressive things about you.'

When Flora was good she was very, very good. It was just his bad luck that over the past few days, she'd been ratty and horrid.

Sam and Munchkin were entwined on the sofa watching a video. A log fire was blazing away and tea was laid on the table. Flora envied them their cosiness.

Not taking his eyes from the screen, Sam sketched a wave. Munchkin smiled coyly. 'Hello, Flora. Had a good day?'

'No, awful.' Flora threw herself down in the armchair. 'A boarder nearly got himself killed in front of me.'

'Poor you. Have some lemon cake. It's delicious. All the chocolate's gone though.'

Miranda had scoffed the lot the night before, comfort eating.

'And you? Nice day?' Flora cut a huge slice. She was ravenous.

'Oh, we just dossed, didn't we?' Munchkin squeezed Sam's hand and smiled.

'What's this?' asked Flora with her mouth full.

'*Misery*'. Brilliant. Have you seen it?'

She nodded. It was horribly apt. Here she was trapped in a house halfway up a snowy mountainside with Martin probably out to murder her.

'Hello, you two,' said Jamie, putting his damp gloves on the radiator. Sam pulled a face. 'Sorry,' he whispered. 'No sign of the others?'

'They didn't make it to Aubrisson,' whispered back Munchkin. 'The Range Rover broke down. Where's Pete?'

'In town.'

'With last night's redhead?' guessed Sam. 'Agnes, isn't it? She's stunning.'

'Isn't she?' agreed Jamie. Munchkin pursed her lips.

Heavy footsteps preceded Giles bursting in. 'Morning campers.' His red headband clashed with his red sunburnt face and white eyelashes. 'What's this? *Misery*? Brilliant.' He hovered in front of the screen blocking the view. 'The best bit is when she whacks his legs with a sledgehammer. Coming up now. Ow.' He turned his head away.

'Shut up, can't you,' said Sam crossly.

James Caan's face filled the screen. He reminded Flora of the boarder being lifted onto the stretcher. Unable to bear it, she went to her room.

Miranda and Anna were fed up. The morning had been a write-off and they'd only managed to ski a couple of runs in the afternoon before the fog had come down. Miranda knew she should be helping Anna make some more tea, but couldn't be fagged.

'Poor you,' said Munchkin, 'you look exhausted. Martin called. Apparently the Range Rover's been fixed.'

'That's something,' Miranda lolled her head back completely uninterested.

'Anyone call for me?' asked Anna, carrying a tray.

Munchkin shook her head. 'Only Martin. And Pete wanting to know what time to link up tonight.' She turned to Jamie. 'Is he bringing this girl along to dinner?'

'Which girl?' Jamie's eyes were fixed on the screen.

'Agnes. From last night. The redhead you all think is so stunning.' Munchkin pinched Sam playfully, then froze, not daring to look at Miranda. Too late.

Jamie winced.

Miranda's mouthful of lemon cake was suddenly as appetising as sand. Muttering that she must have a shower, she scrambled to her feet.

Just as the film was finishing, Nikki and Martin arrived. They were flushed with triumph from a successful shopping trip. He was brandishing a pair of bright yellow and black skis. 'No beers? Slacking a bit, aren't you?'

'How's the Range Rover?' asked Munchkin.

'Good as new. Garage blokes were brilliant. Worked double hard because they fancied Nikki of course.' She beamed at him as he patted her behind.

'Guess what?' she said. 'Martin was asked for his autograph in the shop just now. The guy said he was one of the best players he'd ever seen. Wasn't that darling?'

Martin was itching for someone to comment on his skis. 'All set to go tomorrow.'

Sam and Giles were so envious that they were determined to keep quiet.

'Very smart,' said Jamie, picking them up and examining them. 'Nice weight. Great balance. Must've set you back a bit.'

'Only money, isn't it? All the Olympic squads are queueing up to be sponsored by this lot. Hot off the production line.'

Nikki turned to Munchkin who was helping Anna stack the crockery. 'Ski today ducks? Thought not. Getting to know Sam, were we?' Munchkin smiled shyly. 'He's such a lovely guy. I told Martin you two were made for each other.'

'Really?' Munchkin's face lit up.

Nikki nodded. 'Enjoy yourself, you deserve it. All that hard work you do. Love the trousers. Armani?'

The telephone rang and Anna dashed across to it. 'Hello. Oh, Pete. Yes. Eight. See you there.' Dejected, she hung up. 'He'll meet us down there.'

'Walk down, shall we?' said Giles, anxious not to put too much wear and tear on the BMW and to be able to drink.

Nikki was alarmed. She'd done enough walking that day to last the whole year.

Seeing her expression, Martin said, 'I'll take the Range Rover. Anyone's welcome to grab a lift.'

The offer was seized on by Giles. 'Terrif. Old bus unlikely to die under us again, is it?'

Sam sniggered. 'Garage will have put in some anti-freeze.'

Catching Jamie's grin, Martin glared. 'Remind me, old chap, how long is it before you're back on the road?'

After her shower, Flora tried to read. Her wedding file remained on the floor, unopened. She hoped the boarder was resting peacefully. Should she call the hospital to check? Her French wasn't up to it. How stupid. The moment she got home she'd enrol for evening classes. Jem had picked up quite a bit of Hebrew from her granite-faced Israeli paratrooper, perhaps Stefan . . . No.

She must stop thinking about him. She must. This Franco-Czech penniless stranger who claimed he was a sculptor mustn't be allowed to invade her head like this. And so what if she'd been so horrible to him, he deserved it. He'd been equally nasty back. How dare he judge her, he didn't know her. He was with Marie-France, she was marrying Jamie.

She picked up her wedding file and began studying paint colour charts.

A few minutes later, Jamie sat on the bed. His blue eyes were concerned, his expression tender. 'What's wrong, Flora? You seem so far away.'

'Just had a bitch of an afternoon, I guess. Sorry about earlier, when we came back.' She pointed to an ivory. 'This for the dining room?'

'Worry about it when we're home. Time to get ready. Martin's offered us a lift.'

It was an unwelcome reminder that she would have to encounter Martin, whom she'd successfully avoided all day. 'Couldn't we walk? There can't be room for everyone. I need the fresh air.'

Jamie was taken aback. Flora's usual idea of fresh air was sitting in non-smoking.

Les Landais was set back from the road. It was a two-storey, wood-clad building with a huge sign over the door in Gothic script. Lining the walls of the entrance leading to the bar were scores of photos of smiling revellers in après ski gear. In the restaurant, red-clothed tables were laid for dinner. A massive stone fireplace stood at the far end, hunting horns and a pair of crossed wooden skis hanging above it. The white walls were rough plastered and the low ceiling covered in knotted pine.

Pete was sitting on a stool at the bar. Martin slapped him on the back and ordered a round of drinks in between telling him about his new skis.

'Thought you had some back home,' said Pete.

'They're for powder,' said Martin quickly. 'Not all rounders.'

'You'll have to give us a demonstration tomorrow. Can't wait.' Pete smiled into his beer. 'Where's Jamie?'

'Walking down with wifey like the good boy he is. Surprised he hasn't got a ring through his nose.'

'You're not still crabby because of the backgammon are you?'

'Course not.'

'Seem a bit down on him. What's the worry?'

'There's no . . .' Martin laughed.

'Good. There shouldn't be. Jamie's the best mate you'll meet. You'd find out if you gave him a chance.'

Martin started to reply but was drowned out by Munchkin's high pitched shrieks as Sam tried to put some ice down her back. As Pete turned round to look, he saw Miranda. 'Like a drink?'

Since she arrived, Miranda had gradually edged closer to him. Having yearned to talk to him for hours, she was suddenly tongue-tied. Only yesterday, they'd been in bed together. Now they were a few feet apart, but distanced by oceans of remorse and wounded pride and suspicion about stunning redheads.

'Gin ton. Thanks.' So anxious to play it cool, Miranda overdid it and sounded fed up. She then overdid it again, answering all his questions about her day in an unfriendly monotone.

Giles butted in. 'Seen the menu? Looks good.' Miranda wished he'd go away. 'Nice afternoon, Pete? Disappear anywhere interesting?'

Pete was curt. 'Played pool.'

'Ran into whatshername from last night? The stunner.'

Miranda stiffened.

'Agnes? Coincidence, eh?' Pete wished he were a million miles away. 'Sorry to hear about Aubrisson.'

'One of those things,' seethed Miranda, tempted to throw her gin ton over him.

'Wait,' he pleaded uselessly, watching her walk away stiff backed. 'Shit, Giles, can't you use your brains before you open your mouth?'

Giles was puzzled. 'Wasn't out of turn, was I? What's eating Mirandy? Very sore about something. Probably the rogering you gave her yesterday.'

'It's not funny,' snarled Pete. 'M.Y.O.B.'

'Mmmyob?'

'Mind your own fucking business from now on.' He shook his head. 'Jamie, at last. Let's go feed.'

The ten trooped through to the restaurant. They took their places on either side of a long table, other diners glancing up at them.

Before a jug-eared waiter had the chance to hand round the menus, Sam ordered more beers and two carafes of wine, vite monsewer. Munchkin was amused.

Flora was dismayed. She found herself sitting opposite Martin. His physicality, his air of can-do, the energy which as usual crackled from him was overwhelming. She felt herself shrinking like Alice in Wonderland. Reflecting on all the friction between them since they'd arrived in the chalet she shrank still further. Her stupid unthinking comment about Nikki's car had set the pattern.

Martin had turned to his right and was telling Miranda about his skis. Miranda was only half-listening. Mouth like a cat's bum, she kept on glancing up the table at Pete.

While Flora pretended to be engrossed in the menu, Giles leant round her and began complaining to Jamie about all-women shortlists for constituencies.

'I mean, why? Political correctness? PC? Stands for pure crap. How can women claim they're equal and then demand special treatment? Typical female logic.'

'If you don't mind,' said Flora.

His white-lashed eyes blinked. 'Oh God, you're not another of these whining feminists? She's not, is she, Jamie?'

'Why ask him?' said Flora, before Jamie could get the words out.

'See. Watch it, Jamie.' Giles hooted with laughter. 'You won't become one of these new men, will you, James?'

'Fat chance,' muttered Flora.

'Phew. That's a relief.' Giles put his arm around Flora's shoulder. 'The joint marital credit card will soon sort out your opinions.'

She lit a cigarette, telling herself it was pointless to try and reason with a pair of burgundy cords, a Viyella shirt and a woollen tie under a bottle green jersey. The hooray uniform hardly suggested an open mind. Giles brayed for everyone to make their minds up. The voice was like a parody of itself. She tried to wriggle away from him, remembering the other night in the kitchen. Luke at me. 'You're not from Manchester, are you?'

'Sorry?' Giles's arm slipped.

'Surrey. Oh.'

Jamie interrupted and suggested they all had a fondue. 'Have five and then share. Agreed? Sam? Anna?' he called down the table. 'Hands up who wants meat. Cheese?'

'I know where I'd like to put my hand up,' guffawed Martin. 'And not there,' he hissed at Flora. He smiled, or rather bared his teeth, making her feel like little Red Riding Hood alone in the woods with the Big Bad Wolf.

As Jamie placed the order with the increasingly harrassed waiter, Sam interrupted to demand five more beers. 'And some more bread. *Encore. Vite. Rapide,*' he called. The waiter nodded sourly.

Cringeing from Martin's hostility, Flora caught a murmur of German. She focussed on two very well-dressed couples in their fifties who were taking their seats. Both men wore caslunere jackets and carried large wallets with straps. They looked as if they should be taking their seats in Lufthansa business class.

'Pete. Pete,' called Martin. 'On for some pool later?'

Miranda winced at his yell. Flora felt sorry for the couples sitting nearby who'd come out for a romantic dinner à deux.

'Can you believe it,' continued Martin volume fortissimo, 'Nikki actually beat me this afternoon, the cow.'

'I did, I did,' she squealed excitedly, smiling at Anna, who tried to force an equally enthusiastic smile back. 'And less of the cow thank you very much Martin.'

'Moo ooo ooo ooo. Moo ooo ooo ooo,' bellowed Sam to the alarm of the other diners, leaning back so his chair was on its back legs. 'Moo ooo ooo ooo.'

'Eee-or. Eee-or. I can do a donkey because I'm hung like one,' roared Martin.

Nikki and Munchkin shrieked. Nikki between laughs ordered Munchkin to oink.

'Oink, Oink.'

'Eee-or. Eee-or.'

'Moo ooo.' Sam's chair toppled backward and he crashed onto the floor amid a chorus of clucks, neighs and baas. Pete and Jamie guffawed so hard, beer shot out of their mouths and across the table. Giles started to sing 'Old MacDonald Had a Farm' and despite Anna's pleas to stop, everyone apart from Miranda and Flora joined in, Jamie and Martin's voices booming above the rest.

'Ee aye ee aye oh. Here we go, here we go, here we go-oh, here we go, here we go, here we go.' Martin led the table banging.

'Here we go again,' muttered Flora, gulping her whisky.

'So embarrassing,' said Miranda, burying her face in her hands, until she was tapped on the shoulder. The elderly *patronne*, whose hair was drawn back in a tight chignon, had abandoned the cash till near the bar and stormed over. Grimfaced she began taking Miranda to task in a volley of abusive French, while gesturing at the others.

'*Je regrette . . .*' stammered Miranda, going scarlet.

'Quiet everyone. Right now,' ordered Anna, her voice like a whipcrack. The singing started to tail off. 'Pete. Shut it. I for one am hungry. Don't want to be chucked out. *Pardon madame.*' She began speaking in fast, fluent French. Madame's fury abated. Trying not to giggle, everyone apologised to Madame, who had one final look round the table to ensure order was restored, then returned to the bar, muttering to herself.

'Phew Anna, you're going to be a brilliant teacher,' said Miranda.

'Mistress. Be mine,' called Martin. 'Any time.'

Flora swapped places with Giles. The fondue dishes were set down. The burners were lit under the enamel bowls.

'Mercy,' said Giles. A huge basket of bread was placed in front of him. 'Dig in, shall we?'

'What's this?' demanded Munchkin, examining the slices of raw meat. 'Beef?'

Sam grinned. 'Moo ooo ooo.'

'Shut up, can't you?' Giles picked up the remains of an ice cube in Flora's glass and lobbed it. It missed Sam, landing with an angry hiss in the bubbling oily fondue dish. Fatty broth splattered into the air. Sam and Munchkin cried out in alarm.

'My jacket,' screamed Nikki, snatching up the salt and pouring it over her lapels.

'Shit,' yelled Pete, leaping up to avoid the shower. He barged backwards into the next table. The two Italians just managed to grab their glasses before they toppled over. 'You dummo, Giles,' said Pete, throwing some bread. It ricochetted off Giles's shoulder and into the lap of one of the Germans, who all began gutteral protests. 'Whoops.' The rest started to giggle. 'Sorry.'

'Sit down and behave, can't you, Pete,' snapped Miranda as unsmiling as Flora opposite her.

'I'm trying to,' he protested. 'Oh no, here comes trouble.' Madame was walking towards him, shaking her head and pointing at his seat, while a stream of invective poured from her. 'What's she on about?'

'Shut up or fuck off, I think,' said Sam, starting a sword fight with Munchkin with his fondue fork.

'On guard,' said Martin and Giles copying them.

A lull ensued while they all concentrated on the food, dipping the raw meat or the bread into the pots.

'I know one should be buying British, but you can't beat the Germans for reliability,' said Giles to Jamie, glancing at Martin. 'BMW every time.'

'Can't rent all your life, Anna,' said Martin, taking a gulp of wine to wash down his food. 'Bricks and mortar. Best investment you'll ever make.'

'Forfeit,' yelled Munchkin, who'd been racing to pick a stray piece of meat in the sauce.

'Take your clothes off,' giggled Nikki.

'Strip fondue, great idea,' laughed Pete. 'Can I play with you, Nikki?'

Miranda and Martin both scowled at him.

'Eat up, Mirandy,' said Giles heartily.

Taking a deep breath, Miranda forced herself to be sociable. 'Eye doesn't look too bad, Martin. Lucky that, isn't it Flora?' Getting no reply she pressed on. 'What a ghastly business. If I saw those Australians, I'd really give them what for. Oiks.'

Martin and Flora stared at one another.

'Flora looked as if she'd definitely give them one.' He was icy. 'Friends of hers.'

'People I met,' she corrected in a low voice.

Miranda wondered how she'd put her foot in it.

'Funny how you seem to meet the scum,' said Martin.

Flora wanted to say funny how Pete meets them too, but kept her mouth shut. She'd make that effort.

'Pass the wine,' ordered Giles.

While Nikki and Munchkin duelled with their fondue forks, Sam loudly demanded more beers and wine from the monsewer. The fondue sets were taken away and the menus handed round at double speed.

'Don't think we're very popular,' said Giles, belching.

Sam and Martin copied him, trying to work out who was the loudest. Exasperated howls came from the neighbouring tables, diners started berating the waiters.

Flora shook her head when the waiter asked her if she wanted any pudding. Her tongue seemed stuck in the roof of her mouth, growing more awkward and bloated as her silence lengthened. Her isolation was complete. Miranda was trying to talk across the table to Anna. His back turned, a braying Giles was cutting into Pete and Jamie's Verbier chitchat, while being out-decibeled by Sam and Martin.

Jamie and Pete ordered Sambucas.

'Jamie.' Nikki screamed in terror. His finger was on fire.

Blue flame burning, he waved his finger round like a conductor before sticking it in his mouth. As Jamie was roaring with laughter, Pete poured Sambuca into the palm of his hand and set it alight. Nikki and Munchkin squealed.

'Fuck,' he yelled in pain and chucked. Blue flames headed towards the Italian couple. The woman leapt up squawking hysterically. 'Sorry, slight miscalculation there. Shit, my hand.' He dunked it into a carafe of water.

Martin stood up and started opening his fly buttons. 'Hey, Jamie, if I set something on fire, will the girls put it out for me?' He laughed gleefully.

'No,' screamed Nikki.

'Sit down, Martin,' ordered Anna.

'I fancy a tart,' announced Sam who yelped as Munchkin hit his arm. 'Look silly, on the menu here. Tarte tatin.'

'I never have sweet,' Nikki said to Anna, who'd ordered crème caramel.

'Swing low, sweet chariot,' sang Sam in a deep bass. The song was taken up immediately by the men and Munchkin, completely out of tune. As the crescendo built up, Flora glanced round the restaurant, sensing the mounting anger. As it ended, cheering and table-banging began.

The Italians had marched up to madame and were demanding a reduction in their bill. Watched anxiously by his three companions, one of the Germans threw down his napkin, pushed back his chair, stalked over and waited for a pause. He caught Jamie's eye. 'Could you please make quiet. My friends and I cannot hear ourselves. This place is not only for you people.'

Jamie stood up, preparing to offer a bottle of wine to make amends. 'Terribly sorry . . .'

'Don't mention ze war,' called Sam.

Snorts of suppressed giggles went round the table. Jamie's

mouth twitched. Every eye in the restaurant was on them and there were multi-lingual shouts of support for the German.

'Love the handbag, darling,' quipped Giles.

'I smell ze gas,' yelled Sam.

Martin stood up, clicked his heels together and did a Nazi salute. 'Heil Hitler.'

Shocked, the German called to his companions that they were leaving.

'That's got rid of him,' called Martin. Humming 'Jingle Bells', he used a spoon as a baton, 'Riding boys.'

Sam, Giles, Pete and Jamie began to sing. 'Riding through the Reich, in a black Mercedes Benz, Shooting lots of kykes, making lots of friends, Rat tat tat tat tat, mow the bastards down, Oh what fun it is to have the Nazis back in town. Lebensraum, Lebensraum . . .'

Listening to the men singing, then break into hoots of laughter, blind fury seized Flora. Grabbing her cigarettes and lighter, she stood up, knocking over the metal ashtray which clattered to the floor. Everyone looked at her.

'What are you doing?' asked Jamie.

'Leaving.'

'Wait, we haven't finished.'

'I've finished.'

'Sit down, old girl. Here,' brayed Giles, waving at his lap. 'Next to hubby. Night's still young.' He tugged at her sleeve.

'My ears are going to start bleeding if I hear another word out of you,' hissed Flora, trying to wrench herself away.

Grinning inanely, his white-lashed eyes glazed, he tightened his grip. 'Now we're not letting you run off.'

'Run orf? Piss orf.' Flora's green eyes flashed. 'Tell me, Giles, in which shop did you buy your horrible accent? I'd take it back and ask for a refund. Now, get off me.' Giles let her go.

The hush was broken by an embarrassed Jamie, urging her to sit down.

'Fuck off, Jamie,' said Flora.

Sam ooohed from the other end of the table. 'Temper, temper. Do as the man tells you.'

Flora glared at him. 'Pity your mouth isn't on the same midget scale as the rest of you, Sam. Still, let's hope it talks you into a job one year. Though I wouldn't hold my breath if I were you.'

'Flora,' thundered Jamie.

There was uncomfortable shifting before Martin laughed. 'It's all right, guys. She's probably had too much to drink. Jamie, tell your wife to shut up, will you. Boring.'

'Boring,' she spat. 'But unlike what you say, it's not complete fantasy, is it? Your fight yesterday. Three of them taken on? Teeth knocked out, blood all over the snow? And you say the Press makes things up. Your backside should be where your mouth is, you talk so much shite.'

Pete sniggered. Martin's face was as red as the table cloth. 'Get this bitch out of here.'

'I'm going.'

'Well hurry up about it,' said Nikki.

'Hear hear,' said Munchkin, stung on Sam's behalf.

'Flora, let's work this out reasonably,' pleaded Anna.

'Quite,' said Miranda.

Flora looked at each one of them. 'You can put up with their attitudes? You don't just stand by a man, you're walking three snivelling paces behind. Doormats? You've got welcome tattooed across your backs. And women threw themselves under racehorses to get you lot the vote. What a waste.' She threw a bundle of notes down and smiled. 'Have fun.'

For the first time that evening there was silence around the table as everyone watched Flora stride towards the door and disappear.

'Sorry about that.' Jamie swallowed the rest of his beer, pressed some notes into Pete's hand and raced across the restaurant.

'Ask her what she's been up to with teacher,' called out Martin. 'Skiing lessons? Huh. Shagging sessions.'

Pete froze. 'What did you say?'

'Her ladyship's been having it off with matey with the earrings.'

'What?'

'Flora and that guy Stefan,' said Martin. 'She hasn't been skiing. She's been sloping off to his apartment.'

'Never.' Disgust crossed Pete's face. 'Pity those nice Aussie blokes didn't finish the job, Martin.' He looked round the table. 'So, you all think it's true.'

'I wouldn't worry about writing your best man's speech,' said Martin.

'I'm getting out of here, the company's really rancid.' Pete slung down some notes in front of Sam and left.

Rage had swept Flora through Les Landais and out into the night, but giving vent to her anger had been a wonderful release. She almost laughed as she skipped down the hill, oblivious to the freezing cold.

'Flora. Flora.' Jamie sounded furious. She stopped and waited for him to catch up. 'What's so funny?'

'Nothing.'

'Well, lose that smile. You've managed to insult everyone in the chalet. What are we going to do the rest of the holiday? We've got another three nights to get through.'

She shrugged.

'They're probably all taking a vote right now and unless you sort things out we'll be told to leave. So, go back and apologise. Grovel if you have to, eat humble pie until it chokes you, but sort it out.'

'No. I didn't want to come on this holiday.'

Jamie let out a deep-throated shout of rage. He grabbed her arms and shook her. 'You've made that fucking obvious from the start. You've done nothing but complain and pull faces. Did you ever once think about me?'

A car drove past illuminating his wrath-filled face.

'Yes, Jamie, I thought about you a lot. How you want a Boy's Own holiday with sex on tap.'

'Rubbish. And what were you thinking about that morning you tried to leave?'

'Look, I admit . . .'

'You made me look a complete tosser. And what were you thinking when you took that money off Martin?'

'I didn't . . .'

'Or when you got chatted up by those fucking Australians last night?'

'They weren't . . .'

'Or when you . . .'

'Will you listen?' shouted back Flora.

'Listen? I listened back there. We all know Sam's out of work and Giles sounds ridiculously ra-ra and . . .'

'And Martin bullshits non-stop.'

'Yes, Flora, that too. We know it. We didn't need you screaming it.'

'I didn't scream. I hardly raised my voice.'

'A perfect performance. Ha. Oscar-winning.' He let her go. 'Why let them get to you? Why did you have to make a scene?'

'Me? Scene?' She was incredulous. 'After everything else that happened?'

'You've burnt your boats. And your bridges. What's next?'

'Don't know. Don't really care.'

'You should care for my sake,' bellowed Jamie. 'You might as well start packing, you'll be as welcome in that chalet as a dose of the clap. Did it occur to you that I might actually want to get on with the people around me?'

'It occurred to me that this is your Boy's Own Holiday with sex on tap.'

'Bullshit. Why can't you make the best of it?' He shook his head in despair. 'You're here now, just enjoy it.'

'Flora must make more effort. Flora must try harder. Ever

thought about being a teacher, Jamie? No. Too badly paid for you. Couldn't pay for the drugs, could it?' She gazed up at the sky. The mist had gone. She wished she recognised more than the Plough.

'For the past few days you've been walking round like a zombie. What the fuck is wrong with you?'

Stefan is, thought Flora.

She gazed and gazed up into the black. Stefan's wrong. A penniless Franco-Czech who tells me to dream beautiful dreams, who's haunted my head and seen inside my soul. Who I've known for a few days but I seem to have known forever, even before I first looked into his green eyes. A man who thinks I'm worthless and who's got a girlfriend called Marie-France. Stefan's wrong.

'If you don't care about me, Flora, let's finish. There's plenty of women who'd be glad to take your place.'

'There will be. Plenty.' All the fight suddenly left her, she hung her head in despair. 'You're a serious catch, aren't you, Jamie? And the irony is that I wasn't even fishing.' She smiled wryly, swiping away her tears. 'Let's finish. End it.'

He flinched. 'You're not serious. You can't be.'

'I don't know anymore.'

'You can't be.'

'Why don't you find someone who'll dress the part, cook the part, act the part, ski the part better than I do. Who won't have to change everything about herself to suit you. Her clothes, her friends, her job.' Her tears wouldn't stop. 'Who won't think twice about quoting you faithfully. How did it go? Naff, noove and something else. I should've apologised to Nikki, it was vile. All because you're such a serious catch.'

'Flora, I love you . . .'

'Do you? Or was I around when you decided you ought to get married? Ought to. Not want to, because you still want a Boy's Own single life.'

'Getting married doesn't mean you have to shut yourself away from the world.'

'But it does mean that you have to take account of your wife's needs and wishes. Or maybe you're such a catch, such a rich catch, such perfect husband material, that you thought you wouldn't have to bother.'

Jamie looked at her in disbelief. 'Don't cry, angel. Please. This holiday was a mistake, I know. I'm so sorry.' He put his arms around her. 'Sssh. My beautiful wife.'

'And she lived happily ever after.' Clinging to Jamie, Flora sobbed and sobbed.

The Porsche pulled up beside them. Pete lowered the window. 'It must be love, love, love,' he sang. Then seeing them, his smile faded away. He winced. 'Tell me to shut up and go.'

Flora wiped her face and wearily shook her head. 'Pete can you give me a lift back to the chalet? Take Jamie out, will you?'

'I want be with you,' he protested.

'And I want you to leave me alone.' She clambered into the back of the Porsche. 'What's wrong? Another Boy's Own night with your best mates Pete and charlie. Go.'

In Les Landais, they watched Pete storm away. Nikki was livid. 'How dare Flora speak to Martin like that?'

Munchkin nodded. 'She must've been drinking.'

'Bit OTT,' sighed Miranda.

'OTT?' said Nikki. 'More like PMT. Except she's got it permanently.'

'I'd like to propose a toast,' said Anna. 'To Flora. Three cheers. She's a jolly good fellow.'

'You're serious?' gasped Martin. 'Sorry, Anna. If this were the Middle Ages, Flora would've been burnt at the stake. I want her out of the chalet first thing tomorrow. Agreed?'

'Still after that bedroom?' snapped Anna. 'No, it's not agreed. As far as I'm concerned you should be the one who leaves.'

'Now just a minute . . .' said Nikki.

'Let's get the bill,' said Miranda. She pretended to reach down for her napkin, but instead swiped away the tears pricking her eyes by the thought of Pete in less rancid company. Like a stunning redhead's company.

Munchkin assumed the mantle of peacekeeper with relish. 'Anna, Martin please don't quarrel. Anna, you must admit, it's been quite obvious that Flora's been unhappy . . .'

Giles was smarting. 'Perhaps it would be for the best if she were to find a hotel for the remaining few nights.'

'I'll get a job soon,' muttered Sam to himself.

'Just make sure she's out of the chalet by the time I get up,' growled Nikki. 'How dare she speak to Martin like that?'

'Listen, let's get out of here,' said Sam suddenly. 'Go to the village.'

'What's the damage, Giles?' asked Martin.

'Service included? Yes. Not too bad.'

'You girlies go along to the car,' said Martin. 'We'll sort it out. Smooth things over with madame.'

'Good idea,' said Nikki. 'Don't like the look of her. Let's leave her to the men.'

Catching sight of the scowl beneath the chignon, the others gratefully handed over their money to Sam and scuttled outside.

The ice crackled under their feet and a bitter wind tore into them. The Range Rover was locked. An occasional pinprick of light shone out miles across the valley from houses on the lower slopes of Les Diables.

Miranda shivered, stamping her feet. 'What are those men doing?'

Munchkin and Nikki were delving on the ground to make snowballs. 'Pack them hard,' said Munchkin. 'We'll get them on the way out.'

'What a ghastly dinner,' said Miranda. 'Those bloody men

and then Flor . . .' She looked over to the road and saw the Porsche racing past. She could've wept.

There was a burst of light as the doors of Les Landais were ripped back. Sprinting towards the Range Rover, Martin aimed his electronic keyring, grabbed Anna's arm and yelled at everyone to get in. 'Now. Hurry.'

Sam and Giles were running after him, and getting pelted with snowballs by Nikki and Munchkin. In the confusion as Martin pushed her and Miranda into the car, Anna heard the faint tinkling of breaking glass, drowned out by the furious revving of the engine and shrieks from Munchkin who was shoved in the back seat and landed on top of her.

'Close the doors,' yelled Martin.

'Fuck. Wait.' Giles swore as he slipped over on the icy ground. He leapt onto the rear bumper and was clinging onto the roof rack. He banged the rear window. 'Move it.'

The Range Rover shot off in a cloud of exhaust fumes, five piled up in the back seat. 'Ow, Sam, that's my foot,' cried Miranda who was being thrown to the right as they lurched round a bend towards St Marie. 'What's going on?'

'Tactical retreat,' laughed Martin. 'Got to put a bit of distance between us and the enemy.'

Giles who had clambered onto the roof rack, banged the roof with his foot.

'Stop. I can't breathe,' coughed Nikki, buried under Sam. 'Slow down, Martin. Move, Munchkin, you fat lump.'

'Someone tell me what's going on,' demanded Anna breathlessly, straightening her spectacles.

'Known in the trade as doing a runner,' laughed Martin, squealing round another corner to more banging from the roof.

'You've left without paying?' Aghast, Anna struggled to sit up. 'Go back right now.'

'No way,' gasped Sam. 'The service was dreadful.'

'Stop, Martin, and let me out. Right now. I'm not having any part in this. It's stealing.'

Anna's words were lost as Sam shoved her aside and reached forward to turn up the volume before landing on top of them all with a thump. Music filled the car, drowning out Anna's indignant protests about theft, Miranda's pleas to slow down and Nikki's moans that she was squashed. Giles banged on the roof in time with the bass.

Martin checked his mirrors in case they'd been followed, then eased off the accelerator. He took his eyes momentarily off the road to adjust the volume and the Range Rover veered. Automatically, he hit the brakes and the car skidded to the left.

'Jesus,' screamed Sam. The headlights were showing up the ever closer crash barriers separating the road from a drop into nothingness. St Marie lay far below. Martin wrenched the steering wheel round to the right and everyone in the back was thrown about.

'Arrrgh.'

'Stop,' screamed Anna and Miranda. Giles had come off the roof and crashed onto a pyramid of snowy gravel piled up at the roadside. 'Stop.'

Martin slammed on the brakes. Everyone was staring out the back window in stunned disbelief.

'No,' whimpered Munchkin.

'Oh God. Giles,' said Miranda.

'Fuck.' Sam turned pale.

Yanking on the handbrake, his heart pounding, Martin jumped out and sprinted over to Giles. Please God he hadn't been killed. Please. Please make him all right. Giles was lying as if he were carved from marble.

'Is he all right?' cried Anna. Like the rest she was scrambling from the car, running through the swirling exhaust fumes. Ashen-faced Martin knelt down. 'Giles. Giles.' His voice was pleading. 'Giles.'

Finally he groaned. In the red glow of the tail lights, Martin saw that he was opening his eyes. His face was screwed up in pain and his forehead was covered in sweat. 'Arm,' he whispered. 'Hurts like fuck.'

'Can you move your legs? Yes.' Martin breathed easier. 'Stand back, can't you?' he ordered the others, who were crowding round. Music was blaring from the Range Rover.

'Is he going to be all right?' Trembling with shock, Munchkin clutched Sam's arm.

Giles teeth were chattering. 'Broken,' he moaned.

'Let's get you to a doctor,' said Martin gently.

'Call an ambulance someone,' said Sam.

'Take too long. The cold will hit him. We'll get him into the car,' said Martin. Thank God he was alive. 'Giles lean on me and try and get up. Very slowly. Easy now. Nikki bring the car closer. Easy. I've got you.' Giles winced in agony as he staggered up onto his feet.

'Easy,' coaxed Martin. 'Hospital any minute. Anna, you'd better come with us, you speak French. Sam, take the girls back to the chalet.'

Everyone was mute, holding their breath as Giles was helped into the Range Rover, teeth still chattering between his groans.

'I'll call you,' said Anna, climbing up onto the front seat.

Miranda watched until the backlights of the Range Rover disappeared round the bend. It was a miracle Giles hadn't been killed. Shivering, she nodded wearily when Sam said they'd better start walking.

They were worn out and deflated, like balloons the morning after a party. They trudged uphill in silence, the air thick with unspoken accusation.

Munchkin, her voice small, kept on saying that Giles could've been killed. She whimpered it the fifth time. 'Or paralysed.'

'We know,' snapped Nikki, skidding on some ice. 'Just stop being such a ghoul. Please, Munchkin. We're all in shock. Upset.'

Sam put his arm round Munchkin's shoulders.

'It's miles back to the chalet,' grumbled Nikki. 'Might as well chuck these Guccis in the bin. Should get some biker boots like Flora.' She sniffed. 'So, Sam, whose idea was it to do a runner?'

'Martin's.'

'Typical,' said Nikki.

'But you and Giles went along with it,' said Miranda exasperated. 'Great.'

'Don't play goody-two-shoes,' protested Sam. 'It's not the end of the world. Giles will be fine.'

'Fine?' exclaimed Miranda

'Sure about that?' said Nikki.

'Come on, Nikki, Miranda,' pleaded Munchkin. 'They didn't mean Giles to end up in hospital. It was only meant to be a bit of fun.'

'Fun?' shrieked Miranda and Nikki.

'Oh God,' said Munchkin. 'We've got to go past the restaurant.'

'Pity the men didn't think of that earlier,' snapped Miranda.

'What happened to Giles was an accident,' said Sam. 'If anyone's to blame, we all are.'

'All?' Miranda was incredulous. 'I didn't plan to leave without paying the bill, I didn't make a disgraceful exhibition of myself at dinner.'

'Didn't notice you objecting. Too busy swooning at Pete.'

'Well, aren't you a little bitch,' snapped Nikki. 'Ignore him, Miranda. Perhaps we should go in and pay.'

'Have you just given your halo a polish?' demanded Sam. 'We can't go back. They're bound to call the filth. I don't fancy spending the night in a frog cell. And there's the window. Good shot, Munchkin.'

'It was an accident.' She was close to tears. 'What a horrible evening. I wish I'd never come on this bloody holiday.'

'Hear hear,' said Miranda and Nikki, then looked at one another in astonishment.

'Shit,' said Nikki, seeing the lights of Les Landais and coming to a halt. She lowered her voice. 'Good shot Munchkin.'

She pointed to where a window near the door had been boarded up.

Munchkin turned pale.

'Come out of the light,' hissed Nikki. 'You two go ahead. Casually. Miranda and I will stay here. As she and Miranda lurked, their hearts pounded. 'Bloody men.'

'Bloody, bloody men,' sighed Miranda.

His feet trembling on the pedals as if he had a fever, Martin drove cautiously into St Marie. Every bump on the road led to groans from the back seat where Giles was slumped, trying to find the least painful position for his battered, bruised body. As usual, the village was packed with people and cars, slowing their progress. Giles's groaning grew louder as his shock wore off. Eventually they drew up outside the tiny hospital near the fire station.

Anna ran inside and explained to the nurse on reception that a friend may have broken his arm and be concussed. She was followed by Martin, staggering under Giles's weight. Both men looked dreadful. As Giles was led away, Anna and Martin went to the deserted, dismal waiting room.

They sat on a wooden bench underneath a crucifix. On the opposite wall was a poster of mountain flowers. The harsh fluorescent light made Martin look worse.

'Where did you learn to speak frog so well?' he asked.

'French.' Anna picked up a dog-eared copy of *Le Figaro*. She hated hospitals.

'Oh for God's sake, you're not a teacher yet.' He wanted to throw up. Getting Giles safely to the hospital had put his thinking on hold. Now the job was done, he was thinking.

'And what's that supposed to mean?'

'It wasn't my fault you know. It's not anyone's fault.'

'Some are more at fault than others,' seethed Anna. 'Did I want to do a runner from a restaurant in which I behaved so appallingly? You said that this was your holiday and you'd enjoy it how you wanted to. Love it or shove it. Charming. Pity you didn't shove yourself.'

Martin bunched his fist to stop the trembling in his fingers. 'What happened to Giles wasn't my fault.'

'Really? It's happened before to you, hasn't it, Martin? Twice looks like carelessness.'

'Thanks, Anna,' Martin's voice was cracking. 'How do you think I felt seeing Giles lying there, not moving, not speaking, wondering if he was dead or paralysed or in a coma?' He buried his head in his hands. 'Brought it all back, every single miserable minute of those six months all those years ago.'

'Which you seem to have learnt nothing from.' Anna was contemptuous.

'Earlier when that guy asked me for my autograph, he said it was better to quit while you're ahead. At the peak. Stupid twat. I was still at base camp. One and a bit seasons. Nineteen years old . . .' He lumbered to his feet, looking haggard, smaller. 'I'll be in the car.'

Almost two hours of miserable silence ticked past before Giles was ushered into the waiting room. 'Broken collarbone.' His arm was in a sausage sling. 'Said it would take weeks to fix.'

'OK, buddy?' asked Martin as a wincing Giles eased himself into the Range Rover.

'Bust collarbone.' He seemed heartbroken. 'Won't be able to ski, won't be able to drive.'

'Look on the bright side. Still be able to wank.'

CHAPTER SIX

Thursday

'Sleeping beauty.' Jamie was gently kissing Flora awake. Outside it was getting light. 'My beautiful wife.'

She opened her eyes to find him sitting on the bed gazing down at her so tenderly. She began to smile, then realised something was wrong. He looked awful. Unshaven, unkempt, circles under his eyes, still in last night's clothes.

'My beautiful wife,' said Jamie. ''Tis pity she's a whore. So. You've been screwing Stefan.'

At first she thought she was dreaming a horrible dream. 'What?'

'Nice apartment?' He stroked her face. She tried not to flinch. He seemed possessed by a cold, calm fury. 'Better than me, is he?'

'Jamie,' she pleaded.

'That's why you said finish it. Fits now.' Flora froze as he leant forward. 'Pete told me.' Jamie kissed her cheek. 'He heard last night. Martin told him. Everyone here has known for days.' He stared into her eyes. 'Good fuck, is he?'

'It's not true.'

Smiling, he took her hair and wrapped it round her neck. 'I could strangle you. I could kill Stefan.'

'Jamie. Please. I promise. I haven't.'

'That's what Pete said. Said you couldn't. That's what he's been telling me all night.'

'You couldn't ask me?' she whispered.

'Pete wouldn't let me near you. Didn't trust what I'd do.' Flora was becoming very frightened. She wondered how much he'd had to drink. 'It's not true is it, angel? My beautiful wife. You are mine, aren't you?'

'That hurts,' she gasped, trying to wrench her wrists free. His hand was like a steel hawser round her twig wrists. 'Jamie, don't.'

'Shut up.' He shoved his other hand over her mouth. 'Open your eyes. Good fuck, is he? Better than me? You're going to keep your eyes open.'

Afterwards, Jamie went for a shower. Flora bundled herself up into a ball, hugging a pillow for comfort and staring at nothing.

Jamie got dressed, occasionally glancing towards the bed, his face moulded with disgust. He came over and took her hand, examining her engagement ring. 'Swear to me that you haven't slept with Stefan.'

'I swear.'

'Why don't I believe you?' He shrugged. 'Boy's Own morning. I'm going skiing with Pete.'

Giles staggered onto his feet and reached for the painkillers with his left hand. He winced at his stiffness. Why had he been so stupid as to ride on the Range Rover's roof? Or to agree to doing a runner in the first place? He'd objected at first, then been goaded into changing his mind. Martin had sneered at him to stop being so wet and Sam had cried chick, chick chicken.

He realised with bitterness there was no such thing as a free dinner.

'Shit. Shit. Shit.' He banged the wardrobe in frustration with his good arm. No skiing, no drinking, no nothing. He'd have to entrust Miranda with his precious BMW for hundreds of nerve-wracking miles.

Why had he gone to all the trouble of arranging this holiday?

No one had thanked him, shown any appreciation. He'd worked his balls off getting a deal on the chalet, sorting out insurance and travel plans. All they had to do was turn up and enjoy themselves. And each other. Pete and Miranda. Even Sam getting it together with Munchkin. They were all having a brilliant time. And here he was, alone and wiped out for the rest of the holiday. If it weren't for the car, he'd be on the next plane out.

He stared out of the window. New Year's Eve promised yet another beautiful day of sunshine and blue skies. Early morning skiers were trekking down the road to Les Pins lift. What was he to do with himself? Sit in the chalet bored rigid while everyone else hit the slopes? So what? He was sick to death of the whole pack of them.

Hearing the twins chattering away making breakfast, he decided to go down, grab some food and go back to bed. There was nothing to get up for.

'Morning, you two,' said Hetty. 'Shocking what happened to Giles, isn't it? Lucky he wasn't killed. Eggs?'

'Please. Where is he?' Anna sat down opposite Miranda.

'Went back to bed. Said he didn't sleep too well.' Hetty put down the teapot. 'You went to Les Landais? Bet you had fondue.'

'Yes,' Miranda scowled. The misery of yesterday had given way to black resentment.

'My favourite. Al and I love it in there. It's so cosy and the waiters are really nice. Scrambled?' She retreated to the kitchen.

'Wonder how cosy it is with that broken window,' said Anna. 'Or how nice the waiters will be if they ever track us down. We should go back and pay.'

Miranda spread some butter on her croissant, but remembering the calories, scraped most of it off again. 'The men can sort it out. Quite frankly, I want to get in the max poss skiing. Yesterday was a complete waste of time.'

'But will they? Anyway, what's happened to our money?'

'Sam's still got it, I guess.'

'Well, he and Martin can go back and pay. Agreed?'

'Whatever.' Anna's insistence was getting tiresome, Miranda just wanted to forget about the whole business. 'It's no big deal. People are always doing it, especially after an Indian. Curry and hurry, Charlie called it.' Not that he'd do it any more, not in the expensive restaurants he took that bitch Emma to. Emma wouldn't tuck into madras with naan bread, she probably only toyed with lobster mousse.

A car roared into the driveway, followed by heavy footsteps taking the stairs two at a time. Pete bounded in.

Miranda stared at him incredulous. He was wearing the same clothes as last night. This was the second morning in a row he'd rolled up to the chalet at breakfast time. Who had he spent the night with? A stunning redhead? Or someone else? The moment she was home, she was going for a check-up. God only knew what she might have picked up.

'Morning, Pete,' said Anna. 'You're up early.'

Hetty bustled out with the scrambled eggs. 'Oh hi, Pete. Did you get your skis waxed OK?'

'Being done now. Need my passport.'

'I thought you got your skis waxed yesterday,' snapped Miranda.

'Well, I didn't.'

Anna was anxious to escape. 'I'll take some tea up to Giles. Did he manage to get any sleep?'

'Wouldn't know,' said Pete. 'What's up with him?'

While Anna explained, Miranda sat rigid with shock. How dare he rub her nose in it like this?

'Poor bastard.' Pete shook his head. 'I had no idea.'

'Odd,' snarled Miranda. 'Very odd. Considering you're meant to be sharing a room.' Her words dropped like ice cubes into a glass.

As Pete looked at them, there was no sunshine in his face. 'If you want to know Miranda, I crashed down here with Jamie.

Jamie. The one who's not best thrilled by these stories that the woman he loves is being unfaithful.'

Anna and Miranda stared up at him, cup and cereal spoon mid-air.

'That's all stupid, wicked nonsense.' Anna squirmed.

'Course it is,' snapped Pete.

'Well, why tell Jamie?' On the defensive, Miranda went on the attack. 'Hardly helpful to stir, is it?'

'I don't hold with letting things fester,' said Pete. 'You should all be ashamed. Why, Miranda? Couldn't bear another couple's happiness?'

She flinched.

'Pete, this is dreadful,' exclaimed Anna. 'Jamie mustn't take these silly stories seriously.'

'That's what I've been telling him all night.'

Miranda huhhed.

Pete heard her and was furious. 'We'll probably be out of here later. Go to a hotel. I wish I could say it's been nice knowing you all. But I can't.'

Just as Giles had finally started to snooze, Pete stomped into their room.

'Anna's just told me what happened. Shit, there must be a hoodoo on this place. Still, at least you're not being taken home in a body bag.'

'Thanks. You're a comfort.'

'Get you anything?'

'How about some peace and quiet?'

'Sorry.' Pete lowered his voice. 'So, no more skiing. Poor bastard. What about getting home? Suppose Sam can drive you.'

Giles looked alarmed. 'No he can't. Miranda can. Though we won't be back for a fortnight, she hunches over the wheel like Mr Magoo.'

'Shit. Where's my passport? Got to get some money out.'

As Giles watched him delve under the bed, shake pillows and toss clothes out of the wardrobe, he wished he were in a single.

'I might be out of here later,' announced Pete, finding his passport in a fleece pocket. 'So will Jamie and Flora. Finding a hotel. Good feeling, is it? Trying to break up a relationship? Your collarbone. Believe in karma, Giles? If you don't, I'd start.'

'What?'

'Let Miranda and Anna explain.' Idly, he picked up Giles's passport lying on top of the chest of drawers and started flicking through it.

'Put that down,' ordered Giles from the bed.

'Strange, eh? The emu and the kangaroo. The lion and the unicorn. Sometimes I wonder what I'm doing in England with all you English.'

'Put that down,' repeated Giles.

'How old are you again?'

'Give it to me.' Giles's white-lashed eyes were furious.

Pete's expression changed from puzzlement to thoughtfulness. 'I see. Giles Thomas born, what did you always say, on the banks of the Test with a fly rod in your hand, isn't quite right is it?'

Giles froze.

'Wayne? Wayne Thomas. Place of birth. Moss Side. Where's that? Manchester, isn't it?'

'Get out. Now,' yelled Giles.

'I'm going.'

Flora pretended to be asleep when Pete knocked on her door. She'd dressed, then crawled back into bed, too miserable and confused to face anyone.

She was curled up in her ball, remorse and self disgust washing through her. How could she have been so weak? Such a bitch to Jamie?

Sam or Giles must have seen her and Stefan in Jimmy's.

Flora pictured one of them dashing past the pool table to blab to the other. Then they'd come back to the chalet and told everyone. She remembered Munchkin's probing at dinner. And Martin in the bar saying he wondered what Jamie was going to make of it when he found out.

She knew what Jamie would make of it when she admitted the truth. Which she must. Jamie would finish with her. He knew his worth. His pride and his self-respect would never let him forgive her for humiliating him so publicly.

'Flora. Flora,' called Hetty, knocking on the door.

She sat up. 'Come in.'

'Morning. Just had a call from the ski school office. Apparently someone called Jacques Neuf is teaching you today. He'll be at La Croix at eleven.'

'What? What about Stefan?'

'They didn't say.' Hetty shrugged. 'Terrible about poor Giles, isn't it? He's feeling awful.'

'Hungover?' asked Flora absentmindedly.

She knew she'd put her foot in it by Hetty's dismayed expression. 'You don't know? He broke his collarbone last night. He was riding on the Range Rover's roof and fell off. He's asked not to be disturbed. Breakfast? Scrambled?'

Flora guessed the twins were anxious to be out on the slopes. 'Thanks.' She knew she ought to eat, she'd scarcely had a mouthful last night. She buckled up her biker boots, too wretched and shellshocked to feel sorry for Giles.

The valley was filled with sunshine, Les Diables seemed to be guarding the village. The peaks looked so pure and pristine wrapped in all their glittering whiteness.

Martin was at the table, munching on cornflakes, tapping on his laptop, mobile phone to his ear. He looked dreadful, as if he hadn't slept much either. The scar on his cheekbone was more pronounced in his tanned face. 'We're not taking that shit. Give me the number, I'll talk to him. Bloody solicitors.'

Glancing at Flora, his scowl deepened. She shrugged. Overnight, it was him who seemed to have shrunk like Alice. He looked older, greyer. The air was suddenly as much hers as his.

Hetty put coffee and eggs in front of her, as he jabbed the off button. 'Morning, Martin. So what happened to Giles?'

'Shouldn't you be packing?'

Flora pulled a face. 'Oh for God's sake. Even now . . .'

'Know something? You should've done us all a favour and fucked off to Vienna days ago.'

'Siena. I wanted to go to Siena. Know something? I wish I had.'

'Would've bought you a ticket. In fact, we all would've coughed up. Munchkin, Sam, Giles, Nikki. Popular girl, aren't you?' He jabbed his finger towards her. 'You're fucking lucky you're not a bloke. You'd never have got away with speaking to me like that last night if you were.'

'And what would you have done?' scoffed Flora. 'Taken care of me like you took care of the Aussies? By the way how is the eye?'

The eye, eyes, narrowed in fury. 'We had a vote in the restaurant last night after your little cabaret turn. You're out. Number for a taxi is on the wall over there. Use it.'

Flora pushed away her scrambled eggs, feeling sick. She gazed out of the window. The valley looked so beautiful. Should she start packing? Perhaps she should get a bus to Annecy rather than wait for Jamie to come back and tell her it was all over. The view was a bit like Jamie. She'd taken both for granted until she was about to be deprived of them.

'I'll use it. Don't worry. Finally get that bedroom after all, won't you? Pity your backgammon skills don't match your capacity for fabrication.'

'I've had a very rough night, Flora.' The teapot crashed down onto the table. 'And right now, I don't need any more lip from you.'

'Where's your next holiday, Martin? Fantasy Island?'

He seemed about to explode. 'And where's yours? The Virgin Islands? Perhaps not, not the way you put it about.'

Flora grew pale.

'Shocked, are you? Everyone knows you've been having it off with your ski instructor. Stefan, isn't it? Talk of the chalet for days, kept us all entertained.'

In the kitchen Hetty and Alice stared at one another open-mouthed.

Flora remembered seeing Stefan's beautiful face reflected in the mirror at Jimmy's and how they'd locked themselves together, overwhelmed by desire, heedless to anything else. Heedless to Sam or Giles.

'Skiing lessons?' scoffed Martin. 'Shagging sessions.'

'That's not true,' she said flatly.

'And just as you were about to get Jamie's ring on your finger and his balls in your handbag.'

'It's not true,' she whispered.

'You were caught redhanded, sweetheart. I'll say one thing, you and Stefan make a very pretty pair.'

She stood up blindly. How could she have been so weak? How could she have wrecked everything between her and Jamie?

'Still, hubby's money wasn't entirely wasted was it? You must've learnt something zooming back to Stefan's apartment for those shagging sessions. Sorry, skiing lessons. Or did you get the lift?'

Flora spun round. 'I really wish those Aussies had hung you out to dry.'

'You thought you were so smart down in that bar, didn't you? Chatting them up.' He eyed her speculatively. 'You weren't having it off with them as well, were you?'

'Not with them. Or with Stefan.' She turned on her heel.

'Smart?' Martin called after her. 'What's so smart about being found out? Though I quite admire your balls, thinking you can get away carrying on with Stefan in front of the whole of St Marie.'

'You'll get that bedroom in an hour,' cried Flora over her shoulder.

'A bit of advice for next time, Flora. Never on your doorstep. The Savoie's hardly the most discreet venue if you must stick your tongue down someone's throat.'

Her head was spinning, she couldn't take any more of him. She wanted to be sick.

'Wonder what Jamie will say when he hears?' taunted Martin. 'Haven't sent out the invitations yet, have you?'

Flora stopped in mid-stride and turned round. Her face was screwed up with misery. 'Jamie's heard. Jamie's going to finish with me.'

'What?' Martin was poleaxed.

'There's no need for any invitations. There'll be no wedding.'

'What do you mean Jamie knows?'

'Pete told him.'

'Pete can't have,' cried Martin.

'Happy now?' She stared and stared out at Les Diables trying to slot everything into place. 'Aussies are like that,' mused Flora, her mind suddenly elsewhere. A hunch was waking up. 'Upfront. Direct. What did you say? Something about skiing back to Stefan's apartment.'

'Look, Flora, I'm sure we can sort this out.' Martin sounded desperate.

'You said.' She frowned at him. 'You said something about the Savoie. Didn't you?'

Martin winced. 'I didn't mean it.'

'The Savoie? Sticking my tongue down his throat.'

'Look, Flora, this joke's gone too far. Not that it was ever very funny.'

'Come on,' coaxed Flora. 'Where else was I caught red-handed, Martin? Where else?' He cringed. 'Nowhere? Nowhere else.'

'Listen, I'm sure we can work this out reasonably,' he pleaded.

White hot rage was filling Flora. She strode towards him. 'Who started this? You?'

'Flora. If you'll just calm down a minute. Please.'

'Did you start these rumours about me and Stefan? Who did?'

'My laptop,' yelped Martin. 'Don't Flora.'

'What happens if I drop it? Delete everything?'

'Jesus. Please Flora don't.'

'Munchkin,' hissed Flora. 'That poison dwarf. Here.' Thrusting the laptop back in his hands, Flora tore up the stairs and along the corridor. Storming into Munchkin's room, she found Sam asleep.

'Munchkin,' yelled Flora, hammering on the bathroom door. 'Come downstairs. Can I have a word with you. Please.'

In his narrow bed, Giles tossed and turned, his brooding interrupted.

Miranda and Anna glanced at one another. Although trying not to eavesdrop, their preparations for a day on the slopes had slowed to a standstill.

Martin watched Flora as she swept back across the sitting room, her expression murderous. 'Flora. I'm sure we can . . .'

'Kindly keep quiet.' She scraped back a dining chair, sat down and lit a cigarette. She'd never been so angry. It was one thing for her to have doubts about her future with Jamie, quite another for him to end things because of chalet tittle-tattle.

Hair wet from the shower, contacts quickly put in, Munchkin padded downstairs. 'Morning.'

The atmosphere was so tense that she assumed Martin had given Flora her marching orders, as he'd threatened the night before. Relishing her role as intermediary, she'd tell the pair of them to stop being silly and would effect a reconciliation. 'Sleep well? Anyone seen Giles yet?'

'Sit down,' ordered Flora.

Munchkin was astounded. 'Do you mind not speaking to me like that? Honestly, the manners of some people.'

'Sit down.'

Munchkin's plan to arbitrate was being torn up. 'Flora, there hasn't been a big conspiracy to get you out, you know. It's just that you don't seem very happy and it might be a good idea . . .'

'You owe me an explanation.'

'I don't owe you anything.' Bewildered, Munchkin appealed to Martin. 'What's all this about?' She sank into a chair beside him.

'It's about these stories going around about me and Stefan. Did you start them?'

Munchkin didn't say anything, but started to blush. Flora was so enraged that she was growing quite frightened.

There was a long pause.

'Listen, Flora, I don't have to take this, you know. You can't speak to me like this. Can she, Martin?'

He sighed heavily. 'How could you be so dumb?'

'If it wasn't you, who was it?' demanded Flora. 'I'll find out. Well, Munchkin? Usually you have no trouble talking.'

Munchkin stared down at the tartan tablecloth, her resistance crumbling. She took a deep breath. 'I think, if I remember right, I mentioned purely in passing to someone that I saw you and Stefan together a couple of days ago. And how nice it was that you seemed to be getting on so well.'

'Up at the Savoie? The day you saw us with our tongues down each other's throats.'

'That wasn't me,' protested Munchkin.

Flora shouted her down, '. . . skiing back arm in arm to have a shagging session at his apartment.'

'Look, all I said is that you seemed to be getting on very well,' pleaded Munchkin. 'Everyone must've read a lot more into it. Like Chinese whispers.'

'These whispers have been whispered round here for days apparently,' hissed Flora. 'Talk of the chalet, according to Martin.'

He cringed.

Munchkin shifted in her seat. 'No one really believed it. You're over-reacting as usual, Flora. Just like last night.'

'I'm over-reacting?' repeated Flora in a low voice.

'Seeing things out of proportion. No one took it seriously.'

'Jamie's taken it seriously.'

'Jamie?' Munchkin's mouth opened like a dead fish. 'He can't. How . . . ? It was only a bit of fun.'

'Bit of fun?' shrieked Flora. 'You wreck everything between Jamie and me and you can explain it away as a bit of fun.'

'Me wreck things?' scoffed Munchkin. 'That's rich. I saw you up at the Savoie and you were doing a good enough job by yourself, Flora.'

'Shut up, Munchkin,' ordered Martin.

'You saw nothing,' spat Flora. 'We were having lunch.'

'Lunch? Pah. Holding hands, gazing into . . .'

'Bullshit.'

'Liar,' screamed Munchkin.

'Girls, please,' appealed Martin.

Trembling with guilt, with indignation, with the injustice of it all, Munchkin spat, 'I wasn't the only one. Ask Giles and Sam. They saw you at the bar with Stefan. Very cosy, weren't you?'

'Such a pity gossiping doesn't burn off calories,' said Flora.

Munchkin blushed scarlet. 'Aside from anything else, hadn't you better think about packing? We don't want you round here for a second longer spoiling the rest of our holiday. Do we, Martin?'

'Munchkin.' He stared at her. 'Shut up for once. Your mouth has caused enough trouble. Nikki always said you should learn to mind your own business.'

Munchkin's chins trembled. Why wasn't Martin backing her up? Had Nikki really said that? She thought they were friends. All the time the three of them had spent together. Martin and her sharing a laugh. Nikki giving her that sweater.

'If I were Flora or Jamie,' said Martin, 'I'd murder you. You stupid, gossiping bitch. Where's Jamie? We've got to straighten this out. Christ, Munchkin, how could you?'

'How could I?' The tartan began to jig as her eyes watered. 'You and Nikki were delighted that madam here was caught out.' Blinking away her tears, she gave Flora a shrewd, chilly stare. 'A good morning's work. Him of all people suddenly on your side. Ask yourself, Flora, how Jamie would've reacted if he'd seen you and Stefan that day?'

'Munchkin . . .' pleaded Martin.

'Suppose it's worth making me look like a piece of dogshit to save your hide.'

'Look . . .' Martin sounded in despair.

'I looked,' spat Munchkin. 'I saw. You might have Jamie's pretty ring on your finger Flora, but honey, you're marrying the wrong man.'

Flora coloured. She noticed her biker boots could do with a polish.

'Munchkin,' warned Martin.

'The other night in the street outside Jimmy's. You and Stefan. Both so jumpy, weren't you?' Munchkin glared at Flora. 'We both know why, don't we?' Seconds ticked away as Flora concentrated hard on folding back the sleeves of her sweater. 'We both know how unfair this is on me,' said Munchkin bitterly.

'I haven't slept with Stefan. I haven't been to his apartment,' said Flora in a small voice.

'The letter of the law and the spirit of the law.' Munchkin leant forward. 'So, I got the letter wrong. Not the spirit, though, did I?' Their eyes met. Flora tried to speak but no words would come out. 'Did I?' Getting to her feet, Munchkin fled towards the stairs.

In the lull that followed Flora buried her head in her hands. She felt as if she'd been in an avalanche.

Martin broke the silence. 'I'm truly sorry, Flora.' He sounded it. 'What can I do? Where's Jamie? I'll explain. Try and sort this mess out.'

'Skiing.'

'With Pete? Probably for the best. Once he's away from this place, he'll realise these stories are rubbish.'

Flora shook her head.

'Don't worry. Pete will talk some sense into him.' He reached forward and squeezed her hand. 'Come on. Don't lose that bottle.'

'Bottle?'

'Bottle. Guts. Spirit.'

'Me? I'm a wet wimp.' She thought about all the times she'd hidden herself away, too cowardly to confront him. 'The wet wimp of a hick hack.' She smiled wanly. All the wariness of him had vanished, all the intimidation she'd felt had gone.

'When we're home, I'll get my mate Jack Mancini to call you. Talk to him about doing some shifts at the *Reporter*,' said Martin.

'Really?' Flora was astonished. This was a whole olive grove, not just a branch. 'Thanks. Listen, I feel as if I ought to explain . . .'

'What about? The grief between us? Boy, can you give as good as you get. Forget it, shall we? New year, new start.' He smiled. 'The priority is you and Jamie getting sorted. Come skiing with me and Nikki and we'll go find him. I'll act as your St Bernard. Or have you got another shagging session at Stefan's apartment?'

'Martin, it's not something to joke about.'

'Wow. I've finally got a proper smile out of you.'

'Oh God. My lesson. What time is it?' Flora scrambled to her feet.

'Relax. I'll give you a lift to Les Pins.'

'That's really kind, but—'

'For once, will you stop arguing? Thank you. Get your shit together. See you outside in five. Here,' he buttered her a croissant and filled it with cheese. 'Eat something for once.'

Her head spinning, Flora went to her room. She couldn't wait to get out in the fresh air and clear her mind. What a morning. And it wasn't even half-past ten.

Pass, money, gloves, scarf, hat, cigarettes, sunglasses.

If only she could talk to Jamie.

She was suddenly relieved that Stefan had decided to ski out of her life the day before. Since she'd first seen him, she'd been like an junkie offered a fix. No matter how wrong, how destructive, she'd craved him. He was the drug that had come close to finishing her and Jamie. Now her supply was cut off. Martin was right. Sorting out herself and Jamie was the priority.

Outside in the drive, Flora stamped her feet. The ice crust crackled. The light bounced off the white layer of snow, which had got thinner by the day.

The sunshine was a spotlight, showing that Martin looked even more haggard. His skin was stretched tight with strain, making his face more hawk-like.

'Anything wrong?' asked Flora, climbing into the Range Rover.

'This deal.' He backed swiftly into the road. 'Ever tried to juggle a couple of million quid? Come across back-to-backs? Don't bother. A site's for sale. Buyer A has first option on it. Buyer B is desperate for it. If buyer A can raise the funds, he buys the site, then immediately sells it on to buyer B. Makes a fortune.'

'Nice.'

'I'm buyer A. Just heard that I'm going to have to raise more money. Shit. All this and Giles. You heard what happened last night?'

Flora nodded. 'Tough on you. Must've stirred up a lot of memories.'

He grimaced. 'Brought a lot back. Thought I'd be getting a one way ticket back to the loony bin again. You know I had a nervous breakdown? After the smash?'

'Years ago though, wasn't it?'

'The smash? Years. Week before the Cup Final. Watched the match in hospital. We lost. Everyone said it would've been different if the boy wonder had been fit.' He reached across and patted her arm. 'Me. Boy wonder. Though you never heard of me.'

'Sorry.'

'Another era. You brought home to me how long ago they were. The glory days.'

'Miss them?'

'Nothing's ever been as good.' He pulled into the lane leading to the lift station. 'If I see Jamie, I'll talk to him. Explain. Don't worry. It'll be fine.'

'Thanks, Martin. Thanks for everything.'

'Come here. God, woman, do as you're told for once.' She leant towards him and he kissed her cheek. 'Cleared the air, haven't we? Apart from your filthy fags. You smoke too much. Peace?'

'Peace.' Flora jumped out of the Range Rover. She frowned. 'Why did you stop playing? You were still so young.'

Waving, he drove off.

Miranda popped her head round Giles's door. She found him a bit off-hand, which she put down to him being in pain. 'Such ghastly luck. Not the best start to the New Year.'

'No.'

'Still, we could all meet up at lunchtime. You don't want to be cooped up in here all day, bored and moping.'

'No.'

'Get you anything? Books? Anna's got hundreds.'

'No.'

'Now, about the car. Am I insured? I think we should check. Will you phone or shall I?'

Why was her voice so jolly? He'd broken his collarbone, not lost his marbles. Why couldn't she just leave him alone? 'I will.'

'Sure I can't get you anything?'

'How about out of here?' said Giles through clenched teeth. 'I need to sleep.'

*　　*　　*

Munchkin was sitting hunched on her bed, staring into space, fingering her avalanche whistle as if it were a set of worry beads. She'd woken up early and mentally rehearsed how she should break her news to Sam. The final run-through had been in the shower, then that lying bitch Flora had hammered on the door and ruined her plans.

Sam had gone for a shower, depriving her of any comfort. When he found out about Flora and Jamie, he'd be as cross with her as everyone else. He'd think she was a stupid, stupid gossiping bitch too. It was all so unfair. Tears pricked her eyes again.

'Now drink this, Munchkin,' said Anna, coming back with a toothmug of water. 'And try to calm down a bit.'

Munchkin gulped it back, her shaking hands spilling it over her Party Animal sweatshirt.

'It's just not fair,' she fumed. 'Everyone thinks I'm to blame about this business with Flora and Stefan. She said I'm trying to wreck things between her and Jamie. She's the one who's destroying them. And she had the cheek to sit there like a duchess and deny everything.'

Anna sighed. 'Even if something were happening with her and Stefan, would you expect Flora to admit it?'

'You see. You believe it too. It's not just me.'

'For goodness sake.' Anna was exasperated.

'All right, so there's no proof that she went back to his place, but something was definitely going on,' protested Munchkin, taking a huge gulp of water. 'Definitely. Body language, it never lies.'

'You claimed you saw them snogging,' said Anna.

'Not exactly.' Munchkin gave a giant sniff.

'Words to that effect,' said Anna. 'Munchkin, I'm afraid whoever said you had a mouth big enough to park a bus in was right.'

Munchkin shook her head. 'Flora and I both know . . .'

'That's enough,' ordered Anna.

Miranda hovered at the doorway. 'Are we skiing?'

'I'll get my stuff,' said Anna, shaking her head and rolling her eyes.

Miranda sat beside Munchkin on the bed. 'Now come on. Buck up. You can explain to Jamie it's all a silly misunderstanding. Grab Sam and let's all go skiing.' Miranda believed skiing had the same magical therapeutic qualities as a nice cup of tea.

'If you'd seen Flora and Stefan, you wouldn't have a shred of doubt.'

'Are you skiing or not? If you are, do get ready. Martin's offered us a lift.'

As usual Nikki kept everyone waiting. Finally, she sashayed to the Range Rover in her Ralph Lauren. 'Forget the gym, I'm taking up walking,' she announced, climbing into the front seat. 'Haven't slept so well in ages. Anyone seen Giles?'

'Grump city,' said Sam. 'He's more pissed off than after the last by-election.'

Anna was sitting between Miranda and Munchkin, both equally taciturn. It was like being in a waxworks museum.

'Cheer up, Munchkin,' said Nikki. 'Jamie will see things straight. When he's sobered up. That guy drinks too much. And once he's got all that stuff out of his system. Must have brought enough drugs to stock a chemists.'

'What?' exclaimed everyone else.

'Him and Pete last night. On the Colombian marching powder. And the whacky baccy. Caught them when I went down for some water.' Peering into the side mirror, she frowned. 'Wicked on the skin to get so dehydrated. Come on, Martin, let's go.'

'What?' whispered Miranda. So Pete had been telling the truth.

As they approached Les Landais, Anna suggested that they go in and pay, but was out-voted.

'Forget it,' said Sam. 'They'll just write it off, bet it happens all the time. Dinner money.' He began handing round the cash from last night.

'Well, I'm not facing madame,' Nikki shivered.

Pocketing the notes reluctantly, Anna resolved to send the money through the post from the safety of home.

Sam laughed as they sped past the restaurant. 'Good shot, Munchkin.' The jug-eared waiter was putting new glass in the window. 'Come on, cheer up. Jamie's forgiving. Anyway, we're all a bit to blame.'

He'd been astounded to come out of the shower to find her in such a state. She'd ranted on almost hysterically about Flora and thingy with the earrings.

'Death corner,' announced Sam as they approached a bend. Martin winced and slowed down almost to a crawl. 'Giles was bloody lucky.'

On the outskirts of the village, Martin was forced to slow down again. Scores of pedestrians ambled in the road, walking awkwardly in their heavy boots towards the lifts. A party of teenagers looked like red Indians, their noses and cheeks scored with fluorescent zinc.

As they drove past the nursery slopes, the air was filled with an excited din. Hundreds of toddlers were revelling on the snow, so thickly wrapped up against the cold they seemed as round as they were tall. Watched over by bored mothers or nannies, some were on minute skis, others pulled toboggans.

'Aren't they sweet?' said Miranda.

Munchkin didn't want to look. She didn't want to think about children.

'Some of the mums certainly are,' leered Martin, blasting his horn, trying to attract the attention of a glamorous mink-swathed blonde in dark glasses. 'She could be a double for Ursula Andrex.'

'Cor,' breathed Sam.

'Perhaps you could borrow a child, give you an excuse to

stand there,' said Nikki icily. 'On second thoughts you act like such kids most of the time, you don't need one.'

Martin winked into the rear-view mirror. 'Nikki always gets grumpy when she's up against some competition.'

'That's not true. I just wish you wouldn't go round with your tongue hanging out.'

Martin turned round, lasciviously stuck his tongue out and wiggled it up and down. 'Boy Scout training.' He winked at Sam. 'Be prepared.'

'Don't be so puerile, Martin,' sighed Nikki.

Sam ooohed.

'What a grown up word,' said Martin. 'Has Anna been giving you lessons?'

Jacques was the bald dwarf the wrong side of sixty whom Flora had assumed must be Stefan that second morning. Humourless and fierce, he reminded her of all the instructors from her childhood. She was tempted to make a run for it.

'*Vous êtes Flora Rose?*' he demanded at the lift station at La Croix, before launching into twenty sentences of impatient-sounding French. He scowled when Flora apologised and said she didn't understand. 'So, you make me talk English.'

'Where's Stefan? Is he ill or something?'

He shrugged. '*Sais pas.* Are you ready? No. Do up your boots.' Jacques pointed with his pole and looked at her disapprovingly. 'You're lazy, I think. You don't want to ski?'

'They're so stiff,' said Flora, trying to squeeze the clips.

'Stiff? What is stiff? A child can do it. *Allez. La bas.* To the lift.'

As she followed him, Jacques barked at her to bend her knees and relax her shoulders.

While they waited for the lift, he pointed out everything she was doing wrong, then asked her if she was listening. Was she serious about learning to ski? Then she must concentrate.

Flora knew that her hat was about to have a big D for Dunce on it.

On the chairlift towards Nabelle, she pulled out her packet of Marlboros.

'You cannot ski and smoke,' exclaimed Jacques. *'C'est fou.* Why come to the fresh air to pollute it?'

Sighing she put them back in her pocket and huddled into her jacket. It was freezing.

Jacques wasted no time in chit-chat. As soon as they were off the lift, he yelled at her to follow him. As she sped across the snow, the wind icing her face, her eyes watering, he bellowed instructions. Head up, knees flexed, arms relaxed, more weight on her lower ski.

Her resentment mounting by the second, she failed to realise he'd led her over a ridge until she found herself flying through the air. Shocked, she screamed. Instinct took over as she hit the ground, she leant forward, crouched over her skis and flexed her legs so they acted as shock absorbers. Wobbling, she just about managed to stay upright. Glancing back to ensure she'd landed safely, he gave her no chance to get her breath back, but pressed on down the piste, shouting at her to lean forwards not backwards.

Instead of the usual zig-zag traverse she was used to with Stefan, Flora found her skis pointing straight ahead down the mountain and gathering speed. She suddenly realised she could find out very painfully why it was called the fall-line.

She was swept on, trees just a green blur to her right, following Jacques as he turned, then traversed, then turned again before they finally reached another chairlift.

She turned her skis uphill and pushed her knees down, coming to a breathless halt beside him.

'*Pas mal,*' he conceded grudgingly. 'We go up.'

Her legs feeling as if they'd collapse under her, Flora glanced at the other people in the lift queue. They all seemed so relaxed, happy and most importantly, enjoying themselves. What was she doing with this humourless tyrant? He was as bad as Mirabête. Why wasn't she dossing on a balcony in the sunshine drinking hot chocolate? Any enthusiasm she had built up for skiing was beginning to crumble. It was all too much like hard work and she had almost three hours to endure.

Beside her on the lift, Jacques started whistling the '*Marseillaise*' and peered down studying two skiers below them. 'Aw-ful. Probably English.'

Flora failed to think of a suitably crushing reply.

After they skied off the lift, Jacques said: 'Now we try to parallel. You listen to me carefully, yes?'

Parallel? Flora felt a surge of excitement run through her.

He drew diagrams in the snow with his pole and explained the theory to her. She frowned, trying to get the sequence sorted out in her mind. 'So mademoiselle, it's just a matter of changing your weight. Simple.'

Over the next hour as they sped from piste to piste and lift to lift, Flora discovered it was anything but simple. She became more and more frustrated, then demoralised and reverted to snowploughs as she grew tired. Her legs were weary and her mind overwhelmed as she tried to talk herself through the technique. She just couldn't get the hang of the weight transference, the way her knees had to roll one way and her body the other. In her confusion she muddled the downhill and the uphill skis. Then she couldn't plant the pole at the right time, it was either too early or too late or in the snow too long or in the wrong place.

Jacques was merciless. He ignored her whimpering pleas for a rest, her protests that other skiers and boarders were putting her off. Flora barely had the chance to brush the snow off when she fell, because he insisted she press on, try one more time.

'Again. To the lift.'

Flora was taken aback to realise there was a glorious view across the valley. She became aware of the sun beating down on her face. If anyone had asked her where she'd skied that day she'd have found it impossible to tell them. Her concentration had been total; Jacques' haranguing about her style relentless. She had tried to improve, if only to shut him up.

'Can't we stop?' she begged. 'I'm exhausted.'

'You shouldn't smoke. *Allez.*'

'Slavedriver,' muttered Flora. She was forced to admit, though, that he was a good teacher, pushing her harder, making her ski faster, better, than she'd ever dreamt was possible. He was serious and dedicated. There'd been no laughs, no cosy breaks for a ciggie and no green eyes or slow lazy smiles to distract her.

On yet another chairlift she tried to get it straight. 'So the downhill ski is on the outside. Yes? Yes. Traverse. Weight on the downhill ski, then coming into the turn, I go down, plant the pole and flatten the skis. Then go up, transferring the weight on the other ski which is now the uphill ski. No, it's not. It's the downhill ski. Is it? Or the uphill? Oh God, I'll never get it right.' She rested her forehead on the safety bar.

Jacques looked at her without a shred of sympathy. 'And you must go faster. You cannot parallel if you ski like an escargot.' Flora smiled. 'Why laugh? Learning to ski is serious. Too many people, stupid English people especially, think they can ski any slope. They don't learn properly. Two days and they're on a black run. *C'est fou.* Cause us many problems.'

He sounded as if Flora were personally to blame. Scowling, she watched a skier dressed in dayglo lime crashing down onto the glittering snow.

'*Anglaise, sans doute.*'

Off the lift, Flora stared intently at her red skis and willed them to obey her. She was going to get it right.

'*Allez*,' called Jacques.

'*Allez*,' Flora told her skis. For the next kilometre she was boss. When she ordered her skis to stem, they stemmed. When she told them to swerve left to avoid a boarder, they swerved. Up ahead Jacques occasionally glanced behind him, but remained silent. He had no need to tell her to flex her knees or turn her shoulders. He couldn't fault her. She knew she was finally doing everything right. As she swept past other skiers, her body seemed relaxed but her mind was totally focussed.

'Parallel,' yelled Jacques, his head swivelling round. 'Good, Flora. Again.'

'Yes.' She'd paralleled. A glorious sense of triumph filled her. She had paralleled.

Mind on her victory rather than on her skis, she went into the next turn too fast. The skis decided to rebel. The left crossed over the right. Three seconds later Flora lost her balance, her pride and her temper. She crashed down in a tangle of skis and poles, before pelting across the white ground on her backside.

'Shit,' she screamed, slithering to a halt. Snow had seeped up inside her jacket and sweater and vest, freezing her skin as it melted.

Jacques had stopped and was shaking his head. 'That will always happen when you don't bend your knees and keep your weight forward.'

Taking a deep breath, she clambered back onto her feet and set off once again.

During the next fifteen minutes, her frustration with herself grew by the second. Each time she approached a turn, she told herself this was the one she'd parallel. Each time, at the very last moment, she ducked it.

Aching and weary, her confidence was being sapped as her concentration ebbed away.

In a style that would have shamed the nursery slope, she followed Jacques along a narrow path in a serpentine snow-plough. He began to yell at her with growing irritation. The path joined a main piste.

'Bend your knees,' he barked, pointing his pole towards the chairlift. '*La bas.*' The slope was so gentle it was almost flat.

Dozens of people were waiting in line behind a red plastic tape.

Flora was totally fed up. With herself, with him, with everything. Anticipating the chance to stop, she forgot she was still skiing. Her skis decided to prove who was boss. They crossed again.

Sprawled on the ground, her ears were filled with mocking whistles and slow hand claps from people in the queue. She lay back, snow filling her hair and gazed up at the blue sky. Ophelia in her stream.

Hearing her name being called, she sat up, her eyes dazzled by the sun.

Jacques was herring-boning his way to her. Furious that she had disgraced him and his professional pride in front of the whole queue, he'd been tempted to abandon her. 'Are you hurt? No? Get up then.'

'Must I?'

'Yes. Up. Up. Up.'

Flora adjusted her hat, now with a giant D for Dunce on it. 'Can't we stop now?'

'No. We take the lift across to La Toit, try, try, try to ski down and then stop. Lesson finished. To both our joys.'

When she was back on her feet, Jacques skied to the queue, muttering to himself in French. He dismissed her apologies. As they moved towards the turnstile, he hung back, so they'd take different chairs.

Finding herself sitting next to an Italian teenager, Flora immediately lit up, trying to angle her cigarette so the smoke was invisible to Jacques in the chair behind. She pulled a face at her skis. How many more times would she fall? Why couldn't she get the lift all the way down?

Maybe it was because she'd had a break, maybe she wanted to spite Jacques, maybe she was resigned to falling and no longer cared. For whatever reason, Flora's mind, body and skis finally harmonised.

Speeding across the piste from the lift exit at La Toit, without thinking she turned, planting her pole and swivelling round it, her skis parallel.

She whooped in delight and sped on, Jacques yelling encouragement. She traversed and paralleled, traversed and paralleled. As she tore across the snow, turning one parallel after another, her screams of joy astounded the other skiers on the piste.

She could parallel. She could do it. She could really do it.

Jamie, Stefan, the chalet, the falls, the cold, the lifts, the aches, the ski boots, the skis, the ice, the rows, the sleepless nights. Everything she'd endured since arriving in St Marie was forgotten as she turned perfect parallel turn after parallel turn.

At the bottom, Jacques allowed himself to give her a small smile and mimed a round of applause. '*Pas mal. C'est tout. Fin.*'

She grinned. 'Wonderful. Thank you. You're a very good teacher.'

'And one day soon you're going to be a very good skier.' He pulled his hat further down over his eyes and they shook hands.

She watched him push off and use his skis like skates, picking up speed as he shot off past the Savoie and down the mountainside.

She decided to celebrate with a hot chocolate. Making her way through to a free table, she was still grinning. The people around her smiled too.

'Flash git,' said Martin, at a slope-side table at Café Neige. His voice was full of admiration for the figure in the middle of the piste, gliding across the snow as if dancing to a waltz. The skier went backwards, jumped up and turned 360 degrees through the air before making a perfect landing. 'Take a look at that.'

'A-mazing,' said Miranda. 'Rarely, rarely a-mazing.'

'Might as well give up,' sighed Sam, then perked up. 'Shit. It's Jamie.'

Munchkin choked on her *vin chaud*.

'And there's Pete,' said Sam excitedly.

Miranda dropped her forkful of spag bog.

'Hey guys,' yelled Sam. 'Over here.' Miranda and Munchkin wanted to slap him. 'Budge up, Anna.'

Jamie's hair looked blonder against his tanned face. Pete in his wake, he strolled up to the table. His blue eyes were hidden behind sunglasses as he studied them all, looking down his aquiline nose. The emperor was at the amphitheatre, weighing up whether a gladiator should be thrown to the lions.

'Wotcha Jamie,' said Sam. 'Good morning?'

'Not too bad.'

Munchkin cringed under his gaze.

'Want a drink, boys?' asked Martin.

'Later,' said Jamie. 'Perhaps.'

'Having lunch, you two?' Anna concentrated on polishing her spectacles.

'Are we having lunch, Pete?' Jamie drawled over his shoulder, continuing to study them all.

Pete pushed the hair out of his eyes, wrinkled up his crooked nose and sniffed. 'Don't know if I want to. Rancid stench round here. What is it?'

Miranda blushed. Anna and Nikki exchanged nervous glances.

'Slander.' Jamie sniffed. 'I smell gossip, mixed up with, what's that, spite? Malice? The stench is this story about my beautiful wife and her ski teacher.'

Munchkin suddenly became fascinated by the bottom of her empty glass of *vin chaud*.

'How does the story go, Martin?'

'Jamie, listen . . .'

'I should fucking kill the lot of you.'

Sam, Martin, Anna and Miranda all squirmed.

'So is it true?'

'Of course it's not true.' Nikki interrupted. 'Rarely as Miranda would say. You're rarely, rarely being a silly billy.' She flicked back her chestnut mane. 'We feel like worms for being such wicked gossips and you've every right to fucking, whoops pardon my French, kill the lot of us. I could do with a manicure. Where was I?' She gazed at Jamie with her huge brown eyes. 'Of course Flora hasn't been having it off with thingy. She adores you, it's obvious. As if anyone would pass you up. Almost the catch of the century. Munchkin, say sorry to Jamie for being such a stupid cow. Not you, Jamie, you're not a stupid cow, Munchkin is.'

'Sorry, Jamie,' said Munchkin in a tiny voice, thick with tears.

'Moo ooo ooo,' bellowed Sam.

'That's better,' said Nikki, seeing Jamie relax. 'Least said, apart from very, very sorry, soonest mended. Put it all behind us. And you give Flora a big kiss to say sorry. Now, sit down. Have some stodgy dinner. Lunch to you, you're posh. Haven't they heard the word salad in this place? Here, Jamie.' She patted the bench. 'If we don't end up with scurvy, I'll be amazed. Should've brought my vitamins.'

As Jamie meekly sat down, the rest gazed at Nikki in astonishment.

Turning to Jamie, Nikki lowered her voice. 'And lay off that cocaine, you.' Jamie was dumbfounded. 'No wonder you smelt funny things. Aside from anything, it ruins the skin.'

Wanting to avoid any grief, Pete sat as far away from Miranda as possible.

Anna went off to find a phone and check how Giles was. 'No reply,' she announced a few minutes later. 'He must be asleep.'

'Giles?' Pete smiled. 'A nose by any other name . . .'

'A rose.' Anna sighed. 'You mean a rose by any other name would smell as sweet.'

'I do?'

'*Romeo and Juliet.*'

'It is?' Pete was blank.

Smiling, Anna shook her head. 'Pete, if your brains matched your looks, you'd be the most devastating man on the planet.'

'Anna,' Pete was astounded. 'You're almost flirting with me.'

Giles stared out across the sunfilled valley towards Les Diables. He ignored the telephone. The view gave him no pleasure, he wished he were on the other side of the world.

What a bastard of a day. First writing off his holiday because of some prattish prank, then getting found out. Back in London why hadn't he insisted on having his own room? He deserved it after all the graft he'd put into arranging the holiday. And being found out by Pete of all people. Sweet Pete, the Aussie playboy with the Porsche, who'd waltzed off with Mirandy. Perhaps it was poetic justice for messing things up between them.

He paced the balcony. Was it such a huge crime to want to put his background behind him, to rise socially as well as professionally? He was much more himself as Giles than he'd ever been growing up as Wayne. His brains, an unimpeachable double first, his ambition, the need to broaden his horizons had isolated him from his family and his school mates.

Often he'd grown up feeling he were a changeling. He understood how transexuals felt, certain they'd been born into the wrong body. He was certain he'd been born into the wrong family and the wrong place and the wrong class.

Class. It still mattered, no matter who pretended otherwise. Easy if you were an outsider like Aussie Pete or Irish Sam. You could get behind those invisible ropes that the English use to cordon off their tribes. You could ignore the totems. The small details on clothes that were worn as a uniform, the tiny nuances of language.

'Not quite PLU. More PLT,' Miranda had once whispered about her boss.

Not quite People Like Us. More Pardon, Lounge, Toilet. Us? What a joke.

He wanted to belong, be one of us. Was it so wrong? He was much more at home with people like Miranda than he was with his parents or their neighbours, with their limited horizons and almost bovine passivity. He hated their constant refrain that 'they' should do something. 'They' meaning the Government, the council, the authorities. Why couldn't they show a bit of gumption and start taking charge of their own lives? Pick up the litter outside their front doors? Use the library to get educated?

He'd been Giles for years now. Since he'd started college, he'd gradually metamorphosed into the person he'd wanted to be. He'd watched and learned and read. It wasn't difficult, he was bright, quick. He'd changed everything. His clothes, the way he held his knife and fork, his accent, which Flora had said he should take back to the shop and ask for a refund.

Early on, he'd thought he'd never get away with it. Parties, trips to the pub, even sharing a flat had been fraught with buttock-clenching anxiety. Well-meaning inquiries such as 'where are you from?' had been avoided by paroxysms of coughing or abrupt changes of subject.

His mam and dad would never understand in a million years why he wanted to be Giles. If they ever telephoned asking for Wayne, he'd tell his lodgers it was the cleaning lady or the garageman probably suffering Alzheimers.

He stared at Les Diables. He thought about the rest, up on the slopes somewhere, enjoying a sunny day's skiing and a good laugh at his expense. He wondered what the Hon Miranda Lake-ffrench would say when Pete told her, and cringed.

He had climbed and climbed over the years, almost reached the summit of his personal mountain. Now, he'd be sliding back again, shoved down to the bottom by an Australian.

* * *

While Jamie had gone to telephone the chalet to try and get hold of Flora, Pete had mentioned that the pair of them had planned to ski Nabelle. 'Let's all go.'

Anna had studied the huge piste chart nailed to the wall and frowned. 'Looks tricky.'

'No worries,' Pete had said airily. 'We can cut through the trees. Avoid that bit. The rest is a very easy red, more like a blue apparently. And Jamie and I can help everyone out.'

A plateful of spag bog, two beers and Nikki's undivided attention helped Jamie's anger subside. She was so incredibly pretty. Sweet too, good at sending herself up. He knew he was being manipulated but quite liked it. If she gave as good a back massage as the dextrous ego massage she was giving him, she must be quite something in bed.

'All of us?' Jamie muttered to Pete, as everyone stood up to go. 'Bit demanding, isn't it? Thought it was just you and me.'

They took a drag lift, then a cable car. Out of the station, they emerged into brilliant sunshine. In the distance, snow-capped peaks seemed to be floating in the sky, islands in a dead-calm sea.

'It's like Shangri-la,' marvelled Anna, thinking of 'Lost Horizon'.

'That place does a brilliant sweet and sour pork,' said Sam.

Pete put on his skis. 'We'll go down and head over there to the right. Then through the trees. Cut out the nasty bit. OK? Fifty to those trees, Jamie?'

Jamie stared down, his mouth watering. Although one part of him said he should keep an eye on the others, the far larger part argued that they'd caused him so much grief, why bother? 'Done. After five.'

Grinning at each other, they counted down. 'Go.' They shot off like thoroughbreds out of their stalls. Leaving serpentine tracks, they swung down towards the trees.

'A-mazing,' sighed Miranda. 'This looks pretty stiff. Can Munchkin cope?'

Munchkin was swallowing hard and breaking out into a sweat of fear. It was so steep. The trees seemed such a long way down. She was tempted to bolt back to the lift.

'We'll look after you.' Martin smiled reassuringly. He didn't like the look of it either.

She nodded her thanks and began a slow snowplough, but after just a few metres her skis seemed to take on a life of their own and began pelting across the snow. Terrified by the speed at which she was being carried, she panicked and tried to stop the only way she could. She threw herself onto the ground.

It was a mistake. Her skis turned into a team of huskies drawing a sledge. She was the sledge and hurtling down faster than ever. She screamed for help as she flew past Nikki and Martin before rolling over onto her side and swinging her skis round to act as brakes.

As she burst into tears, she heard Nikki calling. Then Martin yelling. Anna was beginning to sidestep up towards her.

Why did they have to make such a fuss? Why did she have to be so useless at everything? Why had she come on holiday when she could be at home in her cosy flat sitting next to a warm fire? Why did she have to get herself pregnant after a one-night-stand with a man whom she didn't dare confide in? Why wasn't that man at her side, taking care of her?

'Munchkin, Munchkin,' called Anna.

A pair of snowboarders tore past, their baggy clothes billowing out behind them as they powered down the piste. She must get up. She couldn't keep the others waiting. And it was freezing. Sniffing back her tears, she dug the edges of her skis into the snow and tried to push herself up with her poles. She got almost halfway up, only to lose her balance and bump down again.

Martin arrived. 'Well, that's one way of getting down a mountain.' He held out his hand, pulling as Munchkin pushed.

'Thanks,' she gulped, wincing as the boots dug into the side of her shins. She reached into her pink jacket pocket for a tissue. The faraway peaks seemed to be longing to touch the cobalt sky, the snow was purest white, a pale moon was rising. Instead of being charmed by all the natural beauty around her, the landscape seemed nothing but a sterile prison.

'All right?' asked Anna, legs aching from the side-stepping.

'Fine, aren't you luvvie,' said Martin. 'We're going to take it nice and easy. Anna in front, Nikki and me behind.'

'I can't,' wailed Munchkin.

'Course you can.'

'I can't.'

'You can.'

Nikki had had enough. He was going to get nowhere like that, they'd be here all night. 'You must and that's that. Now come on. It's freezing.'

Nikki's exasperation startled Munchkin out of her misery. Their progress was slow. Martin, whose style Jamie described as hit, run and hope for the best, fell three times. Eventually they made it to the trees, where the other four were waiting.

Sensing that Pete was trying to avoid her, Miranda was determinedly talking Verbier with Sam.

'Took your time,' said Sam.

'Well, excuse us,' spat Nikki. 'Easy red? My arse. Munchkin's had a bad fall.'

'She OK?' asked Sam alarmed.

'She'll live.'

Pete got out his battered map, which Giles had faxed to the bar a week earlier and frowned.

'What?' asked Martin.

'The run through the trees has been closed.'

'So?'

'So, the other one was icy the other day, and there was a long, long drop. Right, Jamie? It's a black by the way,' said Pete. Munchkin paled at hearing icy, long drop, black. 'I vote we stick to the original which is much easier and links up with this motorway piste here. That takes us straight to Nabelle.'

'But it must've been closed for a reason,' objected Miranda.

'Doubtful.' Pete shrugged. 'They're usually shut in case of an avalanche, but there's no chance of that. Never been one here. Probably the ski patrols are feeling lazy and can't be bothered to hack down there. It's up to you lot.'

Martin and Sam were quite taken with the idea. They could claim it was off-piste, which sounded expert, adventurous and would be something to boast about back home. Neither Nikki nor Anna liked the idea of icy, long drop and black. Miranda was out-voted.

Pete threw away his cigarette, to Anna's disapproval. 'Right, I'll lead the way and . . .'

'Jamie can come up the rear.' Winking, Sam nudged Nikki who almost overbalanced.

'Pathetic,' muttered Miranda. 'Let's go. It's freezing.'

A path leading down between an avenue of pine trees was cordoned off. Jamie smiled encouragingly at Munchkin. 'This should be nice and easy. He lifted up the red plastic rope, ignoring the sign: *Fermé. Interdit.*

Jamie was wrong. Snow hung from the branches, which the sun had failed to reach, but barely covered the ground. It was rutted with tree roots and rocks.

Pete had shot off and was nowhere in sight. Anna had fallen after she turned into a tree stump. She skied gingerly, anxious about more hazards under her skis. Miranda brushed against a small branch which swung back and swiped Nikki who came to an abrupt halt. Cursing, she rubbed her cheek.

'Where the hell is this motorway?' called Martin after fifteen minutes, finding himself on little more than pine needles. His new skis would be wrecked.

'And where the hell is Pete?' muttered Jamie, furious with

him. It was so bloody irresponsible to bring the rest of them up here. He'd known it was a bad idea back at the restaurant. Was Pete absolutely certain they were in the right place? It seemed more like a path for summer ramblers, which would've been marked in yellow. Of course, he wouldn't have known that from his black and white fax.

'Is this never going to end?' wailed Nikki.

Jamie was relieved when the trees started to thin out. The motorway must be close now.

The strain of negotiating such rough terrain was showing on their faces. Because they were going so slowly, the cold was seeping into them, tightening their muscles, making the skiing even tougher.

'I feel like Hansel and Gretel,' called Jamie.

'And Pete is definitely the wicked witch,' said Anna.

At last they entered a clearing. The trees thinned out, giving way to a bank of snow-covered boulders to their right. Above, an expanse of sky was visible. From somewhere they could just hear the faint whoosh of skis cutting across snow and a French voice shouting something.

'Must stop for a breather,' said Miranda. She rubbed her hands together, trying to warm her frozen fingers, damp in their gloves. She turned to Nikki. 'Sorry about that branch.'

'Not your fault. Bloody men, we should've listened to you.' Frowning, she examined her skis for scratches. 'Blimey. How are we going to get down this?'

The path ahead of them was less than ten feet wide and steep. It was grooved with small rocks and stones peeking through a thin crust which was more ice than snow. To the left was a sheer drop, down down down onto thin treetops.

Looking at it stretched out in front of her ski tips, Munchkin grew frightened again. She was tempted to pretend she'd twisted her ankle, so the blood wagon would come to her rescue.

'Keep well over to the right,' ordered Jamie.

'I don't like the look of this,' said Nikki.

Martin didn't either, but wasn't going to admit it.

'Jamie, go first. Show us how it's done,' pleaded Anna. 'On second thoughts, to hell with it. Walkies.' She took off her skis.

'Good idea,' said Munchkin gratefully.

'It's easier on skis,' warned Jamie.

'Not for me, it's not,' said Anna. She turned sideways and went down like a crab. She dug in one boot to ensure she had a foothold and used her skis like a cumbersome walking stick.

The others watched her undecided. Martin and Sam were worried about losing face, especially when Jamie offered to take Munchkin and Anna's skis for them.

'I'll wait for you just down there,' Jamie called as he moved off, two sets of skis slung over his shoulders. There was no way this was any sort of run, Pete was such an idiot. He wove down the path and felt a thrill of excitement when he was jolted by the stones under his skis as he sideslipped. Scree running was one of his favourite memories of a training exercise on Dartmoor.

Jamie slid over to the left and found himself on better snow. He pressed on in a series of tight turns, narrowly avoiding a tree stump and some boulders at the edge. It was quite a drop, he realised, peering down onto the balding treetops. Better take it easy. Up ahead, just beyond the bend, the trees gave way to an expanse of white piste.

He stopped and threw the two pairs of skis down onto the ground. 'Not too easy. Keep well to the right.'

Ahead of Sam, Miranda was side-slipping, taking it three inches at a time. Her heart pounded. This was vile. She knew she should never have listened to Pete.

Martin and Nikki still hadn't made up their minds whether or not to walk.

Eager to show off to Munchkin, determined not to be shown up too much by Jamie, Sam flattened the edges of his skis and tried to emulate Jamie's pace.

A heart-stopping scream rang out, echoing off the grey rockface.

Miranda watched Sam career past her out of control, tumble to the ground and slither sideways towards the drop. Loose stones clattered, following him. Miranda screamed again, seeing Sam clutching handful after handful of nothing trying to brake his slide, his skis grating and scratching on the ice. His face was mummified in helplessness, his mouth open in silent appeal as he was swept away from her. She could do nothing in those few seconds when he was carried towards the edge, his poles ripped from his wrists.

Instinctively, unable to watch, Miranda closed her eyes. And prayed. There was silence. Then a long despairing cry.

Sam was still on the path. Just. His fall was broken by a boulder, which he'd grabbed and clung onto as he dug his skis into the snow inches away from the edge.

'Move to the right,' yelled Jamie. 'Sam. Move.'

Sam couldn't move. Would the feathery green of the trees break his fall? The branches would splinter when he crashed onto them, as he plunged down and down and down . . . He heard voices; Jamie telling him to move, then Munchkin pleading with Jamie to hurry, Martin telling Nikki to take his skis.

'Hang on. Literally. What a fucking stupid thing to say.' Jamie's expression was grim. He'd never side-stepped and herringboned so fast in his life. His breath streamed around him in a white mist. 'Sam. Move your legs. Towards me.'

'Can't move.' Sam's eyes were shut tight, but he sensed a shadow crossing him for a brief second as Jamie drew closer. He was shaking, he felt one of his skis trembling up and down on the snow's surface. Clutching the boulder, his arms were being stretched on a rack. 'Help me. Jamie. Help.'

Jamie ripped at his ski bindings. A shower of stones kicked up by Martin ran past him. Freeing his skis from his boots, he pushed them out of the way and scrambled onto his knees. The skis clattered down the path. The slope was like an ice-rink, freezing his legs. If he weren't careful, they'd both go over.

He dug in the edge of his boots, trying to get some purchase.

'Sam, we've got to take off your skis.' Half sitting, half lying, Jamie went onto his side and reached. His fingers were a few inches from Sam's bindings. He reached again. Still not far enough. He'd have to move down the slope a fraction.

'Careful,' screamed Miranda.

Jamie felt himself sliding before he managed to jam his boots into the icy ground. He stopped. Jesus Christ. Sweat ran down his back.

He tried to scramble back up towards Sam, but kept on slipping. It was a nightmare game of snakes and ladders. He drew level with Sam's skis. His hands were frozen, making it difficult to move his fingers. He tugged. A ski was freed.

'That's one. Now the other. Come on, you bastard.' Jamie's face was screwed up in concentration as he wrenched at the heel clip. Beside him Sam shook feverishly. 'Bastard.' The ski was freed and shot away down over the edge onto the trees below.

'Listen,' gasped Jamie, snaking up alongside Sam. 'I'm going to hold onto you and after the count of three, you've got to let go, grab me and we roll to our right. OK? OK, Sam? Look at me. Don't look down. At me.'

As Jamie's arms grabbed him round the waist, Sam opened his eyes. The edge was less than six inches away. The soft branches would break his fall, he'd land on a green feathery mattress. Under his gloves, he felt the rough stone. He must keep hold of it, otherwise he'd slide over the ice and over the edge. Jamie's breath was on his face, telling him to answer, telling him they'd both go over if he didn't do what he was told. Did he understand? Don't look down. He was so cold, that must be why he was shaking. Let go? He didn't want to, couldn't, mustn't. Didn't want to, didn't want to. Was he saying it or was someone else?

'Shut up,' ordered Jamie. 'After three. Understand?' Jamie's boots started to slip, he counted down, the panic rising in him. 'Roll.'

Jamie's jacket tightened round his neck, strangling him as Sam grabbed it. He threw himself over to the right and rolled

Sam on top of him, and then rolled again and again. Snow, rockface, the green of the trees, the blue of the sky went past until they came to a stop on the right hand side of the path.

Breathless, Jamie lay on his back, eyes shut until the adrenalin rush had died away. 'We can't go on meeting like this.'

Brushing the snow off him, he waved up at the others.

Sam turned his head and retched. If he had nine lives, he'd just lost one of them. His body trembled. 'Thanks.'

He tried to smile at Miranda, up the path. Her legs collapsing under her, she had sunk to the ground. Anna and Munchkin were clutching one another. Nikki had buried her head in Martin's shoulder and was being comforted by him. Sam wiped his mouth on his sleeve.

Jamie knew Sam was in shock. Even if his ski could be found, there was no way he could get back on them. 'You must move. We'll get you to the piste, then I'm going for the bloodwagon.' He got to his feet. 'We've got to get out of here,' he called up to the five. 'It'll be dark soon.'

In fact it was only just after three, but the last few minutes had seemed like forever.

'Can you make it? We'll go on,' yelled Jamie. He yanked Sam to his feet, thanking God that the other man was such a midget. Slipping and sliding across the rutted icy snow, he half dragged him to the bend.

'Finally.' They'd reached the end of the path. Beyond the red plastic rope lay an expanse of piste. Jamie retrieved his skis. A kindergarten class was playing follow my leader. 'Sam. Have my jacket. Walk.'

Jamie wondered what sort of reception he'd get from the hard-faced pisteurs. Sam wasn't actually injured. He was shocked, dazed, but conscious and walking. They'd be none too sympathetic or willing to bring out the blood wagon when told that a load of inexpert Brits had got themselves into trouble attempting to ski an out-of-bounds Interdit area. They'd probably tell him to stop wasting their time.

On the other side of the rope, Jamie heaved a huge sigh of relief. About two hundred metres away was a lift station. A beacon on their journey back to warmth and safety. 'You can make it down there easy. Good man. I'm going to find your ski.'

Jamie needed an excuse to get some space. He trudged up the piste, alongside the trees to his left. How fucking stupid could they get? His sleepless night was catching up with him. Worn out, he longed to see Flora, to put everything right again. Why had he brought her on this bloody holiday with all these strangers? Apart from Pete, he didn't give a toss for any of them.

In less than two minutes, he spotted the ski among some branches. Jumping up, he swung on a branch until it was released. He looked up and up and could just make out the curve of the path through the trees. Christ, Sam was lucky.

Anna was doling out chocolate. They were all huddled together on the side of the piste and seemed to have lost their will to think or to move.

Seeing them, Jamie rebelled. The scum who'd caused him and Flora such grief deserved nothing. But like sheep frightened by dogs, they were waiting for their shepherd.

Flora's gloat lasted as long as her first hot chocolate. Waiting for the second, without a book to distract her, she began to grow self conscious about sitting on her own. Everyone else around her in the Savoie seemed to be in jolly, laughing groups like something out of *Friends*. Why hadn't Chalet Juliette been like that?

She gazed down at the piste. Next time, she'd make sure Jem and Fred came along too, though she couldn't quite picture Fred on skis. He could stay on a balcony admiring the light or something. They'd stay in a beautiful chalet with a massive hot water tank so they could all have baths. And it would be close to the lifts. Not a trek away where sherpas and oxygen supplies should be on standby. And she'd conquer black runs. Perhaps.

Maybe. Well, at least she'd make sure she looked good 50 metres either side of a restaurant.

Flora almost dropped her lighter. Next time? What had happened to her? Oh God, she was turning into Miranda. Soon she'd be wearing a headband and ironing her jeans and writing thank you letters.

Her expression changed. If there were a next time, would she be Flora Rose or Mrs James Naze? She should be thinking about her wedding, the happiest day of her life, not making plans for holidays with Jem and Fred.

She rubbed her engagement ring on a napkin. Everything would come right between her and Jamie once they were home. Wouldn't it? Her supply cut off, the memory of a green-eyed, penniless Franco-Czech would fade away to nothing. It would. Jamie was her future. Her doubts last night had been silly, just a reaction to that horrible, horrible dinner.

A group to her left broke into laughter. Suddenly she wanted to get back to the chalet, see Jamie, sort things out. Put it right between them. She'd behaved appallingly to him, jeopardising their happiness, their whole future together, by giving in to a few moments of lust.

Shivering, she got up abruptly to pay.

Lost in thought, she walked across to the lift station, oblivious to the figures around her. As the lift began its descent, a bitter wind tore into her face, stinging her eyes. The piste was crowded. Everyone was being driven home early by the cold and wanted to get ready to celebrate the new year.

Wrapping her scarf round her face like a bank robber, she gazed down across the valley trying to find the landmarks of St Marie. The peaks of Les Diables glowed gold in the low, slanting sun. Jamie was right, it was so beautiful.

The chalet seemed deserted. Flora planned to have something to eat and an illicit bath. Looking in a kitchen cupboard for some cake, she jumped. 'Giles. Didn't realise you were here. Sorry about your arm.' Her heart sank, she wanted to be on her own. 'Like some tea?'

'Thanks.'

Filling the kettle, Flora glanced at the book on the last general election which Giles was holding in his left hand. 'Interesting?'

'No.'

He did seem down. 'Shall I make a fire?'

Giles followed her into the sitting room, watching her lay kindling and firelighters. 'Enjoyed your holiday, Flora?'

'Um.' She screwed up some paper and reached for her lighter. 'Thank you for organising everything.'

He gazed at the paper which was twisting as it burned. 'Sussed out me, didn't you? Is that why you got pretty boy Pete to snoop at my passport?'

'What?' Flora held a bunch of twigs in mid-air.

'Had a good laff did you at Wayne's expense?'

'Giles, what are you on about?'

'Easy for people like you to rip the piss, isn't it?' His voice was flat northern. 'You don't know what it's like to sweat and work every inch of the way for any success. Easy for you, wasn't it, Miss Rosehagen? You were brought up with it and now you're going to marry it big time.'

Flora was utterly bewildered. 'Rose,' she corrected automatically. 'The kettle must've boiled. I'll get you some tea and you can start from the beginning.' She went to the kitchen. 'Sugar?'

Giles had disappeared.

On the road winding up from the village, Martin drove slowly and as far away from the edge of the road as he could. They all shuddered when Munchkin pointed out the spot where Giles had fallen and added how they'd almost had two bad accidents in a day.

'Thank Christ you were there, Jamie,' said Martin. 'We were mad to listen to Pete. Then the selfish bastard just shoots off.'

'Typical Pete,' snapped Miranda.

They found Giles staring into the embers of a dying fire, his book lying on his lap. His face was forlorn, his jowls more than usually pronounced. Not lifting his eyes, he answered their questions about how he was feeling in a monotone.

'Flora around?' asked Jamie.

'Miss Rosehagen? Came back an hour ago.'

'Rose,' corrected Jamie.

'She had a bath. Nicked all the hot water.'

Jamie sighed. Why couldn't Flora be more considerate?

'Rosehagen,' insisted Giles. 'As in Rosehagen Bank. As in a seat on the board of Rosehagen Bank.' He smiled nastily.

Jamie frowned. 'Did Pete come back?'

'No. In town chasing skirt, isn't he?'

Helping Anna make tea in the kitchen, Miranda almost dropped the sugar bowl.

'Your office rang, Martin,' Giles sounded bored. 'Had problems getting through on the mobile. Some hassle with a deal.'

'What?' yelped Martin. 'When? What did they say?'

'I'm not your answering service.'

'Anyone call for me?' asked Anna from the kitchen.

'I'm not a fucking message service. I only organise holidays.' Giles scowled.

Martin dashed up the stairs, taking them two at a time.

'Enjoyed your week, Sam?' asked Giles. 'Taken your mind off being such a loser?'

'Aren't we a crosspatch?' Sam pulled a face, and gestured to Munchkin that they should go upstairs.

Jamie and Nikki exchanged glances. He went off to the storeroom to fetch some more logs.

She sat down and flicked her chestnut mane over her shoulders. 'Got the glums, haven't you, Giles? Sorry about your collarbone.' Putting on some lipsalve, she pouted. 'But for your information, we've had an awful afternoon, thank you very much.'

'Sure,' Giles scoffed.

'Sam was almost killed.'

'What happened? Munchkin sat on him?'

'I'm not listening to you be unkind. Where's my *Vogue*?'

From under his white lashes, a half smile on his face, Giles watched Jamie come back. 'Flora been having another shagging session with matey, has she?'

'Giles,' protested Nikki. 'We all know that's not . . .'

Jamie had dropped the log basket and pounced within a few inches of Giles.

'What are you going to do?' sneered Giles. 'Have me horsewhipped on the steps of your club?'

'Wouldn't sully the club,' hissed Jamie, white with anger.

Giles slumped back in his chair. 'How long did Flora have me sussed? Suppose you and her had a good laff about it for days, didn't you, old chap. And pretty boy Pete told the rest of them? Have a good crow, did you?'

Manicured hands folded on her lap, Nikki's pretty face was perplexed. 'That hospital must've given you some funny drugs. I've got some brilliant stuff upstairs, left over from my wisdom teeth. Harley Street. Safe.'

'Tea's up,' called Miranda from the kitchen.

'What a treat,' sneered Giles. 'The Honourable Miranda Lake-ffrench skivvying around after the likes of me.'

'What are you on about?' demanded Jamie.

'It's about you and her and the rest of them and me.'

Nikki frowned. 'What about you?'

'You know very well,' spat Giles. 'Wayne.'

'John Wayne?' asked Jamie.

'Me. Wayne Thomas. Pete told you, didn't he?'

'No,' said Nikki and Jamie. Nikki pouted. 'You mean you've changed your name? So?'

'So I'm Wayne Thomas from Moss Side.'

'And?'

'Dad a bin man, mam a cleaner.'

'You mean that's why you're pissed off? You think it matters?' Jamie tutted. 'For God's sake Giles, stop being so bloody chippy.'

'Chippy?' Giles turned on him in fury. 'Easy for you to say isn't it, James Algernon Henry Naze. Giles passes muster. Wayne from a sink estate and a sink school, parents with an allotment, wouldn't get through your front door.'

'You're so wrong.'

'Sure.' Giles was bitter.

Nikki flicked through the pages of *Vogue*. 'For someone who's so clever, you're another silly billy. You must be clever, Giles. University, partner in an accountants, future MP.' She looked up. 'So, you didn't have the best start. Well, not many of us did. We're not all toffs like Jamie and Miranda.'

'I'm not a toff,' said Jamie indignantly.

'Course you are.' Nikki rolled her eyes. 'You wanted to put your past behind you, Giles? Good for you. No one else's business.'

'Pete made it everyone's business,' muttered Giles.

'No.' Nikki sighed. 'He didn't.'

'He didn't?'

'Like the rest of us, he doesn't give a stuff. This mag is very heavy. If I hit you with it, will it knock some sense into you? You should've met us for lunch, instead of sitting here moping.' Nikki picked at a furball on her white sweater. 'Apart from anything, this central heating ruins the skin. Shrivels it.'

'It does?' said Giles faintly.

'Remember, cream indoors and nothing less than factor fifteen outside.'

Jamie marvelled at Nikki sitting on the sofa looking like something out of her magazine. Was her inane chatter quite so inane?

Giles looked downcast. 'I thought—'

'What?' Nikki sounded impatient. 'That anyone cared? They don't. So you've got no excuse for being so snide and bitchy, have you?'

Giles slumped further into the chair. 'You wouldn't know . . .'

'Wouldn't I?' Nikki raised an eyebrow. 'I'm so posh, am I, Giles? You live once, live it as you're most comfortable. Though personally, I can't see why you want to be a hooray. Not more cake.' She groaned, seeing Anna come in with a tray. 'I'm going to be tied to that stairmaster when I get back. Now come with me, Giles and let's find those pills. They'll make you sleep for a bit, but that's probably a good idea.'

Amazed, Jamie watched Giles obediently get to his feet and follow Nikki up the stairs like a puppy.

'Oh dear,' sighed Miranda, pouring out tea. 'Is all that news to you? One of Giles's lodgers told me yonks ago. And Sam knew from day one. I've never let on. Always thought it was up to Giles to tell me.'

'He should be proud of what he's achieved,' said Anna.

Jamie cut some cake. 'Course he should.'

'Giles has been a good friend to me,' continued Miranda. 'Shugg? Put himself out. Spent ages researching the best mortgage when my sister and I bought the flat. We were clueless.'

'Look at the trouble he took to arrange this week,' said Anna.

'Answer,' muttered Martin, coming down the stairs, lines of strain etched round his mouth. 'Shit.' He jabbed the off button. 'They can't have gone home already. Idle bastards.'

'Problem?' asked Jamie.

'Your bank do loans? Martin hurled the mobile onto the sofa in frustration. 'I'm relying on this deal.' He began to dial again.

'*Where Eagles Dare*?' asked Jamie, looking through the stack of videos. 'I'll just check on Flora.' She was fast asleep.

✻   ✻   ✻

The fire was roaring away in the grate and the curtains closed against the twilight. As everyone tucked into tea and watched the video, Pete strode in. 'What happened to you lot?'

Eight pairs of eyes looked at him reproachfully.

Jamie got up and dragged him away explaining exactly what had happened. Pete listened in appalled incredulity.

'She's a bit of all right,' said Giles, his mouth full of cake, ogling Ingrid Pitt whose cleavage filled the screen. 'Quick you two, look at the tits on that.'

Martin whistled.

'Wouldn't kick her out of bed,' said Sam.

Miranda and Anna pulled faces. Normal service had obviously been resumed.

They sat in harmony warmed by the blazing fire, munching cake and slurping tea, eyes glued to the film.

'Perhaps not the happiest of choices,' said Anna, wincing as a fight broke out on the top of a cable car.

'I can't watch. Just like Sam.' Munchin covered her face with a cushion. 'Sam? Where's Sam gone?'

The sound of retching came from the bathroom.

Flora had crashed out two minutes after her bath and had a glorious dreamless sleep. The chalet was so quiet that she assumed it must be about five in the morning. The clock said six. No music. No mayhem. Had she missed New Year's Eve?

She stretched indolently, smiling as she remembered her triumph. She had paralleled. Jacques had been a monster, but by pushing her and pushing her, he'd made her do it. But what had happened to Stefan? It was for the best that her supply had been cut off, that she'd never see him again. As soon as she'd set eyes on him, she should've filed him under F for Forbidden.

Hearing footsteps, Flora gave a guilty start. Why hadn't she been thinking about Jamie? She must put things right between them.

'Hello, Flora,' said Jamie, striding in. He closed the door. 'Good sleep?' His face was tanned, making his hair look blonder, his eyes bluer.

'Yes, thank you.'

Emptying his pockets with his back to her, they studied each other's reflection in the mirror. Jamie stacked his francs into different piles.

'I didn't sleep with Stefan,' she said quietly.

'That's what they've all been telling me.' He turned round. 'Sorry, Jamie, for stirring the shit. Sorry, Jamie, for causing you grief. Well, let them eat crow.'

'See, they all admit . . .' She was too hasty.

'See? I've got perfect eyesight,' hissed Jamie. 'Yesterday I saw the pair of you together. How you touched him as you put on your skis.'

Flora quailed. 'I was only trying to keep my balance.'

'I expect my wife, like Caesar's, to be above suspicion.' His words cracked like a whip. She flinched. 'You've convinced them. Not me, though. Tomorrow I'm going to find out exactly what you've been up to with Stefan. I'm taking you skiing.'

'Fine,' said Flora. 'I can parallel.'

'You, parallel?' Jamie smiled scornfully.

'I can.' She glared at him.

'Bullshit.' He began taking off his clothes. 'I need a few zeds.'

'It's all right, I'm getting up.' She didn't want to be in bed with him. 'So. Pistols, or rather skis at dawn.'

Nikki was by the fire reading *Vogue*, wearing dusty pink suede jodhpurs and a pale pink shirt. 'Flora. Can you do something for me?'

What? Jump off Les Diables? Theirs hadn't been the easiest of weeks together and as usual, Flora felt intimidated by Nikki's stunning appearance.

'Let me see your ring.'

Disarmed, Flora moved closer. The diamonds glittered in the firelight as Nikki examined the ring with an expert eye. 'Wonderful stones. Beautifully cut. Bet you've become very left handed. And you never take it off.'

'Too careless. Once found it in the bin swimming in a load of Chinese takeaway.'

Nikki laughed. 'Look after it. You're a very lucky girl. You heard about this afternoon?' Flora nodded. 'Sam was inches from going over and we all stood around like dummies. Thank God Jamie was there, no way anyone else could've got there in time. You know, he was brilliant. Completely calm. Makes you think, doesn't it? First Giles, then Sam. Could've both ended up brown bread dead.'

Flora wished she could've put things right with the brilliant, completely calm Jamie. After a tepid shower and giving her a lecture on being selfish for being one of Miranda's hot hogs, he'd crashed out.

'I'm still in shock. Despite the herbals. Glad you and me and Martin are sorted. Least said. Sometimes I think this aroma whatsit is a complete load of old rubbish. Give me a decent doctor anyday. Giles had a funny turn this afternoon. Jamie tell you? I told him, Giles, I take as I find. Ever thought of using henna?'

Like everyone else, Flora was bemused. It was as if Nikki had decided to step out of the shadow that Martin had cast over her all week.

Nikki finished off her vodka and tonic. 'Fancy a game of backgammon?'

'I wondered what was wrong,' said Sam glumly. He was sitting on Munchkin's bed, arm round her shoulders. 'Come on, cheer up.'

'Part of me aches for a baby sometimes, so much I could burst.' She folded and refolded her Party Animal sweatshirt. 'But not . . .'

'Not the result of a one-night-stand with the loser from Limerick.' Sam sighed. 'Shit, I can't even ski. Look what happened this afternoon.'

She squeezed his fingers. 'Don't say no one would've missed you. That's not true.' She sighed. 'Bubbly not blubbery. Bit more PMA from both of us in the new year.'

'Is that related to pre thingy thingy? Female whatsit?'

'Sam, you're hopeless. Well, you're not. Positive Mental Attitude.' Munchkin pushed back her shoulders. 'Anyway, sorry about burdening you.'

'It's not a burden. I'm involved, Munchkin. Why didn't you tell me sooner? Days and days of worrying by yourself.'

'Because I thought you'd run a mile. Me trying to trap you.'

Sam shook his head. 'Perhaps I want to be trapped, silly.' He kissed the tip of her nose.

She managed a smile. 'Anyway, doesn't matter now. False alarm.'

'Put all problems on hold tonight, agreed?' asked Martin, opening a bottle of champagne. Flora glanced at Jamie. Miranda glanced at Pete. Anna glanced at the phone, wondering why the cats hadn't called. 'Party time.'

Munchkin had been taken aback to come downstairs to find Nikki and Flora playing backgammon.

Giles was cosseted by Miranda, who ran round refilling his glass, fetching more cushions and listening to his loud and detailed analysis of the general election results in East Midlands constituencies. 'Our voters didn't rat, they simply stayed at home,' he brayed, adjusting his sausage sling. He was planning to tell his work colleagues that he'd wiped out on a black run.

'Thanks is a bit inadequate for helping me out earlier, but thanks,' said Sam. They were standing by the fire.

'Least I could do,' said Jamie.

'Think of a way of making it up to you when I'm less skint.'

'Tip for the Cheltenham Gold Cup will do.'

'Don't encourage Sam to gamble, Jamie,' reproved Giles. 'Rather than studying form, he should be filling them in.'

Sam curled his lip. 'Where's that tambourine?'

'You all right, cute boots?' asked Pete in a low voice, setting out the backgammon counters.

'Fine.' Flora wished she didn't feel as far from Jamie as a nursery slope separating a black run. She wore her biker boots under her black silk skirt. Why was she as pathetically mixed up and confused as her clothes? She'd chuck them out the moment she got home.

Jambon au gratin was followed by chicken in mustard. The candles burned lower, the bottles of champagne piled up on the sideboard and the volume and merriment grew round the table. As they raised their glasses, they agreed it was a wonderful evening.

'You're coming down to the village to watch the procession?' asked Hetty. Anxious to meet up with their fellow chalet girls, the twins made the earliest possible escape.

'Do they drink that much back home?' muttered Alice on the stairs.

'Probably. That's why they're so wrinkly. Boozing really ages you.'

'Do you think we'll be like that?'

'No way.' Hetty was smug.

'Right,' announced Nikki, as they finished their brandies. 'St Marie is to chic what Chanel is to Woolworths. When in Rome. Let's watch the procession, then we'll all go and play pool.'

'We will?' asked Martin astonished.

'Yes, we will. Anna, upstairs now. Sam and Munchkin, will you stop snogging?'

'And I thought I was the bossy one,' marvelled Miranda.

'No. You're the gorgeous bit of posh,' said Nikki. 'As Pete will tell you.'

The pair of them glanced at one another, then looked away quickly.

Outside it was soberingly cold and clear. Hundreds of stars and a pale moon were etched onto the black of the sky. Waiting by the Range Rover, Miranda heard laughter and trickles. 'You men. Rarely. Must you?'

'Got to write your name in the snow,' chortled Sam. 'Tradition, isn't it?'

Giles froze, expecting Sam to make some crack about Wayne. It reminded him of those early years, when he'd been taut with nerves in case he got found out.

Jamie held out his arm. 'Very icy. Grab me, Giles. Don't want you breaking the other one.'

Anna came out wearing a violet suede parka. Her hair was different, softer, and Miranda could swear there were touches of make-up behind her glasses. And a bit of lipstick?

'I've told her she can be a feminist and still be pretty,' said Nikki.

St Marie was having a party. Thousands of fairy lights were hanging above the streets making them as bright as day. The whole village had braved the cold to line the pavements. Cars were crammed full of people leaning out and blasting klaxons and whistles. Tinsel and streamers trailed from balconies, car aerials, lampposts. To a percussion of firecrackers, singing rang out from the square.

High up on the blackness of Les Pins, a minute glow of flickering light appeared. Seconds later it was followed by another, and then another and then dozens more. A huge cheer went up from the crowds gathered at the lift station. The magical snake of light on the inky mountainside was bewitching. Gradually it grew closer. The flames of the flickering torches bathed the snow in gold. The crowd went wild as the leader skied to a halt and doused his torch in triumph.

Jamie and Pete grabbed Flora's hands and ran her through the throngs of people towards the packed market square. Fire crackers exploded around their feet, whistles blew. Breathless, they caught up with the rest. The church's clock face showed one minute to twelve. The crowd gazed up, stamping their feet excitedly. Children were hoisted onto shoulders. The countdown began.

As the church bell tolled, a deafening cheer went up and a tide of goodwill surged round. Everyone joined hands, hugging and kissing. Streamers were thrown, horns sounded. The ten linked arms and burst into an ear-shattering 'Auld Lang Syne,' almost drowning out the fireworks.

'Happy New Year,' said Jamie to Flora, hugging her. 'My beautiful wife.'

She hugged him back with all her might. 'Happy New Year, Jamie.'

After visiting five different bars, each more packed than the last, it was almost two a.m. when they headed for Jimmy's. The entrance was blocked by a crush of people, barmen sounded klaxons, the floor was sticky with spilt drinks.

Losing Jamie in the chaos, Flora was grabbed by some teenage boys who played pass the parcel with her, kissing her on the cheek and wishing her Bonne Année.

'You're doing well,' said Nikki as Flora pushed her way to the bar.

'Some of them are rarely yummy,' called Miranda above Bob Marley, gazing at a goatee-bearded nineteen-year-old with cropped blond hair. 'Let's play stick the phone number on the toyboy.'

Giles frowned, overhearing her.

'Table,' screamed Munchkin, seeing a group leaving and shooting towards it like a guided missile. 'Quick, everyone.'

After buying two bottles of champagne, Jamie and Martin decided to play pool. 'Don't mind, do you, angel?' He kissed Flora's cheek.

'Flora, grab some chairs,' called Munchkin.

'Well done, Munch,' said Giles as everyone settled themselves. He'd been anxious about his arm getting knocked. He looked round and saw Pete standing at the bar. 'Over here, Pete,' he shouted above the blast of a klaxon. 'Bring the grotty totty.'

Miranda's eyes swivelled round. Beyond a group of French girls, she saw the grotty totty. A tall ethereal figure with a mane of red hair. Agnes. She instinctively pulled in her stomach. How old? Eighteen? The alabaster skin was so perfect. Miranda felt every line and wrinkle gouged onto her face, clownlike with make-up compared to all that naturalness.

'Lovely looking,' admired Nikki. 'What a figure.'

'Flat chested,' yawned Sam.

'Too skinny,' agreed Munchkin eagerly. 'Probably anorexic.'

Flora saw Miranda bite her lip.

'Wonder if she's got a sister,' speculated Giles.

'Don't let her stand near me,' said Nikki. 'Can't compete with that, can we, Miranda?'

Miranda wished Nikki would take a flying fuck back to Aspen. As she jumped to her feet and disappeared, Nikki asked: 'Was it something I said?'

'That's Agnes,' said Munchkin in a stage whisper.

'Who?'

Munchkin explained.

'Oh shit,' said Nikki. She leapt to her feet and barged her way through the crush. 'Very pretty? You'll find I've got a very pretty left hook,' she hissed at a Fulham hooray, who was taking advantage of the crush to pinch her bottom. She dived outside, then came back and scooted round the pool table and the bar.

She found Miranda in the calm of the loo in front of the mirror, scrubbing at her smudged mascara with a damp tissue.

'Drink this.' She handed her a glass of champagne. 'Medicine. Need a dose myself.'

'Happy New Year,' said Miranda flatly. 'Sorry. Being a tad pathetic. Not that great at coping with Pete rubbing my nose in it like that.'

The door was thrown back, letting in noise and Bob Marley from the bar. A teenage couple ended up in a giggling heap on the floor before running out.

'God, this place makes me feel old,' said Miranda. She looked in the mirror and only saw the lines etched on her face. She realised she was ageing, feared that she was past the best she'd ever look. 'Past my sell-by date and stuck on the shelf.'

'You're neither,' said Nikki.

'Yes I am.' Miranda's self control began to falter. 'Charlie, who dumped me? The bastard who finished with me over the phone. He's getting married to a little rich babe called Emma, who's just like Pete's Agnes. Very young and extremely pretty.' Miranda screwed up her face. 'And now I'm fucking crying and I'll look even worse.'

Nikki fumbled in her pocket and handed Miranda some tissues.

Miranda blew her nose and took a deep breath. 'Sorry. Pathetic. First Charlie, now sweet, sweet Pete.' She sniffed and took a slug of champagne. 'Hours after we went to bed together he was screwing that, that child. Doesn't do much for a girl's faith in herself. Any more tissues?'

'Here and here,' said Nikki, delving in her Prada bag. 'My box of tricks. I'll get us another drink.' She pressed her make-up bag into Miranda's hands.

When she returned Miranda had calmed down. 'Think you should go and talk to Pete.'

'Nice make-up,' said Miranda. 'Anna looks different.'

'She's just given the brush off to a couple of Italians who were chatting her up. In Italian.' Nikki put on some more lipstick. 'If I'd put the time into languages that I've wasted on men, I'd be fluent in about a hundred by now.'

'You would?'

'This Charlie?' Nikki blotted her lips. 'Sounds a right selfish, gutless creep to finish it over the phone. Useless in bed as well, was he?'

'Nikki . . .' Miranda blushed.

'Thought so.' She pouted into the mirror. 'Soon you'll be so glad you're not stuck with him. Now drink up and let's have another. God, this bag is heavy. Amount of make-up I cart around, I should get a fork-lift.'

They wandered back into the heat and the noise and the music and the smoke. Martin and Jamie were at the pool table. Nikki challenged them to a game, declaring she could beat either of them blindfolded. 'Or blind drunk, the way I'm carrying on.'

Arriving at the table, Miranda found Pete talking to Flora. Giving him a cool look, she wondered where the totty had got to. As he smiled back at her, she was struck again by how gorgeous he was. How he and Agnes made such a perfect couple. 'Sorry?'

Because of the music Pete had to lean forward and repeat himself. 'I said it would be a far happier new year if you weren't so cross with me.'

Feeling his breath on her ear, despite herself, Miranda's insides began to thaw. 'Where's the totty? I mean, Agnes.'

'Gone.' Pete shrugged.

'Gone? Oh? Oh.' She watched him push his hair out of those green-blue eyes. At least she'd had one afternoon with him. More than most would ever get. The memory might keep her warm over the coming winter nights.

'Miranda, Flora's been telling me it's time you and I had a talk. Get a few things straight.'

'Sit here, Miranda. I'll get another bottle.' As Bob Marley was replaced by the Rolling Stones, Flora went off to the bar.

' "I can't get no . . ." Where's our grog?' said Giles, peering through the gloom and the crush to the bar.

'Flora's got distracted by those toyboys,' said Sam.

She was talking to Miranda's rarely yummy blond and his friends.

'Krauts,' said Giles, his jowls almost quivering in disapproval. 'She really ought to concentrate.'

'Well, well, well,' said Munchkin, craning her neck in Flora's direction. 'Look who's just arrived.'

She nudged Sam and Giles as Flora froze, staring up at the tall figure, dark hair pulled back in a ponytail. Even in the gloom they could see her shock. She reached past the Germans and touched the sleeve of his jacket. He turned and returned her stare, before breaking into a slow, lazy smile.

'Don't tell me there's nothing going on between those two,' hissed Munchkin. 'Anna, look.'

'What?' Anna glanced in Flora's direction. 'Munchkin. Don't.'

The joy was wiped from Flora's face. She must've said something because Stefan glanced in the direction of the table. They all looked away quickly. The pair turned their backs and faced the bar.

'Body language. It never lies,' stormed Munchkin. 'I rest my case. How dare she have the cheek to say I make things up? I should sue.'

'Munchkin,' hissed Anna.

'Something definitely put that smile on her face,' said Sam.

'Think you're right,' said Giles out of the corner of his mouth. 'For one moment there, she looked as if her knickers were about to go into meltdown.'

* * *

At the bar, Flora asked Stefan to get the barman's attention for her. File under F for Forbidden, she ordered herself, glancing up at his profile. Seconds later as his green eyes met hers and he broke into another of his slow, lazy smiles, Flora's filing began to get muddled. Perhaps F for Friends? No.

Determined to keep her distance from Stefan, aware that Jamie was so close and that Munchkin and the rest were eyeing her, she tried to look bored. Stefan was a maths lesson where differential calculus was being explained.

He glanced over at the pool table. 'So why isn't the rich husband taking care of his beautiful wife?'

'The wife can take care of herself,' snapped Flora. Just then, she was almost knocked off her feet by one of the German boys and crashed into the bar. Feeling like one of Jamie's pool balls, she overheard two Sloane girls saying yum yum as they gazed at Stefan.

Munchkin kept glancing towards the bar, intrigued and indignant. Flora and Stefan were obviously wrapped up in each other, eyes locked onto eyes, able to ignore the mayhem and the noise and the crowd pushing past them. 'Look at that body language.'

Giles followed her gaze. 'Obviously he speaks the right sort of language to get a drink.'

'It's called French,' snapped Anna.

Bemused, Flora arrived at the table clutching an ice bucket. Her heart was lurching, she felt giddy. 'Sorry it took so long.'

What was Stefan playing at, going off and cosying up to Jamie? She glanced across at the pool table. They were shaking hands, slapping one another on the back, a picture of warm fraternity. Martin was cueing up, Miranda was looking on, Pete had disappeared. Nervous and confused, Flora fiddled with her engagement ring.

'Are you all right?' asked Anna, pouring out the champagne.

'Too hot in here,' shivered Flora. What the hell was Jamie

saying to Stefan? While Sam and Giles talked cars, clearly Munchkin was wondering the same thing.

Stefan pushed his way back and drew up a chair next to Flora. She wished she were a million miles away.

'We met the other night. Giles and Sam? Yes?' said Stefan. 'Happy New Year.'

'And this is Munchkin and Anna,' said Flora, sounding strained. She was careful to keep her distance, her hands in view and her eyes off him.

Anna smiled and, to Munchkin's displeasure, broke into some beautiful-sounding French.

'Show off,' said Sam. 'Impressive though.'

'Very.' Stefan smiled.

He looked relaxed, at ease, never more desirable and never more dangerous. Flora could smell the leather of beaten-up jacket, the faintest citrus of aftershave. She must go and watch Jamie play pool. Stefan wasn't her salvation, he was her damnation. He was sending her to hell, wrecking everything. Why? What was he doing turning up here and torturing her like this?

He turned to her. 'So how was your lesson today, Flora?'

She couldn't look at him. 'Fine thanks.'

'Don't you know?' asked Munchkin puzzled.

Stefan shook his head. 'No. Jacques took Flora today. The rudest and toughest man in the ski school. She needed to be taught a lesson.'

'Oh?' Munchkin was curious. 'We thought that's what you were doing.'

Stefan lit a cigarette. 'Another sort of lesson.'

'Well, tomorrow we're going to be finding out exactly how much progress Flora's made with you.' Munchkin smiled her sweetest smile. Giles and Sam exchanged glances. Flora froze. 'We can't wait.'

Flora stood up. She couldn't take another second of this. She must find Jamie. She turned round and collided with Pete.

'Stefan? Pete Logan. Good to meet you. You've been looking after the princess?'

A klaxon was blasted again. 'Gimme Shelter' was pouring from the speakers. Flora shoved her way through the throng to the pool table, getting splashed by a French girl's glass of beer. Jamie and Martin were playing Miranda and Nikki. A drunk Italian blew a whistle into Flora's ear. She winced.

'Hello angel,' called Jamie.

'Can we go?' asked Flora. 'Please, Jamie. Please.'

'Course not. Not until after this game.'

'Monster game,' called Nikki.

Jamie ruffled Flora's hair. 'Then I'm playing Pete. Have another drink. Talk to Stefan. Pete should be sorting him out right now.'

'Your shot, Jamie,' yelled Miranda.

'Sorting what out?' Flora thought her head would explode. She had nothing to say to Stefan, she didn't want to talk to him, why did Jamie want her to? Was he testing her? Proving to everyone that he thought she was above suspicion? Or had he just got chummy with his old mate charlie and wanted to concentrate on playing pool?

'Out of the way, angel,' said Jamie. 'My shot.'

Flora felt like the blind man in a game of blind man's buff. Blindfolded, she was being pushed away by Jamie.

'Knew it,' said Munchkin half standing up.

Flora had wandered outside, then driven in by the cold, had gone to seek sanctuary in the loo.

Munchkin tracked Stefan through the crowd on the other side of the horseshoe bar as if he were an enemy force on a radar screen. 'Coincidence my foot, Anna. He's following her.'

'Rubbish.' Anna rolled her eyes.

Munchkin squeezed Sam's hand. 'Must just pop to the ladies.'

'Actually, time to point Percy.' Giles was reminded of his uncomfortably full bladder.

'Give them a few minutes.' Munchkin was convinced vindication was in the bag.

Following Giles like a tracker dog on a promising scent, Munchkin bustled round the bar, tiptoed into the loo and lurked by the washbasin where Miranda and Nikki had talked. Behind the locked cubicle, she heard low voices.

Munchkin darted out into the corridor, grabbed Giles by his good arm and pointed at the cubicle. Behind the door came a sharp sssh.

'Bloody hell,' mouthed Giles. 'You're right.'

Their eyes widened as they heard Flora say this was vile, uncomfortable and wasn't there anywhere else they could go. Another sssh of rebuke was followed by the movement of bodies. Munchkin took out her comb and slunk over to the mirror to give herself an alibi.

'Wonderful,' breathed Flora, sighing ecstatically.

'My God,' whispered Giles.

Straining her ears and holding her breath, Munchkin heard him order Flora to open her mouth. An ummm of pleasure followed.

'Good?' asked Stefan. 'Get closer.'

Giles pulled a face at Munchkin and pointed at the bar, but she shook her head. There was more movement and an incredulous Flora gasped that it must still be Christmas.

The door was opened. Noise and music poured from the bar. Giles darted over to the washbasin and ran the tap with his good hand, Munchkin frantically started tugging a comb through her hair. A drunk teenager stumbled in, then out again.

'The best. Thank you,' breathed Flora

'I must thank Jamie,' said Stefan.

'I was right all along,' hissed Munchkin.

'Think you were, Munch,' said Giles.

The door swung back, crashing against the wall. 'Where's Flora?' demanded Jamie. His eyes were glazed.

Giles was poleaxed. 'No idea.'

Jamie hammered on the cubicle door. 'Open up. Right now. Know you're in there.'

Giles and Munchkin looked at one another with uneasy excitement.

The lock drew back. Flora peered out, a furtive-looking Stefan behind her. Her eyes narrowed, there was no mistaking Munchkin's smug expression of triumph.

'What the fuck have you been doing?' asked Jamie.

Munchkin held her breath. Things were going to get nasty, she wasn't prepared to act as mediator, she was preparing to bolt.

'Took your time,' he added.

'Your turn, Jamie,' said Flora kissing his cheek. 'Thanks.'

Giles and Munchkin watched open mouthed as Jamie disappeared into the cubicle, slamming the door behind him. 'Best ever,' she said, checking her reflection in the mirror, before sauntering towards the door.

'Jamie?' whispered Giles. 'Jamie? Queer? One of them? Bloody hell. I need a drink.'

Bursting to tell, they pressed urgently through the crowd and made their way back to the table. Flora was at the bar.

'Bloody hell. You're never going to believe this,' said Giles sitting down with a thud. He winced as his arm bounced.

'Proved,' declared Munchkin, bosom heaving inside her Powder and Glory sweatshirt. 'Giles is my witness. We've just caught them. Shagging.'

'Who?' chorused Sam, Anna and Miranda.

'Flora and Stefan.'

'What?'

'Just now. Can you believe it? After everything she said this morning. She's just admitted it, hasn't she, Giles?'

'Yes.' He was emphatic.

'No,' cried Anna and Miranda, eyes swivelling in Flora's direction.

'Yes,' said Munchkin, gulping her drink and nodding vigorously. 'And that's not all. She and Jamie are obviously some sort of sick perverts.'

'What?' cried Sam.

'Unbelievable.' Giles shook his head. 'Quite unbelievable. She said Johnny Frog was the best she's ever had and now it's Jamie's turn. A bender. Jamie.'

'You what? What did you say?' Pete arrived with another bottle. 'Jamie?'

'Chutney ferret. Homo. Sorry to disillusion you, old chap.'

'Sorry?'

'He and Stefan. At it as we speak.' Munchkin squirmed. 'In the ladies loo.'

'Never,' cried Miranda.

'Over there.' Munchkin pointed, pulling a face. 'Quite disgusting. Pete, are you OK?' He'd buried his head in his hands. 'No idea, had you? Well, none of us had. Not a whisper. Real shock to realise your best friend is that way. Not that I've got anything against gays, of course,' she added hastily. 'And I think Flora owes me a huge apology.' She glowered in the direction of the bar, then laid a consoling hand on Pete's arm. 'Awful for you. I always knew there was something well, weird about Flora, but Jamie. He appeared so straight in every way.'

There was a hoot of hysteria from behind Pete's hands, which she put down to him being in shock. 'Poor Pete.'

He threw his head back and laughed. Watching him bend over double and almost fall off his chair, everyone grew puzzled. 'I can't . . .' he spluttered. 'I can't believe you thought . . .'

'What?' Munchkin grew uneasy as tears streamed down his face.

'Snow.'

'What?' Why was he talking about the weather? 'Shock,' she mouthed to the others.

'Charlie,' said Pete, trying to straighten his face.

'Miranda's Charlie?'

'Coke,' he hissed.

'You want a drink?' demanded Munchkin, utterly bemused.

'Wake up.' He whispered in her ear.

'Cocaine . . .' she squawked.

'Fuck. Keep it down.' Looking round, he sniffed hard. 'What else? You thought Flora and Stefan? And then Stefan and Jamie?' He burst into another peel of laughter. 'And you as well, Giles?' He clutched his stomach, roaring his head off.

Standing beside Flora at the bar, Stefan glanced through the crowd across at the table. 'At last I can talk to you.'

Blind man's buff had continued when she'd been grabbed by him as she had stood next to the wash basin and been hustled into the cubicle, saying that Jamie had given him a perfect alibi to get her alone. 'Couldn't you just talk?'

'Not with your friends eavesdropping.' Stefan glanced towards the pool table. 'How much of that shit does your rich husband take?'

'Not much. Enough. A lot. I don't know.'

'How much of that shit do you take?'

'As much as you,' said Flora. 'Zero. Though Munchkin and Giles would never believe it after that charade.' She smiled ruefully. 'Still, better they think that, than . . .'

Because of the crowd, he was standing so close they were almost touching. They kept on being shoved together by the people milling around them, waving money, trying to attract the attention of the barmen.

'Than what?' asked Stefan.

Flora blushed. She told herself to keep her distance.

'Pete,' shouted Jamie above 'Jumping Jack Flash'. 'We're on.'

Pete was shoving his way through the scrum. 'Stefan, playing pool?'

'Soon.' Stefan smiled back. 'Nice guy,' he said, watching Pete disappear. He looked at Flora. 'I'm going back to Paris tomorrow.'

'You are?' Despite trying to stand her ground, she was knocked into him.

He held her arm, steadying her. 'Come with me.'

'What?' She stared up at him in shock. 'Paris? Sure,' she scoffed. 'Jamie will be so pleased. What do I say? I'm buying my trousseau?'

'Never mind Jamie.'

'Never mind?' Flora gasped. 'I'm marrying him in April.' She told herself to say goodbye to Stefan and walk away. Walk over to Jamie and back to sanity.

'Why? For the money?'

'No,' she cried.

'Because you love him so much. You don't.'

'I do.'

'No. You wouldn't have looked at me twice, you wouldn't be talking to me now. And you wouldn't have done what you did the other night. Over there.' He pointed across the bar. 'Remember?'

Flora looked down, watching her finger trace through some spilt beer on the counter. 'I'd better go.' She forced a smile.

'Or have you forgotten?'

She wished she could forget how she'd clung to him, how his mouth had bruised hers and how his stubble had rubbed her skin raw and how much she'd wanted him. How she still wanted him.

'Remember?' His low voice was insistent.

She was jolted back to the reality of the crowded bar, of 'Jumping Jack Flash' being a gas, gas, gas and Jamie by the pool table. 'I remember. Another of your great lines, wasn't it?'

'What?'

'You give great dialogue, Stefan. Come to Paris, meet me in Amsterdam. I can't let you get married. The voice helps of course. As seductive and beguiling as the rest of you.'

'What are you saying?'

'I'm saying you should go now. You'll be back with Marie-France tomorrow.'

'It's over.'

Flora shrugged. 'Sorry.' She must go. She must. 'But not really my concern, is it?'

'Isn't it?' Stefan was bitter. 'You'd do it again, wouldn't you? Right now.'

Bruise her mouth again, rub her skin raw on his, hold him as if she'd never let him go? Beside her, the Fulham hooray was yelling at the barman for three beers. She must find Jamie. Stefan must be filed under F for Forbidden. Farewell. Forgotten.

'Thanks for everything. So.' She tried to smile. 'So long. Farewell. Goodbye.'

'Don't go.'

'I must.'

'Why? Flora?'

'Because. Because.' She stared up at his beautiful face and took a deep breath. 'Because I would do it again. Right now. And more. Because I'm so weak. Because instead of thinking about Jamie and my wedding or anything real, for days there's been nothing in my head but you.' She gazed up into those green eyes. She had nothing to lose. She'd lost it all anyway. 'Because I've really fallen for you, Stefan. So. So long.'

She tried to shove herself past the hooray.

'Early wedding present, Flora?' Stefan grabbed her arm. 'One broken heart.'

'Yes.' She couldn't believe it could hurt so much. 'Mine.'

'No. Mine.'

'What?'

'I've fallen in love with an English brat who I hardly know, who can be as ugly as she's beautiful, who even expects me to carry her skis. And who's getting married in April.'

'You can't have,' gasped Flora. Suddenly the riddle that had been teasing her for days, its answer so tantalisingly close was solved. Waves of happiness broke over her. 'You have? Fallen?'

'Why else would I spend all morning searching the mountainside for you and Jacques? Why spend all evening going everywhere in St Marie trying to find you? Look in my sketchbook, Flora, page after page after page of you.'

'Squeeze past, can I?' demanded the hooray.

'Have you?' Elation was coursing through Flora. 'Fallen?'

'Yes. Haven't you?'

'Yes.' She gazed up at him, laughing with joy. 'Yes. Completely. Utterly. Uncontrollably. Head over heels. At first sight. Although I'm supposed to be getting married.'

'You are getting married. To me.'

Feeling as if she were on a roller coaster, Flora glanced towards the pool table. 'It will be different when you're back in Paris.'

Stefan shook his head and pointed at her left hand. 'It might be when you're home. You've got more to lose. Diamonds suit you.'

'Less and less.'

'Come to Paris with me. We'll get a sleeper from Annecy. I want to spend the night hearing you breathing and telling me how much you love me and how I'm your salvation.'

She looked across and saw Jamie sharing a joke with Pete. She could feel Munchkin's eyes boring into her back. 'I do love you. You are my salvation. But I can't come with you tomorrow. You want me brave. The brave thing is to confront. Not to run away. I've got a wedding to cancel.'

'And a wedding to arrange. What did you say the other day? An inch is as good as a mile? We're inches apart but unable to touch.' He laughed. 'When can I?'

'Soon,' sighed Flora longingly. 'Very soon. I hope.'

'And I hope you'll have sleepless nights missing me.'

'I think I already have.'

'Good. So have I. You'll write me long romantic love letters?'

'Every day. You won't change your mind about me?'

'No. I can't. I tried. Especially after telling me you don't sleep with the staff, especially after you ordered me to carry your skis.'

'They were so heavy,' she protested. 'I've got bruises on my shoulders.'

'I'll kiss them better.' He smiled his slow smile. 'Or give you more.'

Flora blushed. 'Will you teach me French?'

'Of course. And Czech and German and Italian and how to ski properly and how to sail a boat.'

'Sail?'

'We're going to sail around the world. After we've driven from Paris to Peking.'

Flora felt dizzier. He was offering the whole world to her, something she'd resigned herself to seeing the tourist's bits of during Jamie's five weeks of expensive holidays a year. The whole world and him too. She'd never been so happy.

Stefan glanced at the table and saw Giles eyeing them. 'We'll sit. You'll be sweet and I'm going to talk to nice Anna. Sssh. You've got a day to get through. I don't want Jamie hurting you.'

She frowned. 'He wouldn't.'

'He would. Despite those perfect English manners, I don't trust him. But then he doesn't trust me. Tell me you love me and I'm your salvation. Then start talking.'

Stefan led the way back to the table. Following him, Flora floated on clouds of bliss rather than walked.

'I love you and you're my salvation,' whispered Flora, then she raised her voice. 'And are you sure my skis aren't the wrong length? Couple of centimetres too long?'

'More champagne?' asked Anna.

'You've not been talking skiing, Flora?' asked Miranda incredulous. 'That's rarely a-mazing.'

'Isn't it?' said Munchkin.

'Miranda, Stefan. Stefan, Miranda,' said Flora.

'You've been teaching Flora?' asked Miranda. 'Good pupil?'

'Alpha,' said Stefan.

'Made a convert?'

'I hope.' He lit a cigarette. 'Let me give you my address, Flora. If you and Jamie are ever in Paris, come and visit the studio.' He reached into his pocket, pulled out a pad and a pen, tore out a sheet of paper, and started scribbling.

'What's that? Sketches?' asked Anna.

Stefan smiled and put the pad back in his pocket.

'Thank you.' Flora picked up the scrap of paper, noticing the mischief on Sam's face. Suddenly she felt an arm on her shoulder. 'Stefan's invited us to look him up if we're ever in Paris.'

'Good idea,' said Jamie. 'Time to make tracks everyone? And if you're in London Stefan, drop by.' He pulled one of his business cards out of his pocket and scribbled down his Chelsea address and number. 'Flora's moving in any day now.'

She was horror-struck but could hardly protest. She'd call Stefan from the cottage with her numbers.

'Thanks for looking after her this week,' said Jamie.

'My pleasure.' Stefan's eyes met Flora's.

'Ready, angel?'

Imprinting every detail of Stefan's beautiful face on her memory, Flora felt as if her heart were breaking. There was nothing sweet in her sorrow. It was like losing part of herself.

She smiled a social smile, trying to disguise her grief. 'Thank you for everything Stefan.' They shook hands and chastely kissed each other farewell under Jamie's watchful gaze. She could feel Stefan's stubble under her lips, smell the faint citrus, hear him saying goodbye.

She tore herself away and followed Jamie into the night. As she walked out the door she allowed herself one final look back at him through the crowded bar. Then Jamie put his arm through hers and led her through the icy streets like a prisoner under guard.

CHAPTER SEVEN

Friday

————◆◇◆◇◆————

While the rest tried to sleep off their hangovers, Anna was downstairs trying to make a telephone call. A huge smile lit up her suddenly tanned face. A smile that stayed although she misdialled three times in her impatience.

'Tom? Happy New Year. And so good to hear you. Where are you? Ambleside? Very last minute. Stolen? Oh God. What did the police say? You called my parents? Tomorrow.' She looked round and lowered her voice. 'I can't wait to get back. Sunny. No. No. Can't. Tell you all about it tomorrow. Better go. Me too, really looking forward to it. Bye.'

'Yes. Yes. Yes.' Grinning in delight, she pirouetted around the room. 'Yes,' she whooped, laughing.

Arriving back shortly after three, she'd found a longed-for message that Tom had called. Happy New Year, tons of love and a strange telephone number.

Anna pulled herself up, realising that in her happy excitement at finally making contact she hadn't bothered to ask about Trotsky and Ortega. Oh well, they were having a nice holiday in a Lake District farmhouse and were probably enjoying themselves far more than she had.

She skipped out onto the balcony and took huge lungfuls of cold, clean air. The relief that Tom hadn't forgotten and still cared was overwhelming. Les Diables should be alive with the sound of music. One more day to get through. Tomorrow, she'd be on her way home. She couldn't wait.

'Oh what a beautiful morning, oh what a wonderful day, I've got . . .'

'Fuck off and die,' growled Nikki, turning over in bed. Even in her sleep her head was pounding.

Flora peeled back her mascara-clogged eyes and immediately squeezed them tight shut again.

'No peace for the wicked,' said Jamie, tearing back the bedclothes from her and leaping up.

'I'm not wicked, I'm hungover,' came a muffled protest from under a pillow.

'Skiing's the best cure.'

'I can't.'

'Oh yes you can, angel.' Jamie pulled back the curtains. 'We're going to find out exactly what you've been up to this week. Skis at dawn, remember?' Hurling the duvet back on top of her, he went for a shower.

Safely alone, Flora tried to think, but her brain was porridge.

An avalanche of anxiety swept through her. The rock-like certainty she'd felt the night before, standing beside Stefan in the bar had shifted during her sleep. Could she turn her life upside-down for a stranger she'd only known for a few hours? In a few days' time when she was back at the cottage, back at work, sitting through a brain and backside-numbing council meeting, how would she feel? Would Stefan be like the ouzo she'd brought back from Greece; ideal for a balmy summer's evening in an Aegean fishing village, untouchable on a cold, wet Tuesday in the cottage?

And what about Jamie? Handsome, successful, charming, English Jamie. She knew Jamie, knew he was good company on those cold, wet Tuesdays. He could be monstrously selfish, but who couldn't? Jamie was a thousand times better than Martin or Sam or Giles.

The consequences of what she was contemplating hit her like a juggernaut. As she imagined telling Jamie it was all over, her insides shrivelled in fear. The wedding cancelled, her family furious. Her brother Jasper going ballistic. Giving up the comfort and security that Jamie had to offer for a penniless Franco-Czech who was more or less a stranger. Was it brave? Or mad?

But if she wanted to be with Jamie enough to make a commitment to him for the rest of her life, what had she done falling in love with Stefan? And she had fallen in love with him. Hadn't she? It was more than an illicit holiday romance. Wasn't it?

Martin crept out of bed. Nikki stirred and pushed off the duvet, showing off her lean body, hair scattered across the pillow like chestnut seaweed. She was so pretty and made him so horny.

He stole across the room and, eyes on her, fished around in her Prada bag. If she asked, he wanted some aspirin. He pulled out a slim leather diary, put it in his track pants and made his way to the bathroom.

He'd called Jack Mancini at the paper on Christmas Eve morning. Might have a little something interesting for him, a little something Jack had thought might be worth five figures, closer to six.

'Course you're not naming names, Mart. But top man, you reckon? One of the great and the good, is he? Knighthood, eh? Sounds promising. Committee man, does lots of charity work? Knows the Royals by any chance? Super. Friends in high places? The PM? Well, don't get much higher, do we? Need oxygen at that altitude. Wife and kids, great. Granddad is he? Bless. Know if matey is into anything kinky in the bedroom department? Find out, there's a love. I'm must say, Mart, I'm liking the sound of this more and more, suddenly I've come over all Christmassy.

Course not. Strictly confidential mate, trappist. No pressure, a little chat between old mates. But if the lady wants to play ball, tell her it could be very worth her while. We're talking well into five figures, closer to six. Young Nicola is a lovely girl. How can I put this, Mart? The course of true love and all that. May I be struck down for such unworthiness, but if you sadly had to part, or if you decided, how shall we put this, decided to go freelance, you realise you're sitting on a teensy weensy goldmine? Just a thought. Be a tad more difficult. We'd need back up. Names, addresses, dates of secret little trysts et cetera. You know how it is. Got to keep the lawyers happy. Listen mate, it's no odds to me. You're making the running here. It's your show, from soup to nuts. Look forward to hearing from you after the hols. Have a good one, mate. Christmas that is.'

Behind the locked door, Martin sat on the edge of the bath and began flicking through the pages, starting at the back. He was pleased to see the name Martin underlined three times, surrounded by exclamation marks and rows of hearts. That must've been the night they met.

The letter M followed by the names of restaurants and films filled the next few pages, interspersed by a few Davids and the names of far more impressive and expensive restaurants. He frowned. So at the start, the sly bitch had been seeing Thone, despite claiming he was in the Far East.

He turned the pages again leading up towards Christmas. Ms were more frequent, here, but one had 'Jack slimy bastard reporter' written next to it. 'Move' was the following entry. The final scribble was under Boxing Day. 'Skiing St Marie.'

Leafing back through the year he saw scores of Davids. David Savoy Grill 8.30pm. David Connaught 9pm. From August there were lots of David lates, David cancelled, David *Swan Lake* crossed out. July 12th Mum's birthday. In June they'd spent a long weekend in Cannes. In May they were in New York. Flown Concorde. A few weeks earlier they'd gone to Paris. David's birthday, collect Cartier. David skiing Aspen was followed by a vertical arrow stretching down ten days in March. And another David skiing Aspen during a week in January.

Apart from Thone, the gym, the dressmaker's and the beautician's, if the diary were a guide, Nikki had a weirdly empty life. He read through the list of phone numbers at the back. There were a few personal ones among those for her garage, her bank, her hairdresser's. David was at the top. HQ, direct, car, mobile, secretary. His own numbers were at the bottom.

Could she be persuaded? If she could, Jack and his editor would move like greyhounds out of a trap. They'd have the thing sewn up in days. And in exchange for a short-term loan, he'd offer Nikki the chance to double that five figures closer to six.

He hadn't liked to press her too hard, but he knew she was intrigued. Wavering.

Getting out a pen and his own diary, Martin quickly copied out the main dates and numbers. For five figures, closer to six, it was worth taking out some insurance.

She was still fast asleep. He put her diary back in her bag and picked up his mobile. He rang his deputy Kelvin's home number. Getting no reply, he left another message at the office.

He stared out at the fir trees. What sort of year would it be if the riverside deal fell through? The roulette wheel was spinning, he'd put everything he had on black and he was now waiting for the ball to drop. He'd lose the lot if red came up.

And what then? Say goodbye to the house, the Range Rover, the business, the lifestyle, Nikki. She wouldn't hang around with someone who was skint. He'd be back to where he started aged twenty. Living with his mum in her semi in Hayes. Washed up but older. Less willing to take a chance. People less willing to give him a chance. In the early days he'd been able to cash in on his celebrity, even the bank manager had wanted to help the fallen hero.

Now? Now, he was largely forgotten. People sometimes looked twice, as if they were trying to place him, wondering why he seemed vaguely familiar. An old school friend? Someone they'd worked with years back? It was a long way from the old days and the nudges and gawps and gasps of 'Martin June' wherever he'd gone. When he'd been mobbed at petrol stations and supermarkets and asked for his autograph. There were whole generations behind him now, people like Flora who'd never heard of him.

If the backers were playing up, someone might come in with a higher offer on the site. It wasn't roulette, it was poker. But to play poker you needed stake money. He was mortgaged to the hilt, his bank already windy, interest payments crippling him.

It would be perfect if Nikki came up with goods for Jack. And if she didn't?

A bit of freelancing?

She made him so horny. He clambered back into bed. 'Happy New Year, lover.'

The peaks of Les Diables were shrouded in iron-grey cloud. The valley seemed wrapped in an eerie gloom. Instead of bright sunshine, electric lights had to be lit.

Flora plodded to the table, burdened by a horrible hangover compounded by confusion. Martin, Sam, Giles and Munchkin were slurping back tea as if their lives depended on it. Hetty announced that snow was forecast.

'Where's Jamie?' asked Flora.

'Gone into St Marie to change some money,' said Munchkin. 'Took the Porsche. Doesn't his ban apply here?'

Flora sighed. 'God knows.'

Sam poured himself some more tea. 'So when can we expect an invite? Should be the mother of all parties.'

'Invite?' Flora did a double take. 'Oh, the wedding. Early March I guess.' Would they be inviting Sam? And the rest? She guessed they'd all make a beeline to sit on Jamie's side of the church.

'Can't wait, can we, Munch?' said Giles.

There wasn't going to be a wedding. Was there? As Flora

imagined herself announcing that she'd changed her mind, a chill ran through her. All that work. All the hurt she'd cause Jamie. All those disappointed people who'd been looking forward to the mother of all parties.

'Right. Are we all skiing today?' asked Martin, revived after his fourth cup of tea.

The merriment died in Sam's eyes. Stomach tightening, he pushed away his plate. Since he'd woken up, he'd had the fear. He didn't want to put his skis back on.

'You'll be taking it easy,' said Giles. 'Flora's going with you.'

'So she is,' said Munchkin, eyeing her speculatively. 'She'll be able to cope?'

'Course she will,' declared Martin.

Munchkin looked unconvinced. 'It's very cold today to be kept hanging around.'

Flora realised they were all looking at her and hastily tore herself away from Paris and Peking and all stops in between.

'You're coming out with us?' said Martin.

'Uh?'

'Ski-ing. We're wond-er-ing if you-'ll be ab-le to cope.' Sam spoke ve-ry slow-ly, as if he were explaining things to a halfwit.

Flora tried to banish all thoughts of Stefan from her mind. 'Think so. If you can put up with me. The chalet tortoise.'

'We're dying to see what Stefan taught you this week,' said Munchkin.

The three men smirked.

Flora's coffee went down the wrong way. That was just what Jamie was dying to see.

Gobbling up the remains of Sam's croissant, Munchkin peered out the window. 'Definitely had the best of the weather, haven't we? Home tomorrow.'

'Mountain of paperwork to catch up on,' said Giles.

'Lucky you.' Sam scowled.

'You'll get another job soon, silly.' Munchkin squeezed his arm. 'PMA, remember.'

'Sure.' Pulling a face, Sam measured out a teaspoon of sugar. 'Remember snakes and ladders?' He began to tip it back in the bowl granule by granule. 'I'm 32. I've spent ten years climbing the ladder and now I'm back down to where I started. Who headhunts the headhunter? No job, no home, no nothing. The loser from Limerick.' He smiled ruefully at the chorus of protests. 'Rubbish, is it? On the first night when you all said you needed a break, you would've taken the piss if I said I needed one too.'

'Would we?' asked Martin.

'According to you lot, I've been having a break. Shit, how can actors call being out of work resting?' He shook his head. 'It's been the most stressful few months ever.'

'But you've been having the time of your life,' spluttered Giles.

'Sure,' said Sam bitterly. 'You of all people should know about the right image,' he paused, 'Giles.' Sugar scattered across the tartan cloth. 'Sorry. Just realised I haven't got much to go home for.'

Up in her bedroom Miranda was getting ready. She darted over to the dressing table. 'Dinner Party Once A Week' was added to her list of resolutions in her shiny new British Field Sports Society diary.

Since she'd met Charlie back in the spring, she'd rather gone to ground. Since he'd dumped her, she'd been completely out of circulation.

For the first time in weeks, she was filled with energy and optimism. Her future didn't have to be a bleak, black empty void. She'd go home and own up to everyone that the gutless, clueless-in-bed wimp Charlie had finished with her.

'French Evening Class'.

'New year, new start.' She smiled at Anna, who was sheepishly applying some mascara that Nikki had given her. 'Wonder if I can get a work permit for Australia?' She was rather off Englishmen.

'Ask Pete,' said Anna.

'Um.' Australia's greatest export. She'd felt so silly when he explained things the night before. In fact, he'd told her he was highly pissed off that she could've misjudged him. Instead of beating herself up, why the fuck hadn't she come straight out and told him about Charlie? Been upfront? Did she think he was the sort of heartless bastard who'd put her down because she'd been badly treated? He'd run a mile, would he? No, Miranda, he wasn't emotionally constipated like her ex and almost every other English boarding school intern.

'Including Jamie?' she'd asked, puzzled.

'Best mate, but yep. Miranda, you need to broaden your vowels and your horizons.'

And he'd kissed her on the cheek as a friend. They'd be friends, she hoped. He was a good man, kind. Something Charlie wasn't. Mummy wouldn't understand, Mummy would have a fit that a postal worker's son from Croydon Park, Sydney was a million times better than Charlie. But then Mummy had always been a bit of a snotty, silly cow who'd insisted on staying in the same room of the same hotel on the exact same week of every year in Mürren.

Romance? It would be lovely, but she needed to get herself sorted out on her own, rebuild her life. She'd had one glorious afternoon with Pete which was more than most would ever get. The memory would keep her warm thoughout the coming cold winter nights.

'Perhaps I should give contact lenses another go,' said Anna.

'Chop, chop, everyone,' called Martin, half an hour later in the drive. 'It's freezing.'

'Could be a blizzard later on,' said Giles. His arm in its sling, he was the Army invalid watching his comrades return to action at the Front. He was taking Nikki's advice to potter around St Marie, rather than spending the day languishing in the chalet. It was nice of them to go out of their way to take him into town, rather than getting the Les Pins lift. 'Better get a move on, or you won't get much skiing in.'

'Shame,' said Flora dryly, wincing as her boots dug into her shins. Compared to the rest of them, her hat was about to have a flashing neon D for Dunce on it.

On the other side of the Porsche, Jamie was pointedly ignoring her as if the sight of her would contaminate him.

'I don't know why she's bothering,' muttered Munchkin to Sam. 'It's far too cold to be hanging around for a beginner.'

'Didn't Stefan the Shag tell her it's easier to carry your skis on your shoulder?'

'Shoes?' asked Martin. 'Have to take the skis and boots back to the hireshop later.'

Flora dashed back into the chalet to get her biker boots.

Munchkin nudged Sam. 'See. Typical. Already holding us up.'

'Amazing they got away with it,' said Pete, changing down a gear as the Porsche followed the Range Rover past Les Landais.

'With what?' asked Jamie flatly.

In the back, Flora quickly closed the European road map. She'd been trying to work out how many miles it was from Jaxley to Paris.

'The runner,' said Pete. 'Didn't you know? They did a runner the other night after we left. That's when Giles did his shoulder in.'

Flora turned round. The jug-eared waiter was sweeping the entrance. He paused and leant on his broom. For a moment his eyes seemed locked onto hers.

'Runner? Isn't it time they grew up?' James Naze Esquire was scornful.

'Pot and kettle.' Pete glanced at him bemused. 'Remember

that chinky in Oxford? That time the door was locked? Shit, heaps of explaining.' He grinned. 'What did you say, Jamie, something about your car alarm going off?'

St Marie was hushed. Few were on the streets and most of the shops were dark and closed. Soggy tinsel, streamers and fire-cracker shells clogged the gutters. It was bitterly cold. The clouds were heavy with unfallen snow.

Pete parked next to the Range Rover outside the chairlift station, which was almost deserted.

Just then Flora caught sight of the back of a black-haired figure in a red ski school jacket. He was waiting for an elderly couple to put on their skis. Her heart pounded. Adrenalin and expectation coursed through her. If she hurried she'd could get over to him, talk, if only for a few seconds. He turned round. Aching with disappointment, she realised she'd made a mistake. Realised that he was on his way to Paris.

'Don't worry,' said Pete, seeing her pinched face and assuming she was nervous. 'We'll look after you.'

'That's the ticket,' boomed Giles. 'Hubby'll be there to help you out. Nothing to fear, but fear itself, as the great man said.'

'If you can manage a snowplough, you'll get down anything,' said Martin.

'Wonder if I can find a *Telegraph*.' Giles adjusted his sling. 'Meet you back at the chalet.'

They trudged up the metal stairs and over to the ice-bound entrance. Flora swore very loudly as she slipped and bumped down onto the ground, her skis clattering beside her.

'That's where we like our women, on their knees and grovelling,' said Martin. He held out his hand and hauled her up. Swiping the ice from her backside, Flora noticed Munchkin was smirking.

'I can't imagine why she's bothering,' hissed Munchkin to Sam, watching Flora struggle to clip up the back of her ski boots.

Neither could Flora.

Jamie's expression matched the temperature

'Come on Munchkin. Get a move on,' said Anna, shuffling forward to the turnstile. 'It's freezing.'

As he waited in the lift queue, Sam got the fear again. Overcome by shaking, he wanted to escape, but with Miranda ahead of him, Munchkin at his side and Jamie behind there was no chance. 'Now I know how it felt to be pressganged.'

On the chairlift up to La Croix, Flora thanked God she was sitting on her own, rather than with Jamie. She could feel the paper with Stefan's number in her skipants' pocket, adding to her guilt. She was so nervous, sweat was breaking out on her palms inside their gloves. She could parallel, she told herself. She could. But suddenly she felt she couldn't even manage a snowplough.

'Home tomorrow,' said Miranda up at La Croix.

'We must exchange numbers and have a get-together really soon,' said Munchkin from under her pink helmet.

'A reunion. Super,' fibbed Miranda. She'd made up her mind that she'd seen quite enough of certain people over the past week to last a long time.

'Don't forget Wednesday, Sam,' said Munchkin coyly.

'A date?' Miranda smiled.

'Dinner.' Munchkin sounded smug. She imagined them sitting in the chic bistro that had recently opened just round the corner from her flat. A romantic dinner à deux, him in a suit, her in the new black dress she'd got in the sales. It would make a nice change to put on something glam.

Sam smiled back at her. He was planning supper at his place, cheap, no taxis and Munchkin was bound to offer to do the cooking, she was a brilliant cook, leaving him in peace to watch the England-Italy match on the box.

Flora gingerly skied off the lift, her body rigid with cold and nerves, her skis as alien as they'd been that first day on the nursery slope. Jamie didn't look at her, but continued to study the piste map he'd borrowed from the twins. He was taking no more chances. He suggested they ski round to a drag-lift, which would take them up higher.

'Fine,' said Pete. 'Any worries, such as getting lost, *you* can take the flak.'

Flora was aghast; for the past week she'd managed to avoid a drag-lift. 'Jamie, I hate those things.'

'Don't be ridiculous,' he snapped back, antarctic cold.

Munchkin muttered to Martin that if anything was a drag around here, Flora was. 'I knew, she shouldn't have come out with us.'

'Still reckon her and matey were more sloping off than nursery slopes,' said Martin out of the corner of his mouth.

'See them last night? Body language. It never lies.'

Searching her pockets, Nikki groaned. 'Forgotten my sunscreen.'

'For God's sake, there's eight eighths cloud cover,' cried Martin. 'We're up a mountain, not in a bloody beautician's.' Playfully he whacked her on the backside, but with more force than he intended, so she shot forward, lost her balance and fell over.

Pete led everyone across the short run to the drag-lift. The piste was almost deserted. Cloud shrouded any view of the peaks. Flora kept well to the back. Having had little chance to melt, the snow was rutted and unyielding under her skis. She was freezing, stiff and found it impossible to establish any sort of rhythm. Arriving at the entrance, she stopped in an unsteady snowplough.

'Very impressive,' said Jamie with crushing sarcasm, resting on his ski poles and watching her. His suggestion that they could all ski through the mogul field had been firmly out-voted. 'The rest are miles ahead. Now what the fuck are you doing?'

She was taking off her gloves and unclipping her boots. She doubled over her thick socks to try and give her raw and tender shinbones some protection.

'Hurry up. We'll have to queue in a minute.'

The lift trail seemed to stretch in a straight line for miles up the mountainside. Far in the distance she could just make out Miranda and Anna, from the clash of lilac and turquoise, the T-shaped wooden bar jammed behind their legs. 'Must I?'

'Yes, and it's easy. So stop making a fuss.'

Flora stuck her pass into the machine at the turnstile. Her face mirrored the expression of fear and misery in the photograph taken that first day. She shuffled up towards the red line, where Jamie motioned to her to stand beside him. 'If you weren't taken on a drag-lift, where else were you taken, my beautiful wife?'

'Now who's being ridiculous?' Flora bit her lip. She was frightened, as scared as she'd been the previous morning. This wasn't the Jamie she knew. It was as if he were possessed by cold malevolence.

'Bend your knees. Poles in your right hand. Skis parallel. Why aren't you taller? These things are easier if you're both the same height.' He reached for the T-bar that was swinging round behind them. 'Don't sit. Lean. Head up.'

Flora felt the wooden bar whack her on the back of the thighs and was dragged forward, Jamie ordering her to bend her knees and hold onto the bar, with one hand not two, for Christ's sake.

'This is horrible,' she hissed after five minutes, trying to keep her knees bent and her skis in the tracks worn into the snow by earlier users. Her thigh muscles felt as if they'd explode.

Refusing to look at her, Jamie kept his eyes on the white wasteland around them. 'Well over a kilometre, so concentrate. Bumps ahead.'

Half a mile? He must be joking. Flora hit a series of mounds and was jolted as if she were inside a washing machine on spin. She almost lost her poles as her skis came close to getting entangled with Jamie's.

'Lean forward and let the lift do the work,' he barked.

Despite the icy cold, she could feel her nose was covered in stress sweat.

'Bend your knees.'

Flora would've glared at him, if she'd dared to take her eyes from the tracks.

'So, angel, a nice gentle red run,' announced Jamie. 'All you have to do is remember everything Stefan taught you.'

She automatically thought of everything Stefan promised he'd teach her, like skiing properly and French and Czech and German and Italian and how to sail.

As Flora's mind wandered, so did her skis. They left the tracks and veered off onto the icy ruts. When she tried to bring them round, they slipped. Despite clinging onto the pole as tight as she could with her left hand and trying to yank herself back, she found that her skis had their own momentum and went right. Jamie tried to grab her but she found herself careering out of his reach.

Crash-landing on the snow she screamed in rage.

'Move to the side and stay there,' Jamie yelled at Flora, a shrinking black figure against the dazzling white.

The enticing bumps and undulations of a deserted mogul field over to his right failed to improve his temper.

Terrified of being run over by whoever was behind her on the lift, Flora hauled herself up and scrambled out of the way. She was furious with herself. And scared. Such a display of complete ineptitude would confirm Jamie's suspicions about Stefan.

Now what? The empty T-bars were far too high for her to reach. Flora looked at the vast, white wilderness around her and felt very small and lonely. Perhaps rather than facing Jamie, perhaps she should ski down alone? But he'd only ask what she'd been running away from.

At the top Jamie skied over to where the others were waiting.

'Where's Flora?' asked Pete.

'Fell off about two-thirds of the way up.'

Martin and Sam sniggered. Munchkin nudged Nikki. 'What did I tell you? She's just not up to it.'

Pete eyed Jamie. 'What's up?'

'You lot go ahead.' He got out the piste map. 'I'll get Flora and we'll ski across and catch up with you here.' He pointed to the start of a run through some trees. 'Fuck it.'

Down the mountain, Flora dug the edges of her skis into the snow. The wind tore through her in icy blasts. She shivered. The few skiers who passed her on the drag-lift stared at her puzzled, before receding into the distance. Maybe she should ski down. This was worse than waiting with the boarder for the blood-wagon. Perhaps Jamie had decided to leave her to rot, hoping she'd get frostbite, that her fingers and toes would snap off one by one.

'Oh God,' she howled, loud enough to start an avalanche. Inside her shrivelled skull, her thoughts chased round like rats in a cage. Jamie, Stefan, calling off the wedding. Like last night, her head would explode.

After what seemed like a week, she was diverted by a lone skier slaloming through the moguls, one pole hitting the ground then the other, as he raced across and through the white hillocks, sometimes turning as he leapt through the air, then crouching low on the back of his skis as they twisted left and right, their tips higher than his head.

She gasped in admiration. Why was she even bothering when there were people that brilliant around? She should've stayed on a balcony under a rug and drunk hot chocolate. The skier hurtled down towards her in a series of sharp turns, the snow kicking out behind him. No. It wasn't? It couldn't be.

'Jamie,' she cried as he stopped beside her. 'I never realised . . .' She felt so proud of him.

'What?'

'That you could ski like that.'

'Can Stefan?'

Flora's smile died. 'I don't know.'

'No. You weren't interested in his performance on skis, were you? And I very much doubt if he cared too much about yours.'

'Jamie, please.'

'Well, let's find out, shall we?' His expression was murderous. '*Allez.*'

She wanted to throw up. Pulse racing, nerves jangling, she pushed off with her poles and began a shaky traverse. In front of her, Jamie skied backwards studying her technique. She realised she had to turn and snowploughed. Badly.

'Come on, angel,' taunted Jamie beckoning her. '*Allez.*'

She told herself to be rational. This was Jamie, her *parfait gentil* knight. The chivalrous English gentleman, who was prepared to swear before God that he would love her and cherish her and protect her. There was no need to be scared.

'He didn't even teach you to snowplough properly?'

'You're putting me off.' She was shaking, cold, distracted, unable to establish any sort of momentum. Her skis seemed stuck in stickiness.

It was as nonsensical as being scared of a teddy bear. This was Jamie, dashing handsome Jamie. A good sportsman in every sense. The man who'd rescued Sam. She snowploughed again and began to traverse.

'Go down. Not across.'

Flora tried to relax, tried to remember how she'd paralleled with Jacques the day before. She wished Jamie would stop staring at her as if she were vermin, she wished there were more people around. The white landscape was as empty as it was bleak. A frozen wilderness of nothing. Her pace slowed.

'How many hours of lessons?' Jamie suddenly turned round and cut in front of her, inches from her ski tips.

'Don't.'

He stemmed, turning again. 'Surely Stefan taught you to

bend your knees?' he hissed, cutting across her path again.

Flora just managed to remain upright. She snowploughed, trying to get away from him. Stefan was right, Jamie could and would hurt her. 'Stop, Jamie.'

'No you don't. The path is that way. Turn.' He skied round behind her and arrived on her right hand side. 'Turn. Bend your fucking knees and relax your shoulders. Head up.'

Close to tears, she went into a wobbly snowplough. She longed to see Pete and the rest.

'Didn't Stefan tell you to bend your knees?' Jamie was skiing backwards again, getting closer. Suddenly he grabbed her left arm. Flora saw her reflection in his sunglasses as she tried to jerk herself free. 'Or just to open your legs?'

And he shoved.

Before she knew it, Flora was down and scudding across the slope. Fast. Her skis were like runaway horses with her on top of them. Her left ski came off, one of her poles was jammed between her and the concrete hard snow, cutting into her ribs. Grey sky, white ground flashed past her eyes as she hurtled down, down, down.

She didn't know how she stopped, but when she did, she just lay there shaking and wanting to be sick. Stefan was right. She felt her ribs. Bruised but not broken.

'Ski school?' Jamie threw her ski down beside her. 'Next time I'll cut out the pimp.'

Flora was too shocked and winded to weep. 'You bastard.'

Jamie bent over her so his face was inches from hers. 'I could tell last night. You've fucked him, haven't you?'

Flora stared into his black sunglasses. 'No.'

'Want to?'

'Why? Like to watch?'

Elbowing him away, she sat up. How far had she tumbled? A long way, she wasn't that far from some trees. She could see Pete, the lilac and the turquoise, Munchkin's pink helmet, Martin's khaki, Nikki's silver fox. She'd never felt so pleased to see them all. She waved. Taking a deep breath, she hauled herself onto her feet. Her whole body felt mugged by the snow, her legs were trembling so much she could hardly put her boot into the binding.

'Come on,' said Jamie studying her. 'You're holding everyone up.'

The final stretch down to the path was steep and icy. Her heart still racing, Flora cautiously snowploughed. Pete had the inevitable fag hanging out of his mouth, Munchkin and Martin were swiping snow from their sleeves.

'Sorry to keep you waiting,' said Jamie.

Munchkin's teeth were chattering. 'Don't worry.' She sounded magnanimous. 'Just a bit cold to be hanging around.'

'You only got here about three seconds ago,' cut in Pete, offering Flora a puff of his cigarette. 'So, had a fight with the lift, did you, princess?'

Flora noticed that everyone was smirking.

'I fought the lift and the lift won,' sang Sam, who'd regained his nerve.

'Caught the tailend of your tailspin,' said Martin. 'You all right? Shouldn't you have walked?'

'Did you? Fine, thanks. Probably,' said Flora.

'Difficult red,' said Pete, chucking away his cigarette. 'The one ahead is much easier, nice and gentle. We'll look after you.'

'If she can't hack it, she can always get the chairlift,' snapped Jamie.

'Give it a bash,' urged Miranda.

'But don't feel under any pressure,' said Anna.

'Right. Shall we go?' demanded Pete. 'Along the path and then hit the motorway.'

'Don't look so worried,' said Nikki to Flora. 'We'll all keep an eye on you.'

'After you,' offered Flora, who wanted to be as far away from Jamie as possible. She was resigned to the fact that her hat was about to have a ginormous flashing neon D for Dunce on it. 'I don't want to hold anyone up.' She caught Munchkin muttering what a blessing.

The path wound its way gently through a pine forest. Flora's pulse quietened. She began to warm up, her limbs became looser and her movements more fluid.

She was astounded to realise that only Jamie, Pete and Miranda showed any sort of elan. All her fears about being the chalet dunce were groundless. Munchkin and Martin were unsteady and all over the shop, with about as much sense of rhythm as a hippopotamus and all the style of a sack of potatoes. Sam and Nikki weren't much better, Anna only a little more competent.

All week, she'd assumed they were paralleling their way down black runs and off-piste.

Jamie was waiting at the foot of the path. Acre after acre of white piste stretched out before them, deserted apart from a few skiers. 'There's the chairlift, Flora.'

She could see her reflection in his sunglasses. She remembered Stefan telling her that Jamie wanted to keep her timid.

'You could always walk down to it,' crowed Sam.

Flora scanned the piste. Any fear, any confusion, any apprehension was being melted by white-hot rage. Jamie had zero excuse for trying to hurt her. She could've been killed. She touched Stefan's paper in her pocket like a talisman. 'No,' she said slowly. 'I think I'll try and ski.'

Jamie shrugged. 'Fine.'

He and Pete flew off, Miranda in pursuit. Anna was behind them, followed by the rest. As Munchkin traversed, she was so close to Sam she was almost standing on his skis. When they both tried to turn, she slammed into him and they ended up in an ungainly tangle on the ground. Judging from their expressions, sharp words were exchanged.

Flora looked down at her skis. Her allies. They'd better not let her down. Pushing off with her poles, she yelled, '*Allez*'.

Munchkin's skis were in a V-shaped snowplough as she inched her way along. She looked up in open-mouthed disbelief as Flora hurtled into a parallel just in front of her.

Flora forgot the cold and the pain in her shins and her ribs as she raced on faster and faster, her face stinging in the wind. Her skis sliced across the snow with a wonderful sssh sound. She headed straight across Sam's path, planted her right pole just inches away from his ski tips and pivoted round it, laughing as he swore at her.

'*Allez*,' she screamed.

Automatically she swung into a succession of parallels, her body banking into the mountainside and then straightening up. She swept past a furious looking Nikki who was waiting for Martin, prostrate on the ground, then passed Anna.

Flora came out of another turn and went into a traverse. She glanced over her shoulder and knew they were all watching her. She turned a perfect parallel. That's for keeping me awake night after night. She traversed and paralleled. That, you men, is for acting like animals, especially in Les Landais. And again. That, you women, is for letting them.

She screamed with joy, her skis searing through the dazzling white. Her skis, her allies, carried her faster, better than she'd ever skied.

'Yes,' she cried, coming to a textbook uphill stop beside Jamie. As she leant over her poles, fighting to get her breath back, she hoped he'd choke on the snow kicked up in her wake.

Jamie was poleaxed. 'I thought— When did you . . . ?'

'I knew what exactly what you thought, Jamie.'

'You said you couldn't ski,' said Miranda, who like Pete, was gawping at her.

'I couldn't,' gasped Flora.

'Well, you can now,' said Pete, offering her a ciggie. 'Brilliant, princess.'

'A-mazing,' said Miranda.

Flora stared into the black of Jamie's sunglasses.

'Oh dear, Martin's down. Again,' said Pete. 'Shame. He should get a toboggan, the amount of time he spends on his arse.'

One by one, the others joined them. Munchkin, last, came to a halt in a juddering snowplough. Her face tightened with displeasure as she heard Flora being congratulated.

'You learnt that in a week?' Anna was delighted for her.

'Stefan was a great teacher,' said Flora, looking at Jamie.

'Obviously,' said Jamie.

'Body language,' said Anna. 'It never lies.'

Munchkin glared at her.

'I told you we should've had lessons, Martin,' snapped Nikki.

'All right, all right, don't go on about it.'

The morning disappeared as they skied run after run. Each time they approached a lift, Pete laughed and told Flora to take it. Jamie winced. Flora had to tell herself not to get too big for her grotesque ski boots.

Shortly after midday, the late night and the biting wind began to take their toll. When Pete suggested they head for the Savoie, all agreed.

The scene outside the Savoie was forlorn, the usually packed tables deserted, the ski racks almost empty.

Jamie took off his sunglasses and gazed at Flora. 'Like Sam saying thanks, my sorry's a bit inadequate, isn't it?'

'After trying to get me killed?' She banged her skis together to get the snow off them. 'Yes.'

'So, I was wrong. I'm surprised your skis didn't spell out a huge "up yours, Jamie" in the snow'.

'They did,' said Flora. 'As they paralleled.'

'But I was right to make you ski? You enjoy it, don't you?'

'Love it. Surprisingly.' She stared at him. 'Your bullying has had one positive outcome. I'll pay you back for the lessons.'

'No need.'

'Every need.' Should she tell him it was over? She didn't trust his reaction. 'Let's eat.'

Inside it was quiet. The normally hard-pressed waitresses were gossiping at the bar.

'This time tomorrow, we'll be on our way,' said Anna, wishing she could be driven by Miranda rather than Pete.

'Flown past, hasn't it?' said Pete, not looking forward to being nagged about his poor miles per gallon rate.

'A week is far too short,' said Munchkin, longing to be home. 'Just as you're relaxed, you're leaving.'

'Could've done with a bit more skiing,' grumbled Nikki.

Martin put his hand on hers. 'Don't worry, lover. We'll go again in March. Somewhere nice like Aspen or St Moritz.'

'Only if we can get a guide.'

'Like Stefan?' Martin winked at Flora, who was stretching like a cat. 'He certainly taught you a thing or two.'

'To ski.' She wondered if he had X-ray vision and could see the slip of paper in her pocket.

'Always worth having lessons, Martin,' said Pete. 'One-to-one preferably. An hour on your own is reckoned to equal about six in a ski school class.'

'You probably did more skiing than any of us, didn't you, Flora?' said Miranda. 'Pretty a-mazing considering you hated the idea.'

'Wonder what made you change your mind,' said Sam with mock innocence.

Flora and Jamie stared at each other.

'Jamie did,' said Flora. 'I'll always be grateful for that.'

A warm cosy fug enveloped them. The windows misted over, shrouding the bleakness outside. The surrounding tables were empty. Over in the corner another party of Brits were complaining about the lack of snow and sunshine, saying it was never this bad in Val.

Miranda ordered croque monsieur and frites, then wailed that her New Year's resolution to eat less fat was out the window.

'Try Michel Montignac, Miranda,' advised Nikki smugly. 'It's fatal to mix proteins and carbo.'

'Miranda's got nothing to worry about,' said Pete gallantly. 'Anyway, eaters are much more fun to be with than neurotic pickers with their lettuce leaves and mineral water. My ex should've lived in a hutch.'

'Really?' said Munchkin, excitement lighting up her face. 'Which ex? The model?'

'That ex.'

Desperate to probe, she was shut up by the unusually grim look on his face.

Miranda defiantly bit into a large crust of bread.

Feeling snubbed, Nikki glanced over at Martin, who'd unzipped his khaki suit and tied the sleeves round his waist. The skin around his eye was vaguely yellow and she could see the quickly forked-up food churning round in his mouth as he talked the state of the property market with Jamie.

She felt a stab of discontent that he'd somehow failed her. He couldn't ski well, they'd been stuck in that pokey bedroom, he hadn't organised any lessons, there had been that business with the car, the scene with the Australians. Was she only with him because he was the first man to come along? Supposing she'd met someone else in the bar that night? What if Pete had been there?

They lingered over lunch, thawed out by jug after jug of *vin chaud*. No one was inclined to move, it was so gloomy and uninviting outside. Even Jamie and Pete had little enthusiasm for getting back on their skis. Chocolate cognacs were ordered.

The wind had died down, but the clouds were low and threatening, cutting them off completely from St Marie. Les Pins was treacherous. In places the rock and yellow tufts of grass were exposed. Apart from Miranda, the women had no appetite to ski. Nikki was weary at the thought of carrying her skis even the short distance to the lift. Munchkin's hands froze immediately when she put on her damp gloves. Flora was a mass of aches and her shinbones felt so raw from her boots, she checked to see if they were bleeding.

Hearing that Pete and Jamie were skiing down and spurred on by the *vins chauds* and the cognacs, Martin felt honour-bound to copy them.

'Are you sure it's a good idea?' asked Nikki doubtfully as they clomped out of the Savoie.

'Just shut up, can't you?' he snapped, picking up his skis from the rack as if he were going into battle.

She shrugged. All the more reason for her to take the lift. She wasn't going to hang around and watch him make a complete jerk of himself yet again.

Anna slung her skis over her shoulder. 'You'll take it easy won't you? A lot of accidents happen on the very last run of the holiday, especially after lunch.'

Pete tutted, deciding that he must have a quiet word with Sam about the drive home. 'See you down at the bottom,' he called to the five, who were almost crawling towards the lift.

'My feet are completely numb,' said Anna. She peered across at the piste, the greying snow seemed in need of a good wash. 'Is Martin going to be OK?'

He was down, less than 50 metres from the Savoie.

'If we go in March, we're definitely having lessons,' said Nikki, her mouth tightening into a pout. 'It's a waste of time going out by yourself if you haven't been taught properly. We should've done what you did, Flora. Apart from anything else, Stefan was absolutely gorgeous, you lucky thing.'

'Bit wasted on me,' fibbed Flora sounding virtuous.

'Oh, come off it. We all know you're engaged, but you can still window shop.' Nikki grinned wickedly. 'You obviously got on well judging from last night. What were you talking about for so long?'

'This and that,' Flora was uneasy.

'And the other?' Giggling, Nikki nudged Anna. 'He was so dreamy. Even Anna thought so. Out with it. You must've been a bit tempted, Flora. No wonder you leapt at the chance of skiing. I would have. In fact I would've leapt on him.'

As they laughed, Nikki peered at the piste. Martin had disappeared. 'Sometimes I think we would've had a far nicer time if the five of us girls had been on our own this week.'

'Agreed.' Anna sighed. 'Still, being around these men is good practice for teaching.'

'Suppose you've got tons of A levels and stuff,' said Nikki wistfully. 'I'd love to do a degree. Nikki Solange BA. Make them think, wouldn't it? I told Martin. He said, "You, study? What? Shopping?" '

Because of the intense cold, all but the most hardy had decided to call it a day. In the lift queue, Sam and Munchkin huddled together for warmth, their noses old boozers' red. Anna envied Nikki her silver fox, then told herself off for giving tacit support for the fur trade.

By the time they were back in St Marie, the five were frozen to the core, their fingers almost too numb to hold their skis and poles. As they trudged out of the lift station, Jamie and Pete cut in front of them and came to a grating halt on the ice. They threw their arms round each other in delight.

'Way to be. Give me five,' cried Pete, the sweat shining on his forehead.

'Five,' said Jamie holding out his palms.

A small boy skied up to his mother and pointed at them. 'Mummy those two men nearly crashed into us.' Mummy had been anxiously waiting for the arrival of her darling. Her far from confident husband was traumatised and complained sourly that those two maniacs obviously didn't have a clue about the mountain code.

'Mummy, they went ever so fast and didn't keep on falling over like daddy did,' said darling to his father's irritation.

Jamie grinned and stepped out of his skis. 'Let me,' he said to Flora, offering to carry hers.

Munchkin was cross that Sam didn't copy him.

Up ahead, at the top of the metal steps Anna called back, asking if Nikki had the keys to the Range Rover.

'Martin's got them.' She sighed.

'We'll be the block of ice that the glacier mint bear stands on by the time he gets here,' shivered Sam. 'If he gets here.'

'There are taxis, you know.' Nikki scanned the piste. No sign of Martin. Why the hell hadn't he got the lift?

The low grey clouds matched the ugly concrete of the lift station. The snow looked greyer, dirty. A dispiriting gloom seemed to have enveloped St Marie. The flashing neon of the shop signs just looked tawdry. When Pete said he was looking forward to hunkering down in front of the fire and a video, everyone agreed.

'Wait for me,' called Miranda, rubbing her bottom. She'd been forced to swerve to avoid an Italian snowboarder who had turned too fast and almost lost it. Infuriatingly, she'd ended up on her backside, while he'd sped on.

'Nikki. Quick,' yelled Anna, who was standing beside the Range Rover.

'What's up?' She was alarmed by Anna's dismayed expression and rushed across as fast as her ski boots would allow. Her eyes followed Anna's pointing finger. 'Oh God, that's all we need.'

The Range Rover's passenger window was smashed, shards of glass covered the seat and the dirty snow by the door.

'*Que passa?*' demanded Sam. Anna stifled her irritation; they were in France not Spain. 'Oh shit,' he sighed, surveying the damage. The others crowded round.

'The door's still locked,' said Jamie. 'Someone's probably whacked their ski through it. Often happens, people are bloody careless.'

'Stereo's still there,' said Anna peering inside.

Nikki looked as if she wanted to cry. 'It's a bank holiday isn't it? Bet we've got no chance of getting it fixed. And we've got to drive all that way tomorrow. It'll be freezing.' She started to pick off the pieces of shattered glass near the seal.

Munchkin's heart sank at the thought of the journey home.

'*Qui est le proprietaire de cette voiture?*'

They all wheeled round in surprise at the authoritative demand. Two gendarmes in their thick blue uniforms and peaked caps had crossed the road. The first was a bison, short and stocky with thick, cropped grey hair and thin mean lips. Flora thought he looked like a chunkier, nastier version of Jacques. He repeated the question. His younger colleague, a prop-forward size giant with a face pitted by acne scars was speaking into a crackling radio.

'What did he say?' asked Nikki.

'*Notre ami,*' cut in Anna.

'*Vous êtes anglaise, mademoiselle?*'

'*Oui.*'

'*Ou-est la proprietaire?*'

'*Il fait le ski, monsieur. La bas. Il arrive.*' Anna pointed towards Les Pins.

Martin had finally made it to the lift station and was taking off his skis. His frozen fingers could scarcely unclip the bindings. Halfway down, he'd made up his mind that skiing was a mug's game. For the same money, he and Nikki could've swanned off to the Caribbean and chilled out on a sunny beach. Seeing the rest gathered round the Range Rover, he took vicious pleasure that he'd kept them waiting in the cold.

'What the . . .' He halted beside the Range Rover, saw the window and punched the door in fury. 'Bastards.'

'A ski probably went through it,' said Munchkin, echoing Jamie.

'*Vous êtes la proprietaire de cette voiture?*' demanded the bison-like gendarme. 'This car is yours?'

'*Oui.*' That was the extent of Martin's French.

'Documents.'

'What?'

'Show me your documents.'

Seeing Martin pull a face, Anna laid a restraining arm on his. 'They'll give you the bumf if you want to claim on insurance.'

Sighing, he reached through the remains of the glass, pulled up the door lock and opened the glove compartment. 'Vehicle registration, insurance, MOT, driving licence.'

Nikki stamped her freezing feet. Frowning, the gendarme slowly scrutinised every document, before passing them to his unsmiling colleague. 'Identification? Passport? Anything with your photograph?' The radio crackled again.

'Only my ski pass.' Martin held it out.

The bison was unamused. 'That does not officially confirm who you are. Your passport please.'

'It's back at the chalet.'

'In St Marie?'

'Yep. Up over there somewhere.' Martin waved vaguely in the direction of Les Pins.

Anna pulled her hood down and rubbed her ears, aching because of the cold. Once again she wished fur wasn't so warm.

'Where exactly?' demanded the bison.

'Chalet Juliette. Up there on the road out of town. What does it matter? You should be looking for the clowns who wrecked my car, not asking me pointless bloody questions.'

The gendarmes stared at him impassively.

'Sssh,' ordered Anna. She explained in French exactly where the chalet was and apologised for her friend who was upset about his car.

Miranda exchanged glances with Flora and sighed. There was little point in Martin being so truculent.

Passers-by were slowing down to stare. Pete got out his cigarettes but faintly remembered something about smoking being outlawed in public places in France. He decided it wasn't worth the risk, these two were alarmingly unfriendly.

'Do you have any official document to prove that you are Martin Eric June?'

'Not with me. No.' Martin glared at them belligerently. 'I haven't stolen the car you know.' He turned to Anna. 'What is this bullshit? Forget the window. Tell them we want to go home.'

Pete had had enough. He got out his keyring. The locks to the Porsche doors sprung up with a clunk. The prop-forward shook his head and gripped Pete's arm. '*Attendez.*'

A police car, white with blue and black stripes along its side, drove up and stopped, parking diagonally across the street.

'You're all staying in the chalet? Together?' The bison stared at them one by one.

They nodded.

Jamie glanced over at two other gendarmes who had got out of their car and were making their way towards them. What was going on?

'Since when?'

'Last Saturday,' said Jamie.

'How many of you?'

'All of us here. Nine. Neuf. Can't you count or something?' said Sam, longing for a hot shower.

Both gendarmes stared at him. 'Anyone else?' asked the bison.

'*Un autre ami,*' said Anna, stabbing Sam's leg with her ski pole. '*Ou est il?*'

'*Chez la chalet. Son bras est cassé.*' She looked uneasily at the two new arrivals, heavy batons swinging from their hips. The radio crackled again and a police van drove down the street, its blue light flashing.

'This is getting a bit heavy,' whispered Pete to Jamie. 'What's going on?'

Jamie shook his head and shrugged. On the other side of the street, people had stopped and were having an unashamed gawp, speculating to one another about the possible reasons for the police presence. The bison nodded to his colleagues. Three in the van jumped out, walked round the back and opened up the double doors.

'You will all come to the Commissariat for questioning. In the van. Now.'

There was an aghast chorus of whys and whats. The seven cops had taken up strategic positions blocking any chance of escape.

'What's this all about?' demanded Flora.

'I'm not getting into any paddy wagon,' bristled Martin, 'I know my rights. And don't even think of laying a finger on me.'

The prop-forward tightened his grip on his baton and growled at him to *allez*.

'Get off,' cried Nikki, trying to free her arms as one of the gendarmes led her towards the doors.

'Sam,' yelled Munchkin, being pulled apart from him as he was shoved in the direction of the van.

Miranda climbed the step up into the windowless interior, as best she could encumbered by her skis, poles and heavy boots. It was useless to protest, this lot weren't Inspector Clouseaus. There was bound to have been some ghastly mix-up and the sooner they sorted it out the better. She sat down on one of the wooden benches that lined each side of the van.

Munchkin and Sam, utterly bewildered, stumbled through the double doors and were ordered to put their skis on the floor and their hands on their laps. Anna translated rapidly.

'What the fuck is happening?' said Sam, rubbing his arm.

Outside Jamie and Pete were both pleading with the bison.

'You're making a big mistake,' shouted Martin. 'And get your hands off me, you.' He tried to struggle free of the prop-forward's grip on his forearm, then yelled in pain as his arm was wrenched round his back. 'Your days are numbered, matey, I'll sue you for assault,' he cried, his skis and poles clattering to the ground.

'*Allez mademoiselle.*'

Flora stood her ground. 'No. You can't just bundle people into vans because you feel like it. It's like something out of Kafka. Questioning about what?'

'*Larcin.* Theft. Fraud.' The bison smiled menacingly.

'Theft?' exploded Flora. 'Theft? Don't be so bloody ridiculous. *C'est fou.*' Behind her Pete laughed. Jamie asked whether they looked like thieves. Two gendarmes drew closer.

'Look,' said Jamie in his most mollifying voice. 'There's obviously been a muddle. Now, we know you have a difficult job to do and we wouldn't dream of pressing charges for wrongful arrest . . .' Flora muttered that she would.

'Theft from Les Landais restaurant on December 30th,' snapped the bison. The three of them looked at one another appalled as his words sunk in. 'Get in the van.'

They needed no further prompting. As she walked towards the doors flanked by two gendarmes, Flora glared at the crowd of curious onlookers.

'Give me the number of the British consul,' screamed Martin inside the van to the gendarme by the door. 'Just you wait till my Euro MP hears about this.'

'Shut up,' ordered Flora, getting into the van. Almost twisting her ankle on the pile of skis and poles piled up in the middle of the floor, she sat down on the narrow bench. Worry, puzzlement and anger were written across everyone's faces.

'Fascist pig,' muttered Sam as Pete was shoved inside. 'Him not you.'

Martin's skis and poles were thrown in. 'They're new,' he yelled.

'What's this all about?' wailed Nikki.

Flora's green eyes narrowed. 'It's about you lot doing a runner from the restaurant the other night.'

Gasps of disbelief were followed by a stunned silence. The doors slammed behind Jamie and someone banged on the outside. In the gloom they all jumped. As the van started to move off, Jamie was thrown to the floor.

'I knew we should've gone back and paid,' said Anna.

'Bit late for that now, isn't it?' snapped Pete. 'Thanks, everyone. I hope you're going to explain that neither me or

Jamie or Flora had anything to do with it. We left before you lot, remember?'

'It was only a bit of fun,' protested Sam.

'What's so bloody funny about it?' demanded Jamie as the van lurched round a corner, causing the skis and poles to slide and everyone to be thrown into the person next to them.

'It was Martin's idea,' said Munchkin.

'And Sam was only obeying orders,' said Jamie.

The van was claustrophobic, with only a tiny skylight in the roof, the atmosphere heavy with stifled argument and silent recrimination. Squashed up, they all wondered how long the journey would take and what would happen at the end of it.

After only a few minutes they stopped. The doors were opened. The prop-forward motioned to them to get out. Climbing down one by one, they found themselves in a walled courtyard. They were told to leave their skis against a wall before they filed through a fire door and into a lino-floored corridor. The harsh fluorescent light drained the little colour left in their faces.

Martin turned to the bison. 'Listen, it had nothing to do with those three.'

'Silence.' The prop-forward stopped and ushered them all into a dingy windowless room, bare apart from the strip light on the ceiling.

Anna translated. 'We must all wait here.'

'Minimalist decor, très hip,' said Miranda. This was awful, supposing they all had to appear in court? Or were sent to gaol? It would be in the papers, her parents would be so ashamed. And she'd have a criminal record, which the Australian immigration people wouldn't look kindly on. Why hadn't she listened to Anna and forced the men to go back and repay the money?

The door was closed behind them. There was nothing to do but wait. A current of anxiety shot through Munchkin. How long would her sentence be for criminal damage?

Flora broke the silence. 'I spy with my little eye something beginning with F.'

'Fuckwit?' suggested Pete looking at Martin.

'Fucked off?' asked Jamie, pacing the room. He hated being in confined spaces.

'Almost. Fed up. Me. Very.' Flora lit up and started blowing smoke rings. Munchkin coughed, but didn't ask her to stub it out.

'I spy with my little eye something beginning with S,' said Pete.

'Stupid?' asked Jamie.

'Sense of humour failure?' said Flora.

'Shit for brains. Your turn, Jamie.' Pete eyed the rest.

'I spy with my little eye something beginning with C.'

'Er,' Flora paused. 'Cross?'

'Cartload of wankers?' said Pete.

'Claustrophobic,' spat Jamie.

'That's enough, you lot,' said Martin. He felt bad enough, there was no need for them to rub in a Siberian mine of salt.

'Don't give me that,' Jamie stopped pacing and spun round. 'We wouldn't be here if it wasn't for you and your pathetic ideas of having a laugh. Now get out of my way, crawl back into your cage and keep your mouth very, very shut.' Martin flinched. 'If we miss our flight tomorrow, you're paying for another one. Got it, old chap?'

Flora went to the door, opened it and peered along the corridor. A gendarme had been posted outside and was reading the paper. He ignored her query of how much longer they'd have to wait and ordered her to get back inside. She took off her ski boots and put her feet in their damp socks on the hot pipe that skirted the room. Nikki shrugged off Martin's arm and sat down next to Anna and Miranda, who were propped up against the wall. She began chewing her nails.

Minutes passed broken only by sighs, yawns and hostile glances.

'Right. Let's get the story straight, shall we?' said Jamie, still pacing. 'What exactly happened that night? Flora and I left, giving our money to Pete. What then?'

'I gave our wad to Sam, then I left. After that? Not all at once,' he said impatiently, as the other six rushed to speak. 'Anna.'

'Martin, Giles and Sam suggested that "us girlies" wait for them outside while they settled up and tried to smooth things over with madame. That awful witch who was like Mrs Danvers in *Rebecca*.'

'Mrs Who? Who's Rebecca?' asked Sam puzzled.

Anna ignored him. 'We gave them our share and went to the Range Rover.' She turned to Miranda who nodded. 'And then the three of them rushed out, screamed at us to get in the car and we tore off with Giles riding on the roof. That's when he fell.'

Sitting against the opposite wall, Martin put his head in his hands.

'So this comes down to more pratting about by Martin, Sam and Giles,' said Jamie. 'Anything else?'

'The window,' wailed Munchkin, eyes filled with anxiety, chins quivering. 'I broke the window. It was a mistake. Nikki and I had a snowball fight. What's going to happen to us?'

'Hangable offence, isn't it?' piped up Flora. 'Sorry. Forgot. The French use the guillotine. Let's hope it's a nice sharp blade. Does anyone know the number for Prisoners Abroad?'

'Oh piss off,' hissed Munchkin, trying to fight back her tears.

'Flora, please,' sighed Jamie.

'It's all right Munchkin,' broke in Martin. 'I'll tell them I did it. I'll explain it was my idea to do a runner and none of you had anything to do with it.' His Sydney Cartonish far, far better feeling of noble self-sacrifice was undermined when Miranda said too right.

'Anna, can you explain all this to Plod?' asked Pete.

While studying Martin and Sam as if they were particularly nasty rodents, she enunciated slowly, 'Explain that we handed over our share of the bill in good faith, waited outside for the men and they decided to scarper without paying? I think so.'

Sam blushed. 'Well, you had no trouble taking the money

back, did you? Don't play Miss High and Mighty with me, Anna.'

'That's true,' said Munchkin.

Anna's loss for words was covered by Miranda whistling 'Stand By Your Man'. Flora's giggles died away when the door opened. Everyone sitting got to their feet as the bison-like gendarme walked to the centre of the room. He ordered Pete to stop smoking and Anna to translate for him.

She listened acutely and waited for his nod. He rattled off a torrent of furious-sounding French, causing them all to wince. 'You are accused of defrauding the owner of Les Landais on December 30th by dining there with the intention of leaving without paying the bill.' . . . 'In effect you have stolen 2,500 francs from madame la patronne.' . . . 'This is a highly serious offence.' . . . 'There is also the matter of criminal damage to the property, namely one broken window.' Munchkin felt her palms sweat. 'We're waiting for la patronne, Madame Blanche to identify you.' . . . 'While this sort of action may be tolerated in England, in France it is dealt with with the utmost severity. I rejoice that you are not my countrymen.'

Each one of them wondered what the utmost severity meant.

Jamie exchanged uneasy glances with Pete. 'This is getting very unamusing.' Neither had a clue about their rights; whether or not they could be held overnight, or whether they could talk to a solicitor.

The bison looked at them all in turn, taking pleasure in the heavy silence and ashamed faces.

Seeing him stalk towards the door, Miranda called out for him to attendez, un moment, monsieur. She was definitely going to French evening classes if she ever got home.

Miranda sounded desperate and fortunately the bison had a weakness for blondes, especially when they begged him to listen. 'Anna, start talking,' hissed Miranda.

The others held their breath and tried to follow as Anna explained exactly what had happened that night, pointing first at

Flora, then at Jamie and Pete. Nikki smiled appealingly at the bison when her name was mentioned and Munchkin raised her downcast eyes in supplication. His expression, like Anna's tone, hardened when it came to Sam and Martin.

'*C'est vrai?*' he asked Miranda, when Anna had finished.

'Truly.' Nodding, she fingered her pearls like a rosary.

They all jumped at an abrupt knock at the door. The gendarme who'd been sitting outside, told his chief that Madame Blanche had arrived.

'You come with me,' he said to Anna. 'The rest wait here. Don't worry.' He patted Miranda's arm.

From the alarm on her face, Anna might have been going to the scaffold. She must have made some progress though, because the bison held the door open for her and allowed her to pass through first.

'Think he's got the hots for you, Miranda,' said Pete. 'Do you think Anna can convince him we're in the clear?'

'Selfish bastard,' muttered Sam. 'Where's Giles?' Giles was equally to blame and should be equally in the shit. Supposing they were sent down? Banged up? Banged up with a load of psychotic French poofters he became more and more panicked as the minutes crawled past.

Everyone jumped up when Anna came back with yet another gendarme, who told Martin and Sam to follow him.

Both feeling utterly sick, they were led away, leaving behind a clamour of demands for Anna to say exactly what was going on.

'Madame was there, wanted to turn me to stone. But she backed me up. One of the waiters saw us giving the men the money. We're to wait here until they decide what to do with them. A fine, probably. Fortunately, Monsieur Lermitte turned out to be extremely nice, speaks excellent English really. His daughter's a teacher.'

'So we're all right. Well done,' said Jamie, giving Anna a hug. 'You were marvellous.' She blushed with pleasure as everyone thanked her.

'A fine, you think?' said Nikki, trying to take her mind off the fact that she needed to visit the loo.

'Probably,' said Anna.

Overcome with relief that she was out of the mire, Miranda could turn her attention to the fate of Sam and Martin. 'They won't go to jug, will they?'

'Unlikely,' said Jamie.

'We could start a campaign to free the Chalet Juliette two,' suggested Flora.

'John MacCarthy had friends,' said Anna. 'We could be Friends of Sam and Martin. Perhaps.' She winked at Flora.

Nikki and Munchkin glowered at them.

Twenty minutes later Sam and Martin returned, almost their old selves again. Martin rubbed at his face, which a livid Madame Blanche had slapped. Munchkin threw her arms round Sam as if he were a freed Nelson Mandela.

'Got to pay back the money, pay for the window and pay a two thousand franc fine.' Sam said over her shoulder, trying to disentangle himself. God, how was he going to afford it? Prison seemed almost appealing. 'You couldn't give me a loan, could you?' he whispered in her ear, as she smothered him in kisses.

'Oh course I can, silly,' she said. 'How much was the window?'

'Seven hundred francs.'

Munchkin grew pale. She hadn't expected it to be that much. No chance of buying all those delicious looking cheeses and charcuterie now.

'You're paying our share of the bill, aren't you, Sam?' said Jamie. 'What happened to our dosh by the way?'

'It's back at the chalet,' said Sam, quickly. He prayed he hadn't spent all of it.

'And let's get this clear. You, Martin and Giles are paying the fine.'

Martin's reception from Nikki was frosty. 'This is a loan, OK?' she warned as she chucked a bundle of notes at him. 'Your mess, your fine, you pay.'

There was a long bad tempered delay while forms had to be filled out in triplicate, money handed over, statements made. Sam, Martin and Anna came and went like characters in a farce, said Jamie, which Miranda said was very apt.

'Now what are they playing at?' he seethed.

'Heard the one about the . . . ?' said Sam.

'No. And I don't want to hear another word out of you,' snapped Pete. 'Or you Martin.' Sam shut up and was forced to listen to the pair's ceaseless grumbling.

Finally, Monsieur Lermitte returned, handed Sam and Martin a wad of paper and said farewell to Anna and a blushing Miranda.

'I wish we'ad met under 'appier circumstances, miss,' he said, kissing her hand. 'What joy it is that a lay-dee like you graces St Marie. Your two friends, 'owever, are not well-come. I think you choose your company more care-full-ee in future.'

They were escorted along the corridor and out of the building by the prop-forward who watched unsmilingly as they picked up their skis. It was almost dark. A side gate was opened and they found themselves out on the street near the hospital.

Martin stared at the prop-forward. 'This is the last time I visit France. Bloody police state.'

Inside his office Monsieur Lermitte got out a bottle of cognac and poured out one for himself and another for Madame Blanche. The window had cost all of 200 francs, but good cousins like him understood the cost of inconvenience.

He tut tutted and warned her that her waiter Michel should be more careful with his skis. One day he might have an accident and they could go through a car window.

Raising her glass, Madame Blanche agreed that would be a pity.

They toasted la belle France.

❋   ❋   ❋

As they trudged towards the lift station, fat flakes of snow began to fall.

Anna and Miranda strode on ahead, complaining about the stupidity of men. Nikki rejected Martin's offer to carry her skis with an angry shake of the silver fox. She almost broke into a sprint to distance herself from him. She wanted to put even more distance between them when she heard Pete loudly telling Jamie that it was dead uncool to be arrested for doing a runner.

'Put a sock in it, will you?' snarled Martin. 'It's done now.'

'So that's all right then.' Jamie was scornful.

'Oh, so you never make a mistake do you, old chap?' Crossly, Martin swiped the snow from his hair. 'Drink-driving doesn't count, I suppose?'

'Now look,' Jamie spun round.

'And neither do drugs, eh? Just as well you weren't searched mate, isn't it? Busted for cocaine? Wouldn't rate your chances for that seat on the Rosehagen board after that. Even if you are married to one of the family.'

Flora was taking a child-like pleasure in the snow. She wanted to skip, play hopscotch. The lights picked out millions of feathery flakes. She broke off from humming 'Walking in a Winter Wonderland.'

'I'm not one of the family.' A pillow in the sky had been shaken, brightening the darkness, softening the harsh man-made edges of the cars and the crash barriers and the buildings under a gentle layer of white.

'Of course you're one of the family, Miss Rosehagen,' scoffed Martin. 'Not a bad wedding present, seat on a board.'

'What?' whispered Flora, slowing to a stop.

'That's what you're giving him, isn't it?'

'I'm sorry?'

'You get your feet under the boardroom table marrying Flora, don't you, Jamie?' said Martin. 'As you keep telling everyone.'

The ground beneath Flora's feet was shifting, her whole

world was doing a somersault, she was giddy as her thoughts got vertigo.

'Flora,' pleaded Jamie. She was statue-still as she stared back at him. As still as Snow White in her glass coffin. 'Flora, it's not what you think.'

She was already running.

Miranda and Anna retrieved their walking boots from the Range Rover and announced they'd be taking a taxi to the chalet. Munchkin and Sam said that they'd also be making their own way back.

'Be like that then,' hissed Martin at their retreating backs.

They'd been walking ahead. Only Pete had seen Jamie punch him.

Her expression set and sullen, Nikki watched Martin sweep the glass off the passenger seat and into the road. They drove back to the chalet in silence.

Nikki sighed as the Range Rover pulled into the drive. A bitter wind brought snow through the gap where the window should've been.

'Well. Another fine mess.' Her voice was as icy as the weather.

Peering out of the sitting room window and seeing the snow fall, Giles wondered if he could drive. In this weather he didn't trust Mirandy to get them safely through the village, let alone all the way home.

He threw another log on the fire, then paced. He was even bored with Jackie Collins, which he'd begun reading hours before, always on the alert for the sound of a car, ready to whip it under a cushion and pick up something more elevating.

Where were they? Probably sitting in some cosy café drinking *vin chaud* and having a laugh.

For weeks after finalising the plans in November, he'd

pictured the holiday. As organiser he'd cast himself in the leading role, hosting an eight day party, conquering mountains by day and St Marie by night. He'd imagined everyone being over-whelmed with gratitude to him, even a possible dalliance with Mirandy. He'd never once thought of a broken collarbone, his past resurrected to haunt him, Mirandy and Pete. Rather than taking centre stage, he'd been elbowed aside to the wings.

Hearing a car, he stuffed Jackie Collins back in the bookcase and grabbed the *Economist*. 'Hello you two.' Nikki stomped upstairs without saying a word. 'Nice day?'

Martin snatched off his gloves and held his frozen hands out to the fire. 'If you call getting the car window bashed in and getting arrested and dragged down to the local pig pen nice.'

'What?' Giles's white-lashed eyes blinked in astonishment. 'Arrested?'

'Talk about police brutality. No chance to see a brief. You missed a treat.'

'Sue for false imprisonment.' His jowls quivered with in-dignation. 'Can't go round picking innocent people off the streets. This isn't a banana republic. Though their colonials will tell you that Johnny Frog's sense of civil liberties leave a lot to be desired. We should inform the consul, get him to make an official complaint.'

'Don't think so,' said Martin.

'False arrest? Course we should. Just the sort of thing that makes me rue the day the Party ever took us into Europe. The Common Agricultural Policy . . .'

'We were picked up for doing the runner,' cut in Martin. 'Pardon?'

Martin threw some logs on the fire. 'Just be glad you were sitting on your fanny up here rather than being down at the cop shop. Wouldn't look too good would it, future MP arrested.'

Giles was horror-struck. 'But it was your idea.'

'So?' Martin shrugged. 'You went along with it. And there's a small matter of a two thousand franc fine, divided three ways.'

'Three? What do you mean three ways?'

'Between me and Sam and you.'

Giles leapt to his feet. 'But it was your idea.' He stalked to the window, his body rigid with anger. This was outrageous. Not only could they have jeopardised his future, but they were expecting him to pay for it. 'Three? What about the others?'

Martin smiled. 'You can try, but you'll be lucky. Pete and the royal couple? Forget it. They'd already left. Pity they hadn't pissed off out of here entirely if you want my opinion. Nikki's already put her tiny foot down. As for the rest, doubtful.'

Giles stabbed at the fire with a poker as Martin went to the kitchen for a beer. 'Have you been keeping a record?' he demanded, seeing him opening the bottle.

'Of what?'

'Everyone's supposed to write down any drinks they have in the honesty book.' Giles went to the sideboard, snatched up the exercise book and opened it. 'Nothing after Tuesday,' he exploded, waving it in front of Martin's nose before throwing it across the room. He dashed to the phone. 'No-one's written down any calls either. And what about the damages? That table, crockery, glasses. Who's responsible? Me. The mug.' Spittle showered out of his mouth.

Martin, swigging beer, watched him impassively. 'Listen, matey,' he said soothingly. 'I'm sure we can work it all out. Don't get so stressed. It's been a long day.'

'Bloody long. Me sitting around here because of your fucking awful driving.'

Beer spurted out onto the rug as Martin snorted in disbelief in mid swig. 'Listen, Giles, you were the one on the roof. You think I could sleep that night? I was too busy puking my guts up.'

'It was your idea . . .'

'A dumb idea. And now we've got to pay for it.'

'I've bloody paid.' Giles adjusted his sausage sling. 'That reminds me, you owe me for the insurance. And let's get one thing straight, shall we? Any money I get from you is cash. OK? No cheques, especially dodgy company ones. Bounce from here to London won't they, from what I've seen of your books. Worse now, if that deal falls through.'

Martin stared at him. 'Nothing wrong with my cheques. Still, suit yourself. I think you'll find I'll be taking my business elsewhere from next week.'

'What business?' scoffed Giles.

'And I'll be reporting you for breaching client confidentiality.'

They were interrupted by voices from downstairs. Anna and Miranda were followed by Sam and Munchkin, their jackets covered in snowflakes from the short walk up the drive. They were taken aback to find the two men glaring at one another and the atmosphere stiff with tension.

'Hello, Giles. How's our wounded soldier?' said Miranda.

As usual, when his wallet might be affected, Giles wasted no time. 'Heard about this fine. I think it's only fair everyone should make some sort of contribution.'

Miranda took off her damp gloves and put them on the radiator, turning her back on him. He sounded so shirty. She had no intention of paying a centime but kept quiet, loathing confrontations about money. Frightfully unpleasant.

'Fair?' Anna bristled. 'No, it's not. It's not fair that we were arrested and dragged to a police station because of you men behaving like children. It wasn't my idea to steal from the restaurant. Don't expect a single franc from me.'

'Told you,' said Martin, seeing Giles's eyes narrow.

'Tea?' asked Munchkin, anxious to escape.

'Please,' said Sam, relieved that Giles was doing his dirty work. He was so skint. It would be nice if the women did cough up, but he was too nervous to press them.

'You all went along with it,' persisted Giles.

'I beg your pardon?' Anna unzipped her turquoise jacket. 'I most certainly did not. If you remember, I told Martin to drive back.'

'I didn't hear you,' snapped Giles.

'Tea, Anna?' cut in Munchkin, sensing a row.

Anna ignored her. 'That's because you were on the roof.'

'Writing off my shoulder and my whole bloody holiday.'

'Well, whose fault was that?' demanded Anna. 'I'm sorry that it happened. But I'm not subsidising you.'

'Munchkin?' said Giles, jowls quivering.

'Tea?' She smiled brightly. 'How's the shoulder?'

'Never mind that. What about the fine?'

Munchkin shifted from one dumpy leg to another. 'Will we have to use chains tomorrow?'

'Are you gong to divvy up or not?'

'Er, don't think so, no. Sorry. Must put the kettle on.' She dived off to the kitchen.

'Miranda?' Giles turned to her, his face brick red.

'Yes?' she hedged.

'Are you with them?'

She avoided his eyes by studying a lock of her sleek blonde hair for non-existent split ends. Must he be quite so aggressive? 'I know it seems unfair with your arm and everything, but the fine's not rarely our problem. Is it, rarely?'

In the silence, Sam's hopes dwindled. Giles snorted in contempt. 'Well, that's that then. Remind me never to organise another holiday.'

Martin threw another log on the fire. 'Nikki agrees with them. Cheque please. On second thoughts, cash,' he called to Giles who was stomping up the stairs, his face twisted in anger.

Anna sighed. Despite everything, they'd manage to avoid any showdowns about money all holiday. Why now? She began searching through the videos.

Munchkin brought in a tray laden with steaming cups and slices of fruit cake. 'He'll calm down in a minute. Just upset about his arm. Where's Nikki?'

Martin threw another log on the fire, sending up a shower of sparks. 'Packing.'

'Any chance of getting the window fixed?' asked Munchkin.

'Doubt it.' Martin scowled. 'Garage was shut when we drove past just now. God knows if anything will be open tomorrow. Holiday weekend.'

'Oh.' She was filled with gloom. 'It'll be freezing.'

'Great. There's gratitude for helping you out with the window business,' Martin had had enough. 'Look, if you're going to moan the whole way, don't bother coming with us. I'd have thought you had enough blubber on you to keep you warm.'

Her mouth stuffed full of fruitcake, Munchkin froze. Then quietly she put down her plate, stood up and disappeared upstairs.

Miranda and Anna stared at Martin in astonishment.

'You unkind bastard,' muttered Sam, slamming down his cup and chasing after her.

'It was a joke,' pleaded Martin uselessly.

'Munchkin's more than welcome to come with us,' said Miranda stiffly.

'We're all getting a little tired of your jokes, Martin,' added Anna, finding the pack of cards hidden among the videos. 'Perhaps we can have a game of something later,' she said to Miranda.

'Old maid perhaps. Or old maids in your case,' sneered Martin, stalking off.

'And then there were two.' Miranda shook her head. This was a madhouse, not a chalet. 'Roll on tomorrow. Although I'm not looking forward to the drive. More cake?'

'Please.' Anna sat down and leant her head back against the cushion, exhausted. 'Just be glad you're not going with Pete.' Miranda wished she were. 'He's an awful driver. Wish I was going with you.'

Miranda leapt at the idea. If Giles was going to be so beastly about this wretched money, it would be a long, dismal drive home. She needed an ally. 'Why don't you? You could swap places with Sam. And you, me and Munchkin could share the driving.'

'Now there's a thought,' said Anna, as if the plan had just occurred to her.

After she'd stomped up to her room, her dark, dingy, pokey room, Nikki had ripped off her silver fox hat and thrown herself down on the bed. Now what?

Being bundled into a van and carted off to a police station was no one's idea of a happy New Year. Is this what the future held? Her life being hijacked by Martin being a prat? What had she let herself in for?

At least with David, there had been style and glamour. Nice flat in a nice address, nice car, nice presents, nice trips to Aspen and to the south of France. And she couldn't deny she'd been fond of the funny old so-and-so. He'd been good to her, certainly at the start, and generous to her to the very end. He was a winner. Dynamic, powerful, with friends in the highest places. She'd been warmed by his reflected glory, not left to freeze in a passenger seat.

She'd given up everything for Martin? The private planes, the chauffeurs, the insider's secrets which a scumbag reporter like Jack Mancini would kill for, the best suites in the best hotels. The assumption that the finest will suffice was a lot for a girl to turn her back on.

Now what? Everything had happened too quickly with Martin. This was worse than being trapped in the flat in the summer.

She stroked her hat as if it were a cat. Now what she should do was get in touch with David the moment she got back, on the pretext of wishing him happy New Year.

It was pushing it, but he might forgive her.

Munchkin lay on her bed, curled up with Sam. How could Martin have been so mean? Despite Sam's reassurances to silence them, the words 'enough blubber', 'enough blubber' echoed round her head. That he was so slight made her feel worse, especially when she realised her splodgy thighs were inches bigger than his.

'Don't worry about him.' Sam pulled her closer. 'He's just uptight because of the car and the police and everything. You should've seen him grovel when they took us away, he was practically on his knees to madame. Begging didn't do much good, she still socked him. When they said they might lock us up, he bricked himself. Almost kissed their feet when it turned out only to be a fine. Sorry to have landed you in it like that.'

'Doesn't matter.' Actually, it gave her another something to tell everyone at work. She'd explain that of course they'd been mistaken for another English group. Enough blubber, enough blubber. Martin had aimed for her Achilles heel and struck it perfectly. 'You think I'm disgustingly fat too, don't you?'

'We've been through all this.' Sam was growing weary. 'No. And you don't need to cart round all those bloody slimming-on-holiday magazines. The ones you've tried to hide under the bed.'

Munchkin managed a small smile. A solicitor she'd once invited back to her place for coffee on the spur of the moment had been amused to find seven calorie counting books in the sitting room. She thought she'd never live down the shame. 'I do.'

'You do what?'

'Inside this size fourteen on a good day is a size twenty-six desperate to get out.' Munchkin reached over to her purse.

'Showing off your gold cards?' asked Sam.

She took out a photo. 'Who's this fat, frumpy tub of lard?'

Sam frowned. 'Dunno.'

'If a bloke was walking past with her, you'd think, huh don't fancy yours. Wouldn't you? Well, that fat, frumpy tub of lard is me.' Munchkin sighed. 'Me. Ten years ago. The all too visible Invisible Woman.'

'Is it?' Sam was amazed. He peered closely at the picture of the middle-aged woman in heavy spectacles and a marquee-sized frock. 'You've changed.'

'Haven't I? Still living at home then, hiding myself away. Few friends, certainly no boyfriends. Then I got ill. Mumps of all things. Typically unglam. But I was so fat it didn't show.' She smiled forlornly. 'But I couldn't eat and I lost a stone. Lying in bed gave me a lot of time to think.'

Sam stared at the photo and then at Munchkin and then back again. Was this truly the same person?

'I started to diet. As I shrank my confidence grew. Got a new job in the post-room of my company. Went to the interview wearing a size twenty suit. I thought that was small then. I was tucked away in the basement, well away from the clients. Image is all. Gradually I got mine right and moved up the building.'

'Found your niche,' said Sam awestruck.

'Yes, and I'm one of the best around.' Munchkin looked at the photo, before putting it back in her purse. 'I'll never forget being the all too visible Invisible Woman though. Not with people like Martin around to remind me.' She suddenly grimaced. 'Not selling myself very well, am I?'

'Munchkin,' Sam kissed the tip of her nose. 'You don't have to. I've already bought. Understand?'

'Damaged goods. Covered in disgusting blubber.'

'You're not disgusting. You mustn't say things like that about yourself, ever. You're kind and cuddly and sweet and good fun.' He was pleased to see the doubt vanish from her eyes. 'And a brilliant cook.' He started tickling her. 'And I'm very lucky. Got a great bargain.'

Miranda approached Munchkin's room with trepidation. She was expecting tears like the other morning. So embarrassing. Instead she heard squeals of mirth. Apologising for the interruption, she told them about her plan for the drive home, which was accepted immediately. Sam relished the thought of being with Pete in the Porsche and Munchkin was delighted that she wouldn't have to play frozen gooseberry in the Range Rover.

Miranda then knocked on Giles's door. 'May I come in?'

'Of course.' He was packing his things.

'Need a hand?'

'Almost there now.' Only a week ago having the Hon. Miranda Lake-ffrench sitting on his bed would've been a prize beyond riches, beyond a partnership in his firm, beyond a safe seat. Blonder, more tanned, looking ten times better than when she arrived, she was no longer his goddess. While putting some contentment back in her eyes, Pete had destroyed her charm.

Miranda fiddled with her pearls. 'About this fine business. I've been thinking. Perhaps I should make a contribution. I don't want us to fall out about money.'

It was Giles's turn to be magnanimous. 'Don't worry. I've been thinking too. Anna was right, it was our idea. I was just a bit pissed off with the way Martin handled it. Between you, me and the bedpost, I rather regret asking him to join us here. He's been a handful throughout.'

'Umm. He's just been completely off to poor Munchkin. And I'm afraid I've done something a little rash.'

'What?' Giles was alarmed. She hadn't beaten Martin to a pulp with the poker had she?

'I've offered her a lift with us. I know it's a cheek, because it's your car, but I felt so sorry for her.'

'Oh.' He did a quick calculation. If Munchkin came with them, he'd save on the cost of the petrol, recouping part of the money for the fine. He was suddenly more cheerful. 'No problem at all. The more the merrier.'

Miranda had casually picked up the passport lying on Pete's bed, hoping to see a photo of him. She met Giles's eyes. 'Yours is it?' He snatched it back. 'Giles, do you think I didn't know? And when I knew, that I cared two hoots? Rarely.'

'But . . .'

'Wonder if we'll need chains? It's coming down fast.' She

went over to the window. 'The fact that you're so successful despite everything is surely something to be rather proud of. Brilliant degree, excellent job, your politics. You've achieved far more than a twit like Charlie. Or me. The typist who arranges plane tickets.' She pulled a face at her reflection in the pane.

'I'm sorry about you and Charlie.'

'Thanks. I was too. Less so now. Thanks for arranging this week. It's helped me get things back in perspective.' She patted his good arm. 'You're a great friend to have.'

Nikki didn't bother to look round when Martin walked into their room. She carried on meticulously folding up her clothes, piled up high on the bed.

'Where's the kitchen sink?' he growled, stepping over her three huge Louis Vuitton bags. 'Why bring so much stuff? We're only away for a week.'

'Excuse me.' She reached past him and grabbed an armful of face-creams.

'What's eating you? It's not my fault about the bloody car window. Let's face it, you can always put on some more clothes if you're cold.'

'It's not the window.' She started to attack her hairbrush with a comb, the teeth becoming filled with long strands of shiny chestnut hair.

'Well, what then?' He stared at her. 'I'm sorry if we haven't lived up to your ladyship's high standards,' he mocked. 'We're not all used to moving in your illustrious circles. Then again, we're not all tarts, are we?'

She blushed. Why had she told him about David? 'Me being a tart doesn't bother you. If it does, leave.'

'Oh I get it,' said Martin. 'Decided my meal ticket doesn't go far enough, have we? Need a richer man to keep you?'

Nikki started putting her clothes in one of the bags. 'I can keep myself.'

'Who are you kidding?' he scoffed. 'One of your jackets would cost most people their month's salary.'

'And who has just paid your fine? Me. Who settled up after your stupid game of backgammon? Me. Who paid for my holiday? Me.' She hurled her shoes into another bag. 'I can keep myself, I don't need to put up with you. Fighting, chucking food, showing off, boasting. The police station was the last straw.' She knelt down and yanked at the zip. Martin grabbed her tiny wrist. 'Fuck off and pick on someone your own size, can't you?'

She was so venomous that he let her go. What had happened to the Nikki he'd arrived with, too nervous to open her mouth? The Nikki who'd used him as a shield to protect her? The vulnerable Nikki, so dependent she wouldn't have dreamt of criticising him, let alone telling him to leave her alone.

He sank down on the bed, knocking a pile of clothes to the floor. 'Sorry,' he said as she cursed and snatched them up. 'Sorry I've acted like a tit. Sorry I ever brought you here.'

'Done now, isn't it?' Her voice was brisk.

'Let's go tonight, shall we?' he pleaded. 'Just get out of here.'

'What's the point? It'll be freezing with that window. Anyway, what about Munchkin? She won't want to go.'

Martin groaned inwardly. He was going to have to make amends there as well. 'I think she's going with Miranda and Giles.'

'So it will just be the two of us. How nice.'

'There's no need to be sarcastic.'

'And there's no need to call me a tart.' She glanced at him. 'What's that mark? Someone else clocked you?'

Martin felt his tender jaw. It was lucky Jamie hadn't broken it. 'Nothing. Dirt, probably.'

'Done.' Nikki zipped up another bag. 'Talking of dirt, your scummy journalist friend Jack Mancini. Don't you ever dare think of breathing a hint about my business to him.'

*　　*　　*

Pete found Flora hidden away in the darkest corner of the Igloo, a shivering, lonely figure in the bar's cosy, fuggy hubbub. Taking shelter, warming themselves with *vins chauds*, everyone was excited about the snow. She had the dazed look of a trauma victim.

'Hello gorgeous. Come here often?' He sat on the bench beside her and put his arm round her. 'What's a nice girl like you doing in a place like this?'

'I'm not a nice girl,' said Flora woodenly, doing origami with her shredded beer mat. 'I'm a scruffy little scrubber from the back-arse of nowhere, who's completely up herself because she's landed a rich toff.'

'Whoever told you that has a premium line in bullshit.'

She shook her head, frowning, eyes fixed on the folding. 'That's me. The hick hack, Flora Rose. But Jamie wants to marry Flora Rosehagen, doesn't he?'

Pete had a glug of her whisky and called to the waiter for two more. 'You're freezing,' he said, rubbing her hands. 'Call this music?' Johnny Haliday was crooning in the background.

'Doesn't he, Pete?' Flora stared into his green-blue eyes. 'Jamie knows his worth. Great catch, charming, handsome, eligible. Jem, Fred, Jasper, everyone was stunned when he asked me to marry him. How could I of all people pull that one off?'

'Because he loves you.'

'Jamie loves someone who doesn't exist.'

The waiter set down their drinks, scowling at the shreds of paper littering the table.

'Don't pay any attention to Martin,' said Pete. 'Shit stirrer. The guy's a heap of creep.'

'That first night.' Flora squeezed her eyes shut. 'I overheard you all. I thought I heard Jamie saying he was marrying me because he'd never get bored. I should've heard seat on the board.'

'Flora, we were pissed up. Macho posturing. We should've just got out our dicks and compared sizes.'

'But Jamie did say he was marrying me for a seat on the board. And I guess it wasn't the first time he said it, either.'

Pete held her hand more tightly. 'It wasn't. Sorry to be brutal.'

'It's all right.' She fiddled with her engagement ring. 'I've already been sick. Retched my guts out. Wondering if my meeting with Jamie at the cottage was the happy coincidence that I'd always imagined.'

'Don't.' Pete gently wiped away her tears and hugged her. 'He's not like that.'

'Isn't he? What was in it for him? He knows his worth. And he knows my worth, not that I knew it. Apparently Julius Rosehagen is intrigued, curious. Natural, I guess, we're cousins, though we've never met. Jamie was going to exploit my family past to promote his future at the bank. He was never marrying me, he was marrying a Rosehagen.'

Pete pushed the hair out of his eyes. 'Flora, sure you're not seeing this all wrong?'

'Sweet Pete.' She smiled wanly. 'Sweet, sweet Pete. If you honestly thought I was wrong, you'd be telling me I was wrong. Not asking. So how come you're not telling me I'm wrong? Maybe because you know that I'm right.'

'I know Jamie loves you.'

'What was the first thing Jamie told you about me, Pete? Weird friends? Awful clothes? Hates skiing? Or my connection with the bank?'

He wanted to deny it so much. His good, kind heart wanted to make it easier on her. He hesitated. Too long.

'Another hug,' he said. 'Tight. Tighter.'

They clung to one another like waifs in a storm, Flora was rocked in his arms.

How could she have been so blind? That meeting at the cottage the first Sunday of spring had never been the happy chance she'd believed. Jamie had known exactly who she was and decided to look her over. Look her over and overlook for the short term the bits of her that didn't fit in. The clothes, the unsettling friends like Fred Quince, the job, all the bits she'd change to please him. She'd been malleable, eager to please, swept off her feet by his looks and his lifestyle and his charm. That graceful, easy-going charm that hid his cynical, calculating heart.

Jamie had wanted to marry Flora Rosehagen and further his career. Even knowing her would have intrigued her distant cousin Julius, set Jamie apart from the scores of his equally ambitious colleagues who were all after that seat on the board. You didn't work at Rosehagen's unless you wanted to succeed very badly.

'I must look like a car crash. Crying my eyes out.'

'You're still beautiful.' He kissed the top of her head.

'Liar.'

'Jamie's my best friend. He's been good to me, so this is difficult.' Pete frowned.

'Difficult to see his cynical, calculating heart,' said Flora bitterly.

'Sssh. Jamie was never going to fall in love and marry . . .'

'A scruffy little scrubber from the back-arse of nowhere.'

'Will you be quiet? He'd never allow himself to end up with someone who couldn't, well, bring something to the party. And why not? He's hosting quite a party. He's got a lot to offer.' Pete shrugged. 'Even if you don't like one of the reasons why he fell in love with you, he loves you Flora.'

'But.'

'But, he does.'

She shook her head. 'Ever been in an earthquake?'

'No. But I've been told often enough I make the earth move.' He grinned, his grip round her tightening.

'Bet you have.' She smiled forlornly. 'Shall we get very drunk together?'

'Love to. But you won't, not in your state. Back to the earthquake.'

'If you're in one,' Flora frowned, playing with his fingers, 'it must take time to trust the ground beneath your feet again. If I could've been so very wrong about Jamie, the man I was meant to spend the rest of my life with, what else, who else, have I been so very wrong about?'

'Zero? Heaps? Everything? Nothing?' Pete shrugged. 'Been there, done it, worn the scars. She didn't do it because of me. Did Jamie tell you?'

'No. He's never said a word.'

'That's good of him. Not that it matters. Well, it does. Trust. There is so much good in Jamie, Flora. She was seeing someone else for months. Acting the drama queen when she was with me in public. Possessive, jealous, almost bashing any woman who came within a five mile radius. Screaming scenes in restaurants, in clubs, in the bar, that I didn't care, that I was cheating on her. And back home, the ice maiden. So when she did it, after he dumped her, I was blamed.'

'Couldn't you put the record straight?' asked Flora.

'What for? Cause more grief and guilt? The guy's married, got kids. Nice bloke, actually. We meet. There's this strange, strong bond between us.' He held her more tightly.

'Cheat on you?' wondered Flora. 'Why?'

Pete whispered a name in her ear. 'You can understand the attraction.'

Flora was stunned.

'Can't bear to hear their music now. Shrinkie says I'll have come to terms with things when I can.'

'Shrinkie?'

'Counseller. Been seeing him twice a week. Sydney sandstone me, looks tough but easily crumbles. Anyway. Enough. Let's fret about you.'

'Sweet Pete.' Flora twisted one of his blond curls. She sighed. 'What happened to Jamie?'

'You ran off and hid; he's still seeking, I guess.'

'He's probably back at the chalet sniffing away his sorrows.'

'Let's go back.' Idly, Pete plaited a lock of her hair. 'Talk to Jamie. Give him a chance to explain.'

They strolled through the snowy streets arm in arm. Both were subdued, pensive. 'Will you come skiing again?' asked Pete, breaking the silence.

'Maybe.' With Stefan? Could she trust him, either? All the certainties she'd felt had been shattered.

'Not a no, then. Something positive's come out of this week.' He squeezed her.

'If nothing else, I can parallel.'

Her skis, along with Pete and Jamie's, were in the Porsche. They had to be taken back. Inside the brightly lit hire shop, the Beach Boys were still playing. Flora eased off her red boots for the last time. Bliss.

'I never want to set foot in them again. All yours,' she said to the Carrot.

He grinned. 'You skied?' She nodded. 'Every day? Honestly? Enjoy? Great.'

'This place must be run by a dominatrix,' said Flora, signing a credit card slip and scowling at her boots. 'Pay for the pleasure of being tortured.'

'Into that, Flora?' Pete winked suggestively. 'Bit of M and S?'

'Marks and Spencer?' she giggled. 'Probably more into S and M. I hate shopping.'

The snow was still falling thickly as Pete drove through St Marie and up the dark mountain road to the chalet. The headlights picked out millions of flakes raining down like white confetti.

Flora eased herself out of the car, the ground under her feet a soft carpet, the icy crystals melting on her face and in her hair. 'It's so beaut—'

'Got you,' yelled Pete. She screamed as he pounced on her and stuffed a handful of snow onto her bare back.

'Stop,' shrieked Flora as he rubbed it in until it was nothing more than water. Struggling to escape, she twisted and turned and finally slipped onto the white ground.

'Howzat,' cried Pete, kneeling down and scouring her face with snow. Laughing, she managed to pick up a handful and shove it into his mouth, then down his neck, then under his fleece.

Hearing the yells and shrieks, Giles pulled back his bedroom curtains and peered out, surprised to see Flora and Pete rolling over and over in the snow. Soaked through, clutching one another, they lay back laughing hysterically as the flakes rained down on them.

He sighed wistfully. They'd clearly been having a great day.

They came into the sitting room, like Arctic explorers at the end of a long march. Nikki briefly smiled up at them and returned to *The Female Eunuch*. Her pink cropped twinset showed off her ironing board stomach, browner and flatter than any of the models' in the copy of *Vogue* at her elbow.

Flora awarded herself a Brownie's badge for being considerate, when she asked if she could have a bath. She lay back in the steaming, scented water.

Stefan seemed so far away, much further than Paris. The scrap of paper with his address that she'd valued more than her engagement ring was meaning less and less. He'd said that he was her salvation, he'd offered her the whole world. Another empty fantasy? Had telling her to dream beautiful dreams been a prophesy?

Obviously she was a giant D for Dunce when it came to judging character.

Someone knocked at the door. 'Can I come in?' said Jamie.

'No. Wait,' called Flora. 'I'll come out.'

Ten minutes later she went into their room and closed the door. He was sitting in the armchair. His blond hair was sleeked back, he was wearing a blue-black cashmere jersey, Guccis. A man wearing success, as at ease as if he were already chairman.

'Have you decided?' He sounded as if it were no more important than if she were choosing a main course from a menu.

Flora took off her engagement ring. 'Catch.'

He caught. 'Pity.'

'Isn't it?' She sat on the bed.

'Yes. I love you so much.'

'Me? Or Flora Rosehagen?'

'I came to see you at the cottage that Sunday because of your link with the bank. So?' Jamie shrugged. 'It was the catalyst for our meeting. You're ending everything because of a catalyst?'

Flora was taken aback. 'There's also the tiny matter of you trying to get me killed today.'

'Don't exaggerate.' Jamie sighed in exasperation. 'I was jealous, more angry than I'd ever been in my life and I over-reacted. Your useless performance on skis seemed to confirm all those vile rumours about you sleeping with Stefan. Later, you proved me wrong. Wrote that massive "up yours Jamie" in the snow. Can't you start seeing things from my point of view?'

Flora hesitated. 'I suppose so.'

'To understand all is to forgive all apparently,' said Jamie. 'I was wrong, I admit it. You can parallel and I can be very sorry. Understand and forgive, Flora.'

'And if I can, what about the rest?'

'Yes, I was intrigued to meet a Rosehagen. I didn't know who was going to be at the cottage. An Anna, a Miranda or, God forbid, a Nikki or a Munchkin. If any of them had been Julius Rosehagen's daughter, let alone some unknown distant cousin, do you honestly think I'd have bothered? Christ, Flora, I might be ambitious, but I'm not Mephistopheles.'

'Faust,' corrected Flora. 'He was the one who sold his soul.'

Jamie laughed. 'See? That's why I love you. The girl at the cottage could easily have turned out to be brain-dead or a dog or boring. Anything.'

'Or a scruffy little scrubber from the back-arse of nowhere.'

'Angel, I don't do scrubbers,' said Jamie loftily. Despite herself, Flora giggled. 'Whoever has been putting that sort of nonsense into your head?'

'Martin actually.' Flora shrugged.

'He's another thing you were right about. Like you were right in saying we should never have come on this holiday. Fucking disaster from start to finish.' Suddenly, he crossed over to her, knelt down and kissed her bare feet. 'I'm so sorry.'

'Stop it.' Flora laughed. 'It tickles.'

'Mwah. Mwah. Mwah.' He looked up at her imploringly. 'Flora. Please. Don't end it now. Things will look very different when we're home. Back in the real world. Please. Give us another chance. No more charlie, chucked it away.'

'Frightened of getting busted by Customs?' asked Flora dryly.

'I don't do getting busted either. No. New year, new nose. New liver too. Please, angel. Let's at least get home so we can both start thinking straight. If, after a week you say it's all over, so be it. But I think we owe each other seven days. Strange things happen when you're away. The unreality of it all. People do stupid things. All those holiday romances that wither into nothing.' Their eyes met for the briefest moment. She wondered how much he guessed. 'Flora. You're deciding something that affects our lives forever. Give it a real week.'

She looked at him. 'But I don't . . .'

He put the engagement ring back on her finger. The diamonds sparkled in the lamplight. 'You do. A week. In exchange for our whole lives.'

He was right. She needed a dose of reality, not a beautiful

dream world conjured up by a beautiful dreamer. She owed it to both of them, to all three of them.

'A week,' agreed Flora quietly.

As everyone gathered by the fireside, Giles cleared himself a space at the table and sat down with a calculator, paper and pen. It was time to work out the figures. He'd been appalled to hear from the twins that more than 200 bottles of beer had been drunk, on top of some duty free and five extra litres of wine each night. 'Are you quite sure?'

'Quite sure,' said Alice in a tone that brooked no argument. 'We've got the receipts and the empties are down in the storeroom. Have to take them to the bottle bank tomorrow, there's no more room. Probably need two trips. Go and count if you don't believe us.'

'No, no. Take your word for it.' He'd backed hurriedly out of the kitchen.

'Take the minutes, shall I?' Miranda sat beside him, prepared to offer comradely help if there was going to be any trouble about money. Her show of bustling efficiency disguised her elation at being ambushed by Pete in the upstairs passageway. He'd made her promise she'd come out to dinner on Friday.

Hugging herself with excitement, she took some paper. 'Now, everyone must write down their telephone calls. Hetty, do you have a list of any breakages?'

Last down, Martin switched on the stereo, but turned it down when Giles and Miranda and Nikki complained they couldn't hear themselves think. He then tried to get back into Munchkin's good books by offering to get her another drink.

'No thanks.' She forced her lips into a smile. 'By the way, I've accepted Miranda's offer of a lift. Giles only lives round the corner from me, so it's so much easier. I'm sure you and Nikki would prefer to be on your own.'

Nikki looked up and glared at Martin.

'About what I said earlier,' Martin lowered his voice, 'no offence, eh?'

'Long forgotten,' said Munchkin airily, enough blubber, enough blubber going through her head. She was wearing slimming navy blue and had taken extra care with her make-up. Bubbly not blubbery she told herself.

'Two hundred beers?' exclaimed Jamie, looking over Giles's shoulder.

'Quite restrained,' said Pete. 'Twenty each.'

'Flora doesn't drink beer.'

'Neither does Nikki,' called Martin quickly.

'I've had three,' said Anna, looking up from *Vogue*. 'Written them down.'

'And I've had two,' piped up Munchkin, wishing she hadn't because they were so calorie laden.

'Are you sure?' Sam sounded suspicious.

'Yes,' she snapped.

'Miranda?' asked Giles.

'Couple if that.'

'Why not divide the total between the five of us men,' suggested Pete.

Giles frowned. 'But Anna's already admitted she's had three and I've only had 17.'

'Bullshit,' declared Sam, standing by the fireplace.

'I've written all mine down.' Giles was indignant. 'Look if you don't believe me.'

'Let's see.' Sam marched across to the dining table and snatched up the exercise book. 'You liar. What about the night we played the flour game. They're not here.'

'Yes they are.'

'One is. One. You had about six.'

'Four,' conceded Giles grudgingly.

'Rubbish,' jeered Sam. 'How can he say he kept a record? Glad you're not my accountant.'

'With the parlous state of your finances, you couldn't possibly afford me.'

The pair of them glared at one another. 'Refill anyone?' asked Munchkin, trying to calm them down. 'Giles? Sam?'

'I think Sam does have a point,' said Pete.

Giles's eyes went from face to face, heart sinking. 'Fine.' He sighed martyr-like. 'We'll divide the beers between five, excluding what the girlies have owned up to.' Scowling he began to stab his calculator buttons.

'Flora. Pete. Jamie.' Miranda tapped the paper with a pen. 'Telephone calls. Local ones count too.'

'Haven't made any,' said Flora.

'What about the airport and the station?' said Giles without looking up.

'Sorry. Forgot.' Her apologetic smile faded when she caught sight of Munchkin's scowl. She knew Munchkin was regretting the fact she hadn't left.

Anna began counting on her fingers. Ten calls, all lasting less than a minute, then the eleventh she'd made that morning. If only those eight reassuring, piece-of-mind minutes had come earlier in the week.

'Smug chops,' said Sam, noticing her grinning to herself.

'Finally made contact?' guessed Miranda, when Anna handed her back the paper.

'Um. This morning.'

'Jolly good,' mumbled Giles, staring at the exchange rates in the *Telegraph*. 'God, the pound is falling through the floor. Contact with whatsisname? Tom?'

'Yes.' Anna took a deep breath. 'With what's-her-name, actually.'

Miranda frowned.

'Her?' Giles's finger hit the clear button by mistake. He stared up at Anna. 'Tom. The boyfriend.'

'Tom. Thomasina. The girlfriend,' corrected Anna, aware that an unnatural quiet had fallen.

'But, but . . . You can't be,' blurted out Munchkin.

'Imogen.' Sam was horrorstruck. 'Jesus, she can't . . .'

'Don't worry,' Anna spun round. 'Your sister's straight.'

'Sure? The parents would get her exorcised.'

'Thanks, Sam,' sighed Anna.

Miranda's fingers flew to her pearls. Anna. One of them. Disgusting. They'd been sharing a room. How many times had she wandered about practically starkers? She could've been pounced on in the middle of the night . . .

'Don't worry,' Anna eyed her defiantly, 'you're not my type.'

'I, um . . . Er . . . Rarely, I, er . . .' Blushing scarlet, Miranda squirmed.

'Bit of girly action, eh?' guffawed Martin, winking at Pete. 'Can we watch?'

'Shut up, you,' ordered Nikki, glaring at him. Anna's defiance was crumbling. 'Ignore him, Anna love, he's a prat. Quite frankly, the way you men have carried on sometimes is enough to turn any girl queer.'

'Hear, hear,' piped up Flora, earning herself a look of horror from Jamie.

Anna began to smile a small smile, then all the fight left her. Standing in the middle of the room, she felt marooned. So alone. They had tried to cover it up, but their reaction had been immediate. Disgust, revulsion.

'Don't cry,' said Pete, putting his arms around her.

'More logs,' said Jamie disappearing downstairs, unable to cope with another scene and yet another weeping woman. It was all far too much.

Hugging Anna, Pete peered over her shoulder. 'Munchkin? Miranda? What's your problem? OK, we all know Giles is a narrow-minded, unenlightened, conformist bigot. That goes with the territory, but . . .'

'Pardon?' protested Giles, white-lashed eyes blinking.

'Well, stop gawping. Anna hasn't got the plague.' Exasperated, Pete pulled a face.

'Haven't I?' Sniffing, Anna took off her glasses and wiped away her tears with the back of her hand. 'That's not what my parents will think. If I ever have the guts to tell them.'

'Perhaps they already know,' suggested Pete gently. 'Is that why you worked in that hostel over Christmas? To avoid them?'

'Partly.' She nodded. 'They'd disown me.'

'Bet they wouldn't. But if they do, next December call me. Orphans' Christmas, OK?' He squeezed her arm.

'Or call me,' offered Nikki. 'Guts? You come out to this bunch of homophobes and you think you're gutless?'

'Homophobe? I've got nothing against gays,' squawked Munchkin. 'Some of my best friends . . .'

'Nikki, rarely,' Miranda interrupted. 'I never said . . .'

Looking from one to the other, Anna wondered what had possessed her to confess. 'Not too long ago you wouldn't have had to pretend that you didn't mind, that you didn't find people like me loathesome. Now you've got to show that you're tolerant. Progress of sorts. I guess.' She sounded bitter.

Sam took a swig. 'How about a bit of tolerance from you, Anna? How long have I known you? Good few years now. Bit of a bombshell, perhaps I need some time to adjust?'

'Adjust to what, Sam?' demanded Nikki. 'Honestly, your mind can't be as small as the rest of you. It's no big deal, is it?'

'It is for me,' said Anna, a picture of desolation. 'Confusing, lonely, feeling a misfit.'

Miranda suddenly felt very sorry. One's love-life could be a nightmare at the best of times, without all the added complications that Anna must have gone through. She got up. 'More drinks anyone?' She squeezed Anna's hand. 'Actually, Anna, I'm dead cross that you don't fancy me. Bring Tom to dins when we get back.'

'Really?' said Anna. 'Or rather rarely?'

'And just because I'm not your type, doesn't mean you can take the piss.' Miranda winked. 'Gin ton? Flora, whisky?'

'Thanks,' said Flora. 'And let's drink to saying it loud, saying it proud. As my friend Fred believes.'

'Good bloke,' said Pete. 'Though I couldn't take up his offer of going on the Pride march.'

'Thank God for that,' hurrumped Giles.

'You? Gay Pride?' called Martin incredulously. 'In your case, Pete, you would've been sued for trespassing. Or for breaking the Trade Descriptions Act.'

Giles looked up in alarm. 'You would, wouldn't you, Pete?' After Anna, things might not be all that they appeared.

'Definitely.' Pete grinned.

'Phew,' said Giles. 'Why these people have to make such a song and dance about their sexual orientation, I don't know.'

'Perhaps because of blinkered, prejudiced people like you,' said Anna.

Coming back with a basket of logs, Jamie grimaced. They weren't still going on about it?

'Like most people, I am neither blinkered nor prejudiced.' Giles sighed. 'Personally Anna, I don't care if you're into men, women or llamas. I don't want you to know what goes on in my bedroom. And I don't want to know what goes on in yours. Doesn't make a jot of difference to me. And I think you'll find most people share my opinion. The British are a tolerant people . . .'

'Here we go.' Sam started humming 'Rule Britannia.'

'The British are a tolerant people,' continued Giles. 'Just don't bother us, rub our noses in it, or frighten the horses or the children. Live and let live. Understood?' Anna looked startled.

'Live and let live,' said Anna in a small voice.

'You've made a brave choice and good luck to you.' His eyes returned to his calculator. 'I mean it.'

'Thanks, Giles.' Anna was touched.

'Not much goes on in your bedroom, mate,' said Sam.

Giles scowled at him. 'Right,' he said, sitting back. 'The beer bill for us five at today's exchange rate in the paper is £35.37.'

'Not bad,' agreed Pete and Jamie.

Sam disagreed, but was comforted that Giles hadn't wriggled out of paying his share.

'Is the phone bill sorted?' asked Giles. 'I think we should divide the wine and the breakages between us. Not the table repair. You'll be sent a bill for that when you get home, Munchkin.'

Munchkin blushed. Flora who was about to protest that she wasn't responsible for any broken anything was silenced by a 'don't start' look from Jamie.

After the figures were totalled and cheques handed over, Giles moved to the sofa and sat beside Anna, who showed him pictures of Japanese designer suits and teased him about buying one.

Giles brushed at his burgundy cords. 'Certainly not. Just look at this chap.' He pointed to a photograph in disgust. 'Hair practically down to his waist, earrings, and my God is he wearing a skirt? No. Thank heavens for that.' He held the magazine out to Flora who studied the opposite page. 'What sort of get up do you call that?'

'Drop-dead gorgeous.'

'Where? Let's see. Oh, isn't he?' Miranda moved next to her. 'A-mazing. Reminds me of thingy, your ski instructor, Flora.'

'Does a bit, doesn't he, Anna?' agreed Nikki. 'Look at those cheekbones.'

Flora stiffened, praying Jamie hadn't heard.

Alice beat the gong and with regret they all tore their eyes from the magazine and sat down giggling.

Wine was poured and bread passed round. Having run out of recipes, the twins decided on jambon au gratin again.

Halfway through the telephone rang. Hetty picked it up. Sticking her finger in her ear, she screwed up her face in concentration. 'Bad line. *Je regrette* . . . *Qui?* . . . Speak up, can't you? . . . *Qui* . . . *Non. Pas ici.*' Her voice became louder. 'Wrong number. You've got the wrong number.'

Shaking her head, she replaced the receiver. 'Mad,' she said. 'Mad Frenchman. Kept on saying he had a message for Saskia and that he loved her so much and they'd meet soon. Sounds as if he was calling from an airport or something. We've never had a Saskia here, have we Al?'

'No,' said Alice from the kitchen. 'Perhaps it's one of the next clients. Unusual name.'

'Rembrandt's wife,' said Anna. 'Rembrandt the painter,' she explained to Sam.

'I know,' he snapped. 'The Nightwatchmen. Saw it in the Riksmuseum in Amsterdam.'

Anna was startled. 'Gosh, I'm impressed.'

'By mistake,' added Sam. 'Stoned off my face and ended up in the wrong place.'

Flora froze. Amsterdam. The call had to be from Stefan. He must have arrived in Paris. Her heart pounded. She glanced at Jamie, wondering if he had guessed.

Giles cut through the ham one handed. 'Hell,' he muttered as sauce splattered onto the table cloth.

'Don't worry,' said Anna, glancing up at the red soup stain on the wall. 'Food seems to go everywhere but men's mouths here.'

'Tuck in.' Jamie nudged Sam. 'Wonder what the grub's like in French prisons.' Sam choked and reached for some water. 'French porridge, yuk. Should've seen or rather heard Anna, Giles. Marvellous. We'd still be stuck there without her.'

She smiled shyly as everyone raised their glasses to her. 'It was nothing. I'd like to propose a toast to Giles who worked so hard to organise everything. Lovely holiday.'

'Hear hear,' said Jamie.

'Well played, Giles,' said Miranda.

He beamed at the circle of smiling faces. Sam led a chorus of Jolly Good Fellow.

'We must all have a get-together when we get back,' said Munchkin, producing a camera. 'Piccy time. Hetty, Alice? Can you come in?'

They stood by the table as Miranda thanked them for an absolutely super week. 'You've looked after us so well, the food's been wonderful and you've kept the chalet beautifully.'

'Surprised sometimes that anything was left standing to be kept so beautifully,' said Hetty.

'What time are you leaving tomorrow?' asked Alice.

'Oh, can't wait to be rid of us, eh?' said Giles heartily. Catching sight of their faces, his smile faded.

Alice cleared the plates and Hetty brought in huge bowls of pasta. 'This time tomorrow we should almost be home,' said Sam. 'Well, we'll be in the Porsche, won't we, Pete? Not sure about you lot.'

'Don't be beastly.' Miranda reproved him. 'There's nothing wrong with my driving.'

'Nothing at all if you learnt to take your foot off the brake.'

'Race you, Miranda,' said Pete grinning. 'Fancy a flutter?'

Miranda blushed, remembering what happened after their last bet.

'Back to work.' Pete yawned, shaking the hair from his eyes.

'Busy week?' asked Jamie.

'Doubt it. No one's boozing in January. Still, should hear about the other place.'

'What's this?' Sam was curious.

'Pub off the Fulham Road. Prime site, but lively as a morgue. Customers are two winos and a dog. Huge potential. Got my eye on it.'

'The Pete Logan empire expands,' said Giles. 'So we can expect an invitation to the opening night, can we?'

'Sure. If it happens.' Wrinkling his crooked nose, Pete turned to Sam. 'I know you're looking for a proper job and this is probably a bit of a come-down, but fancy doing a bit of managing for me? Until you can find something?'

'Seriously?' gasped Sam.

'Hopefully, I'm going to be busy with this new place,' said Pete. 'Slim's leaving next week and I need someone I can trust until I find a replacement.'

'You trust me?'

'Course I do. Will you think about it?'

'You'd be great at it,' said Munchkin, squeezing Sam's arm. 'Could make some contacts.'

'Thanks, Pete.' Sam smiled. 'Thanks a bloody million. I'd love to. Help pay the rent, eh, Rachman? I mean Giles.'

Finishing his pudding Jamie got up and went to the window. The snow had stopped falling, but Les Diables were invisible, swallowed up by the black of the night. He threw another log on the fire and settled down in an armchair, a glass of brandy at his side.

'Night.' Martin went up to bed.

'He's been quiet. Not ill, is he Nikki?' asked Munchkin.

Nikki shrugged.

'Music anyone?' She curled up next to Sam on the sofa, deciding to have an early night. She was exhausted, her body aching from all the skiing.

'Something gentle,' pleaded Nikki, returning to *The Female Eunuch*.

Pete pulled up a chair next to Jamie and set up the backgammon pieces. Munchkin rummaged through the CDs. 'How about some Mozart? Yours isn't it, Flora?'

She nodded. The haunting sound of the violin concerto was all the more welcome as she'd been bracing herself for a blast of techno.

Miranda spotted the pack of cards. 'Anyone play bridge?'

'Marvellous idea,' said Giles. 'I do. Anna does. Flora? Up for a rubber, as they say?'

She looked at the three of them doubtfully. 'I haven't played for ages. And I was always useless.'

'Nonsense,' said Miranda. 'That's what you said about your skiing. Let's cut for partners.' She glanced across at Pete. Flora looked at Jamie.

As the flames from the fire danced to the music, peace broke out in Chalet Juliette.

Thursday Night, March

❦

The new red Ferrari reversed noisily into the space outside the bar off the Fulham Road. Their chatter faltering, some of those near the windows peered out into the rain-drenched street to admire it. Others turned their backs, determined not to give the owner the chance to gloat.

Munchkin waved a canapé in greeting to someone across the room, then hastily re-focussed on the woman beside her. 'Where were we?'

'Cannes.' Wendy White, a *Capital Chronicle* diarist fanned herself, praying that her foundation was holding up in the heat. The place was packed with far too many beautiful people. 'Well, you were.'

'Oh, just for a boring day's research,' said Munchkin, noting the tone of slight resentment. 'I'm organising a launch down there in May. Awayday for the press. Fly to Nice, taxi along the coast, have lunch. Shall I ink you in? Call you tomorrow and confirm. We must do lunch. Any chance that tonight gets a teensy weensy mention?'

Wendy held out her glass to a passing waiter for a refill. 'Nice place, nice party, but to be honest . . .' She shook her head.

'Feature on London's most gorgeous bar owners?' pressed Munchkin.

'The most gorgeous.' Sighing, Wendy gazed longingly in Pete's direction. 'Definitely.' Her eyes widened. 'Look who's here.'

The chatter hushed momentarily as Martin strode through the throng. Deeply tanned, wearing a perfectly cut black suit, eyes shrewd in his hawk face, he had the air of a mafia boss who could buy the place fifty times over. Which he could.

'Hello, Munchkin. Lovely as ever.' Smiling, he gave her a hug. 'Bloody Sam beat me to the prize. How was the States?'

'Busy.' Turning pink, Munchkin gingerly hugged him back. 'Didn't expect to see you here.'

'Giles mentioned something at his office the other day. Invite probably got lost in the move. You must come down. Spend the weekend. Play some tennis. Have a swim.'

'Lovely,' said Munchkin. 'Oh by the way, Martin June, Wendy White.' She added casually, 'Wendy works on the *Capital Chronicle*.'

Wendy smiled as if she were in a toothpaste ad. 'Been anywhere nice?'

Martin stiffened. 'Must go and grab a drink. Excuse me.'

'Have I got bad breath or something?' Watching him disappear through the crowd, Wendy bristled.

'He doesn't like the Press.' Munchkin was apologetic.

'Loves us if he's earning out of us. Must've got a fortune for the story about his girlfriend.' She got out her notebook. 'Didn't realise you knew him. Any idea where he's been?'

Alarmed, Munchkin choked on another canapé. 'Sorry, Wend.'

'What about Nikki Solange? Where's she gone to ground?'

'No idea.'

Wendy's overplucked eyebrows shot up like Tintin's. 'You know her then?'

'Um. We've met.' This wasn't the sort of publicity Munchkin had had in mind.

'Come on,' wheedled Wendy, notebook back in her bag. 'Off the record. Just to satisfy my curiosity. What's she really like?'

'Well,' Munchkin lowered her voice. 'Strictly entre nous . . .'

*　　*　　*

Miranda caught sight of Martin advancing towards her, went into reverse and slalomed round a waiter. What was he doing here? PNG, he was meant to be NFIed. Mentally she heard Pete telling her to stop speaking Sloane. Persona Non Grata, Martin was Not Fucking Invited. Gatecrashing. The gall.

Pete did a double-take as Martin grabbed his sleeve. 'Didn't expect to see you here. Thought you were sunbaking in the Caribbean.'

'Got bored,' said Martin. 'Should've gone skiing. Anyway, the car was delivered on Tuesday.' Grinning, he held out his keyring with the prancing horse on it.

'Nice.' Pete sounded unimpressed.

'Fancy a test drive?'

'Heard you've got yourself a new place.'

'Um. Didn't realise a pool needs so much upkeep. How about you and Mirandy coming down this weekend? Swim, play some tennis . . .'

'Thanks. But we're going away.' Pete glanced round and smiled fondly at Miranda, who'd escaped to the other side of the room. She looked five years younger and ten times better. Out were the headband, the pearls, the loafers and the gilt buttoned navy blazer. Her hair was blonder, longer. Her LBD, (Sloane was catching) her little black dress showed off her excellent legs.

'The Pete Logan empire expands, just as Giles predicted,' said Martin.

'Um.' He whispered to a passing waiter to refill some glasses. His jaw hurt from smiling at people who congratulated him as they swooped past. It had been a gruelling few months, finalising the lease, sorting out the licence, refurbishing the place which hadn't been touched for decades. Of course, everyone was enjoying themselves tonight, it was a free party. Would they be back as paying punters?

Martin scowled at Wendy. 'See you're hoping for some free publicity.'

'Munchkin is organising the marketing. She's been brilliant.

Came up with a stack of ideas.' Pete stared down at Martin. 'Anyway, we can't all get paid a Ferrari for getting our name in the papers.'

Martin's eyes narrowed. 'I didn't.'

They were interrupted by one of the waitresses saying the cigarette machine was playing up. 'Better sort it out,' said Pete.

'Some weekend soon?' called out Martin, but Pete ignored him.

Sam and Giles were standing by the bar, catching up on their news. They'd seen little of one another in recent weeks. Since they'd got back from skiing, Sam had spent most of his time at Munchkin's, when he wasn't managing Pete's place in the City.

'Got my rent cheque, Rachman? I mean Giles.' Sam grinned.

'Yes,' sighed Giles. His white-lashed eyes lit up as he caught sight of a tall rangy blonde in an ultra-short, black suit. Better pins than Mirandy's. Noticing a photographer approach through the throng, he rearranged his features and hastily lowered his glass. Having just done a presentation course for Prospective Parliamentary Candidates, he knew how to pose.

'You've got that constipated Giles Thomas MP face on again,' said Sam.

Giles glared. Would Sam always take the piss? Disappointingly, the camera was raised in the direction of the blonde and the snapper pressed past him to get her name.

'Oh come on.' Sam smiled. 'Seriously Giles, well done. Can I come and have lunch at the Commons?'

'Years yet. If we make it.'

'Come off it. Nice safe seat in true-blue Hampshire. You'll need a fleet of juggernauts to deliver your votes to the count. In fact, why bother counting them?'

Giles was shocked. 'Democracy would hardly be best served . . .'

'Only joking.' Sam pulled a face. 'You're not on *Newsnight* yet.'

'No. Not yet.' Giles smiled elatedly. For the past week he'd been hugging himself with joy since the gruelling selection. A tricky part had been when a terrifying biddy wanted to know why he wasn't married, declaring that stable family life was the foundation of the nation and the Party couldn't afford any further episodes such as the unfortunate Thone scandal. Fortunately a buffer had shouted her down and pointed out that David Thone was supposed to have been happily married.

Another buffer had harrumphed that Giles was hardly the most local of candidates and what possible use could he be to the constituency?

'Madam chairman, ladies and gentlemen, if only I'd been privileged enough to have grown up on the Test with a fly rod in my hand, but . . .' Giles had launched on his well rehearsed but impassioned speech about Britain, the land of opportunity, impressing the committee with his fervour. He had played up his background and childhood, so that the levels of deprivation had sounded like something out of Dickens.

Giles's face lit up again as Miranda bustled over.

'Hello, you two. Mwah, mwah. Got enough to drink?' Assuming the role of hostess, Miranda was anxious. 'How do you think it's going?'

'It'll be fine, if the City's anything to go by,' said Sam. 'Takings are through the roof.'

Miranda smiled at him fondly. 'Thanks to you. Honestly Sam, you were wasted being a boring headhunter.'

'Wasted is right. Permanently pissed.' Sam grinned. 'Hi babe, I've got access to all these international financiers, want a bottle of poo? Anyway, the bar's earning enough for Pete to spoil you on that long weekend in Gstaad.'

'He's told you about it?' Miranda grinned delightedly. 'He needs a break, poor thing, he's ab-so-lute-ly ex-haust-ed.'

Her eyes followed him across the other side of the room. Some of her friends kept warning her that she was on the rebound and should be careful. She wondered what sort of friends they were, especially the friends who'd called up out of the blue to ask if she'd seen Charlie's news in the paper. Their feigned concern was almost as sickening as Charlie's announcement of his engagement on St Valentine's day.

But the whole business had washed over her, because she'd been so blissed out with the arrival of Pete's three dozen red roses. 'Can you come to dins on Saturday, Giles?'

'Sorry.' He shook his head. 'Spending the day with my folks, then shooting down to the constituency.' He'd seen quite a bit of his parents since returning from France. 'How's the new job?'

'Brilliant. I'm so glad I moved.' Miranda seemed as sparkling as the champagne in her glass. 'Nils wants me to go to Copenhagen with him on Monday.'

'Private jet set.' Giles was impressed. 'Nils is it now?'

'Oh, he's not a bit stuffy. Actually, serious sweetie.'

'Well, watch it with these tycoons,' advised Sam. 'Look what happened to Nikki.'

'You know he's here?' hissed Miranda.

'Your boss? Do introduce.' Giles immediately thought he might make a useful contact.

'Not Nils. Martin.'

'What?' Giles was alarmed.

'Really?' said Sam. 'Thought he'd want to lie low for a bit. Like, forever.'

'Awful business.' Giles gave a disapproving hurrumph. 'Thone's a huge contributor to Party funds.'

' "In the Rough", remember?' asked Sam. 'The caption under the photo of him and the Prime Minister playing golf?'

Giles winced.

'Well, I thought it was appalling that the Royal Family got dragged into it,' said Miranda. 'They've got quite enough on their plate.'

'That bit about the chocolate éclairs.' Sam sniggered. 'And Madame Puss, the hooker. My cane stroked Thone until he purred.'

'Shares in Thone Corp have taken another tumble after his interview last night,' said Giles sagely. 'Can't think what he was playing at. Never complain, never explain. My sources think he'll have to resign.'

'Your sources?' scoffed Sam. 'It was in tonight's paper.'

'Poor Nikki,' clucked Miranda.

'Changed your tune, haven't you?' Sam raised an eyebrow. 'Rarely. Model, indeed. Didn't cross my mind that she was that sort of model.' He mimicked Miranda's accent. 'No wonder she has all those clothes and a Mercedes. How could she? How could the cheap, nasty trollop sell her story? Daddy goes shooting with Thone, he'll go ballistic.'

Miranda looked sheepish.

'No poor Nikkis then. Come on, Miranda, admit it,' said Sam.

She thought back to her reaction a month ago. 'That was before Flora . . .'

'Hi, guys. Miranda.'

As Martin kissed her, Miranda's blush deepened.

'Martin.' Giles looked at him, then at the photographer. Agitated, he edged away slightly.

There was an awkward silence. The three were struck by how prosperous Martin appeared. His hands gripped the glass. His nails seemed manicured, which made Miranda feel slightly queasy.

'Well, well, Mr Kiss, tell and sell,' said Sam coldly. 'I should be a poet.'

'Like Pete,' said Giles distractedly, worried in case the snapper caught him and Martin together, which would be seriously bad for his image.

'How's the Ferrari?' cut in Miranda, nervous at the way Martin and Sam were scowling at one another. 'Très flash.'

'Blood red, isn't it?' asked Sam. 'As in blood money.'

'And business?' asked Miranda, fingers reaching up for her absent pearls.

'Great,' said Martin tersely. He'd done three more back-to-back deals since the riverside one came off so spectacularly. 'I didn't sell out Nikki.'

'Sure,' said Sam. 'Former soccer star speaks of his love for shamed stunner. The Nikki I knew by Martin June.'

'I was set up,' said Martin.

'The Mancini chap. Chum of yours, isn't he?' said Giles.

'Was. What the fuck do I need a paltry few grand for? I was set up.'

The three watched him impassively.

'To use one of your phrases, Martin,' said Miranda. 'Bollocks.'

As the guests started to drift away, Pete felt himself relax. It had been a success. Everyone assured him that the bar would take off like a rocket.

After yelling at Wendy, Martin had shoved his way to the door, jumped into the Ferrari and roared off into the night. She assured Pete that the place was likely to get a mention the next day. 'Might make it onto the news pages if Thone resigns. Don't know if Martin June telling me exactly where I can stuff my notebook actually passes for an exclusive interview, but it's something. Bye.'

Pete was uneasy. Did he want to trade off the back of the Thone scandal? 'Munchkin, your glass is empty.' He beckoned a waiter.

She reached out for a canapé, then wished she hadn't. Not only was it at least 120 empty calories, but it was soggy.

'So, you and Miranda are off skiing,' said Munchkin. She and Sam were planning to go to Paris for Easter.

'Today week. Can't wait.'

She took a slurp of her Chardonnay. 'How's Jamie?'

'Settling in. He called earlier, hoped tonight would go well. Wish he was here.' Pete sounded forlorn. 'The bank's got him this huge apartment overlooking Central Park. I'm going over in three weeks.'

'Isn't that when the wedding . . . ?' blurted out Munchkin. 'That's why I'm going,' said Pete quietly.

Munchkin wandered over to join Sam and Giles, telling them that Pete was off to New York. 'Poor Jamie. Practically jilted at the altar like that. Wonder if Flora kept the ring? Probably. She struck me as a gold-digger. I always said it would end in tears.'

'Pity to have missed out on the mother of all parties. I was looking forward to that wedding.' Giles sounded gloomy.

Munchkin's eyes lit up at the approach of a fresh tray of canapés. 'Bonking her ski instructor. You know, that guy with the earrings. It was obvious something was going on between them. Despite what she claimed. Body language, it never lies. I should sue. Entre nous, Jamie's better off without her. Good riddance to bad rubbish if you ask my opinion.'

'I didn't.' The rangy blonde turned round. 'So keep quiet.'

Jaws dropping, Giles straightened his tie and Sam his spine.

'Flora didn't keep the ring. Or have shagging sessions with Stefan.' The blonde looked Munchkin up and down. 'Munchkin, the chalet motormouth. Right?'

Blushing furiously, being made to feel short, fat and inadequate, wanting to kill Sam and Giles for gawping with such obvious lust, Munchkin spluttered, 'If you don't mind, this is a private conversation.'

'Is it? By the way, I'm Jem Cate. Flora's best friend.' She beckoned the waiter. Taking the tray of canapés from him, she handed it to Munchkin. 'Work your way through these. They'll shut you up.'

Two hundred miles away, Nikki was opening a tin. Chutney and Pickle, Anna's renamed cats, mewed round her feet. Spread out on the kitchen counter was a month old copy of a tabloid paper, headlined 'PM Pal's Pervy Pleasures'. She studied the front page, although she knew it off by heart.

The Prime Minister's closet chum, top industrialist David Thone, dressed in nappies during spanking sessions with his secret mistress and a string of call girls.

Thone, 63, a confidante of leading Royals, for more than a year passed off gorgeous Nikki Solange, 31, ex-fiancée of former soccer hero Martin June, as a secretary who only took down his dictation.

After days on the golf course with the PM, the tycoon romped his nights away with the stunning brunette in their hideaway lovenest in London's exclusive Knightsbridge.

The granddad of three, a lay preacher, would tell his charity worker wife Marjory, 60, he was at Chequers, the Premier's country retreat, advising on the economy.

Thone, head of Thone Corp, is tonight starring in UK plc, the TV series on Britain's leading business bosses. What the programme won't be revealing is the multi-millionaire's secret vices including

- *Dressing up in baby clothes and being beaten with a rattle*
- *Three-in-a-bed sexploits with prostitutes*
- *Snorting amyl nitrate and cocaine*

Thone was made a peer in the New Year's Honours list for his services to industry.

Only last week, the self-confessed God-fearing family man urged a return to traditional values. Recently he called for new privacy laws to curb the media.

Lord Thone was unavailable last night. He and his wife are believed to be in South Africa. Staff at his 2,000 acre estate in Aldswick, Yorks, refused to comment.

Downing Street was remaining tight-lipped about this latest scandal to rock the Government. The PM's official spokesman said: 'The Prime Minister is in Brussels. His main concern is securing a reduction to our budget contribution.'

Continued Pages 2,3,4,5,7. Special Report. See Centre Pages.

Watching the cats gobbling up their food, Nikki realised they were getting fatter. Must be all the tidbits she was feeding them. When she'd fled to Anna's after the story broke, she'd spent hours slumped in the armchair stroking them for comfort.

'Time to start packing,' she told them. 'Wish I could take you two.'

Time to go back to the tiny studio in Holland Park that she'd rented when she left Martin, two days after they came back from France. The holiday had made up her mind. She didn't want to be with him.

Is that why he'd wanted revenge? To pay her back for sneaking off, for vanishing without trace?

Back in January, she'd been unable to cope with the storm that would follow if she told him face-to-face that she must leave. She just wanted out. Fast. No fuss, no muss.

Martin would have assumed she'd gone back to David. Ironically, although she thought about it in France, she hadn't bothered contacting him. Life was suddenly too full of possibilities and she had wanted to move on, not go backwards.

How she'd relished her independence. Sweet freedom. She'd enjoyed working again, even if it was only temping. With Anna's help, she'd found out about doing a degree and was applying for access courses. Half the time she was engrossed in library books, from the list she'd badgered Anna and Tom into making for her. She'd even got a bicycle, paid for out of the money she'd got when she'd sold her jewellery and two thirds of her clothes.

She'd been taken out a lot too. Insisted on paying her way. No sex, no strings. A film and a pizza was a long way from the Savoy Grill, but ten times more enjoyable. She realised that being with an older man for so long had almost made her old. She wanted friends, not a boyfriend. But on St Valentine's Day the studio was filled with more flowers than Kew Gardens, which she'd visited for the first time the previous Sunday.

Why hadn't she jettisoned her gym membership along with the rest of her old life?

Nikki watched the cats licking their paws.

Frankie had followed her into the sauna after the step class and they'd got talking. They'd talked and talked. Then fun, pretty Frankie had suggested they go to the bar round the corner. Over numerous Martinis, fun, pretty Frankie had opened up her heart about being in love with a married man.

Mellow with vodka, warming to her sweet, well-dressed companion, eager to make new friends, Nikki had enjoyed herself. Then, spurred on by Frankie's tales about being lonely, bored and let down at the last minute by her lover, tales which uncannily mirrored her own experience, Nikki confessed to having been in a similar situation.

So you think I should get out? Frankie had asked her. They never leave their wives? But he promised.

Frankie's giggling candour about her man's bizarre sexual preferences inspired similar confidences.

Frankie wasn't a gold-digger, she had assured Nikki, but these days a girl has to be realistic. He's taking me to Aspen. Another drinkie, go on. What do you mean, it's not worth it, ditch him? You got a flat? In Knightsbridge, wow. And a Mercedes? Perhaps we should form Mistresses Anonymous.

Much later, having exchanged numbers and addresses, Nikki had stumbled into a cab. Frankie had promised to be in touch in a couple of weeks when she got back from Aspen.

Only two days later, however, at Saturday lunchtime after she'd come back from the library, Nikki had waited by the studio's front door, smiling in anticipation at the thought of a cosy girls' lunch as Frankie had panted her way round the landing and up the stairs.

'What happened to Aspen?' The words had died on her lips and she had frozen in horror at the sight of those cold turquoise eyes.

'Hello Nicola. As gorgeous as ever,' said Jack Mancini.

'How do you know him?' She had stared at Frankie, her mind groping for an answer, an answer she'd immediately dismissed as too terrible to consider, but an answer she knew was correct a nano-second later.

'Francesca and I go back a long way. Don't be like that.'

Darting inside, Nikki had slammed the door on them.

She had hidden herself in the bathroom, stomach churning, trembling with shock. After half an hour of pounding on the door, peering through the letter box and calling out questions, they'd left. Even after they'd gone, the studio which had been her sanctuary had felt violated, as if it had been burgled. She sensed unknown eyes watching her from out in the street.

For however long she wondered what she could do and who she could turn to.

Eventually, she had plucked up the courage to call David Thone on his mobile. Between sobs, she had told him what had happened and begged for his advice.

'Get a razor, cut out your tongue, then slash your wrists.'

Sunday Reporter journalists had tried to visit Thone's house at breakfast time. The security guards had barred them from the estate. Then the bastards had been on the phone. There were no grounds for an injunction. His lawyers had told him he might as well try to stop an avalanche. He was on his way now to the airport to join Marjory in Cape Town. Shocked, bitter, furious, he had accused Nikki of selling the story.

'Like everyone else, eh, cats?' said Nikki sadly. 'You and Anna and Tom were the only ones who believed me.'

Perhaps a few more would now, since she'd had her chance to put her side of things. Anna had suggested that she call Flora at the *Jaxley Standard* and offer her an exclusive.

'Nikki, are you sure?' Flora had asked down the telephone. 'Go to one of the nationals. You're a huge story. We can't pay you a penny. And Knoxxy, my editor, is bound to quibble that you're not a local.'

'Money is the last thing I want, you silly sausage, Flora. I want to explain that I didn't get any money. I was conned. Please. The hick hack is the only reporter I can trust.'

'Call you back in five minutes.'

'He quibbled.' Flora then suggested Nikki stay at her cottage for a couple of nights. 'That sorts out the local angle,' she sighed. 'Knoxxy reckons the nationals will pick it up. Sure you don't want to go to them direct?'

Flora had collected her from Jaxley station in her Fiat 500 and driven to the tucked-away cottage, so idyllic it looked as if it should've been made out of gingerbread. Canvases covered almost every crooked wall. Fred, who painted them, was away. They'd talked through the evening. Jamie, Martin, St Marie, Miranda and Pete, Munchkin and Sam. Anna and Tom, Giles and his con- stituency. For someone who'd changed the course of her life, Flora although thinner, seemed happy enough. The only time she'd faltered was when Nikki made a joke about ski instructors.

Nikki threw the cat food tin into the recycling bag. She looked at the photo of herself in the *Reporter*. The picture had been snatched by someone, who?, in the bar, while Frankie was taping her words. She had been beautiful, glamorous. Perhaps she could've been a model after all. Not now though, not with all her hair hacked off and her make-up-free face.

'Another life, Pickle,' she said, picking up the cat and showing it the image.

She heard the key in the lock. Anna and Tom walked in. They'd been to a Reclaim the Night meeting.

Later, as the three women finished off their pasta, Anna offered to let Nikki stay on. 'The cats can look after you. Why not work here? I can stay with Tom.'

'Thanks.' Nikki was grateful. 'But it's time to go back. The fuss has died down now. David will have to resign, I guess. Anyway, I'll be back to do my degree.'

Tom popped her head round the door, waving the *Sunday Reporter*. As much as she hated to admit it, it was a more entertaining read than her usual leftish broadsheet, full of worthy accounts of obscure African states. 'Want this? Could use it for the litter tray.'

'Hang on.' Nikki jumped up and turned to the page which carried Martin's interview. There was a huge photo of the former soccer idol turned property magnate. Giggling, she carefully folded the pages and handed back the paper. 'This way up please. Chutney, Pickle, do your worst.'

Martin sped through London, taking little pleasure in his new toy. No one believed that he hadn't stitched up Nikki, especially after she had given her side of the story, saying that she could only assume that he had wanted revenge after she ditched him. Her account of how she'd been betrayed by him, then been duped by his journalist friends, had left everyone shocked. They were all on her side.

No one believed that he'd been conned too.

Martin had seen Jack a few days before St Valentine's Day in the same Soho pub they'd met up in before Christmas. He was still engulfed in black misery, the same black misery that had started when Nikki left, a depression that the successful property deals had failed to lift.

They were meant to be discussing Martin's idea about a chain of soccer schools. But all he had really wanted to talk about was Nikki.

After the pub, he'd spent the night at Jack's place where they had got through almost a bottle of whisky. Jack had tut-tutted with sympathy and warned him about the perfidy of women.

'So, the lovely walked. You want her back. Come off it Mart, why? All right, ours not to reason why. Find her then, matey. The Lady Vanishes might be a nice little title for a film, but it doesn't cut the mustard in real life. No one vanishes. Trust me. I know. Where there's a will. Call her friends, family, the ex. No, of course I don't think the babe has gone back to him, but she might want a nice, platonic shoulder to cry on. Often happens.'

'Can hardly call Lord Thone.'

If Martin hadn't been so maudlin drunk, he would have noticed the flicker of excitement in those cold turquoise eyes.

'Where does she hang out? *Cherchez la femme.* You just haven't been applying the grey matter, have you? Clubs, hairdresser, gym. Sort who belongs to a swank gym, isn't she? Which one?'

A few days had passed before he heard from Jack again. 'We do like your idea. Former soccer ace turned tycoon Martin June setting up a charity to fund after-school sports clubs. Good stuff, although I had to tell the features editor who you were. She'd never heard of you. And we've tracked down the bloke involved in the smash all those years ago. The one in the coma. Nice touch, eh? He gives you his blessing. You vowing to sacrifice your career in exchange for him pulling through. Life for life. Rather Old Testament that, I thought. Raises the tone.'

'What? Who told you about that?' Martin had felt the first stabs of unease.

'You did, mate, the other night. Life's mysteries, the Marie Celeste, the Bermuda Triangle and why Martin June threw in the towel and ended his glittering career. Now solved.'

'You don't have to include that. It's too personal.'

'Human interest.' Jack had laughed. 'We don't want our readers to think you're another fat cat businessman doing his cynical bit for charity just to get a few tax breaks. Do we? Come on, Mart, it's a brilliant idea. You'll want lottery funding. How about some pix? All in a good cause. You can't deprive those deprived kids.'

A few days later, a Saturday, he had gone to a studio to get his photograph taken. He had assumed it was for the feature. A motorcycle courier had interrupted the session, asking for Martin's signature on a disclaimer. He had made a hasty scribble on a contract without reading it.

Afterwards, Martin had called Jack at the *Reporter*'s offices. 'Have you got enough?'

'Ta. Plenty.' Smiling, feet on his desk, Jack was examining Martin's signature. 'Thanks for your autograph. Keep the lawyers happy. And I trust that lots of nice, doleful snaps of Mr Heart-broken are winging their way down the wires as we speak.'

'What?'

'Well,' Jack sniffed. 'You looking as smug as fuck hardly helps the "jilted ex tells of love for shamed stunner" angle, does it? Oh, didn't I explain?' Jack sniffed again. 'Sorry, more dodgy sulphate, have to give my dealer his marching orders. Marching powder orders.'

'Jilted ex? What are you on about?'

'Where was I? The shamed stunner. Well, Mart, sorry and all that, but to be honest, I haven't actually played a very straight bat with you. Sorry, that's cricket. You're footie, aren't you? Is there a way I can break this gently? Thinking about it, there isn't. A couple of weeks back a couple of slags, we are talking dog rough, wanted to dish some dirt on the esteemed Lord Thone. Pillar of the community, family man. Friend of the Premier. Thought it was a wind-up, so we sent them packing. Madame Puss and Estelle the Swedish schoolgirl. She won't see forty again. And then the other night. Your little yarn about the stunner. Nikki Solange. Well, tied in a treat, didn't it? Actually, thinking about it, that's just what chummy's into, according to the lovely Nicola.'

Martin jabbed at the CD button. The music died. What was he doing, driving aimlessly through London's streets? He had no one to see. Turning the Ferrari round, he retraced his route west. There was nowhere to go but home. Home? Nothing much to do there, except rattle around in the huge place and fiddle with the chemicals for the pool.

Passing the bar, he saw them huddled together on the wet pavement. Sam, Giles, Munchkin and Pete, with his arm round Miranda. Laughing, they were working out where to have dinner to celebrate.

Knowing that he'd be unwelcome, he accelerated away.

The night he'd pulled off the riverside deal, he planned to ask Nikki to marry him. Only she'd gone. No trace of her remained, apart from the skis he'd given her, propped up against the hall wall and a note saying she needed to think things out. He had kept a copy of the *Sunday Reporter*, it was the one photo he had of her.

He sped past a church noticeboard in Putney. There was a poster with a verse from St Mark which caught his eye. 'What profit is there for a man who wins the whole world but loses his soul?'

Jamie's office was on the thirtieth floor of a Wall Street skyscraper. He peered out of the window, overawed by the Manhattan skyline. He was getting to know New York, slowly finding his way about. It would take time to settle in. American girls just wanted to hear him speak, they adored his drawling English voice. Things were looking up, one of his new colleagues had a lodge in Vermont and had invited him skiing for the weekend.

How different would his life be now if he hadn't dragged Flora to France? They'd probably be getting married in three weeks' time. Whose fault was it that they weren't? Hers? His? Theirs?

When she'd put the engagement ring back on her finger that last night of the holiday, he'd believed they had a future together. Once safely home, he thought that her doubts and their disagreements would melt like snow in the spring.

How much was Stefan to blame? Seeing them together in the bar on New Year's Eve, he knew that Stefan had wanted more than to teach Flora how to parallel turn. Not only had the bastard taken his charlie, he had wanted his woman. And Flora? What had she wanted? He'd watched and waited, not wanting to humiliate himself by playing the jealous boyfriend, not wanting to lend weight to those rumours. He had given her a long leash that night, confident that if he waited, he would find a way of tugging her back to where she belonged.

He hadn't had to wait too long. On the Saturday, that very last morning in the chalet, he'd found the piece of paper with Stefan's address and number on their bedroom floor. It had dropped out of the pocket of Flora's ski pants, which she'd left hanging over the back of a chair. After copying out the numbers into his diary, he'd gone out onto the balcony. Using her lighter, he'd set fire to the rumpled paper watching it blacken and curl until it was ash.

Even when they were home, he'd suspected that Flora was straying. He'd sensed that Stefan was somehow threatening his position. His unease grew when Flora mentioned on the phone that she had started working on a French language tape.

Then she had called on that first Friday morning, saying she couldn't see him after all, she'd be spending the weekend in the cottage rather than in Chelsea. She'd also be visiting her parents. No, he couldn't come. She was having a fitting for her wedding dress. She had made it sound as if she were being measured for a shroud. A knife of suspicion had twisted inside him.

That lunchtime, he had called Stefan at the studio. He'd said he was meeting clients in Paris. Could Stefan suggest anywhere for dinner? Money no object. Of course. As soon as he could, Stefan had asked how Flora was.

'Marvellous,' he'd replied, doodling a Union Jack on his notepad. 'Got some wonderful news today. Perhaps she shouldn't have gone skiing.'

'Why not?'

'She's expecting.'

'Expecting?' Stefan's husky voice had been puzzled.

'A baby. Around July. It's all a bit of a shock, but a very nice one. Sorry about this, booked in for a conference call, so I'd better push off. I won't have time to link up next week, but whenever you're in London you must look us up. Come and stay. We'd both be delighted to see you. In fact, all three of us would be.'

He'd felt rather sorry for Stefan. The poor chap had sounded so shattered.

The weekend had passed, then the following week. Flora had sounded more and more remote with each passing day. No, she couldn't see him, she had to work. No, he couldn't come down to the cottage. No, she didn't want to look at fucking carpets or wallpaper. No, she was spending this weekend at the cottage too. Fred and Jem would be there.

That second weekend, Jem and Fred had obviously talked some sense into Flora. By the Sunday, she was calling, begging him to leap on the train and come down for dinner. He'd assumed that the Stefan hurdle had been safely cleared, because the French language tape hadn't got beyond lesson *deux*. The wedding file was dusted off and they'd spent a happy evening going through menus. She'd even talked about the cooking course.

For weeks, all had been fine until that awful Sunday when the Thone story broke. Pete and Miranda had come down for lunch at the cottage. While they played Monopoly, there had been some joke about one of Fred's pictures and from that moment, Flora had huddled on the sofa, not saying a word.

He had got a lift back to Chelsea with Pete, and realised Wednesday would be a bad time for Flora to come up and sort out the invitations because it was UEFA cup tie night. Couldn't the mother of all parties be arranged another day?

There was nothing to arrange. The phone was ringing as he walked through the door. It was Flora. Crying her heart out, she'd whispered, sorry, sorry, sorry.

The shock had lasted for days. He'd never loved Flora as much as when he had lost her. What he hadn't lost was his chance for that seat on the board.

'One hears that you and the rebel have called things off.' Julius Rosehagen had said. 'A great pity. Bright young man like you with excellent prospects. Girl's obviously as feckless as her grandfather. Still, ambitious men don't get sidetracked by their emotional lives. What you need is a challenge, a focus. New York for two years. Our board members must know their way around Wall Street.'

Deep down, there had been something else. It had taken him until he'd got to New York to realise it. Reprieve. That noose of little Flamies and their nannies and school fees and my little ponies and four-door estate cars with child seats had frayed and then snapped. He was still a free man.

Jamie's computer screen showed the latest stock prices. He tapped at the keyboard, calling up the snow reports. Vermont was looking good. This trip, there would be no need to draw a hanged man with his ski pole.

Flora let herself into the cottage and threw herself down on the tatty sofa. As she expected, the planning meeting had been brain and backside numbing. She wondered how Jamie was in New York and how the party at the bar had gone. Had Jem called for a goss?

She pressed play on the answering machine, surprised to hear Fred, sounding jubilant, telling her he'd call back later. He was at Billy's. So his trip round European ports was over. What had he been up to in Tallinn and Hamburg and Lisbon? Sailors stupid, Jem had scoffed.

Exhausted, Flora yawned, glancing down at her left hand. She wasn't used to it being ringless and kept on getting panic attacks that she'd lost three times her salary. The diamonds should've been joined by a slim gold band in three weeks time.

Since that awful Sunday when she'd called off the wedding, she'd never worked so hard, arriving at the *Standard* before seven in the morning, volunteering for every evening job going. When she did get home, the machine was full of how-could-you messages.

Whenever she wasn't working, she missed Jamie. It was like losing a part of herself. When he had written saying he was taking a job in New York for two years, she had wept. But not once did she regret her decision. She felt she'd been dragged to the safety of the shore after almost drowning. She might be in shock, coughing, spluttering and needing time to recover, but she was alive.

Earlier that day, Knoxxy the editor had asked her about her week off. 'You've earned it. Just had the figures. Highest ever after your interview with that Nikki Solange woman. Jaxley's most famous resident, even if it was only for a few days.' He had given Flora a shrewd glance. 'The *Standard* scooping the nationals. And it didn't cost us a penny.'

'No pay rise for me then?'

'Certainly not.' Affronted, he peered over his half-moon spectacles. 'If you're so concerned about money, what were you doing chucking your rich toff? You can have tomorrow off. So what about your hols? You're looking peaky.'

'Thinking of going to Siena with my friend Jem.'

'Vienna?'

'Siena, Italy.'

'What for? To look at pictures and things?' Knoxxy had given a disapproving sniff. 'Trail round musty old churches? Went to Florence once, couldn't stick it. Nearly had a coronary going up the Duomo. Give me Florida anyday. What about skiing? Or is it too late?'

The cottage needed a good tidy in honour of Fred's arrival. Lighting the fire, Flora thought back to her last few days in St Marie, when she had paralleled her way down the mountainsides, her skis speeding across the snow, her sense of exhilaration and joy.

It was probably the last skiing holiday of her life.

If she hadn't gone skiing, would she still be getting married? That week away had brought home the reality of life with Jamie, a man who wanted a Boy's Own life with sex on tap.

And Stefan? He had been a catalyst, hadn't he? Nothing but a tiny episode in her past, who had made her confront her doubts about the future. He was right. He had been her salvation, even if he'd put her in hell for weeks.

The bleakness of early January had mirrored Flora's despair.

A sorcerer, Stefan had cast a magical spell over her and then vanished forever, leaving a void, which nothing filled. She had tried to settle down, but nothing worked. She couldn't see Jamie and she couldn't forget Stefan. No matter what she did, wherever she went, even when she had the first fitting for her wedding dress, his beautiful face appeared.

Alone at the cottage, she had sat huddled in apathy reliving the time with the man who'd promised her the world, who'd told her to dream beautiful dreams. His low voice echoed round her head. A loop tape, his words went round in her mind. I want to listen to your breathing. Yes, you are getting married. To me.

As she promised she wrote him long love letters every day. Not that she could send them. The cottage had become ever more slumlike and chaotic after her repeated and ever more frantic ransackings for the piece of paper with his address. She called international directory inquiries a dozen times, but there was no number under his name. She tried his parents in Annecy but they were unlisted. She called Amsterdam, for information about art galleries, but no exhibition by Stefan Kovak was scheduled.

Weight fell off her. She couldn't eat, couldn't sleep. Imagining him with Marie-France was a torture. Unopened, the wedding file gathered dust.

Her work suffered badly. The contacts she had worked so hard to build up were taken aback by her indifference when they called with a tip-off. For days, there were no Flora Rose by-lines, no exclusives.

'You haven't left yet,' bellowed Knoxxy, one morning in front of the whole newsroom. 'We know you're preoccupied with your wedding, but I've got a paper to get out. Either pull your weight, Flora Rose, or collect your P45 right now.'

Like everything else, the rant washed over her. Flora was numb. She could touch, but she couldn't feel.

Jem and Fred had put her right that second weekend. They knew about Stefan, but not about the extent of Flora's continuing obsession.

Jem had been firm. 'You're never going to see him again. Ever. No, he was not, not, not, made for you. He's back with his girlfriend and the hoards of other women swooning at his skiboots. Yes hoards. Because pretty men are pretty rare. Him being in love, him wanting to marry you, I can't believe you fell for it. Don't you see, losing his number was fate? If he wanted you so much, he could've found you. Called Jamie, of course, found out where you worked. *Le Jaxley Standard, et voilà.* So how come he hasn't? You've got to forget about Stefan and get on with Jamie. You love Jamie. He tried to kill you? Flora, don't be pathetic. So, he was furious and isn't that a surprise? Eligible he may be, dumb he isn't. He guessed something was up. Jamie is going to be a perfect husband. He's not only interested in you because of the Rosehagen thing. That's nonsense, and even if it's not, why's it such a big deal? Get real. Guys like Jamie look for a trade off. It's two-way traffic. Handsome, charming, ambitious, generous. Have you sorted out the wedding list yet? Why not? You mean you were thinking of chucking everything away for a few memories of a half baked holiday romance? Half baked. Yes. Let's face it, you didn't even sleep with Stefan. He might be a complete, you know, inadequate. Brilliant? How do you know? Well, you're never, ever going to find out, so stop obsessing and start focussing on Jamie.'

'Forget Stefan, darling.' Fred had shaken his curls in despair. 'I know I had my doubts about you and Jamie, but I've come round. We'll have so much fun when you're rich. Now, I'm looking forward to a proper trad wedding and chatting up Jamie's divine best man. You look dreadful. If this is the effect Stefan has had on you, he's hardly a force for good. Salvation? Sweetpea, anyone would need saving from all those butch hearties of darkness. No wonder you collapsed into the first pair of strong masculine arms that came along. I warned you not to go skiing.'

Between them, they helped Flora recover her sense of perspective. Her despair had lifted. She'd assured Jamie she'd just been suffering from prenuptial nerves. For weeks everything was fine. Her wedding file had been permanently open, they'd even gone to choose carpets.

The Sunday the Thone story broke, she'd invited Pete and Miranda down to the cottage for lunch. Fred had just gone away again. Playing Monopoly, Flora had gone bankrupt first. The others divided her assets and she went to make some tea. Re-reading the *Sunday Reporter* in the kitchen, she had studied Martin's photograph. The Jack Mancini by-line leapt out from the page. The story was brilliantly written.

Martin's hawk face stared back at her. Nikki's wariness at the chalet had suddenly made sense. She'd been sitting on the scandal of the year, wary of letting anything slip out. Flora had assumed the story must've earned Nikki a fortune. Perhaps she needed one of her own. From the paper it sounded as if things between her and Martin were over. The split must've been recent, but there was no way of knowing. No one had seen either of them since they got back from St Marie.

The week in France had replayed in Flora's head. A video tape fast-forwarding. The view from the balcony of Les Diables, Mirabête, Jacques, the cable car, the chair lifts, Les Landais, the police station, the Savoie, the nursery slope, parallel turning, that horrible last morning when Jamie shoved her down the piste. A kaleidoscope of images had appeared. The most vivid was Stefan. His beautiful face, his green eyes were as real as if he were standing beside her. That first time she'd seen him at La Croix when she had shaded her sun-dazzled eyes to that last moment in Jimmy's when she had dragged herself away from him, her heart breaking.

'Mine,' Jamie had called out in the sitting room.

'Everything of Flora's will be once you're married and vice versa,' said Pete.

'Including these paintings?' Miranda asked. 'Rarely, er, interesting.'

'Quince the Mince's junk? He's given some to Flora.' Jamie had groaned. 'God knows how I'm going to live with them.

They'll fight with Tiger.' Tiger was a pastel of his beloved childhood labrador, which hung above the mantlepiece in Jamie's drawing room. 'Poor thing, he'll hate them. Have to bribe the removal men to lose them. If I'm lucky, perhaps they'll lose Quince the Mince too.'

That had been the moment when Flora had realised it would never work with Jamie. Now, she held out her hands to the fire to warm them up, smiling up at one of the paintings. They might yet win Fred the Turner prize.

Just as she was about to go and make herself some scrambled eggs, the telephone rang.

'Fred. I've missed you so much.' Flora smiled in delight. 'No, I didn't change my mind. He's in New York. Two years. The bank said he needed the experience to get that seat on the board. Where are you? Billy's? Guess what. No, I haven't got a new man. Julius Rosehagen's invited me to lunch. Where have you been?'

Fifty miles away, in Billy's Aladdin's cave of a flat, Fred sipped his tea. 'That's better. Can't remember the last time I had a decent cuppa. Never mind what I've been up to, I want you to listen. Has my present turned up yet? No? Gawd, these rail people can't run a bath. I've brought you something back from my travels. You know that a thing of beauty is a joy forever? The joy you're going to have, my darling, the joy. No, I can't keep it. It's yours, alas, all yours. I found it in a gallery in Amsterdam. Describe it? About six foot two, green eyes, made in Paris and Prague. Flora? Flora? Speak to me . . .'

But Flora had gone, running to answer a knock at the door.